THE CITY OF MIRRORS

could they slay the Twelve, nor find the places wherein they dwelled. For such was not the will of GOD at that time.

8 And in this manner did the years pass, five in sum.

9 And at the end of that time, Amy received a sign; and this sign was a dream. And in that dream Wolgast came to her, appearing as a man. And Wolgast said:

10 "My master is waiting; and the place of his waiting is a great ship in which he dwells. For a change is upon the land. Soon I will come for you, to show you the way."

11 And that man was Carter, Twelfth of Twelve, who was to be called Carter the Sorrowful; a man righteous in his generation, and beloved of GOD.

12 And thus did Amy wait for Wolgast's return.

CHAPTER SIX

1 But there was also in that time another city of mankind, in the place of Iowa. And this was known as the Homeland.

2 And in that place abided a race of men who had drunk the blood of a viral, so that they might live, ruling for many generations. And these were called Redeyes. And the greatest of these was Guilder the Director, a man of the Time Before.

3 And the viral from which they took their sustenance was Grey, called the Source. For in his blood was the seed of Zero, father of the Twelve. And Grey abided in chains, wherein he suffered greatly.

4 And in that place the people lived as captives to serve the Redeyes, doing all they wished. And one of these captives was Sara the Healer, taken at the place of Roswell, whose friends knew not that she lived.

5 And Sara had a daughter, Kate; but the child was taken away. And the Redeyes told Sara that her daughter had not survived, causing a great woe in her heart.

6 And it came to pass that the child was given to a woman of the Redeyes. And this was Lila, wife of Wolgast.

7 For Lila's daughter had died in the Time Before; and though many years had passed, the wound was still sharp in her mind. And she took comfort in Kate, imagining her to be the daughter she had lost.

8 And it came to pass that certain people of the Homeland rose up against their oppressors; and these were the Insurgents. And Sara joined with them. And she was sent to Lila to serve her in the Dome, wherein the Redeyes dwelled, that she might learn more about their ways. And in this manner did she discover that her daughter yet lived.

PROLOGUE

From the Writings of the First Recorder ("The Book of Twelves")
Presented at the Third Global Conference
  on the North American Quarantine Period
Center for the Study of Human Cultures and Conflicts
University of New South Wales, Indo-Australian Republic
April 16–21, 1003 A.V.
[Excerpt 2 begins.]

CHAPTER FIVE

1 Thus did it come to pass that Amy and her fellows returned to Kerrville, in the place of Texas.

2 And there they were to learn that three among them had been lost. And these were Theo and Mausami, his wife; and Sara, who was called Sara the Healer, wife of Hollis.

3 For in the place of Roswell, where they had taken shelter, a great army of virals had laid siege, killing every kind. And only two of their company survived. And these were Hollis the Strong, husband of Sara, and Caleb, son of Theo and Mausami.

4 And a great sadness was upon them all, for the friends that they had lost.

5 And in the place of Kerrville, Amy went to live among the Sisters, who were women of GOD. And likewise did Caleb do the same, to be cared for by Amy.

6 And in that same period, Alicia, who was Alicia of Blades, and Peter, the Man of Days, took up arms with the Expeditionary, who were soldiers of Texas, to search for the Twelve. For they had learned that to kill one of the Twelve was to kill his Many also, sending their souls unto the LORD.

7 And many battles were joined; and many lives were lost. But neither

CONTENTS

CONTENTS

And how am I to face the odds
Of man's bedevilment and God's?
I, a stranger and afraid
In a world I never made.

—A. E. HOUSMAN, *LAST POEMS*

For my family

First published in Great Britain in 2016
by Orion Books,
an imprint of The Orion Publishing Group Ltd,
Carmelite House, 50 Victoria Embankment
London EC4Y 0DZ

An Hachette UK company

1 3 5 7 9 10 8 6 4 2

A CIP catalogue record for this book
is available from the British Library.

ISBN (Hardback) 978 0 7528 9789 9
ISBN (Export Trade Paperback) 978 0 7528 9791 2

Printed in Great Britain by Clays Ltd, St Ives plc

www.orionbooks.co.uk

THE CITY
OF
MIRRORS

JUSTIN CRONIN

9 And in that same time also, Alicia and Peter discovered the lair of Martínez, Tenth of Twelve, in the place of Carlsbad; and there they did battle with his Many. But they did not find Martínez, who had fled from that place.

10 For Zero had commanded Guilder the Director to build a mighty fortress, wherein the Twelve should reside, to feed upon the blood of beasts and the blood of the Homelanders also. For their Many had devoured nearly every living thing upon the earth, making it a wasteland, fit neither for man nor viral, nor any kind of animal.

11 And in accordance with this design, the Twelve told their Many to leave their places of darkness; and they died. And this was known as the Casting Off.

12 And the Twelve commenced their journeys to the Homeland, a distance of many miles, so that they might preside over the earth.

CHAPTER SEVEN

1 But there was one who did not heed Zero's words; and this was Carter the Sorrowful, Twelfth of Twelve. And he instructed Wolgast to guide Amy to the place wherein he dwelled, that they two might join against his fellows.

2 And Amy heeded this command and left the place of Kerrville for the place of Houston. And in her company was Lucius the Faithful, who was a helpmate to her, and a man righteous in the eyes of GOD.

3 And in the place of Houston, Amy found the ship, which was the *Chevron Mariner;* and in its belly Carter dwelled. And many things passed between them. And when Amy emerged, her body was no longer that of a child, but of a woman; and in the company of Lucius she set out for the Homeland, to do battle with the Twelve.

4 And in that time also, Peter, the Man of Days; and Michael, who was called Michael the Clever; and Hollis, husband of Sara, likewise journeyed to the Homeland, to learn what was there. For they had come to believe that Sara was held captive in that place and many others also.

5 And with them were two companions. And the first of these was Lore, who was Lore the Pilot. And the second was a criminal, called Tifty the Gangster.

6 And in that same period, Alicia likewise made her way to the place of Iowa, pursuing Martínez, Tenth of Twelve, whom she had vowed to slay. For Martínez was the most evil of these demons, a killer of many women, and a scourge upon the earth.

7 But Alicia was taken captive at the Homeland, and endured many tribulations at the hands of the Redeyes and their helpmates, who were called Cols. And the worst of the Cols was Sod. But Alicia was strong and did not yield.

8 And when one night Sod came to her cell, so that he might have his dark way with her again, Alicia said: "Loosen my chains, so that you may take your pleasure more easily." And she wrapped the chains around his neck, killing him in this manner. And she made her escape, slaying many others.

9 And in the wilderness beyond the walls of the Homeland, Amy appeared to her; and Alicia saw that she was now a woman in body as well as mind. And Amy comforted her; for they were sisters in blood.

10 But Alicia had a secret; and this was the blood-hunger. For the seed of the Twelve was growing strong within her, making her a viral. And this was a great heaviness in her heart, for she loved her fellows deeply, and did not wish to be apart from them.

11 And in that same time, Sara was discovered by the Redeyes; and she was made a captive, and suffered many violations. For Guilder the Director desired that all who had risen up against him should know his wrath in fullest measure.

12 But the hour of reckoning was at hand; for Amy and Alicia had joined with the Insurgents, to take arms against the Redeyes. And among them a plan was hatched to liberate the people of the Homeland and destroy the Twelve and rescue Sara also.

CHAPTER EIGHT

1 And it came to pass that Peter and his fellows arrived in the place of Iowa, so that all were in attendance, making a mighty force. And the greatest of these was Amy.

2 For she had surrendered to the Redeyes, saying: "I am the leader of the Insurgents; do with me as you will." For it was her design that Guilder in his fury should unleash the Twelve to kill her.

3 And all did come to pass as Amy had foreseen; and the hour of her execution was established. And this would occur in the Stadium, a great amphitheater from the Time Before, so that the people of the Homeland might see.

4 And Alicia and the others concealed themselves in that place, so that when the Twelve were revealed, they could use their weapons upon them and upon the Redeyes also.

5 And Amy was brought before the crowd, and bound in chains; and upon an armature of metal she was made to hang. And Guilder took great delight in her suffering, exhorting the multitudes to do likewise.

6 But Amy would not give him satisfaction. And Guilder commanded the Twelve to devour her, so that all in attendance might know his power, bowing down before him.

7 But Amy saw that she was not alone; for among the Twelve was Wolgast, who had taken Carter's place, so that he might protect her. And Amy said to the Twelve:

8 "My brothers, hello. It is I, Amy, your sister." And no more words were spoken by her.

9 For she began to shake, and her body became as a bright light shattering the darkness; and with a furious roar Amy became as one of them, taking the form of a viral, mighty to behold. And this was the Letting Go. And one to see was Peter, and another Alicia, and a third Lucius, and all the others also.

10 And the chains were broken, and a great battle joined; and a great victory was won. And many lives were lost. And one of these was Wolgast, who sacrificed himself to save Amy; for his love for her was like unto a father's for his child.

11 And in this manner the Twelve perished from off the face of the earth, freeing all its people.

12 But of Amy's fate, her friends knew nothing; for she was nowhere to be found.

I

THE DAUGHTER

98–101 A.V.

There is another world but it is this one.

—PAUL ÉLUARD

I

CENTRAL PENNSYLVANIA
August 98 A.V.
Eight months after the liberation of the Homeland

The ground yielded easily under her blade, unlocking a black smell of earth. The air was hot and moist; birds were singing in the trees. On her hands and knees, she stabbed the dirt, chopping it loose. One handful at a time, she scooped it away. Some of the weakness had abated but not all. Her body felt loose, disorganized, drained. There was pain, and the memory of pain. Three days had passed, or was it four? Perspiration beaded on her face; she licked her lips to taste the salt. She dug and dug. The sweat ran in rivulets, falling into the earth. That's where everything goes, Alicia thought, in the end. Everything goes into the earth.

The pile beside her swelled. How deep was enough? Three feet down, the soil began to change. It became colder, with the odor of clay. It seemed like a sign. She rocked back on her boots and took a long drink from her canteen. Her hands were raw; the flesh at the base of her thumb had peeled back in a sheet. She placed the web of her hand to her mouth and used her teeth to sever the flap of skin and spat it into the dirt.

Soldier was waiting for her at the edge of the clearing, his jaws loudly working on a stand of waist-high grass. The grace of his haunches, his rich mane and blue roan coat, the magnificence of his hooves and teeth and the great black marbles of his eyes: an aura of splendor surrounded him. He possessed, when he chose, an absolute calm, then, in the next moment, could perform remarkable deeds. His wise face lifted at the sound of her approach. *I see. We're ready.* He turned in a slow arc, his neck bent low, and followed her into the trees to the place where she had pitched her tarp. On the ground beside Alicia's bloody bedroll lay the small bundle, swaddled in a stained blanket. Her daughter had lived less than an hour, yet in that hour Alicia had become a mother.

Soldier watched as she emerged. The baby's face was covered; Alicia drew back the cloth. Soldier bent his face to the child's, his nostrils flaring, breathing in her scent. Tiny nose and eyes and rosebud mouth, startling in their humanness; her head was covered in a cap of soft red hair. But there was no life, no breath. Alicia had wondered if she would be capable of loving her—this child conceived in terror and pain, fathered by a monster. A man who had beaten her, raped her, cursed her. How foolish she'd been.

She returned to the clearing. The sun was directly overhead; insects buzzed in the grass, a rhythmic pulsing. Soldier stood beside her as she laid her daughter in the grave. When her labor had started, Alicia had begun to pray. *Let her be all right.* As the hours of agony dissolved into one another, she had felt death's cold presence inside her. The pain pounded through her, a wind of steel; it echoed in her cells like thunder. Something was wrong. *Please, God, protect her, protect us.* But her prayers had fallen into the void.

The first handful of soil was the hardest. How did one do it? Alicia had buried many men. Some she'd known, and some she hadn't; only one she'd loved. The boy, Hightop. So funny, so alive, then gone. She let the dirt sift through her fingers. It struck the cloth with a pattering sound, like the first spits of rain upon leaves. Bit by bit her daughter disappeared. *Goodbye,* she thought, *goodbye, my darling, my one.*

She returned to her tent. Her soul felt shattered, like a million chips of glass inside her. Her bones were tubes of lead. She needed water, food; her stores were exhausted. But hunting was out of the question, and the creek, a five-minute walk down the hillside, felt like miles away. The needs of the body: what did they matter? Nothing mattered. She lay on her bedroll and closed her eyes, and soon she was asleep.

She dreamed of a river. A wide, dark river, and above it the moon was shining. It laid its light across the water like a golden road. What lay ahead Alicia did not know, only that she needed to cross this river. She took her first cautious step upon its glowing surface. Her mind felt divided: half marveled at this unlikely mode of travel; the other half did not. As the moon touched the far shore, she realized she had been deceived. The shining pathway was dissolving. She broke into a run, desperate to reach the other side before the river swallowed her. But the distance was too great; with every step she took, the horizon leapt farther away. The water sloshed around her ankles, her knees, her waist. She had no strength to fight its pull. *Come to me, Alicia. Come to me, come to me, come to me.* She was sinking, the river was taking her, she was plunging into darkness . . .

She awoke to a muted orange light; the day had nearly passed. She lay motionless, assembling her thoughts. She had grown accustomed to these nightmares; the pieces changed but never the feeling of them—the futility, the fear. Yet this time something was different. An aspect of the dream had traveled into life; her shirt was sopping. She looked down to see the widening stains. Her milk had come in.

*　　*　　*

Staying was not a conscious decision; the will to move on was simply absent. Her strength returned. It approached with small steps; then, like a guest long awaited, it arrived all at once. She constructed a shelter of deadfall and vines, using the tarp as a roof. The woods abounded with life: squirrels and rabbits, quail and doves, deer. Some were too quick for her but not all. She set traps and waited to collect her kill or took them on her cross: one shot, a clean death, then dinner, raw and warm. At the end of each day when the light had faded, she bathed in the creek. The water was clear and shockingly cold. It was on such an excursion that she saw the bears. A rustling ten yards upstream, something heavy moving in the brush; then they appeared at the edge of the creek, a mother and a pair of cubs. Alicia had never seen such creatures in the flesh, only in books. They prowled the shallows together, pushing the mud with their snouts. There was something loose and half-formed about their anatomy, as if the muscles were not firmly stitched to the skin beneath their heavy, twig-tangled coats. A cloud of insects sparkled around them, catching the last of the light. But the bears did not appear to notice her or, if they did, did not think she was important.

The summer faded. One day, a world of fat green leaves, dense with shadow; then the woods exploded with riotous color. In the morning, the floor of the forest crunched with frost. Winter's cold descended with a feeling of purity. Snow lay heavy on the land. The black lines of the trees, the small footprints of birds, the whitewashed sky, bleached of all tone: everything had been pared to its essence. What month was it? What day? As time wore on, food became a problem. For hours, whole days even, she barely moved, conserving her strength; she hadn't spoken to a living soul in nearly a year. Gradually it came to her that she was no longer thinking in words, as if she had become a creature of the forest. She wondered if she was losing her mind. She began to talk to Soldier, as if he were a person. *Soldier,* she would say, *what should we have for dinner? Soldier, do you think it's time to gather wood for the fire? Soldier, does the sky look like snow?*

One night she awoke in the shelter and realized that for some time she'd been hearing thunder. A wet spring wind was blowing in directionless gusts, hurling around in the treetops. With a feeling of detachment, Alicia listened to the storm's approach; then it was suddenly upon them. A blast of lightning forked the sky, freezing the scene in her eyes, followed by an earsplitting clap. She let Soldier inside as the heavens opened, ejecting raindrops heavy as bullets. The horse was shivering with terror. Alicia needed to calm him; just one panicked movement in the tiny space and his massive body would blow the shelter to pieces. *You're my good boy,* she murmured, stroking his flank. With her free hand she slipped the rope around his neck. *My good, good boy. What do you say? Keep a girl company on a rainy night?* His body was tense with fear, a wall of coiled muscle, and yet when she applied slow force to draw him downward, he allowed it. Beyond the walls of the shelter, the lightning flashed, the heavens rolled. He dropped to his knees with a mighty sigh, turned onto his side beside her bedroll, and that was how the two of them slept as the rain poured down all night, washing winter away.

She abided in that place for two years. Leaving was not easy; the woods had become a solace. She had taken its rhythms as her own. But when Alicia's third summer began, a new feeling stirred: the time had come to move on. To finish what she'd started.

She passed the rest of the summer preparing. This involved the construction of a weapon. She left on foot for the river towns and returned three days later, hauling a clanking bag. She understood the basics of what she was attempting, having watched the process many times; the details would come through trial and error. A flat-topped boulder by the creek would serve as her anvil. At the water's edge, she stoked her fire and watched it burn down to coals. Maintaining the right temperature was the trick. When she felt she had it right, she removed the first piece from the sack: a bar of O1 steel, two inches wide, three feet long, three-eighths of an inch thick. From the sack she also withdrew a hammer, iron tongs, and thick leather gloves. She placed the end of the steel bar in the fire and watched its color change as the metal heated. Then she got to work.

It took three more trips downriver for supplies, and the results were crude, but in the end she was satisfied. She used coarse, stringy vines to wrap the handle, giving her fist a solid purchase on the otherwise smooth metal. Its weight was pleasant in her grip. The polished tip shone in the sun. But the first cut would be the true test. On her final trip downriver, she had wandered upon a field of melons, the size of human heads. They grew in a dense patch, tangled with vines of grasping, hand-shaped leaves. She'd selected one and carried it home in the sack. Now she balanced it atop a fallen log, took aim, and brought the sword down in a vertical arc. The severed halves rocked lazily away from each other, as if stunned, and flopped to the ground.

Nothing remained to hold her in place. The night before her departure, Alicia visited her daughter's grave. She did not want to do this at the last second; her exit should be clean. For two years the place had gone unmarked. Nothing had seemed worthy. But leaving it unacknowledged felt wrong. With the last of her steel, she'd fashioned a cross. She used the hammer to tap it into the ground and knelt in the dirt. The body would be nothing now. Perhaps a few bones, or an impression of bones. Her daughter had passed into the soil, the trees, the rocks, even the sky and animals. She had gone into a place beyond knowing. Her untested voice was in the songs of birds, her cap of red hair in the flaming leaves of autumn. Alicia thought about these things, one hand touching the soft earth. But she had no more prayers inside her. The heart, once broken, stayed broken.

"I'm sorry," she said.

Morning dawned unremarkably—windless, gray, the air compacted with mist. The sword, sheathed in a deer-hide scabbard, lay across her back at an angle; her blades, tucked in their bandoliers, were cinched in an X over her chest. Dark, gogglelike glasses, with leather shields at the temples, concealed her eyes. She fixed the saddlebag in place and swung onto Soldier's back. For days he'd roamed restlessly, sensing their imminent departure. *Are we doing what I think we're doing? I rather like it here, you know.* Her plan was to ride east along the river, to follow its course through the mountains. With luck, she'd reach New York before the first leaves fell.

She closed her eyes, emptying her mind. Only when she had cleared this space would the voice emerge. It came from the same place dreams did, like wind from a cave, whispering into her ear.

Alicia, you are not alone. I know your sorrow, because it's my own. I'm waiting for you, Lish. Come to me. Come home.

She tapped Soldier's flanks with her heels.

2

The day was just ending when Peter returned to the house. Above him, the immense Utah sky was breaking open in long fingers of color against the deepening blue. An evening in early autumn: the nights were cold, the days still fair. He made his way homeward along the murmuring river, his pole over his shoulder, the dog ambling at his side. In his bag were two fat trout, wrapped in golden leaves.

As he approached the farmstead, he heard music coming from the house. He removed his muddy boots on the porch, put down his bag, and eased inside. Amy was sitting at the old upright piano, her back facing the door. He moved in quietly behind her. So total was her concentration that she failed to notice his entry. He listened without moving, barely with breath. Amy's body was swaying slightly to the music. Her fingers moved nimbly up and down the keyboard, not so much playing the notes as calling them forth. The song was like a sonic embodiment of pure emotion. There was a deep heartache inside its phrases, but the feeling was expressed with such tenderness that it did not seem sad. It made him think of the way time felt, always falling into the past, becoming memory.

"You're home."

The song had ended without his noticing. As he placed his hands on her shoulders, she shifted on the bench and tilted her face upward.

"Come here," she said.

He bent to receive her kiss. Her beauty was astonishing, a fresh discovery every time he looked at her. He tipped his head at the keys. "I still don't know how you do that," he said.

"Did you like it?" She was smiling. "I've been practicing all day."

He told her he did; he loved it. It made him think of so many things, he said. It was hard to put into words.

"How was the river? You were gone a long while."

"Was I?" The day, like so many, had passed in a haze of contentment. "It's so beautiful this time of year, I guess I just lost track." He kissed the top of her head. Her hair was freshly washed, smelling of the herbs she used to soften the harsh lye. "Just play. I'll get dinner going."

He moved through the kitchen to the back door and into the yard. The garden was fading; soon it would sleep beneath the snow, the last of its bounty put up for winter. The dog had gone off on his own. His orbits were wide, but Peter never worried; always he would find his way home before dark. At the pump Peter filled the basin, removed his shirt, splashed water on his face and chest, and wiped himself down. The last rays of sun, ricocheting off the hillsides, lay long shadows on the ground. It was the time of day he liked best, the feeling of things merged into one another, everything held in suspension. As the darkness deepened he watched the stars appear, first one and then another and another. The feeling of the hour was the same as Amy's song: memory and desire, happiness and sorrow, a beginning and an ending joined.

He started the fire, cleaned his catch, and set the soft white meat in the pan with a dollop of lard. Amy came outside and sat beside him while they watched their dinner cook. They ate in the kitchen by candlelight: the trout, sliced tomatoes, a potato roasted in the coals. Afterward they shared an apple. In the living room, they made a fire and settled on the couch beneath a blanket, the dog taking his customary place at their feet. They watched the flames without speaking; there was no need for words, all having been said between them, everything shared and known. When a certain time had passed, Amy rose and offered her hand.

"Come to bed with me."

Carrying candles, they ascended the stairs. In the tiny bedroom under the eaves they undressed and huddled beneath the quilts, their bodies curled together for heat. At the foot of the bed, the dog exhaled a windy sigh and low-ered himself to the floor. A good old dog, loyal as a lion: he would remain there until morning, watching over the two of them. The closeness and warmth of their bodies, the common rhythm of their breathing: it wasn't happiness Peter felt but something deeper, richer. All his life he had wanted to be known by just one person. That's what love was, he decided. Love was being known.

"Peter? What is it?"

Some time had passed. His mind, afloat in the dimensionless space between sleep and waking, had wandered to old memories.

"I was thinking about Theo and Maus. That night in the barn when the viral attacked." A thought drifted by, just out of reach. "My brother never could figure out what killed it."

For a moment, Amy was silent. "Well, that was you, Peter. You're the one who saved them. I've told you—don't you remember?"

Had she? And what could she mean by such a statement? At the time of the attack, he had been in Colorado, many miles and days away. How could he have been the one?

"I've explained how this works. The farmstead is special. Past and present and future are all the same. You were there in the barn because you needed to be."

"But I don't remember doing it."

"That's because it hasn't happened yet. Not for you. But the time will come when it does. You'll be there to save them. To save Caleb."

Caleb, his boy. He felt a sudden, overwhelming sadness, an intense and yearning love. Tears rose to his throat. So many years. So many years gone by.

"But we're here now," he said. "You and me, in this bed. That's real."

"There's nothing more real in the world." She nestled against him. "Let's not worry about this now. You're tired, I can tell."

He was. So very, very tired. He felt the years in his bones. A memory touched down in his mind, of looking at his face in the river. When was that? Today? Yesterday? A week ago, a month, a year? The sun was high, making a sparkling mirror of the water's surface. His reflection wavered in the current. The deep creases and sagging jowls, the pockets of flesh beneath eyes dulled by time, and his hair, what little remained, gone white, like a cap of snow. It was an old man's face.

"Was I . . . dead?"

Amy gave no answer. Peter understood, then, what she was telling him. Not just that he would die, as everyone must, but that death was not the end. He would remain in this place, a watchful spirit, outside the walls of time. That was the key to everything; it opened a door beyond which lay the answer to all the mysteries of life. He thought of the day he'd first come to the farmstead, so very long ago. Everything inexplicably intact, the larder stocked, curtains on the windows and dishes on the table, as if it were waiting for them. That's what this place was. It was his one true home in the world.

Lying in the dark, he felt his chest swell with contentment. There were things he had lost, people who had gone. All things passed away. Even the earth itself, the sky and the river and the stars he loved, would, one day, come to the end of their existence. But it was not a thing to be feared; such was the bittersweet beauty of life. He imagined the moment of his death. So forceful was this vision that it was as if he were not imagining but remembering. He would be lying in this very bed; it would be an afternoon in summer, and Amy would be holding him. She would look just as she did now, strong and beautiful and full of life. The bed faced the window, its curtains glowing with diffused light. There would be no pain, only a feeling of dissolution. *It's all right, Peter,* Amy was saying. *It's all right, I'll be there soon.* The light would grow larger and larger, filling first his sight and then his consciousness, and that was how he would make his departure: he would leave on waves of light.

"I do love you so," he said.

"And I love you."

"It was a wonderful day, wasn't it?"

She nodded against him. "And we'll have many more. An ocean of days."

He pulled her close. Outside, the night was cold and still. "It was a beautiful song," he said. "I'm glad we found that piano."

And with these words, curled together in their big, soft bed beneath the eaves, they floated off to sleep.

I'm glad we found that piano.

That piano.

That piano.

That piano . . .

Peter ascended to consciousness to find himself naked, wrapped in sweat-dampened sheets. For a moment, he lay motionless. Hadn't he been . . . ? And wasn't he . . . ? His mouth tasted like he'd been eating sand; his bladder was dense as a rock. Behind his eyes, the first stab of his hangover was making its presence felt.

"Happy birthday, Lieutenant."

Lore lay beside him. Not so much *beside* as coiled around, their bodies knotted together, slick with perspiration where they touched. The shack, just two rooms with a privy out back, was one they'd used before, though its ownership wasn't clear to him. Beyond the foot of the bed, the small window was a gray square of predawn summer light.

"You must be mistaking me for somebody else."

"Oh, believe me," she said, placing a finger against the center of his chest, "there's no mistaking you. So how does it feel to be thirty?"

"Like twenty-nine with a headache."

She smiled seductively. "Well, I hope you liked your present. Sorry I forgot the card."

She unwound herself, swiveled to the edge of the bed, and snatched her shirt from the floor. Her hair had grown long enough to need tying back; her shoulders were wide and strong. She wrenched herself into a pair of dirty gaps, shoved her feet into her boots, and turned her upper body to face him again.

"Sorry to run, *mi amigo,* but I've got tankers to move. I'd make you breakfast, only I seriously doubt there's anything here." She leaned forward to kiss him, quickly, on the mouth. "Give my love to Caleb, okay?"

The boy was spending the night with Sara and Hollis. Neither ever asked Peter where he was going, though certainly they had guessed the kind of thing it was. "I'll do that."

"And I'll see you the next time I'm in town?" When Peter said nothing, she cocked her head and looked at him. "Or . . . maybe not."

He didn't really have an answer. What passed between them wasn't love— the subject had never come up—but it was also more than physical attraction. It fell into the gray space between the two, neither one thing nor the other, and that was where the problem lay. Being with Lore reminded him of what he couldn't have.

Her face fell. "Well, shit. And I was so damn *fond* of you, Lieutenant."

"I don't know what to say."

She sighed, looking away. "I guess it's not like this could have lasted. I just wish I'd thought to dump you first."

"I'm sorry. I shouldn't have let things go so far."

"Believe me, it'll pass." She lifted her face toward the ceiling and took a long, steadying breath, then touched a tear away. "Fuck it all, Peter. See what you made me do?"

He felt awful. He hadn't planned this; up until a minute ago, he'd expected that the two of them would just drift in the current of whatever-this-was until they lost interest or new people came along.

Lore asked, "This isn't about Michael, is it? Because I told you, that's over."

"I don't know." He paused, shrugged. "Okay, maybe a little. He's going to find out if we keep this up."

"So he finds out—so what?"

"He's my friend."

She wiped her eyes and gave a quiet, bitter laugh. "Your loyalty is admirable, but trust me, I'm the last thing on Michael's mind. He'd probably thank you for taking me off his hands."

"That's not true."

She shrugged. "You're only saying that because you're being nice. Which is maybe why I like you so much. But you don't have to lie—we both know what we're doing. I keep telling myself I'll get him out of my system, but of course I never do. You know what kills me? He can't even tell me the truth. That goddamn redhead. What is it with her?"

For a moment Peter felt lost. "Are you talking about . . . Lish?"

Lore looked at him sharply. "Peter, don't be dense. What do you think he's doing out in that stupid boat of his? Three years since she's gone, and he still can't get her out of his head. Maybe if she were still around, I'd stand a chance. But you can't compete with a ghost."

It took Peter another moment to process this. A mere minute ago he wouldn't have said that Michael even *liked* Alicia; the two used to quarrel like a couple of cats over a clothesline. But underneath, Peter knew, they were not so unlike—the same cores of strength, the same resolve, the same stubborn refusal to be told no when an idea stuck in their teeth. And, of course, a long history was there. Was that what Michael's boat was all about? That it was his way of mourning the loss of her? They'd all done it in their own fashion. For a time, Peter had been angry with her. She had abandoned them without explanation, not even saying goodbye. But a lot had changed; the world had changed. Mostly what he felt was a pure ache of loneliness, a cold, empty place in his heart where Alicia had once stood.

"As for you," Lore said, rubbing her eyes with the back of her wrist, "I don't know who she is, but she's a lucky girl."

There was no point in denying it. "I really am sorry."

"So you've said." With a pained smile, Lore clapped her palms on her knees. "Well, I've got my oil. A girl could hardly ask for more. Do me a favor and feel like shit, okay? You don't have to drag it out or anything. A week or two is fine."

"I feel like shit now."

"Good." She leaned forward and took his mouth with a deep kiss that tasted of tears, then pulled abruptly away. "One for the road. See you around, Lieutenant."

The sun was just rising as Peter made his way up the stairs to the top of the dam. His hangover had settled in for the long haul, and a day spent swinging a hammer on a blazing rooftop wasn't going to improve it any. He could have done with an extra hour of sleep, but after his conversation with Lore, he wanted to clear his head before reporting to the jobsite.

The breaking day met him when he reached the top, softened by a low-hanging stratum of clouds that would burn off within the hour. Since Peter's resignation from the Expeditionary, the dam had become a site of totemic importance in his mind. In the days leading up to his fateful departure for the Homeland, he had brought his nephew here. Nothing especially noteworthy had occurred. They had taken in the view and talked about Peter's journeys with the Expeditionary and about Caleb's parents, Theo and Maus, then gone down to the impoundment to swim, something Caleb had never done before. An ordinary outing, yet by the end of that day, something had changed. A door had opened in Peter's heart. He had not understood it at the time, but on the far side of this door lay a new way of being, one in which he would assume the responsibilities of being the boy's father.

That was one life, the one that people knew about. Peter Jaxon, retired officer of the Expeditionary turned carpenter and father, citizen of Kerrville, Texas. It was a life like anybody else's, with its satisfactions and travails, and he was glad to live it. Caleb had just turned ten. Unlike Peter, who at that age was already serving as a runner of the Watch, the boy was experiencing a childhood. He went to school, he played with his friends, he did his chores without much prodding and only occasional complaint, and every night after Peter tucked him in, he drifted into dreams on the cushioning knowledge that the next day would be just like the last. He was tall for his age, like a Jaxon; the little-boy softness had begun to leave his face. Every day he looked a little bit more like his father, Theo, though the subject of his parents never came up anymore. Not that Peter was avoiding it; the boy just didn't ask. One evening, after Peter and Caleb had been living on their own for six months, the two of them were playing chess when the boy, hovering over his next move, said, simply, with no more weight than if he were inquiring about the weather, *Would it be okay if I called you Dad?* Peter was startled; he had failed to see this coming. *Is that what you want to do?* Peter asked, and the boy nodded. *Uh-huh,* he said. *I think that would be good.*

As for his other life: Peter could not say quite what it was, only that it existed, and that it happened at night. His dreams of the farmstead included a range of days and events, but the tone was always the same: a feeling of belonging, of home. So vivid were these dreams that he awoke with the sensation that he had actually traveled to another place and time, as if his hours of waking and sleeping were two sides of the same coin, neither one more real than the other.

What were these dreams? Where did they come from? Were they the product of his own mind, or was it possible that they derived from an outside source—even from Amy herself? Peter had told no one about the first night of the evacuation from Iowa when Amy had come to him. His reasons were many, but most of all he couldn't be sure the whole thing had actually happened. He had entered the moment from deep sleep, Sara and Hollis's daughter out cold on his lap, the two of them bundled up in the Iowa cold beneath a sky so drunk with stars he had felt himself to be floating among them, and there she was. They had not spoken, but they didn't need to. The touch of their hands was enough. The moment had lasted forever and was over in a flash; the next thing Peter knew, Amy was gone.

Had he dreamed that, too? The evidence said so. Everyone believed that Amy had died in the stadium, killed in the blast that had killed the Twelve. No trace of her had been found. And yet the moment had felt so real. Sometimes he was convinced that Amy was still out there; then the doubts would creep in. In the end, he kept these questions to himself.

He stood awhile, watching the sun spread its light over the Texas hills. Below him, the face of the impoundment was as still and reflective as a mirror. Peter would have liked a swim to shake off his hangover, but he needed to fetch Caleb and take him to school before reporting to the jobsite. He wasn't much of a carpenter—he'd really only ever learned to do one thing, which was be a soldier—but the work was regular and kept him close to home, and with so much construction going on, the Housing Authority needed all the warm bodies they could get.

Kerrville was busting at the seams; fifty thousand souls had made the journey from Iowa, more than doubling the population in just a couple of years. Absorbing so many hadn't been easy and still wasn't. Kerrville had been built on the principle of zero population growth; couples weren't allowed to have more than two children without paying a hefty fine. If one did not survive to adulthood, they could have a third, but only if the child died before the age of ten.

With the arrival of the Iowans, the whole concept had gone out the window. There had been food shortages, runs on fuel and medicine, sanitation problems—all the ills that went with too many people wedged into too little space, with more than enough resentment on both sides to go around. A hastily erected tent city had absorbed the first few waves, but as more arrived, this temporary encampment had quickly descended into squalor. While many of the Iowans, after a lifetime of enforced labor, had struggled to adjust to a life in which not every decision was made for them—a common expression was "lazy as a Homelander"—others had gone in the opposite direction: violating curfew, filling Dunk's whorehouses and gambling halls, drinking and stealing and fighting and generally running amok. The only part of the population that seemed happy was the trade, which was making money hand over fist, operating a black market in everything from food to bandages to hammers.

People had begun to openly talk about moving outside the wall. Peter supposed this to be just a matter of time; without a single viral sighting in three years, drac or dopey, the pressure was mounting on the Civilian Authority to open the gate. Among the populace, the events in the stadium had become a thousand different legends, no two exactly the same, but even the most hardcore doubters had begun to accept the idea that the threat was really over. Peter, of all people, should have been the first to agree.

He turned to look out over the city. Nearly a hundred thousand souls: there was a time when this number would have knocked him flat. He had grown up in a town—a world—of fewer than a hundred people. At the gate, the transports had gathered to take workers down to the agricultural complex, chuffing diesel smoke into the morning air; from everywhere came the sounds and smells of life, the city rising, stretching its limbs. The problems were real but small when compared to the promise of the scene. The age of the viral was over; humankind was finally on the upswing. A continent stood for the taking, and Kerrville was the place where this new age would begin. So why did it seem so meager to him, so frail? Why, standing on the dam on an otherwise encouraging summer morning, did he feel this inward shiver of misgiving?

Well, thought Peter, so be it. If being a parent taught you one thing, it was that you could worry all you wanted, but it wouldn't change a thing. He had a lunch to pack and "be good"s to say and a day of honest, simple work to wrestle to the ground, and twenty-four hours from now, he'd start it all over again. *Thirty,* he mused. *Today, I turn thirty years old.* If anyone had asked him a decade ago if he'd live to see it, let alone be raising a son, he would have thought they were crazy. So maybe that was all that really mattered. Maybe just being alive, and having someone to love who loved you back, was enough.

He had told Sara that he didn't want a party, but of course the woman would do something. *After all we've been through, thirty means something. Come by the house after work. It'll just be the five of us. I promise it won't be any big deal.* He picked up Caleb at school and went home to wash, and a little after 1800 they arrived at Sara and Hollis's apartment and stepped through the door and into the party that Peter had refused. Dozens of people were there, crammed into two tiny, airless rooms—neighbors and co-workers, parents of Caleb's friends, men he had served with in the Army, even Sister Peg, who, in her dour gray frock, was laughing and chatting away like everybody else. At the door Sara hugged him and wished him happy birthday, while Hollis put a drink in his hand and clapped him on the back. Caleb and Kate were giggling so fiercely they could barely contain themselves. "Did you know about this?" Peter asked Caleb. "And what about you, Kate?" "Of course we knew!" the boy exclaimed. "You should see your face, Dad!" "Well, you're in big trouble," Peter said, using his cross-dad voice, though he was laughing, too.

There was food, drink, cake, even some presents, things people could make or scrounge, some of them jokes: socks, soap, a pocketknife, a deck of cards, a huge straw hat, which Peter put on so everybody could enjoy a laugh. From Sara and Hollis, a pocket compass, a reminder of their journeys together, though Hollis also slipped him a small steel flask. "Dunk's latest, something special," he said with a wink, "and don't ask me how I got it. I still have friends in low places."

When the last presents had been opened, Sister Peg presented him with a large piece of paper rolled into a tube. *Happy Birthday to Our Hero,* it read, with the signatures—some legible, some not—of all the children in the orphanage. A lump rising in his throat, Peter put his arms around the old woman, surprising them both. "Thank you, everyone," he said. "Thank you one and all."

It was close to midnight when the party broke up. Caleb and Kate had fallen asleep on Sara and Hollis's bed, the two of them piled together like a couple of puppies. Peter and Sara sat at the table while Hollis cleaned up.

"Any word from Michael?" Peter asked her.

"Not a peep."

"Are you worried?"

She frowned sharply, then shrugged. "Michael's Michael. I don't get this thing with the boat, but he's going to do what he wants to do. I sort of thought Lore might settle him down, but I guess that's done."

Peter felt a stab of guilt; twelve hours ago he'd been in bed with the woman. "How are things at the hospital?" he asked, hoping to change the subject.

"It's a madhouse. They've got me delivering babies. Lots and lots of babies. Jenny's my assistant."

Sara was speaking of Gunnar Apgar's sister, whom they'd found at the Homeland. Pregnant, Jenny had returned to Kerrville with the first batch of evacuees and arrived just in time to deliver. She'd gotten married a year ago to another Iowan, though Peter didn't know if the man was actually the father. A lot of the time, these things were improvised.

"She's sorry she couldn't make it," Sara continued. "You're sort of a big deal to her."

"I am?"

"To lots of people, actually. I can't tell you how many times people have asked me if I know you."

"You're kidding."

"I'm sorry, didn't you read that poster?"

He shrugged, embarrassed, though part of him was pleased. "I'm just a carpenter. Not too good at it, either, if you want to know the truth."

Sara laughed. "Whatever you say."

The hour was long past curfew, but Peter knew how to avoid the patrols. Caleb's eyes barely opened as he hoisted him onto his back and headed home. He had just tucked the boy into bed when he heard a knock on the door.

"Peter Jaxon?"

The man in the doorway was a military officer, with the epaulets of the Expeditionary on his shoulders.

"It's late. My boy's asleep. What can I do for you, Captain?"

He offered Peter a sealed piece of paper. "Have a good night, Mr. Jaxon."

Peter quietly closed the door, cut the wax with his new pocketknife, and opened the message.

Mr. Jaxon:

Might I ask you to pay me a call in my office on Wednesday at 0800? Arrangements have been made with your work supervisor to excuse your late arrival at the jobsite.

Sincerely,
Victoria Sanchez
President, Texas Republic

"Dad, why was there a soldier at the door?"

Caleb had wandered into the room, rubbing his eyes with his fists. Peter read the message again. What could Sanchez want with him?

"It's nothing," he said.

"Are you in the Army again?"

He looked at the boy. Ten years old. He was growing so fast.

"Of course not," he said, and put the note aside. "Let's get you back to bed."

3

RED ZONE
Ten Miles West of Kerrville, Texas
July 101 A.V.

Lucius Greer, the Man of Faith, took his position on the platform in the hour before dawn. His weapon: a bolt-action .308, meticulously restored, with a polished wooden stock and an optical sight, its glass clouded by time but still usable. He was down to four rounds; he'd have to return to Kerrville soon, to trade for more. But on this morning of the fifty-eighth day, this was no concern. A single shot was all he'd need.

A gentle mist had settled overnight in the glade. His trap—a bucket of crushed apples—was a hundred yards upwind, nestled in the tall grass. Sitting motionless, his legs folded under him and his rifle resting on his lap, Lucius lay in wait. He had no doubt that his quarry would make an appearance; the smell of fresh apples was irresistible.

To pass the time, he offered a simple prayer: *My God, Lord of the Universe, be my guide and solace, give me the strength and wisdom to do Your will in the days ahead, to know what is required of me, to be worthy of the charge You have placed in my care. Amen.*

Because something was coming; Lucius could feel it. He knew it the same as he knew his own heartbeat, the wind of breath in his chest, the carriage of his bones. The long arc of human history was headed toward the hour of its final test. When this hour would come there was no knowing, but come it surely would, and it would be a time for warriors. For men like Lucius Greer.

Three years had passed since the liberation of the Homeland. The events of that night were still with him, indelible memories flashed upon his consciousness. The bedlam of the stadium, and the virals making their entrance; the insurgency's unleashing of their firepower upon the redeyes and Alicia and Peter advancing on the stage, guns drawn, firing again and again; Amy in chains, a meager figure, and then the roar that rose from her throat as she'd released the power within herself; her body transforming, shedding its human shape, and then the snap of the chains as she freed herself and her bold leap, quick as lightning, upon the monstrous enemies; the chaos and confusion of battle, and Amy trapped beneath Martínez, Tenth of Twelve; the bright flash of destruc-

tion, and the absolute quiet of aftermath, the whole world arrested into stillness.

By the time Lucius had returned to Kerrville, the following spring, he knew
he could no longer dwell among people. The meaning of that night was clear;
he had been called to a solitary existence. Alone, he had constructed his modest hut along the river only to feel the pull of something deeper, summoning
him into the wilderness. *Lucius, lay yourself bare. Put down your lendings;
cast aside all worldly comforts that you may know me.* With nothing but a
blade and the clothes on his back, he had ventured into the dry hills and beyond, no destination but the deepest solitude he could find so that his life
might find its true shape. Days without food, his feet torn and bloody, tongue
thick in his mouth from thirst: as the weeks went by, with only the rattlesnakes
and cacti and scorching sun for company, he had begun to hallucinate. A stand
of saguaros became rows of soldiers at attention; lakes of water appeared
where there were none; a line of mountains took the form of a walled city in
the distance. He experienced these apparitions uncritically, with no awareness
of their falsehood; they were real because he believed them to be so. Likewise
did the past and present blend in his mind. At times he was Lucius Greer,
major of the Expeditionary; at others, a prisoner of the stockade; at still others,
a young recruit, or even his boyhood self.

For weeks he wandered in this condition, a being of multiple worlds. Then
one day he awoke to discover himself lying in a gully beneath an obliterating
midday sun. His body was grotesquely emaciated, covered with scratches and
sores; his fingers were bloody, some of the nails torn away. What had happened?
Had he done this to himself? He possessed no recollection, only a sudden, overwhelming awareness of the image that had come to him during the night.

Lucius had received a vision.

He had no sense of where he was, only that he needed to walk north. Six
hours later, he found himself on the Kerrville Road. Mad with thirst and hunger, he continued to walk until just before nightfall, when he saw the sign with
the red X. The hardbox was amply stocked: food, water, clothes, gas, weapons
and ammo, even a generator. Most welcome of all to his eyes was the Humvee.
He washed and cleaned his wounds and spent the night on a soft cot, and in the
morning he fueled up the vehicle, charged the battery and filled the tires, and
headed east, reaching Kerrville on the morning of the second day.

At the edge of the Orange Zone he abandoned the Humvee and made his
way into the city on foot. There, in a dark room in H-town, among men he did
not know and whose names were never offered, he sold three of the carbines
from the hardbox to buy a horse and other supplies. By the time he arrived at
his hut, night was falling. It stood modestly among the cottonwoods and

swamp oaks at the edge of the river, just one room with a packed-dirt floor, yet the sight of it filled his heart with the warmth of return. How long had he been away? It seemed like years, whole decades of life, and yet it was just a matter of months. Time had come full circle; Lucius was home.

He unsaddled, tied up his horse, and entered the hut. A nest of fluff and twigs on the bed indicated where something had made its home in his absence, but the sparse interior was otherwise unaltered. He lit the lantern and sat at the table. At his feet was the duffel bag of supplies: the Remington, a box of cartridges, fresh socks, soap, a straight razor, matches, a hand mirror, a half dozen quill pens, three bottles of dewberry ink, and sheets of thick, fibrous paper. At the river he filled his washbasin, then returned to the house. The image in the mirror was neither more nor less shocking than he expected: cheeks cratered, eyes sunk way back in his skull, skin scorched and blistered, a tangle of madman's hair. The lower half of his face was buried beneath a beard that a family of mice would gladly live in. He had just turned fifty-two; the man in the mirror was an easy sixty-five.

Well, he said to himself, if he was going to be a soldier again, even an old, broken-down one, he damn well ought to look the part. Lucius hacked away at the worst of his hair and beard, then used the straight razor and soap to shave himself clean. He tossed the soapy water out the door and returned to the table, where he'd laid out his paper and pens.

Lucius closed his eyes. The mental picture that had come to him that night in the gully wasn't like the hallucinations that had dogged him during his sojourn in the desert. It was more like a memory of something lived. He brought its details into focus, his mind's eye roaming its visual expanse. How could he ever hope to capture something so magnificent with his amateur's hand? But he would have to try.

Lucius began to draw.

A rustling in the brush: Lucius drew the riflescope to his eye. There were four of them, rooting through the dirt, snuffling and grunting: three sows and a boar, reddish brown, with large, razor-sharp tusks. A hundred and fifty pounds of wild pig for the taking.

He fired.

While the sows scattered, the boar staggered forward, shuddered with a deep twitch, and went down on its front legs. Lucius held the image in his scope. Another twitch, deeper than the first, and the animal flopped on its side.

Lucius scrambled down the ladder and went to where the animal lay in the grass. He rolled the boar onto the tarp, dragged it to the tree line, looped the animal's hind legs together, set the hook, and began to hoist him up. When the boar's head reached the height of Lucius's chest, he tied off the rope, positioned the basin beneath the hog, drew his knife, and slashed the animal's throat.

A gush of hot blood splattered into the basin. The boar would produce as much as a gallon. When the boar had emptied out, Lucius funneled the blood into a plastic jug. With more time on his hands, he would have gutted and butchered the animal and smoked the meat for trade. But it was day fifty-eight, and Lucius needed to be on his way.

He lowered the corpse to the ground—at least the coyotes would get the benefit—and returned to the hut. He had to admit it: the place looked like a madman lived there. A little over two years since Lucius had first put pen to paper, and now the walls were covered with the fruits of his labor. He'd branched out from ink to charcoal, graphite pencil, even paint, which cost a bundle. Some were better than others—viewing them in chronological order, one could trace his slow, at times frustratingly inept self-education as an artist. But the best ones satisfyingly captured the image Lucius carted around in his head all day like the notes of a song he couldn't shake except by singing.

Michael was the only person who'd seen the pictures. Lucius had kept his distance from everyone, but Michael had tracked him down through somebody on the trade, a friend of Lore's. One evening over a year ago Lucius had returned from setting his traps to find an old pickup parked in his yard and Michael sitting on the open tailgate. Over the years Greer had known him, he had grown from a rather meek-looking boy to a well-made specimen of manhood in its prime: hard and sleek, with strong features and a certain severity around the eyes. The sort of companion you could count on in a bar fight that began with a punch to the nose and ended with running like hell.

"Holy damn, Greer," he said, "you look like shit on a biscuit. What does a man have to do to get a little hospitality around this place?"

Lucius got the bottle. At first it wasn't quite clear what Michael wanted. He seemed changed to Lucius, a little at loose ends, a bit sunk down into himself. One thing Michael had never been was quiet. Ideas and theories and various campaigns, however cockeyed and half-baked, shot from the man like bullets. The intensity was still there—you could practically warm your hands on the man's skull—but it had a darker quality, the feel of something caged, as if Michael were chewing on something he didn't have words for.

Lucius had heard that Michael had quit the refinery, split from Lore, built some kind of boat and spent most of his time on it, sailing out alone into the Gulf. What the man was looking for in all that empty ocean, he never got around to saying, and Lucius didn't press; how would he have explained his own hermitic existence? But over the course of the evening they passed together, getting drunker and drunker on a bottle of Dunk's Special Recipe

No. 3—Lucius wasn't much of a drinker these days, though the stuff came in handy as a solvent—he came to think that Michael didn't really *have* a reason for appearing at his doorstep beyond the basic human urge to be around another person. Both of them were doing their time in the wilderness, after all, and maybe what Michael really wanted, when you boiled away the bullshit, was a few hours in the company of someone who understood what he was going through—this profound impulse to be alone just when all of them should have been dancing for joy and having babies and generally celebrating a world where death didn't reach down from the trees and snatch you just for the hell of it.

For a while they caught up on news of the others: Sara's job at the hospital and her and Hollis's long-awaited move out of the refugee camps into permanent housing; Lore's promotion to crew chief at the refinery; Peter's resignation from the Expeditionary to stay home with Caleb; Eustace's decision, which surprised no one, to resign from the Expeditionary and return with Nina to Iowa. A tone of optimistic good cheer glazed the surface of the conversation, but it only went so deep, and Lucius wasn't fooled; always lurking beneath the surface were the names they weren't saying.

Lucius had told nobody about Amy—only he knew the truth. On the matter of Alicia's fate, Lucius had nothing to offer. Nor, apparently, did anybody else; the woman had vanished into the great Iowa emptiness. At the time, Lucius had been unconcerned—Alicia was like a comet, given to long, unannounced absences and blazing, unanticipated returns—but as the days went by with no sign of her, Michael trapped in his bed with his casted leg in a sling, Lucius watched the fact of her disappearance burning in his friend's eyes like a long fuse looking for a bomb. *You don't get it,* he told Lucius, practically levitating off his bed with frustration. *This isn't like the other times.* Lucius didn't bother to contradict him—the woman needed absolutely nobody—nor did he try to stop Michael when, twelve hours after the cast came off, the man saddled up and rode into a snowstorm to look for her—a highly questionable move, considering how much time had passed, and the fact that he could barely walk. But Michael was Michael: you didn't tell the man no, and there was something oddly personal about the whole thing, as if Alicia's leaving was a message just for him. He returned five days later, half-frozen, having run a one-hundred-mile perimeter, and said no more about it, not that day or all the days after; he'd never even said her name.

They had all loved her, but there existed a kind of person, Lucius knew, whose heart was unknowable, who was born to stand apart. Alicia had stepped into the ether, and with three years gone by, the question in Lucius's mind wasn't what had become of her but if she'd really been there in the first place.

It was well past midnight, after the last glasses had been poured and tossed back, when Michael finally raised the subject that, in hindsight, had been plaguing him all night.

"Do you really think they're gone? The dracs, I mean."

"Why would you ask that?"

Michael cocked an eyebrow. "Well, do you?"

Lucius framed his answer carefully. "You were there—you saw what happened. Kill the Twelve and you kill the rest. If I'm not mistaken, that was your idea. It's a little late to change your mind."

Michael glanced away and said nothing. Had the answer satisfied him?

"You should come sailing with me sometime," he said finally, brightening somewhat. "You'd really like it. It's a big wide world out there. Like nothing you've ever seen."

Lucius smiled. Whatever was eating the man, he wasn't ready to talk about it. "I'll give it some thought."

"Consider it a standing invitation." Michael got to his feet, one hand clutching the edge of the table for balance. "Well, I, for one, am completely hammered. If it's all right with you, I think it's time for me to go throw up and pass out in my truck."

Lucius gestured toward his narrow cot. "The bed's yours if you want it."

"That's sweet of you. Maybe when I get to know you better."

He stumbled to the door, where he turned to cast his bleary gaze around the tiny room.

"You're quite the artist, Major. Those are interesting pictures. You'll have to tell me about them sometime."

And that was all; when Lucius awoke in the morning, Michael was gone. He thought he might see the man again, but no more visits were forthcoming; he supposed Michael had gotten what he was looking for, or else he'd decided that Lucius didn't have it. *Do you really think they're gone . . . ?* What would his friend have said if Lucius had actually answered his question?

Lucius put these disconcerting thoughts aside. Leaving the jug of boar's blood in the shade of the hut, he walked down the hillside to the river. The water of the Guadalupe was always cold, but here it was colder; where the river made a bend there was a deep hole—twenty feet to the bottom—fed by a natural spring. Tall banks of white limestone encircled the edge. Lucius stripped off his boots and trousers, grabbed the rope he'd left in place, took a deep breath, and dove in a clean arc into the water. With every foot of his descent the temperature dropped. The satchel, made of heavy canvas, was secured beneath an overhang, protected from the current. Lucius tied the rope to the satchel's handle, tugged it free of the overhang, blew the air from his lungs, and ascended.

He climbed out on the opposite shore, walked downstream to a shallow spot, crossed the river again, and followed a path to the top of the limestone wall. There he sat at the edge, took the rope in his hands, and hauled up the satchel.

He dressed again and carried the satchel back to the hut. There, at the table, he removed the contents: eight more jugs, for nine gallons total—the same amount of blood, more or less, that coursed through the circulatory systems of half a dozen human adults.

Once it was out of the river, his prize would quickly spoil. He strung the jugs together and gathered his supplies—three days' worth of food and water, the rifle and ammo, a blade, a lantern, a length of sturdy rope—and carried them out to the paddock. Not even 0700, but already the sun was blazing. He saddled his horse, slid the rifle into its holder, and slung the rest over the horse's withers. He never bothered with a bedroll; he'd be riding through the night, arriving in Houston on the morning of the sixtieth day.

With a tap of his heels to the horse's flanks, he was off.

4

GULF OF MEXICO

Twenty-two Nautical Miles South-southeast of Galveston Island

0430: Michael Fisher awoke to the pattering of rain on his face.

He drew his back upright against the transom. No stars but, to the east, a narrow transect of ditchwater dawn light hovered between the horizon and the clouds. The air was dead calm, though this wouldn't last; Michael knew a storm when he smelled one.

He unfastened his shorts, jutted his pelvis over the stern, and released a urine stream of satisfying volume and duration into the waters of the Gulf. He wasn't especially hungry, hunger being something he'd taught his body to ignore, but he took a moment to go below and mix a batch of powdered protein and drink it down in six throat-pumping gulps. Unless he was mistaken, and he almost never was, the morning would bring its share of excitement; best to face it with a full belly.

He was back on deck when the first jag of lightning forked the horizon. Fifteen seconds later, the thunder arrived in a long, rolling peal, like a grumpy god clearing its throat. The air had picked up, too, in the disorganized manner of an approaching squall. Michael unhooked the self-steerer and took the tiller in his fist as the rain arrived in earnest: a hot, needling, tropical rain that soaked him in a second. About the weather, Michael lacked any strong opinion. Like everything else, it was what it was, and if this was to be the storm that finally sent him to the bottom, well, it wasn't like he hadn't asked for it.

Really? Alone? In that thing? Are you crazy? Sometimes the questions were kindly meant, an expression of genuine concern; even total strangers tried to talk him out of it. But more often than not, the speaker was already writing him off. If the sea didn't kill him, the barrier would—that blockade of floating explosives said to encircle the continent. Who in his right mind would tempt fate like that? And especially now, when not a single viral had been seen for, what, going on thirty-six months? Wasn't a whole continent sufficient space for a restless soul to roam around in?

Fair enough, but not every choice came down to logic; a lot came from the gut. What Michael's gut was telling him was that the barrier didn't exist, that it had never existed. He was raising his middle finger to history, a hundred years of humanity saying, *Not me, no way, you go on ahead without me.* That or playing Russian roulette. Which, given his family history, wasn't necessarily out of the question.

His parents' suicide wasn't something he liked to think about, but of course he did. In some room in his brain, a movie of that morning's events was constantly running. Their gray, empty faces, and the tautness of the ropes around their necks. The slight creaking sound they made. The elongated shapes of their bodies, the absolute, unoccupied looseness of them. The darkness of their toes, bloated with pooled blood. Michael's initial reaction had been complete incomprehension: he'd stared at the bodies for a good thirty seconds, trying to parse the data, which came to him in a series of free-floating words he couldn't stick together (*Mom, Dad, hanging, rope, barn, dead*), before an explosion of white-hot terror in his eleven-year-old brain sent him dashing forward to scoop their legs into his arms to push their bodies upward, all the while screaming Sara's name so she could come and help him. They'd been dead for many hours; his efforts were pointless. Yet one had to try. A lot of life, Michael had learned, came down to trying to fix things that weren't fixable.

So, the sea, and his solo wanderings upon it. It had become a home of a kind. His boat was the *Nautilus.* Michael had taken the name from a book he'd read years ago, when he was just a Little in the Sanctuary: *Twenty Thousand Leagues Under the Sea,* an old yellowed paperback, pages popping loose, and on its cover the image of a curious, armor-plated vehicle that seemed like a cross between a boat and an undersea tank, entwined in the suctioning tentacles of a sea monster with one huge eye. Long after the details of the story had fallen away from his mind, the image had stayed with him, seared into his retinas; when it came time to christen his craft, after two years of planning and execution and plain old guesswork, *Nautilus* had seemed a natural. It was as if he'd been storing the name in his brain for later use.

Thirty-six feet from stern to bowsprit with a six-foot draft, one main and one headsail, masthead-rigged, with a small cabin (though he almost always slept on the deck). He'd found it in a boatyard near San Luis Pass, tucked away in a warehouse, still standing on blocks. The hull, made of polyester resin, was sound, but the rest was a mess—deck rotted, sails disintegrated, anything metal fatigued beyond use. It was, in other words, perfect for Michael Fisher, first engineer of Light and Power and oiler first class, and within a month he'd quit the refinery and cashed in five years of unspent paychecks to buy the tools he needed and hire a crew to bring them down to San Luis. *Really? Alone? In that thing?* Yes, Michael told them, unfolding his drawing on the table. Really.

How ironic that after all those years of blowing on the embers of the old world, trying to relight civilization with its leftover machines, in the end it should be the most ancient form of human propulsion that seized him. The wind blew, it back-eddied along the edge of the sail, it created a vacuum that the boat forever tried to fill. With every voyage he took, he went a little longer, a little farther, a little more crazily *out there.* He'd traced the coasts at the start, getting the feel of things. North and east along the coast to oil-mucked New Orleans and its depressing plume of gooey, river-borne, chemical stink. South to Padre Island, with its long, wild stretches of sand as white as talc. As his confidence grew, his trajectories expanded. From time to time he came across the anachronistic leavings of mankind—clumps of rusted wreckage piled along the shoals, ersatz atolls of bobbing plastic, derelict oil rigs bestriding massive slicks of pumped-out sludge—but soon he left all of these behind, driving his craft deeper into the heart of an oceanic wilderness. The water's color darkened; it contained incredible depths. He shot the sun with his sextant, plotting his course with a stub of pencil. One day it occurred to him that beneath him lay nearly a mile of water.

The morning of the storm, Michael had been at sea for forty-two days. His plan was to make Freeport by noon, restock, rest for a week or so—he really needed to put on some weight—and set out again. Of course, there would be Lore to contend with, always an uncomfortable business. Would she even speak to him? Just glare at him from a distance? Grab him by the belt and drag him into the barracks for an hour of angry sex that, against his better judgment, he couldn't make himself refuse? Michael never knew what it would be or which made him feel worse; he was either the asshole who had broken her heart or the hypocrite in her bed. Because the one thing he couldn't find the words to explain was that she had nothing to do with any of it: not the *Nautilus,* or his need to be alone, or the fact that, although she was in every way deserving, he could not love her in return.

His thoughts went, as they often did, to the last time he'd seen Alicia—the last time anyone had, as far as he knew. Why had she chosen him? She had come to him in the hospital, on the morning before Sara and the others had left the Homeland to return to Kerrville. Michael wasn't sure what time it was; he was asleep and awoke to see her sitting by his bed. She had this . . . *look* on her face. He sensed that she'd been sitting there for some time, watching him as he slept.

—Lish?

She smiled.

—Hey, Michael.

That was it, for at least another thirty seconds. No *How are you feeling?* or *You look kind of ridiculous in that cast, Circuit,* or any of the thousand little barbs that the two of them had fired at each other since they were little kids.

—Can you do something for me? A favor.

—Okay.

But the thought went unfinished. Alicia looked away, then back again.

—We've been friends a long time, haven't we?

—Sure, he said. Absolutely we have.

—You know, you were always so damn smart. Do you remember . . . now, when was this? I don't know, we were just a couple of kids. I think Peter might have been there, Sara, too. We all snuck up to the Wall one night, and you gave this speech, an actual speech, I swear to God, about how the lights worked, the turbines and the batteries and all the rest of it. You know, up until then, I thought that they just came on by themselves? Seriously. God, I felt so dumb.

He shrugged, embarrassed.

—I was kind of a showoff, I guess.

—Oh, don't apologize. I thought it right then: That kid's really got something. Someday, when we need him, he's going to save our sorry asses.

Michael hadn't known what to say. Never had he seen anyone who looked so lost, so weighed down by life.

—What did you want to ask me, Lish?

—Ask you?

—You said you needed a favor.

She frowned, as if the question didn't quite make sense to her.

—I guess I did, didn't I?

—Lish, are you okay?

She rose from her chair. Michael was about to say something else, he wasn't sure what, when she leaned forward, brushed his hair aside, and, amazing him utterly, kissed him on the forehead.

—Take care of yourself, Michael. Will you do that for me? They're going to need you around this place.

—Why? Are you going somewhere?

—Just promise me.

And there it was: the moment when he'd failed her. Three years later and still he was reliving it over and over, like a hiccup in time. The moment when she told him she was leaving for good, and the one thing he could have said to keep her there. *Somebody loves you, Lish. I love you. Me, Michael. I love you and I've never stopped and never ever will.* But the words got tangled up somewhere between his mouth and his brain, and the moment slipped away.

—Okay.

—Okay, she said. And then was gone.

But the storm, on the morning of his forty-second day at sea: lost in these thoughts, Michael had let his attention drift—had noted, but failed to fully process, the sea's growing hostility, the absolute blackness of the sky, the accumulating fury of the wind. Too quickly it arrived with an earsplitting blast of thunder and a massive, rain-saturated gust that slapped the boat like a giant hand, heeling it hard. *Whoa,* thought Michael, scrambling up the transom. *What the holy fuck.* The moment had passed to reef the sail; the only thing to do was take the squall head-on. He tightened the mainsheet and steered his boat close to the wind. Water was pouring in—foaming over the bow, dumping from the heavens in sheets. The air was lit with voltage. He locked the main in his teeth, pulled it as tight as it could go, and snapped it down in the block.

All right, he thought. *At least you let me take a piss first. Let's see what you've got, you bastard.*

Into the storm he went.

Six hours later he emerged, his heart soaring with victory. The squall had blown through, carving a pocket of blue air behind it. He had no idea where he was; he had been thrown far off course. The only thing to do was head due west and see where he made landfall.

Two hours later, a long gray line of sand appeared. He approached it on a rising tide. Galveston Island: he could tell from the wreckage of the old seawall. The sun was high, the winds fair. Should he turn south for Freeport—home, dinner, a real bed, and all the rest—or something else? But the events of the morning made this prospect seem depressingly tame, a too-meager conclusion to the day.

He decided to scout the Houston Ship Channel. He could anchor for the night there, then proceed to Freeport in the morning. He examined his chart. A narrow wedge of water separated the north end of the island from the Bolivar

Peninsula; on the far side lay Galveston Bay, a roughly circular basin, twenty miles wide, leading at its northeastern edge to a deep estuary, lined with the wreckage of shipyards and chemical plants.

Running before the wind, he made his way into the bay. Unlike the brown-tinged surf of the coastline, the water was clear, almost translucent, with a greenish cast. Michael could even see fish, dark shapes running below the surface. In places the shoreline was clotted with huge masses of debris, but elsewhere it seemed scrubbed clean.

The afternoon had begun to fade as he approached the estuary's mouth. A large, dark shape stood in the channel. As he neared, the image came into focus: a massive ship, hundreds of feet long. It had come to rest midway between two stanchions of a suspension bridge that traversed the channel. He guided his craft closer. The ship was listing slightly to port, bow-down, the tops of its massive propellers just visible above the waterline. Was it aground? How had it gotten there? Probably the same way he had, pulled by the tides through Bolivar Pass. Across the stern, dripping with rust, was written the vessel's name and registry:

BERGENSFJORD

OSLO, NORWAY

He drew the *Nautilus* alongside the closest stanchion. Yes, a ladder. He tied off, dropped his sails, then went below to fetch a pry bar, a lantern, an assortment of tools, and two one-hundred-yard lengths of heavy rope. He put his supplies in a backpack, returned to the deck, took a steadying breath, and began to climb.

Michael didn't care for heights. Not much else got to him, except for that. At the refinery, circumstances often placed him somewhere far above the ground—swinging from a harness on the towers, chipping off the rust—and over time he'd become more brave about it, insofar as his crew could tell. But exposure went only so far in its curative effects. The ladder, steel rungs set into the concrete of the stanchion, was not, on close inspection, anywhere near as sturdy as it had appeared from below. Some of the rungs seemed barely attached. By the time he reached the top, his heart felt like it was stuffed against the back of his throat. He lay on his back on the suspension bridge's roadway, just breathing, then peered over the edge. He guessed it was a hundred and fifty feet down to the ship's deck, maybe more. Jesus.

He tied the rope to the railing and watched it fall. The trick would be using his feet to control his descent. Taking the rope in his hands, he leaned backward over the edge, swallowed hard, and stepped off.

For half a second he believed he had made the biggest mistake of his life. What a stupid idea! He was going to plummet like a rock to the deck. But then his feet found the rope, wrapping it in a death grip. Hand over hand, he made his way down.

Michael guessed the boat had been some kind of freight vessel. He headed for the stern, where an open metal staircase led to the pilothouse. At the top of the stairs he came to a heavy door with a handle that refused to move. He popped the handle loose with the pry bar and inserted the tip of a screwdriver into the mechanism. A bit of jiggling, tumblers clacking, and with a second pop of the pry bar the door swung free.

An eye-watering ammoniac funk filled the air—air that nobody had breathed for a century. Beneath the broad windshield, with its view of the channel, was the ship's control panel: rows of switches and dials, flat-panel displays, computer keyboards. In one of the three high-backed chairs that faced the panel was a body. Time had turned it into little more than a shrunken brown stain encased by the moldy tatters of its clothing. Military-style epaulets with three stripes decorated the shoulders of its shirt. An officer, Michael thought, perhaps the captain himself. The cause of death was apparent: a hole in his skull, no bigger than the tip of Michael's pinkie, marked the spot of the bullet's entry. On the floor, beneath the man's outstretched right hand, lay a revolver.

Michael found other bodies below decks. Nearly all were in their beds. He didn't linger, merely added them to the count, forty-two corpses in all. Had they killed themselves? The orderliness of the bodies said so, yet the method was not apparent. Michael had seen this sort of thing before, but never so many, all in one place.

Traveling downward into the ship, he came to a room that was different from the others, with not one or two beds but many—narrow bunks attached two high on the bulkheads, the space bisected by a slim corridor. The crew's quarters? Many of the cots were empty; he counted only eight bodies, including two that were naked, their limbs wound together in the cramped space of a lower bunk.

This space was more cluttered than the others. Rotted articles of clothing and miscellaneous objects covered much of the floor. Many of the walls beside the bunks were decorated: faded photographs, religious images, postcards. He gently freed one of the photographs and held it up to his lantern. A dark-haired woman, smiling for the camera, cradling an infant in her lap.

Something caught his eye.

A large sheet of paper, thin as tissue, taped to the bulkhead: at the top, in ornate lettering, were the words INTERNATIONAL HERALD TRIBUNE. Michael loosened the tape and laid the paper across the bunk.

HUMANITY IN PERIL

Crisis Deepens as Death Toll Soars Worldwide
Virus extends its deadly reach to all continents
Ports and borders overrun as millions
flee the spread of infection
Major cities in chaos as massive blackouts darken Europe

ROME (AP), May 13—The world stood on the edge of chaos Tuesday night as the disease known as the Easter Virus continued its deadly march across the globe.

Although the disease's rapid spread makes estimates of the dead difficult, U.N. health officials say the toll numbers in the hundreds of millions.

The virus, an airborne variant of the one that decimated North America two years ago, emerged in the Caucasus region of central Asia just fifty-nine days ago. Health officials have been at pains to identify either a source of the virus or an effective treatment.

"What we can say at this point is that this pathogen is unusually vigorous and highly lethal," said Madeline Duplessis, Chairman of the World Health Organization's Executive Board, speaking from its headquarters in Geneva. "Morbidity rates are running very close to 100 percent."

Unlike the North American strain, the Easter Virus does not require close physical contact to pass from person to person and can travel great distances attached to dust motes or respiratory droplets, causing many health officials to liken it to the Spanish influenza epidemic of 1918, which killed as many as 50 million people worldwide. Travel bans have done little to slow its spread, as have attempts by officials in many cities to prevent people from congregating in public places.

"I fear we are on the verge of losing control of the situation," said Italian Health Minister Vincenzo Monti in an extended press briefing, during which coughing could be heard throughout the room. "I cannot stress enough the importance that people stay indoors. Children, adults, the elderly—none has been spared the effects of this cruel epidemic. The only way to survive this disease is not to catch it."

Absorbed through the lungs, the Easter Virus acts swiftly to overwhelm the body's defenses, attacking the respiratory system and digestive tracts. Early symptoms include disorientation, fever, headache, coughing, and vomiting with little or no warning. As the pathogen takes hold, victims experience massive internal hemorrhaging, typically leading to death within 36 hours, though some cases have been reported in which healthy adults have succumbed within as little as two hours. In rare instances, victims of the illness have exhibited the transformative effects of the North American strain, including a marked increase in aggressiveness, but whether any of these individuals have survived past the 36-hour threshold is not known.

"This appears to be happening in a small percentage of cases," Duplessis told reporters. "Why these individuals are different, we simply don't know at this time."

WHO officials have speculated that the disease may have traveled from North America via ship or aircraft, despite the international quarantine imposed by the United Nations in June two years ago. Other theories of the pathogen's origins include an avian source, connected to the massive die-off of several species of migrating songbirds in the southern Ural Mountains just prior to the disease's appearance.

"We're looking at everything," Duplessis said. "We're leaving no stone unturned."

A third theory is that the epidemic is the work of terrorists. Responding to continued speculation in the press, Interpol Secretary-General Javier Cabrera, the former United States Secretary of Homeland Security and a member of the U.S. government in exile in London, told reporters, "At this time, no group or individual has claimed responsibility that we are aware of, though our investigation continues." Cabrera went on to state that the international law enforcement organization, with 190 member states, possesses no evidence that any terrorist group or sponsoring country has the capability to create such a virus.

"Despite the many challenges, we continue to coordinate our efforts with law enforcement and intelligence agencies around the world," Cabrera said. "This is a global crisis warranting a global response. Should any credible evidence arise that the epidemic is man-made, rest assured that we will bring the perpetrators to justice."

With most of the globe now under some form of martial law, riots have engulfed hundreds of cities, with fierce fighting reported in Rio de Janeiro, Istanbul, Athens, Copenhagen, Prague, Johannesburg, and Bangkok, among many others. Responding to the rising tide of violence, the United Nations, meeting in an emergency session at its headquarters in The Hague, urged the nations of the world to exercise restraint in the use of deadly force.

"Now is not the time for humankind to turn upon itself," said U.N. Secretary-General Ahn Yoon-dae in a printed statement. "Our common humanity must be a guiding light in these dark days."

Power outages throughout Europe continue to hamper relief efforts and add to the chaos. As of Tuesday night, darkness extended from as far north as Denmark to southern France and northern Italy. Similar failures have been reported throughout the Indian subcontinent, Japan, and Western Australia.

Landline and cellular communications networks have also been adversely affected, cutting many cities and towns off from the outside world. In Moscow, water shortages and high winds are being blamed for the unchecked fires that have left much of the city in ashes and killed thousands.

"The whole thing is gone," said one eyewitness. "Moscow is no more."

Also on the rise are reports of mass suicides and so-called "death cults." Early Monday in Zurich, police officers, responding to reports of a suspicious smell, discovered a warehouse containing more than 2,500 bodies, including children and infants. According to police, the group had used secobarbital, a powerful barbiturate, mixing it with a powdered fruit drink to make a lethal cocktail. Though the majority of victims appeared to have taken the drug voluntarily, some of the bodies had been bound at the ankles and wrists.

Speaking to the press, Zurich Chief of Police Franz Schatz described the scene as one of "unspeakable horror."

"I cannot imagine the despair that led these people to end not only their own lives but those of their children," Schatz said.

Around the globe, huge crowds have flocked to houses of worship and important religious sites to seek spiritual comfort during the unprecedented crisis. In Mecca, Islam's holiest city, millions continue to gather despite food and water shortages that have added to the suffering. In Rome, Pope Cornelius II, whom many eyewitnesses claimed appeared ill, addressed the faithful Tuesday evening from the balcony of the papal residence, exhorting them to "place your lives in the hands of an almighty and merciful God."

As bells tolled throughout the city, the pontiff said, "If it is God's will that these should be the last days of humanity, let us meet our heavenly father with peace and acceptance in our hearts. Do not abandon yourselves to despair, for ours is a living and loving God, in whose hands of mercy his children have rested since time's beginning and will rest until its end."

As the death toll rises, health officials worry that the unburied remains of the deceased may be accelerating the spread of infection. Struggling to keep pace, officials in many European locales have employed open pit graves. Others have resorted to mass burials at sea, moving the bodies of the deceased by freight cars to coastal sites.

Yet despite the risks, many of the bereaved are taking matters into their own hands, using any available patch of ground to bury their loved ones. In a scene typical of cities around the world, Paris's famed Bois de Boulogne, one of Europe's most storied urban parks, is now the site of thousands of graves.

"It is the last thing I could do for my family," said Gerard Bonnaire, 36, standing by the freshly dug grave of his wife and young son, who had succumbed within six hours of each other. After fruitless attempts to notify officials, Bonnaire, who identified himself as an executive with the World Bank, asked neighbors to help him move the bodies and dig a grave, which he had marked with family photographs and his son's stuffed parrot, a beloved toy.

"All I can hope is to join them as soon as possible," Bonnaire said. "What is left for any of us now? What can we do but die?"

It took Michael a moment to realize he had come to the end. His body felt numb, almost weightless. He raised his eyes from the paper and looked around the compartment, as if searching for someone to tell him that he was mistaken, that it was all a lie. But there was no one, only bodies, and the great, creaking weight of the *Bergensfjord.*

Good God, he thought.

We're alone.

5

The woman in bed 16 was making a ruckus. With each contraction, she released a volley of curses at her husband that would make an oiler blush. Worse, her cervix was barely dilated, just two centimeters.

"Try to keep calm, Marie," Sara told her. "Yelling and screaming won't make it any better."

"Goddamnit," Marie screeched at her husband, "you did this to me, you son of a bitch!"

"Is there anything you can do?" her husband asked.

Sara wasn't sure if he meant to ease his wife's pain or to shut her up. From the cowed look on his face, she guessed that the verbal abuse was nothing new. He worked in the fields; Sara could tell by the crescents of dirt under his fingernails.

"Just tell her to breathe."

"What do you call *this*?" The woman puffed up her cheeks and blew out two sarcastic breaths.

I could hit her with a hammer, Sara thought. *That would do the trick.*

"For God's sake, tell that woman to zip it!" The voice came from the next bed, occupied by an old man with pneumonia. He finished his plea with a spasm of wet coughing.

"Marie, I really need you to work with me here," Sara said. "You're upsetting the other patients. And there's really nothing I can do at this point. We just have to let nature take its course."

"Sara?" Jenny had come up behind her. Her brown hair was askew, lacquered to her forehead with sweat. "A woman's come in. She's pretty far along."

"Just a second." Sara gave Marie a firm look: *No more nonsense.* "Are we clear on this?"

"Fine," the woman huffed. "Have it your way."

Sara followed Jenny to admissions, where the new woman lay on a gurney, her husband standing beside her, holding her hand. She was older than the patients Sara was used to seeing, maybe forty, with a drawn, hard face and crowded teeth. Shocks of gray ran through her long, damp hair. Sara quickly read her chart.

"Mrs. Jiménez, I'm Dr. Wilson. You're thirty-six weeks along, is that correct?"

"I'm not sure. About that."

"How long have you been bleeding?"

"A few days. Just spotting, but then this morning it got worse and I started to hurt."

"I told her she should have come sooner," her husband explained. He was a large man in dark blue coveralls; his hands were big as bear paws. "I was at work."

Sara checked the woman's heart rate and blood pressure, then drew up the gown and placed her hands on her belly, gently pressing. The woman winced in pain. Sara moved her hands lower, touching here and there, searching for the site of the abruption. That was when she noticed the two boys, young teenagers, sitting off to the side. She exchanged a look with the man but said nothing.

"We have a birthright certificate," the man said nervously.

"Let's not worry about that now." From the pocket of her coat, Sara withdrew the fetoscope and pressed the silver disk against the woman's abdomen, holding up a hand for silence. A strong, swishing click filled her ears. She recorded the baby's heart rate on the chart, 118 bpm—a little low, but nothing too concerning yet.

"Okay, Jenny, let's get her into the OR." She turned to the woman's husband. "Mr. Jiménez —"

"Carlos. That's my first name."

"Carlos, everything's going to be fine. But you'll want your children to wait here."

The placenta had separated from the uterine wall; that's where the blood was coming from. The tear might clot on its own, but the fact that the baby was in a breech position complicated matters for a vaginal delivery, and at thirty-six weeks, Sara saw no reason to wait. In the hall outside the OR, she explained what she intended to do.

"We could hold off," she told the woman's husband, "but I don't think that's wise. The baby might not be getting enough oxygen."

"Can I stay with her?"

"Not for this." She took the man by the arm and looked him in the eye. "I'll take care of her. Trust me, there'll be lots for you to do later."

Sara called for the anesthetic and a warmer while she and Jenny washed up and put on their gowns. Jenny cleaned the woman's belly and pubic area with iodine and bound her to the table. Sara rolled lights into place, snapped on her gloves, and poured the anesthetic into a small dish. Using forceps, she dipped a sponge into the brown liquid, then placed this into the compartment of the breathing mask.

"Okay, Mrs. Jiménez," she said, "I'm going put this on your face now. It will smell a little strange."

The woman looked at her with helpless terror. "Is this going to hurt?"

Sara smiled to reassure her. "Believe me, you won't care. And when you wake up, your baby will be here." She positioned the breather on the woman's face. "Just take slow, even breaths."

The woman was out like a light. Sara rolled the tray of instruments, still warm from the boiler, into place and drew up her mask. With a scalpel she cut a transverse incision at the top of the woman's pubic bone, then a second to open the uterus. The baby appeared, coiled head-down in the amniotic sac, its fluid tinged pink with blood. Sara carefully punctured the sac and reached inside with forceps.

"Okay, get ready."

Jenny moved beside her with a towel and a basin. Sara drew the baby through the incision, sliding her hand beneath its head as it emerged and hooking her thumb and pinkie beneath its shoulders. *Her* arms; the baby was a girl. One more slow pull and she came free. Holding her in the towel, Jenny suctioned her mouth and nose, rolled her onto her stomach, and rubbed her back; with a wet hiccup, the child began to breathe. Sara clamped the umbilicus, snipped it with a pair of shears, drew out the placenta, and dropped it into the basin. While Jenny put the baby in the warmer and checked her vitals, Sara sutured the woman's incisions. Minimal blood, no complications, a healthy baby: not bad for ten minutes' work.

Sara drew the mask off the woman's face. "She's here," she whispered into her ear. "Everything's fine. She's a healthy baby girl."

Her husband and sons were waiting outside. Sara gave everyone a moment together. Carlos kissed his wife, who had begun to come around, then lifted the baby from the warmer to hold her. Each of the sons took a turn.

"Do you have a name for her?" Sara asked.

The man nodded, his eyes shining with tears. Sara liked him for this; not all the fathers were so sentimental. Some seemed barely to care.

"Grace," he said.

Mother and daughter were wheeled down the hall. The man sent his boys away, then reached into the pocket of his jumpsuit and nervously handed Sara the piece of paper she was expecting. Couples who were going to have a third baby were allowed to purchase the right to do so from a couple who had had fewer than their legal allotment. Sara disliked the practice; it seemed wrong to her, buying and selling the rights to making a person, and half the certificates she saw were forgeries, purchased on the trade.

She examined Carlos's document. The paper was government-issue stock, but the ink wasn't even close to the correct color, and the seal had been embossed on the wrong side.

"Whoever sold you this, you should get your money back."

Carlos's face collapsed. "Please, I'm just a hydro. I don't have enough to pay the tax. It was totally my fault. She said it wasn't the right day."

"Good of you to admit, but I'm afraid that's not the issue."

"I'm begging you, Dr. Wilson. Don't make us give her to the sisters. My sons are good boys, you can see that."

Sara had no intention of sending baby Grace to the orphanage. On the other hand, the man's certificate was so palpably false that somebody in the census office was bound to flag it.

"Do us both a favor and get rid of this. I'll record the birth, and if the paperwork bounces back, I'll make something up—tell them I lost it or something. With any luck, it'll get misplaced in the shuffle."

Carlos made no move to accept the certificate; he seemed not to comprehend what Sara was telling him. She had no doubt that he had mentally rehearsed this moment a thousand times. Not once, in all that time, had he imagined that somebody would simply make his problem go away.

"Go on, take it."

"You'd really do that? Won't you get in trouble?"

She pushed the paper toward him. "Tear it up, burn it, shove it in a trash can somewhere. Just forget we had this conversation."

The man returned the certificate to his pocket. For a second, he seemed about to hug her but stopped himself. "You'll be in our prayers, Dr. Wilson. We'll give her a good life, I swear."

"I'm counting on it. Just do me a favor."

"Anything."

"When your wife tells you it's not the right day, believe her, okay?"

At the checkpoint, Sara showed her pass and made her way home through darkened streets. Except for the hospital and other essential buildings, the electricity was shut off at 2200. Which was not to say that the city went to bed the minute the power was cut; in darkness, it acquired a different kind of life. Saloons, brothels, gaming halls—Hollis had told her plenty of stories, and after two years in the refugee camp, there wasn't much that Sara hadn't seen herself.

She let herself into the apartment. Kate had long since been put to bed, but Hollis was waiting up, reading a book by candlelight at the kitchen table.

"Anything good?" she asked.

With Sara working so many late hours at the hospital, Hollis had become quite a reader, checking out armfuls of books from the library and reading them from a stack he kept by his side of the bed.

"It's a little heavy on the mumbo jumbo. Michael recommended it a while ago. It's about a submarine."

She hung her coat on the hook by the door. "What's a submarine?"

Hollis closed the book and removed his reading glasses—another new development. Little half-moon lenses, cloudy and scratched, set in a black plastic frame: Sara thought they made him look distinguished, though Hollis said they made him feel old.

"Apparently, it's a boat that goes underwater. Sounds like bullshit to me, but the story's not bad. Are you hungry? I can fix you something if you want."

She was, but eating felt like too much effort. "All I want to do is go to bed."

She checked on Kate, who was sound asleep, and washed up at the sink. She paused to examine herself in the mirror. No doubt about it, the years were starting to show. Fans of wrinkles had formed around her eyes; her blond hair, which she now wore shorter and pulled back, had thinned somewhat; her skin was beginning to lose its tightness. She'd always thought of herself as pretty and, in a certain light, still was. But sometime in the midst of life she had passed the apex. In the past, when she'd looked at her reflection, she had still seen the little girl she'd once been; the woman in the mirror had still been an extension of her girlhood self. Now it was the future she saw. The wrinkles would deepen; her skin would sag; the lights of her eyes would dim. Her youth was fading, easing into the past.

And yet this thought did not disturb her, or not very much. With age came authority, and with authority came the power to be useful—to heal and comfort and bring new people into the world. *You'll be in our prayers, Dr. Wilson.* Sara heard words like these nearly every day, but she had never become inured to them. Just that name, Dr. Wilson. It still amazed her to hear someone say it and know they were speaking to her. When Sara had arrived in Kerrville, three years ago, she'd reported to the hospital to see if her nurse's training could be of any use. In a little windowless room, a doctor by the name of Elacqua quizzed her at length—bodily systems, diagnostics, treatments for illness and injury. His face showed no emotion as he responded to her answers with marks on a clipboard. The grilling lasted over two hours; by its conclusion, Sara felt like she was stumbling blind in a windstorm. What use could her meager training be to a medical establishment that was so far ahead of the homespun remedies of the Colony? How could she have been so naïve? "Well, I guess that about covers it," Dr. Elacqua said. "Congratulations." Sara was knocked flat; was he being ironic? "Does this mean I can be a nurse?" she asked. "A nurse? No. We have plenty of nurses. Report back here tomorrow, Ms. Wilson. Your training starts at oh-seven-hundred sharp. My guess is twelve months should do it." "Training for what?" she asked, and Elacqua, whose lengthy inquisition was a mere shadow of things to come, said, with unconcealed impatience, "Perhaps I'm not being clear. I don't know where you learned it, but you know twice as much as you have any right to. You're going to be a doctor."

And then, of course, there was Kate. Their beautiful, amazing, miraculous Kate. Sara and Hollis would have liked to have had a second child, but the violence of Kate's birth had inflicted too much damage. A disappointment, and not without irony, as day by day new babies traveled into the world beneath her hands, but Sara was hardly entitled to complain. That she should have found her daughter at all, and that the two of them should have been reunited with Hollis and escaped the Homeland to travel back to Kerrville to be a family together—*miracle* was hardly the word. Sara was not religious in the churchgoing sense—the sisters all struck her as good people, if a bit extreme in their beliefs—but only an idiot would fail to feel the actions of providence. You couldn't wake up each day in a world like that and not spend a solid hour just thinking of ways to be grateful.

She thought rarely of the Homeland, or as rarely as she could. She still had dreams about it—though, strangely, these dreams did not focus on the worst things that had happened to her there. Mostly they were dreams of feeling hungry and cold and helpless, or the endlessly turning wheels of the grinder in the biodiesel plant. Sometimes she was simply looking at her hands with a feeling of perplexity, as if trying to remember something she was supposed to be holding; from time to time she dreamed about Jackie, the old woman who had befriended her, or else Lila, for whom Sara's complex feelings had distilled over time to a kind of sorrowful sympathy. Once in a while, her dreams were flat-out nightmares—she was carrying Kate in blinding snow, the two of them being chased by something terrible—but these had abated. So that was one more thing to be thankful for: eventually, perhaps not soon but someday, the Homeland would become just one more memory in a life of memories, an unpleasant recollection that made the others all the sweeter.

Hollis was already out cold. The man slept like a fallen giant; his head hit the pillow, and soon he was snoring away. Sara extinguished the candle and slid beneath the covers. She wondered if Marie had delivered her baby yet, and if she was still yelling at her husband; she thought of the Jiménez family and the look on Carlos's face as he lifted baby Grace into his arms. Maybe *grace* was the word she was looking for. It was possible they'd still get flagged by the census office, but Sara didn't think so. Not with so many babies being born. Which was the thing. That was the heart of the matter. A new world was coming; a new world was already here. Maybe that was what getting older taught you, when you looked in the mirror and saw the passage of time in your face, when you looked at your sleeping daughter and saw the girl you once were and would never be again. The world was real and you were in it, a brief part but still a part, and if you were lucky, and maybe even if you weren't, the things you'd done for love would be remembered.

6

The sky over Houston released the night slowly, darkness easing to gray. Greer made his way into the city. Where the Katy Freeway met the 610 in a tangle of collapsed ramps and overpasses, he arced north, away from the bayous and swamps, with their sucking mud and impenetrable foliage, bypassing the liquefied inner neighborhoods for higher ground, then followed a wide avenue of junked cars south to the downtown lagoon.

The rowboat was where he'd left it two months ago. Greer tied up his horse, dumped out the mosquito-infested rainwater, and dragged the craft to the water's edge. Across the lagoon, the *Chevron Mariner* lay at its improbable angle, a great temple of rust and rot lodged among the listing towers of the city's central core. He laid his supplies in the bottom of the boat, set it afloat, and rowed away from shore.

In the lobby of One Allen Center, he tied off at the base of the escalators and ascended, the duffel bag with its sloshing contents slung over his shoulder. The ten-story climb through mold-befouled air left him dizzy and short of breath. In the empty office, he pulled up the rope he'd left in place and lowered the bag to the deck of the *Mariner,* then climbed down behind it.

He always fed Carter first.

On the port side, just about amidships, a hatch lay flush with the deck. Greer knelt beside it and removed the jugs of blood from the bag. He tied three together by their handles with one of the ropes. The sun was angled behind him, raking the deck with light. With a heavy wrench he unscrewed the safety bolts, turned the handle, and opened the hatch.

A shaft of sunshine spilled into the space below. Carter lay curled in a fetal position near the forward bulkhead, his body in shadow, away from the light. Old jugs and coils of rope were piled in a heap on the floor. Hand over hand, Greer lowered the jugs. Only when they reached bottom did Carter stir. As he scuttled on all fours toward the blood, Greer released the rope, closed the hatch, and replaced the safety bolts.

Now, Amy.

Greer moved to the second hatch. The trick was to move fast but not with panicked recklessness. The scent of blood: for Amy, it could not be contained by something as meager as the thin plastic membrane of the jugs; her hunger was too strong. Greer set his supplies within quick reach, unwrenched the bolts, and placed them to the side. A deep breath to calm his nerves; then he opened the hatch.

Blood.

She leapt. Lucius dropped the jugs, slammed the hatch, and shoved the first bolt into place as Amy's body made contact. The metal clanged as if hit by a giant hammer. He threw his body across it; another blow came, knocking the wind from his chest. The hinges were bending; unless he could get the remaining bolts in place, the hatch wouldn't hold. He'd managed to get two more into their holes when Amy struck again; Greer watched helplessly as one of the bolts jogged free and rolled across the deck. His hand stabbed outward and seized it at the very edge of his reach.

"Amy," he yelled, "it's me! It's Lucius!" He shoved the bolt into place and smacked it with the head of the wrench, driving it home. "The blood is there! Follow the scent of the blood!"

Three turns on the wrench and the bolt locked down, bringing the fourth hole back into alignment. He rammed its bolt into place. One last pound on the underside of the hatch, halfhearted; then it was over.

Lucius, I didn't mean it . . .

"It's all right," he said.

I'm sorry . . .

He picked up his tools and put them in the empty duffel. Below him, in the hold of the *Chevron Mariner,* Amy and Carter were drinking their fills. It always happened like this; Greer should have been used to it by now. Yet his heart was pounding, his mind and body flying with adrenaline.

"I'm yours, Amy," he said. "I always will be. Whatever comes, you know that."

And with these words, Lucius made his way across the deck of the *Mariner* and climbed back through the window.

7

Amy returned to awareness to find herself on all fours in the dirt. Her hands were gloved; a plastic flat of impatiens rested on the ground close by and, beside it, a rusty trowel.

"You all right there, Miss Amy?"

Carter was sitting on the patio, legs akimbo beneath the wrought-iron table, fanning his face with his big straw hat. On the table were two glasses of iced tea.

"That man takes good care of us," he said, and sighed with satisfaction. "Haven't eaten my fill like that since I don't remember when."

Amy rose unsteadily to her feet. A deep lassitude enveloped her, as if she had just awoken from a long nap.

"Come and sit a minute," Carter said. "Give the body a chance to digest. Feeding day like a day off round here. Them flowers can wait."

Which was true; there were always more flowers. As soon as Amy finished planting a flat, a new one would appear by the gate. It was the same with the tea: one minute the table was bare; in the next, two sweating glasses awaited. By what unseen agency these things arrived, Amy did not know. It was all part of this place and its own particular logic. Every day a season, every season a year.

She removed her gloves and crossed the lawn to sit across from Carter. The greasy taste of blood lingered in her mouth. She sipped the tea to clear it away.

"It's good to keep your strength up, Miss Amy," Carter said. "Ain't no prize for starving yourself."

"I just don't . . . like it." She looked at Carter, who was still fanning himself with his hat. "I tried to kill him again."

"Lucius knows the situation well enough. I doubt he takes it personal."

"That's not the point, Anthony. I need to learn to control it the way you do."

Carter frowned. He was a man of compact expression, small gestures, thoughtful pauses. "Don't be so hard on yourself. You ain't had but three years to get used to things. You still just a baby in the way of being what we are."

"I don't feel like a baby."

"What you feel like then?"

"A monster."

She'd spoken too sharply; she glanced away, feeling ashamed. After feeding, she always passed through a period of doubt. How strange it all was: she was a body in a ship, but her mind lived here, with Carter, among the plants and flowers. Only when Lucius brought the blood did these two worlds touch each other, and the contrast was disorienting. Carter had explained that this place was nothing particular to the two of them; the difference was that they could see it. There was one world, of flesh and blood and bone, but also another— a deeper reality that ordinary people could glimpse only fleetingly, if at all. A world of souls, both the living and the dead, in which time and space, memory and desire, existed in a purely fluid state, the way they did in dreams.

Amy knew this to be so. She felt as if she'd always known it—that even as a little girl, a purely *human* girl, she had sensed the existence of this other realm, this world-behind-the-world, as she had come to call it. She supposed that many children did the same. What was childhood if not a passage from light to dark, of the soul's slow drowning in an ocean of ordinary matter? During her time in the *Chevron Mariner,* a great deal of the past had become clear. Vivid recollections had inched their way back to her, approaching on memory's delicate feet, until things that had happened ages past felt like recent occurrences. She recalled a time, long ago, in the innocent period she thought of as "before"—before Lacey and Wolgast, before Project NOAH, before the Oregon mountaintop where they had made their home and then her long, solo wanderings in a peopleless world with only the virals for company—when animals had spoken to her. Larger animals, like dogs, but also smaller ones that nobody paid attention to—birds and even insects. She'd thought nothing of this at the time; it was simply the way things were. Nor did it trouble her that nobody else seemed to hear them; it was part of the world's arrangement that the animals spoke only to her, always addressing her by name, as if they were old friends, telling her stories about their lives, and it made her happy to be the recipient of the special gift of their attention when so much else in her life seemed to make no sense at all: her mother's lurching emotions and long absences, their drifting from place to place, the strangers that came and went with no apparent purpose.

All this had gone on without repercussion until the day Lacey had taken her to the zoo. At the time, Amy did not yet fully comprehend that her mother had deserted her—that she would never see the woman again—and she'd welcomed the invitation; she'd heard of zoos but had never been to one. She entered the grounds to an animal buzz of welcome. After the confusing events of the previous day—her mother's abrupt departure and the presence of the nuns, who were nice but in a slightly stilted way, as if they were reciting their kindnesses off a card of instructions—here was a familiar comfort. In a burst of energy, she broke away from Lacey and dashed to the polar bear tank. Three were basking in the sun; a fourth was swimming under the water. How magnificent they were, how amazing! Even now, so many years later, it gave her pleasure to remember them, their wonderful white fur and great muscular bodies and expressive faces, which seemed to contain all the wisdom of the universe. As Amy approached the glass, the one in the water paddled toward her. Though she knew that her communication with the creatures of the natural world was best conducted in private, her excitement could not be contained. She felt suddenly sorry that such a stately creature should be forced to live like a prisoner, sunning himself on phony rocks and being gawked at by people who did not appreciate him. "What's your name?" she asked the bear. "I'm Amy."

His answer was a collision of incompatible consonants, as were the names of the other bears, which he courteously offered. Were these things real? Had she, a little girl, simply imagined them? But no; all of it had happened, she believed, precisely as she recalled. As she stood at the glass, Lacey came up beside her. She was wearing a look of deep concern. "There now, Amy," Lacey advised. "Not so close." To put her unease at bay, and because Amy had detected in this kindly woman with her melodious accent an openness to extraordinary phenomena—the zoo, after all, had been her idea—she explained the situation as simply as she knew how. "He has a bear name," she told Lacey. "It's something I can't pronounce."

Lacey frowned. "The bear has a name?"

"Of course he does," said Amy.

She returned her attention to her new friend, who was bumping his nose against the glass. Amy was about to ask him about his life, if he missed his Arctic home, when the water was rocked by a tremendous splash. A second bear had leapt into the tank. With paws big as hubcaps he swam toward her, taking his place beside the first bear, who was licking the glass with his immense pink tongue. A collective exhalation of oohs and aahs ascended from the crowd; people began to snap pictures. Amy placed her hand against the glass in greeting, but something felt wrong. Something was different, and it wasn't very good. The bears' great black eyes seemed to be looking not at her but *through* her, with a gaze of such intensity that she could not look away. She felt herself dissolving into it, as if she were melting, and with this came a falling sensation, like putting her foot on a step that wasn't there.

Amy, the bears were saying. *You're Amy Amy Amy Amy Amy . . .*

Things were happening. Some sort of commotion. As Amy's awareness widened, she became conscious of other sounds, other voices, coming from all around—not human but animal. The hoots of monkeys. The shrieks of birds. The roars of jungle cats and the concussing hooves of elephants and rhinoceroses stamping the ground in panic. As the third and then the fourth bear leapt into the tank, displacing its contents with their white-furred tonnage, a wall of frigid water bulged over the lip. It crashed down upon the crowd, unleashing mayhem.

It's her, it's her, it's her, it's her . . .

She was kneeling by the glass, soaked to the bone, her head bowed to its slick surface. Her mind swirled with the voices, a chorus of black dread. She felt as if the universe were bending around her, swathing her in darkness. They would die, all these animals. That is what her presence meant to them. The bears and monkeys and birds and elephants: all of them. Some would starve in their cages; others would perish by more violent means. Death would take them all, and not just the animals. The people, too. The world would die around her, and she would be left standing at the center, alone.

It's coming, death is coming, you're Amy, Amy, Amy . . .

"You remembering, ain't you?"

Amy's mind returned to the patio. Carter was looking at her pointedly.

"I'm sorry," she said. "I didn't mean to snap at you."

"'Sall right. I felt the same, there at the beginning. Took some getting used to."

The feeling of summer had faded; autumn would soon come. In the blue-green water of the pool, the body of Rachel Wood would rise. Sometimes, when Amy was tending flowers near the gate, she would see the woman's black Denali slowly cruising past. Through the tinted windows she could make out Rachel in her tennis clothes, staring at the house. But the car never stopped, and when Amy waved at her, the woman never waved back.

"How much longer do you think we have to wait?"

"That depends on Zero. Man got to show his hand sooner or later. So far as he knows, I'm gone with the rest of them."

It was the water, Carter had explained, that protected them. Its cold embrace was nothing Fanning's mind could penetrate. As long as they stayed where they were, Fanning couldn't find them.

"But he'll come," said Amy.

Carter nodded. "He's bided his time a good while, but the man wants this thing done. It's what he's wanted from the start. Everything over."

The wind was picking up—an autumn wind, damp and raw. Clouds had moved in, denuding the light. It was the time of day when a certain silence always fell.

"We're quite a pair, aren't we?"

"That we are, Miss Amy."

"I was wondering if maybe you could drop the 'miss.' I should have said that long ago."

"I just meant it respectful. But as long as you're asking, I'd like that."

The leaves were spinning down. They fluttered across the lawn, the patio, the pool deck, tossing in the wind like skeletal hands. Amy thought of Peter, how she missed him. Wherever he was now, she hoped that happiness would find him in his life. That was the price she'd paid; she had given him up.

She took a last sip of tea to clear the blood taste from her mouth and drew on her gloves. "Ready?"

"Right you are." Carter donned his hat. "We best get to work on them leaves."

8

"Michael!"

His sister took her last two steps at a jog and wrapped him in a hug that made his ribs crunch.

"Whoa. I'm glad to see you, too."

The nurse at the desk was staring at them, but Sara couldn't be contained. "I can't believe it," she said. "What are you doing here?" She stepped back and looked him over with a motherly eye. One part of him felt embarrassed; another part would have been disappointed if she hadn't. "God, you're thin. When did you get here? Kate will be thrilled." She glanced at the nurse, an older woman in a boiled smock. "Wendy, this is my brother, Michael."

"The one with the sailboat?"

He laughed. "That's me."

"Please tell me you're staying," Sara said.

"Just a couple of days."

She shook her head and sighed. "I guess I'll have to take what I can get." She was clutching his upper arm as if he might float away. "I'm off in an hour. Don't go *anywhere,* okay? I know you, Michael. I mean it."

He waited for her, and together they walked to the apartment. How odd it was to be back on dry land, with its disconcerting stillness underfoot. After three years mostly alone, the hum of so much packed humanity felt like something scraping his skin. He did his best to conceal his agitation, believing it would pass, though he also wondered if his time at sea had wrought a fundamental change in his temperament that would bar him from ever living among people again.

With a stab of guilt, he noted how much Kate had changed. The baby in her was gone; even her curls had straightened. The two of them played go-to with Hollis while Sara made supper; when dinner was over, Michael got into bed with her to tell her a story. Not a story from a book: Kate demanded something from real life, a tale of his adventures at sea.

He chose the story of the whale. This was something that had happened about six months before, far out in the Gulf. It was late at night, the water calm and gleaming beneath a full moon, when his boat began to lift, as if the sea were rising. A dark bulge emerged off his port side. At first he didn't know what it was. He had read about whales but never seen one, and his sense of such a creature's dimensions was vague, even disbelieving. How could something so big be alive? As the whale slowly breached the surface, a spout of water shot from its head; the creature rolled lazily onto its side, one massive flipper lifting clear. Its flanks, shiny and black, were encrusted with barnacles. Michael was too amazed to be afraid; only later did it occur to him that with one slap of its tail, the whale could have shattered his boat to pieces.

Kate was staring at him, wide-eyed. "What happened?"

Well, Michael went on, that was the funny thing. He had expected the whale to move on, but it didn't. For nearly an hour it ran alongside the *Nautilus*. Occasionally it would duck its enormous head beneath the surface, only to reappear a few moments later with a spout from its blowhole, like a big wet sneeze. Then, as the moon was setting, the creature descended and did not reappear. Michael waited. Was it finally gone? Several minutes passed; he began to relax. Then, with an explosion of seawater, it reared upward off his starboard bow, hurling its massive body high into the air. It was, Michael said, like watching a city lift into the sky. *See what I can do? Don't mess with me, brother.* It crashed back down with a second detonation that blasted him broadside and left him drenched. He never saw it again.

Kate was smiling. "I get it. He was playing a joke on you."

Michael laughed. "I guess maybe he was."

He kissed her good night and returned to the main room, where Hollis and Sara were putting up the last of the dishes. The power had been cut for the night; a pair of candles flickered on the table, exuding greasy trails of smoke.

"She's quite a kid."

"Hollis gets the credit," Sara said. "I'm so busy at the hospital I sometimes feel like I barely see her."

Hollis grinned. "It's true."

"I hope a mat on the floor is all right," Sara said. "If I'd known you were coming, I could have gotten a proper cot from the hospital."

"Are you kidding? I usually sleep sitting up. I'm not even sure I actually sleep anymore."

Sara was wiping down the stove with a cloth. A little too aggressively— Michael could sense her frustration. It was an old conversation.

"Look," Michael said, "you don't have to worry about me. I'm fine."

Sara exhaled sharply. "Hollis, talk to him. I know I won't get anywhere."

The man shrugged helplessly. "What do you want me to say?"

"How about 'People love you, stop trying to get yourself killed.'"

"It's not like that," Michael said.

"What Sara is trying to say," Hollis interjected, "is we all hope you're being careful."

"No, that's not at all what I'm saying." She looked at Michael. "Is it Lore? Is that the reason?"

"Lore has nothing to do with it."

"Then tell me, because I'd really like to understand this, Michael."

How should he explain himself? His reasons were so tangled together that they weren't anything he could assemble into an argument. "It just feels right. That's all I can say."

She resumed her overzealous scrubbing. "So you *feel* like you should be scaring the hell out of me."

Michael reached for her, but she shook him away. "Sara—"

"Don't." She refused to look at him. "Don't tell me this is okay. Don't tell me any of this is okay. Goddamnit, I told myself I wouldn't do this. I have to get up early."

Hollis moved in behind her. He placed one hand on her shoulder, the other on the rag, bringing it to a halt and gently taking it from her hand. "We've talked about this. You've got to let him be."

"Oh, listen to you. You probably think it's just great."

Sara had begun to cry. Hollis turned her around and drew her into him. He looked past her shoulder at Michael, who was standing awkwardly by the table. "She's just worn out is all. Maybe you could give us a minute?"

"Sure, yeah."

"Thank you, Michael. The key's right by the door."

Michael let himself out of the apartment and exited the complex. With no-where to go, he took a seat on the ground near the entrance where nobody would bother him. He hadn't felt this bad in a long time. Sara had always been a worrier, but he didn't like upsetting her; it was one of the reasons he came to the city so rarely. He would have liked to make her happy—find someone to marry, settle down with a job just like everybody else, have kids. His sister deserved some peace of mind after all she'd done, stepping in to look after him when their parents had died, though she'd just been a kid herself. Everything they did and said to each other contained this unspoken fact. If things had happened differently, they might have been just like any other brother and sister, their importance to one another fading over time as new connections took precedence. But not the two of them. New people would take the stage, but there would always be a room in their hearts in which only the two of them resided.

When he felt like he'd waited a suitable time, he returned to the apartment. The candles were doused; Sara had left a mat and pillow for him. He un-dressed in the dark and lay down. Only then did he notice the note that Sara had propped on his pack. He lit a candle and read.

I'm sorry. I love you. All eyes.—S

Just three sentences, but they were all he needed. They were the same three sentences that the two of them had been saying to each other every day of their lives.

He awoke to see Kate's face just inches from his own.

"Uncle Michael, *wake . . . up.*"

He drew himself up on his elbows. Hollis was standing by the door. "Sorry. I told her to leave you alone."

It took Michael a moment to gather himself. He wasn't used to sleeping so late. He wasn't used to sleeping at all. "Is Sara here?"

"Gone for hours." He beckoned to his daughter. "Let's go—we're going to be late."

Kate rolled her eyes. "Daddy's scared of the sisters."

"Your daddy's a smart man. Those ladies make my insides twist."

"Michael," said Hollis, "you're not helping."

"Right." He looked at the girl. "Do as your daddy says, sweetheart."

Kate surprised him with a sudden, forceful hug. "Will you be here when I get back?"

"Sure I will."

He listened to their footsteps descending the stairs. You had to hand it to the kid. Pure emotional blackmail, but what could he do? He dressed and washed up at the sink. Sara had left rolls for breakfast, but he wasn't really hungry. He could find something later if he needed to, assuming he actually felt like eating.

He grabbed his pack and headed out.

Sara was finishing her morning rounds when one of the nurses fetched her. She made her way to the reception area to find Sister Peg standing at the desk.

"Sister, hello."

Sister Peg was one of those people who changed any room she entered, tightening every screw. Her age was anybody's guess—at least sixty, though it was said that she'd looked exactly the same for twenty years. A figure of legendary cantankerousness, though Sara knew better; beneath the stern exterior was a woman devoted completely to the children in her care.

"Might I have a word with you, Sara?"

Moments later, they were headed to the orphanage. As they drew near, Sara could hear the whoops and cries of children; morning recess was in full swing. They entered through the garden gate.

"Dr. Sara, Dr. Sara!"

Sara didn't make it five steps onto the playground before the children descended. They knew her well, but part of their excitement, she understood, was the presence of any visitor. She extricated herself with promises to stay longer next time and followed Sister Peg into the building.

The girl was sitting on the table in the little room Sara used for exams. Her eyes flicked up as Sara entered. She could have been twelve or thirteen; it was difficult to tell through the layers of filth. She was wearing a grimy burlap frock, knotted over one shoulder; her feet, blackened with dirt and covered with scabs, were bare.

"Domestic Security brought her in late last night," Sister Peg said. "She hasn't spoken a word."

The girl had been caught trying to break into an ag storehouse. Sara could see why: she looked half-starved.

"Hello, I'm Dr. Sara. Can you tell me your name?"

The girl, peering intently at Sara from under the hood of her matted hair, gave no reply. Her eyes—the only part of her body that had moved since Sara entered the room—darted to Sister Peg, then back at Sara.

"We tried to find out who her parents are," Sister Peg said, "but there's no record of anybody looking for her."

Sara guessed there wouldn't be. She removed her stethoscope from her bag and showed the girl. "I'm going to listen to your heart—would that be okay?"

No words, yet the girl's eyes said she could. Sara slid the knotted side of the frock from her shoulder. She was thin as a reed, but her breasts had just begun to show. At the feel of the cold disk on her skin, the girl flinched slightly, but that was all.

"Sara, you should look at this."

Sister Peg was staring at the girl's back. It was covered with burns and lash marks. Some were old, others still weeping. Sara had seen it before, but never like this.

She looked at the girl. "Honey, can you tell me who did this to you?"

"I don't think she can talk," Sister Peg said.

Sara had begun to grasp the situation. The girl allowed Sara to hold her chin. Sara moved her other hand beside the girl's right ear. She snapped her fingers three times; the girl did not react. She swapped hands to test the other ear. Nothing. Looking into the girl's eyes, Sara then pointed to her own ear and slowly shook her head, meaning no. The girl nodded.

"That's because she's deaf."

Then a surprising thing happened. The girl reached for Sara's hand. With her index finger, she began to draw a series of lines in Sara's upturned palm. Not lines, Sara realized. Letters. P. I. M.

"Pim," Sara said. She glanced at Sister Peg, then looked back at the girl. "Pim—is that your name?"

She nodded. Sara took the girl's palm. SARA, she wrote, and pointed at herself. "Sara." She looked up. "Sister, can you get me something to write with?"

Sister Peg departed the room, returning moments later with one of the handheld chalkboards the children used for their lessons.

WHERE ARE YOUR PARENTS? Sara wrote.

Pim took the board. She erased Sara's words with her palm, then gripped the chalk awkwardly in her fist.

—DED

—WHEN?

—MOM THEN DAD LONG TIM

—WHO HURT YOU?

—MAN

—WHAT MAN?

—DONT KNW GOT AWAY

The next question pained her, but it had to be asked.

—DID HE HURT YOU ANYWHERE ELSE?

The girl hesitated, then nodded. Sara's heart sank.

—WHERE?

Pim took the board.

—GIRLPLACE

Without taking her eyes off the girl, Sara said, "Sister, can you give us a minute?"

When Sister Peg was gone, Sara wrote, MORE THAN ONCE?

The girl nodded.

—NEED TO LOOK. WILL BE CAREFUL.

Pim's whole body clenched. She shook her head vigorously back and forth.

—PLEASE, wrote Sara. HAVE TO MAKE SURE YOU ARE OK.

Pim took the chalkboard and quickly scribbled, MY FALT PROMISST NOT TO TELL

—NO. NOT YOUR FAULT.

—PIM BAD

Sara didn't know if she wanted to cry or be sick. She'd seen some things in her life—terrible things—and not just at the Homeland. You couldn't walk the hospital halls without encountering the worst of human nature. A woman with a broken wrist and an excuse about falling down a flight of stairs, reciting how it had happened while her husband looked on, coaching her with his eyes. An old man with advanced malnutrition dumped at the door by relatives. One of Dunk's whores, her body ravaged with disease and misuse, clutching a fistful of Austins to rid herself of the baby she was carrying so she could get back on the stool. You hardened your heart because there was no other way to get through the day, but the children were the worst. The children you couldn't look away from. In Pim's case, it wasn't hard to reconstruct the story. Her parents dead, somebody had offered to take the girl in, a family member or neighbor, everyone thinking how kind and generous that person was, to assume responsibility for this poor orphan who couldn't hear or talk, and after that nobody had bothered to check.

"No, honey, no." Sara took Pim's hands and looked into her eyes. There was a soul in there, tiny, terrified, discarded by the world. There wasn't anybody more alone on the face of the earth, and Sara understood what was being asked of her, just for being human.

Not even Hollis knew the story. It wasn't that Sara was afraid to tell him; she knew the kind of man he was. But silence was a decision she'd made long ago. At the Homeland, it was said, everybody had taken their turn, and Sara's had come in due course. She had endured it as best she knew how, and when it was over, she imagined a box, made of steel with a strong lock. Then she took the memory and put it in the box.

She took the board and wrote:

—SOMEBODY HURT ME THERE ONCE TOO.

The girl studied the board with the same guarded expression. Perhaps ten seconds passed. She took up the chalk again.

—SECRET?

—YOU ARE THE ONLY PERSON I EVER TOLD.

The girl's face was changing. Something was letting go.

Sara wrote: WE ARE THE SAME. SARA IS GOOD. PIM IS GOOD. NOT OUR FAULT.

A film of tears appeared in the surface of the girl's eyes. A single drop edged over the barrier and spilled down her cheek, cutting a river in the dirt. Her lips were closed; the muscles of her neck and jaw grew taut, then began to quiver. A strange new sound entered the room. It was a kind of growl, like an animal's. It felt like something fighting to get out.

And then it did. The girl opened her mouth and released a howl that seemed to shatter the very idea of human language, distilling it to a single sustained vowel of pain. Sara wrapped her in a tight embrace. Pim was wailing, shaking, fighting to break free, but Sara wouldn't let her. "It's all right," she said. "I won't let you go, I won't let you go." And she held her that way until the girl was quiet again, and for a long time after.

9

The capitol building, housed in what had once been Texas First Trust Bank—the name was still engraved in the building's limestone fascia—was just a short walk from the school. A directory in the lobby listed the various departments: Housing Authority, Public Health, Agriculture and Commerce, Printing and Engraving. Sanchez's office was located on the second floor. Peter ascended the stairs, which opened onto a second open area with a desk, behind which sat a Domestic Security officer in an unnaturally clean uniform. Peter felt suddenly embarrassed to be dressed in his ratty work clothes, carrying a bag full of rattling tools and nails.

"Help you?"

"I'm here to see President Sanchez. I have an appointment."

"Name?" His eyes had returned to his desk; he was filling out some kind of form.

"Peter Jaxon."

It was like a light going on in the man's face. "You're Jaxon?"

Peter dipped his head.

"Holy smokes." The man just sat there, awkwardly staring. It had been some time since Peter had gotten this kind of reaction. On the other hand, he rarely met anybody new these days. Never, in fact.

"Maybe you could let somebody know?" Peter said finally.

"Right." The officer popped from his chair. "Just a second. I'll tell them you're here."

Peter noted the word "them." Who else would be attending the meeting? For that matter, why was he here at all? In the hours of mulling over the president's note, he'd come up empty. Maybe it was just as Caleb had suggested and they really *did* want him back in the Army. If so, it was going to be a short conversation.

"You can come right back, Mr. Jaxon."

The officer took Peter's tool bag and led him down a long hallway. Sanchez's door was open. She rose from behind her desk as Peter entered: a small woman with mostly white hair, sharp features, and a strong gaze. A second person, a man with a tight, bristly beard, was seated across from her. He looked familiar, though Peter couldn't place him.

"Mr. Jaxon, it's good to see you." Sanchez stepped around her desk and extended her hand.

"Madam President. It's an honor."

"Please," she said, "it's Vicky. Let me introduce you to Ford Chase, my chief of staff."

"I believe we've met, Mr. Jaxon."

Now Peter remembered: Chase had attended the inquest after the destruction of the bridge on the Oil Road. The memory was unpleasant; he'd taken an instant disliking to the man. Compounding Peter's distrust, Chase was wearing a necktie, the most incomprehensible article of clothing in the history of the world.

"And of course you know General Apgar," Sanchez said.

Peter turned to see his former commanding officer rising from the couch. Gunnar had aged a little, his clipped hair gone gray, his brow more deeply furrowed. A bit of a paunch stretched the buttons of his uniform. The urge to salute was strong, but Peter held it in check, and the two men shook.

"Congratulations on the promotion, sir." To the surprise of no one who had served under the man, Apgar had been named general of the Army after Fleet had stepped down.

"I regret it every day. Tell me, how's your boy?"

"He's doing well, sir. Thanks for asking."

"If I wanted you to call me 'sir,' I wouldn't have accepted your resignation. Which is my second-biggest regret, by the way. I should have put up more of a fight."

Peter liked Gunnar; the man's presence put him at his ease. "It wouldn't have done you any good."

Sanchez led them to a small sitting area with a sofa and a couple of leather armchairs surrounding a low table with a stone top, on which rested a long tube of rolled paper. For the first time Peter had a chance to look at his surroundings: a wall of books, a curtainless window, a chipped desk piled high with paper. A pole stood behind it bearing the Texas flag, the only ceremonial object in the room. Peter took one of the chairs, across from Sanchez. Apgar and Chase sat to the side.

"To begin, Mr. Jaxon," Sanchez said, "I'm sure you're wondering why I asked you to come see me. I'd like to request a favor. To put this in context, let me show you something. Ford?"

Chase unrolled the paper on the table and weighed down the corners. A surveyor's map: Kerrville stood at the center, its walls and perimeter lines clearly marked. To the west, along the Guadalupe, three large areas were blocked off with cross-hatching, each with a notation: SP1, SP2, SP3.

"At the risk of sounding grandiose, what you're looking at is the future of the Texas Republic," Sanchez said.

Chase explained, "SP stands for 'settlement parcel.'"

"These are the most logical areas for moving out the population, at least to start. There's water, arable soil in the bottoms, good land for grazing. We're going to proceed in stages, using a lottery system for people who want to leave."

"Which will be a lot of them," Chase added.

Peter looked up. Everyone was waiting for his reaction.

"You don't seem pleased," Sanchez said.

He searched for the words. "I guess . . . I never really thought this day would come."

"The war is over," Apgar said. "Three years without a single viral. It's what we've been fighting for, all these years."

Sanchez was leaning forward. There was something tremendously attractive about the woman, an undeniable force. Peter had heard this about her— she was said to have been a great beauty in her youth, with a list of suitors a mile long—but it was an entirely different matter to experience it.

"History will remember you, Peter, for all you've done."

"It was more than just me."

"I know that, too. There's more than enough congratulations to go around. And I'm sorry about your friends. Captain Donadio is a great loss. And Amy, well . . ." She paused. "I'll be honest with you. The stories about her—I was never quite sure what to believe. I'm not sure I completely understand them now. What I do know is that none of us would be having this conversation if not for Amy, and for you. You're the one who brought her to us. That's what the people know. And it makes you very important. You could say there's no one like you." Her eyes remained fixed on his face; she had a way of making it feel as if they were the only two people in the room. "Tell me, how do you like working for the Housing Authority?"

"It's all right."

"And it gives you the chance to raise your boy. To be around for him."

Peter sensed a strategy unfolding. He nodded.

"I never had children," Sanchez said, somewhat regretfully. "One of the costs of the office. But I understand your feelings. So let me say right off that I'm sensitive to your priorities, and nothing about what I'm proposing would get in the way of that. You'll be there for him, just as you are now."

Peter knew a half-truth when he heard one. On the other hand, Sanchez's approach was so carefully laid he couldn't help but admire it.

"I'm listening."

"What would you say, Peter, to joining my staff?"

The notion was so ludicrous he almost laughed. "Forgive me, Madam President—"

"Please," the woman cut in with a smile, "it's Vicky."

He had to admit it, the woman was masterful. "There's so much wrong with the idea I don't even know where to begin. Just for starters, I'm not a politician."

"And I'm not asking you to be one. But you are a leader, and the people know it. You're too valuable a resource to sit on the sidelines. Opening the gate isn't just about making more room, though we absolutely need it. This represents a fundamental change in how we do just about everything. A lot of details have to be hammered out, but within the next ninety days I'm planning to suspend martial law. The Expeditionary is going to be recalled from the territories to assist with resettlement, and we'll be transitioning to a full civilian government. It's a big adjustment, giving everybody a place at the table, and it's going to be messy. But it absolutely has to happen, and this is the right moment."

"With all due respect, I don't see what this has to do with me."

"It has everything to do with you, actually. Or at least I hope so. Your position is unique. The military respects you. The people love you, especially the Iowans. But those are only two legs of the tripod. The third is the trade. They're going to have a field day with this. Tifty Lamont may be dead, but your previous relationship with him gives you access to their chain of command. There's no question of shutting them down, we couldn't if we tried. Vice is a fact of life—an ugly fact, but a fact nonetheless. You know Dunk Withers, yes?"

Peter nodded. "We've met."

"More than met, if what my sources tell me is correct. I've heard about the cage. That was quite a stunt."

She was referring to Peter's first encounter with Tifty at his underground compound north of San Antonio. As a cathartic entertainment, members of the trade leadership would face off against virals in hand-to-hand combat, the others betting on the outcome. Dunk had gone into the cage first, dispatching a dopey with relative ease, followed by Peter, who had taken on a full-blown drac in order to secure Tifty's agreement to escort them to Iowa.

"It seemed like the thing to do at the time."

Sanchez smiled. "That's my point. You're a man who does what needs to be done. As for Dunk, the man's not half as smart as Lamont was, and I wish he were. Our agreement with Lamont was a simple one. The man was sitting on some of the best-preserved military hardware we'd seen in years. We couldn't have outfitted the Army without him. Keep the worst stuff in check, we told him, keep the guns and ammo coming, and you can go about your business. He understood the sense of it, but I doubt Dunk will. The man's a pure opportunist, and he has an ugly streak."

"So why not just put him in the stockade?"

Sanchez shrugged. "We could, and it may come to that. General Apgar thinks we should round up the lot of them, seize the bunker and the gambling halls, and put an end to it. But somebody else would slide into his spot before the ink was dry, and we'd be back to square one. It's a case of supply and demand. The demand is there—who will supply the goods? The card tables, the lick, the prostitutes? I don't like it, but I'd rather deal with a known quantity, and for now that's Dunk."

"So you want me to talk to him."

"Yes, in time. Corralling the trade is important. So is keeping the military and the civilian population fully on board during the transition. You're the one man who has stock with all three. Hell, you could probably have my job if you asked for it, not that I'd wish it on my worst enemy."

Peter had the unsettling feeling that he had already agreed to something. He looked at Apgar, whose face said, *Believe me, I've been down this road.*

"What exactly are you asking?"

"For now, I'd like to name you as a special adviser. A go-between, if you like, between the stakeholders. We can come up with a more specific title later. But I want you out in front, where everyone can see you. Your voice should be the first one people hear. And I promise you that you'll be home for supper every day with your boy."

The temptation was real: no more sweltering days swinging a hammer. But he was also tired. Some essential energy had left him. He'd done enough, and what he wanted now was a quiet, simple life. To take his boy to school and do a day of honest labor, and put his boy to bed at night and spend eight sweet hours someplace else entirely—the only place where he had ever been truly happy.

"No."

Sanchez startled; she wasn't used to being denied so succinctly. "No?"

"That's it. That's my answer."

"Surely there's something I can say that will change your mind."

"I'm flattered, but this has to be somebody else's problem. I'm sorry."

Sanchez didn't seem angry, merely puzzled. "I see." The disarming smile returned. "Well, I had to ask."

She rose to her feet, everyone else following suit. Now it was Peter's turn to be surprised; he realized he'd expected her to put up more of a fight. At the door, she shook his hand in parting.

"Thank you for taking the time to meet with me, Peter. The offer stands, and I hope you'll reconsider. You could do a lot of good. Promise me you'll think about it?"

There seemed no harm in agreeing. "I'll do that."

"General Apgar can show you out."

So that was it. He felt a little amazed, and wondered, as one always did when a door closed, if he had made the right choice.

"Peter, one last thing," Sanchez said.

He turned at the threshold. The woman had returned to her desk.

"I was meaning to ask. How old is your boy?"

The question seemed harmless enough. "He's ten."

"And it's Caleb, yes?"

Peter nodded.

"It's a wonderful age. His whole life ahead of him. When you stop to think about it, it's the children we're really working for, isn't it? We'll be long gone, but our decisions in the next few months will determine the kind of world they're going to live in." She smiled. "Well. Food for thought, Mr. Jaxon. Thank you again for coming."

He followed Gunnar out the door. Halfway down the hall, Peter heard the man chuckling under his breath.

"She's good, isn't she?"

"Yeah," said Peter. "She's good all right."

10

Michael had three things in his bag. The first was the newspaper. The second was a letter.

He had found it in the breast pocket of the captain's uniform. The envelope was unmarked; the man had never intended to send it. The letter, less than a page, was written in English.

> *My darling boy,*
> *I know now that you and I are never to meet in this life. Our fuel is nearly exhausted; our last hope of reaching the refuge is gone. Last night, the crew and passengers took a vote. The result was unanimous. Death by dehydration is a fate none desires. Tonight will be the last we share on earth. Entombed in steel, we will drift in the currents until such time as almighty God chooses to take us to the bottom.*
>
> *I obviously have no hope that these last words will reach you. I can only pray that you and your mother have been spared the devastation and somehow survived. What awaits me now? The Holy Quran says: "To Allah belongeth the Mystery of the heavens and the earth. And the Decision of the Hour of Judgment*

*is as the twinkling of an eye, or even quicker: for Allah hath
power over all things." Surely we are His and to Him we shall
return. In spite of all that has happened, I have faith that my
immortal soul will pass into His hands, and that when at last we
meet, it shall be in paradise.*

My final thoughts in life are with you. Baraka Allahu fika.

Your loving father,
Nabil

Michael mused on these words as he made his way through the streets of
H-town. He was accustomed to scenes of abandonment and devastation; he
had crossed ruined cities that contained skeletons by the thousands. But never
before had the dead spoken so directly to him. In the captain's quarters, he had
found the man's passport. His full name was Nabil Haddad. He had been born
in the Netherlands, in a city called Utrecht, in 1971. Michael found no further
evidence of the boy in the cabin—no photographs or other letters—but the
emergency contact named in his passport was a woman named Astrid Keeble,
with a London address. Perhaps she was the boy's mother. Michael wondered
what had happened between the three of them, that the captain never should
have seen his son. Perhaps the boy's mother wouldn't allow it; perhaps for
some reason the man did not feel worthy. Yet he had felt the need to write to
him, knowing that in a few hours he would be dead and the letter would travel
no farther than his own pocket.

But that wasn't all the letter told him. The *Bergensfjord* had been going
somewhere; it had had a destination. Not "a refuge," "*the* refuge." A safe
haven where the virus could not reach them.

Hence the third thing in Michael's bag, and his need for the man they called
the Maestro.

If the man had a real name, Michael didn't know it. The Maestro also had
the habit of speaking in disconcertingly butchered sentences while always referring to himself in the third person; it took some getting used to. He was
quite old, possessing a sinewy twitchiness that made him seem less like a man
than some kind of overgrown rodent. He had once been an electrical engineer
for the Civilian Authority; long retired, he had become Kerrville's go-to man
for electronic antiquities. Crazy as a caged bird, and not a little paranoid, but
the man knew how to make an old hard drive confess its secrets.

The Maestro's shed was unmissable; it was the only building in H-town
with solar panels on the roof. Michael knocked loudly and stepped back for the
camera; the Maestro wanted a good look at you first. A moment passed, and
then a series of heavy locks opened.

"Michael." The Maestro stood in a narrow wedge of open door, wearing a work apron and a plastic visor with flip-down lenses.

"Hello, Maestro."

The man's eyes darted up and down the street. "Quickly," he said, waving Michael inside.

The shed's interior was like a museum. Old computers, office machines, oscilloscopes, flat-panels, huge bins of handhelds and cellphones: the sight of so much circuitry always gave Michael a tingly thrill.

"How can the Maestro be of assistance?"

"I've got an antique for you."

Michael removed the third thing from his bag. The old man took it in his hand and examined it quickly.

"Gensys 872HJS. Fourth generation, three terabytes. Late prewar." He looked up. "Where?"

"I found it on a derelict ship. I need to recover the files."

"A closer look, then."

Michael followed him to one of several workbenches, where he laid the drive on a cloth mat and flipped down the lenses of his visor. With a minuscule screwdriver he removed the case and perused the interior parts.

"Moisture damage. Not good."

"Can you fix it?"

"Difficult. Expensive."

Michael removed a wad of Austins from his pocket. The old man counted it on the bench.

"Not enough."

"It's what I've got."

"The Maestro doubts that. Oil man like yourself?"

"Not anymore."

He studied Michael's face. "Ah. The Maestro remembers. He has heard some crazy stories. True?"

"Depends on what you heard."

"Hunting for the barrier. Sailing out alone."

"More or less."

The old man pursed his rubbery lips, then slid the money into the pocket of his apron. "The Maestro will see what he can do. Come back tomorrow."

Michael returned to the apartment. In the meantime he'd been to the library, adding a heavy book to his satchel: *The Reader's Digest Great World Atlas.* It wasn't one that people were permitted to check out. He'd waited for the reference librarian to be distracted, concealed it in his bag, and slipped outside.

Once again, he was called upon for a bedtime story. This one was about the storm. Kate listened with tense excitement, as if the story might end with him drowned in the sea, despite the fact that he was sitting right in front of her. With Sara, the subject of the previous night did not come up. This was their way; a lot was said by saying nothing. She also seemed distracted. Michael assumed that something had happened at the hospital and let it go at that.

In the morning he left the apartment before anyone else was awake. The old man was waiting for him.

"The Maestro has done it," he declared.

He led Michael to a CRT. His hands scurried over the keyboard; a glowing map appeared on the screen. "The ship. Where?"

"I found it in Galveston Bay, at the mouth of the ship channel."

"Long way from home."

The Maestro walked Michael through the data. Departing from Hong Kong in mid-March, the *Bergensfjord* had sailed to Hawaii, then passed through the Panama Canal into the Atlantic. According to the time line Michael had established from the newspaper, that much would have occurred before the outbreak of the Easter Virus. They had made port in the Canary Islands, perhaps to refuel, then continued north.

At this point, the data changed. The ship had traveled in circles up and down the coast of northern Europe. A brief foray to the Strait of Gibraltar, then it reversed course without entering the Mediterranean and returned to Tenerife. Several weeks elapsed, and they set sail again. The epidemic would have been widespread by this time. They passed through the Strait of Magellan and headed north toward the equator.

In midocean, the ship appeared to stop. After two motionless weeks, the data ended.

"Can we tell where they were headed?" Michael asked.

Another screen of data appeared: these were course plottings, the Maestro explained. He scrolled down the page and directed Michael's attention to the last one.

"Can you back that up for me?" Michael asked.

"Already done." The old man produced a flash drive from his apron; Michael put it in his pocket. "The Maestro is curious. Why so important?"

"I was thinking of taking a vacation."

"The Maestro has already checked. Empty ocean. Nothing there." His pale eyebrows lifted. "But something, perhaps?"

The man was no fool. "Perhaps," said Michael.

*   *   *

He left Sara a note. *Sorry to run. Visiting an old friend. Hope to be back in a few days.*

The second transport to the Orange Zone left at 0900. Michael rode it to the end of the line, got off, and waited as the bus drove away. The posted sign read:

YOU ARE ENTERING THE RED ZONE.
PROCEED AT OWN RISK.
WHEN IN DOUBT, RUN.

If you only knew, he thought. Then he began to walk.

11

Sara returned to the orphanage before the start of her morning shift. Sister Peg greeted her at the door.

"How is she doing?" Sara asked.

The woman looked more harried than usual; it had been a long night for her. "Not very well, I'm afraid."

Pim had woken up screaming. Her howls were so loud that they had awakened the entire dormitory. For the time being, they had put her in Sister Peg's quarters.

"We've had abused children before, but nothing so extreme. Another night like that . . ."

Sister Peg led Sara to her room, a monastic space with just the bare-bones necessities. The only decoration was a large cross on the wall. Pim was awake and sitting on the bed with her knees tight to her chest. But as Sara entered, some of the tension released from her face. *Here is an ally, someone who knows.*

"I'll be outside if you need me," Sister Peg said.

Sara sat on the bed. The grime was gone, the mats in her hair teased straight or cut away. The sisters had dressed her in a plain wool tunic.

—HOW ARE YOU FEELING TODAY? Sara wrote on the chalkboard.

—OK

—SISTER SAID YOU COULDN'T SLEEP.

Pim shook her head.

Sara explained to Pim that she needed to change her dressings. The girl flinched as Sara eased away the bandages but made no sound. Sara applied antibiotic salve and a cream of cooling aloe and rewrapped her.

—I'M SORRY IF THAT HURT.

Pim shrugged.

Sara looked her in the eye. IT WILL BE OK, she wrote. Then, when the girl did nothing: IT GETS BETTER.

—NO MOR NITEMERES?

Sara shook her head. "No."

—HOW?

There was, of course, the easy thing to say: *Give it time.* But that wasn't the truth, or at least not the whole truth. What took the pain away, Sara knew, was other people—Hollis, and Kate, and being a family.

—IT JUST DOES, she wrote.

It was nearly 0800; Sara had to leave, though she didn't want to. She packed up her kit and wrote:

—I HAVE TO GO NOW. TRY TO REST. THE SISTERS WILL TAKE CARE OF YOU.

—COME BACK? Pim wrote.

Sara nodded.

—DO YU SWEAR?

Pim was looking at her intently. People had been throwing her away her entire life; why should Sara be different?

"Yes," she said, and crossed her heart. "I swear."

Sister Peg was waiting for Sara in the hall. "How is she?"

The day had only just started, yet Sara felt completely drained. "The wounds on her back aren't the real problem. I wouldn't be surprised if she has more nights like that."

"Is there any chance of finding a relative? Somebody who can take her in?"

"I think that would be the worst thing for her."

Sister Peg nodded. "Yes, of course. That was stupid of me."

Sara gave the woman a roll of gauze, boiled cloth pads, and a jar of ointment. "Change her dressings every twelve hours. There's no sign of infection, but if anything starts to look worse, or she gets a fever, send for me right away."

Sister Peg was frowning at the objects in her hand. Then, brightening a little, she looked up. "I meant to thank you for the other night. It was nice to get out. I should do it more often."

"Peter was happy to have you there."

"Caleb has grown so much. Kate, too. Sometimes it's easy to forget how lucky we are. Then you see something like this . . ." She let the thought pass.

"I'd better get back to the children. Where would they be without mean old Sister Peg?"

"It's a good act, if you don't mind my saying so."

"Does it show? I'm really just an old softie at heart."

She walked Sara out. At the doorway, Sara paused. "Let me ask you something. In the course of a year, say, how many children get adopted?"

"In a year?" The woman seemed startled by the question. "Zero."

"None at *all*?"

"It happens, but very rarely. And it's never the older children, if that's what you're asking. Sometimes a baby will be left here and a relative will come and claim it within a few days. But once a child has been here awhile, the odds are good they'll stay."

"I didn't know."

Her eyes searched Sara's face. "The two of us aren't so very different, you know. Ten times a day our jobs give us good reason to cry. And yet we can't. We wouldn't be any use to anyone if we did."

It was true; but it didn't make Sara's heart feel any less heavy. "Thank you, Sister."

She headed for the hospital. Her mood was bleak. As she entered the building, Wendy urgently waved her over to the desk.

"There's somebody waiting for you."

"A patient?"

The woman looked around to make sure she wasn't overheard. She lowered her voice to a whisper. "He says he's from the *census office.*"

Uh-oh, thought Sara. *That was fast.* "Where is he?"

"I told him to wait, but he went to look for you on the ward. Jenny's with him."

"You let *Jenny* talk to him? Are you nuts?"

"There wasn't anything I could do! She was standing right there when he asked for you!" Wendy lowered her voice again. "It's about that woman with the abruption, isn't it?"

"Let's hope not."

At the door to the ward, Sara took a clean smock from the shelf. Two things worked in her favor. The first was her rank. She was a doctor, and although she didn't like to do it, she could throw her weight around if she had to. A certain peremptory tone; veiled or not-so-veiled references to unnamed persons of substantial influence; the mantle of the higher calling, busy day, lives to save: Sara had learned the tricks. Second, she hadn't done anything illegal. Failing to file the proper paperwork was not a crime—more like an error. She was safe, more or less, but this wouldn't help Carlos or his family. Once the fraud was discovered, Grace would be taken away.

She stepped into the ward. Jenny was standing with a man who possessed the unmistakable look of a bureaucrat: soft, balding, and flat-footed, with pasty skin that rarely saw sunshine. Jenny's glance met hers with a look of barely concealed panic: *Help!*

"Sara," she began, "this is—"

She didn't let the girl finish. "Jenny, could you please check the laundry for blankets? I think we're running low."

"We are?"

"Now, please."

She scurried away.

"I'm Dr. Wilson," Sara said to the man. "What is this about?"

The man cleared his throat. He seemed a little nervous. Good. "There was a woman who delivered a girl here four nights ago." He fumbled through the papers he was holding. "Sally Jiménez? I believe you were the doctor on duty."

"And you are?"

"Joe English. I'm from the census office."

"I have a lot of patients, Mr. English." She pretended to think. "Oh, yes, I remember. A healthy girl. Is there an issue?"

"No birthright certificate was filed with the census form. The woman has two sons."

"I'm sure I took care of it. You'll have to check again."

"I spent all yesterday looking for it. It definitely wasn't sent to my office."

"Your office never makes mistakes? Loses paperwork?"

"We're very thorough, Dr. Wilson. According to the nurse at the desk, Mrs. Jiménez was released three days ago. We always talk to the family first, but they don't seem to be home. Her husband hasn't been to work since the birth."

Dumb move, Carlos, Sara thought. "I can't be responsible for people once they leave here."

"But you *are* responsible for filing the proper documentation. Without a valid birthright, I'm going to have to move her case up the line."

"Well, I'm sure there was one. You're mistaken. Is that all? I'm very busy here."

He regarded her for an uncomfortably long moment. "For now, Dr. Wilson."

Wherever the Jiménez family had gone, Sara knew it wouldn't take long for the census office to track them down. There were only so many places to hide.

She tried to put them out of her mind. She'd done her best to help, and the situation was out of her hands. Sister Peg was right; she had a job to do. It was important, and she was good at it. That was what mattered most.

In the middle of the night, she awoke with the feeling that a powerful dream had ejected her from sleep. She rose and checked on Kate. She felt certain that her daughter had been in this dream, if peripherally; she had not been the focus—rather, a witness, almost a judge. Sara sat on the edge of her daughter's cot and watched the night pass through her. The girl was deeply asleep, her lips slightly parted, her chest expanding and contracting with long, even breaths, filling the air with her unmistakable scent. At the Homeland, in the time before Sara had found her again, it was Kate's smell that had given her the strength to go on. She'd kept a baby curl in an envelope, hidden away in her bunk, and each night she had taken it out and pressed it to her face. This act was, Sara knew, a form of prayer—not that Kate was still alive, because she'd believed absolutely that her daughter was dead, but that wherever she was, wherever her spirit had gone, it felt like home.

"Is everything okay?"

Hollis was standing behind her. Kate stirred, rolled over, and then was quiet again.

"Come back to bed," he whispered.

"I can sleep in. I'm on second shift."

Hollis said nothing.

"All right," she said.

When dawn came, Sara was wide awake. Hollis told her to stay in bed, but she got up anyway; she wouldn't return from the hospital until after dinner and wanted to take Kate to school. She was half-drunk with exhaustion, although this fact did not seem like a compromising influence on her judgment but a source of clarity. At the door of the school, she hugged her daughter tightly. It did not seem so long ago that Sara had needed to kneel to do this; now the crown of Kate's head reached Sara's chest.

"Mom?"

The hug had gone on for some time. "Sorry." Sara released her. The other children were streaming past. She realized what she was feeling. She was happy; a weight had lifted from her heart. "Go on, kiddo," she said. "I'll see you later."

The records office opened at nine o'clock. Sara waited on the steps in the dappled shade of a live oak. It was a pleasant summer morning; people were striding past. How quickly life could change, she thought.

When the clerk unlocked the door, Sara rose and followed the woman inside. She was older, with a pleasant, weathered face and a row of bright false teeth. She took her time situating herself behind the counter before looking Sara's way, pretending to notice her for the first time.

"Can I help you?"

"I need to transfer a birthright."

The clerk licked her fingers and removed a form from a slotted shelf, then placed it on the counter and dipped her quill in a bottle of ink. "Whose?"

"Mine."

The woman's pen halted over the paper. She raised her face with an expression of concern. "You seem young, honey. Are you sure?"

"Please, can we just do this?"

Sara sent the form to the census office with a note attached—*Sorry! Found it after all!*—and went to the hospital. The day passed quickly; Hollis was still awake when she got home. She waited until they were in bed to make her announcement.

"I want to have another child."

He rose on his elbows and turned toward her. "Sara, we've been through this. You know we can't."

She kissed him, long and tenderly, then drew back to meet his eyes. "Actually," she said, "that's not exactly true."

12

Ten moves, and Caleb had Peter completely boxed in. A feint with a rook, a knight cruelly sacrificed, and the enemy forces swarmed over him.

"How the heck did you do that?"

Peter didn't really mind, though it would be nice to win once in a while. The last time he'd beaten Caleb, the boy had had a nasty cold and had dozed off midway through the game. Even then, Peter had barely eked out the victory.

"It's easy. You think I'm on defense, but I'm not."

"Laying a trap."

The boy shrugged. "It's like a trap in your head. I make you see the game the way I need you to." He was setting up the pieces again; one victory was not enough for the night. "What did the soldier want?"

Caleb had a way of changing the subject so abruptly that sometimes Peter struggled to keep up. "It was about a job, actually."

"What kind?"

"To tell you the truth, I'm not really sure." He shrugged and looked at the board. "It's not important. Don't worry about it—I'm not going anywhere."

They were listlessly moving pawns.

"I still want to be a soldier, you know," the boy said, "like you were."

From time to time, the boy brought this up. Peter's feelings were mixed. On the one hand, he had a parent's intense desire to keep Caleb away from any danger. But he also felt flattered. The boy was, after all, expressing interest in the same life he had chosen.

"Well, you'd be good at it."

"Do you miss it?"

"Sometimes. I liked my men, I had good friends. But I'd rather be here with you. Plus, it looks like those days are over. Not much need for an army when there's nobody to fight."

"Everything else seems like it would be boring."

"Boredom is underrated, believe me."

They played in silence.

"Somebody asked me about you," Caleb said. "A kid at school."

"What was the question?"

Caleb squinted at the board, reached toward his bishop, stopped, and moved his queen one space forward. "Just, what it's like, you being my dad. He knew a lot about you."

"Which kid was this?"

"His name is Julio."

He wasn't one of Caleb's usual friends. "What did you tell him?"

"I told him you worked on roofs all day."

For once, Peter held Caleb to a draw. He put the boy to bed and poured himself a drink from Hollis's flask. Caleb's words had stung a little. Peter wasn't truly tempted by Sanchez's offer, but the whole thing had left a bad taste in his mouth. The woman's manipulation was transparent, as it was meant to be—that was the genius of it. She had simultaneously aroused his natural sense of duty and made it clear that she was not a woman to be messed with. *I'll have you in the end, Mr. Jaxon.*

Just you try, he thought. I'll be right here, reminding my kid to brush his teeth.

They were reroofing an old mission close to the center of town. Empty for decades, it was now being converted to apartments. Peter's crew had spent two weeks dismantling the rotted belfry and had begun to strip off the old slates. The roof was steeply pitched; they worked on twelve-inch-wide horizontal boards, called cleats, anchored by metal brackets nailed into the sheeting and spaced at six-foot intervals. A pair of ladders, lying flush with the roof at the ends of the cleats, acted as staircases connecting them.

All morning they worked shirtless in the heat. Peter was on the uppermost cleat with two others, Jock Alvado and Sam Foutopolis, who went by the name Foto. Foto had worked construction for years, but Jock had been there just a couple of months. He was young, seventeen or so, with a narrow, acned face and long greasy hair he wore in a ponytail. Nobody liked him; his movements were too sudden, and he talked too much. It was an unwritten rule of the roofing crews not to remark on the danger. It was a form of respect. Looking down, Jock liked to say stupid things like "Wow, that would hurt" and "That would most definitely fuck a person *up.*"

At noon they broke for lunch. Climbing down was too much trouble, so they ate where they were. Jock was talking about a girl he had seen in the market, but Peter was barely listening. The sounds of the city drifted upward in an aural haze; from time to time a bird floated past.

"Let's get back to it," Foto said.

They were using pry bars and mallets to chip out the old tiles. Peter and Foto moved to the third cleat; Jock was working below them to the right. He was still talking about the woman—her hair, a certain way she walked, a look that passed between them.

"Will he ever shut up?" Foto said. He was a thick, muscular man, his black beard sprinkled with gray.

"I think he just likes the sound of his own voice."

"I'm going to throw his ass off this roof, I swear." Foto glanced up, squinting into the sun. "Looks like we missed a couple."

Several tiles remained along the ridgeline. Peter slid his bar and mallet into his tool belt. "I'll go."

"Forget it, lover boy can do it." He yelled down, "Jock, get up there."

"I'm not the one who missed those. That was Jaxon's section."

"It's yours now."

"Fine," the boy huffed. "Whatever you say."

Jock unclipped his harness, scrambled up the ladder to the uppermost cleat, and wedged his pry bar under one of the tiles. As he lifted the mallet to strike, Peter realized he was straight above them.

"Wait a sec—"

The tile popped free. It sang past, narrowly missing Foto's head.

"You idiot!"

"Sorry, I didn't see you there."

"Where did you *think* we were?" Foto said. "You did that on purpose. And clip in, for Christ's sake."

"It was an accident," Jock said. "Calm down. You'll have to move."

They shifted to the side. Jock finished up and had begun to climb down when Peter heard a pop. Jock let out a yelp. A second pop, and with a loud clatter the ladder rocketed down the roof with Jock still attached. At the last second he lunged clear and began to slide down the roof on his belly. After his first cry, he hadn't made a sound. His hands were madly searching for something to grab hold of, his toes digging into the tiles to slow his descent. Nobody had ever fallen that Peter knew of. Suddenly this seemed not possible but inevitable; Jock was the one chosen.

Ten feet from the edge his body halted. His hand had found something: a rusty spike.

"Help!"

Peter unclipped and scrambled down to the lowest cleat. Gripping a bracket, he leaned out. "Take my hand."

The boy was frozen with terror. His right hand was clutching the spike, his left gripping the edge of a tile. Every inch of him was pressed to the surface.

"If I move I'll fall."

"No, you won't."

Far below, people had stopped on the street to look.

"Foto, toss me my safety line," Peter said.

"It won't reach. I'll have to reset the anchor."

The spike was bending under Jock's weight. "Oh God, I'm slipping!"

"Stop squirming. Foto, hurry up with that rope."

Down it came. Peter had no time to clip in; the boy was about to fall. As Foto pulled the line taut through the block, Peter wrapped it around his forearm and lunged toward Jock. The spike broke loose; Jock began to slide.

"I've got you!" Peter yelled. "Hold on!"

Peter had him by the wrist. Jock's feet were inches from the edge.

"Find something to grip," Peter said.

"There's nothing!"

Peter didn't know how much longer he could hold him. "Foto, can you pull us up?"

"You're too heavy!"

"Tie it off and get down here with some brackets."

A small crowd had gathered on the street. Many were pointing upward. The distance to the ground had enlarged, becoming an infinite space that would swallow them whole. A few seconds passed; then Foto was moving across the cleat above them.

"What do you want me to do?"

Peter said, "Jock, there's a small lip at the edge just below you. Try to find it with your feet."

"It's not there!"

"Yes, it is—I'm looking right at it."

A moment later, Jock said, "Okay, got it."

"Take a deep breath, okay? I'm going to have to let you go for a second."

Jock tightened his grip on Peter's wrist. "Are you kidding me?"

"I can't get you up unless I do. Just lie still. I guarantee, the lip will hold you if you don't move."

The man had no choice. Slowly he released his grip.

"Foto, toss me a bracket."

Peter caught it with his free hand, wedged it under a seam in the tiles, removed a nail from his tool belt, and pressed it into the gap until it bit. Three strokes of the mallet drove it home. He set the second nail, then lowered himself a few feet.

"Toss me another."

"Please," Jock moaned, "hurry."

"Deep breaths. This will all be over in a minute."

Peter set three more brackets in place. "Okay, carefully reach up and to your left. Got it?"

Jock's hand gripped the bracket. "Yeah. Jesus."

"Now pull yourself up to the next one. Take your time—there's no hurry."

Bracket by bracket, Jock ascended. Peter followed him up. Jock was sitting on the cleat, gulping water from a canteen. Peter crouched beside him.

"Okay?"

Jock nodded vaguely. His face was pale, his hands trembling.

"Just take a minute," Peter said.

"Hell, take the whole day," said Foto. "Take the rest of your life."

Jock was staring into space. Though he wasn't really seeing anything, Peter guessed.

"Try to relax," Peter said.

Jock glanced down at Peter's harness. "You weren't clipped in?"

"There wasn't time."

"So you just . . . did all that. Holding the rope."

"It worked, didn't it?"

Jock looked away. "I thought I was dead for sure."

"You know what gets me?" Foto said. "That little shit didn't even thank you."

They'd knocked off early; the two of them were sitting on the front steps, passing a flask. They'd seen the last of Jock; he'd turned in his tool belt and walked off.

"That was smart, with the brackets," Foto continued. "I wouldn't have thought of that."

"You might have. I just got there first."

"That kid is fucking lucky, is all I have to say. And look at you, not even rattled."

It was true: he'd felt invincible, his mind perfectly focused, his thoughts clear as ice. In fact, there was no lip at the edge of the roof; the surface was perfectly smooth. *I make you see the game the way I need you to.*

Foto capped the flask and got to his feet. "So I guess I'll see you tomorrow."

"Actually, I think that's it for me," Peter said.

Foto stared at him, then gave a quiet chuckle. "Anybody else, I'd figure they were worried about getting killed. You'd probably like it if somebody fell every day so you could catch them. What will you do instead?"

"Somebody's offered me a job. I thought I wasn't interested, but maybe I am."

The man nodded evenly. "Whatever it is, it's got to be more interesting than this. It's true what they say about you." They shook hands. "Good luck to you, Jaxon."

Peter watched him go, then walked to the capitol. As he entered Sanchez's office, she glanced up from her papers.

"Mr. Jaxon. That was fast. I thought I was going to have to work a little harder."

"Two conditions. Actually, three."

"The first is your son, of course. I've given you my word. What else?"

"I want direct access to you. No middlemen."

"What about Chase? The man's my chief of staff."

"Just you."

She thought only a moment. "If that's what it takes. What's the third?"

"Don't make me wear a necktie."

The sun had just set when Michael knocked on the door of Greer's cabin. There was no light inside, no sound. *Well, I've walked too long to wait out here,* he thought. *I'm sure Lucius won't mind.*

He put his bag on the floor and lit the lamp. He looked around. Greer's pictures: How many were there? Fifty? A hundred? He stepped closer. Yes, his memory had not betrayed him. Some were hasty sketches; others had obviously required hours of focused labor. Michael selected one of the paintings, untacked it from the wall, and laid it on the table: a mountainous island, bathed in green, seen from the bow of a ship, which was just visible at the bottom edge. The sky above and behind the island was a deep twilight blue; at its center, at forty-five degrees to the horizon, was a constellation of five stars.

The door flew open. Greer stood at the threshold, pointing a rifle at Michael's head.

"Flyers, put that *down*," Michael said.

Greer lowered the gun. "It's not loaded anyway."

"Good to know." Michael tapped the paper with his finger. "Remember when I said you should tell me about these?"

Greer nodded.

"Now would be the time."

The constellation was the Southern Cross—the most distinctive feature of the night sky south of the equator.

Michael showed Greer the newspaper, which the man read without reaction, as if its contents came as no surprise to him; he described the *Bergensfjord* and the bodies he'd found; he read the captain's letter aloud, the first time he had done this. It felt very different to speak the words, as if he were not overhearing a conversation but enacting it. For the first time, he glimpsed what the man had intended by writing a letter that could never be sent; it imparted a kind of permanence to the words and the emotions they contained. Not a letter but an epitaph.

Michael saved the data from the *Bergensfjord*'s navigational computer for last. The ship's destination had been a region of the South Pacific roughly halfway between northern New Zealand and the Cook Islands; Michael used the atlas to show Greer. When the ship's engines had failed, they had been fifteen hundred miles north-northeast of their goal, traveling in the equatorial currents.

"So how did it end up in Galveston?" Greer asked.

"It shouldn't have. It should have sunk, just like the captain said."

"Yet it didn't."

Michael frowned. "It's possible the currents could have pushed it here. I don't really know much about it. I'll tell you one thing it means. There's no barrier and never was."

Lucius looked at the newspaper again. He pointed midway down the page. "This here, about the virus having an avian source—"

"Birds."

"I'm familiar with the word, Michael. Does it mean the virus could still be out there?"

"If they're carriers, it might be. Sounds like the people in charge never figured it out, though."

"'In rare instances,'" Greer read aloud, "'victims of the illness have exhibited the transformative effects of the North American strain, including a marked increase in aggressiveness, but whether any of these individuals have survived past the thirty-six-hour threshold is not known.'"

"That got my attention, too."

"Are they talking about virals?"

"If so, they're a different strain."

"Meaning they could still be alive. Killing the Twelve wouldn't have affected them."

Michael didn't say anything.

"Good God."

"You want to know what's funny?" Michael said. "Maybe *funny*'s not the right word. The world quarantined us and left us to die. In the end, it's the only reason we're still here."

Greer rose from the table and fetched a whiskey bottle from the shelf. He poured two glasses, handed one to Michael, and sipped. Michael did the same.

"Think about it, Lucius. That ship traveled halfway around the world, never bumping into anything, never running aground, never downflooding in a storm. Somehow it manages to make its way perfectly intact, into Galveston Bay, right under our noses. What are the odds?"

"Not good, I'd say."

"So you tell me what it's doing here. You're the one who drew those pictures."

Greer poured more into his glass but didn't drink it. He was silent for a moment, then said, "It's what I saw."

"What do you mean, 'saw'?"

"It's difficult to explain."

"None of this is easy, Lucius."

Greer was staring into his glass, turning it around on the tabletop. "I was in the desert. Don't ask me what I was doing there—it's a long story. I hadn't had anything to eat or drink for days. Something happened to me in the night. I'm not really sure what to call it. I guess it was a dream, though it was stronger than that, more real."

"This image, you mean. The island, the five stars."

Lucius nodded. "I was on a ship. I could feel it moving under me. I could hear the waves, smell the salt."

"Was it the *Bergensfjord*?"

He shook his head. "All I know is, it was big."

"Were you alone?"

"There may have been other people there, but I couldn't see them. I couldn't turn around." Greer looked at him pointedly. "Michael, are you thinking what I think you're thinking?"

"That depends."

"That the ship is meant for us. That we're supposed to go to the island."

"How else can you explain it?"

"I can't." He frowned skeptically. "This isn't at all like you. To put so much faith in a picture drawn by a crazy man."

For a moment, neither man spoke. Michael sipped his whiskey.

"This ship," Greer said. "Will it float?"

"I don't know how much damage there is below the waterline. The lower decks are flooded, but the engine compartment's dry."

"Can you fix it?"

"Maybe, but it'd take an army. And lots of money, which we don't have."

Greer drummed his fingers on the table. "There are ways around that. Assuming we had the manpower, how long would we need?"

"Years. Hell, maybe decades. We'd have to drain her, build a drydock, float her in. And that's just for starters. The damn thing's six hundred feet long."

"But it could be done."

"In theory."

Michael studied his friend's face. They had yet to touch on the missing piece, the one question from which all the rest descended.

"So how much time do you think we have?" Michael asked.

"Until what?"

"Until the virals come back."

Greer didn't answer right away. "I'm not sure."

"But they *are* coming."

Greer looked up. Michael saw relief in the man's eyes; he had been alone with this for too long. "Tell me, how did you figure it out?"

"It's the only thing that makes sense. The question is, how did *you*?"

Greer drained his whiskey, poured another, and drank that, too. Michael waited.

"I'm going to tell you something, Michael, and you can never tell anybody what you know. Not Sara, not Hollis, not Peter. *Especially* not Peter."

"Why him?"

"I don't make the rules, I'm sorry. I need your word on this."

"You have it."

Greer drew a long breath and let the air out slowly. "I know the virals are coming back, Michael," he said, "because Amy told me."

13

Rain was falling as Alicia approached the city. Seen from above in the soft morning light, the river was as she'd imagined it: wide, dark, ceaselessly flowing. Beyond it rose the spires of the city, dense as a forest. Ruined piers jutted from the banks; wrecks of ships were washed against the shoals. In a century, the sea had risen. Parts of the island's southern tip looked submerged, water lapping against the sides of the buildings.

She picked her way north, hopscotching through the detritus, searching for a way across. The rain stopped, started, stopped again. It was late afternoon when she reached the bridge: two massive struts, like giant twins, holding the decks aloft with cables slung over their shoulders. The thought of crossing it filled Alicia with a profound anxiety she dared not show, but Soldier sensed it anyway. The smallest notch of reluctance in his gait: *This again?*

Yes, she thought. This.

She veered inland and located the ramp. Barricades, gun emplacements, military vehicles stripped bare by a century of weather, some overturned or lying on their sides: there had been a battle here. The upper deck was choked with the carcasses of automobiles, painted white by the droppings of birds. Alicia dismounted and led Soldier through the wreckage. With every step her apprehension increased. The feeling was automatic, like an allergy, a sneeze barely held in abeyance. She kept her eyes forward, putting one foot in front of the next.

About mid-span they came to a place where the roadway had collapsed. Cars lay in a twisted heap on the deck below. A narrow ledge along the guard-rail, four feet wide at the most, presented the only viable pathway.

"No big deal," Alicia said to Soldier. "Nothing to it."

The height was irrelevant; it was the water she feared. Beyond the edge lay a swallowing maw of death. Step by step, gelid with dread, she led Soldier across. How strange, she thought, to fear nothing but this.

The sun was behind them when they reached the far side. A second ramp guided them to street level, into an area of warehouses and factories. She re-mounted Soldier and headed south, along the backbone of the island. The numbered streets ticked down. Eventually the factories gave way to blocks of apartments and brownstones, interspersed with vacant lots, some barren, others like miniature jungles. In some places the streets were flooded, dirty river water bubbling up through the manholes. Never had Alicia been in such a place; the island's sheer density astounded her. She was aware of the tiniest sounds and movements: pigeons cooing, rats scurrying, water dripping down the walls of the buildings' interiors. The acrid spore-smell of mold. The funk of rot. The stench of the city itself, death's temple.

Evening came on. Bats flittered in the sky. She was on Lenox Avenue, in the 110s, when a wall of vegetation rose in her path. At the heart of the abandoned city, a woodland had taken root, flowering to massive dimensions. At its edge she brought Soldier to a halt and tuned her thoughts to the trees; when the virals came, they came from above. It wasn't her they'd want, of course; Alicia was one of them. But there was Soldier to consider. She allowed a few minutes to go by, and when she was satisfied that they would pass in safety, tapped her heels to his flanks.

"Let's go."

Just like that, the city vanished. They could have been in the mightiest of ancient forests. Night had fallen in full, lit by a waning rind of moon. They came to a wide field of feathered grass tall enough to swish against her thighs; then the trees again staked their claim upon the land.

They emerged up a flight of stone steps onto Fifty-ninth Street. Here the buildings had names. Helmsley Park Lane. Essex House. The Ritz-Carlton. The Plaza. She jogged east to Madison Avenue and headed south again. The buildings grew taller, towering above the roadway; the street numbers continued their relentless decline. Fifty-sixth. Fifty-first. Forty-eighth. Forty-third.

Forty-second.

She dismounted. The building was like a fortress, smaller than the great towers that surrounded it but with a royal aspect. A castle, fit for a king. High, arched windows gazed darkly upon the street; along the roofline, at the center of the facade, a stone figure stood with his arms outstretched in welcome. Beneath this, etched into the building's face, chiseled in moonlight, were the words GRAND CENTRAL TERMINAL.

Alicia, I'm here. Lish, I'm so glad that you have come.

She could feel her brothers and sisters plainly now. They were everywhere beneath her, a vast repository curled in slumber in the bowels of the city. Did they sense her presence also? There was, Alicia realized, a single hour that all the days since your birth pointed you toward. What you thought was a maze of choices, all the possibilities of what your life might become, was, in fact, a series of steps you took along a road, and when you reached your destination and looked back, only one path—the one chosen for you—was visible.

She clipped a rope to Soldier's bridle. Two nights before, camped on the outskirts of Newark, she'd prepared a pine-knot torch. Now, crouched on the sidewalk, she shaved a pile of tinder, ignited it with her firesteel, and dipped the end of the torch in the flames until the pitch began to burn. She rose, holding it aloft. The torch, which would burn for hours, gave off a smoky orange light. She cinched her bandoliers tight to her chest, then reached her right hand over the opposite shoulder to withdraw her sword from its sheath. Bright-edged, hard-tipped, the cords at the handle worn from hours of practice, the object had no symbolic meaning for her; it was simply a tool. She swooped it slowly back and forth, feeling its power meld with her own. Soldier was watching her. When the moment felt right, Alicia resheathed her weapon and opened the door to the terminal.

"It's time."

She led him inside. Broken glass crunched underfoot; she heard the squeaks of rats. Ten feet past the door, two options: straight ahead, down a sloping hallway to the station's lower level, or left, through an arched portal.

She went left.

Space expanded around her. She was in the main room of the station, but it did not seem like a station—more like a church. A place where vast crowds gathered to commune with one another in the company of some higher presence. Shafts of moonlight pulsed from the high windows onto the floor, spreading like a pale yellow liquid. The silence was intense; she could hear the blood swishing in her ears. Looking up, she saw what she thought was the sky until she realized it was a painting. Stars were strewn across the ceiling, and in their midst were figures—a bull, a ram, a man pouring water from a pitcher.

"Alicia. Hello."

She startled. It was his voice. An audible, distinctly human-sounding voice.

"I'm over here."

The sound came from the far end of the room. Alicia moved toward it, guiding Soldier beside her. Ahead she saw a structure. It looked like a small house. Positioned on top, like a crown, was a large, four-faced clock. As she approached, the clock was the first thing to capture the glow of her torch, not so much reflecting the light as absorbing it, causing its faces to shine with an orange luster.

"Up here, Lish."

A broad flight of stairs ascended to a balcony. She released the rope and placed her hand against Soldier's neck. His coat was damp with sweat. She pressed her palm against it with a calming gesture: *Wait here.*

"Don't worry, your friend will be safe. He's a magnificent companion, Lish. More than I even imagined. Every inch a soldier, like you. Like my Lish."

She ascended the stairs, making no effort to conceal herself—there was no point. What form of creature awaited her? The voice was human, meager in a way, but the body surely wouldn't be. He would be a giant, a monster of gargantuan dimensions, a titan of his race.

She reached the top. To her right was a bar with stools, straight ahead an area of tables, some overturned, others still set with china and silverware.

Sitting at one of the tables was a man.

Was it a trick? Had he done something to her mind? He was sitting at ease, his hands folded on his lap, wearing a dark suit, a white shirt, collar undone at his throat. Sandy hair, almost red, with a sharp widow's peak; a slight sag around the jowls; eyes with a certain indefinable intensity. Suddenly nothing around her seemed real. It was all a gigantic joke. He was like any man, a figure in a crowd, no one a person would notice.

"Does my appearance surprise you?" he asked. "Perhaps I should have warned you."

His voice aroused her to action. She dropped the torch and the sword came out as she strode toward him; she swung it away from her body, cocked her hip, transferring energy to the large muscle groups—shoulders, pelvis, legs— and brought it around, halting its flight just inches from his neck.

"What the hell are you?"

Not a muscle had flinched. Even his face was relaxed. "What do I look like?"

"You're not human. You can't be."

"You might ask yourself the same thing. What it means, to be human." He tipped his head toward her blade. "If you're going to use that, I suggest you get on with it."

"Is that what you want?"

He angled his face toward the ceiling. At the corners of his mouth, dagger-like incisors revealed themselves. They were the teeth of a predator, and yet the face before her was mild. "I've been waiting here rather a long time, you know. In a hundred years, you get around to thinking about pretty much everything. All the things you did, the people you knew, the mistakes you made. The books you read, the music you listened to, how the sun felt, the rain. It's all still there inside you. But it's not enough, is it? That's the thing. The past is never enough."

The sword was still poised at his neck. How simple he was making this, how easy. He was looking at her with an expression of perfect calm. One swift blow, and she would be free.

"We're two of a kind, you see." His voice was placid, almost teacherly. "So much regret. So many things lost."

Why hadn't she done it? Why had she failed to strike? A strange immobility had taken hold—not a physical paralysis; more a dimming of her will.

"I have no doubt you're more than capable." He touched a spot on his neck. "Right about here, I think. That should do the trick."

Something was wrong. Something was terribly wrong. All she had to do was pull back the sword and let fly, yet she could not make herself do it.

"You can't, can you?" He frowned; his tone was almost regretful. "Patricide goes against the grain after all."

"I killed Martínez. I watched him die."

"Yes, but you did not belong to him, Lish. You belong to me. The viral that bit you was one of mine. Amy is but one part of you; I am the other. You could no more use that sword on me than you could on her. I'm surprised you hadn't figured that out."

She felt the truth of his words. The sword, the sword; she could not move the sword.

"But I don't think you came to kill me. I don't think that's why you're here at all. I can see it. You have questions. There are things you want to know."

She answered through gritted teeth: "I don't want anything from you."

"No? Then I'll ask you something instead. Tell me, Alicia, what did being human ever get you?"

She felt disoriented; none of this made sense.

"It's a simple question, really. Most things are, in the end."

"I had friends," she said, and heard the shakiness in her voice. "People who loved me."

"Did they? Is that why you left them?"

"You don't know what you're talking about."

"I think I do. Your mind is an open book to me. Peter, Michael, Sara, Hollis, Greer. And Amy. The great and powerful Amy. I know all about them. Even the boy, Hightop, who died in your arms. You promised him you would keep him safe. But in the end you could not save him."

Her being was dissolving; the sword was like an anvil in her hand, incomparably dense.

"What would your friends say to you now? I'll answer for you. They would call you a monster. They would hound you from their midst, if they didn't kill you first."

"Shut up, goddamnit."

"You're not one of them. You never have been, not since the day the Colonel took you outside the walls and left you there. You sat there under the trees and cried all night. Isn't that so?"

How could he know these things?

"Did he comfort you, Alicia? Did he tell you he was sorry? You were just a little girl, and he left you all alone. You have always been . . . alone."

The last of her resolve was failing; it was all she could do to hold the sword aloft.

"I know, because I know *you*, Alicia Donadio. I know your secret heart. Don't you see? That's why you've come to me. I'm the only one who does."

"Please," she begged. "Please stop talking."

"Tell me. What did you name her?"

She was undone; she had nothing left. Whoever she'd been, or wanted to be, she felt that person leaving her.

"Tell me, Lish. Tell me your daughter's name."

"Rose." The word came out with a choking sound. "I named her Rose."

She had begun to sob. At some uncharted distance, the sword fell clattering to the floor. The man had risen and put his arms around her, drawing her into a warm embrace. She made no resistance, having none to offer. She cried and cried. Her little girl. Her Rose.

"That's why you came here, isn't it?" His voice was soft, close to her ear. "That's what this place is for. You came to speak your daughter's name."

She nodded against him. She heard herself say, "Yes."

"Oh, my Alicia. My Lish. Do you know where you are? All your journeys are ended. What is home but a place where you are truly known? Say it with me. 'I've come home.'"

A flicker of resistance; then she let it go. "I've come home."

"'And I am never leaving here.'"

How easy it suddenly was. "And I am never leaving here."

A moment passed; he stepped away. Through her tears, she looked at his kind face, so full of understanding. He pulled a chair from the table.

"Now, sit with me," he said. "We have all the time in the world. Sit with me, and I will tell you everything."

II

THE LOVER

28–3 B.V.
(1989–2014)
*from Morn
To Noon he fell, from Noon to dewy Eve,
A Summers day; and with the setting Sun
Dropped from the Zenith like a falling Star.*

—MILTON, *PARADISE LOST*

14

Behind every great hatred is a love story.

For I am a man who has known and tasted love. I say "a man" because that is how I know myself. Look at me, and what do you see? Do I not take the form of a man? Do I not feel as you do, suffer as you do, love as you do, mourn as you do? What is the essence of a man, if not these things? In life I was a scientist, called Fanning. Fanning, Timothy J., holder of the Eloise Armstrong Distinguished Chair in Biochemical Sciences, Columbia University. I was known and respected, a figure of my times. My opinions were sought on many subjects; I walked the hallways of my profession with my head held high. I was a man of connections. I shook hands, kissed cheeks, made friends, took lovers. Fortune and treasure flowed my way; I supped at the flower of the modern world. City apartments, country houses, sleek automobiles, good wine: all of these were things I had. I dined in fine restaurants, slept in upscale hotels; my passport was fat with visas. Thrice I wooed and thrice I wed, and although these unions came to naught, each was, in its final measure, no matter of regret. I worked and rested, danced and wept, hoped and remembered— even, from time to time, prayed. I lived, in sum, a life.

Then, in a jungle in Bolivia, I died.

You will know me as Zero. Such is the name that history has bestowed upon me. Zero the Destroyer, Great Devourer of the World. That this history shall never be written is a circumstance of ontological debate. What becomes of the past when there is no man to record it? I died and then was brought to life, the oldest tale there is. I arose from the dead, and what did I behold? I was in a room of the bluest light—pure blue, cerulean blue, the blue the sky would be if it were married to the sea. My arms, legs, even my head were bound; I was a captive in that place. Scattered images lit my mind, flashes of light and color that refused to gather into meaning. My body was humming. That is the only word. I was to learn that I had just emerged from the final stages of my trans-formation. I had yet to see my body, being inside it.

Tim, can you hear me?

A voice, coming from everywhere and nowhere. Was I dead? Was this the voice of God, addressing me? Perhaps the life I'd lived had been not so wor-thy, and things had gone the other way.

Tim, if you can hear me, lift a hand.

This did not seem too much for God, any god, to ask.

That's it. Now the other one. Excellent. Well done, Tim.

You know this voice, I said to myself. You are not dead; it is the voice of a human being, like you. A man who calls you by name, who says "well done."

That's it. Just breathe. You're doing fine.

The nature of the situation was becoming clear. I had been ill in some manner. Perhaps I had suffered seizures; that would explain the restraints. I could not yet recall the circumstances, how I had come to be in this place. The voice was the key. If I could identify its owner, all would be revealed.

I'm going to undo the straps now, okay?

I felt a release of pressure; triggered by some remote mechanism, my bindings had surrendered their hold.

Can you sit up, Tim? Can you do that for me?

It was also true that, whatever my ailment was, the worst had passed. I did not feel ill—quite the contrary. The humming sensation, which originated in my chest, had enlarged to an orchestral, whole-body vibrato, as if all the molecules of my anatomy were playing a single note. The sensation was deeply, almost sexually pleasurable. My loins, the tips of my toes, even the roots of my hair—never had I experienced anything so exquisite.

A second voice, deeper than the first: *Dr. Fanning, I'm Colonel Sykes.*

Sykes. Did I know a man named Sykes?

Can you hear us? Do you know where you are?

A hole had opened inside me. Not a hole: a maw. I was hungry. Deeply, madly hungry. Mine was the appetite not of a human being but of an animal. A hunger of claws and teeth, of burrowing in, of soft flesh beneath the jaws and hot juices exploding upon the palate.

Tim, you've got us pretty worried in here. Talk to me, buddy.

And just like that the gates of memory opened, releasing a flood. The rain forest, with its steamy air and dense green canopy full of hooting animals; the stickiness of my skin and the omnipresent swarm of insects around my face; the soldiers, scanning the trees with their rifles as we walked, their faces streaked with jungle paint; the statues, manlike figures of monstrous form, warning us away even as they called us forward, summoning us deeper into the heart of this vile place; the bats.

They'd come at night, swarming our encampment. Bats by the hundreds, the thousands, the ten thousands, a flapping multitude. They blotted out the heavens. They took the sky by storm. The gates of hell had opened and this was its disgorgement, its black vomitus. They seemed not to fly but to swim, moving in organized waves, like a school of airborne fish. They fell upon us, all wings and teeth and vicious little squeaks of joy. I remembered the shots, the screams. I was in a place of blue light and a voice that knew my name but in my mind I was running for the river. I saw a woman, writhing on the banks.

Her name was Claudia; she was one of us. The bats had covered her like a cloak. Imagine it, the horror. Almost no part of her was visible. She twitched in a demonic dance of agony. In truth, my first instinct was to do nothing. I did not possess the heart of a hero. Yet sometimes we discover things about ourselves we never knew. I took two great leaps and tackled her, sending the two of us plunging into the fetid jungle water. I felt the hot stab of the bats' teeth in the flesh of my arms and neck. The water boiled with blood. Such was their fury that even the water did not deter them; they would feed upon us even as they drowned. I locked Claudia's neck in my elbow and dove down, though I knew this would come to nothing; the woman was already dead.

I remembered all these things, and then one more. I remembered a man's face. It hovered above me, framed by jungle sky. I was insensate, burning with fever. The air around me throbbed with the din of the helicopter's blades. The man was yelling something. I tried to focus on his mouth. *It was alive,* he was saying—my friend, Jonas Lear, was saying—*it was alive, it was alive, it was alive . . .*

I lifted my head and looked. The room was barren, like a cell. On the wall across from me, a wide, dark window showed my reflection.

I saw what I'd become.

I did not rise. I launched. I rocketed across the room and hit the window with a thud. Behind the glass, the two men lurched backward. Jonas and the second one, Sykes. Their eyes were wide with fear. I pounded. I roared. I opened my jaws to display my teeth so they would know the measure of my rage. I wanted to kill them. No, not kill. "Kill" is too dull a word for that which I desired. I wanted to annihilate them. I wanted to tear them limb from limb. I wanted to crack their bones and bury my face in the wet remains. I wanted to reach inside their chests and yank out their hearts and devour the bloody meat as the last stray current twitched the muscle and watch their faces as they died. They were yelling, screaming. I was not what they'd bargained for. The glass was bowing, shuddering beneath my blows.

A blast of white-hot brightness engulfed the room. I felt as if I'd been shot by a hundred arrows. I stumbled backward and fell curling to the floor. A clattering of gears above, and with a bang the bars fell, sealing me away.

Tim, I'm sorry. This was never my intention. Forgive me . . .

Perhaps he was. It made no difference. Even then, huddled in agony, I knew that their advantage was temporary; it held no weight. The walls of my prison could not help but eventually yield to my power. I was the dark flower of mankind, ordained since time's beginning to destroy a world that had no God to love it.

*   *   *

From one, we became Twelve. That, too, is a matter of record. From my blood the ancient seed was taken and passed into others. I came to know these men. At first, they alarmed me. Their human lives had been very different from my own. They possessed no conscience, no pity, no philosophy. They were like brute animals, their bestial hearts full of the blackest of deeds. That such men existed I had long understood, but evil, to be truly comprehended, must be felt, experienced. One must enter into it, as into a lightless cave. One by one they came into my mind, and I into theirs. Babcock was the first. What terrible dreams he possessed—though they were, in truth, no worse than my own. The others followed in due course, each added to the fold. Morrison and Chávez. Baffes and Turrell. Winston and Sosa, Echols and Lambright, Reinhardt and Martínez, vilest of all. Even Carter, whose memories of suffering blew upon the dying embers of compassion in my heart. Over time, in the company of these troubled souls, I underwent an expanding sense of mission. They were my heirs, my acolytes; alone among them, I possessed the capacity to lead. They did not despise the world, as I did; to such men, the world is nothing, as everything is nothing. Their appetites knew no moderation; unguided, they would bring down swift and total destruction upon us all. They were mine to command, but how to make them follow?

What they needed was a god.

Nine and one, I commanded them, in my best god voice. *Nine are yours but one is mine, as you are mine. Into the tenth shall be planted the seed so that we will be Many, millions-fold.*

A reasonable person might ask, Why did you do it? If I possessed the power to lead them, surely I could have put a stop to everything. The rage was part of it, yes. All that I loved had been taken from me, and that which I did not love as well, which was my human life. So, too, did the biological imperatives of my remanufactured self; could you ask a hungry lion to ignore the bounty of the veldt? I do not note these things to seek the pardon of any person, because my actions are unpardonable, nor to say I'm sorry, although I am. (Does that surprise you to hear? That Timothy Fanning, called Zero, is sorry? It's true: I'm sorry about everything.) I merely wish to set the stage, to place my mental contours in their proper context. What did I desire? To make the world a wasteland; to bring upon it the mirrored image of my wretched self; to punish Lear, my friend, my enemy, who believed he could save a world that was not savable, that never deserved saving in the first place.

Such was my wrath in those early days. Yet I could not ignore the metaphysical aspects of my condition indefinitely. As I boy, I spoke often to the Almighty. My prayers were shallow and childish, as if I were speaking to Santa Claus: spaghetti for dinner, a new bike at my birthday, a day of snow and no school. "If, Lord, in your infinite mercy, it would not be too much trouble . . ." How ironic! We are born faithful and afraid, when it should be the opposite; it is life that teaches us how much we stand to lose. As a grown man, I mislaid the impulse, like many people. I would not say I was a nonbeliever; rather, that I gave little if any thought to celestial concerns. It did not seem to me that God, whoever he was, would be the sort of god to take an interest in the minutiae of human affairs, or that this fact released us from the duty to go about our lives in a spirit of decency to others. It is true that the events of my life brought me into a state of nihilistic despair, yet even in the darkest hours of my human life—the hours that, to this day, I dwell in—I blamed no one but myself.

But as love turns to grief, and grief becomes anger, so must anger yield to thought, in order to know itself. My symbolic properties were inarguable. Made by science, I was a perfect industrial product, the very embodiment of mankind's indefatigable faith in itself. Since our first, furry ancestor scraped flint on stone and banished night with fire, we have climbed heavenward on a ladder made of our own arrogance. But was that all? Was I the final proof that humanity dwelled in an unwatched cosmos of no purpose, or was I something more?

Thus did I contemplate my existence. In due course, these ruminations led me to but one conclusion. I had been made for a purpose. I was not the author of destruction; I was its instrument, forged in heaven's workshop by a god of horrors.

What could I do but play the part?

As to my present, more human-seeming incarnation: all I can say is that Jonas was right about one thing after all, though the bastard never knew it. The events I am about to describe occurred just a few days after my emancipation, in a certain benighted prairie hamlet by the name (I was later to learn) of Sewanee, Kansas. To this day my recollections of that early period are drowned in joy. What soaring liberty! What bountiful slaking of my appetites! The world of night seemed a glorious banquet to my senses, an infinite buffet. Yet I moved with a certain caution. No roadhouse-tavern massacres. No families slaughtered whole in their beds. No fast-food emporia painted red, patrons strewn willy-nilly in bloody dismemberment. These things would come eventually; but for the time being, I sought to leave a lighter footprint. Each night, as I made my way east, I dined upon only a handful, and only in situations in which I could do so at my ease, and swiftly dispose of the remains.

Thus my heart sang an aria of delight at the sight of the truck.

The vehicle, a preposterously bloated and overappointed quad cab pickup— smokestacks, duallies, lights on the roll bar, Confederate-flag decal on the bumper—was parked nose-in at the lip of a flooded quarry. Its isolation was ideal, as was the distracted state of its occupants: a man and a woman in full passionate flagrante, enjoying each other as much as I was about to enjoy them. For a time, I merely watched. My gaze was not carnal; rather, I observed with the curiosity of the scientist. Why this crummy place to do the deed? Why the awkward confines of a pickup (the man was practically crushing his beloved against the dashboard) to unleash their animal splendor? Surely there were enough beds in the world to go around. They were not young, far from it—he bald and rather portly, she scrawny and loose-skinned, the two of them a spectacle of aging flesh. What about this place had called out to them? Was it nostalgia? Had they come here when they were young? Was I witnessing a reenacted glory of youth? Then it came to me. They were married. They just weren't married to each other.

I took the woman first. Astride her companion on the wide bench seat, so wildly was she pumping upon his anatomy—fists gripping the headrest, skirt bunched around her waist and underpants swinging from a bony ankle, her face angled toward the ceiling like a supplicant—that as I yanked open the door she seemed more irritated than alarmed, as if I had interrupted her in the midst of a particularly important train of thought. This, of course, did not last long, no more than a couple of seconds. It is an interesting truth that the human body, liberated from its head, is in essence a bag of blood with a built-in straw. Holding her headless torso upright, I positioned my mouth around this jetting orifice and gave it a long, muscular suck. I wasn't expecting anything much. It seemed likely that her small-town diet, rich in preservatives, would give her blood a chemical taste. But this turned out not to be the case. The woman was, in fact, delicious. Her blood was a veritable bouquet of complex flavors, like a well-aged wine.

Two more robust sucks and I cast her aside. By this time her associate, pants puddled around his ankles, gleaming penis in rapid deflation, had gathered the wherewithal to shimmy toward the driver's side of the cab, where he was frantically attempting to isolate the truck's key from a ring of them. The ring was enormous. It was positively janitorial. Fingers trembling, he jammed one key into the slot and then another, all to no avail, muttering a chain of "oh God"s and "holy fuck"s that were only a lightly retooled rendition of the ecstatic sounds and filthy encouragements he'd been breathing into his companion's ear mere seconds ago.

The comedy was exquisite. Speaking frankly, I couldn't get enough of it.

Which was my grand mistake. Had I killed him more quickly, not pausing to savor this risible display, the world we know would be a different place. As it was, my delay gave him time to locate the correct key, shove it into the ignition, turn the engine over, and reach for the gearshift before I shot into the cab, grabbed his head, tipped it to the side, and crushed his windpipe under my jaws with a gristly crunch. So enraptured was I with the bloody feast of my hapless victim that I failed to notice what was happening—that he had put the truck in gear.

Our species' aversion to water is well known; water is death to us. We sink like stones, our bodies lacking the buoyancy of adipose tissue. Of my plunge into the quarry I possess only a fractured recollection. The truck's slow progress to the lip of the abyss; the snatch of gravity and the inevitable plunge; water all around me, a cocoon of cold death, engulfing my eyes and nose and lungs. From small mistakes come great catastrophes; invincible in most other aspects, I had found the quickest way to die. As the truck touched down with a soft thump upon the quarry's watery floor, I extricated myself from the cab and began to crawl along the bottom. Even in my panicked state, the irony was not lost on me. Subject Zero, World Destroyer, scuttling like a crab! My only hope was to feel my way to the edge of the pit and scale my way to freedom. Time was my enemy; I had but one bottled breath with which to save myself. A wall of rock met my desperate grasp; I began to climb. Hand over hand I made my ascent. My vision swirled with darkness, the end was closing in . . .

How I came in due course to find myself on hands and knees—pink-fleshed, inarguably human-looking hands and knees—whilst gagging out great volumes of boggy vomitus is a question I shall leave to the theologians. For die I surely did; the body remembers these things. Having freed myself from the quarry's waters, I had yet succumbed and for some period of time lain as a drowned corpse upon the rocks, only to be shot back into existence.

Death's doorway, it seemed, was not marked EXIT ONLY after all.

The last of the quarry's waters expelled, I managed, in a state of dazed astonishment, to rise. Where was I? When was I? *What* was I? Such was my disorientation that it seemed that I might have dreamed it all—then, conversely, that I was dreaming *this.* I held up a hand before the moon. It was, in every visible aspect, the hand of a human being—the hand of Timothy Fanning, holder of the Eloise Armstrong Chair, et cetera. I looked down upon the rest of me; with tremulous digits I probed my face, my chest and stomach, my pale legs; naked by moonlight, I investigated each feature of my physical person like a blind man reading braille.

I'll be goddamned, I thought.

I had come to rest on a rocky shelf jutting from the quarry wall; a narrow switchback led me to the top, where I emerged into an area of rusted machinery half-buried by weeds. The hour was unknown to me. Save for the moon, no lights burned anywhere. The landscape was one of such uninhabited desolation the world might have ended already.

The quarry's waters would conceal my second victim, but there was the woman to consider; the last thing I wanted was a police manhunt to complicate matters. I circled the quarry to the parking area. The sight of her aroused no remorse, just the sort of perfunctory, quickly dispatched pity one might feel reading a newspaper account of some distant catastrophe over one's second slice of morning toast. Two distant splashes—body, head—and into the watery deep she went.

None of which did anything to solve the problem of being a naked, full-grown man at large in an unknown countryside. I needed clothes, shelter, a story. Also, a certain mental agitation, like an inaudible siren in my brain, told me that, should daybreak find me in the open, nothing happy would ensue.

The main highway was too risky. I headed for the woods, hoping that I might eventually come to some lesser-traveled thoroughfare. At length I emerged into a landscape of freshly planted fields bisected by a dirt road. In the distance I saw a light and headed toward it. A small, rather dilapidated one-story house of nondescript design, little more than a box in which to store a human life: the light I'd seen was a lamp in one of the two front windows. There was no car in the driveway, suggesting that the house was unoccupied, the light left burning in anticipation of its owner's return.

The door obediently opened onto a living room of particleboard furniture, country-themed bric-a-brac, and a television the size of a Jumbotron. A quick survey of the interior—four rooms and a kitchen—confirmed my impression that no one was home. My inspection further revealed that the occupant was a woman, had attended nursing school at Wichita State, was in her late forties, possessed a soft, moonlike face and gray hair she didn't do much with, wore a size twenty, was frequently photographed in a state of rosy-cheeked inebriation in ethnic-themed restaurants (wearing a plastic lei, flirting shamelessly with the mariachis, holding up a flaming fondue spike), and that she lived alone. From her wardrobe I selected the most neutral things I could find—a pair of sweatpants, voluminous on my midsized masculine frame, a hooded sweatshirt, likewise huge, and a pair of flip-flops—and entered the bathroom.

The sight that greeted me in the mirror was not wholly unexpected. By this time it had become apparent to me that the physical act of drowning had not wholly restored me to my human state but wrought upon my person something more like costumery. The virus remained; my death had merely excited it into some new interaction with its host. Many attributes had been preserved. Vision, hearing, smell: all had retained their supercharged acuteness. Though I had yet to put them to a proper test, my limbs—indeed, my entire physical carriage, bones to blood—hummed with bestial strength.

Yet these things hardly prepared me for what I saw. My complexion was unnaturally pale, almost cadaverous. My hair, which had miraculously grown back, triangulated at my forehead to a comically perfect widow's peak. My eyes possessed the alien rosiness of an albino's. But the final detail was the one that stopped me flat. At first I thought it was a joke. Behind the corners of my upper lip, amidst otherwise ordinary dentition, two white points dripped like icicles—or, more precisely, fangs.

Dracula. Nosferatu. Vampyre. I can barely utter the names without a roll of the eyes. Yet here I was, Jonas Lear's fantasy incarnate, a legend come to life.

The crunch of tires on gravel aroused me; as I emerged from the lavatory, a pair of headlights raked the room. I ducked behind a coat tree just in time for the door to fling open with a gust of spring air. The woman, whose name was Janet Duff—I'd gotten this from the framed diploma hung above the bill-cluttered desk in her bedroom—lumbered inside, wearing the flowered smock, white polyester trousers, and sensible shoes of a nurse coming off the late-night shift. Without missing a beat she deposited her ring of keys on the table by the door, kicked off her shoes, flung her overstuffed purse onto a chair, and made her way back to the kitchen, from whence ensued the sound of an open-ing refrigerator and the splash and glug of a tumbler being filled. A moment in which to down a soul-soothing quantity of wine (I could smell it: cheap Cha-blis, from a box, probably), and Nurse Duff returned to the living room bear-ing a glass the approximate size of a paint can, turned on the giant TV, and plopped down on the sofa, settling into its cushions like a punctured parade float.

How she had failed to notice me behind the coat tree I couldn't guess, except to say that my new condition had afforded me the ability to stand with a still-ness that functioned as a kind of camouflage, rendering me nearly invisible to the casual, world-weary eye. I watched her flick through various programs—a cop drama, the Weather Channel, a prison documentary—until she settled on a reality show about, what else, competitive cupcake making. Her back was to me. Sip by sip, the wine went down. I guessed it wouldn't be long before the alcohol-anesthetized Nurse Duff began to snore. But with dawn's blade sliding toward me, and my various needs pressing down—cash, an automobile, a safe place to wait out the daylight hours—I saw no reason for delay. I emerged from my concealment and stepped behind her.

"Ahem."

I did not kill her immediately. Again, I seek not pardon but patience with my tale. There was data to collect, and for that, Nurse Duff needed to be alive.

A taste and the deed was done. At once, the woman fell into a swoon—eyes rolled back, breath expelled, every inch gone flabbily slack. Like an eager groom I picked her up and carried her to the bedroom, where I lay her on the comforter, then retreated to the bathroom and filled the tub. By the time I returned, the change had commenced. A white froth bubbled from her lips. Her fingers began to twitch, her hands. She began to moan, then grunt, then fell silent as a series of hard spasms shook her frame so violently I thought dear Nurse Duff would snap like a cracker.

Then it happened. The closest visual approximation I can offer is a time-accelerated video of a flower breaking into blossom. With a cartilaginous crunch, her fingers commenced their elongation. Her hair suddenly detached from her skull and fell fanlike onto the pillow. As if doused by acid, her facial features blandified until no trace of personality remained. By this time her convulsions had ceased; her eyes were closed, her face almost peaceful. I sat on the bed beside her, murmuring gentle encouragements. A green light had begun to emanate from her, bathing the room in a nursery-soft glow. Her jaw unhinged; with something like a dog's sneeze, her teeth shot from her mouth like a handful of corn kernels, making way for the barricade of lances that ascended bloodily from her gums.

It was ghastly. It was beautiful.

She opened her eyes. For a long moment, she stared at me. What pathos in that gaze! We are, each of us, a character in our own story; that is how we make sense of our lives. But the woman who had been Nurse Duff—help maid to the sick and suffering, collector of quilts and butter churns, drinker of mai tais, margaritas, and Bahama Mamas; daughter, sister, dreamer, healer, spinster—had become unknown to herself. She was a part of me now, an extension of my will; had I desired, I could have made her hop on one foot while playing an invisible ukulele.

"You don't have to be afraid," I said, taking her hand in mine. "It's all for the best, you'll see."

Once again, I lifted her into my arms. My strength was such that her considerable bulk seemed toylike. A memory came to me—I had carried a woman like this once. Though the circumstances were very different, she, too, had seemed to weigh almost nothing. The recollection aroused a feeling of tenderness so overwhelming that for a moment I doubted my actions. But there were things to learn, and the duty I was about to perform was, in its backhanded way, a kindness.

I carted Nurse Duff to the bathroom and suspended her body above the tub. Through some lingering womanly instinct, she had looped her arms around my neck; she had yet to notice the water, as was my hope. I was gazing deep into her eyes, beaming thoughts of reassurance. Her trust in me was absolute. What was I to her? Father? Lover? Deliverer? God?

The spell was broken the moment her body touched the water. She began to thrash wildly, fighting to free herself. But her strength was far outmatched by mine. Pressing her by the shoulders, I forced her gargoyle's face below the surface. Her panic and confusion rippled through me. What betrayal! What incomprehensible deceit! Others would have been moved to mercy, yet these feelings only strengthened my resolve. I felt her take the first breath of water. It ricocheted through her like a hiccup. She took a second, then a third, filling her lungs. A last agonal spasm and she was gone.

I stepped back. The first test had been passed; here was the second. Waiting for the restoration of her human form, I counted off the seconds; when nothing happened, I hoisted her from the water and arranged her facedown on the floor, thinking this might encourage the process. But more minutes ticked away, and I was forced to concede that no change was forthcoming; Nurse Duff had permanently departed from this life.

I retreated from the room and sat on the woman's bed to ponder the situation. The only conclusion I could draw was that the transformative effect of death by water was for me alone—that my descendants possessed no such gift of resurrection. Yet why this should be so—why I should be sitting there, looking altogether like the man I'd once been, while she should be lying dead on the bathroom floor like a beached sea monster—was beyond my power to explain. Was I simply a more robust version of our species, being the alpha, the original, the Zero? Or could the difference be one not of body but of mind? That I had wanted to live, while she had not? I considered my emotions. I didn't really have any. I had drowned an innocent woman in a bathtub, yet my feelings were utterly colorless. From the moment I'd sunk my incisors into the soft meat of her neck and taken the first, candy-sweet sip, she had ceased to exist as an entity distinct from myself; rather, she'd been a kind of appendage. Killing her had seemed no more morally noteworthy than trimming a fingernail. So perhaps that was where the difference lay. In the only way that really mattered, Nurse Duff was already dead when I'd shoved her in the water.

Simultaneously, alarm bells were ringing inside me. The light in the room was changing; daybreak, my nemesis, was at hand. I moved hastily through the house, drawing every drape and shade, locking doors both front and back. For the next twelve hours, I was going nowhere.

I awoke in delicious darkness, having discovered the most refreshing dreamfree sleep I had ever known. No knock on the door had aroused me; Nurse Duff's departure from the world had yet to be noticed, though surely this would come. I made my preparations quickly. On America's byways, even a vampire, especially one who wishes to fly beneath the radar, needs money to get by. In a cat-shaped cookie jar, I discovered twenty-three hundred dollars in soft bills, more than enough, and a .38 revolver, which no person in the history of the planet needed less than I.

My plan was to zigzag my way east, avoiding major highways. The journey would take five, perhaps six nights. Nurse Duff's well-worn Corolla, with its detritus of candy wrappers, pop cans, and worthless scratch-offs, would suffice for the time being but would have to be discarded soon; somebody was bound to catch wind of the dead demon in the bathroom and note her missing automobile. I also felt—and looked—ridiculous in the woman's oversized sweat suit and shower shoes; a more suitable costume was in the offing.

Eight hours later I was in southern Missouri, where I commenced the pattern that would organize my life for the duration. Each new daybreak found me safely ensconced in an off-brand motel behind closed drapes, duct-taped cardboard panels, and a Do Not Disturb sign; once night fell, I would set out again and drive without stopping until an hour or two before dawn. In Carbondale, Illinois, I decided to ditch the Corolla. I was also very hungry. I lingered at my hotel past dark, sitting in my parked car, so that I might observe the comings and goings of my fellow travelers and identify an appropriate provider of nutrition, clothes, and transport. The man I selected was my approximate height and weight; he also seemed, conveniently, inebriated. As he entered his room I pushed in behind him, killed him tidily before he could utter more than a drunken whimper—he tasted rancidly of nicotine and bar-pour whiskey—wrapped his body in the shower curtain to conceal the stench of putrefaction, shoved him in the closet, helped myself to the contents of his wallet and suitcase (Dockers, no-iron sport shirts of obnoxious plaid, six sets of underpants and a pair of "novelty" boxers with the words KISS ME, I'M IRISH stenciled on the crotch), and skedaddled in his plushly appointed, thoroughly American sedan. The business cards in his wallet identified him as a regional sales manager for a manufacturer of industrial air-circulation equipment. I might as well have been him.

In this manner I hunt-and-pecked my way across the great featureless slab of the American Middle West. As the nights and miles slithered by, road hypnosis cast my mind into the past. I thought of my parents, long dead, and the town where I was raised—a doppelgänger to the many anonymous hamlets that I, King of Destruction, passed through unremarkably, just a pair of headlights drifting downstream in the dark. I thought of people I'd known, friends I'd made, women I'd bedded. I thought of a table with flowers and crystal and a view of the sea, and a night—a sad and beautiful night—when in falling snow I had carried my beloved home. I thought of all these things, and many more besides, but most of all, I thought of Liz.

The lights of New York rose from wretched New Jersey on the evening of the sixth day. Eight million souls: my senses were singing like a soprano. I entered Manhattan via the Lincoln Tunnel, abandoned the car on Eighth Avenue, and set out on foot. I stopped in the first tavern I came to, an Irish pub with a heavily lacquered bar and sawdust on the floor. Among the patrons, nothing seemed out of the ordinary; such is the insularity of New Yorkers that what was happening in the middle of the country had yet to coalesce into a feeling of general crisis. Seated alone at the bar, I ordered a Scotch, not intending to drink it, but discovered that I wanted to and, more interestingly, that it caused no ill effects. It was delicious, its most subtle flavors dancing upon my palate. I was on my third when I realized two other things: I was not the least drunk, and I badly needed to piss. In the men's room my body released a stream so powerfully percussive it made the porcelain chime. This, too, was immensely satisfying; it seemed there was no bodily pleasure that had not been amplified a hundred-fold.

But the real object of my attention was the television above the bar. A Yankees game was on. I waited until the last pitch was thrown and asked the bartender if he would switch to CNN.

I did not have to wait long: "Colorado Killing Spree," read the chyron at the bottom of the screen. The madness was spreading. Reports were coming in from locales throughout the state: whole families obliterated in their beds, towns without a man or woman left alive, a roadside restaurant of patrons gutted like trout. But there were also survivors—bitten, but alive. *It just looked at me. It wasn't human. It gave off this kind of glow.* The ravings of the traumatized or something more? No one had done the math yet, but I did. Per my instructions, for every nine killed, one had been called into the fold. The hospitals were filling with the sick and injured. Nausea, fever, spasms, then . . .

"That's some creepy shit."

I turned to the man sitting next to me. When had the adjacent stool become occupied? A certain urban type, manufactured by the thousands: balding and lawyerish, with an intelligent, slightly pugnacious face, a speckling of day-old beard, and a little paunch he kept meaning to do something about. Wingtips and a blue suit and starched white shirt, necktie loose around his throat. Somebody was waiting for him at home, but he couldn't quite bring himself to face them yet, not after the day he'd just had.

"Don't I know it."

On the bar before him sat a glass of wine. Our eyes met for what seemed an unusually long time. I noted the overwhelming odor of nervous perspiration he'd attempted to cloak with cologne. His eyes traveled the length of my torso, pausing at my mouth on the upswing. "Haven't I seen you in here before?"

Ah, I thought. I darted my eyes around the room. There were no women at all. "I don't think so. I'm new."

"Are you meeting anyone?"

"Not until now."

He smiled and put out his hand—the one without the wedding ring. "I'm Scott. Let me buy you a drink."

Thirty minutes later, wearing his suit, I left him in an alleyway, twitching and frothing.

I thought of visiting my old apartment but discarded the idea; it was not, had never been, home. What is home to a monster? To anyone? There exists for each of us a geographical fulcrum, a place so saturated with memory that within its precinct the past is always present. It was late, after two A.M., when I entered the main hall at Grand Central Terminal. The restaurants and shops had long since closed, sealed behind their grates; the board above the ticket windows listed only morning trains. Just a few souls lingered: the ubiquitous transit police in their Kevlar vests and creaking leather accoutrements, a couple in evening wear racing for a train that had long since departed, an old black man pushing a dust mop, earphones stuffed in his head. At the center of the marbled hall stood the information booth with its legendary timepiece. *Meet me at the kiosk, the one with the four-faced clock* . . . It was New York's most celebrated rendezvous point, perhaps the most famous in the world. How many fateful encounters had occurred in this place? How many assignations had commenced, what nights of love? How many generations walked the earth because a man and a woman had arranged to meet here, beneath this storied timepiece of gleaming brass and opalescent glass? I tilted my face toward the barrel-vaulted ceiling, 125 feet overhead. In my young adulthood, its beauty had been muted by layers of coal soot and nicotine, but that was the old New York; a thorough cleaning in the late nineties had restored its gold-leaf astrological images to their original luster. Taurus, the bull; Gemini, the twins; Aquarius, bearing his water; a milky smear of galactic arm, as one sees only on the clearest of nights. A little-known fact, though not unacknowledged by my scientist's eye, is that the ceiling of Grand Central is actually backward. It is a mirror image of the night sky; lore holds that the artist was working from a medieval manuscript that showed the heavens not from within but from without—not mankind's view but God's.

I took a seat at the top of the west balcony steps. One of the transit cops gave me a quick eyeball, but as I was now dressed for the part of respectable white-collar professional and was neither asleep nor visibly drunk, he left me alone. I took logistical stock of my surroundings. Grand Central was more than a train station; it was a principal nexus of the city's substrata, its vast underground world of tunnels and chambers. People by the hundreds of thousands flowed through this place each and every day, most never looking beyond the tips of their own shoes. It was perfect, in other words, for my purpose.

I waited. The hours moved by, and then the days. No one seemed to notice me or, if they did, to care. Too much else was going on.

And then after some unknown interval of time had passed, I heard a sound I had not heard before. It was the sound that silence makes when there is no one left to listen. Night had fallen. I rose from my place on the steps and walked outside. There were no lights burning anywhere; the blackness was so complete I might have been at sea, miles from any shore. I looked up and beheld the most curious of sights. Stars by the hundreds, the thousands, the millions, locked in their slow turning above the empty world, as they had done since time's beginning. Their pins of light fell upon my face like pattering drops of rain, streaming out of the past. I did not know what I was feeling, only that I felt it; and I began, at last, to weep.

15

And thus to my woeful tale.

Observe him, a capable young man of passable looks, slender and shaggy-haired, tan from a summer of honest outdoor work, good with math and things mechanical, not without ambition and bright hopes and possessing a solitary, inward-looking personality, alone in his bedroom beneath the eaves as he packs his suitcase of folded shirts and socks and underwear and not much else. The year is 1989; our setting is a provincial town named Mercy, Ohio—famous, briefly, for its precision brassworks, said to produce the finest shell casings in the history of modern warfare, though that, like much else of the town, is long faded. The room, which is to be unoccupied within the hour, is a shrine to the young man's youth. Here is the display of trophies. Here are the soldier bedside lamp and matching martial-themed curtains; here the shelves of serial novels featuring intrepid trios of underappreciated teenagers whose youthful intellects enable them to solve crimes their elders cannot. Here, tacked to the neutral plaster walls, are the pennants of sports teams and the conundrumous M. C. Escher etching of hands drawing each other and, opposite the sagging single bed, the era-appropriate poster of the erect-nippled *Sports Illustrated* swimsuit model, beneath whose lubricious limbs and come-hither gaze and barely concealed pudenda the boy has furiously masturbated night after adolescent night.

But the boy: he undertakes his packing with the puzzled solemnity of a mourner at a child's funeral, which is the scene's appropriate analogue. The problem is not that he cannot make his belongings fit—he can—but the opposite: the meagerness of the bag's contents seems mismatched with the grandeur of his destination. Tacked above his cramped little-boy's desk, a letter gives the clue. *Dear Timothy Fanning,* it reads on elaborately decorated letterhead with a crimson, shield-shaped emblem and the ominous word VERITAS bespeaking ancient wisdoms. *Congratulations, and welcome to the Harvard class of 1993!*

It is early September. Outside, an earthbound, misting rain, tinged by summer's green, hugs the little hamlet of houses and yards and storefront commercial concerns, one of which belongs to the boy's father, the town's lone optometrist. This places the boy's family in the upper reaches of the town's constricted economics; they are, by the standards of that time and place, well-off. His father is known and appreciated; he walks the streets of Mercy to a chorus of amiable hellos, because who is more admirable and worthy of gratitude than the man who has placed the spectacles upon your nose that enable you to see the things and people of your life? As a child, the boy loved to visit his father's office and try on all the eyeglasses that decorated the racks and display cases, longing for the day when he would need a pair of his own, though he never did: his eyes were perfect.

"Time to go, son."

His father has appeared in the door: a short, barrel-chested man whose gray flannel trousers, by gravitational necessity, are held aloft by clip-on suspenders. His thinning hair is wet from the shower, his cheeks freshly scraped by the old-fashioned safety razor he favors despite modern innovations in shaving technology. The air around him sings with the smell of Old Spice.

"If you forget anything, we can always send it to you."

"Like what?"

His father shrugs amiably; he is trying to be helpful. "I don't know. Clothes? Shoes? Did you take your certificate? I'm sure you'll want that."

He is speaking of the boy's second-place award in the Western Reserve District 5 Science Day competition. "The Spark of Life: Gibbs-Donnan Equilibrium and Nernst Potential at the Critical Origin of Cell Viability." The certificate, in a plain black frame, hangs on the wall above his desk. The truth is, it embarrasses him. Don't all Harvard students win first prize? Nevertheless, he makes a show of gratitude for being reminded and places it atop the pile of clothing in the open suitcase. Once in Cambridge, it will never make it out of his bureau drawer; three years later, he will discover it beneath a pile of miscellaneous papers, regard it with a quick, bitter feeling, and pitch it into the trash.

"That's the spirit," his father says. "Show those Harvard smarties who they're dealing with."

From the base of the stairs, his mother's voice ascends in an insistent song: "Tim-o-thy! Are you ready yet?"

She never calls him "Tim"; always it is "Timothy." The name embarrasses him—it feels both courtly and diminutive at the same time, as if he were a little English lord on a velvet cushion—though he also secretly likes it. That his mother vastly prefers him to her husband is no secret; the reverse is also true. The boy loves her far more easily than he loves his father, whose emotional vocabulary is limited to manly pats on the back and the occasional boys-only camping trip. Like many only children, the boy is aware of his value in the household economy, and nowhere is this value more lofty than in his mother's eyes. *My Timothy,* she likes to say, as if there are others not hers; he is her only one. *You are my special Timothy.*

"Haaa-rold! What are you doing up there? He's going to miss the bus!"

"For Pete's sake, just a minute!" He returns his eyes to the boy. "Honestly, I don't know what she's going to do without you to worry about. That woman's going to drive me crazy."

A joke, the boy understands, but in his father's voice he detects an undertone of seriousness. For the first time he considers the full emotional dimensions of the day. His life is changing, but his parents' lives are changing, too. Like a habitat abruptly deprived of a major species, the household will be wrenched into realignment by his departure. Like all young people, he has no idea who his parents really are; for eighteen years he has experienced their existence only insofar as it has related to his own needs. Suddenly his mind is full of questions. What do they talk about when he's not around? What secrets do they hold from each other, what aspirations have been left to languish? What private grievances, held in check by the shared project of child rearing, will now, in his absence, lurch into the light? They love him, but do they love each other? Not as parents or even husband and wife but simply as people—as surely they must have loved each other at one time? He hasn't the foggiest; he can no more grasp these matters than he can imagine the world before he was alive.

Compounding the difficulty is the fact that the boy has never been in love himself. Though the social patterns of Mercy, Ohio, are such that even a modestly attractive person can find opportunities in the sexual marketplace, and the boy, although a virgin, has been from time to time its beneficiary, what he has experienced is merely love's painless presage, the expression without the soul. He wonders if this is a lack within himself. Is there a part of the brain from which love comes that in his case has drastically malfunctioned? The world is awash in love—on the radio, in movies, in the pages of novels. Romantic love is the common cultural narrative, yet he seems immune to it. Thus, though he has yet to taste the pain that comes with love, he has experienced pain of a different, related sort: the fear of facing a life without it.

They meet the boy's mother in the kitchen. He expects to find her dressed and ready to go, but she is wearing her flowered housecoat and terry-cloth slippers. Through some unspoken agreement it has been determined that his father alone will accompany him to the station.

"I packed you a lunch," she declares.

She thrusts a paper sack into his hands. The boy unfolds the crinkled top: a peanut butter sandwich in waxed paper, cut carrots in a baggie, a pint of milk, a box of Barnum's Animal Crackers. He is eighteen: he could devour the contents of ten such bags and still be hungry. It's a meal for a child, yet he finds himself absurdly grateful for this small present. Who knows when his mother will make him lunch again?

"Do you have enough money? Harold, did you give him any cash?"

"I'm fine, Mom. I have plenty from the summer."

His mother's eyes have begun to pool with tears. "Oh, I said I wouldn't do this." She waves her hands in front of her face. "Lorraine, I said, don't you dare cry."

He steps into her warm embrace. She is a substantial woman, good to hug. He breathes in the smell of her—a dusty, fruit-sweet aroma, tinged with the chemical scent of hairspray and the off-gassing nicotine of her breakfast cigarette.

"You can let him go now, Lori. We're going to be late."

"Harvard. My Timothy is going to Harvard. I just can't believe it."

The ride to the bus station, in a neighboring town, takes thirty minutes along rural highways. The car, a late-model Buick LeSabre with a soft suspension and seats of crushed velour, makes the roadway beneath them seem vague, as if they are levitating. It is his father's one self-indulgence: every two years a new LeSabre appears in the driveway, all but indistinguishable from the last. They pass the last houses and ease into the countryside. The fields are fat with corn; birds wheel over the windbreaks. Here and there a farmhouse, some pristinely kept, others in disrepair—paint flaking, foundations tipping, upholstered furniture on the porches and abandoned toys in the yards. Everything the boy sees touches his heart with fondness.

"Listen," his father says, as they are approaching the station, "there's something I wanted to say to you."

Here it comes, the boy thinks. This impending announcement, whatever it is, is the reason they've left his mother behind. What will it be? Not girls or sex; apart from one awkward conversation when he was thirteen, the subject has never been raised. Study hard? Keep your nose to the grindstone? But these things, too, have already been said.

His father clears his throat. "I didn't want to say this before. Well, maybe I did. I probably should have. What I'm trying to say is that you're destined for big things, son. *Great* things. I've always known that about you."

"I'll do my best, I promise."

"I know you will. That's not really what I'm saying." His father hasn't looked at the boy once. "What I'm saying is, this isn't the place for you anymore."

The remark is deeply unsettling. What can his father intend?

"It doesn't mean we don't love you," the man continues. "Far from it. We only want what's best."

"I don't understand."

"The holidays, okay. It wouldn't make sense for you not to be here for Christmas. You know how your mother is. But otherwise . . ."

"You're telling me you don't want me to come home?"

His father is speaking rapidly, his words not so much spoken as unleashed. "You can call, of course. Or we can call you. Every couple of weeks, say. Or even once a month."

The boy has no idea what to make of any of this. He also detects a note of falsehood in his father's words, a manufactured rigidity. It is as if he's reading them off a card.

"I don't believe what you're saying."

"I know this is probably hard to hear. But it really can't be helped."

"What do you mean, it can't be helped? Why can't it be?"

His father draws a breath. "Listen, you'll thank me later. Trust me on that, okay? You might not think so now, but you've got your whole life ahead of you. That's the point."

"That's not the goddamned point!"

"Hey, let's watch the language. There's no reason for that kind of talk."

Suddenly the boy is on the verge of tears. His departure has become a banishment. His father says nothing more, and the boy understands that a border has been reached; he'll get nothing more from the man. *We only want what's best. You've got your whole life.* Whatever his father is actually feeling lies hidden behind this barricade of clichés.

"Dry your tears, son. There's no reason to make a mountain out of a molehill."

"What about Mom? Is this her idea, too?"

His father hesitates; the boy detects a flash of pain on the man's face. A hint of something genuine, a deeper truth, but in the next instant it's gone.

"You don't have to worry about her. She understands."

The car has come to a halt; the boy looks up, amazed to discover that they've arrived at the station. Three bays, one with a bus awaiting; passengers are filing aboard.

"You've got your ticket?"

Speechless, the boy nods; his father extends his hand. He feels like he's being fired from a job. When they shake, his father squeezes before he does, mashing his fingers together. The handshake is awkward and embarrassing; they're both relieved when it's over.

"Go on now," his father urges with false cheer. "You don't want to miss your bus."

There is no rescuing the moment. The boy gets out, still clutching his paper sack of lunch. It feels totemic, the last vestige of a childhood not so much departed as obliterated. He hoists his suitcase from the trunk and pauses to see if his father will emerge from the Buick. Perhaps in a gesture of last-minute conciliation the man will carry his bag to the bus, even send him away with a hug. But no such thing happens. The boy advances to the bus, places his bag in one of the open bays, and takes his place in line.

"Cleveland!" the driver bellows. "All aboard for Cleveland!"

There is some confusion at the head of the line. A man has lost his ticket and is attempting to explain. While everyone waits for the matter to be sorted out, the woman just ahead of the boy turns toward him. She is maybe sixty, with neatly pinned hair, shimmering blue eyes, and a bearing that strikes him as grand, even aristocratic—someone who should be boarding an ocean liner, not a dirty motor coach.

"Now, I bet a young man like you is off somewhere interesting," she says merrily.

He doesn't feel like talking—far from it. "College," he explains, the word thick in his throat. When the woman doesn't respond, he adds, "I'm going to Harvard."

She reveals a smile of absurdly false teeth. "How *marvelous.* A Harvard man. Your parents must be very proud."

His turn comes; he hands his ticket to the driver, moves down the aisle, and selects a seat at the rear because it is as far away from the woman as possible. In Cleveland he will change buses for New York; after a night sleeping on a hard bench in the Port Authority station, his suitcase tucked under his legs, he will catch the first bus to Boston, departing at five A.M. As the big diesel rumbles to life, he finally turns his face toward the window. The rain has returned, dotting the glass. The spot where his father parked is empty.

As the bus backs away, he opens the bag in his lap. It's surprising, how hungry he is. He tears into the sandwich; six bites and it's gone. He downs the milk without removing the carton from his lips. The carrots are next, devoured in an instant. He barely tastes any of it; the point is simply to eat, to fill an empty space. When all else is done, he opens the little box of cookies, pausing to regard its colorful illustrations of caged circus creatures: the polar bear, the lion, the elephant, the gorilla. Barnum's Animal Crackers have been a staple of his childhood, yet it is only now that he notices that the animals are not alone in their cages; each is a mother with her baby.

He places a cookie on his tongue and lets it melt, coating the walls of his mouth with its vanilla sweetness, then another and another, until the box is empty, then closes his eyes, waiting for sleep to come.

Why do I relate this scene in the third person? I suppose because it's easier. I know my father meant well, but it took me many years to process the pain of his decree. I have forgiven him, of course, but absolution is not the same as understanding. His unreadable face, his casually declarative tone: all these years later, I still puzzle over the apparent ease with which he dispatched me from his life. It seems to me that one of the great rewards of raising a son would be the simple enjoyment of his company as he moves into the real business of adulthood. But having no son of my own, I can neither confirm nor deny this.

So it was that I arrived at Harvard University in September 1989—the Soviet Union on the brink of collapse, the economy in a state of general decline, the national mood one of weary boredom with a decade of drift—friendless, orphaned in all but name, with few possessions and no idea what would become of me. I had never set foot on the campus or, for that matter, traveled east of Pittsburgh, and after the past twenty-four hours in transit, my mind was in such a state that everything around me possessed an almost hallucinatory quality. From South Station I took the T to Cambridge (my first ride on a subway) and ascended from the cigarette-strewn platform into the hubbub of Harvard Square. It appeared that the season had changed during my journey; muggy summer had yielded to tart New England autumn, the sky so shockingly blue it was practically audible. In my jeans and slept-in T-shirt, I shivered as a dry breeze moved over me. The hour was just shy of noon, the square thick with people, all of them young, all apparently at perfect ease with their surroundings, moving purposefully in pairs or packs, the talk and laughter passing between them with the crisp assuredness of batons in a relay race. I had entered an alien realm, but this was home to them. My destination was a dormitory named Wigglesworth Hall, though, reluctant to ask anyone for directions— I doubted they'd even stop to talk to me—and discovering that I was famished, I made my way up the block away from the square, looking for someplace inexpensive to eat.

I was to learn later that the restaurant I chose, Mr. and Mrs. Bartley's Burger Cottage, was a beloved Cambridge landmark. I stepped inside to an eye-watering assault of weaponized onion smoke and the roar of a crowd. Half the city appeared to have shoved itself into the cramped space, filling the long tables, everyone trying to talk over everybody else, including the cooks, who were shouting out their orders like quarterbacks calling signals. On the wall above the grill was an enormous blackboard bearing elaborate descriptions in colored chalk of the most off-puttingly garnished burgers I had ever heard of: pineapple, blue cheese, fried egg.

"Just you?"

The man addressing me looked more like a wrestler than a waiter—a huge, bearded fellow wearing an apron as stained as a butcher's. I nodded dumbly.

"Singles at the counter only," he commanded. "Grab a stool."

A place had just come free. As the waitress behind the counter whisked away the previous occupant's dirty plate, I slid my suitcase against the base of the counter and took a seat. It wasn't very comfortable, but at least my luggage was hidden from view. I took my map out of my pocket and began to look it over.

"What'll you have, hon?"

The waitress, a harried-looking older woman with sweat stains at the armpits of her Burger Cottage T-shirt, stood before me, pad and pencil poised.

"A cheeseburger?"

"Lettuce, tomato, onion, pickle, ketchup, mayo, mustard, Swiss, cheddar, provolone, American, what kind of bun, toasted or plain?"

It was like trying to catch bullets from a machine gun. "Everything, I guess."

"You want four different kinds of cheese?" She had yet to lift her eyes from her pad. "I'll have to charge you extra."

"I didn't mean that. Sorry. Just the cheddar. Cheddar is fine."

"Toasted or plain?"

"I'm sorry?"

Her eyes, weary with boredom, rose at last. "Do . . . you . . . want . . . your bun . . . toasted . . . or . . . plain?"

"Jesus, Margo, take it easy on the guy, will you?"

The voice had come from the man sitting to my right. I had studiously kept my eyes forward, but now I turned to look. He was tall, broad-shouldered but not overtly muscular, with the sort of well-proportioned face that gives the impression of having been made more carefully than most people's. He was dressed in a rumpled oxford shirt tucked into faded Levi's; a pair of sunglasses was perched on his head, held in place by the folds of his wavy brown hair. One ankle, his right, was propped on the opposite knee, showing a scuffed penny loafer without a sock. In the periphery of my vision he had registered as a full-fledged adult, but I now saw that he couldn't have been more than a year or two older than I was. The difference was one not of age but of bearing.

Everything about him radiated an aura of belonging, that he was a scion of the tribe and fluent in its customs.

He closed his book, placed it on the counter next to his empty coffee cup, and gave me a disarming smile that said, *Don't worry, I've got this.*

"The man wants a cheeseburger with the works. Toasted bun. Cheddar cheese. Fries with that, I think. How about a drink?" he asked me.

"Um, milk?"

"And a milk. No," he said, correcting himself, "a shake. Chocolate, no whip. Trust me."

The waitress looked at me doubtfully. "Okay with you?"

The whole exchange had left me baffled. On the other hand, a shake did sound good, and I was in no mood to turn away a kindness. "Sure."

"Attaboy." My neighbor climbed down from his stool and tucked his book under his arm in a way that suggested all books should be carried in precisely this manner. I saw but did not understand the title: *Principles of Existential Phenomenology.* "Margo here will take good care of you. The two of us go way back. She's been feeding me since I was in short pants."

"I liked you better then," Margo said.

"And you wouldn't be the first to say so. Now, chop-chop. Our friend looks hungry."

The waitress left without another word. Their repartee suddenly became clear to me. Not the banter of friends but something rather like a precocious nephew and his aunt. "Thanks," I said to my companion.

"*De nada.* Sometimes this place is like a big rudeness contest, but it's worth the hassle. So where did they put you?"

"I'm sorry?"

"What dorm. You're an incoming freshman, aren't you?"

I was amazed. "How did you know that?"

"The powers of my mind." He tapped his temple, then laughed. "That and the suitcase. So, which is it? I hope they didn't put you in one of the Union dorms. You want to be in the Yard."

The distinction meant nothing to me. "Someplace called Wigglesworth."

My answer obviously pleased him. "You're in luck, friend. You'll be right in the middle of the action. Of course, what qualifies as action around this place can be a little staid. It's usually people tearing their hair out at four A.M. over a problem set." He gave my shoulder a manly clap. "Don't worry. Everybody feels a little lost at first."

"I kind of get the feeling you didn't."

"I'm what you'd call a special case. Harvard brat from birth. My father teaches in the philosophy department. I'd tell you who he is, but then you might feel you should take one of his courses out of gratitude, which would be, pardon me, a huge fucking mistake. The man's lectures are like a bullet to the brain." For the second time in as many days, I was to receive a handshake from a man who seemed to know more about my life than I did. "Anyway, good luck. Out the door, take a left, go down a block to the gate. Wigglesworth is on your right."

With that, he was gone. Only then did I realize that I had neglected to get his name. I hoped I might see him again, though not too soon, and that when I did, I could report that I had ably inserted myself into my new life. I also made a note that at the earliest opportunity I would go shopping for a white oxford shirt and loafers; at least I could look the part. My cheeseburger and fries arrived, shimmering deliciously with grease, and beside it the promised chocolate shake, standing tall in an elegant, fifties-era glass. It was more than a meal; it was an omen. I was so thankful that I might have said grace, and nearly did.

College days, Harvard days: the feeling of time itself changed in those early months, everything rushing past at a frenetic pace. My roommate was named Lucessi. His first name was Frank, though neither I nor anyone I knew ever used it. We were friends of a sort, thrust together by circumstances. I had expected everyone at the college to be some version of the fellow I'd met at the Burger Cottage, with a quick-talking social intelligence and an aristocrat's knowledge of local practices, but, in fact, Lucessi was more typical: weirdly smart, a graduate of the Bronx High School of Science, hardly the winner of any prizes for physical attractiveness or personal hygiene, his personality laden with tics. He had a big, soft body, like a poorly filled stuffed animal's, large damp hands he had no idea what to do with, and the roving, wide-eyed gaze of a paranoiac, which I thought he might be. His wardrobe was a combination of a junior accountant's and a middle schooler's: he favored high-waisted pleated pants, heavy brown dress shoes, and T-shirts emblazoned with the emblem of the New York Yankees. Within five minutes of our meeting he had explained to me that he had scored a perfect 1600 on his SATs, intended to double major in math and physics, could speak both Latin and ancient Greek (not just read: actually *speak*), and had once caught a home run launched from the bat of the great Reggie Jackson. I might have viewed his companionship as a burden, but I soon saw the advantages; Lucessi made me appear well-adjusted by comparison, more confident and attractive than I actually was, and I won not a few sympathy points among my dormitory neighbors for putting up with him, as one might have for tending to a farty dog. The first night we got drunk together—just a week after our arrival, at one of the countless freshman keg parties that the administration seemed content to overlook—he vomited so helplessly and at such extended duration that I spent the night making sure he didn't die.

My goal was to be a biochemist, and I wasted no time. My course load was crushing, my only relief a distribution course in art history that required little more than sitting in the dark and looking at slides of Mary and the baby Jesus in various beatific poses. (The class, a legendary refuge for science majors meeting their humanities requirement, bore the nickname "Darkness at Noon.") My scholarship was generous, but I was used to working and wanted pocket money; for ten hours a week, at a wage just above minimum, I shelved books at Widener Library, pushing a wobbly cart through a maze of stacks so isolated and byzantine that women were warned against visiting them alone. I thought the job would kill me with boredom, and for a while it nearly did, but over time I came to like it: the smell of old paper and the taste of dust; the deep hush of the place, a sanctuary of silence broken only by the squeaking wheels of my cart; the pleasant shock of pulling a book from the shelves, removing the card, and discovering that nobody had checked it out since 1936. A twinge of anthropomorphic sympathy for these underappreciated volumes often inspired me to read a page or two, so that they might feel wanted.

Was I happy? Who wouldn't be? I had friends, my studies to occupy me. I had my quiet hours in the library in which to woolgather to my heart's content. In late October, I lost my virginity to a girl I met at a party. We were both very intoxicated, didn't know each other at all, and though she didn't say as much—we barely spoke, beyond the usual preliminary blather and a brief negotiation over the mechanically baffling mechanism of her brassiere—I suspected she was a virgin, too, and that her intention was simply to get the thing done as expeditiously as possible so that she could move on to other, more satisfying encounters. I suppose I felt the same. When it was over, I left her room quickly, as if from the scene of a crime, and in four years I laid eyes on her only twice more, both times at a distance.

Yes, I was happy. My father was right: I had found my life. I dutifully telephoned every two weeks, reversing the charges, but my parents—indeed, my whole small-town Ohio childhood—began to fade from my mind, the way dreams do in the light of day. Always these calls were the same. First I would speak with my mother, who usually answered—the suggestion being that she had spent two weeks waiting by the phone—and then my father, whose jovial tone seemed contrived to remind me of his parting edict, and finally both together. I could easily imagine the scene: their faces angled close together with the receiver between them as they called out their valedictory "I love you"s and "I'm proud of you"s and "be good"s, my father's eyes locked in an optic death grip on the clock above the kitchen sink, watching his money drain away at thirty cents a minute. Their voices aroused great feelings of tenderness in me, almost of pity, as if I were the abandoner and they the abandoned, yet I was always relieved when these calls ended, the click of the receiver releasing me back into my true existence.

Before I knew it, the leaves had turned, then fallen, their desiccated carcasses everywhere underfoot, suffusing the air with a sweet smell of decay; the week before Thanksgiving the first snow fell, my inaugural New England winter, damp and raw. It felt like one more baptism in a year of them. There had been no discussion of my returning home for the Thanksgiving break, and Ohio was too far in any case—I'd have wasted half the time on the bus—so I accepted an invitation to spend the holiday with Lucessi in the Bronx. Stupidly, I had expected a scene of Italian life straight out of Hollywood: a cramped apartment above a pizza parlor, everyone yelling and screaming at one another, his father leaking armpitty garlic sweat through his undershirt and his mustached mother, in a housecoat and slippers, throwing up her hands and wailing *"Mamma mia"* every thirty seconds.

What I found couldn't have been more different. They lived in Riverdale, which, though technically the Bronx, was as tony as any neighborhood I'd ever seen, in a huge stone Tudor that looked as if it had been hijacked from the English countryside. No spaghetti and meatballs here, no household shrines to the Madonna, no arm-waving drama of any sort; the house was as stultifying as a tomb. Thanksgiving dinner was served by a Guatemalan housemaid in an aproned uniform, and afterward, everybody repaired to a room they actually called "the study," to listen to a radio broadcast of Wagner's interminable *Ring* cycle. Lucessi had told me that his family was in "the restaurant business" (thus the pizza parlor of my imagination), but in fact his father was chief financial officer of the restaurant division of Goldman Sachs, to whose Wall Street offices he commuted every day in a Lincoln Continental the size of a tank. I'd known that Lucessi had a younger sister; he had failed to mention that she was a bona fide Mediterranean goddess, quite possibly the most beautiful girl I'd ever laid eyes on—regally tall, with lustrous black hair, a complexion so creamy I wanted to drink it, and a habit of traipsing into a room wearing nothing more than a slip. Her name was Arianna. She was home from boarding school, someplace in Virginia where they rode horses all day, and when she wasn't lounging around in her underwear, reading magazines and eating buttered toast and talking loudly on the phone, she was striding through the house in tall riding boots and clanking spurs and tight breeches, a costume no less powerful than the slip in its ability to send the blood dumping to my loins. Arianna was completely out of my league, in other words, a fact as obvious as the weather, yet she went out of her way to remind me of it, calling me "Tom" no matter how many times her brother corrected her and nailing me with looks of such dismissive contempt it was like being doused by cold water.

My final night in Riverdale, I awoke sometime after midnight to discover that I was hungry. I had been instructed to treat the house "as if it were my own"—laughably impossible—yet I knew I would not sleep unless I put something in my stomach. I slipped on a pair of sweatpants and crept downstairs to the kitchen, where I discovered Arianna at the table in a flannel bathrobe, paging through *Cosmopolitan* with her elegant hands and spooning cereal into her flawlessly formed, generously lipped mouth. A box of Cheerios and a gallon of milk sat on the counter. My first instinct was to retreat, but she had already noticed me, standing like an idiot in the doorway.

"Do you mind?" I asked. "I thought I'd get a snack."

Her attention had already returned to her magazine. She took a bite of cereal and gave a backhanded wave. "Do what you want."

I helped myself to a bowl. There was no place else to sit, so I joined her at the table. Even in the flannel bathrobe, her face without makeup and her hair uncombed, she was magnificent. I had no idea what to say to such a creature.

"You're looking at me," she said, turning a page.

I felt the blood rushing to my cheeks. "No, I wasn't."

She said nothing more. I had no place to put my eyes, so I looked at my cereal. The crunch of my chewing seemed intensely loud.

"What are you reading?" I asked finally.

She sighed irritably, closed her magazine, and looked up. "Okay, fine. Here I am."

"I was just trying to make conversation."

"Can we not? Please? I've seen you watching me, Tim."

"So you know my name."

"Tim, Tom, whatever." She rolled her eyes. "Oh, all right. Let's get this over with."

She parted the top of her robe. Beneath it she was wearing only a bra of shimmering pink silk. The sight aroused me indescribably.

"Go on," she urged.

"Go on what?"

She was looking at me with an expression of bored mockery. "Don't be dense, Harvard boy. Here, let me help you."

She took my hand and placed it, rather mechanically, against her left breast. A magnificent breast it was! I had never touched a goddess before. Its spherical softness, sheathed in high-dollar silk with a scallop of delicate lace at the edges, filled my palm like a peach. I sensed she was making fun of me, but I hardly cared. What would happen now? Would I be permitted to kiss her?

Apparently not. As I was constructing a complete sexual narrative in my head, the wonderful things we might do together, culminating in breathy intercourse upon the kitchen floor, she abruptly pulled my hand away and let it fall on the table with the same contemptuous gesture one might use for dropping trash into a bin.

"So," she said, reopening her magazine, "did you get what you wanted? Did that satisfy you?"

I was utterly flummoxed. She turned a page, then another. What the hell had just happened?

"I don't understand you at all," I said.

"Of course you don't." She looked up again, wrinkling her nose in distaste. "Tell me something. Why are you even friends with him? I mean, all things considered, you seem sort of normal."

This was, I supposed, what passed for a compliment. It also aroused in me a fiercely protective instinct toward her brother. Who was she to talk about him like that? Who did she think she was, teasing me this way?

"You're awful," I said.

She gave a nasty little laugh. "Sticks and stones, Harvard boy. Now, if you'll excuse me, I'm trying to read."

And that was the end of it. I returned to bed, so sexually charged I barely slept, and in the morning, before anybody else in the house was awake, Lucessi's father drove us to the train station in his monstrous Lincoln. As we disembarked, in an awkward reversal of customary courtesy, he thanked me for coming in a manner that suggested that he, too, felt a little baffled by my friendship with his son. A picture was emerging: Lucessi was the runt of the litter, an object of family-wide pity and embarrassment. I felt profoundly sorry for him, even as I recognized his situation's similarity to my own. We were a couple of castaways, the two of us.

We boarded the train. I was exhausted and didn't feel like talking. For a while we bumped along in silence. Lucessi was the first to speak.

"Sorry about all that." He was drawing meaningless shapes on the window with his index finger. "I'm sure you were hoping for something more exciting."

I hadn't told him what had happened and, of course, never would. It was also true that my anger had softened, replaced by a budding curiosity. Something altogether unexpected about the world had been glimpsed. This life his family led; I had known that such wealth existed, but that is not the same as sleeping under its roof. I felt like an explorer who'd stumbled upon a golden city in the jungle.

"Don't worry about it," I said. "I had a great time."

Lucessi sighed, settled back, and closed his eyes. "They can be the stupidest people on earth," he said.

*   *   *

What fascinated me, of course, was money. Not just because of the things it could buy, though these were appealing (Lucessi's sister being Exhibit A). The deeper attraction lay in something more atmospheric. I had never been around wealthy people but had not felt this as a lack; I had never been around Martians, either. There were plenty of rich kids at Harvard, of course, the ones who'd gone to exclusive prep schools and addressed each other with preposterous nicknames like "Trip" and "Beemer" and "Duck." But in day-to-day existence, their affluence was easily overlooked. We lived in the same crappy dormitories, sweated through the same papers and tests, ate the same atrocious food in the dining hall, like co-residents of a kibbutz. Or so it seemed. Visiting Lucessi's house had opened my eyes to a hidden world that lay beneath the egalitarian surface of our lives, like a system of caves under my feet. Except for Lucessi, I actually knew very little about my friends and classmates. It seems improbable to say so now, but the thought had never occurred to me that there could be something so fundamentally different about them.

In the weeks after Thanksgiving, I took clearer stock of my surroundings. There was a boy who lived down the hall whose father was the mayor of San Francisco; a girl I knew slightly, who spoke with a heavy Spanish accent, was said to be the daughter of a South American dictator; one of my lab partners had confided to me, apropos of nothing, that his family owned a summer house in France. All this information coalesced into a whole new awareness of where I was, and the thought made me incredibly self-conscious, even as I longed to learn more about it, to penetrate its social codes and see where I might fit.

Equally fascinating to me was the fact that Lucessi himself wanted nothing to do with any of it. Throughout the weekend, he had made no secret of his contempt for his sister, his parents, even the house, which he called, in typical Lucessian fashion, "an idiotic pile of rock." I attempted to draw him out on this subject but got nowhere; my overtures actually made him angry and snappish. What I had begun to discern in my roommate was the price of being too smart. He possessed an intellect capable of calculating reams of data without taking pleasure in any of it. To Lucessi, the world was a collection of interlocking systems divorced from all meaning, a surface reality governed only by itself. He could, for instance, recite the batting averages of every player on the New York Yankees, but when I asked him who his favorite was, he had no answer. The only emotion he seemed capable of was disdain for other people, though even that possessed a quality of childish bewilderment, as if he were a bored toddler in a man's body, forced to sit at the grown-ups' table and listen to incomprehensible conversations about the price of real estate and who was divorcing whom. I believe this pained him—he wasn't aware what the problem was, only that it existed—resulting in a kind of nihilistic loneliness: he both despised and envied everybody else, except for me, to whom he attributed a similar vision of the world, simply because I was always around and didn't make fun of him.

As for his unhappy fate: perhaps I didn't value him enough as a friend. Sometimes I think I might have been the only friend he ever had. And it is strange, after so many years, that from time to time my thoughts still turn to him, even though he was, after all, but a minor actor in my life. Probably it is the idleness of my circumstances that draws me to the recollection. With so many years to fill, one inevitably gets around to everything, opens each drawer of the mind to rustle around inside it. I did not know Lucessi well; no man could. Yet the failure to know a person does not rule out his importance in our lives. I wonder: how would Lucessi regard me now? Were he to wander, miraculously alive, into this prison of my own making, this becalmed memorial to things lost, ascend the marble staircase with his graceless Lucessian gait and stand before me in his clunky shoes and ill-fitting trousers and Yankees' jersey stinking of unwashed Lucessian sweat, what would he tell me? *See?* he might say. *Now you get it, Fanning. Now you really get it, after all.*

I returned to Ohio for Christmas. I was glad to be home, but mine was the exile's gladness; none of it seemed to pertain to me anymore, as if I'd been gone for years, not months. Harvard was not my home, at least not yet, but neither was Mercy, Ohio. The very idea of home, of one true place, had become odd to me.

My mother did not appear well. She had lost a great deal of weight, and her smoker's cough had worsened. A glaze of sweat appeared on her brow at the smallest exertion. I paid this little mind, accepting at face value my father's explanation that she had overdone it making ready for the holidays. I dutifully went through the sentimental motions: tree trimming and pie baking, a trip to Midnight Mass (we never attended church otherwise), opening my presents while my parents looked on—an awkward ceremony that is the bane of all only children—but my heart was nowhere in this, and I departed two days early, explaining that with exams still ahead of me, I needed to get back to my studies. (I did, but that wasn't the reason.) Just as he'd done in September, my father drove me to the station. The rains of summer had been replaced by snow and biting cold, the warm wind through open windows by a blast of desiccated air from the dashboard vents. It would have been the perfect time to say something meaningful, if either of us could have imagined what such a thing might be. When the bus pulled away, I did not look back.

About the remainder of that first year, there is not much else to say. My grades were good—better than good. Though I knew I had done well, I was still astonished to see my first-semester report with its barricade of A's, each emphatically embossed into the paper by the old-fashioned dot matrix printer. I did not use this as an opportunity to slack off but redoubled my efforts. I also, for a brief time, acquired a girlfriend, the daughter of the South American dictator. (He was actually the Argentine minister of finance.) What she saw in me I have no idea, but I wasn't going to interrogate the point. Carmen possessed a good deal more sexual experience than I did—a *great* deal. She was the kind of woman who used the word "lover," as in "I have taken you as my," and she applied herself to pleasure's project with greedy abandon. She was blessed with a single room, rare for a freshman, and in that hallowed precinct of draped scarves and female aromas she introduced me to what might have passed for actual, grown-up eroticism, working her way through the full menu of bodily delights, appetizers to dessert. We did not love each other—that sainted emotion still eluded me, and Carmen had little use for it—nor was she what I would call conventionally attractive. (I can say this because I wasn't, either.) She was a little heavy, and her face possessed a slightly masculine bulk around the jawline, which looked like a boxer's. But unclothed, and in the heat of passion, crying out naughty things in her Argentine-inflected Spanish, she was the most sensual creature who ever walked the earth, a fact magnified a hundred-fold by her own awareness of it.

Between these carnal escapades—Carmen and I would often race back to her room between classes for an hour of furious copulation—and my voluminous classwork and, of course, my hours at the library—time well spent replenishing myself for our next encounter—I saw less and less of Lucessi. He'd always kept odd hours, studying through the night and living on naps, but as the semester wore on, his comings and goings became more erratic. When I slept over at Carmen's, I might not see him for several days in a row. By this time I had widened my society beyond the walls of Wigglesworth to include a number of Carmen's friends, all of them far more cosmopolitan than I was. Lucessi obviously resented this, but any effort to pull him into the circle was sternly rebuffed. His hygiene took another dip; our room stank of socks and the trays of moldy food he brought back from the cafeteria and never removed. Many times I entered to find him sitting on his bed, barely dressed, muttering to himself and making odd, twitchy hand gestures, as if involved in earnest conversation with some unseen party. At bedtime—whenever he decided that was, even if it was the middle of the day—he would smear his face with a layer of acne cream as thick as a mime's makeup; he began to sleep with a scuba diver's knife in a rubber sheath strapped to his leg. (This should have disturbed me more than it did.)

I worried about him, but not very much; I was simply too busy. Despite my new, more interesting circle of friends, I had always assumed that the two of us would continue to room together. At the end of the year, all freshmen entered a lottery to determine which of the Harvard houses they would live in for the next three years. This was regarded as a rite of passage as socially determinant as whom one married, and it possessed two aspects. The first was which house one sought to live in. There were twelve, each with its own reputation: the preppy house, the artsy house, the jock house, and so forth. The most desirable were the ones located along the Charles River—extremely fancy real estate for the price of an undergraduate tuition. The least were the ones in the old Radcliffe Quad, far up Garden Street. To be "quadded" was tantamount to exile, one's life forever chained to a schedule of shuttle buses that, inconveniently, stopped running long before the party had ended.

The second aspect was, of course, who would room with whom. This made for an uncomfortable few weeks as people sorted out their allegiances and prioritized their friendships. Rejecting one's freshman roommate in favor of other parties was common but no less awkward than a divorce. I considered having this very conversation with Lucessi, then found that I didn't have the heart. Who else would be willing to room with him? Who else would tolerate his quirks, his doleful personality, his unhealthful aromas? On top of which, come to think of it, nobody else had asked me. Lucessi, it seemed, was mine.

As the day of the lottery approached, I sought him out to see what he wanted to do. I told him I thought we might go in for Winthrop House, or else Lowell. Quincy, maybe, as a backup. They were river houses but without the distinct social slant of some of the others. This conversation occurred in the middle of the afternoon of a warm spring day that Lucessi had apparently slept through. He was sitting at his desk, wearing only briefs and an undershirt, fussing with a calculator as I spoke, punching in meaningless digits with the eraser end of a pencil. A white crust of dried toothpaste ringed his mouth.

"So what do you think?"

Lucessi shrugged. "I already entered."

His words made no sense. "What are you talking about?"

"I asked for a single in the quad."

Psycho singles, they were called. Housing for the maladjusted; rooms for people who couldn't handle roommates.

"It's pretty nice up there, actually," Lucessi went on. "Quieter. You know. Anyway, it's done."

I was dumbfounded. "Lucessi, what the hell? The lottery's next week. I thought we were going to go together."

"I just kind of assumed you didn't want to. You have lots of friends. I thought you'd be happy."

"*You're* supposed to be my friend." I strode furiously around the room. "Is that what this is about? I can't believe you're doing this. Look at this place. Look at *you*. Who else do you have? And you're doing this to *me*?"

These awful, unrecallable words: Lucessi's face crumpled like a wad of paper. "Christ, I'm sorry. I didn't mean—"

He didn't let me finish. "No, you're right. I really am pretty pathetic. Believe me, it's nothing I haven't heard before."

"Don't talk about yourself like that." My guilt was excruciating. I sat on his bed, trying to get him to look at me. "I shouldn't have said what I did. I was just upset."

"That's okay. Forget it." A moment went by, Lucessi frowning at the calculator. "Did I ever tell you I was adopted? I'm not even related to her. Not technically, anyway."

The comment came from so far out of left field it took me a moment to realize that he was talking about Arianna.

"Everybody always thinks it's the other way around," he continued. "I mean, God, just look at her. But no. My parents got me out of some orphanage. They didn't think they could have kids. Eleven months later, wouldn't you know, along comes Miss Perfect."

I had never heard a confession of such absolute misery. What was there to say? And why was he telling me this now?

"She really hates me, you know. I mean *hates*. You should hear the things she calls me."

"I'm sure that's not true."

Lucessi shrugged hopelessly. "They all do it. They think I don't know, but I do. Okay, I'm king of the dorks. It's not like I haven't figured that out. But Arianna. You've seen her—you know what I'm talking about. Jesus, it just kills me."

"Your sister is a total bitch. She probably treats everybody like that. Just forget about her."

"Yeah, well. That's not really the issue." He lifted his gaze from the calculator and looked me dead in the eye. "You've been really nice to me, Tim, and I appreciate it. I mean that. Promise me we'll stay friends, okay?"

I realized what Lucessi was doing. What I'd thought was jealousy or self-pity was actually a kind of backhanded generosity. Just as my father had done, Lucessi was severing his ties to me because he thought I'd be better off. The worst part was, I knew he was right.

"Sure," I said. "Of course we will."

He held out his hand. "Shake on it? So I know you're not too mad."

We shook, neither of us believing it meant a thing.

"So that's it?" I said.

"I guess so, yeah."

*   *   *

He was in love with her, of course. Though he'd told me as much, this was the part of the story that took me a long time—too long—to figure out. He loved the thing he also hated, and it was destroying him. The other thing Lucessi had told me, without actually saying it, was that he was in the process of flunking all his courses. His living arrangements were moot, because he wouldn't be returning.

In the meantime, this left me with the problem of finding a place to live. I felt betrayed, and angry with myself for having so badly misunderstood the situation, but also resigned to my fate, which seemed somehow deserved. It was as if I'd lost some cosmic game of musical chairs; the song had stopped, I was left standing, and there was simply nothing to be done about it. I called around to see if anybody I knew was looking for a third or a fourth to round out a suite, but no one was, and rather than dig deeper into my list of acquaintances and embarrass myself further, I stopped asking. There were no singles in any of the River Houses, but it was still possible to enter the lottery as a "floater"; I'd be placed on a waiting list for each of the three houses I chose, and if a student dropped out over the summer, the university would give me his slot. I put in for Lowell, Winthrop, and Quincy, no longer caring which one I got, and waited to hear.

The year came to an end. Carmen and I went our separate ways. One of my professors had offered me a job working in his lab. The pay was negligible, but it was an honor to be asked, and it would keep me in Cambridge for the summer. I rented a room in Allston from a woman in her eighties who favored Harvard students; except for her collection of cats, which was voluminous—I was never quite sure how many there were—and the overwhelming stink of the litter boxes, the situation was close to ideal. I left early and returned late, usually taking my meals at one of the many cheap eateries on the fringes of Cambridge, and the two of us rarely saw each other. All my friends were gone for the summer, and I expected to be lonely, but it didn't turn out that way. The year had left me enervated and overstuffed, as if by a too-rich meal, and I was glad for the quiet. My job, which involved collating reams of data on the structural biology of plasma cells in mice, could be conducted virtually without interaction with another human being. Sometimes I barely spoke for days.

It shames me to say this, but during that silent summer, I forgot all about my parents. I do not mean that I ignored them. I mean that I forgot that they existed at all. I had told them in a letter where I would be staying and why but hadn't given them the phone number, because I didn't know it at the time—an omission I never got around to correcting. I did not call them and they could not call me, and as the summer wore on, this casual oversight became a psychological buffer that eradicated them from my thoughts. Doubtless, in some pocket of my mind I knew what I was doing, and I would need to contact them before the fall to file the proper paperwork for my scholarship; but at the level of conscious awareness, they simply ceased to matter.

Then my mother died.

My father informed me of this in a letter. Suddenly, a great deal was made clear to me. A month before I'd left for Harvard, my mother had been diagnosed with uterine cancer. She had delayed surgery—a total abdominal hysterectomy—until after my departure, not wanting to cast a shadow over this occasion. Postoperative biopsies had revealed that the cancer was an aggressive and rare adenosarcoma that left her with no hope of recovery. By winter, she had metastases in her lungs and bones. There was simply nothing to be done. It was, my father said, her dying desire that the son she loved so much should suffer no interruption in his progress toward the fulfillment of all her proud hopes: in other words, that I should go about my life and know nothing. She had died two weeks previously, her ashes buried without funereal pageant, in accordance with her wishes. She had not suffered much, my father wrote, rather coldly, and it was on loving thoughts of me that she had traveled into the life to come.

He wrote in closing, *Probably you're angry with me, with both of us, for keeping this secret from you. If it's any consolation, I wanted you to know, but your mother wouldn't hear of it. When I told you that day at the bus to leave us behind, those were her words, not mine, though she eventually made me see the wisdom of them. Your mother and I were happy together, I believe, but never for a moment did I doubt that you were the great love of her life. She wanted only what was best for you, her Timothy. You may wish to return home, but I encourage you to wait. I am doing reasonably well, under the circumstances, and can see no reason for you to interrupt your studies for what would be, in the end, a painful distraction that would serve no purpose. I love you, son. I hope you know that, and that you can forgive me—forgive us both—and that when we next meet, it will be not to mourn your mother's passing but to celebrate your triumphs.*

I read this letter standing in the front hallway of the house of a woman I barely knew, cats nosing around my feet, at ten o'clock on a warm night in early August when I was nineteen years old. What I experienced is nothing I have words for, and I will not make the attempt. The urge to telephone him was strong; I wanted to scream at him until my throat ripped open, until my words were blood. So was the urge to get on a bus to Ohio, go straight to the house, and strangle him in his bed—the bed he had shared with my mother for nearly thirty years and where, no doubt, I had been conceived. But I did neither. I realized I was hungry. The body wants what it wants—a useful lesson—

and I availed myself of the old woman's larder to make myself a cheese sandwich on stale bread with a glass of the same milk she left in saucers all around the house. The milk had turned, but I drank it anyway, and that is what I remember most vividly of all: the taste of sour milk.

16

The remainder of the summer passed in an emotionless haze. At some point I received a letter informing me that I had been placed in Winthrop House with an as-yet-unnamed roommate who was returning from a year abroad. That I cared nothing about this news is a gross understatement. As far as I was concerned, I could have gone on living with the old woman and her dirty litter boxes. About my mother, I told no one. I worked at the lab right up until the first day of the new semester, leaving no transitional interval in which I might find myself with nothing to distract me. My professor asked me if I wanted to continue working with him during the academic year, but I turned him down. Perhaps this was unwise, and he seemed shocked that I should decline such a privilege, but it would leave no time for the library, whose consoling silence I missed.

I come now to the part of the story in which my situation changed so radically that I recall it as a kind of plunge, as if I had been merely floating on the surface of my life until then. This commenced the day I moved into Winthrop House. Lucessi and I had sold off our Salvation Army furniture, and I arrived with little more than the same suitcase I'd brought to Harvard a year ago, a desk lamp, a box of books, and the impression that I had once again slipped into an anonymity so pure that I could have changed my name if I wanted to with nobody the wiser. My quarters, two rooms arranged railroad-apartment-style with a bathroom at the rear, was on the fourth floor facing the Winthrop quadrangle, with a view of Boston's modest skyline behind it. There was no sign of my roommate, whose name I was yet to learn. I spent some time mulling over which space to choose as my own—the interior room was smaller but more private; on the other hand, I would have to endure my roommate trooping through at all hours to the toilet—before deciding that, to get things off on the right foot, I would await his arrival, so that we might decide together.

I had finished carting the last of my belongings up the stairs when a figure appeared in the doorway, his face obscured by the stack of cardboard boxes in his arms. He advanced into the room, groaning with effort, and lowered them to the floor.

"You," I said.

It was the man I'd met at the Burger Cottage. He was wearing frayed khaki pants and a gray T-shirt that said HARVARD SQUASH, with crescents of sweat under the arms.

"Wait," he said, peering at me. "I know you. How do I know you?"

I explained our meeting. At first he professed no recollection; then a look of recognition dawned.

"Of course. The guy with the suitcase. I'm guessing this means you found Wigglesworth." A thought occurred to him. "No offense, but wouldn't that make you a sophomore?"

It was a fair question, with a complicated answer. Though I'd been admitted as a freshman, I had enough AP credits to graduate in three years. I'd given this matter little thought, always expecting to hang around for the full four. But in the weeks since receiving my father's letter, the option to bang out my education at a quickstep and skedaddle had grown more appealing. Evidently the Harvard higher-ups had thought so, too, since they'd housed me with an upperclassman.

"I guess that makes you a real smarty-pants, doesn't it?" he said. "So, let's have it."

He had a way of speaking that was both elusively sarcastic and somehow complimentary at the same time. "Have what?"

"You know. Name, rank, serial number. Your major, place of origin, that sort of thing. The history of yourself, in other words. Keep it simple—my memory is for shit in this heat."

"Tim Fanning. Biochemistry. Ohio."

"Nicely done. Though if you ask me tomorrow I probably won't remember, so don't be offended." He stepped forward, hand extended. "Jonas Lear, by the way."

I did my best to respond with a manly grip. "Lear," I repeated. "Like the jet?"

"Alas, no. More like Shakespeare's mad king." He glanced around. "So, which of these luxury compartments have you selected as your own?"

"I thought it would be fair to wait."

"Lesson number one: Never wait. Law of the jungle and so forth. But since you're determined to be a nice guy, we can flip for it." He pulled a coin from his pocket. "Call it."

Up the coin went before I could respond. He snatched it from the air and slapped it to his wrist

"I guess . . . heads?"

"Why does everybody call heads? Someone should do a study." He lifted his hand. "Well, what do you know, it's heads."

"I guess I was thinking of the smaller one."

He smiled. "See? How hard was that. I would have gone the same way."

"You never told me what you were studying."

"Right you are. That was rude of me." He tossed a pair of finger quotes into the air. "Organismic and Evolutionary Biology."

I'd never heard of it. "That's an actual major?"

He'd bent to open one of the boxes. "So my transcript tells me. Plus, it's fun to say. It sounds a little dirty." He glanced up and smiled. "What? Not what you expected?"

"I would have said—I don't know—something more lively. History, maybe. Or English."

He removed an armload of textbooks and began loading them onto the shelves. "Let me ask you something. Of all the possible subjects in the world, why did you choose biochemistry?"

"I suppose because I'm good at it."

He turned, hands on his hips. "Well, there you have it. The truth is, I'm just crazy about amino acids. I put them in my martini."

"What's a martini?"

His face drew back. "James Bond? Shaken, not stirred? They don't have these movies in Ohio?"

"I know who James Bond is. I mean, I don't know what's in one."

His mouth curved into a mischievous grin. "Ah," he said.

We were on our third drink when we heard a girl's voice calling his name and the sound of footsteps coming up the stairs.

"In here!" Lear yelled.

The two of us were seated on the floor with the tools of Lear's enterprise spread before us. I have never met anyone else who traveled with not only a fifth of gin and a bottle of vermouth but the sort of bartending gizmos—jiggers, shakers, tiny, delicate knives—one sees only in old movies. A bag of ice swooned in a puddle of meltwater beside an open jar of olives from the market up the street. Ten-thirty in the morning, and I was completely hammered.

"Jesus, look at you."

I hauled my addled eyes into focus on the figure in the doorway. A girl, wearing a summer dress of pale blue linen. I note the dress first because it is the easiest thing to describe about her. I do not mean to say that she was beautiful, although she was; rather, I wish to make a case that there was about her something distinctive and therefore unclassifiable (unlike Lucessi's sister, whose ice-pick perfection was a dime a dozen and had left no lasting mark on me). I could note the particulars—her figure, slender and small-breasted, almost boyish; the petite formation of her sandaled toes, darkened by street grime; her heart-shaped face and damp blue eyes; her hair, pale blond, unmanaged by clips or barrettes, cut to her shining, sun-touched shoulders—but the whole, as they say, was greater than the sum of its parts.

"Liz!" Lear made a big show of getting to his feet, trying not to spill his drink. He threw his arms around her in a clumsy hug, which she pushed back from with a look of exaggerated distaste. She was wearing small, wire-framed eyeglasses, perfectly round, that on another woman might have seemed mannish but in her case didn't at all.

"You're drunk."

"Not in the least. More like in the most. Not as bad as my new roomie here." He propped his free hand against the side of his mouth and spoke in an exaggerated whisper: "Don't tell him, but a minute ago he appeared to be melting." He lifted his glass. "Have one?"

"I have to meet my adviser in half an hour."

"I'll take that as a yes. Tim, this is Liz Macomb, my girlfriend. Liz, Tim. Don't recall his last name, but I'm sure it'll come to me. Say your hellos while I fix this girl a cocktail."

The polite thing to do would have been to stand, but somehow this seemed too formal, and I decided against it. Also, I wasn't sure I could actually accomplish this.

"Hi," I said.

She sat on the bed, folded her slender legs beneath herself, and drew the hem of her dress over her knees. "How do you do, Tim? So you're the lucky winner."

Lear was sloppily pouring gin. "Tim here is from Ohio. That's about all I remember."

"Ohio!" She spoke this word with the same delight she might have used for Pago Pago or Rangoon. "I've always wanted to go there. What's it like?"

"You're kidding."

She laughed. "Okay, a little. But it's your home. Your *patria.* Your *pays natal.* Tell me anything."

Her directness was totally disarming. I struggled to come up with something worthy of it. What was there to say about the home I'd left behind?

"It's pretty flat, I guess." I winced inwardly at the lameness of the remark. "The people are nice."

Lear handed her a glass, which she accepted without looking at him. She took a tiny sip, then said, "Nice is good. I like nice. What else?"

She had yet to avert her eyes from my face. The intensity of her gaze was unsettling, though not unwelcome—far from it. I saw that she had a faint swirl of peach fuzz, dewy with sweat, above her upper lip.

"There really isn't very much to tell."

"And your people? What do they do?"

"My father's an optometrist."

"An honorable profession. I can't see past my nose without these things."

"Liz is from Connecticut," Lear added.

She took a second, deeper sip, wincing pleasurably. "If it's all right with you, Jonas, I'll speak for myself."

"What part?" I said, as if I knew the first thing about Connecticut.

"Little town called Greenwich, dah-ling. Which I'm supposed to hate, there's probably no place more hateable, but I can't seem to manage it. My parents are angels, and I adore them. Jonas," she said, gazing into her glass, "this is really *good.*"

Lear dragged a desk chair to the center of the room and lowered himself onto it backward. I made a mental note that this would be how I sat from now on.

"I'm sure you can describe it better than that," he said, grinning.

"This again. I'm not some dancing monkey, you know."

"Come on, pumpkin. We're totally wasted."

"'Pumpkin.' Listen to you." She sighed, puffing out her cheeks. "Fine, just this once. But to be clear, I'm only doing this because we have company."

I had no idea what to make of this exchange. Liz sipped again. For an unnervingly long interval, perhaps twenty seconds, silence gripped the room. Liz had closed her eyes, like a medium at a séance attempting to conjure the spirits of the dead.

"It tastes like—" She frowned the thought away. "No, that's not right."

"For God's sake," Lear moaned, "don't be such a tease."

"Quiet." Another moment slipped by; then she brightened. "Like . . . the air of the coldest day."

I was amazed. She was exactly right. *More* than right: her words, rather than functioning as a mere decoration of the experience, actually deepened its reality. It was the first time that I felt the power of language to intensify life. The phrase was also, coming from her lips, deeply sexy.

Lear gave an admiring whistle through his teeth. "That's a good one."

I was frankly staring at her. "How did you do that?"

"Oh, just a talent I have. That and twenty-five cents will get you a gumball."

"Are you some kind of writer?"

She laughed. "God, no. Have you met those people? Total drunks, every one."

"Liz here is one of those English majors we were talking about," Lear said. "A burden on society, totally unemployable."

"Spare me your crass opinions." She directed her next words to me: "What he's not telling you is that he's not quite the self-involved bon vivant he makes himself out to be."

"Yes, I am!"

"Then why don't you tell him where you were for the last twelve months?"

In my state of information overload, and under the influence of three strong drinks, I had overlooked the most obvious question in the room. Why had Jonas Lear, of all people, needed a floater for a roommate?

"Okay, I'll do it," Liz said. "He was in Uganda."

I looked at him. "What were you doing in Uganda?"

"Oh, a little of this, a little of that. As it turns out, they've got quite a civil war going on. Not what the brochure promised."

"He was working in a refugee camp for the U.N.," Liz explained.

"So I dug latrines, handed out bags of rice. It doesn't make me a saint."

"Compared to the rest of us, it does. What your new roommate hasn't told you, Tim, is that he has serious designs on saving the world. I'm talking major savior complex. His ego is the size of a house."

"Actually, I'm thinking of giving it up," Lear said. "It's not worth the dysentery. I've never shat like that in my life."

"Shit, not 'shat,'" Liz corrected. "'Shat' is not a word."

These two: I could barely keep up, and the problem wasn't merely that I was smashed, or already half in love with my new roommate's girlfriend. I felt like I had stepped straight from Harvard, circa 1990, into a movie from the 1940s, Spencer Tracy and Katharine Hepburn duking it out.

"Well, I think English is a great major," I remarked.

"Thank you. See, Jonas? Not everyone is a total philistine."

"I warn you," he told her, wagging a finger my direction, "you're talking to another dreary scientist."

She made a face of exasperation. "Suddenly in my life it's raining scientists. Tell me, Tim, what kind of science do you do?"

"Biochemistry."

"Which is . . . ? I've always wondered."

I found myself strangely happy to be asked this question. Perhaps it was just a matter of who was asking it.

"The building blocks of life, basically. What makes things live, what makes them work, what makes them die. That's about all there is to it."

She nodded approvingly. "Well, that's nicely said. I'd say there's a bit of the poet in you after all. I'm beginning to like you, Tim from Ohio." She polished off her drink and set it aside. "As for me, I'm really here to form a philosophy of life. An expensive way to do it, but it seemed like a good idea at the time, and I've decided to go with it."

This luxurious ambition—four years of college at twenty-three grand a pop to amass a personality—struck me as another alien aspect of her that I was hoping to learn more about. I say alien, but what I mean is angelic. By this point, I was utterly convinced that she was a creature of the spheres.

"You don't approve?"

Something in my face must have said so. I felt my cheeks grow warm. "I didn't say that."

"You didn't say anything. Piece of advice. 'That man that hath a tongue, I say, is no man, if with his tongue he cannot win a woman.'"

"I'm sorry?"

"Shakespeare, *Two Gentlemen of Verona*. In plain English, when a woman asks you a question, you better answer."

"If you want to get her into bed," Lear added. He looked at me. "You'll have to excuse her. She's like the Shakespeare channel. I don't understand half the things she says."

I knew almost nothing about Shakespeare. My experience of the bard was limited, like many people's, to a dutiful slog through *Julius Caesar* (violent, occasionally exciting) and *Romeo and Juliet* (which, until that moment, I'd found patently ridiculous).

"I just meant I've never met anybody who thinks that way."

She laughed. "Well, if you want to hang around with me, bub, better bone up. And with that," she said, rising from the bed, "and speaking of which, I must be off."

"But you're not *half* as drunk as we are," Lear protested. "I was hoping to have my way with you."

"Weren't you just." At the doorway, she looked back at me. "I forgot to ask. Which are you?"

One more question I had no answer for. "Come again?"

"Fly? Owl? A.D.? Tell me you're not Porcellian."

Lear answered in my stead: "Actually, our boy here, though technically a junior, has yet to experience this aspect of Harvard life. It's a complicated story I'm much too drunk to explain."

"So, you're not in a club?" she said to me.

"There are clubs?"

"*Final* clubs. Somebody pinch me. You really don't know what they are?"

I had heard the term, but that was all. "Are they some kind of fraternity?"

"Um, not exactly," Lear said.

"What they are," Liz explained, "are anachronistic dinosaurs, elitist to the core. Which also happen to throw the best parties. Jonas is in the Spee Club.

Like his daddy and his daddy's daddy and all the Lear daddies since fish grew legs. He's also the whattayacallit. Jonas, what *do* you call it?"

"The punchmaster."

She rolled her eyes. "And what a title that is. Basically, it means he's in charge of who gets in. Honeybunch, do something."

"I only just met the guy. Maybe he's not interested."

"Sure I am," I said, though I wasn't sure at all. What was I letting myself in for? And what did something like that cost? But if it meant spending more time in Liz's company, I would have walked through fire. "Absolutely. I'd definitely be interested in something like that."

"Good." She smiled victoriously. "Saturday night. Black tie. See, Jonas? It's settled."

I had no doubt that it was.

The first problem: I didn't own a tuxedo.

I had worn one once in my life, a powder-blue rental with navy velvet accents, paired with a ruffled shirt that only a pirate could have loved and a clip-on bow tie fat as a fist. Perfect for the island-themed senior prom at Mercy Regional High School ("A Night in Paradise!") but not the rarefied chambers of the Spee Club.

I intended to rent one, but Jonas convinced me otherwise. "Your tuxedo life," he explained, "has only just begun. What you need, my friend, is a *battle tux*." The shop he took me to was called Keezer's, which specialized in recycled formal wear cheap enough to vomit on without compunction. A vast room, unfancy as a bus station, with moth-eaten animal heads on the walls and air so choked with naphthalene it made my sinuses sting: from its voluminous racks I selected a plain black tux, a pleated shirt with yellow stains under the arms, a box of cheap studs and cuff links, and patent leather dress shoes that hurt only when I walked or stood. In the days leading up to the party, Jonas had adopted a persona that was somewhere between a wise young uncle and a guide dog for the blind. The selection of the tux was mine, but he insisted on choosing my tie and cummerbund, examining dozens before settling on pink silk with a pattern of tiny green diamonds.

"Pink?" Needless to say, it wasn't anything that would have flown in Mercy, Ohio. A powder-blue tux, yes. A pink tie, no. "Are you sure about this?"

"Trust me," he said. "It's the kind of thing we do."

The party, as I understood it, would be a sort of elaborate first date. Members would have the chance to look over fresh prospects, called "punchees." I was worried that I didn't have anyone to bring, but Jonas assured me that I was better off alone. That way, he explained, I would have the opportunity to impress the flotilla of unescorted women imported for the occasion from other colleges.

"Get two of them into bed, and you're definitely in."

I laughed at the absurdity. "Why only two?"

"I mean at the same time," he said.

I had not seen Liz since my first day in Winthrop House. This did not seem strange to me, as she lived in Mather, far down the river, and moved in an artsier crowd. I had, however, through discreet, well-spaced questioning, managed to learn more about her connection to Jonas. They were not, in fact, a strictly Harvard couple but had known each other since childhood. Their fathers had been prep school roommates, and the two families had vacationed together for years. This made sense to me; in hindsight, their verbal jousting had sounded as much like an exchange between two precocious siblings as a romantic twosome's. Jonas claimed that for many years, they actually couldn't stand each other; it wasn't until they were fifteen, and forced to endure two foggy weeks with their parents on a remote island off the coast of Maine, that their mutual antipathy had boiled over into what it really was. They'd kept this from their families—even Jonas confessed that there was something vaguely incestuous about the whole thing—confining their passions to secret, summer-time trysts in barns and boathouses while their parents got drunk on the patio, not really thinking of themselves as boyfriend-girlfriend until they'd both wound up at Harvard and discovered that they actually liked each other after all.

This account also explained, at least partly, the oddness of their relationship. What else but shared history could bond two people who possessed such fundamentally incompatible temperaments, such divergent visions of life? The more I grew to know them both, the more I came to understand how truly different they were. That they had traveled in the same social circles as children, attended virtually interchangeable country day and boarding schools, and been able to navigate the New York subway system, the Paris Métro, and the London tube by the time they were twelve said nothing about who they really were as people. It is possible for the same circumstances that draw two souls together to keep them forever at arm's length. Herein lies the truth of love, and the essence of all tragedy. I was not yet wise enough to understand this, nor would I be, until many years had passed. Yet I believe that from the start I sensed this, and that it was the source of my affinity, the force that pulled me to her.

The day of the party arrived. The daylight hours were all desultory preamble; I got nothing done. Was I nervous? How does the bull feel when he is marched into the ring and notices the cheering crowds and the man with his cape and sword? Jonas had gone off for the day—I didn't know where—and as the clock neared eight, the appointed hour, he had yet to show himself. The midwesterner in me was forever disturbed by the regional differences in what was and was not considered late, and by nine-thirty, when I decided to dress (I had entertained the girlish fantasy that Jonas and I would do this together), my anxiety was such that it verged on anger. It seemed likely that his promise had been forgotten and I would spend the evening like a jilted groom, watching TV in a tuxedo.

The other difficulty lay in the fact that I did not know how to tie a bow tie. Probably I couldn't have accomplished this in any event; my hands were actually shaking. Managing the studs and cuff links felt like trying to thread a needle with a hammer. It took me ten full minutes of cursing like a longshoreman to lodge them in their proper holes, and by the time I was done, my face was damp with sweat. I mopped it away with a bad-smelling towel and examined myself in the full-length mirror on the bathroom door, hoping for some encouragement. I was an unremarkable-looking sort of boy, neither one thing nor the other; although naturally slender, and without significant blemishes, I had always felt my nose was too big for my face, my arms too long for my body, my hair too bulky for the head it sat atop. Yet the face and figure I beheld in the mirror did not look so unpromising to me. The sleek black suit and shiny shoes and starch-hardened shirt—even, against my expectations, the pink cummerbund—did not appear unnatural on me. Instantly I regretted the powder-blue getup I'd worn to prom; who knew that something as simple as a black suit could gentrify one's appearance so thoroughly? For the first time, I dared to think that I, this plain boy from the provinces, might pass through the doors of the Spee Club without an alarm going off.

The door sailed open; Jonas charged into the outer room. "Fuck, what time is it?" He marched straight past me to the bathroom and turned on the shower. I followed him to the door.

"Where have you been?" I said, realizing too late how peevish this sounded. "No big deal, but it's almost ten."

"I had a lab due." He was peeling off his shirt. "This thing doesn't really get going until eleven. Didn't I tell you?"

"No."

"Oh. Well, sorry."

"How do you tie a bow tie?"

He had stripped to his boxers. "Hell if I know. Mine's a clip-on."

I retreated to the outer room. Jonas called out over the water, "Has Liz been here?"

"Nobody's been here."

"She was supposed to meet us."

My anxiety had now focused entirely on the matter of my tie. I returned to the mirror and withdrew it from my pocket. The gist, I'd heard, was to tie it like a pair of shoes. How much harder could it be? I'd been tying my own shoes since I was two.

The answer was: a lot harder. Nothing I did made the ends come out even close to the same length. It was as if the silk were possessed.

"Now, don't you look spiffy."

Liz had come in through the open door. Or, rather, a woman who *resembled* Liz; in her place stood a creature of pure understated glamour. She was wearing a slender black cocktail dress scooped low at the neck and high-heeled shoes of shiny red leather; she had added something to her hair, making it full and rich, and exchanged her glasses for contacts. A long string of pearls, no doubt real, dangled deep into her décolletage.

"Wow," I said.

"And *that*," she said, tossing her clutch on the sofa, "is the very syllable that every woman longs to hear." A cloud of complex scent had followed her into the room. "Having some troubles with your neckwear, I see?"

I held out the villainous article. "I have no idea what I'm doing."

"Let's have a look." She stepped toward me and took it from my hand. "Ah," she said, examining it, "here's the problem."

"What?"

"It's a bow tie!" She laughed. "As it so happens, you've come to the right person. I do this for my father all the time. Hold still."

She draped the tie around my neck and positioned it under the collar. In her heels, she was nearly as tall as I was; our faces were inches apart. With her eyes intently focused on the base of my throat, she engaged in her mysterious business. I had never been so close to a woman I was not about to kiss. My gaze instinctively went to her lips, which looked soft and warm, then downward, following the path of the pearls. The effect was like a low-voltage current passing through each cell of my body.

"Eyes up here, buster."

I knew I was blushing. I looked away. "Sorry."

"You're a man, what can you do? You're like pull toys. It must be awful." A final adjustment; then she stepped back. That heat in her cheeks: was she blushing, too? "There you go. Have a look."

She retrieved a compact from her clutch and gave it to me. It was made of a material that was smooth to the touch, like polished bone; it felt warm in my hand, as if it were radiating a pure, womanly energy. I opened it, revealing its bay of flesh-toned powder and small round mirror, in which my face looked back at me, floating above the flawlessly knotted pink bow tie.

"Perfect," I said.

The shower shut off with a groan, widening my awareness. I had forgotten all about my roommate.

"Jonas," Liz called, "we're late!"

He bounded into the room, clutching a towel around his waist. I had the feeling of being caught doing something I shouldn't have.

"So, are you two going to stand around and watch me dress? Unless—" Looking at Liz, he gave his towel a suggestive jostle, like an exotic dancer teasing an audience. *"Ça te donne du plaisir, mademoiselle?"*

"Just hurry it up. We're late."

"But I asked in French!"

"You'll want to work on your accent. We'll meet you outside, thank you very much." She gripped me by the arm, steering me toward the door. "Come on, Tim."

We took the stairs to the courtyard. A college campus on a Saturday night follows principles of its own: it awakens just as the rest of the world is readying for slumber. Music came from everywhere, pouring out of the windows; laughing figures moved through the darkness; voices lit the night from all directions. As we stepped through the breezeway, a girl hurried past, holding the hem of her dress with one hand, a bottle of champagne in the other.

"You'll do fine," Liz assured me.

We were standing just beyond the gate. "Do I look worried?" Though, of course, I was.

"All you have to do is act like you belong. That's really the whole point. Of most things, actually."

Away from Jonas, she had become somebody slightly different: more philosophical, even a little world-weary. I sensed that this was closer to the truth of her.

"I forgot to mention," Liz said, "I've got somebody I'd like you to meet. She'll be at the party."

I wasn't sure what I thought of this.

"We're cousins," she went on. "Well, second cousins. She goes to B.U."

The offer was disorienting. I had to remind myself that what had transpired upstairs had been an innocent flirtation, nothing more—that she was somebody else's girlfriend.

"Okay."

"Try not to sound too excited."

"What makes you think we'd hit it off?"

The remark came off too blunt, even a little resentful. But if she took offense, she didn't show it. "Just don't let her drink too much."

"Is that a problem?"

She shrugged. "Steph can be a bit of a party girl, if you know what I mean. That's her name, Stephanie."

Jonas caught up with us, all grins and apologies. We made our way to the party, which was just three blocks away. Previously, he had pointed out the Spee Club building to me, a brick townhouse with a walled side garden I had passed a thousand times. A college party is usually a loud affair, belching out a wide perimeter of sound, but not this one. There was no evidence that anything was going on inside, and for a second I thought Jonas might have gotten the night wrong. He stepped up to the door and withdrew a single key on a fob from the pocket of his tux. I had seen this key before, lying on his bureau, but had not connected it to anything until now. The fob was in the form of a bear's head, the symbol of the Spee.

We followed him inside. We were in an empty foyer, the floor painted in alternating black and white squares, like a chessboard. I did not feel as if I were going to a party—parachuting at night into an alien country was more like it. The spaces I could see were dark and masculine and, for a building inhabited by college students, remarkably neat. A clack of ivory: nearby, someone was playing pool. On a pedestal in the corner stood a large stuffed bear—not a teddy bear, an actual bear. It was rearing up on its hind legs, clawed hands reaching forward as if it were going to maul some invisible attacker. (That, or play the piano.) From overhead came a swell of liquor-loosened voices.

"Come on," Jonas said.

He led us back to a flight of stairs. Seen from the street, the building had appeared deceptively modest in its dimensions, but not inside. We ascended toward the noise and heat of the crowd, which had spilled from two large rooms onto the landing.

"Jo-man!"

As we made our entry, Jonas's neck was clamped in the elbow of a large, red-haired man in a white dinner jacket. He had the florid complexion and thickened waist of an athlete gone to seed.

"Jo-man, Jo-Jo, the big Jo-ster." Unaccountably, he gave Jonas a big smooch on the cheek. "And Liz, may I say you are looking *especially* tasty tonight."

She rolled her eyes. "So noted."

"Does she love me? I'm asking, does this girl just love me?" With his arm still draped around Jonas, he looked at me with an expression of startled concern: "Sweet Jesus, Jonas, tell me this isn't the guy."

"Tim, meet Alcott Spence. He's our president."

"And roaring drunk, too. So tell me, Tim, you're not gay, are you? Because, no offense, you look a little gay in that tie."

I was caught totally off guard. "Um—"

"Kidding!" He roared with laughter. We were being pressed on all sides now, as more partygoers ascended the stairs behind us. "Seriously, I'm just messing with you. Half the guys in here are *huge* fags. I myself am what you call a sexual omnivore. Isn't that right, Jonas?"

He grinned, playing along. "It's true."

"Jonas here is one of my most special friends. *Very* special. So you just go ahead and be as gay as you feel you need to be."

"Thanks," I said. "But I'm not gay."

"Which is also totally fine! That's what I'm saying! Listen to this guy. We're not the Porcellian, you know. Seriously, those guys can*not* stop fucking each other."

How much did I want a drink at that moment? Very, very much.

"Well, I've enjoyed our little chat," Alcott merrily continued, "but I must be off. Hot date in the sauna with a certain sophomore from the University of Loose Morals and some *cocaina más excelente*. You kids run along and have fun."

He faded into the throng. I turned to Jonas. "Is everybody here like that?"

"Actually, no. A lot of them can come on pretty strong."

I looked at Liz. "Don't you dare leave me."

She laughed wryly. "Are you kidding?"

We fought our way to the bar. No lukewarm keg beer here: behind a long table, a white-shirted bartender was frantically mixing drinks and passing out bottles of Heineken. As he shoveled ice into my vodka tonic—I'd learned my freshman year to stick to clear liquor when I could—I had the urge to send him some clandestine message of Marxist-inspired fellowship. "I'm actually from Ohio," I might have told him. "I shelve books at the library. I don't belong here any more than you do." ("P.S. Stand ready! The Glorious Workers' Revolution commences at the stroke of midnight!")

Yet as he placed the drink in my hand, a new feeling came upon me. Perhaps it was the way he did it—automatically, like a high-speed robot, his attention already focused to the next partygoer in line—but the thought occurred to me that I'd done it. I'd passed. I had successfully snuck into the other world, the hidden world. This was where I had been headed, all along. I gave myself a moment to soak in the sensation. Joining the Spee: what I had believed utterly impossible just moments before suddenly seemed like a fait accompli, a thing of destiny. I would take my place among its membership, because Jonas Lear would pave the way. How else to explain the extraordinary coincidence of our second meeting? Fate had put him in my path for a reason, and here it was, in the rich atmosphere of privilege that radiated from everywhere around me. It was like some new form of oxygen, one I'd been waiting all my life to breathe, and it made me feel weirdly alive.

So caught up was I in this new line of thought that I failed to notice Liz standing right in front of me. With her was a new person, a girl.

"Tim!" she yelled over the music that had erupted in the room behind us. "This is Steph!"

"Pleased to meet you!"

"Likewise!" She was short, hazel-eyed, with a spray of freckles and glossy brown hair. Unremarkable compared to Liz, but pretty in her own way—*cute* would be the word—and smiling at me in a manner that told me Liz had laid the groundwork. She was holding a nearly empty glass of something clear. Mine was empty, too. Was it my first or my second?

"Liz says you go to B.U.!"

"Yeah!" Because the music was so loud, we were standing very close. She smelled like roses and gin.

"Do you like it?"

"It's okay! You're a biochem major, right?"

I nodded. The most banal conversation in history, but it had to be done. "What about you?"

"Poli-sci! Hey, do you want to dance?"

I was an awful dancer, but who wasn't? We made our way to the light-confettied ballroom and began our awkward attempt to perform this intimate act, pretending we hadn't met each other thirty seconds ago. The dance floor was already full, the music having been strategically withheld until everybody was adequately liquored; I glanced around for Liz but didn't find her. I supposed she was too cool to make a fool of herself in this way and hoped she didn't see me. Stephanie, not to my surprise, was an enthusiastic dancer; what I hadn't banked on was that she'd be so good at it. Whereas my moves were an ungainly mimicry of actual dancing, wholly unrelated to this song or any other, hers possessed a lithe expressiveness that verged on actual grace. She spun, twirled, gyrated. She did things with her hips that elsewise might have looked indecent but under the circumstances seemed ordained by a different, less constricted morality. She also managed to keep her attention on me the whole time, wearing a warmly seductive smile, her eyes focused like lasers. What had Liz called her? A "party girl"? I was beginning to see the advantages.

We broke after the third song for yet another drink, slung them back like sailors on leave, and returned to the floor. I'd eaten no dinner, and the booze was doing its work. The evening dissolved into a haze. At some point I found myself talking to Jonas, who was introducing me to other members of the club, and then playing pool with Alcott, who was not such a bad fellow after all. Everything I did and said seemed charmed. More time passed, and then Stephanie, whom I'd briefly lost track of, was pulling me by the hand back toward the music, which pumped without ceasing like the night's own heartbeat. I had no idea what time it was and didn't care. More fast dancing, the song downshifted, and she wrapped her arms around my neck. We'd barely spoken, but now this warm, good-smelling girl was in my arms, her body pressed against mine, the tips of her fingers stroking the hairs at the back of my neck. Never had I received such an undeserved present. What was happening to my anatomy was nothing she could have missed; nor did I want her to. When the song ended, she placed her lips against my ear, her breath a sweet exhalation that made me shudder.

"I have coke."

I found myself, then, sitting beside her on a deep leather couch in a room that looked like something in a hunting lodge. From her purse she produced a small packet made of notebook paper, sealed by complex folding. She used my Harvard ID to arrange the coke in two fat lines on the coffee table and rolled a dollar bill into a tube. Cocaine was an aspect of college life that I had not experienced but did not see the harm of. She bent to the table, sucked the powder deep into her sinuses with a delicate, girlish snort, and passed me the bill so that I might do the same.

It wasn't bad at all. It was, in fact, very good. Within seconds of the powder's purchase, I experienced a Roman-candle rush of well-being that seemed not a departure from reality but a deeper entry into truth. The world was a fine place full of wonderful people, an enchanted existence worthy of the utmost enthusiasm. I looked at Stephanie, who was quite beautiful now that I had eyes to see, and sought the words to explain this revelation on a night of many.

"You're a really good dancer," I said.

She leaned forward and took my mouth with hers. It was not a schoolgirl's kiss; it was a kiss that said there were no rules if I didn't want there to be. It did not take long before our bodies were a confusion of tongues and hands and skin. Things were being slid aside, unlatched, unzipped. I felt like I had plummeted into a vortex of pure sensuality. It was different than it had been with Carmen. It had no edges, no roughness. It felt like being melted. Stephanie was astride my lap and drawing her panties aside and down she went, enveloping me; she began to move in a wondrous, aquatic fashion, like an anemone undulating on the tides, rocking and rising and plunging, each variation accompanied by the creak of leather upholstery. Mere hours since I'd been pacing my room, consigned to a night of humiliated loneliness, and here I was, fucking a girl in a cocktail dress.

"Whoa. Sorry, bud."

It was Jonas. Stephanie was off me like a shot. A moment of frantic activity as the pants were yanked upward, the dress downward, various articles of underclothing rammed into adjustment. Standing in the doorway, my roommate was in a state of barely contained hilarity.

"Jesus," I said. I was pulling up my fly, or trying to. My shirttail was stuck in the zipper. More comedy. "You could have knocked."

"And you could have locked the door."

"Jonas, did you find her?" Liz appeared behind him. As she stepped into the room, her eyes widened. "Oh," she said.

"They were getting better acquainted," Jonas offered, laughing.

Stephanie was smoothing down her hair; her lips were swollen, her face flushed with blood. I had no doubt mine was the same.

"I can see that," Liz said. Her mouth was set in a prim line; she didn't look at me. "Steph, your friends are waiting for you outside. Unless you want me to tell them something else."

This was clearly impossible; the balloon of passion had been punctured. "No, I guess I should go." She fetched her shoes from the floor and turned to me. I was, ridiculously, still sitting on the sofa. "Well, thanks," she said. "It was really nice to meet you."

Should we kiss? Shake hands? What was I supposed to say? "You're welcome" didn't seem like it would cut it. In the end, the gap between us was too wide; we didn't even touch.

"You, too," I said.

She followed Liz from the room. I felt miserable—not only because of my painfully blockaded loins, but also because of Liz's unmistakable disappointment in me. I had revealed myself to be just like every other guy: a pure opportunist. It wasn't until that moment that I fully realized how important her opinion of me had become.

"Where is everybody?" I asked Jonas. The building was remarkably quiet.

"It's four o'clock in the morning. Everybody's gone. Except for Alcott. He's passed out in the pool room."

I looked at my watch. So it was. Whether from the adrenaline or the coke counteracting the booze, my thoughts had cleared. Cringe-inducing snippets of the night came back to me: knocking a drink onto a member's date, attempting a Cossack dance to the B-52's "Love Shack," laughing too loudly at a joke that was actually somebody's sad story about his disabled brother. What had I been thinking, getting so drunk?

"Are you okay? You want us to wait?"

I'd never wanted anything less in my life. I was already calculating which park bench I could sleep on. Did people do that anymore? "You guys go ahead. I'll be along."

"Don't worry about Liz, if that's what you're thinking. This was totally her idea."

"It was?"

Jonas shrugged. "Well, maybe not that you'd actually bone her cousin on the couch. But she wanted you to feel . . . I don't know. Included."

This made me feel even worse. Stupidly, I had assumed that Liz was doing her cousin a favor, when it was the other way around.

"Listen, Tim, I'm sorry—"

"Forget it," I said, and waved my roommate away. "I'm fine, really. Go home."

I waited ten minutes, gathered myself together, and left the building. Jonas hadn't said where he and Liz were going; back to her place, probably, but I couldn't chance it. I made my way down to the river and began to walk. I had no destination in mind; I suppose I was performing a kind of penance, though for what, precisely, I could not say. I had, after all, done exactly what was expected of me by the standards of that time and place.

Gray dawn found me, a pathetic figure in his tuxedo, five miles away on the Longfellow Bridge, overlooking the Charles River Basin. The first rowers were out, carving the waters with their long, elegant oars. It is at such moments that revelations are said to come, but none did. I had wanted too much and embarrassed myself; there wasn't anything more to say than that. I was badly hungover; blisters had formed on both feet from my too-tight shoes. The thought occurred to me that I hadn't spoken to my father in a very long time, and I was sorry about that, though I knew I would not call him.

By the time I got back to Winthrop, it was nearly nine o'clock. I keyed the lock and found Jonas freshly shaved and sitting on his bed, shoving his legs into a pair of jeans.

"Jesus, look at you," he said. "Did you get mugged or something?"

"I went for a walk." Everything about him radiated cheerful urgency. "What's going on?"

"We're leaving, is what's going on." He got to his feet, shoving his shirt into the waistband of his jeans. "You better change."

"I'm exhausted. I'm not going anywhere."

"Better rethink that. Alcott just phoned. We're driving down to Newport."

I had no idea what to make of this ridiculous claim. Newport was at least two hours away. All I wanted to do was climb into my bed and sleep. "What are you talking about?"

Jonas snapped on his watch and stepped to the mirror to brush his hair, still damp from the shower. "The after-party. Just members and punchees this time. The ones who, you know, passed. Which would include you, my friend."

"You're joking."

"Why would I joke about a thing like that?"

"Gee, I don't know. Maybe because I made a total jackass of myself?"

He laughed. "Don't be so hard on yourself. You got a little wasted, so what? Everybody really liked you, especially Alcott. Apparently, your escapade in the library made quite an impression."

My stomach dropped. "He knows?"

"Are you serious? Everybody knows. It's Alcott's house we're going to, by the way. You should see this place. It's like something in a magazine." He turned from the mirror. "Earth to Fanning. Am I talking to myself here?"

"Um, I guess not."

"Then for fucksake, get dressed."

17

The fall was a marathon of parties, each more extravagant than the last. Nights at restaurants I could never afford, strip clubs, a harbor cruise on a sixty-foot boat owned by an alumnus who never came out of his cabin. Bit by bit, the candidates dropped away, until only a dozen remained. Just after the Thanksgiving holiday, an envelope appeared under my door. I was to report to the club at midnight. Alcott met me in the entryway, instructed me not to speak, and handed me a pewter cup of powerful rum, which he told me to down. The building seemed empty; all the lights were out. He led me to the library, blindfolded me, and told me to wait. Some minutes passed. I was feeling quite drunk and having trouble maintaining my balance.

Then I heard, from behind me, an alarming sound—a low, animal growling, like a dog about to attack. I spun, stumbling, and whipped off the blindfold as the bear reared up before me. It seized me bodily, hurled me to the ground, and pounced on top of me, pushing the wind from my chest. In the dark room all I could make out was its great black bulk and gleaming teeth, poised above my neck. I screamed, utterly convinced that I was about to die—a prank, intended to be harmless, had obviously gone terribly wrong—until I realized that the bear, rather than tearing my throat open, had begun to hump me.

The lights came on. It was Alcott, wearing a bear suit. All the members were there, including Jonas. An explosion of general hilarity, and then the champagne came out. I had been accepted.

The dues were a hundred and ten dollars a month—more than I had to spare, less than I could do without. I signed on for extra hours at the library and found I could make up the difference easily enough. I had spent Thanksgiving at Jonas's house in Beverly, but Christmas was a problem. I had told him nothing about my situation, and did not want to be the object of his pity. A semester of nonstop parties had also put me badly behind in my studies. I was at a loss as to what to do until I hit upon the idea of calling Mrs. Chodorow, the woman whose house I had lived in for the summer. She agreed to let me stay, even offered to let me have my room for free—it would be nice, she said, to have a young person around for the holidays. On Christmas Eve, she invited me downstairs, and the two of us passed the afternoon together, baking cookies for her church and watching the Yule log on TV. She'd even bought me a present, a pair of leather gloves. I had thought I was immune to holiday sentiment, but I was so touched that my eyes actually welled with tears.

It wasn't until February that I decided to call Stephanie. I felt bad about what had happened and had meant to apologize sooner, but the longer I'd waited, the more difficult this had become. I assumed that she'd just hang up on me, but she didn't. She seemed genuinely happy to hear from me. I asked her if she wanted to meet for coffee, and the two of us discovered that, even sober, we liked each other. We kissed under an awning in the falling snow— a much different kind of kiss, shy, almost courtly—and then I put her in a cab to Back Bay, and when I returned to my room, the phone was already ringing.

Thus were the terms established for the next two years of my life. Somehow, the universe had forgiven me my trespasses, my vain ambitions, my casual, self-interested cruelties. I should have been happy and for the most part was. The four of us—Liz and Jonas, Stephanie and I—became a quartet: parties, movies, weekend ski trips to Vermont, and lusty, drunken outings to Cape Cod, where Liz's family had a house left conveniently unoccupied during the off-season. I did not see Stephanie during the week, nor did Jonas see much of Liz, whose life did not seem otherwise to intersect with his own, and the rhythms appeared to work. From Monday to Friday, I worked my tail off; come Friday night, the fun began.

My grades were excellent, and my professors took notice. I was encouraged to begin thinking about where I would pursue my doctoral work. Harvard was at the top of my list, but there were other considerations. My adviser was lobbying for Columbia, the chairman of the department for Rice, where he had taken his PhD and still had close professional connections. I felt like a racehorse up for auction but hardly minded. I was in the gate; soon the bell would ring, and I would commence my mad dash down the track.

Then Lucessi killed himself.

This was in the summer. I'd remained in Cambridge, staying at Mrs. Chodorow's, and had resumed working at the lab. I hadn't spoken to Lucessi since the last day of our freshman year—indeed, had barely thought of him beyond a mild curiosity, never acted on, as to his fate. It was his sister, Arianna, who telephoned me. How she'd tracked me down, I didn't think to ask. She was clearly in shock; her voice was flat and emotionless, laying out the facts. Lucessi had been working in a video store. He appeared, at first, to have taken his expulsion more or less in stride. The experience had chastened but not broken him. There were vague plans about his attending the local community college, perhaps reapplying to Harvard in a year or two. But across the winter and spring, his tics had gotten worse. He became sullen and uncommunicative, refusing to talk to anyone for days. The low-grade muttering became more or less continual, as if he were engaged in conversation with imaginary persons. A number of disturbing obsessions took hold. He would spend hours reading the daily newspaper, underlining random sentences in wholly unrelated articles, and claimed that the CIA was watching him.

Gradually it became apparent that he was in the throes of a psychotic episode, perhaps even full-blown schizophrenia. His parents made arrangements to have him admitted to a psychiatric hospital, but the night before he was to leave, he disappeared. Apparently he had taken the train to Manhattan. With him, in a canvas bag, was a length of sturdy rope. In Central Park, he had selected a tree with a large rock beneath its boughs, flung the rope over one of the branches, put the noose in place, and stepped off. The distance was not enough to break his neck; he could have regained a foothold on the boulder at any time. But such was his determination that he hadn't done this, and death had been caused by slow strangulation—a horrendous detail I wished Arianna had not shared with me. In his pocket was a note: *Call Fanning.*

The funeral was scheduled for the following Saturday. Under the circumstances, the family wanted to proceed quietly, with a brief service confined to close family and friends. That I was to be among them was ordained by his note, although I told Arianna that I didn't know what to make of it, which was true. We'd been friends, but not great friends. Our bond had hardly gone deep enough to earn my inclusion in his final thoughts. I wondered if he intended this note as a punishment of some kind, though I could not think what sin I had committed to warrant it. The other possibility was that he was sending me a message of an altogether different nature—that his death was, in a way only he could understand, a demonstration for my benefit. But what it could mean, I hadn't the foggiest.

Jonas was spending the summer on an archaeological dig in Tanzania; Stephanie had won a coveted internship in Washington, working on Capitol Hill, but at the time of Lucessi's death was traveling with her parents in France and could not be reached. I did not think that Lucessi's death had shaken me all that badly, but of course it had—my emotions, like Arianna's, were blunted by shock—yet I showed the good sense to call the one person I trusted whom I could actually get on the phone. Liz's family was on the Cape, but she was working at a bookshop in Connecticut. I'm sorry about your friend, she said. You shouldn't be alone. Meet me at Grand Central at the main kiosk, the one with the four-faced clock.

My train got into Penn Station early Friday morning. I took the 1 train uptown to Forty-second Street, changed to the 7, and arrived at Grand Central at the height of the rush. Except to change buses at Port Authority in the middle of the night, I had never been to New York City, and as I ascended the ramp into the terminal's main concourse, I was, like many a traveler through the ages, bowled over by the majesty of its dimensions. I felt as though I'd entered the grandest of cathedrals, not some mere way station but a destination in its own right, worthy of pilgrimage. Even the tiniest sound seemed magnified by the sheer size of the place. The smoke-stained ceiling, with its images of constellated stars, soared so majestically overhead it seemed to rewrite the dimensions of the world. Liz was waiting for me at the kiosk, wearing a light summer dress and carrying an overnight bag. She hugged me far longer and more tightly than I was prepared for, and it was in the shelter of her embrace that I suddenly felt the weight of Lucessi's death, like a cold stone at the center of my chest.

"We're staying at my parents' apartment in Chelsea," she said. "I won't take no for an answer."

We took a cab downtown, through streets clogged with traffic and great walls of pedestrians that surged forward at every intersection. This was early 1990s New York, a time when the city seemed on the verge of unmanageable chaos, and although I was, later in life, to live in a very different Manhattan— safe, tidy, and affluent—my first impression of the city was so indelible, so charged with heat and light, that it remains my truest vision of the place. The apartment was on the second floor of a brownstone just off Eighth Avenue— two small rooms, compactly furnished, with a view across Twenty-eighth Street of a small theater known for incomprehensible avant-garde productions and a men's haberdashery called World of Shirts and Socks. Liz had explained that her parents only used the place when they came into the city to shop or take in a show. Probably nobody had been there in months.

The funeral was at ten the next morning. I called Arianna to tell her where I was staying, and she said that she'd arrange for a car to meet us in the morning and drive us to Riverdale. There was no food in the apartment, so Liz and I went up the street to a small café with tables on the sidewalk. She told me what she knew of Jonas, which wasn't very much. She'd received only three letters, none very long. I'd never quite understood what he was doing there—he was a biologist, or wanted to be, not an archaeologist—though I knew it had to do with extracting fossilized pathogens from the bones of early hominids.

"Basically," she said, "he's squatting in the dirt all day long, dusting rocks with a paintbrush."

"Sounds like fun."

"Oh, to him it is."

I knew this to be so. Sharing a room with the man had taught me that, despite his fun-loving exterior, Jonas was deeply serious about his studies, sometimes verging toward obsession. The core of his passion lay in the idea that the human animal was a truly unique organism, evolutionarily distinct. Our powers of reason, of language, of abstract thought—none of these was matched anywhere else in the animal kingdom. Yet despite these gifts, we remained chained to the same physical limitations as every other creature on the earth. We were born, we aged, we died, all of it in a relatively short span of time. From an evolutionary point of view, he said, this simply made no sense. Nature craved balance, yet our brains were completely out of sync with the short shelf life of the bodies that housed them.

Think about it, he said: What would the world be like if human beings could live two hundred years? Five hundred? How about a thousand? What leaps of genius would a man be capable of, with a millennium of accumulated wisdom on which to draw? The great mistake of modern biological science, he believed, was to assume that death was natural, when it was anything but, and to view it in terms of isolated failures of the body. Cancer. Heart disease. Alzheimer's. Diabetes. Trying to cure them one by one, he said, was as pointless as swatting at a swarm of bees. You might get a couple, but the swarm would kill you in the end. The key, he said, lay in confronting the whole *question* of death, to turn it on its head. Why should we have to die at all? Could it be that somewhere within the deep molecular coding of our species lay the road map to a next evolutionary step—one in which our physical attributes would be brought into equilibrium with our powers of thought? And wouldn't it make sense that nature, in its genius, intended for us to discover this for ourselves, employing the unique endowments it had afforded us?

He was, in short, making a case for immortality as the apotheosis of the human state. This sounded like mad science to me. The only things missing from his argument were a slab of reassembled body parts and a lightning rod, and I'd told him as much. For me, science wasn't about the big picture but the small one—the same modestly ambitious, hunt-and-peck investigations that Jonas decried as a waste of time. And yet his passion was attractive—even, in its own crackpot way, inspiring. Who wouldn't want to live forever?

"The thing I don't get is why he thinks the way he does," I said. "He seems so sensible otherwise."

My tone was light, but I could tell I'd hit on something. Liz called the waiter over and asked for another glass of wine.

"Well, there's an answer for that," she said. "I thought you knew."

"Knew what?"

"About me."

This was how I came to learn the story. When Liz was eleven, she had been diagnosed with Hodgkin's disease. The cancer had originated in the lymph nodes surrounding her trachea. Surgery, radiation, chemotherapy—she'd had it all. Twice she'd gone into remission, only to have the disease return. Her current remission had lasted four years.

"Maybe I'm cured, or so they tell me. I guess you never know."

I had no idea how to respond. The news was deeply distressing, but anything I might have offered would have been an empty platitude. Yet in a way I could not put my finger on, the information did not seem entirely new to me. I had felt it from the day we'd met: there was a shadow over her life.

"I'm Jonas's pet project, you see," she continued. "I'm the problem he wants to solve. It's pretty noble, when you think about it."

"I don't believe that," I said. "He worships you. It's totally obvious."

She sipped her wine and returned it to the table. "Let me ask you something, Tim. Name one thing about Jonas Lear that isn't perfect. I'm not talking about the fact that he's always late or picks his nose at traffic lights. Something important."

I searched my thoughts. She was right. I couldn't.

"This is what I'm saying. Handsome, smart, charming, destined for great things. That's our Jonas. Since the day he was born, everybody's loved him. And it makes him feel guilty. *I* make him feel guilty. Did I tell you he wants to marry me? He tells me all the time. *Say the word, Liz, and I'll buy the ring.* Which is ridiculous. Me, who might not live past twenty-five, or whatever the statistics say. And even if the cancer doesn't come back, I can't have children. The radiation took care of that."

It was getting late; I could feel the city changing around me, its energies shifting. Down the block, people were stepping from the theater, hailing cabs, going in search of drinks or food. I was tired and overloaded by the emotions of the last few days. I signaled the waiter for the bill.

"I'll tell you something else," Liz said as we were paying the tab. "He really admires you."

This was, in some ways, the strangest news of all. "Why would he admire *me*?"

"Oh, a lot of reasons. But I think it comes down to the fact that you're something he can't ever be. Authentic, maybe? I'm not talking about being modest, although you are. Too modest, if you ask me. You underestimate yourself. But there's something . . . I don't know, pure about you. A resilience. I saw it the moment I met you. I don't mean to put you on the spot, but the one good thing about cancer, and I mean the *only* thing, is it teaches you to be honest."

I felt embarrassed. "I'm just a kid from Ohio who did well on his SATs. There's nothing interesting about me at all."

She paused, gazing into her glass, then said, "I've never asked you about your family, Tim, and I don't mean to pry. All I know is what Jonas has told me. You never mention them, they never call, you spend all your breaks in Cambridge with this woman and her cats."

I shrugged. "She's not so bad."

"I'm sure she isn't. I'm sure she's a saint. And I like cats as much as the next person, in the right quantity."

"There's not really much to tell."

"I doubt that very much."

A silence followed. I discovered that swallowing took a great deal of effort; my windpipe felt as if it had constricted. When at last I spoke, the words seemed to come from another place entirely.

"She died."

Behind her glasses, Liz's eyes were intently fixed on my face. "Who died, Tim?"

I swallowed. "My mother. My mother died."

"When was this?"

It would all come out now; there was simply no stopping it. "Last summer. It was just before I met you. I didn't even know she was sick. My father wrote me a letter."

"And where were you?"

"With the woman and her cats."

Something was happening. Something was coming undammed. I knew that if I didn't move immediately—stand up, walk around, feel the beating of my heart and the action of air in my lungs—I would fall apart.

"Tim, why didn't you tell us?"

I shook my head. I felt suddenly ashamed. "I don't know."

Liz reached across the table and gently took my hand. Despite my best efforts, I had begun to cry. For my mother, for myself, for my dead friend Lucessi, whom I knew I had failed. Surely I could have done something, said something. It wasn't the note in his pocket that told me so. It was the fact that I was alive and he was dead, and I of all people should have understood the pain of living in a world that didn't seem to want him. I did not want to take my hand away—it felt like the only thing anchoring me to the earth. I was in a dream in which I was flying and could not make myself land were it not for this woman who would save me.

"It's all right," Liz was saying, "it's all right, it's all right . . ."

Time moved then; we were walking, I didn't know where. Liz was still holding my hand. I sensed the presence of water, and then the Hudson emerged. Decrepit piers jutted long fingers into the water. Across the river's broad expanse, the lights of Hoboken made a diorama of the city and its lives. The air tasted of salt and stone. There was a kind of park along the water's edge, filthy and abandoned-looking; it did not seem safe, so we headed north along Twelfth Avenue, neither of us speaking, before turning east again. I had given no thought at all to what would happen next but now began to. In the last hour, Liz had spoken of things that I felt certain she had told no other person, just as I had done with her. There was Jonas to think of, but we were also a man and a woman who had shared the most intimate truths, things that, once said, could never be unsaid.

We arrived at the apartment. No words of consequence had passed between us for many minutes. The tension was palpable—surely she could feel it, too. I couldn't say for certain what I wanted, only that I didn't want to be away from her, not for a minute. I was standing dumbly in the middle of the tiny room, searching my mind for the words to capture how I felt. Something needed to be said. And yet I could say nothing.

It was Liz who broke the silence. "Well, I'm going to turn in. The sofa folds out. There are sheets and blankets in the closet. Let me know if you need anything else."

"Okay."

I could not make myself move toward her, though I wanted to, very badly. On the one hand there was Liz, and all we had shared, and the fact that, in every way, I loved her and probably had since the day we'd met; on the other, there was Jonas, the man who'd given me a life.

"Your friend Lucessi. What was his first name?"

I actually had to think. "Frank. But I never called him that."

"Why do you think he did it?"

"He was in love with somebody. She didn't love him back."

Not until that moment had this chain of thought, in all its starkness, come clear to me. *Call Fanning,* my friend had written. *Call Fanning to tell him that love is all there is, and love is pain, and love is taken away.*

"What time is the car?" she asked.

"Eight o'clock."

"I'm going with you, you know."

"I'm glad you are."

A frozen moment passed.

"Well," Liz said, "I guess that's it." She retreated to the bedroom door, where she paused and turned to face me again. "Stephanie is a lucky girl, you know. I'm just saying that in case you haven't figured it out."

Then she was gone. I stripped to my boxers and lay on the couch. Under different circumstances, I might have felt foolish, daring to think that such a woman would take me into her bed. But I actually felt relieved; Liz had chosen the honorable route, making the decision for both of us. It occurred to me that not once, neither at the restaurant nor as we'd walked, had I thought of Stephanie in the context of any betrayal I might have contemplated. The day felt like a year; through the windows, I heard the wash of the city, an oceanic sound. It seemed to creep into my chest, where it matched itself to the rhythm of my breathing. Exhaustion poured through my bones, and soon I drifted off.

Sometime later, I awoke. I had the unmistakable sense of being watched. A sensation, vaguely electrical, lingered on my forehead, as if I had been kissed. I rose onto my elbows, expecting to see someone standing over me. But the room was empty, and I thought I must have dreamed this.

About the funeral, there is little to say. To describe it in detail would be a violation of its confidential grief, its closed circuit of pain. During the service, I kept my eyes on Arianna, wondering what she was feeling. Did she know? I wanted her to know, but I also didn't; she was just a girl. No good could come of it.

I declined the family's invitation to lunch; Liz and I returned to the apartment to retrieve my luggage. On the platform at Penn Station she hugged me, then, revising her thoughts, kissed me quickly on the cheek.

"So, okay?"

I didn't know if she meant me or the two of us. "Sure," I said. "Never better."

"Call me if you get too blue."

I stepped aboard. Liz was watching me through the windows as I made my way down the car to find an empty seat. I remembered boarding the bus to Cleveland, that long-ago September day—the drops of rain on the window, my mother's crinkled bag in my lap, looking to see if my father had stayed to watch my departure, finding him gone. I took a seat beside the window. Liz had yet to move. She saw me, smiled, waved; I waved back. A deep mechanical shudder; the train began to move. She was still standing there, following my carriage with her gaze, as we entered the tunnel and disappeared.

18

May 1992: The last of my coursework had been completed. I was to graduate summa cum laude; offers of generous graduate fellowships had come my way. MIT, Columbia, Princeton, Rice. Harvard, which had decided it had not seen the last of me if I cared to stay on. It was the obvious choice, one I felt bound to make in the end, though I had not committed, preferring to savor the possibilities for as long as I could. Jonas would be going back to Tanzania for the summer, then heading to the University of Chicago to start his doctoral work; Liz would be going to Berkeley for her master's in Renaissance literature; Stephanie was returning to Washington to work for a political consulting firm. The graduation ceremony itself would not happen until the first week of June. We had entered a nether time, a caesura between what our lives had been and what they would become.

In the meanwhile, there were parties—lots of them. Roiling keggers, black-tie balls, a garden fete where everyone drank mint juleps and all the girls wore hats. In my trusty battle tux and pink tie—wearing it had become a trademark—I danced the Lindy, the Electric Slide, the Hokey Pokey, and the Bump; at any given hour of the day, I was either drunk or hungover. An hour of triumph, but it came at a cost. For the first time in my life, I felt the pain of missing people I had not yet left.

The week before graduation, Jonas, Liz, Stephanie, and I drove down to the Cape, to Liz's house. No one was talking about it, but it seemed unlikely that the four of us would be together again for some time. Liz's parents were there, having just opened the house for the season. I had met them before, in Connecticut. Her mother, Patty, came across as a bit of a society doyenne, with a brisk, somewhat phony graciousness and a lock-jawed accent, but her father was one of the most likable and easygoing people I'd ever met. A tall, bespectacled man (Liz had gotten his vision) with an earnest face, Oscar Macomb had been a banker, retired early, and now, in his words, spent his days "noodling around with money." He worshipped his daughter—that was plain to anyone with eyes; less apparent, though undeniable, was that he vastly preferred her to his wife, whom he regarded with the bemused affection one might give to an overbred poodle. With Liz, the man was all smiles—the two of them would frequently chatter away in French—and his warmth extended to anybody in her circle, including me, whom he had nicknamed "Ohio Tim."

The house, in a town called Osterville, stood on a bluff overlooking Nantucket Sound. It was enormous, room upon room, with a wide back lawn and rickety stairs to the beach. No doubt it was worth many millions of dollars, just for the land alone, though in those days I had no ability to calculate such things. Despite its size, it had a homey, unfussy feel. Most of the furniture looked like you could pick it up for pennies at a yard sale; in the afternoons, when the wind swung around, it tore through the house like the offensive line of the New York Giants. The ocean was still too cold for swimming, and because it was so early in the season, the town was mostly deserted. We spent our days lying on the beach, pretending not to be freezing, or lazing around on the porch, playing cards and reading, until evening arrived and the drinks came out. My father might have had a beer before dinner while he watched the news on television, but that was the extent of it; my mother never drank at all. In the Macomb household, cocktail hour was religion. At six o'clock everyone would gather in the living room or, if the evening was pleasant, on the porch, whereupon Liz's father would present us with a silver tray of the evening's concoction—whiskey old-fashioneds, Tom Collinses, vodka martinis in chilled glasses with olives on sticks—accompanied by dainty porcelain cups of nuts warmed in the oven. This was followed by ample quantities of wine with dinner and sometimes whiskey or port afterward. I had hoped our days on the Cape would give my liver a chance to recuperate; there was no chance of that.

Jonas and I were sharing a bedroom, the girls another, located at opposite ends of the house with Liz's parents in between. When we'd come here during the academic term, we'd had the place, and our choice of sleeping arrangements, to ourselves. But not this time. I'd expected that the situation would lead to a certain amount of creeping around in the wee hours, but Liz forbade it. "Please do not shock the grown-ups," she said. "We'll all be shocking them soon enough."

Which was just as well. By this time, I had begun to tire of Stephanie. She was a wonderful girl, but I did not love her. There was nothing about her that made this so; she was in every way deserving. My heart was simply elsewhere, and it made me feel like a hypocrite. Since the funeral in New York, Liz and I had not spoken of my mother, or her cancer, or the night when we had walked the city streets together but in the end had chosen to step back from the abyss and keep our allegiances intact. Yet it was clear that the night had left its mark on both of us. Our friendship, until that time, had flowed through Jonas. A new circuit had been opened—not through him but around him—and along this pathway pulsed a private current of intimacy. We knew what had happened; we had been there. I had felt it, and I was sure she'd felt it too, and the fact that we'd done nothing only deepened this connection, even more than if we'd fallen into bed together. We would be sitting on the porch, each of us reading one of the mildew-smelling paperbacks left behind by other guests; we would look up at just the same moment, our eyes would meet, an ironic smile would flash at the corners of her mouth, which I'd return in kind. *Look at us,* we were saying to each other, *aren't we the trusty twosome. If only they knew how loyal we are. We should get a prize.*

I intended to do nothing about this, of course. I owed Jonas that much and more. Nor did I think Liz would have welcomed the attempt. The connection she shared with Jonas, one of long history, ran deeper than ours ever could. The house, with its endless warren of rooms and ocean views and shabbily genteel furnishings, reminded me how true this was. I was a visitor to this world, welcomed and even, as Liz had told me, admired. But a tourist nonetheless. Our night together, though indelible, had been just that: a night. Still, it thrilled me just being around her. The way she held her drink to her lips. Her habit of pushing her glasses to her forehead to read the smallest print. How she smelled, which I will not attempt to name, because it wasn't like anything else. Pain or pleasure? It was both. I wanted to bathe in her existence. Was she dying? I tried not to think about it. I was happy to be near her at all and accepted the situation as it stood.

Two days before our departure, Liz's father announced that we would be eating lobsters for dinner. (He did all the cooking; I'd never seen Patty so much as fry an egg.) This was for my benefit; he had learned, to his alarm, that I had never eaten one. He returned from the fish market in the late afternoon bearing a sack of squirming red-black monsters, removed one with a carnivore's grin, and made me hold it. No doubt I looked horrified; everyone had a good laugh, but I didn't mind. I loved her father a little for it, in fact. A lazy rain had been falling all day, sapping our energy; now we had a purpose. As if in acknowledgment of this fact, the sun emerged in time for the festivities; Jonas and I carried the dining table out to the back porch. I had noticed something about him. In the last couple of days, he had adopted a manner I could only describe as secretive. Something was afoot. At the cocktail hour, we drank bottles of dark beer (the only proper accompaniment, Oscar explained); then on to the main event. With great solemnity, Oscar presented me with a lobster bib. I had never understood this infantile practice; no one else was wearing one, and I felt a bit resentful until I cracked a claw and sprayed lobster juice all over myself, to an explosion of table-wide hilarity.

Imagine the perfection of the scene. The table with its red-checkered cloth; the ridiculous bounty of the feast; the golden sunset streaming toward us across the sound, then sinking into the sea with a final flash like an elegant gentleman tipping his hat in farewell. The candles came out, polishing our faces with their flickering glow. How had my life led me to such a place, among such people? I wondered what my parents would have said. My mother would have been pleased for me; wherever she was, I hoped its rules included the power to observe the living. As for my father, I didn't know. I had severed all ties completely. I saw now how unfair I'd been and vowed to get in touch. Perhaps it was not too late for him to make my graduation.

When we'd finished dessert—a strawberry-rhubarb pie—Jonas clinked his glass with his fork.

"Everybody, if I could have your attention."

He rose and moved around the table so that he was standing next to Liz. With a little grunt of effort, he turned her chair so she was facing him.

"Jonas," she said with a laugh, "what the hell are you doing?"

His hand fumbled in his pocket, and I knew. My stomach plunged, then the rest of me. As he bent to one knee, my friend withdrew the small velvet box. He opened the lid and held it before her. A huge, nervous grin was on his face. I saw the stone. It was enormous, made for a queen.

"Liz, I know we've talked about it. But I wanted to make it official. I feel like I've loved you all my life."

"Jonas, I don't know what to say." She looked up and laughed uneasily. Her cheeks were flushed with embarrassment. "This is so corny!"

"Say yes. That's all you have to do. I promise to give you everything you want in life."

I wanted to be ill.

"C'mon," Stephanie said. "What are you waiting for?"

Liz looked at her father. "At least tell me he asked you first."

The man was smiling, a conspirator. "That he did."

"And what did you tell him, O wise man?"

"Honey, it's really your decision. It's a big step. But I'll say I'm not opposed."

"Mom?"

Ever so slightly, the woman was crying. She nodded ardently, speechless.

"God," Stephanie moaned, "I can't stand the suspense! If you don't marry him, I will."

As Liz looked back at Jonas, did her eyes pause at my face? My memory says she did, though perhaps I imagined this.

"Well, I, um—"

Jonas removed the ring from the box. "Put it on. That's all you have to do. Make me the happiest man alive."

She stared at it, expressionless. The damn thing was fat as a tooth.

"Please," said Jonas.

She looked up. "Yes," she said, and nodded. "My answer is yes."

"You really mean it?"

"Don't be dense, Jonas. Of course I mean it." At last she smiled. "Get over here."

They embraced, then kissed; Jonas slid the ring onto her finger. I looked out over the water, unable to bear the scene. But even its broad blue expanse seemed to mock me.

"Oh!" Liz's mother cried. "I'm so happy!"

"Now, no sneaking around tonight, you two," her father laughed. "You're in separate rooms for the duration. Save it for the wedding night."

"Daddy, don't be gross!"

Jonas turned to her father and extended his hand. "Thank you, sir. Thank you from the bottom of my heart. I'll do everything in my power to make her happy."

They shook. "I know you will, son."

Out came the champagne, which Liz's father had kept in the wings. Glasses were filled, then raised.

"To the happy couple," Oscar said. "Long lives, happiness, a house full of love."

The champagne was delicious. It must have cost a bundle. I could barely swallow it down.

I couldn't sleep. I didn't want to.

As soon as I was sure Jonas was out cold, I snuck from the house. It was well after midnight; the moon, fat and white, had risen over the sound. I had no plan, only the desire to be alone with my feelings of desolation. I removed my shoes and took the stairs to the beach. Not a breath of wind blew; the world felt stuck. The tiniest of waves lapped upon the shore. I began to walk. The sand beneath my feet was still damp from the day of rain. The houses above me were all dark, some still boarded up, like tombs.

At a distance I saw someone sitting in the sand. It was Liz. I halted, uncertain what to do. She was holding a champagne bottle. She lifted it to her mouth and took a long drink. She noticed me, then looked away, but the damage was done; I couldn't turn back now.

I sat on the sand beside her. "Hey."

"Of course it would be you," she said, slurring her words.

"Why 'of course'?"

She took another swig. The ring was on her finger. "I noticed you didn't say anything tonight. It's considered polite, you know, to congratulate the bride-to-be."

"Okay, congratulations."

"You say that with such conviction." She sighed mournfully. "Jesus, am I drunk. Get this away from me."

She passed me the bottle. Just the dregs remained; I wished there were more. There were times to be sober, and this wasn't one of them. I polished it off and tossed it away.

"If you didn't want to, why did you say yes?"

"With everyone staring at me? You try it."

"So back out. He'll understand."

"No, he won't. He'll ask and ask, and I'll eventually give in and be the luckiest woman on earth, to be married to Jonas Lear."

We were quiet for a time.

"Can I ask you something?" I said.

She laughed sarcastically. Her gaze was cast over the sea. "Why not? Everybody's doing it."

"That night in New York. I was asleep, and something happened. I felt something."

"Did you now."

"Yes, I did." I waited. Liz said nothing. "Did you . . . kiss me?"

"Now, why would I do a thing like that?"

She was looking right at me. "Liz—"

"Shhh." A frozen moment followed. Our faces were just a foot apart. Then she did something puzzling. She took off her glasses and put them in my hand.

"You know, without these, I can't see anything. What's funny is that it's like nobody can see me, either. Isn't that strange? I kind of feel invisible."

I absolutely could have done it. *Should* have done it, long before. Why hadn't I? Why hadn't I taken her in my arms and pressed my mouth to hers and told her how I felt, consequences be damned? Who's to say I couldn't give her just as good a life? *Marry me,* I thought. *Marry me instead. Or don't marry anyone at all. Stay just as you are, and I will love you forever, as I do now, because you are the other half of me.*

"Oh, God," she said. "I think I'm going to throw up."

Then she did; she turned her face away and retched onto the sand. I held her hair back as all the lobster and champagne came up and out of her.

"I'm sorry, Tim." She was crying a little. "I'm so sorry."

I lifted her to her feet. She was mumbling more apologies as I draped her arm over my shoulders. She was close to dead weight now. Somehow I managed to haul her up the stairs and prop her in a chair on the divan on the porch. I was at a total loss; how would this look? I couldn't take her up to her room, not with Stephanie there. I doubted I could have gotten her up the stairs anyway without waking the entire house. I drew her upright again and carried her to the living room. The sofa would have to do; she could always say she'd had trouble sleeping and come downstairs to read. A crocheted blanket lay across the back of the sofa; I pulled it over her. She was fast asleep now. I got a glass of water from the kitchen and put it on the coffee table where she could find it, then took a chair to watch her. Her breathing became deep and even, her face slack. I allowed some more time to pass to be certain she would not be sick again, and got to my feet. There was something I needed to do. I bent over her and kissed her on the forehead.

"Good night," I whispered. "Good night, goodbye."

I crept up the stairs. Dawn wasn't far off; through the open windows, I could hear the birds beginning to sing. I made my way down the hall to the room I shared with Jonas. I gently turned the handle and stepped inside, but not before I heard, behind me, the snap of a closing door.

The cab rolled up the drive at six A.M. I was waiting on the porch with my bag.

"Where to?" the driver asked.

"The bus station."

He glanced up through the windshield. "You really live in this place?"

"No chance of that."

I was putting my bag in the trunk when the door of the house opened. Stephanie came striding down the walk, wearing one of the long T-shirts she slept in. It was actually one of mine.

"Sneaking off, are you? I saw the whole thing, you know."

"It wasn't what you thought."

"Sure it wasn't. You're a total asshole, you know that?"

"I'm aware of that, yes."

She rocked her face upward, hands on her hips. "God. How could I be so blind? It was totally obvious."

"Do me a favor, will you?"

"Are you kidding me?"

"Jonas can't ever know."

She laughed bitterly. "Oh, believe me, the last thing I want is to get mixed up with this mess. It's your problem."

"Feel free to think of it that way."

"What do you want me to tell them? As long as I'm being such a fucking liar."

I thought for a moment. "I don't care. A sick relative. It doesn't really matter."

"Just tell me: did you ever think about *me* in any of this? Did I even once cross your mind?"

I didn't know what to say.

"Fuck you," she said, and strode away.

I lowered myself into the cab. The driver was filling out a slip of paper on a clipboard. He glanced at me through the rearview. "Kinda rough, pal," he said. "Trust me, I've been there."

"I'm not really in the mood to talk, thanks."

He tossed his clipboard onto the dash. "I was only trying to be nice."

"Well, don't," I said, and with that we drove away.

19

I left them all behind.

I did not attend graduation. Back in Cambridge, I packed my belongings—three years later, there still wasn't much—and telephoned the biochemistry department at Rice. Of all the programs I had been accepted to, it possessed the virtue of being the farthest away, in a city I knew nothing about. It was a Saturday, so I had to leave a message, but yes, I told them, I'd be coming. I thought about abandoning my tuxedo; perhaps the next occupant would get some use out of it. But this seemed peevish and overly symbolic, and I could always throw it out later. Waiting outside, double-parked, was a rental car. As I closed my suitcase, the phone began to ring, and I ignored it. I carried my things downstairs, dropped off my key at the Winthrop House office, and drove away.

I arrived in Mercy in the middle of the night. I felt as if I'd been gone for a century. I slept in my car outside the house and awoke to the sound of tapping on the window. My father.

"What are you doing here?"

He was wearing a bathrobe; he had come out of the house to get the Sunday paper and noticed the car. He had aged a great deal, in the manner of someone who no longer cared much about his appearance. He had not shaved; his breath was bad. I followed him into the house, which seemed eerily the same, though it was very dusty and smelled like old food.

"Are you hungry?" he asked me. "I was going to have cereal, but I think I have some eggs."

"That's all right," I said. "I wasn't really planning on staying. I just wanted to say hello."

"Let me put some coffee on."

I waited in the living room. I had expected to be nervous, but I wasn't. I wasn't really feeling much of anything. My father returned from the kitchen with two mugs and sat across from me.

"You look taller," he said.

"I'm actually the same height. You must remember me wrong."

We drank our coffee.

"So, how was college? I know you just graduated. They sent me a form."

"It was fine, thank you."

"That's all you've got to say about it?" The question wasn't peevish; he merely seemed interested.

"Mostly." I shrugged. "I fell in love. It didn't really work out, though."

He thought for a moment. "I suppose you'll want to visit your mother."

"That would be nice."

I asked him to stop at a grocery store so I could pick up some flowers. They didn't have much, just daisies and carnations, but I did not think my mother would mind, and I told the girl behind the counter to wrap them with some greens to make them nice. We drove out of town. The interior of my father's Buick was full of fast-food trash. I held up a bag from McDonald's. A few dried-out fries rattled inside it.

"You shouldn't eat this stuff," I said.

We arrived at the cemetery, parked, and walked the rest of the way. It was a pleasant morning. We were passing through a sea of graves. My mother's headstone was located in the area for cremations: smaller headstones, spaced close together. Hers had just her name, Lorraine Fanning, and the dates. She had been fifty-seven.

I put the flowers down and stepped back. I thought about certain days, things we'd done together, about being her son.

"It's not bad to be here," I said. "I thought it might be."

"I don't come all that much. I guess I should." My father took a long breath. "I really screwed this up. I know that."

"It's all right. It's all over now."

"I'm kind of falling apart. I have diabetes, my blood pressure's through the roof. I'm forgetting things, too. Like yesterday, I had to sew a button on my shirt, and I couldn't find the scissors."

"So go to a doctor."

"It seems like a lot of trouble." He paused. "The girl you're in love with. What's she like?"

I thought for a moment. "Smart. Beautiful. Kind of sarcastic, but in a funny way. There wasn't one thing that did it, though."

"I think that's how it's supposed to be. That's how it was with your mother."

I looked up, into the spring day. Seven hundred miles away, in Cambridge, the graduation ceremony would be just getting rolling. I wondered what my friends were thinking about me.

"She loved you very much."

"I loved her, too." I looked at him and smiled. "It's nice here," I said. "Thanks for bringing me."

We returned to the house.

"If you want I can make up your room," my father said. "I left it just as it was. It's probably not very clean, though."

"Actually, I need to get going. I have a long drive."

He seemed a little sad. "Well. All right then." He walked me to my car. "Where are you off to?"

"Texas."

"What's there?"

"Texans, I guess." I shrugged. "More school."

"Do you need any money?"

"They're giving me a stipend. I should be all right."

"Well, let me know if you need more. You're welcome to it."

We shook hands and then, somewhat awkwardly, embraced. If I'd had to guess, I would have said my father wasn't going to live much longer. This turned out to be true; we would see each other only four more times before the heart attack that killed him. He was alone in the house when it happened. Because it was a weekend, several days would pass before anybody noticed he was missing and thought to look.

I got into the car. My father was standing above me. He motioned with his hand for me to roll down the window. "Call me when you get there, okay?"

I told him I would, and I did.

In Houston, I rented the first apartment I looked at, a garage studio with a view of the back of a Mexican restaurant, and got a job shelving books at the Rice library to tide myself over for the summer. The city was strange-looking and hotter than the mouth of hell, but it suited me. We search for ourselves in our surroundings, and everything I saw was either brand-new or falling apart. Most of the city was quite ugly—a sea of low-rise retail, shabby apartment complexes, and enormous, overcrowded freeways piloted by maniacs—but the area around the university was rather posh, with large, well-kept houses and wide boulevards flanked by live oaks so perfectly manicured they looked less like trees than sculptures of trees. For six hundred dollars, I bought my first car, a snot-yellow 1983 Chevy Citation with bald tires, 230,000 miles on the odometer, and a sagging vinyl ceiling I used a staple gun to reattach. I'd heard nothing from Liz or Jonas, but of course they had no idea where I was. There was a time in America when it was still possible to disappear by going left when everybody expected you to go right. With a little digging, they probably could have found me—a few well-placed calls to a few department chairs—but this presupposed that they would want to. I had no idea what they would want. I didn't think I ever had.

Classes began. About my studies, there is not much to say except that they occupied me utterly. I made friends with the department secretary, a black woman in her fifties who basically ran the place; she confided to me that nobody in the department had actually expected me to come. I was, in her words, "a prize thoroughbred they had bought for pennies on the dollar." To describe my fellow graduate students as antisocial would be the understatement of the century; no lawn parties here. Their minds were utterly unfettered by thoughts of fun. They also despised me for the naked favoritism shown me by my professors. I kept my head down, my nose to the stone. I adopted the practice of taking long drives in the Texas countryside. It was windblown, flat, without meaningful demarcation, every square of dirt the same as every other. I liked to pull the car to the side of the road someplace completely arbitrary and just look at it.

The one eastern habit I retained was reading *The New York Times,* and in this manner I learned that Liz and Jonas had made it official. This was in the fall of '93; a year had passed. "Mr. and Mrs. Oscar Macomb, of Greenwich, Connecticut, and Osterville, Massachusetts, are pleased to announce the marriage of their daughter, Elizabeth Christina, to Jonas Abbott Lear of Beverly, Massachusetts. The bride, a graduate of Harvard, recently completed a master's degree in literature at the University of California, Berkeley, and is currently a doctoral student in Renaissance studies at the University of Chicago, where the groom, also a Harvard graduate, is pursuing a PhD in microbiology."

Two days later, I received a large manila envelope from my father. Inside was another envelope, to which he'd affixed a sticky note, apologizing for taking so long to forward it. It was an invitation, of course, postmarked the previous June. I put it aside for a day, then, the next night, in the company of a bottle of bourbon, sat at the kitchen table and peeled back the flap. Ceremony to be held September 4, 1993, St. Andrew's-by-the-Sea, Hyannis Port. Reception to follow at the home of Oscar and Patricia Macomb, 41 Sea View Avenue, Osterville, Massachusetts. In the margin was a message:

> *Please please please come. Jonas says so too. We miss you*
> *terribly.*

> *Love, L*

I looked at this for some time. I was sitting in the window of my apartment, facing the alley behind the restaurant, with its reeking dumpsters. As I watched, a kitchen worker, a small, round-bellied Hispanic man in a stained apron, came through the door. He was carrying a garbage bag; he opened one of the dumpsters, tossed the bag inside, and closed the lid with a clang. I expected him to go back inside, but instead he lit a cigarette and stood there, inhaling the smoke with long, hungry drags.

I rose from the table. I kept them in my bureau, wrapped in a sock: Liz's glasses. I had put them in my pocket that night on the beach and forgotten all about them until I was in the cab, by which time it was too late to return them. Now I put them on; they were a little small for my face, the lenses quite strong. I sat back down at the window and watched the man smoke in the alleyway, the image distorted and far away, as if I were looking through the wrong end of a telescope or sitting at the bottom of the sea, gazing upward through miles of water.

20

Here I must leap ahead in time, because that is what time did. I finished my degree at a quickstep; this was followed by a postdoc at Stanford, then a faculty appointment at Columbia, where I was tenured in due course. Within professional circles, I became well known. My reputation increased; the world came calling. I traveled widely, speaking for lucrative fees. Grants flowed my way without difficulty; such was my reputation, I barely had to fill out the forms. I became the holder of multiple patents, two purchased by pharmaceutical concerns for outrageous sums that set me up for life. I refereed important journals. I sat on elite boards. I testified before Congress and was, at various times, a member of the Senate Special Commission on Bioethics, the President's Council on Science and Technology, the NASA advisory board, and the U.N. Task Force on Biological Diversity.

Along the way, I married. The first time, when I was thirty, lasted four years, the second half that. Each woman had, at one time, been my student, a matter of some awkwardness—chummy glances from male colleagues, raised eyebrows from the higher-ups, frosty exchanges with my female co-workers and the wives of friends. Timothy Fanning, that lothario, that dirty old man (though I had not turned forty). My third wife, Julianna, was just twenty-three the day we married. Our union was impulsive, forged in the furnace of sex; two hours after she graduated, we attacked each other like dogs. Though I was very fond of her, I found her bewildering. Her tastes in music and movies, the books she read, her friends, the things she thought important: none made a lick of sense to me.

I was not, like many a man of a certain age, trying to prop up my self-esteem with a young woman's body. I did not mourn the years' unraveling, or fear death unduly, or grieve my waning youth. To the contrary, I liked the many things my success had brought me. Wealth, esteem, authority, good tables at restaurants and hot towels on planes—the whole kit and caboodle that history awards the conquerors: for all of these, I had time's passage to thank. Yet what I was doing was obvious, even to me. I was trying to recapture the one thing I had lost, that life had denied me. Each of my wives, and the many women in between—all far younger than I was, the age gap widening with every one I took into my bed—was a facsimile of Liz. I speak neither of their appearances, though all belonged to a recognizable physical type (pale, slender, myopic), nor of their temperaments, which possessed a similar brainy combativeness. I mean that I wanted them to *be* her, so I could feel alive.

That Jonas and I should cross paths was inevitable; we belonged to the same world. Our first reunion occurred at a conference in Toronto in 2002. Enough time had gone by that we both managed to make no reference to my abrupt severing of the relationship. We were all "how the hell are you" and "you haven't changed a bit" and vowed to keep in better touch, as if we'd been in touch at all. He had returned to Harvard, of course—it ran in the family. He felt himself to be on the verge of some kind of breakthrough, though he was secretive about this, and I didn't press. Of Liz, he offered only the bare-bones professional data. She was teaching at Boston College; she liked it, her students worshipped her, she was working on a book. I told him to say hello for me and let it go at that.

The following year, I received a Christmas card. It was one of those photograph cards that people use to parade their beautiful children, though the image showed only the two of them. The shot had been taken in some arid locale; they were dressed head to foot in khaki and wearing honest-to-God pith helmets. A note from Liz was written on the back, penned in a hurried script, as if added at the last second: *Jonas said he ran into you. Glad you're doing well!*

Year by year, the cards kept coming. Each showed them in a different exotic setting: atop elephants in India, posing before the Great Wall of China, standing at the bow of a ship in heavy parkas with a glacial coastline in the background. All very cheery, yet there was something depressing about these photos, a mood of compensation. *What a great life we're having! Really! Swear to God!* I began to notice other things. Jonas was the same hale specimen he'd always been, but Liz was aging precipitously, and not just physically. In previous pictures, her eyes had been distracted in a manner that made the photo seem incidental to the moment. Now she looked at the camera dead-on, like a hostage made to pose with a newspaper. Her smile felt manufactured, a product of her will. Was I imagining this? Furthermore, was it fancy on my part that her darkening gaze was a message meant for me? And what of their bodies? In the first photograph, taken in the desert, Lear was standing behind her, wrapping her with his arms. Year by year, they separated. The last one I received, in 2010, had been taken at a café beside a river that was unmistakably the Seine. They were sitting across from each other, far out of arm's reach. Glasses of wine stood on the table. My old roommate's was nearly empty. Liz had touched hers not at all.

At the same time, rumors began to swirl about Jonas. I had always known him to be a man of ardent if somewhat outlandish passions, but the stories I heard were disturbing. Jonas Lear, it was said, had gone off the deep end. His research had drifted into fantasy. His last paper, published in *Nature,* had danced around the subject, but people had begun to use the V-word in connection to him. He hadn't published anything since, or appeared at the usual conferences, where a good deal of barroom hilarity transpired at his expense. Some of his colleagues even went so far as to conjecture that his tenure was in jeopardy. A certain amount of schadenfreude was built into our profession, the theory being that one man's fall was another man's rise. But I became genuinely worried for him.

It was not long after Julianna tossed in the towel on our ersatz marriage that I received a call from a man named Paul Kiernan. I had met him once or twice; he was a cell biologist at Harvard, a junior colleague of Jonas's, with an excellent reputation. I could tell that the conversation made him uncomfortable. He had learned of our long association; the gist of his call was his concern that his tenure case might be adversely affected by his connection to Jonas. Might I write a letter on his behalf? My initial instinct was to tell him to grow up, that he was lucky to even know such a man, gossip be damned. But given the ignominious workings of tenure committees, I knew he had a point.

"A lot of it has to do with his wife, actually," Paul said. "You've got to feel for the guy."

I practically dropped the phone. "What are you talking about?"

"I'm sorry, I thought you knew, being such good friends and all. She's very sick, it doesn't look good. I guess I shouldn't have said anything."

"I'll write your letter," I said, and hung up.

I was completely at a loss. I looked up Liz's number at Boston College and began to dial, then put the phone back in its cradle. What would I say, after so many years? What right did I have at this late date to reinsert myself into her life? Liz was dying; I'd never stopped loving her, not for a second, but she was another man's wife. At a time like this, their bond was paramount; if I had learned anything from my parents, it was that the journey of death was one that spouses took together. Maybe it was just the old cowardice returning, but I did not pick up the phone again.

I waited for news. Every day I checked the *Times'* obituary page, in a grim death watch. I was short with colleagues, avoided my friends. I had turned the apartment over to Julianna and sublet a one-bedroom in the West Village, making it easy to disappear, to recede into the fringes of life. What would I do when my Liz was gone? I realized that in some drawer of my brain I had kept the idea that someday, somehow, we would be together. Perhaps they would divorce. Perhaps Jonas would die. Now I had no hope.

Then one night, close to Christmas, the phone rang. It was nearly midnight; I had just settled into bed.

"Tim?"

"Yes, this is Tim Fanning." I was annoyed by the lateness of the call and did not recognize the voice.

"It's Liz."

My heart crashed into my ribs. I could not form words.

"Hello?"

"I'm here," I managed to say. "It's good to hear your voice. Where are you?"

"I'm in Greenwich, at my mother's."

I noted that she did not say "my parents'." Oscar was no more.

"I need to see you," she said.

"Of course. Of course you can." I was madly fumbling in the drawer for a pencil. "I'll drop everything. Just tell me where and when."

She would be taking the train into the city the next day. She had something to do first, and we planned to meet at Grand Central at five o'clock, before she returned to Greenwich.

I left my office well ahead of time, wanting to arrive first. It had rained all day, but as the early winter darkness fell, the rain changed to snow. The subway was jammed; everything felt like it was moving in slow motion. I arrived at the station and took my position beneath the clock with minutes to spare. The heedless crowds streamed by—commuters in raincoats with umbrellas tucked under the arms, the women wearing running shoes over their stockings, snow clinging to everyone's hair. Many were carrying shopping bags brightly decorated for the season. Macy's. Nordstrom. Bergdorf Goodman. Just the thought of these happy, hopeful people irritated me more than I can say. How could they think about Christmas at a time like this? How could they think about anything at all? Didn't they know what was about to happen in this place?

Then she appeared. The sight of her nearly undid me; I felt as if I were awakening from a long sleep. She was wearing a dark trench coat; a silk scarf covered her hair. She threaded her way toward me through the hurrying mobs. It was absurd, but I was afraid that she would never make it, that the crowds would swallow her, as in a dream. She caught my eye, smiled, and made a "move along" gesture behind the back of a man who was blocking her path. I pushed my way to her.

"And there you are," she said.

What followed was the warmest, most deeply felt hug of my life. Just the smell of her drowned my senses in joy. Yet happiness was not the only thing I felt. Every bone, every edge of her pressed against me; it was as if I were holding a bird.

She pulled away. "You look great," she said.

"So do you."

She gave a little laugh. "You're such a liar, but I do appreciate the sentiment." She removed her scarf, revealing a scrim of pale hair, the kind that grows back after chemo. "What do you think of my new holiday 'do? I'm guessing you know the story."

I nodded. "I got a call from a colleague of Jonas's. He told me."

"That would be Paul Kiernan, that little weasel. You scientists are such gossips."

"Are you hungry?"

"Never. But I could use a drink."

We climbed the stairs to the bar on the west balcony. Even this small effort seemed to enervate her. We took a table near the edge with a view of the grand hall. I ordered a Scotch, Liz a martini and a glass of water.

"Do you remember when you met me here the first time?" I asked.

"You had a friend, wasn't it? Something awful had happened."

"That's right. Lucessi." I hadn't said the name in years. "It meant a lot to me, you know. You really took care of me."

"Comes with the service. But if I remember correctly, it was at least half the other way around. Maybe more than half." She paused, then said, "You really do look good, Tim. Success suits you, but I always knew it would. I've kind of kept tabs. Tell me one thing. Are you happy?"

"I'm happy now."

She smiled. Her lips were thin and white. "An excellent dodge, Dr. Fanning."

I reached across the table and took her hand. It was cold as ice. "Tell me what's going to happen."

"I'm going to die, that's what."

"I can't accept that. There has to be something they can do. Let me make some calls."

She shook her head. "They've all been made. Believe me, I'm not going down without a fight. But it's time to raise the white flag."

"How long?"

"Four months. Six if I'm lucky. That's where I was today. I've been seeing a doc at Sloan Kettering. It's all over the place. His words."

Six months: it was nothing. How had I let all the years go by? "Jesus, Liz—"

"Don't say it. Don't say you're sorry, because I'm not." She squeezed my hand. "I need a favor, Tim."

"Anything."

"I need you to help Jonas. I'm sure you've heard the stories. They're all true. He's in South America right now, on his great goose chase. He can't accept any of this. He still thinks he can save me."

"What can *I* do?"

"Just talk to him. He trusts you. Not just as a scientist but as his friend. Do you know how much he still talks about you? He follows your every move. He probably knows what you ate for breakfast this morning."

"That makes no sense. He should hate me."

"Why would he hate you?"

Even then, I couldn't say the words. She was dying, and I couldn't tell her.

"Leaving the way I did. Never telling him why."

"Oh, he knows why. Or thinks he does."

I was shocked. "What did you tell him?"

"The truth. That you finally figured out you were too good for us."

"That's insane. And it wasn't the reason."

"I know it wasn't, Tim."

A silence passed. I sipped my drink. Announcements were being made; people were hurrying to their trains, riding into the winter dark.

"We were a couple of good soldiers, you and I," Liz said. She gave a brittle smile. "Loyal to a fault."

"So he never figured out that part."

"Are we talking about the same Jonas here? He couldn't even imagine such a thing."

"How has it been with him? I don't just mean now."

"I can't complain."

"But you'd like to."

She shrugged. "Sometimes. Everyone does. He loves me, he thinks he's helping. What else could a girl ask for?"

"Somebody who understood you."

"That's a tall order. I don't think I even understand myself."

I felt suddenly angry. "You're not some high school science project, damnit. He just wants to feel noble. He should be here with you, not trooping around, where was it? South America?"

"It's the only way he has of dealing with this."

"It's not fair."

"What's fair? I have cancer. That isn't fair."

I understood, then, what she was saying to me. She was afraid, and Jonas had left her alone. Maybe she wanted me to bring him home; maybe what she really needed was for me to tell him how he'd failed her. Maybe it was both. What I knew was that I'd do absolutely anything she asked.

I became aware that neither of us had spoken for a while. I looked at Liz; something was wrong. She'd begun to perspire, though the room was quite cold. She took a shuddering breath and reached weakly for her glass of water.

"Liz, are you all right?"

She sipped. Her hand was shaking. She returned the glass to the table, nearly spilling it, dropped her elbow, and braced her forehead against her palm.

"I don't think I am, actually. I think I'm going to faint."

I rose quickly from my chair. "We need to get you to a hospital. I'll get a cab."

She shook her head emphatically. "No more hospitals."

Where then? "Can you walk?"

"I'm not sure."

I threw some cash onto the table and helped her to her feet. She was on the verge of collapse, giving me nearly all of her weight.

"You're always carrying me, aren't you?" she murmured.

I got her into a cab and gave the driver my address. The snow was falling heavily now. Liz leaned back against the seat and closed her eyes.

"The lady okay?" the driver asked. He was wearing a turban and had a heavy black beard. I knew he meant, Is she drunk? "The lady looks sick. No puking in my cab."

I handed him a hundred-dollar bill. "Does this help?"

The traffic was like glue. It took us nearly thirty minutes to get downtown. New York was softening under the snow. A white Christmas: how happy everyone was going to be. My apartment was on the second floor; I would have to carry her. I waited for a neighbor to come through the door and asked him to hold it open, guided Liz out of the cab, and lifted her into my arms.

"Wow," my neighbor said. "She doesn't look too good."

He followed us to my apartment door, took the key from my pocket, and opened that as well. "Do you want me to call 911?" he asked.

"It's okay, I've got this. She had a little too much to drink is all."

He winked despicably. "Don't do anything I wouldn't do."

I got her out of her coat and carried her into the bedroom. As I lay her on my bed, she opened her eyes and turned her face toward the window.

"It's snowing," she said, as if this were the most amazing thing in the world.

She closed them again. I removed her glasses and shoes, draped a blanket over her, and doused the lights. There was an overstuffed chair close to the window where I liked to read. I sat down and waited in the dark to see what would happen next.

Sometime later, I awoke. I looked at my watch: it was nearly two A.M. I went to Liz and placed my palm to her forehead. She felt cool, and I believed that the worst had passed.

Her eyes opened. She looked around cautiously, as if she wasn't quite sure where she was.

"How are you feeling?" I asked.

She didn't answer right away. Her voice was very soft. "Better, I think. Sorry to scare you."

"That's perfectly all right."

"It happens sometimes like that, but it goes away. Until sometime when it doesn't, I guess."

I had nothing to say to that. "Let me get you some water."

I filled a glass in the bathroom and brought it to her. She lifted her head off the pillow and sipped. "I was having the strangest dream," she said. "The chemo is what does it. The stuff's like LSD. I thought that was over, though."

A thought occurred to me. "I have a present for you."

"You do?"

"Wait here."

I kept her glasses in my desk. I returned to the bedroom and placed them in her hand. She studied them for a long moment.

"I was wondering when you'd get around to giving these back."

"I like to put them on sometimes."

"And here I didn't get you anything. I'm just appalling." She was crying, just a little. She looked up, meeting my eye. "You're not the only one who blew it you know."

"Liz?"

She reached out her hand and touched my cheek. "It's funny. You can live your whole life and then suddenly know that you didn't do it right at all."

I wrapped her fingers with my own. Outside, the snow fell upon the sleeping city.

"You should kiss me," she said.

"Do you want me to?"

"I think that's the dumbest thing you've ever said."

I did. I brought my mouth to hers. It was a soft, quiet kiss—*peaceful* would be the word—the kind that obliterates the world and makes all time turn around it. Infinity in a moment, the hem of creation brushing the face of the waters.

"I should stop," I said.

"No, you shouldn't." She began to unbutton her blouse. "Just please be careful with me. I'm kind of breakable, you know."

21

We became lovers. I don't think I'd ever truly understood the word. I don't mean just sex, though there was that—unhurried, meticulous, a form of passion I had never known existed. I mean that we lived as richly as two people ever could, with a feeling of absolute rightness. We left the apartment only to walk. A deep cold had followed the snow, sealing the city in whiteness. Jonas's name was never mentioned. It wasn't a subject we were avoiding. It had simply ceased to matter.

We both knew she would have to return eventually; she could not simply step out of her life. Nor could I imagine the two of us being apart for one minute of the time she had left. I believed she felt the same. I wanted to be there when it happened. I wanted to be touching her, holding her hand, telling her how much I loved her as she faded away.

One morning the week after Christmas, I awoke in bed alone. I found her in the kitchen, sipping tea, and knew what she was about to tell me.

"I have to go back."

"I know," I said. "Where?"

"Greenwich first. My mother must be worried. Then Boston, I suppose." She didn't have to say more; her meaning was plain. Jonas would be home soon.

"I understand," I said.

We took a cab to Grand Central. Few words had been spoken since her announcement. I felt like I was being taken to face a firing squad. Be brave, I told myself. Be the sort of man who stands tall with his eyes open, waiting for the guns' report.

Her train was called. We walked to the platform where it awaited. She put her arms around me and began to cry. "I don't want to do this," she said.

"Then don't. Don't get on the train."

I felt her hesitancy. Not just the words; I felt it in her body. She couldn't make herself let go.

"I have to."

"Why?"

"I don't know."

People were hurrying past. The customary announcement crackled overhead: *All aboard for New Haven, Bridgeport, Westport, New Canaan, Greenwich* . . . A door was closing; soon it would be sealed.

"Then come back. Do what you have to do, and then come back. We can go someplace."

"Where?"

"Italy, Greece. An island in the Pacific. It doesn't matter. Somewhere nobody can find us."

"I want to."

"Say yes."

A frozen moment; then she nodded against me. "Yes."

My heart soared. "How long do you need to tie things up?"

"A week. No, two."

"Make it ten days. Meet me here, under the clock. I'll have everything ready."

"I love you," she said. "I think I did from the start."

"I loved you even before that."

A last kiss, she stepped toward the train, then turned and embraced me again.

"Ten days," she said.

I made ready. There were things I needed to do. I composed a hasty email to my dean, requesting a leave of absence. I wouldn't be around to know if it had been accepted, but I hardly cared. I could imagine no life beyond the next six months.

.I called a friend who was an oncologist. I explained the situation, and he told me what would happen. Yes, there would be pain, but mostly a slow receding.

"It's not something you should manage on your own," he said. When I didn't reply, he sighed. "I'll phone in a prescription."

"For what?"

"Morphine. It will help." He paused. "At the end, you know, a lot of people take more than they should, strictly speaking."

I said I understood and thanked him. Where should we go? I had read an article in the *Times* about an island in the Aegean where half the population lived to be a hundred. There was no valid scientific explanation; the residents, most of whom were goat herders, took it as a fact of life. A man was quoted in the article as saying, "Time is different here." I bought two first-class tickets to Athens and found a ferry schedule online. A boat traveled to the island only once a week. We would have to wait two days in Athens, but there were worse places. We would visit the temples, the great, indestructible monuments of a lost world, then vanish.

The day arrived. I packed my bags; we would be going straight from the station to the airport for a ten P.M. flight. I could barely think straight; my emotions were an indescribable jumble. Joy and sadness had fused together in my heart. Foolishly, I had planned nothing else for the day and was forced to sit idly in my apartment until late afternoon. I had no food on hand, having cleaned out the refrigerator, but doubted I could have eaten anyway.

I took a cab to the station. Five o'clock was, once again, the appointed hour. Liz would be taking an Amtrak train to Stamford, to see her mother, in Greenwich, one last time, then a local to Grand Central. With each passing block my feelings annealed into a pure sense of purpose. I knew, as few men did, why I had been born in the first place; everything in my life had called me forward to this moment. I paid the cabbie and went inside to wait. It was a Saturday, the crowds light. The opalescent clock faces read 4:36. Liz's train was due in twenty minutes.

My pulse quickened as the announcement came over the speakers: *Now arriving at track 16* . . . I considered going to the platform to head her off, but we might lose each other in the crowd. Passengers surged into the main hall. Soon it became clear that Liz was not among them. Perhaps she had taken a later train; the New Haven line ran every thirty minutes. I checked my phone, but there were no messages. The next train came, and still no Liz. I began to worry that something had happened. It did not occur to me yet that she had changed her mind, though the idea was waiting in the wings. At six o'clock I called her cell, but it went straight to voicemail. Had she shut it off?

Train by train, my panic grew. It was now obvious that Liz would not be coming, and yet I continued to wait, to hope. I was hanging by my fingertips over an abyss. Time and again I tried her cell, with the same result. *This is Elizabeth Lear. I'm not available to take your call.* The clocks' hands mocked me with their turning. It was nine, then ten. I had waited five hours. What a fool I'd been.

I left the station and began to walk. The air was cruel; the city seemed like a huge dead thing, some monstrous joke. I did not button my coat or put on my gloves, preferring to feel the pain of the wind. Sometime later I looked up to find I was on Broadway, near the Flatiron. I realized I had left my suitcase at the station. I thought to go back and retrieve it—surely somebody would have turned it in—but the flame of this impulse quickly extinguished itself. A suitcase—who cared? Of course there was the morphine to consider. Perhaps whoever found it would enjoy themselves.

Drinking myself blind seemed like the next logical step. I entered the first restaurant I came to, in the lobby of an office building—sleek and upscale, full of chrome and stone. A few couples were still eating, though it was after midnight. I took a place at the bar, ordered a Scotch, finished it before the bartender had returned the bottle to the rack, and requested a refill.

"Excuse me. You're Professor Fanning, aren't you?"

I turned to the woman sitting a few stools away. She was young, a little heavy but quite striking, Indian or Middle Eastern, with raven-black hair, full cheeks, and a bow-shaped mouth. Above her generically sexy black skirt she wore a filmy top the color of cream. A glass of something with fruit in it sat on the bar in front of her, its rim stained with crescents of rust-colored lipstick.

"I'm sorry?"

She smiled. "I guess you don't remember me." When I didn't reply, she added, "Molecular Biology 100? Spring 2002?"

"You were my student."

She laughed. "Not much of one. You gave me a C minus."

"Oh. Sorry about that."

"Trust me, no offense taken. The human race has a lot to thank you for, actually. Many people are alive today because I didn't go to med school."

I had no recollection of her; hundreds of young women like her came and went from my classes. It is also not the same thing to see someone from the distance of a podium at eight o'clock in the morning, wearing sweatpants and furiously tapping a laptop, as to find them sitting three stools away in a bar, dressed for a night of adventure.

"So, where did you end up?" A dull remark; I was simply looking for something to say, since conversation was now inevitable.

"Publishing, where else?" She leveled her gaze at me. "You know, I had the biggest crush on you. I'm talking *major*. A lot of the girls did."

I realized she was drunk, making such a confession without even telling me her name.

"Miss—?"

She moved to the stool next to mine and extended her hand. Her nails were perfectly manicured, painted to match her lips. "Nicole."

"It's been a long night for me, Nicole."

"I could sort of tell, the way you put away that Scotch." She touched her hair for no reason. "What do you say, Professor? Buy a girl a drink? It's your chance to make up for that C."

She was plainly amusing herself, a woman who knew what she had, what it could do. I glanced past her; just a handful of other people were in the room. "Aren't you—?"

"With anyone?" She gave a little laugh. "Like, did my date step out for a smoke?"

I felt suddenly flustered; I hadn't meant the question as a come-on. "I mean, a pretty girl like you. I just assumed."

"Well, you assumed wrong." With the tips of her fingers she picked a cherry from her glass and raised it slowly to her lips. Her eyes locked onto my face; she placed it on her tongue, balancing it there for a half second before popping the stem and curling the red meat into her mouth. It was the hokiest thing I'd ever seen.

"Don't you know, Professor? Tonight I'm all yours."

We were in a taxi. I was very drunk. The cab was bouncing through narrow streets and we were kissing like teenagers, drinking each other's mouths in furious gulps. I appeared to have lost all volition; things were simply happening of their own accord. There was something I wanted, I didn't know what. One of my hands had found its way up her skirt, lost in a feminine country of skin and lace; the other was lifting her buttocks toward me, pulling our hips together. She unlatched my trousers and eased me free, then dropped her head to my lap. The cabbie glanced back, said nothing. Up and down she went, my fingers entwined in the lush mane of her hair. My head was spinning, I could hardly breathe.

The taxi halted. "Twenty-seven fifty," the driver said.

It was like being splashed by cold water. I hurriedly rearranged myself and paid. When I exited the car, the girl—Natalie? Nadine?—was already waiting on the steps to her building, smoothing down the front of her skirt. Something loud and large was rattling overhead; I thought we might be in Brooklyn, near the Manhattan Bridge overpass. More grappling at the door and she pushed me away.

"Wait here." Her face was flushed; she was breathing very fast. "I have something to take care of. I'll buzz you in."

She was gone before I could object. Standing on the sidewalk, I tried to reassemble the order of the night's events. Grand Central, the hours of hopeless waiting. My desolate walk through the icy streets. The warm oasis of the bar, and the girl—Nicole, that was it—smiling and moving closer and putting her hand on my knee and the two of us making our hasty, inevitable exit. I could remember these things, yet none of them seemed completely real. Abandoned in the cold, I felt a rush of panic. I did not want to be alone with my thoughts. How could she have done it? How could Liz have left me standing there, train after train? If the door didn't buzz soon, I knew, I would literally detonate.

A few agonizing minutes passed. I heard the door open and turned in time to see a woman emerge from the building. She was older, heavyset, perhaps Hispanic. Her body, buried in a bunchy down coat, was hunched against the wind. She had failed to notice me standing in the shadows; I slid behind her and grabbed the door just before it closed.

The lobby encased me with its sudden warmth. I scanned the mailboxes. Nicole Forood, apartment zero. I descended the stairs to the basement, where a single door awaited. I knocked with my knuckles, then, when no one responded, with my fist. My frustration was indescribable. My feelings had annealed to a pure desperation, almost like anger. My fist was raised again when I heard footsteps inside. The complicated unlocking of a New York apartment door commenced; then it opened just enough for me to see the girl's face on the other side of the chain. She had taken off her makeup, revealing an otherwise plain face, flawed by traces of acne. Another man would have understood the meaning, but my agitation was such that my brain could not compute the data.

"Why did you leave me?"

"I don't think this is a good idea. You should go."

"I don't understand."

Her face was as rigid as a blind man's. "Something's come up. I'm sorry."

How could this be the same girl who had laid siege to me in the bar? Was this some kind of game? I wanted to blow the chain off its anchors and burst through the door. Maybe that was what she wanted me to do. She sort of seemed the type.

"It's late. I shouldn't have left you out there, but I'm going to shut the door now."

"Please, just let me warm up for a minute. I promise I'll go after that."

"I'm sorry, Tim. I had a good time. Maybe we can do it again sometime. But I really have to go."

I'll admit it: part of my mind was computing the strength of the chain that held the door. "You don't trust me, is that the reason?"

"No, that's not it. It's just—" She didn't finish.

"I swear I'll behave. Whatever you want." I offered a sheepish smile. "The truth is, I'm still a little drunk. I really need to sober up."

I could see the indecision in her face. My appeal was doing its work.

"Please," I said. "It's freezing out there."

A moment passed; her face relaxed. "Just a few minutes, okay? I have to be up early."

I held up three fingers. "Scout's honor."

She closed the door, undid the chain, and opened it again. Disappointingly, the skirt and filmy top had been replaced by a robe and a shapeless flannel nightgown. She stepped aside to let me enter.

"I'll put on some coffee."

The apartment had a dingy look: a small living area with high-set windows facing the street, a galley kitchen with dishes teetering in the sink, a narrow hallway that led, presumably, to the bedroom. The couch, which faced an old tube-style television, was heaped with laundry. There were few books in sight, nothing on the walls except a couple of cheap museum posters of water lilies and ballerinas.

"Sorry it's such a mess," she said, and waved at the sofa. "Just shove that stuff aside if you want."

Nicole's back was to me. She filled a pot at the tap and began to pour the water into a stained coffee machine. Something peculiar was happening to me. I can only describe it as a kind of astral projection. It was as if I were a character in a movie, observing myself from a distance. In this divided state, I watched myself approach her from behind. She was sifting ground beans into the machine. I was about to put my arms around her when she sensed my presence and spun toward me.

"What are you doing?"

My body was pressing her against the counter. I began to kiss her neck. "What do you think I'm doing?"

"Tim, stop. I mean it."

I was burning from within. My senses were swarming. "God, you smell so good." I was licking, tasting. I wanted to drink her.

"You're scaring me. I need you to leave."

"Say you're her." Where were these words coming from? Who was talking? Was it me? "Say it. Tell me how sorry you are."

"Goddamnit, stop!"

With surprising strength, she shoved me away. I fell against the counter, barely staying on my feet. When I looked up, she was pulling a long knife from a drawer. She aimed it at me like a pistol.

"Get out."

Darkness was spreading inside me. "How could you do it? How could you leave me standing there?"

"I'll scream."

"You bitch. You fucking bitch."

I lurched toward her. What were my intentions? Who was she to me, this woman with the knife? Was she Liz? Was she even a person, or merely a mirror in which I beheld the image of my wretched self? To this day, I do not know; the moment seems the property of another man entirely. I do not say this to exonerate myself, which is impossible, only to describe events as accurately as I can. With one hand I reached to cover her mouth; with the other I grabbed her arm, jerking the knife downward. Our bodies collided in a soft crash, and then we were falling to the floor, my body on top of hers, the knife between us.

The knife. The knife.

As we hit the floor, I felt it. There was no mistaking the sensation, or the sound it made.

The events that followed are no less strange to my memory, benighted by horror. I was in a nightmare in which the great, unrecallable act had been committed. I rose from her body. A pool of blood, rich and dark, almost black, was spreading beneath it; more was on my shirt, a crimson splash. The blade had entered just below the girl's sternum, driven deep into her thoracic cavity by my falling weight. She was looking at the ceiling; she let out a little gasp, no louder than a person would make who had suffered a mild surprise. *Is my life over? Is that all? This stupid little thing and that's the end?* Bit by bit, her eyes lost focus; an unnatural stillness eased across her face.

I turned to the sink and vomited.

The decision to hide my tracks was not one I recall making. I did not have a plan; I merely enacted one. I did not yet think of myself as a killer; rather, I was a man who had been involved in a serious accident that would be misunderstood. I stripped to my undershirt; the girl's blood had not seeped through. I cast my eyes around for the things I might have touched. The knife of course; that would have to be disposed of. The front door? Had I touched the knob, the frame? I had seen the shows on television, the ones with the good-looking detectives combing crime scenes for the minutest evidence. I knew their prowess to be wildly overstated for dramatic purposes, but they were my only reference. What invisible traces of me were, even now, touching down upon the surfaces of the woman's apartment, awaiting collection and study, pointing to my guilt?

I rinsed my mouth and washed the knobs and sink with a sponge. The knife I cleaned as well, then wrapped it in my shirt and deposited it carefully in the pocket of my coat. I did not look at the body again; to do so would have been unbearable. I scrubbed the counters and turned to appraise the rest of the apartment. Something seemed different. What was I seeing?

I heard a sound, coming from down the hall.

What is the worst thing? The deaths of millions? A whole world lost? No: the worst thing is the sound I heard.

Details I had failed to notice emerged in my vision. The pile of laundry, full of tiny pink garments. The bright toys of plush and plastic strewn across the floor. The distinctive, fecal aroma masked by sweet powder. I remembered the woman I had seen coming from the building. The timing of her departure had been no accident.

The sound came again; I wanted to flee but could not. That I had to follow it was my penance; it was the stone I would carry for life. Slowly I moved down the hall, terror accompanying my every step. A pale, vigilant light shone through the partly open door. The odor grew stronger, coating my mouth with its taste. At the threshold I paused, petrified, yet knowing what was required of me.

The little girl was awake and looking about. Six months, a year—I was not a good judge of these things. A mobile of cardboard-cutout animals dangled above her crib. She was waving her arms and kicking her legs against the mattress, causing the animals to jostle on their strings; she made the sound again, a joyful little squeal. *See what I can do? Mama, come look.* But in the other room her mother lay in a pool of blood, her eyes staring into time's abyss.

What did I do? Did I fall before her and beg her forgiveness? Did I pick her up with my unclean hands, the hands of a killer, and tell her I was sorry for her motherless life? Did I call the police and take my shameful vigil beside her crib to wait for them?

None of these. Coward that I was, I ran.

And yet the night does not end there. You could say it never has.

A flight of stairs led from Old Fulton Street to the Brooklyn Bridge walkway. At the midpoint of the bridge, I removed the knife and bloody shirt and dropped them into the water. The hour was approaching five A.M.; soon the city would arise. Already the traffic was thickening—early commuters, taxis, delivery trucks, even a few bicyclists, their faces masked against the cold, whizzing past me like wheeled demons. There is no being who feels more anonymous, more forgotten, more alone than a New York pedestrian, if he so chooses, but this is an illusion: our comings and goings are tracked to a fault. In Washington Square I bought a cheap baseball cap from a street vendor to hide my face and found a pay phone. Calling 911 was out of the question, as the call would be instantly traced. From information I got the number for the *New York Post,* dialed it, and asked for the city desk.

"Metro."

"I'd like to report a murder. A woman's been stabbed."

"Hang on a second. Who am I speaking to?"

I gave the address. "The police don't know yet. The door's unlocked. Just go look," I said and hung up.

I made two more calls, to the *Daily News* and the *Times,* from different pay phones, one on Bleecker Street, the other on Prince. By this time, the morning was in full swing. It seemed to me I should return to my apartment. It was the natural place for me to be and, more to the point, I had no place else to go.

Then I remembered my abandoned suitcase. How this might connect me to the girl's death I could not foresee, but it was, at the very least, a thread best cut quickly. I took the subway uptown to Grand Central. At once I became aware of the station's heavy police presence; I was now a murderer, sentenced to a preternatural awareness of my surroundings, a life of constant fear. At the kiosk, I was directed to the lost and found, located on the lower level. I showed my driver's license to the woman behind the counter and described the bag.

"I think I left it in the main concourse," I said, attempting to sound like one more flustered traveler. "We just had so much luggage, I think that's how I forgot it."

My story didn't interest her even vaguely. She disappeared into the racks of luggage and returned a minute later with my suitcase and a piece of paper.

"You'll need to fill this out and sign at the bottom."

Name, rank, serial number. It felt like a confession; my hands were shaking so badly I could barely hold the pen. How absurd I was being: one more filled-out form in a city that generated a felled forest of paper every day.

"I need to photocopy your license," the woman said.

"Is that really necessary? I'm in a bit of a hurry."

"Honey, I don't make the rules. You want your bag or don't you?"

I handed it over. She ran it through the machine, gave it back, and stapled the copy to the form, which she shoved into a drawer under the counter.

"I bet you get a lot of bags," I remarked, thinking I should say something.

The woman rolled her eyes. "Baby, you should see the stuff that comes in here."

I took a cab to my apartment. Along the way, I inventoried my situation. The girl's apartment, as far as I could tell, was clean; I'd washed every surface I'd touched. No one had seen me enter or leave, except the cabbie; that could be a problem. There was the bartender to consider, as well. *Excuse me. You're Professor Fanning, aren't you?* I couldn't recall if he'd been within earshot, though he'd certainly had a good look at both of us. Had I paid with cash or a credit card? Cash, I thought, but I couldn't be sure. The trail was there, but could anyone follow it?

Upstairs, I opened the suitcase on my bed. No surprise, the morphine was gone, but everything else was there. I emptied my pockets—wallet, keys, cell-phone. The battery had died in the night. I plugged it into the charger on the nightstand and lay down, though I knew I would not sleep. I didn't think I would ever sleep again.

My phone chirped as the battery awoke. Four new messages, all from the same number, with a 401 area code. Rhode Island? Who did I know in Rhode Island? Then, as I was holding it, the phone rang.

"Is this Timothy Fanning?"

I didn't recognize the voice. "Yes, this is Dr. Fanning."

"Oh, you're a doctor. That explains it. My name is Lois Swan. I'm a nurse in the ICU at Westerly Hospital. A patient was brought here yesterday afternoon, a woman named Elizabeth Lear. Do you know her?"

My heart lurched into my throat. "Where is she? What happened?"

"She was taken off an Amtrak train from Boston and brought here by ambulance. I've been trying to reach you. Are you her physician?"

The nature of the call was becoming clear to me. "That's right," I lied. "What's her condition?"

"I'm afraid that Mrs. Lear has passed away."

I didn't say anything. The room was dissolving. Not just the room, the world.

"Hello?"

I made an effort to swallow. "Yes, I'm here."

"She was unconscious when they brought her in. I was alone with her when she woke up. She gave me your name and number."

"Was there a message?"

"I'm sorry, no. She was very weak. I wasn't even sure I heard the number right. She died just a few minutes later. We tried to reach her husband, but apparently he's overseas. Is there anybody else we should notify?"

I hung up. I placed a pillow over my face. Then I began to scream.

22

The story of the girl's death was plastered on the front pages of the tabloids for several days, and in this manner I learned more about her. She was twenty-nine, from College Park, Maryland, the daughter of Iranian immigrants. Her father was an engineer, her mother a school librarian; she had three siblings. For six years she had worked at Beckworth and Grimes, ascending to the rank of associate editor; she and the baby's father, an actor, were recently divorced. Everything about her was ordinary and admirable. A hard worker. A devoted friend. A beloved daughter and doting mother. For a time, she had wanted to be a dancer. There were many photos of her. In one, she was just a child herself, wearing a leotard and performing a little-girl plié.

Two days later I received a call from Jonas, relaying the news of Liz's death. I did my best to act surprised and discovered that I actually was a little, as if, hearing his broken voice, I were experiencing the loss of her for the first time all over again. We talked awhile, sharing stories of the past. From time to time we laughed over something funny she had done or said; at others, the phone went silent for long intervals in which I heard him crying. I listened to the spaces in the conversation for any indication that he'd known, or suspected, about the two of us. But I detected nothing. It was just as Liz had said: his blindness was total. He couldn't even imagine such a thing.

I was still slightly amazed that nothing had happened to me: no knock on the door, no dark men in suits standing beyond the chain, displaying their badges. *Dr. Fanning, mind if we have a word with you?* None of the stories mentioned the bartender or the cabbie, which I took to be a good sign, though eventually, I believed, the law would come calling. My penance would be extracted; I would fall to my knees and confess. The universe could simply make no sense otherwise.

I took a shuttle to Boston for the funeral. The ceremony was held in Cambridge, within sight of Harvard Yard. The church was packed. Family, friends, colleagues, former students; in her too-short years, Liz had been much loved. I took a pew in back, wanting to be invisible. I knew many, recognized others, felt the weight of all. Among the mourners was a man whom, beneath his puffy alcoholic's face, I knew to be Alcott Spence. Our eyes met briefly as we followed Liz's casket outside, though I do not think he remembered who I was.

After the burial, the inner circle repaired to the Spee Club for a catered lunch. I had told Jonas that I needed to return early and couldn't make it, but he insisted so ardently that I had little choice. There were toasts, remembrances, a great deal of drinking. Every second was torture. As people were leaving, Jonas pulled me aside.

"Let's go out to the garden. There's something I need to talk to you about."

So here it was, I thought. The whole mess was about to come out. We exited through the library and sat on the steps that led down to the courtyard. The day was unusually warm, a mocking foretaste of spring—a spring I believed I would not see. Surely I would be living in a cell by then.

He reached into the inside pocket of his jacket and removed a flask. He took a long pull and passed it to me.

"Old times," he said.

I didn't know how to respond. The conversation was his to steer.

"You don't have to say it. I know I fucked up. I should have been there. That may be the worst thing."

"I'm sure she understood."

"How could she?" He drank again and wiped his mouth. "The truth is, I think she was leaving me. Probably I deserved it."

I felt my stomach drop. On the other hand, if he'd known it was me, he would have already said so. "Don't be ridiculous. She was probably just going to see her mother."

He gave a fatalistic shrug. "Yeah, well, last time I checked, you don't need a passport to go to Connecticut."

I had failed to consider this. There was nothing to say.

"That's not the reason I asked you out here, though," he went on. "I'm sure you've heard the stories about me."

"A little."

"Everybody thinks I'm a big joke. Well, they're wrong."

"Maybe this isn't the day for this, Jonas."

"Actually, it's the perfect day. I'm close, Tim. Very, very close. There's a site in Bolivia. A temple, at least a thousand years old. The legends say there's a grave there, the body of a man infected with the virus I've been searching for. It's nothing new—there are lots of stories like that. Too many for all this to be nothing, in my opinion, but that's another argument. The thing is, I've got hard evidence now. A friend at the CDC came to me a few months back. He'd heard about my work, and he'd happened across something he thought would interest me. Five years ago, a group of four American tourists showed up at a hospital in La Paz. All of them had what looked like hantavirus. They'd been on some kind of ecotour in the jungle. But here's the thing. They all had terminal cancer. The tour was one of those last-wish things. You know, do the stuff you always wanted to do before you check out."

I had no idea where he was headed. "And?"

"Here's where it gets interesting. All of them recovered, and not just from the hanta. From the cancer. Stage four ovarian, inoperable glioblastoma, leukemia with full lymphatic involvement—not a trace of it was left. And they weren't just cured. They were *better* than cured. It was as if the aging process had been reversed. The youngest one was fifty-six, the oldest seventy. They looked like twenty-year-olds."

"That's quite a story."

"Are you kidding? It's *the* story. If this pans out, it will be the most important medical discovery in history."

I was still skeptical. "So why haven't I heard about it? It isn't in any of the literature."

"Good question. My friend at the CDC suspects the military got involved. The whole thing went over to USAMRIID."

"Why would they want it?"

"Who knows? Maybe they just want the credit, though that's the optimistic view. One day you have Einstein, puzzling over the theory of relativity, the next you've got the Manhattan Project and a big hole in the ground. It's not like it hasn't happened before."

He had a point. "Have you examined them? The four patients."

Jonas took another pull of the whiskey. "Well, that's a bit of a wrinkle. They're all dead."

"But I thought you said—"

"Oh, it wasn't the cancer. They all seemed to kind of . . . well, speed up, like their bodies couldn't handle it. Somebody took a video. They were practically bouncing off the walls. The longest any of them lasted was eighty-six days."

"That's a mighty big wrinkle."

He gave me a hard look. "Think about it, Tim. Something's out there. I couldn't find it in time to save Liz, and that'll haunt me the rest of my days. But I can't stop now. Not just in spite of her; *because* of her. A hundred and fifty-five thousand human beings die every day. How long have we been sitting here? Ten minutes? That's over a thousand people just like Liz. People with lives, families who love them. I need you, Tim. And not just because you're my oldest friend, and the smartest guy I know. I'll be honest: I'm having a hard time with the money. Nobody wants to back this anymore. Maybe your credibility could, you know, grease the gears a bit."

My credibility. If he only knew how little that was worth. "I don't know, Jonas."

"If you can't do it for me, do it for Liz."

I'll admit, the scientist in me was intrigued. It was also true that I wanted nothing to do with this project, or with Jonas, ever again. In the slender ten minutes in which a thousand human beings had perished, I had come, very profoundly, to despise him. Perhaps I always had. I despised his obliviousness, his monstrous ego, his self-aggrandizing pomp. I despised his naked manipulation of my loyalties and his unwavering faith that the answer to everything lay within his grasp. I despised the fact that he didn't know one goddamn thing about anything at all, but most of all, I despised him for letting Liz die alone.

"Can I give it some thought?" An easy dodge; I had no such intentions.

He began to say something, then stopped himself. "Got it. You have your reputation to consider. Believe me, I know how it goes."

"It's not that. It's just a big commitment. I have a lot on my plate these days."

"I'm not going to let you off easy, you know."

"I was pretty sure you wouldn't."

We were silent for a time. Jonas was looking at the garden, though I knew he wasn't seeing it.

"It's funny—I always knew this day would come. Now I can't believe it.

It's like it's not even happening, you know? I feel like I'll go back to the house and there she'll be, grading papers at her desk or stirring something in the kitchen." He blew out a breath and looked at me. "I should have been a better friend to you, all these years. I shouldn't have let so much time pass."

"Forget it," I said. "It was my fault, too."

The conversation ended there. "Well," Jonas said, "thank you for being here, Tim. I know you'd come anyway, just for her. But it means a lot to me. Let me know what you decide."

I sat awhile after he'd gone. The building was quiet; the mourners had left, returning to their lives. How lucky they were, I thought.

I heard nothing more from Jonas. Winter yielded to spring, then summer, and I began to believe that the dots hadn't been connected after all and I would remain a free man. Bit by bit, the girl's death ceased to hang over my every thought and action. It was still there, of course; the memory touched down often and without warning, paralyzing me with guilt so deep I could hardly draw a breath. But the mind is nimble; it seeks to preserve itself. One particularly clement summer day, cool and dry with a sky so crisp it looked like a great blue dome snapped down over the city, I was walking to the subway from my office when I realized that for a full ten minutes I hadn't felt utterly ruined. Perhaps life could go on, after all.

I returned to teaching in the fall. A bevy of new graduate assistants awaited me; as if the administration took delight in torturing me, most were female. But to say that those days were over for me would be the understatement of the century. Mine was a monk's existence, as it would be henceforth. I did my work, I taught my classes, I sought the company of no one, man or woman. I heard, secondhand, that Jonas had found funding for his expedition after all and was gearing up for Bolivia. Good riddance, I thought.

On a day in late January, I was grading labs in my office when there was a knock on the door.

"Come."

Two people, a man and a woman: I instantly knew who, and what, they were. My face probably betrayed my guilt in a heartbeat.

"Got a minute, Professor Fanning?" the woman said. "I'm Detective Reynaldo, this is Detective Phelps. We'd like to ask you a few questions, if you don't mind."

"Of course." I feigned surprise. "Sit down, Detectives."

"We'll stand, if that's all right."

The conversation lasted barely fifteen minutes, but it was enough to let me know that the noose was tightening. A woman had come forward—the babysitter. She was an illegal, which explained the long delay. Though she had glimpsed me quickly, the description she provided matched the bartender's. He did not recall my name but had overheard the part of our conversation in which she confessed her crush on me, using the phrase "a lot of the girls did." This led them to Nicole's college transcript and eventually to me, who bore a remarkable resemblance to the sitter's description of the suspect. A *very* remarkable resemblance.

I made the customary denials. No, I had never been to the bar in question. No, I did not recall the girl from my classes; I had seen the story in the papers but had made no connection. No, I could not recall my whereabouts that night. When, exactly? Probably I was in bed.

"Interesting. In bed, you say?"

"Perhaps I was reading. I'm a bit of an insomniac. I really don't recall."

"That's strange. Because according to the TSA, you were scheduled to be on a flight to Athens. Any thoughts on that you'd care to share at this point, Dr. Fanning?"

The cold sweat of the criminal dampened my palms. Of course they would know this. How could I have been so dumb?

"Very well," I said, doing my best to seem annoyed. "I wish this hadn't had to come out, but since you insist on prying into my personal life, I was going away with a friend. A *married* friend."

A single eyebrow lasciviously lifted. "Care to tell us her name?"

My mind was racing. Could they connect us? I'd paid for the tickets in cash and bought them separately to cover our tracks. Our seats weren't even next to each other's; I'd planned to sort it out before we boarded.

"I'm sorry, I can't do that. It's not my place."

"A gentleman doesn't kiss and tell, huh?"

"Something like that."

Detective Reynaldo smiled imperiously, enjoying herself. "A gentleman who runs off with another man's wife. Doubt you'll win any prizes for that."

"I don't claim to, Detective."

"So why didn't you go?"

I gave my most innocent shrug. "She changed her mind. Her husband is a colleague of mine. It was a stupid idea to begin with. That's really all there is to it."

For ten full seconds neither of us spoke—a gap I was obviously meant to fill, incriminating myself.

"Well, that's all for now, Dr. Fanning. Thank you for taking time out of your busy day." She gave me her card. "You think of anything else, you call me, all right?"

"I'll do that, Detective."

"And I do mean anything."

I waited thirty minutes to make sure they were well clear of the building, then took the subway home. How long did I have? Days? Hours? How much paperwork did they need to get me into a lineup?

I could think of only one option. I called Jonas's office, then his cell, but got no answer. I would have to risk an email.

> *Jonas—I've given some thought to your proposal. Sorry it took*
> *me so long. Not sure how much I can offer at this late date, but*
> *I'd like to sign on. When do you leave?—TF*

I waited at my computer, hitting the Refresh button over and over. Thirty minutes later his reply came.

> *Delighted. We leave in three days. Have already cleared your*
> *visa with State. Don't ever say I'm not a man with connections.*
> *How many more do you need for your team? Knowing you, you'll*
> *bring a flotilla of attractive female grad assistants, which we*
> *could sure use to brighten up the place.*
>
> *Move your ass, buddy. We're going to change the world.—JL*

23

There is not much more to say. I went. I was infected. Of those infected, I alone survived. And thus was built a race to establish dominion over the earth.

There was a night when Jonas came to see me in my chamber. This was long after my transformation, by which time I had adjusted to my circumstances. I could not know what the hour was, such things having lost all meaning in my captive state. My plans were well under way. I and my co-conspirators had identified the avenue of our escape. The weak-minded men who watched over us: day by day we had infiltrated their thoughts, filling their minds with our black dreams, bringing them into the fold. Their flabby souls were collapsing; soon they would be ours.

His voice came over the speaker: "Tim, it's Jonas."

This was not his first visit. Many was the time I had seen his face behind the glass. Yet he had not addressed me directly since the day of my awakening.

The last years had wrought startling changes to his appearance. Long-haired, wild-bearded, crazed-eyed, he had become the very image of the mad scientist I had always thought him to be.

"I know you can't talk. Hell, I'm not even sure you can understand me."

I felt a confession coming. I was, I admit, only vaguely interested in what he had to say. His disturbed conscience—what did I care? His visit had also interrupted my feeding schedule. Though in life I had not much cared for the taste of wild game, I had come to enjoy raw rabbit very much.

"Something bad is happening. I'm really losing control of this thing."

Indeed, I thought.

"God, I miss her, Tim. I should have listened to her. I should have listened to *you*. If only you could talk to me."

You will hear from me soon enough, I thought.

"I've got one more chance, Jonas. I still believe this can work. Maybe if I pull it off, I can get the military to back away. I can still turn everything around."

Hope springs eternal, does it not?

"The thing is, it has to be a child." He was silent for a moment. "I can't believe I'm saying this. They just brought her in. I don't even want to know what they did to get her here. Jesus, Tim, she's just a little kid."

A child, I thought. Here was an intriguing wrinkle; no wonder Jonas despised himself. I delighted in his misery. I had learned how low a man could sink; why shouldn't he?

"They're calling her Amy NLN. No last name. They got her from some orphanage. God almighty, she doesn't even have a proper name. She's just some girl from nowhere."

I felt my heart go out to this unlucky child, plucked from her life to become the last pitiable hope of a crazy man. Yet even as I considered this, a new thought was bearing fruit inside me. A little girl, bathed in the innocence of youth: of course. The symmetry was undeniable; it was a message, meant for me. To face her, that would be the test. I heard the rumble of distant armies joining. This girl from nowhere. This Amy NLN. Who was alpha, who omega? Who the beginning and who the end?

"Did you love her, Tim? You can tell me."

Yes, I thought. Yes and yes and yes. She was the only thing that ever mattered. I loved her more than any man could. I loved her enough to watch her die.

"The police came to me, you see. They knew the two of you were supposed to be on the same plane. You know what's funny? I was actually happy for her. She deserved someone who could love her the way she needed. The way I never could. I guess what I'm saying is, I'm glad it was you."

Was it possible? Had my eyes—the eyes of a beast, a demon—begun to shed tears?

"Well." Jonas cleared his throat. "I guess that's what I came to say. I'm sorry about all this, Tim. I hope you know that. You were the best friend I ever had."

Now it is dark. Stars soar above the vacant city, heaven's diadem. A century since the last person walked here, and still one cannot travel its streets, as I do, without seeing one's face reflected a thousand-fold. Shop windows. Bodegas and brownstones. The mirrored flanks of skyscrapers, great vertical tombs of glass. I look, and what do I see? Man? Monster? Devil? A freak of cold nature or heaven's cruel utensil? The first is intolerable to think, the second no less so. Who is the monster now?

I walk. Listen closely, and one still hears the footfalls of a throng, engraved in stone. At the center has grown a forest. A forest in New York! A great green eruption, alive with animal sounds and smells. There are rats everywhere, of course. They grow to fantastic dimensions. Once I saw one that I thought might be a dog, or a wild pig, or something brand-new to the world. The pigeons wheel, the rain falls, the seasons turn without us; in winter, all is dressed with snow.

City of memories, city of mirrors. Am I alone? Yes and no. I am a man of many descendants. They lie hidden away. Some are here, those who once called this island home; they slumber beneath the streets of the forgotten metropolis. Others lie elsewhere, my ambassadors, awaiting final use. In slumber they become themselves again; in dreams, they relive their human lives. Which world is the real one? Only when they're aroused does the hunger obliterate them, taking them over, their souls spilling into mine, and so I leave them as they are. It is the only mercy I can offer.

Oh, my brothers, Twelve in sum, you were sorely used by this world! I spoke to you like the god you thought I was, though in the end I could not save you. I would not say I failed to see this coming. From the start, your fates were written; you could not help being what you were, which was the truth of us. Consider the species known as man. We lie, we cheat, we want what others have and take it; we make war upon each other and the earth; we harvest lives in multitudes. We have mortgaged the planet and spent the cash on trifles. We may have loved, but never well enough. We never truly knew ourselves. We forgot the world; now it has forgotten us. How many years will pass before jealous nature reclaims this place? Before it is as if we never existed at all? Buildings will crumble. Skyscrapers will come crashing to the ground. Trees will sprout and spread their canopies. The oceans will rise, rinsing the rest away. It is said that one day all will be water again; a vast ocean will blanket the world. *In the beginning, God created the heaven and the earth. And the earth was without form, and void; and darkness was upon the face of the deep. And the Spirit of God moved upon the face of the waters.* How will God, if there is a God, remember us? Will he even know our names? All stories end when they have returned to their beginnings. What can we do but remember in his stead?

I go abroad, into the streets of the empty city, always returning. I take my place upon the steps, beneath the inverted heavens. I watch the clock; its mournful faces stay the same. Time frozen at the moment of man's departure, the last train exiting the station.

III

THE SON

TEXAS REPUBLIC

POP. 204,876

MARCH 122 A.V.

TWENTY-ONE YEARS AFTER

THE DISCOVERY OF THE *BERGENSFJORD*

All the world's a stage,
And all the men and women merely players:
They have their exits and their entrances,
And one man in his time plays many parts.

—SHAKESPEARE, *AS YOU LIKE IT*

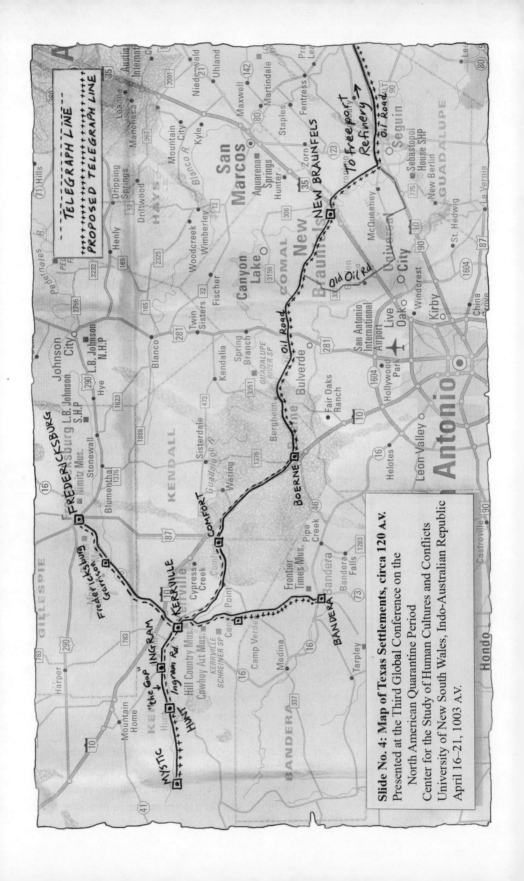

Slide No. 4: **Map of Texas Settlements, circa 120 A.V.**
Presented at the Third Global Conference on the
North American Quarantine Period
Center for the Study of Human Cultures and Conflicts
University of New South Wales, Indo-Australian Republic
April 16–21, 1003 A.V.

24

Peter Jaxon, age fifty-one, president of the Texas Republic, stood at the Kerrville gate in the pale dawn light, waiting to say goodbye to his son.

Sara and Hollis had just arrived; Kate was working at the hospital but had promised that her husband, Bill, would bring the girls. Caleb was loading the last of their gear into the wagon while Pim, in a loose cotton dress, stood nearby, holding baby Theo. Two strong horses, fit for plowing, idled in their harnesses.

"I guess that's it," Caleb said, as he finished lashing the final crate. He was wearing a long-sleeved work shirt and overalls; he'd let his hair grow long. He checked the load on his rifle, a lever-action .30-06, and put it up on the seat. "We really should get moving if we're going to make Hunt by dark."

They were headed to one of the outer settlements, a two-day ride on the buckboard. The land had only just been incorporated, though people had been homesteading there for years. Caleb had spent most of two years preparing the place—framing the house, digging the well, laying out fences—before returning for Pim and the baby. Good soil, the clear water of the river, woods heavy with game: there were worse places, Peter thought, to start a life.

"You can't go yet," Sara said. "The girls will be heartbroken if you leave without seeing them."

Sara had, simultaneously, signed these words for Pim, who now turned to her husband with a stern look.

You know how Bill is, Caleb signed. *We could be here all day.*
No. We wait.

There was no point in arguing when Pim had made up her mind. Caleb always said it was the woman's stubbornness that had kept them together while he was stationed with the Army on the Oil Road, and Peter didn't doubt it. The two of them had married the day after Caleb had finally capitulated and resigned his commission—not, as he often pointed out, that there was much of an Army remaining to resign from. Like nearly everything else in Kerrville, the Army had scattered to the winds; barely anyone remembered the Expeditionary, disbanded twenty years ago, when the Texas Code had been suspended. It had been one of the great disappointments of Caleb's life that there was nobody left to fight anymore. He'd spent his years in the service as a glorified ditch digger, assigned to the construction of the telegraph line between Kerrville and Boerne. It was a different world than the one Peter had known. The city walls went unmanned; the perimeter lights had gone out one by one and never been repaired; the gate hadn't been shut in a decade. A whole generation had grown to adulthood thinking the virals were little more than exaggerated boogeymen in scary stories told by their elders, who, in the fashion of all old people since the dawn of time, believed theirs had been the vastly harder and more consequential life.

But it was like Kate's husband, Bill, to be late. The man had his positive qualities—he was far more easy-going than Kate, counterbalancing her often humorless maturity—and there was no question that he adored their daughters. But he was scattered and disorganized, liked the lick and cards, and lacked anything approximating a work ethic. Peter had tried to bring him into the administration as a favor to Sara and Hollis, offering him a low-level job with the Bureau of Taxation that required little more than the ability to use a stamp. But as with Bill's brief forays into carpentry, farriering, and driving a transport, it wasn't long before he drifted away. Mostly he seemed content to look after his daughters, make Kate the occasional meal, and sneak out to the tables at night—both winning and losing but, according to Kate, always winning just a little more.

Baby Theo had begun to fuss. Caleb used the delay to pick the horses' hooves while Sara took Theo from Pim to change his diaper. Just when it had begun to seem that Bill wouldn't show, Kate appeared with the girls, Bill bringing up the rear with a sheepish look on his face.

"How did you get away?" Sara asked her daughter.

"Don't worry, Madam Director—Jenny's got it covered. Plus, you love me too much to fire me."

"You know, I really hate it when you call me that."

Elle and her younger sister, Merry, who everybody called Bug, dashed to Pim, who knelt and hugged them together. The girls' signing abilities were limited to simple phrases, and all exchanged *I love you,* circling their hearts with a flat palm.

Visit me, Pim signed, then glanced up at Kate, who explained what she was asking.

"Can we?" Bug asked eagerly. "When?"

"We'll see," Kate said. "Maybe after the baby is born."

This was a sore subject; Sara had wanted Pim to delay their departure until after the birth of their second child. But that wouldn't be until nearly the end of the summer, far too late to plant. Nor did Pim, in her obstinate way, plan to return alone for the birth. *I've done it before,* she said. *How hard can it be?*

"Please, Mom?" Elle begged.

"I said, we'll see."

Hugs all around. Peter glanced at Sara; she was feeling it, too. Their children were leaving for good. It was what you were supposed to want, the thing you worked for, yet facing it was a different matter.

Caleb shook Peter's hand, then pulled him into a masculine embrace. "So I guess this is it. Mind if I say some stupid things? Like, I love you. You're still a terrible chess player, though."

"I promise to practice. Who knows? Maybe you'll find me out there before too long."

Caleb grinned. "See? That's what I've been telling you. No more politics. It's time to find a nice girl and settle down."

If you only knew, Peter thought. *Every night I close my eyes and do just that.*

He lowered his voice slightly. "Did you do like I asked?"

Caleb sighed indulgently.

"Humor your old man."

"Yeah, yeah, I dug it."

"And you used the steel framing I sent out? It's important."

"I did it just like you said, I promise. At least I've got someplace to sleep when Pim kicks me out."

Peter looked up at his daughter-in-law, who had climbed onto the bench. Baby Theo, worn out by all the attention, had passed out in her arms.

Look after him for me, Peter signed.

I will.

The babies, too.

She smiled at him. *The babies, too.*

Caleb lifted himself onto the buckboard.

"Be safe," Peter said. "Good luck."

The indelible moment of departure: everyone stepped back as the wagon moved through the gate. Bill and the girls were the first to leave, followed by Kate and Hollis. Peter had a full schedule ahead of him, but he couldn't quite bring himself to start his day.

Nor, apparently, could Sara. They stood together without speaking, watching the wagon bearing their children away.

"Why do I feel sometimes like they're parenting us?" Sara said.

"They will be, soon enough."

Sara snorted. "Now *there's* something to look forward to."

The wagon was still in sight. It was crossing the old fence line to the Orange Zone. Beyond it, only a fraction of the fields had been plowed for planting; there simply wasn't enough manpower. Nor were there that many mouths remaining to feed; the population of Kerrville itself had shrunk to just about five thousand. Make that 4,997, thought Peter.

"Bill's a mess," Peter said.

Sara sighed. "And yet Kate loves him. What's a mother to do?"

"I could try again with a job."

"I'm afraid he's a lost cause." She glanced at him. "Speaking of which, what's this about you not running for reelection?"

"Where did you hear that?"

She shrugged coyly. "Oh, just around the halls."

"Meaning Chase."

"Who else? The man is chomping at the bit. So, is it true?"

"I haven't decided. Maybe ten years is enough, though."

"People will miss you."

"I doubt they'll even notice."

Peter thought she might ask him about Michael. What had he heard? Was her brother okay at least? They avoided the details, a painful reality. Michael on the trade, rumors of some crazy project, Greer in cahoots with Dunk, an armed compound on the ship channel with trucks full of lick and God knew what else leaving every day.

But she didn't. Instead Sara asked, "What does Vicky think?"

The question pierced him with guilt. He'd been meaning to visit the woman for weeks, months even.

"I need to go see her," he said. "How is she doing?"

The two of them were still standing shoulder to shoulder as their eyes traced the course of the wagon. It was little more than a speck now. It crested a small rise, began to sink, then was gone. Sara turned toward him.

"I wouldn't wait," she said.

His day dissolved into the customary duties. A meeting with the collector of taxes to decide what to do about homesteaders who refused to pay; a new judicial appointment to make; an agenda to set for the upcoming meeting of the territorial legislature; various papers to sign, which Chase placed in front of him with only cursory description. At three o'clock, Apgar appeared in Peter's door. Did the president have a minute? Everybody else on the staff simply called him by his first name, as he preferred, but Gunnar, a stickler for protocol, refused. Always he was "Mr. President."

The subject was guns—specifically, a lack of them. The Army had always run on a combination of reconditioned civilian and military weaponry. A lot had come from Fort Hood; plus, the old Texas had been a well-armed place. Virtually every house, it seemed, had a gun cabinet in it, and there were weapon-manufacturing facilities throughout the state, offering a bountiful supply of parts for repair and reloading. But a lot of time had passed, and certain guns lasted longer than others. Metal-framed pistols, like the old Browning 1911, SIG Sauer semiautos, and army-issue Beretta M9s, were close to indestructible with adequate maintenance. So were most revolvers, shotguns, and bolt-action rifles. But polymer-framed pistols, like Glocks, as well as M4 and AR-15 rifles, the bread and butter of the military, did not enjoy the same indefinite shelf life. As their plastic casings cracked with fatigue, more and more were retired; others had leaked via the trade into civilian hands; some had simply vanished.

But that was only part of the problem. The more pressing issue was a dwindling supply of ammunition. Decades had passed since a prewar cartridge had been fired; except for the stockpiles in Tifty's bunker, which were vacuum-sealed, the primer and cordite didn't last more than twenty years. All of the Army's rounds had been either reloaded from spent brass or manufactured with empty casings taken from two munitions plants, one near Waco and a second in Victoria. Casting lead for bullets was easy; far trickier was engineering a propellant. Weapons-grade cordite required a complicated cocktail of highly volatile chemicals, including large quantities of nitroglycerine. It could be done, but it wasn't easy, and it necessitated both manpower and expertise, both of which were in very short supply. The Army was down to just a couple thousand soldiers—fifteen hundred spread throughout the townships, and a garrison of five hundred in Kerrville. They had no chemists at all.

"I think we both know what we're talking about here," Peter said.

Apgar, seated across the paper-stacked expanse of Peter's desk, was looking at his nails. "I didn't say I liked it. But the trade has the manufacturing capacity, and it's not like we haven't dealt with them before."

"Dunk's not Tifty."

"What about Michael?"

Peter frowned. "Sore subject."

"The guy was an OFC. He knows how to cook oil—he can do this."

"What about this boat of his?" Peter asked.

"He's *your* friend. You tell me what it's all about."

Peter took a long breath. "I wish I could. I haven't seen the guy in over twenty years. On top of which, we tell the trade we're out of ammo, we've tipped our hand. Dunk will be sitting in this chair in a weekend."

"So threaten him. He comes through for us or that's it, the deal's off, we storm the isthmus and put him out of business."

"Across that causeway? It'd be a bloodbath. He'll smell a bluff before I stop talking."

Peter leaned back in his chair. He imagined himself laying out Apgar's terms to Dunk. What could the man do but laugh in his face?

"This is all stick. There's no way it's going to work. What can we offer him?"

Gunnar scowled. "What, besides money, guns, and whores? Last time I checked, Dunk had all of those in plentiful supply. Plus, the guy's practically a folk hero. You know what happened last Sunday? Out of the blue, a five-ton full of women shows up at the encampment in Bandera where they're housing the road crews. The driver has a note. 'Compliments of your good friend Dunk Withers.' On a fucking *Sunday.*"

"Did they send them away?"

Gunnar snorted through his nose. "No, they took them to church. What do you think?"

"Well, there has to be something."

"You could ask him yourself."

A joke, but not entirely. There was also Michael to consider. Despite everything, Peter liked to think that the man would at least agree to talk to him.

"Maybe I'll do that."

As Gunnar rose, Chase appeared in the doorway.

"What is it, Ford?" Peter asked.

"We've got another sinkhole. A big one. Two houses this time."

This had been happening all spring. A rumbling in the earth; then, within moments, the ground would collapse. The largest hole had been over fifty feet wide. *This place really is falling apart,* Peter thought.

"Anybody hurt?" he asked.

"Not this time. Both houses were empty."

"Well, that's lucky." Ford was still looking at him expectantly. "Is there something else?"

"I'm thinking we should make a statement. People are going to want to know what you're doing about it."

"Such as what? Telling the ground to behave itself?" When Ford said nothing, Peter sighed. "Fine, write something up, and I'll sign it. Engineering on the case, situation in hand, et cetera." He raised an eyebrow at Ford. "Okay?"

Apgar looked like he was about to laugh. *Jesus,* Peter thought, *it never ends.* He got to his feet.

"Come on, Gunnar. Let's get some air."

He had become president not because he desired the job particularly but as a favor to Vicky. Right after her election to a third term, she had developed a tremor in her right hand. This was followed by a series of accidents, including a fall on the capitol steps that had broken her ankle. Her handwriting, always precise, decayed to a scrawl; her speech adopted a weirdly monotonic quality, lacking all inflection; the tremors spread to her other hand, and she began to make involuntary rocking motions with her neck. Peter and Chase had managed to hide the situation by keeping her public schedule to a minimum, but halfway into her second year, it became clear that she could no longer continue. The Texas Constitution, which had superseded the Code of Modified Martial Law, allowed her to name a president pro tem.

At the time, Peter was serving as secretary of territorial affairs, a position he had taken on midway through her second term. It was one of the most visible jobs in the cabinet, and Vicky made no secret of the fact that she was grooming him for something more. Still, he had assumed that Chase would be the one to step in; the man had been with her for years. When Vicky called Peter to her office, he wholly expected a meeting to discuss the transition to Chase's administration; what he found was a judge with a Bible. Two minutes later, he was president of the Texas Republic.

This was, he came to understand, what the woman had intended from the start: to create her successor from the ground up. Peter had stood for election two years later, won easily, and ran unopposed for his second term. Some of this was his personal popularity as a chief executive; as Vicky had predicted, his stock was very high. But it was also true that he had assumed the office at a time when it was easy to make people happy.

Kerrville itself was on its way to becoming irrelevant. How long before it was just one more provincial town? The farther out people settled, the less the idea of centralized authority held sway. The legislature had relocated to Boerne and almost never met. Financial capital had followed human capital to the townships; people were opening businesses, trading commodities at market-established prices, negotiating life on their own terms. In Fredericksburg, a group of private investors had pooled their money to open a bank, the first of its kind. There were still problems, and only the federal administration possessed the resources for major infrastructure projects: roads, dams, telegraph lines. But even this wouldn't last indefinitely. When Peter was being honest with himself, he understood that he was not so much running the place as guiding it into port. Let Chase have his chance, he thought. Two decades in public life, with its endless closed-door bickering, was plenty for any man. Peter had never farmed; he'd never so much as planted a tomato. But he could learn, and best of all, a plow had no opinions.

Vicky had retired to a small, wood-frame house on the east side of town. A lot of the neighborhood was empty, folks having cleared out long ago. It was getting dark when he stepped onto the porch. A single light was burning in the front parlor. He heard footsteps; then the door opened to reveal Meredith, Vicky's partner, wiping her hands on a cloth.

"Peter." About sixty, she was a petite woman with sharp blue eyes. She and Vicky had been together for years. "I didn't know you were coming."

"I'm sorry, I should have sent word."

"No, come in, of course." She stepped back. "She's awake—I was just about to feed her some supper. I know she'll be happy to see you."

Vicky's bed was in the parlor. As Peter entered, she glanced in his direction, her head jerking side to side against the elevated pillows.

"Ssss . . . bout tahm . . . Misss . . . ter . . . P . . . p . . . reeee . . . sa . . . dent."

It was as if she were swallowing the words, then spitting them out again. He drew a chair to the side of her bed. "How are you feeling?"

"Toooo . . . day . . . n . . . not ssso . . . b . . . b . . . a-duh."

"I'm sorry I've been away."

Her hands were moving about restlessly on the blanket. She gave a crooked smile. "Thasss . . . oh . . . k . . . *kay.* Aaas you . . . caaan see . . . I . . . fff . . . been . . . bizzz . . . ee."

Meredith appeared in the door with a tray, which she placed on the bedside table. On the tray were a bowl of clear broth and a glass of water with a straw. She cupped the back of Vicky's head to lift it forward from the pillow and tied a cotton bib around her neck. Night had fallen, making mirrors of the windows.

"Do you want me to do it?" Peter asked Meredith.

"Vicky, do you want Peter to help you with dinner?"

"W . . . w . . . why . . . n . . . n . . . not."

"Small sips," Meredith told him, and patted him on the arm. She gave him the faintest of smiles; her face was heavy with fatigue. The woman probably hadn't slept a solid night in months and was simply grateful for the help. "If you need me, I'll be in the kitchen."

Peter began with the water, holding the straw to Vicky's lips, which were flaked with dryness, then moved on to the broth. He could see the tremendous effort it required for her to swallow even the tiniest amount. Most of it dribbled from the corners of her mouth; he used the bib to wipe her chin.

"Sss . . . sss . . . fun . . . neee."

"What's that?"

"You . . . ffff . . . fff . . . eed . . . ing . . . me. Like . . . a . . . bay . . . beeee."

He gave her more of the broth. "The least I could do. You spoon-fed me more than once."

Her neck made a sinewy pumping motion as she tried to swallow. It exhausted him, just watching it.

"How . . . ssss . . . the . . . cam . . . p . . . p . . . aign?"

"Not really gotten started yet. Been a bit tied up."

"Yyyyy . . . you're . . . f . . . full of . . . sh . . . sh . . . shit."

She had him dead to rights, but of course she always did. He fed her another spoonful, without much luck. "Caleb and Pim left for the townships today."

"You're . . . j . . . j . . . ust . . . blue. It . . . will . . . lll . . . passss."

"What? You don't think I can farm?"

"I . . . I kn . . . know . . . you . . . P . . . eter. You'lllll . . . go . . . c . . . c . . . craze . . . ee."

She said nothing else. Peter put the bowl aside; she'd consumed only a fraction. When he looked up again, Vicky's eyes were closed. He doused the lamp and watched her. Only in sleep did the restless turmoil of her body cease. A few minutes passed; he heard a sound behind him and saw Meredith standing in the kitchen doorway.

"It happens like that," the woman said quietly. "One minute she's there, the next . . ." She left the thought unfinished.

"Is there anything I can do?"

Meredith placed one hand on his arm and met his eye. "She was so proud of you, Peter. It made her so happy, watching all you've done."

"Will you call me if you need me? Anything at all."

"I think this was a perfect visit, don't you? Let's let it be the last one."

He returned to Vicky's bedside and lifted one of her hands from the blanket. The woman didn't stir. He held it for a minute, thinking about her, then leaned down and kissed her on the cheek, something he had never done before.

"Thank you," he whispered.

He followed Meredith to the porch. "She loved you, you know," the woman said. "It wasn't the kind of thing she said very often, not even to me. That's just how she was. But she did."

"I loved her, too."

"She knows you did." They embraced. "Goodbye, Peter."

The street was silent, no lights burning. He touched a finger to his eye; it came away wet. Well, he was the president, he could cry if he wanted to. His son was gone; others would follow. He had entered the era of his life when things would drop away. Peter tipped his face to the sky. It was true, what they said about the stars. The more you looked, the more you saw. They were a comfort, their watchful presence a force of reassurance; yet this had not always been so. He stood and looked at them, remembering a time when the sight of so many stars had meant something else entirely.

25

They spent the night in Hunt, sleeping on the ground by the wagon, and arrived in Mystic Township on the second afternoon. The town was a threadbare outpost: a small main street with just a few houses, a general store, and a government building that acted as everything from the post office to the jail. They passed through and followed the river road west through a tunnel of thickening foliage. Pim had never been to the townships before; everything she saw seemed to fascinate her. *Look at the trees,* she signed to the baby. *Look at the river. Look at the world.*

The day had begun to fade when they reached the homestead. The house stood on a rise looking down toward the Guadalupe, with a paddock for the horses, fields of black soil between, and a privy in the rear. Caleb stepped down from the buckboard and reached up for Theo, who was sleeping in a basket.

"What do you think?"

Since Theo's birth, Caleb had made it his habit to speak and sign simultaneously whenever the boy was present. With nobody else around, he would grow up thinking that talking and signing were really no different from each other.

You did all this?

"Well, I had help."

Show me the rest.

He led her inside. There were two rooms on the main floor, with real glass windows and a kitchen with a stove and a pump, and a flight of stairs that led to a loft where the three of them would sleep. The floor, of sawn oak planks, felt solid underfoot.

"It'll be too hot to sleep inside in the summer, but I can build a sleeping porch out back."

Pim was smiling; she looked as if she couldn't believe her eyes. *When will you have time for that?*

"I'll do it, don't worry."

They unloaded a night's worth of gear. In a few days, Caleb would have to return to town, an eight-mile ride, to begin the process of securing stock: a milk cow, a goat or two, chickens. His seeds were ready to plant; the soil had been turned. They would be growing corn and beans in alternating rows, with a kitchen garden out back. The first year would be a race against time. After that, he hoped, things would settle into a more predictable rhythm, though life would never be easy, by any means.

They ate a simple dinner and lay down on the mattress he had moved inside from the wagon to the floor of the main room. He'd wondered if Pim would be afraid or at least anxious, being out here, just the three of them. She'd never spent a night beyond the city walls. But the opposite seemed true; she appeared completely at ease, eager to see how their situation unfolded. Of course, there was a reason. The things that had happened to her when she was a young girl had become for her a source of strength.

Pim had crept up on his life slowly. At the beginning, when Sara had brought her home from the orphanage, she had hardly seemed like a person to him. Her blunt gestures and guttural groans unnerved him. Extending even the simplest kindness was met with incomprehension, even anger. The situation had started to change when Sara taught Pim sign language. They moved through this improvisationally, beginning by spelling out every word, then advancing to whole phrases and ideas that could be captured with a single swoop of the hand. A book from the library had been involved, but later, when Kate gave it to Caleb to study, he realized that many of the gestures Pim used were made up: a bubble of private language that only she and her mother—and, to a degree, Kate and her father—shared. Caleb was, by this point, fourteen or fifteen. He was a clever boy, unused to problems he could not solve. Also, Pim had begun to seem interesting to him. What sort of person was she? The fact that he could not communicate with her as he could with everybody else was both frustrating and attractive. He made a point of carefully observing Pim's interactions with members of her family to encode these gestures into memory. Alone in his room, he practiced in front of a mirror for hours, signing both sides of dialogues on arbitrary topics. *How are you today? I am very well, thank you. What do you think of the weather? I enjoy the rain but am looking forward to warmer days.*

It became important that he delay the unveiling of his new abilities until he had acquired the confidence to engage her on a range of subjects. The opportunity presented itself on an afternoon outing their families had taken together to the spillway. While everyone else was enjoying their picnic by the water, he had climbed to the top of the dam. There he saw Pim, sitting on the concrete, writing in her journal. She was always writing; Caleb had wondered about this. She glanced up as he made his approach, her dark eyes narrowing on him in their intense way, then looked away dismissively. Her brown hair, long and glossy and tucked behind her ears, flared with captured sunshine. He stood for a moment, observing her. She was three years older than he was, basically an adult in his eyes. She had also become very pretty, though in a no-nonsense way that came across as condescending, even a little icy.

His presence was obviously unwelcome, but it was too late to back out. Caleb walked up to her. She regarded him with her head slightly cocked to the side, wearing an expression of bored mirth.

Hello, he signed.

She closed her book around her pencil. *You want to kiss me, don't you?*

The question was so unexpectedly direct that he actually startled. Did he? Was that what this was all about? Now she really *was* laughing at him— laughing with her eyes.

I know you know what I'm saying, she signed.

He found the answer with his hands: *I learned.*

For me or for yourself?

He felt caught. *Both.*

Have you kissed anyone before?

He hadn't. It was something he had been meaning to get around to. He knew he was blushing.

A few times.

No, you haven't. Hands don't lie.

He recognized the truth of this. All his study and practice, yet he'd failed to notice the obvious fact, which Pim had laid bare to him in mere seconds: signing was a language of complete forthrightness. Within its compact rhetoric, little space remained for evasion, for the self-protecting half-truths that were most of what people said to one another.

Do you want to?

She stood and faced him. *Okay.*

So they did. He closed his eyes, thinking this was something he should do, tilted his head slightly, and leaned forward. Their noses bumped, then passed each other, their lips meeting in a soft collision. It was over before he knew it.

Did you like it?

He barely believed this was actually happening. He spelled out his answer: *Lots.*

Open your mouth this time.

That was even better. A soft pressure entered his mouth that he realized was her tongue. He followed her lead; now they were kissing for real. He had always imagined the act to be a simple grazing of surfaces, lips upon lips, but kissing was, he now understood, far more complex. It was more a mingling than a touching. They did this for a while, exploring one another's mouths, then she backed away in a manner that indicated that the kissing was over. Caleb wished it weren't; he could have done it for a long while more. Then he understood the nature of the interruption. Sara was calling to them from the bottom of the dam.

Pim smiled at him. *You're a good kisser.*

And that was all, at least for a time. In due course, they had kissed again, and done different things as well, but it hadn't amounted to much, and other girls had come along. Yet always those slender minutes on the dam remained in his mind as a singular point in his life. When he joined the Army, at eighteen, his CO said he should find someone back home to write to. He chose Pim. His letters were all cheerful nonsense, complaints about the food and lighthearted stories of his friends, but hers were unlike anything he'd ever read, richly observant and full of life. At times they read like poetry. A single phrase, even describing something trivial—how the sun looked on leaves, a passing remark by an acquaintance, the smell of cooking food—would catch his mind and linger for days. Unlike sign language, with its unequivocal compactness, Pim's words on the page seemed to overflow with feeling—a richer kind of truth, closer to the heart of her. He wrote to Pim as often as he could, hungering for more of her. It was her voice he was hearing—hearing at last— and it wasn't long before he began to fall in love with her. When he told her, not in a letter but in person when he returned to Kerrville on a three-day pass, she laughed with her eyes, then signed, *When did you finally figure it out?*

To these memories, Caleb drifted into sleep. Sometime later he awoke to find her gone. He didn't worry; Pim was something of a night owl. Theo was still asleep. Caleb slid into his trousers, lit the lantern, got his rifle from its place by the door, and stepped outside. Pim was sitting with her back against the stump he used for splitting.

Everything okay?

Douse the light, she signed. *Come sit.*

She was wearing only her nightgown, though it was actually quite chilly; her feet were bare. He took his place beside her and extinguished the lantern. In the dark, they had a system. She took his hand and in his palm signed in miniature: *Look.*

At what?

Everything.

He understood what she was saying, between the lines. This is ours.

I like it here.

I'm glad.

Caleb detected movement in the brush. The sound came again, a grassy rustling to their left. Not a raccoon or possum—something larger.

Pim sensed his sudden alertness. *What?*

Wait.

He relit the lantern, casting a pool of light on the ground. The rustling was coming from several places now, though generally in the same direction. He positioned the rifle under his arm and clenched it to his side with his elbow. Holding the lantern in one hand, the rifle in the other, he crept forward, toward the heart of the sounds.

The light caught something: a flash of eyes.

It was a young deer. It froze in the light, staring at him. He saw the others, six in all. For a moment nothing moved, man and deer regarding one another with mutual astonishment. Then, as if guided by a common mind, the herd turned as one and burst away.

What could he do? What else could Caleb Jaxon do but laugh?

26

"Okay, Rand, try it now."

Michael was lying on his back, wedged into the slender gap between the floor and the base of the compressor. He heard the valve opening; gas began to move through the line.

"What's it say?"

"Looks like it's holding."

Don't you dare leak, Michael thought. *I've given you half my morning.*

"Nope. Pressure's dropping."

"God*damn*it." He'd checked every seal he could think of. Where the hell was the gas coming from? "The hell with it. Shut it off."

Michael wriggled free. They were on the lower engineering level. From the catwalk above came the sounds of metal striking metal, the crackling hiss of arc welders, men calling to one another, all of it amplified by the acoustics of the engine compartment. Michael hadn't seen sunshine for forty-eight hours.

"Any ideas?" he asked Rand.

The man was standing with his hands in the pockets of his trousers. There was something equine about him. He had small eyes, delicate-seeming in his strong face, and black wavy hair that, despite his age—somewhere north of forty-five—failed to show more than scattered threads of gray. Calm, reliable Rand. He had never spoken of a wife or girlfriend; he never visited Dunk's whores. Michael had never pressed, the matter being one of supreme unimportance.

"It could be someplace in the charger," Rand suggested. "Tight fit, though."

Michael looked up at the catwalk and yelled, to whomever might hear him, "Where's Patch?"

Patch's real name was Byron Szumanski. The nickname came from the anomalous square of white in his otherwise coal-black stubble. Like many of Michael's men, he had been raised in the orphanage; he'd done a stint in the military, learning a thing or two about engines along the way, then worked for the civilian authority as a mechanic. He had no relatives, had never married and professed no desire to do so, possessed no bad habits Michael knew of, didn't mind the isolation, wasn't a talker, took orders without complaint, and liked to work—perfect, in other words, for Michael's purposes. A wiry five foot three, he spent whole days in pockets of the ship so cramped that another man wouldn't have been able to draw a breath. Michael paid him accordingly, though nobody could complain about the wages. Every cent Michael made from the stills went straight to the *Bergensfjord.*

A face appeared above: Weir's. He drew his welder's mask up to his forehead. "I think he's on the bridge."

"Send somebody to get him."

As Michael bent for his tool bag, Rand rapped him on the arm. "We've got company."

Michael looked up; Dunk was coming down the stairs. Michael needed the man, just as Dunk needed him, but their relationship was not an easy one. Needless to say, Dunk knew nothing of Michael's true purpose; he regarded the *Bergensfjord* as an eccentric distraction, an elaborate pastime on which Michael wasted his time—time better spent putting more money in Dunk's pockets. That the man had never bothered to wonder just why Michael needed to refloat a six-hundred-foot freighter was just more evidence of his limited intelligence.

"Great," Michael said.

"You want me to get some guys together? He looks pissed."

"How can you tell?"

Rand moved away. At the base of the stairs Dunk halted, propped his hands on his hips, and surveyed the room with an expression of weary irritation. The tattoos on his face ended abruptly at his former hairline. A lifetime of hard living had done him few favors in the aging department, but he was still built like a tank. For entertainment, he liked to lift a truck by its bumper.

"What can I do for you, Dunk?"

He had a way of smiling that made Michael think of a cork in a bottle. "I really should get down here more often. I don't know what half this stuff is. Take those things over there." He wagged a meaty finger, thick as a sausage.

"Water jacket pumps."

"What do they do?"

The day was getting away without much to show for it; now he had to deal with this. "It's kind of technical. Not really your thing."

"Why am I here, Michael?"

Guessing games, as if they were five years old. "A sudden interest in marine repair?"

Dunk's eyes hardened on Michael's face. "I'm here, Michael, because you're not meeting your obligation to me. Mystic's open for settlement. That means demand. I need the new boiler up and running. Not later. Today."

Michael aimed his voice at the catwalk. "Has anybody found Patch yet?"

"We're looking!"

He turned toward Dunk again. What an ox the man was. He should've been strapped to a plow. "I'm kind of busy at the moment."

"Allow me to remind you of the terms. You do your magic with the stills, I give you ten percent of the profits. It's not hard to remember."

Michael yelled up to the catwalk again. "Sometime today would be nice!"

The next thing Michael knew, he was rammed up against the bulkhead, Dunk's forearm pressing against his throat.

"Do I have your attention now?"

The man's broad, pitted nose was inches from Michael's; his breath was sour as old wine.

"Easy, amigo. We don't have to do this in front of the kids."

"You work for *me,* goddamnit."

"If I could point something out. Breaking my neck might feel good in the moment, but it won't get you any more lick."

"Everything okay, Michael?"

Rand was standing behind Dunk with two others, Fastau and Weir. Rand was clutching a long wrench; the other two had lengths of pipe. They were holding these implements in an offhand manner, as if they'd merely picked them up in the course of a day's work.

"Just a little misunderstanding," Michael replied. "How about it, Dunk? We don't need to have a problem here. You've got my attention, I promise."

Dunk's arm pressed tighter against his throat. "Fuck you."

Michael glanced over Dunk's shoulder at Weir and Fastau. "You two, go check on the stills, see what the situation is, then report back to me. Got it?" He returned his attention to Dunk. "Got this covered. I'm hearing you loud and clear."

"Twenty years. I've had it with your bullshit. This . . . hobby of yours."

"Totally understand your feelings. I spoke out of turn. New boilers up and running, no problem."

Dunk kept glowering at him. It was hard to say how things were going to go. Finally, giving Michael a last hard shove against the bunker, Dunk backed away. He turned toward Michael's men and nailed them with a hard look.

"You three should be more careful."

Michael withheld his coughing until Dunk was out of sight.

"Jesus, Michael." Rand was staring at him.

"Oh, he's just having a bad day. He'll cool off. You two, back to work. Rand, you're with me."

Weir frowned. "You don't want us to go to the stills?"

"No, I don't. I'll look in on them later."

They walked away.

"You shouldn't goad him like that," Rand said.

Michael paused to cough again. He felt a little foolish, though on the other hand, the whole thing had been strangely gratifying. It was nice when people were themselves. "Have you seen Greer anywhere?"

"He took a launch up the channel this morning."

So, feeding day. Michael always worried—Amy still tried to kill Greer every time—but the man took it in stride. Except for Rand, who'd been with them from the beginning, none of Michael's men knew about that part of things: Amy, Carter, the *Chevron Mariner,* the jugs of blood that Greer dutifully delivered every sixty days.

Rand glanced around. "How long do you think we have before the virals come back?" he asked quietly. "It's got to be close by now."

Michael shrugged.

"It's not that I'm not grateful. We all are. But people want to be ready."

"If they do their damn jobs, we'll be long gone before it happens." Michael hitched his tool bag onto his shoulder. "And for fucksake, will somebody *please* go find Patch. I don't want to wait around all morning."

It was evening when Michael finally emerged from the bowels of the ship. His knees were killing him; he'd done something to his neck, too. He'd never found the leak, either.

But he would; he always did. He would find it, and every other leak and rusty rivet and frayed wire in the *Bergensfjord*'s miles of cables and wires and pipes, and soon, in a matter of months, they would charge the batteries and test-fire the engines, and if all went as it should, they'd be ready. Michael liked to imagine that day. The pumps engaging, water pouring into the dock, the retaining wall opening, and the *Bergensfjord,* all twenty thousand tons of her, sliding gracefully from her braces into the sea.

For two decades, Michael had thought of little else. The trade had been Greer's idea—a stroke of genius, really. They needed money, a lot of it. What did they have to sell? A month after he'd shown Lucius the newspaper from the *Bergensfjord,* Michael had found himself in the back room of the gambling hall known as Cousin's Place, sitting across a table from Dunk Withers. Michael knew him to be a man of extraordinary temper, lacking all conscience, driven by only the most utilitarian concerns; Michael's life meant nothing to him, because no one's did. But Michael's reputation had preceded him, and he'd done his homework. The gates were about to open; people would be flooding into the townships. The opportunities were many, Michael pointed out, but did the trade possess the capacity to meet a rapidly growing demand? What would Dunk say if Michael told him that he could triple—no, *quadruple*— his output? That he could also guarantee an uninterrupted flow of ammunition? And furthermore, what if Michael knew about a place where the trade could operate in complete safety, beyond the reach of the military or the domestic authority but with quick access to Kerrville and the townships? That, in sum, he could make Dunk Withers richer than he could imagine?

Thus was the isthmus born.

A great deal of time was wasted at the start. Before Michael could so much as tighten a single bolt on the *Bergensfjord,* he had to win the man's confidence. For three years he had overseen the construction of the massive stills that would make Dunk Withers a legend. Michael was not unaware of the costs. How many fistfights would leave a man bloodied and toothless, how many bodies would be dumped into alleyways, how many wives and children would be beaten or even killed, all because of the mental poison he provided? He tried not to think about it. The *Bergensfjord* was all that mattered; it was a price she demanded, paid in blood.

Along the way, he laid the groundwork for his true enterprise. He began with the refinery. Cautious inquiries: Who seemed bored? Dissatisfied? Restless? Rand Horgan was the first; he and Michael had worked the cookers together for years. Others followed, recruited from every corner. Greer would leave for a few days, then return with a man in a jeep with nothing but a duffel bag and his promise to stay on the isthmus for five years in exchange for wages so outrageous they would set him up for life. The numbers accumulated; soon they had fifty-four stout souls with nothing to lose. Michael noticed a pattern. The money was an inducement, but what these men really sought was something intangible. A great many people drifted through their lives without a feeling of purpose. Each day felt indistinguishable from the last, devoid of meaning. When he unveiled the *Bergensfjord* to each new recruit, Michael could see a change in the man's eyes. Here was something beyond the scope of ordinary days, something from before the time of mankind's diminishment. It was the past Michael was giving these men and, with it, the future. *We're actually going to fix it?* they always asked. *Not "it,"* Michael corrected. *"Her." And no, we're not going to fix her. We're going to wake her up.*

It didn't always take. Michael's rule was this: At the three-year mark, once Michael was certain of a man's loyalty, he took him to an isolated hut, sat him in a chair, and gave him the bad news. Most took it well: a moment of disbelief, a brief period of bargaining with the cosmos, requests for evidence Michael declined to provide, resistance eventually yielding to acceptance and, finally, a melancholy gratitude. They would be among the living, after all. As for those who didn't last three years, or failed the test of the hut, well, that was unfortunate. Greer was the one to take care of this; Michael kept his distance. They were surrounded by water, into which a man could quietly vanish. Afterward, his name was never mentioned.

It took two years to repair the dock, another two to pump and refloat the hull, a fifth to back her in. The day they set her hull in the braces, sealed the doors, and drained the water from the dock was the most anxious of Michael's life. The braces would hold, or not; the hull would crack, or it wouldn't. A thousand things could go wrong, and there would be no second chances. As a layer of daylight appeared between the receding water and the bottom of the hull, his men erupted in cheers, but Michael's emotions were different. He felt not elation but a sense of fate. Alone, he took the stairs to the bottom of the dock. The cheers had quieted; everyone was watching him. With water pooling around his ankles, he stepped toward her cautiously, as if approaching some great, holy relic. Clear of the water, she had become something new. The sheer size of her, her indomitable bulk—it staggered the mind. The curvature of her hull below the waterline possessed an almost feminine softness; from her bow jutted a bulbous shape, like a nose or the front of a bullet. He moved under her; all her weight was above him now, a mountain suspended over his head. He reached up and placed a hand against her hull. She was cold; a humming sensation met the tips of his fingers. It was as if she were breathing, a living thing. A deep certainty flowed into his veins: here was his mission. All other possibilities for his life dropped away; until the day he died, he would have no purpose but this.

Except to sail the *Nautilus,* Michael had not left the isthmus since. A show of solidarity, politically wise, but in his heart he knew the real reason. He belonged nowhere else.

He walked to the bow to look for Greer. A damp March wind was blowing. The isthmus, part of an old shipyard complex, jutted into the channel a quarter mile south of the Channel Bridge. A hundred yards offshore, the *Nautilus* lay at anchor. Her hull was still tight, her canvas crisp. The sight made him feel disloyal; he had not sailed her in months. She was the forerunner; if the *Bergensfjord* was his wife, then the *Nautilus* was the girl who had taught him to love.

He heard the launch before he saw it, churning under the Channel Bridge in the silvery light. Michael descended to the service dock as Greer guided the boat in. He tossed Michael a line.

"How did it go?"

Greer tied off the stern, passed Michael his rifle, and climbed onto the pier. Just past seventy, he had aged the way bulls did: one minute they'd be huffing and snorting, looking to gore you; the next you'd find them lying in a field, covered in flies.

"Well," Michael offered, "she didn't kill you—that's a plus."

Greer didn't answer. Michael sensed that the man was troubled; the visit had not gone well.

"Lucius, did she say something?"

"Say? You know how this works."

"Actually, I've never really known."

He shrugged. "It's a feeling I have. *She* has. Probably it's nothing."

Michael decided not to press. "There was something else I wanted to bring up with you. I had a little run-in with Dunk today."

Greer was coiling rope. "You know how he gets. This time tomorrow he'll have forgotten all about it."

"I don't think he's going to let this one go. It was bad."

Greer looked up.

"It was my fault. I was egging him on."

"What happened?"

"He came down to the engine room. The usual bullshit about the stills. Rand and a couple of guys practically had to pull him off me."

Greer's brow furrowed. "There's been too much of this."

"I know. He's getting to be a problem." Michael paused, then said, "It may be time."

Greer was silent, taking this in.

"We've talked about it."

Greer thought for a moment, then nodded. "Under the circumstances, you may be right."

They went over the names: who they could count on, who they couldn't, who was somewhere in between and would have to be carefully handled.

"You should lie low for now," Greer said. "Rand and I will make the arrangements."

"If you think that's best."

The spotlights had come on, drenching the dock with light. Michael would be working most of the night.

"Just get that ship ready," said Greer.

Sara glanced up from her desk; Jenny was standing in the doorway.

"Sara, you need to see something."

Sara followed her downstairs to the wards. Jenny pulled back the curtain to show her. "The DS found him in an alley."

It took Sara a moment to recognize her own son-in-law. His face had been beaten to a pulp. Both of his arms were in casts. They moved back outside.

Jenny said, "I only just saw the chart and realized who it was."

"Where's Kate?"

"She's on the evening shift."

It was nearly four o'clock. Kate would be walking in the door any second.

"Head her off."

"What do you want me to say?"

Sara took a moment to think. "Send her to the orphanage. Aren't they due for a visit?"

"I don't know."

"Figure it out. Go."

Sara entered the ward. As she approached, Bill looked up with the eyes of a man who knew his day was about to get worse.

"Okay, what happened?" she asked.

He turned his face away.

"I'm disappointed in you, Bill."

He spoke through split lips: "I kinda figured."

"How much do you owe them?"

He told her. Sara dropped into a chair by the bed. "How could you be so goddamned stupid?"

"It wasn't like I planned this."

"You know they'll kill you. Probably I should just let them."

He surprised her by starting to cry.

"Cripes, don't do that," she said.

"I can't help it." Snot was running from his thickened nose. "I love Kate, I love the girls. I'm really, really sorry."

"Sorry doesn't help. How much time have they given you to come up with the money?"

"I can earn it all back. Just stake me for one night. I won't need much, just enough to get started."

"Does Kate fall for stuff like this?"

"She doesn't have to know."

"It was a rhetorical question, Bill. How much time?"

"The usual. Three days."

"What's usual about it? On second thought, don't tell me." She got to her feet.

"You can't tell Hollis. He'll kill me."

"He might."

"I'm sorry, Sara. I screwed up, I know that."

Jenny appeared, a little breathless. "Okay, looks like she bought it."

Sara glanced at her watch. "That gives you about an hour, Bill, before your wife shows up. I suggest you come clean and beg for mercy."

The man looked terrified. "What are you going to do?"

"Nothing you deserve."

27

Caleb was building a chicken coop when he saw a figure walking up the dusty road. It was late in the afternoon; Pim and Theo were resting in the house.

"Saw your smoke." The man who stood before him had a pleasant, weathered face and a thick, woolly beard. He was wearing a wide straw hat and suspenders. "Since we're going to be neighbors, thought I'd come by to say hello. Phil Tatum's the name."

"Caleb Jaxon." They shook.

"We're just on the other side of that ridge. Been there a bit, before most folks. There's me and my wife, Dorien. We got a grown boy just started his own place up toward Bandera. Did you say Jaxon?"

"That's right. He's my father."

"I'll be damned. What are you doing way out here?"

"Same as everyone, I guess. Making do." Caleb removed his gloves. "Come in and meet my family."

Pim was sitting in a chair by the cold hearth with Theo on her lap, showing him a picture book.

"Pim," Caleb said, signing along, "this is our neighbor, Mr. Tatum."

"How do you do, Mrs. Jaxon?" He was holding his hat against his chest. "Please, don't get up on my account."

I'm very pleased to meet you.

Caleb realized his error. "I should have explained. My wife is deaf. She says she's pleased to meet you."

The man nodded evenly. "Got a cousin like that, passed a while back. She learned to read lips a little, but the poor thing just lived in her own world." He raised his voice, the way a lot of people did. "That's a fine-looking boy you have, Mrs. Jaxon."

What's he saying?

You're beautiful and he wants to go to bed with you. He turned to their guest, who was still fingering the brim of his hat. "She says thank you, Mr. Tatum."

Don't be rude. Ask him if he wants something to drink.

Caleb repeated the question.

"Have to be home before supper, but I reckon I could sit for a bit, thank you."

Pim filled a pitcher with water, added slices of lemon, and placed it on the table, where the two men sat. They talked about little things: the weather, other homesteads in the area, where Caleb should get his livestock and at what price. Pim had gone off with Theo; she liked to take him down to the river, where the two of them would just sit quietly. It became clear to Caleb that the man and his wife were a little lonely. Their son had gone off with a woman he'd met at a dance in Hunt, barely saying goodbye.

"Couldn't help notice your wife is expecting," Tatum said. They had finished the water; now they were just talking.

"Yes, she's due in September."

"There's a doc in Mystic when the time comes." He gave Caleb the information.

"That's very kind. Thank you." Caleb sensed the presence of a sad history in the man's offer. The Tatums had had another child, perhaps more than one, who had failed to survive. This was all far in the past, but not really.

"Much obliged to you both," Tatum said at the door. "It's nice to have some young people around."

That night, Caleb replayed the conversation for Pim. She was bathing Theo in the sink. He had fussed at the start but now seemed to be enjoying himself, batting the water around with his fists.

I should call on his wife, Pim signed.

Do you want me to go with you? He meant to translate for her.

She looked at him like he had lost his mind. *Don't be ridiculous.*

This conversation stayed with him for several days. Somehow, in all his planning, Caleb had failed to consider that they would need other people in their lives. Some of this was the fact that with Pim he shared a private richness that made other relationships seem trivial. Also, he was not innately social; he preferred his own thoughts to most human interaction.

It was true, as well, that Pim's world was more limited than most people's. Beyond her family, it was confined to a small group of those who, if they could not sign, were able to intuit her meanings. She was often alone, which did not seem to trouble her, and she filled much of this time by writing. Caleb had peeked at her journals a few times over the years, unable to resist this small crime; like her letters, her entries were wonderfully written. While they sometimes expressed doubts or concern over various matters, generally they communicated an optimistic view of life. They also contained a number of sketches, though he had never seen her draw. Most depicted familiar scenes. There were a great many drawings of birds and animals, as well as the faces of people she knew, although none of him. He wondered why she had never let him see them, why she had drawn them in secret. The best ones were the seascapes—remarkable, because Pim had never seen the ocean.

Still, she would want friends. Two days after Phil had stopped by, Pim asked Caleb if he would mind looking after Theo for a few hours; she wanted to visit the Tatums and planned to bring a johnnycake. Caleb spent the afternoon working in the garden while Theo napped in a basket. He began to worry as the day drew to a close, but just before dark Pim returned in high spirits. When Caleb asked her how they had been able to carry on a conversation for close to five hours, Pim smiled. *It doesn't matter with women,* she signed. *We always understand each other just fine.*

The next morning, Caleb took the buckboard into town for supplies and to reshoe one of the horses, the big black gelding they called Handsome. Pim had also written a letter to Kate and asked him to post it. Besides these errands, he wanted to establish contact with more people from the area. He could ask the men he met about their wives, with the hope of expanding Pim's circle, so that she would not feel lonely.

The town was not encouraging. Just a few weeks had passed since he and Pim had passed through on their way to the farmstead; at the time there had been people about, but now the place seemed lifeless. The town office was closed, as was the farrier. But he had better luck at the mercantile. The owner was a widower named George Pettibrew. Like many men on the frontier, he had a taciturn manner, slow to warm up, and Caleb had never managed to learn much about him. George followed him as he moved through the cluttered space, placing his order—a sack of flour, beet sugar, a length of heavy chain, sewing thread, thirty yards of chicken wire, a sack of nails, lard, cornmeal, salt, oil for the lanterns, and fifty pounds of feed.

"I'd also like to buy some ammo," Caleb said, as George was tallying the bill at the counter. "Thirty-aught-six."

The man made a certain expression: *You and everybody else.* He continued jotting figures with a stub of pencil. "I can give you six."

"How many in a box?"

"Not boxes. Rounds."

It seemed like a joke. "That's all? Since when?"

George poked his thumb over his shoulder. Tacked to the wall behind the counter was a sign.

$100 BOUNTY

MOUNTAIN LION

PRESENT CARCASS AT HUNT TOWNSHIP OFFICE TO COLLECT.

"Folks cleaned me out, not that I had much to begin with. Ammo's scarce these days. I'll give 'em to you for a buck apiece."

"That's ridiculous."

George shrugged. Business was business; it was all the same to him. Caleb wanted to tell him to stick it, but on the other hand, a mountain lion was nothing to mess with. He rolled off the bills.

"Think of it as an investment," George said, depositing the money in his lockbox. "You bag that cat, this won't seem so much, will it?"

Everything went into the wagon. Caleb surveyed the empty street. It really *was* awfully damn quiet for the middle of the day. He found it a little unnerving, though mostly he felt disappointed that he would return with so little to show for his visit.

He was about to drive out of town when he remembered the doctor Tatum had told him about. It would be good to introduce himself. The doctor's name was Elacqua. According to Tatum, he had once worked at the hospital in Kerrville and retired to the townships. There weren't many houses, and the doctor's was easy to find: a small frame structure, painted a cheerful yellow, with a sign that read, BRIAN ELACQUA, M.D. hanging off the porch. A pickup truck with rusted fenders was parked in the yard. Caleb tied up the horses and knocked. A single eye peeked through the curtain on the door's window.

"What do you want?" The voice was loud, almost hostile.

"Are you Dr. Elacqua?"

"Who's asking?"

Caleb regretted coming; there was obviously something wrong with the man. He thought he might be drunk. "My name is Caleb Jaxon. Phil Tatum is my neighbor, he said you were the doctor in town."

"Are you sick?"

"I just wanted to say hello. We're new out here. My wife is expecting. It's all right—I can come back later."

But as Caleb stepped off the porch, the door opened. "Jaxon?"

"That's right."

The doctor had the look of a derelict, thick at the waist, with a wild mane of snow-white hair and a beard to match. "You might as well come in."

His wife, a nervous woman in a shapeless housedress, served them some kind of bad-tasting tea in the parlor. No explanation was offered for Elacqua's curt behavior at the door. Maybe that was just how things were done out here, Caleb thought.

"How far along is your wife?" Elacqua asked, after they'd gotten past the formalities. He had, Caleb noted, put a little something in his tea from a pocket flask.

"About four months." Caleb saw an opening. "My mother-in-law is Sara Wilson. Maybe you know her."

"Know her? I trained her. I thought her daughter worked at the hospital, though."

"That's Kate. My wife is Pim."

He thought for a moment. "I don't remember a Pim. Oh, the mute." He shook his head sadly. "The poor thing. Nice of you, to marry her."

Caleb had heard statements like this before. "I'm sure she thinks it's the other way around."

"On the other hand, who wouldn't want a wife who couldn't talk? I can barely put two thoughts together around here."

Caleb just looked at him.

"Well," Elacqua said, and cleared his throat, "I can pay a call if she'd like, just to see how things are going."

At the door, Caleb remembered Pim's letter. He asked Elacqua if he would mind posting it for him when the office opened.

"I can try. Those people are never there."

"I was wondering about that," Caleb said. "The town seems kind of empty."

"I didn't notice." He frowned doubtfully. "Could be the mountain lion, I guess. That happens out here."

"Has anyone been attacked?"

"Not that I've heard, just livestock. With the bounty, a lot of folks are out looking. Stupid, if you ask me. Those things are nasty."

Caleb rode out of town. At least he'd tried to post the letter. As for Elacqua, he seriously doubted Pim would want anything to do with the man. The mountain lion didn't concern him unduly. It was simply the price one paid for life on the frontier. Still, he would tell Pim not to take Theo to the river for a while. The two of them should stay near the house until the matter was resolved.

They ate their supper and went to bed. Rain was falling, making a peaceful pattering on the roof. In the middle of the night, Caleb awoke to a sharp cry. For a terrifying second he thought something had happened to Theo, but then the sound came again, from outside. It was fear he was hearing—fear and mortal pain. An animal was dying.

In the morning he searched the brush behind the house. He came to an area of broken branches; tufts of short, stiff hair, tacky with blood, were spread over the ground. He thought it might have been a raccoon. He scanned the area for tracks, but the rain had washed them away.

The next day he walked over the ridge to the Tatums'. Their operation was much larger than his own, with a good-sized barn and a house with a standing-seam metal roof. Boxes of bluebonnets hung beneath the front windows. Dorien Tatum greeted him at the door, a plump-cheeked woman with gray hair in a bun; she directed him to the far edge of the property, where her husband was clearing brush.

"A mountain lion, you say?" Phil removed his hat to mop his brow in the heat.

"That's the word in town."

"We've had 'em before. Long gone by now, I'd guess. They're restless sons of bitches."

"I thought so, too. Probably it's nothing."

"I'll keep a lookout, though. Thank your wife for the johnnycake, won't you? Dory really enjoyed her visit. Those two were writing messages to each other for hours."

Caleb made to leave, then stopped. "What's it usually like in town?"

Tatum was drinking from a canteen. "What you mean?"

"Well, it was pretty quiet. It seemed odd, in the middle of the day." Now that he'd said it, he felt a little silly. "The town office was shut, the farrier, too. I was hoping to get one of the horses reshod."

"Folks are usually around. Maybe Juno's taken sick." Juno Brand was the farrier.

"Maybe that's it."

Phil smiled through his beard. "Go round in a day or two. I bet you'll find him. But you get hard up for something, you let us know."

Caleb had decided not to tell Pim about what he'd found in the woods; there seemed no good reason to alarm her, and a dead raccoon meant nothing. But that night as they were cleaning up the dishes, he repeated his request that she and Theo stay close to the house.

You worry too much, she signed.

Sorry.

Don't be. She turned at the sink to surprise him with a lingering kiss. *It's one of the reasons I love you.*

He wagged his eyebrows cornily. *Does this mean what I think it does?*

Let me get Theo down first.

But there was no need. The boy was already asleep.

28

She began the night, as she began all nights, atop the partially constructed office tower at the corner of Forty-third and Fifth Avenue. The air was blustery, with a hint of warmth; stars bedecked the heavens, thick as dust. The shapes of great buildings crenellated the sky in silhouettes of perfect blackness. The Empire State. Rockefeller Center. The magnificent Chrysler Building, Fanning's favorite, soaring above everything around it with its graceful art deco crown. The hours after midnight were the ones Alicia liked best. The quiet was richer somehow, the air purer. She felt closer to the core of things, the world's rich chroma of sound and scent and texture. The night flowed through her, a coursing in the blood. She breathed it in and out. A darkness indomitable, supreme.

She crossed the roof to the construction crane and began to climb. Attached to the exposed girders of the building's upper floors, it soared another hundred feet above the roof. There were stairs, but Alicia never bothered, stairs being a thing of the past, a quaint feature of a life she barely recalled. The boom, hundreds of feet long, was positioned parallel with the building's west face. She made her way down the catwalk to the boom's tip, from which a long hooked chain dangled in the darkness. Alicia winched it up, released the brake, and drew the hook backward along the boom. Where the boom met the mast was a small platform. She laid the hook there, returned to the tip, and reset the chain's brake. Then, back to the platform. A keen anticipation filled her, like a hunger about to be slaked. Standing erect, head held high, she gripped the hook in her fists.

And stepped off.

She plunged down and away. The trick was to release the hook at just the right moment, when her speed and upward momentum existed in perfect balance. This would occur roughly two-thirds up the back side of the hook's arc. She swung through the bottom, still accelerating. Her body, her senses, her thoughts—all were attuned, at one with speed and space.

She released the hook. Her body inverted; she tucked her knees to her chest. Three aerial rolls and she uncoiled. The flat-topped roof across the street: that was the target. It rose in greeting. *Welcome, Alicia.*

Touchdown.

Her powers had expanded. It was as if, in the presence of her creator, some powerful mechanism within her had been fully unleashed. The aerial spaces of the city were trivial; she could vault vast distances, alight on the narrowest ledges, cling to the tiniest cracks. Gravity was a toy to her; she ranged above Manhattan like a bird. In the glass faces of skyscrapers her reflected image dove and darted, plunged and swooped.

She found herself, sometime later, above Third Avenue, near the demarcation between land and sea; a few blocks south of Astor Place, the encroaching waters began, bubbling up from the island's flooded underworld. She descended, ping-ponging between buildings, to the street. Broken shells lay everywhere among the dried husks of ocean weeds swept inward by storm surges. She knelt and pressed her ear to the pavement.

They were definitely moving.

The grate pulled away easily; she dropped into the tunnel, lit her torch, and began to walk south. A ribbon of dark water sloshed at her feet. Fanning's Many had been eating. Their droppings were everywhere, rank, ureic, as were the skeletal remains of their feeding—mice, rats, the small creatures of the city's clammy substratum. Some of the droppings were fresh, a few days old at the most.

She passed through the Astor Place station. Now she could feel it: the sea. The great bulge of it, always pressing, seeking to enlarge its domain, to drown the world with its cold blue weight. Her heart had quickened; the hairs stood up along her arms. *It's only water,* she told herself. *Only water . . .*

The bulkhead appeared. A thin spray of water, almost a mist, shot from its edges. She stepped toward it. A moment's hesitation; then she extended a hand to touch its frigid face. On the other side, untold tons of pressure lay in stasis, stalemated for a century by the weight of the door. Fanning had explained the history. The entire Manhattan subway system lay below sea level; it had been a disaster waiting to happen. After Hurricane Wilma had flooded the tunnels, the city fathers had constructed a series of heavy doors to hold the water in check. In the throes of the epidemic, when the electricity had failed, a fail-safe mechanism had sealed them. There they had rested for over a century, holding the encroaching ocean at bay.

Don't be afraid, don't be afraid . . .

She heard a skittering behind her. She spun, raising her torch. At the edge of the darkness, a pair of orange eyes flared. A large male but skinny, the bumps of his ribs showing; he squatted, froglike, between the tracks, a rat gripped in his mouth with the very tips of his teeth. The rat squirmed and squeaked, its bald tail whipping.

"What are you looking at?" Alicia said. "Get out of here."

The jaws clamped shut. An arcing pop of blood and a sucking sound and the viral spat the empty bag of bones and fur to the ground. Alicia's stomach tumbled, not with nausea but hunger; she hadn't eaten for a week. The viral extended its claws, petting the air like a cat. It cocked his head: *What sort of being is this?*

"Go on." She waved the torch like a pike. "Shoo. Scat."

A last look, almost fond. It darted away.

Fanning had already prepared for daybreak by drawing the shades. He was sitting at his usual table on the balcony above the main hall, reading a book by candlelight. His eyes lifted as she approached.

"Good hunting?"

Alicia took a chair. "I wasn't hungry."

"You should eat."

"So should you."

His attention returned to his book. Alicia glanced at the title: *The Tragedy of Hamlet, Prince of Denmark.*

"I went to the library."

"So I see."

"It's a very sad play. No, not sad. Angry." Fanning shrugged. "I haven't read it for years. It seems different to me now." He found a certain page, looked at her, and raised a professorial finger. "Have a listen."

The spirit I have seen
May be the devil, and the devil hath power
T' assume a pleasing shape; yea, and perhaps
Out of my weakness and my melancholy,
As he is very potent with such spirits,
Abuses me to damn me. I'll have grounds
More relative than this. The play's the thing
Wherein I'll catch the conscience of the king.

When Alicia said nothing, he raised an eyebrow at her. "You're not a fan?"

Fanning's moods were like this. He could go silent for days, brooding incessantly, then, without warning, would emerge. Lately he had adopted a tone of dry cheerfulness, almost smug.

"I can see why you like it."

"'Like' may not be the word."

"The end doesn't make sense, though. Who's the king?"

"Precisely."

Wedges of sunlight peeked through the drapes, making pale stripes on the floor. Fanning seemed unperturbed by them, though his sensitivity was far greater than her own. For Fanning, the sun's touch was deeply painful.

"They're waking up, Tim. Hunting. Moving through the tunnels."

Fanning continued reading.

"Are you listening?"

He looked up with a frown. "Well, what of it?"

"That's not our agreement."

His attentions had returned to his book, though he was only pretending to read. She got to her feet. "I'm going to see Soldier."

He yawned, showing his fangs, and gave her a pale-lipped smile. "I'll be here."

Alicia cinched on her goggles, exited onto Forty-third, and headed north on Madison Avenue. Spring had come on sluggishly; only a few trees were budding out, and pockets of snow still lay in the shadows. The stable was located on the east side of the park at Sixty-third, just south of the zoo. She removed Soldier's blanket and led him out of his stall. The park felt static, as if caught between the seasons. Alicia sat on a boulder at the edge of the pond and watched the horse graze. He had taken on the years with dignity; he tired more easily, but only a little, and was still strong, his gait firm. Strands of white had appeared in his tail and whiskers, more on the feathers at his feet. She watched him eat his fill, then saddled him and climbed aboard.

"A little exercise, boy, what do you say?"

She guided him across the meadow, into the shade of the trees. A memory came to her of the day she'd first seen him, all that coiled wildness inside him, standing alone outside the wreckage of the Kearney garrison, waiting for her like a message. *I am yours as you are mine. For each of us there will always be one.* Past the trees she brought him to a trot, then a canter. To their left lay the reservoir, a billion gallons, lifeblood of the city's green heart. At the Ninety-seventh Street Transverse, she dismounted.

"Back in a jiff."

She made her way into the woods, removed her boots, and scaled a suitable tree at the edge of the glade. There, balanced on her haunches, she waited.

Eventually her wish was granted: a young doe tiptoed into view, ears flicking, neck bent low. Alicia watched the animal approach. Closer. Closer.

Fanning hadn't moved from the table. He looked up from his book, smiled. "What's this I see?"

Alicia heaved the doe off her shoulders, onto the bar top. Its head hung with the looseness of death, the pink tongue unspooling from its mouth like a ribbon.

"I told you," she said. "You really need to eat."

29

The first gunshots rang out on schedule, a series of distant pops from the end of the causeway. It was one A.M. Michael was concealed with Rand and the others outside the Quonset hut. The door swung open with a blaze of light and laughter; a man stumbled out, his arm draped over the shoulders of one of the whores.

He died with a gurgle. They left him where he fell, blood darkening the earth from the wire's incision around his neck. Michael stepped up to the woman. She wasn't one he knew. Rand's hand was covering her mouth, dampening her terrified shrieks. She couldn't have been a day over eighteen.

"Nothing's going to happen to you, if you keep quiet. Understand?"

She was a well-fed girl with short, red hair. Her eyes, heavily made up, were open very wide. She nodded.

"My friend is going to uncover your mouth, and you're going to tell me what room he's in."

Cautiously, Rand drew his hand away.

"The last one, at the end of the hall."

"You're certain?"

She nodded vigorously. Michael gave her a list of names. Four were playing cards in the front room; two more were back in the stalls.

"Okay, get out of here."

She dashed away. Michael looked at the others. "We go in in two groups. Rand with me; the rest of you hover in the outer room until everybody's ready."

Eyes flicked up from the tables as they entered, but that was all. They were comrades, no doubt stopping by the hut for the same reasons everyone did: a drink, some cards, a few minutes of bliss in the stalls. The second group spread out across the room while Michael and the others faded to the hallway and took their positions outside the doors. The signal was passed, the doors were flung open.

Dunk was on his back, naked, a woman busily rocking astride his hips. "Michael, what the fuck?" But when he saw Rand and the others, his expression changed. "Oh, give me a break."

Michael looked at the whore. "Why don't you take a walk?"

She snatched her dress from the floor and ran out the door. From elsewhere in the building came an assortment of screams and shouts, the sound of glass breaking, a single gunshot.

"It was going to happen sooner or later," Michael said to Dunk. "Might as well make the best of it."

"You think you're so fucking smart? You'll be dead the minute you walk out of here."

"We've pretty much cleaned house, Dunk. I was saving you for last."

Dunk's face lit with a phony smile; beneath the bluster, the man knew he was looking into an abyss. "I get it. You want a bigger share. Well, you've certainly earned it. I can make that happen for you."

"Rand?"

The man moved forward, gripping the wire in his fists. Three others grabbed Dunk as he attempted to rise and shoved him hard onto the mattress.

"For fucksake, Michael!" He was squirming like a fish. "I treated you like a son!"

"You have no idea how funny that is."

As the wire slipped around Dunk's neck, Michael stepped from the room. The last of Dunk's lieutenants was putting up a bit of a struggle in the second stall, but then Michael heard a final grunt and the thump of something heavy striking the floor. Greer met him in the front room, where bodies lay strewn amid overturned card tables. One of them was Fastau; he'd been shot through the eye.

"Are we done?" Michael asked.

"McLean and Dybek got away in one of the trucks."

"They'll stop them at the causeway. They aren't going anywhere." Michael looked at Fastau, lying dead on the floor. "We lose anyone else?"

"Not that I've heard."

They loaded the bodies into the five-ton that waited outside. Thirty-six corpses in all, Dunk's inner circle of murderers, pimps, thieves: they'd be carted to the dock, loaded onto a launch, and dumped in the channel.

"What about the women?" Greer asked.

Michael was thinking of Fastau—the man had been one of his best welders. Any loss at this point was a concern.

"Have Patch put them under guard in one of the machine sheds. Once we're ready to move, get them on a transport out of here."

"They'll talk."

"Well, consider the source."

"I see your point."

The truck with the bodies drove away.

"I don't mean to press," Greer said, "but have you decided about Lore?"

The question had preoccupied Michael for weeks. Always he came back to the same answer. "I think she's the only one I trust enough to do this."

"I agree."

Michael turned toward Greer. "Are you sure you don't want to be the one to run things around here? I think you'd be good at it."

"That's not my role. The *Bergensfjord* is yours. Don't worry, I'll keep the troops in line."

They were quiet for a time. The only lights burning were the big spots on the dock. Michael's men would be working through the night.

"There's something I've been meaning to bring up," Michael said.

Greer cocked his head.

"In your vision, I know you couldn't see who else was on the ship—"

"Just the island, the five stars."

"I understand that." He hesitated. "I'm not sure how to put this. Did it . . . *feel* like I was there?"

Greer seemed perplexed by the question. "I really couldn't say. That wasn't part of it."

"You can be honest with me."

"I know I can."

The sound of gunfire from the causeway: five shots, a pause, then two more, deliberate, final. Dybek and McLean.

"I guess that's that," said Greer.

Rand walked up to them. "Everybody's assembled at the dock."

Suddenly Michael felt the weight of it. Not ordering the deaths of so many; that had been easier than expected. He was in charge now—the isthmus was his. He checked the magazine on his sidearm, decocked the hammer, and slid the pistol back into its holster. From now on, he would never be apart from it.

"All right, that oil ships in thirty-six days. Let's get this show on the road."

30

IOWA FREESTATE
(Formerly the Homeland)
Pop. 12,139

Sheriff Gordon Eustace began the morning of March 24—as he did every March 24—by hanging his holstered revolver on the bedpost.

Because carrying a weapon wouldn't be right. It wouldn't be respectful. For the next few hours, he'd be just a man, like any man, standing in the cold on aching joints to think about the way things might have been.

He kept a room at the back of the jail. For ten years, since the night he couldn't make himself return to the house, that was where he'd slept. He'd always considered himself the sort of man who could pick himself up and get on with things, and it wasn't as if he was the first person whose luck had turned bad. But something had gone out of him and never come back, and so this was where he lived, in a cinder-block box with nothing but a bed and a sink and a chair to sit in and a toilet down the hall, nobody but drunks sleeping it off for company.

Outside the sun was rising in a halfhearted, March-in-Iowa way. He heated a kettle on the stove and carried it to the basin with his straight razor and soap. His face looked back in the old cracked mirror. Well, wasn't that a pretty sight. Half his front teeth gone, left ear shot off to a pink nub, one eye clouded and useless: he looked like something in a children's story, the mean old ogre under the bridge. He shaved, splashed water on his face and under his arms, and dried himself off. All he had on hand for breakfast were some leftover biscuits, hard as rocks. Sitting at the table, he worked them over with his back teeth and washed them down with a shot of corn liquor from the jug beneath the sink. He wasn't much of a drinker, but he liked one in the morning, especially this morning of all mornings, the morning of March 24.

He put on his hat and coat and stepped outside. The last of the snow had melted, turning the earth to mud. The jailhouse was one of the few buildings in the old downtown that anybody still used; most had been empty for years. Blowing on his hands, he made his way past the ruins of the Dome—nothing left of it now but a pile of rocks and a few charred timbers—and down the hill into the area that everybody still called the Flatland, though the old workers' lodges had long since been dismantled and used as firewood. Some folks still lived down here, but not many; the memories were too bad. The ones who did were generally younger, born after the days of the redeyes, or else very old and unable to break the psychological chains of the old regime. It was a squalid dump of shacks without running water, miasmatic rivers of sewage running in the streets, and a roughly equivalent number of dirty children and skinny dogs picking through the trash. Eustace's heart broke every time he saw it.

It wasn't supposed to be this way. He'd had plans, hopes. Sure, a lot of people had accepted the offer to evacuate to Texas in those first years; Eustace had expected that. *Fine,* he'd thought, *let them go.* The ones who remained would be the hearty souls, the true believers who viewed the end of the redeyes not merely as a liberation from bondage but something more: the chance to right a wrong, start over, build a new life from the bottom up.

But as he'd watched the population drain away, he'd begun to worry. The people who stayed behind weren't the builders, the dreamers. Many were simply too weak to travel; some were too afraid; others so accustomed to having everything decided for them that they were incapable of doing much of anything at all. Eustace had made a run at it, but nobody had the slightest idea how to make a city work. They had no engineers, no plumbers, no electricians, no doctors. They could operate the machines the redeyes left behind, but nobody knew how to fix them when they broke. The power plant had failed within three years, water and sanitation within five; a decade later, almost nothing functioned. Schooling the children proved impossible. Few of the adults could read, and most didn't see the sense of it. The winters were brutal—people froze to death in their own houses—and the summers were almost as bad, drought one year and drenching rains the next. The river was foul, but people filled their buckets anyway; the disease that everyone called "river fever" killed scores. Half the cattle had died, most of the horses and sheep, and all of the pigs.

The redeyes had left behind all the tools to build a functioning society but one: the will to actually do it.

The road through the Flatland joined the river and took him east to the stadium. Just beyond it was the cemetery. Eustace made his way through the rows of headstones. A number were decorated—guttered candles, children's toys, the long-desiccated sprigs of wildflowers exposed by the retreating snow. The arrangement was orderly; the one thing people were good at was digging graves. He came to the one he was looking for and crouched beside it.

NINA VORHEES EUSTACE

SIMON TIFTY EUSTACE

BELOVED WIFE, BELOVED SON

They had perished within a few hours of each other. Eustace was not told of this until two days later; he was roiling with fever, his mind adrift in psychotic dreams he was glad to have no memory of. The epidemic had cut through the city like a scythe. Who lived and who died seemed random; a healthy adult was as likely to succumb as an infant or someone in their seventies. The illness came on quickly: fever, chills, a cough from deep in the lungs. Often it would seem to run its course only to come roaring back, overwhelming the victim within minutes. Simon had been three years old—a watchful boy with intelligent eyes and a joyful laugh. Never had Eustace felt a love so deep for anyone, not even for Nina. The two of them joked about it—how, by comparison, their affection for each other seemed minor, though of course that wasn't quite true. Loving their boy was just another way of loving each other.

He spent a few minutes by the grave. He liked to focus on little things. Meals they'd shared, snippets of conversation, quick touches traded for no reason, just to do it. He hardly ever thought about the insurgency; it seemed to have no bearing anymore, and Nina's ferocity as a fighter made up but one small part of the woman she was. Her true self was something she had shown only to him.

A feeling of fullness told him it was time to go. So, another year. He touched the stone, letting his hand linger there as he said goodbye, and made his way back through the maze of headstones.

"Hey, mister!"

Eustace spun around as a chunk of ice the size of a fist sailed past his head. Three boys, teenagers, stood fifty feet away among the headstones, guffawing like idiots. But when they got a look at him, the laughter abruptly ceased.

"Shit! It's the sheriff!"

They dashed away before Eustace could say a word. It was too bad, really; there was something he wanted to tell them. *It's okay,* he would have said. *I don't mind. He would have been about your age.*

When he returned to the jail, Fry Robinson, his deputy, was sitting at the desk with his boots up, snoring into his collar. He was just a kid, really, not even twenty-five, with a wide, optimistic face and a soft round jaw he barely had to shave. Not the smartest but not the dumbest either; he'd stayed on with Eustace longer than most men did, which counted for something. Eustace let the door bang behind himself, sending Fry jolting upright.

"Jesus, Gordo. What the hell did you do that for?"

Eustace strapped on his gun. It was mostly for show; he kept it loaded, but the ammunition the redeyes had left behind was nearly gone, and what remained was unreliable. On more than one occasion, the hammer had fallen on a dud.

"Did you feed Rudy yet?"

"I was just about to before you woke me up. Where'd you go? I thought you were still back there."

"Went to visit Nina and Simon."

Fry gave him a blank stare; then he understood. "Shit, it's the twenty-fourth, isn't it?"

Eustace shrugged. What was there to say?

"I can look after things here if you want," Fry offered. "Why don't you take the rest of the day off?"

"And do what?"

"Sleep or something. Get drunk."

"Believe me, I've thought about it."

Eustace carried Rudy's breakfast back to his cell: a couple of stale biscuits and a raw potato cut into slices.

"Rise and shine, partner."

Rudy lifted his emaciated frame off his bunk. Thieving, fighting, being a general, all-around pain in the ass: the man was in jail so often he actually had a favorite cell. This time the charge was drunk and disorderly. With a lurid snort he excavated a wad of phlegm, hawked it into the bucket that served as a toilet, and shuffled to the bars, beltless pants hoisted in his fist. Maybe I should let him keep his belt next time, Eustace thought. The man might do us all a favor and hang himself. Eustace slid the plate through the slot.

"That's it? Biscuits and a potato?"

"What do you want? It's March."

"The service isn't what it used to be around this place."

"So stay out of trouble for once."

Rudy sat on the bunk and took a bite of one of the biscuits. The man's teeth were disgusting, brown and wobbly-looking, though Eustace was hardly one to talk. Crumbs spurted from his mouth as he spoke. "When's Abel coming?"

Abel was the judge. "How should I know?"

"I need a clean bucket, too."

Eustace was halfway down the hall.

"I'm serious!" Rudy yelled. "It stinks in here!"

Eustace returned to the front and sat behind his desk. Fry was wiping down his revolver, something he did about ten times a day. The thing was like his pet. "What's his problem?"

"Didn't care much for the cuisine."

Fry frowned with contempt. "He should be grateful. I didn't get much more than that myself." He stopped and sniffed the air. "Jesus, what's that smell?"

"Hey, assholes," Rudy yelled from the back, "got a present for you!"

Rudy was standing in his cell holding the now-empty bucket with a triumphant look on his face. Shit and piss were running down the hallway in a brown river.

"This is what I think of your fucking potato."

"Goddamnit," Fry yelled, "you're cleaning this up!"

Eustace turned to his deputy. "Hand me the key."

Fry unhooked the ring from his belt and passed it to Eustace. "I mean it, Rudy." He jabbed a finger in the air. "You're in a heap of trouble, my friend."

Eustace unlocked the door, stepped into the cell, closed the door behind himself, reached with the keys back through the bars, and locked the door again. Then he deposited the ring deep in his pocket.

"What the hell is this?" Rudy asked.

"Gordon?" Fry looked at him cautiously. "What are you doing?"

"Just give me a sec."

Eustace drew his revolver, spun it around in his hand, and slapped the butt across Rudy's face. The man stumbled backward and toppled to the floor.

"Are you out of your mind?" Rudy scrabbled backward until he was against the wall of the cell. He worked his tongue around and spat a bloodied tooth into his palm. He held it up by its long, rotten root. "Look at this! How am I supposed to eat now?"

"I doubt you'll miss it much."

"You had that coming, you piece of shit," Fry said. "Come on, Gordo, let's get this asshole a mop. I think he's learned his lesson."

Eustace didn't think so. *Teach the man a lesson*—what did that actually mean? He wasn't sure what he was feeling, but it was coming to him. Rudy was holding out his tooth with a look of righteous indignation on his face. The sight of it was thoroughly disgusting; it seemed to encapsulate everything wrong with Eustace's life. He reholstered his gun, letting Rudy think the worst was over, then hauled him to his feet and slammed his face against the wall. A damp crunch, like a fat cockroach popping underfoot: Rudy released a howl of pain.

"Gordon, seriously," Fry said. "Time to open that door."

Eustace wasn't angry. Anger had left him, years ago. What he felt was relief. He hurled the man across the cell and got to work: his fists, the butt of the revolver, the points of his boots. Fry's pleas for him to stop barely registered in his consciousness. Something had come uncorked inside him, and it was elating, like riding a horse at full gallop. Rudy was lying on the floor, his face protectively buried in his arms. *You pathetic excuse for a human being. You worthless waste of skin. You are everything that's wrong with this place, and I am going to make you know it.*

He was in the process of lifting Rudy by his collar to slam his head against the edge of the bunk—what a satisfying crack that was going to make—when a key turned in the lock and Fry grabbed him from behind. Eustace connected with an elbow to Fry's midriff, knocking him away, and wrapped Rudy's neck in the crook of his arm. The man was like a big rag doll, a fleshy sack of loosely organized parts. He tightened his biceps against Rudy's windpipe and shoved his knee into his back for leverage. One hard yank and that would be the end of him.

Then: snowflakes. Fry was standing over him, heaving for breath, holding the fire poker he'd just used on Eustace's head.

"Jesus, Gordo. What the hell was *that*?"

Eustace blinked his eyes; the snowflakes winked out one by one. His head felt like a split log; he was a little sick to his stomach, too.

"Got a little carried away, I guess."

"It wasn't like the guy didn't deserve it, but what the fuck."

Eustace turned his head to get a look at the situation. Rudy was curled into a fetal ball with his hands jammed between his legs. His face looked like raw meat.

"I really did a number on him, didn't I?"

"The man never traded on his looks anyway." Fry directed his voice at Rudy. "You hear me? You breathe one word of this, they're going to find you in a ditch, you asshole." Fry looked at Eustace. "Sorry, I didn't mean to hit you so hard."

"That's okay."

"Don't mean to rush you, but it's probably best if you vacate the premises for the time being. Think you can stand?"

"What about Abel?"

"I'll handle it. Let's get you on your feet."

Fry helped him up. Eustace had to hold on to the bars for a second to make the floor feel solid. The knuckles of his right hand were bloody and swollen, skin split along the bone. He tried to close it into a fist, but the joints wouldn't go that far.

"Okay?" Fry was looking at him.

"I think so, yeah."

"Just go clear your head. You might want to take care of that hand, too."

At the door of the cell, Eustace stopped. Fry was easing Rudy into a seated position. His shirt was a bib of blood.

"You know, you were right," Eustace said.

Fry glanced up. "How's that?"

Eustace didn't feel sorry about what he'd done, though he supposed he might later on. A lot of things were like that; the reaction you were supposed to have took its time getting there.

"Maybe I should have taken the day off after all."

31

Alicia began to spend her nights in the stable.

Fanning took little notice of her absence. *That horse of yours,* he might comment, barely lifting his eyes from one of the books that now completely occupied his waking hours. *I don't see why you feel the need, but it's really none of my business.* His mind seemed distant, his thoughts veiled. Yes, he was different; something had shifted. The change felt tectonic, a rumbling from deep in the earth. He wasn't sleeping, there was that—if indeed their kind could be said to sleep. In the past, the daylight hours had brought forth in him a kind of melancholy exhaustion. He would fade into a trancelike state—eyes closed, hands folded in his lap with his fingers tidily meshed. Alicia knew his dreams. The clocks' hands remorseless turning. The anonymous crowds streaming past. His was a nightmare of infinite waiting in a universe barren of pity—without hope, without love, without the purpose that only hope and love could bear upon it.

She had a dream like that of her own. Her baby. Her Rose.

She sometimes thought about the past. "New York," Fanning liked to say, "has always been a place of memory." She missed her friends as the dead might miss the living, citizens of a realm she had permanently departed. What did Alicia remember? The Colonel. Being a little girl in the dark. Her years on the Watch, how true they felt. There was a night that came back to her often; it seemed to define something. She had taken Peter up to the roof of the power station to show him the stars. Side by side they had lain on the concrete, still warm with the day's crushing heat, the two of them just talking, beneath a night sky made more remarkable by the fact that Peter had never seen it before. It brought them out of themselves. *Have you ever thought about it?* Alicia had asked him. *Thought about what?* he'd asked; and she'd said, nervously—she couldn't seem to stop herself—*You're going to make me say it? Pairing, Peter. Having Littles.* She understood, much later, what she was really asking of him: to save her, to lead her into life. But it was too late; it had always been too late. Since the night the Colonel had abandoned her, Alicia hadn't really been a person anymore; she had given it up.

So, the years. Fanning said time was different for their kind, and it was. The days' ceaselessly melding, season into season, year into year. What were they to each other? He was kind. He understood her. *We have traveled the same road,* he said. *Stay with me, Lish. Stay with me, and all of it is ended.* Did she believe him? There were times when he seemed to know the deepest truths of her. What to say, what to ask, when to listen and for how long. *Tell me about her.* How soft his voice was, how gentle. It was like no voice she had ever heard; it felt like floating in a bath of tears. *Tell me about your Rose.*

Yet there was another part of him, veiled, impenetrable. His long, brooding silences disturbed her, as did instances of a slightly off-key cheerfulness that seemed wholly manufactured. He began to venture out at night, something he had not done in years. He made no announcement; he would simply be gone. Alicia decided to follow him. For three nights he wandered without apparent destination, a forlorn figure haunting the streets; then, on the fourth night, he surprised her. With deliberate strides he made his way downtown, into the West Village, and halted before a nondescript residential building, five stories tall, with a flight of steps connecting the front door to the street. Alicia concealed herself behind a rooftop parapet at the top of the block. Several minutes passed, Fanning studying the building's face. Suddenly it came to her: Fanning had lived here once. Something seemed to click inside him, and he marched up to the door, forced it with his shoulder, and disappeared inside.

He was gone for a long while. An hour, then two. Alicia began to be concerned. Unless Fanning appeared soon, there would not be time for him to return to the station before sunrise. Finally he emerged. At the bottom of the steps, he stopped. As if sensing her presence, he cast his eyes around the street, then looked straight toward her. Alicia ducked below the parapet and pressed her body to the rooftop.

"I know you're there, Alicia. But it's all right."

When she looked again, the street was empty.

He made no mention of the night's events, and Alicia did not press. She had glimpsed something, a clue, but its meaning eluded her. Why, after all this time, would he make such a pilgrimage?

He never left again.

What was going to happen next, Fanning must have anticipated; Alicia was obviously meant to do it. The building was a wreck on the inside. Black spatters of mold scaled the walls, and the floors were soft underfoot. In the stairwell, water dripped from a leak in the ceiling, high above. She ascended to the second floor, where a door stood open in invitation. The interior of the apartment had been largely spared the destruction. The furniture, though caked with dust, was all neatly arranged; books and magazines and various decorative objects still occupied their places, just as, Alicia supposed, they had been in the final hours of Fanning's human life. As she moved through the fastidious rooms she became aware of what she was feeling. Fanning wanted her to know the man he'd been. A new, deeper intimacy had been offered her.

She entered the bedroom. It seemed different from the other spaces of the apartment, possessing an intangible sense of more recent occupation. The furniture was simple: a desk, a dresser, an upholstered chair by the window, a bed, neatly made. Bisecting the center of the mattress was a depression of distinctly human dimensions. A similar divot marked the pillow.

A pair of eyeglasses rested on the bedside table. Alicia knew whom they'd belonged to; they were part of the story. She gently picked them up. They were petite, with wire frames. The cratered bed, the linens, the glasses within reach. Fanning had lain here. And he had left all of this for her to see.

To see, she thought. What did he want her to see?

She lay on the bed. The mattress was formless beneath her, its internal structure long collapsed. Then she put on the glasses.

She could never explain it; the moment she had looked through the lenses, it was as if she had *become* him. The past poured through her, the pain. The truth hit her heart like voltage. Of course. Of course.

Daybreak found her at the bridge. Her fear of the churning waters, though strong, seemed trivial; she pushed it aside. The sun cast its long, golden rays behind her. Upon Soldier's back she made her way across, following her shadow.

32

They found Bill in the retaining pool at the bottom of the spillway. The night before, he'd slipped out of the hospital, taking his clothes and shoes. After that, the trail went cold. Someone said they had seen him at the tables, although the man demurred; he could be thinking of a different night, he said. Bill was always at the tables. It would have been more remarkable if he weren't.

It was the fall that had killed him: a hundred feet from the top of the dam, then the long slide to the pool, where his body had wedged against a drain. His legs were shattered, his chest caved in; otherwise, he looked the same. Had he jumped or was he pushed? His life was not what they had thought it to be; Sara wondered how much Kate had kept from her. But it was not a question to ask.

The matter of his debts remained. Pooling their savings with Kate's, Sara and Hollis could assemble less than half the amount owed. Three days after the burial, Hollis took the money to the building in H-town that everyone still called Cousin's Place, though Cousin himself had been dead for years. Hollis hoped that this token of good faith, combined with his old connections, would square the matter. He returned, shaking his head dispiritedly. The players had changed; he had no clout. "This is going to be a problem," he said.

Kate and the girls were bedding down at Sara and Hollis's house. Kate seemed benumbed, a woman who had accepted a fate she had long seen coming, but the girls' grief was shattering to witness. In their young eyes, Bill was simply their father. Their love for him was uncolored by the knowledge that he had, in a sense, shunned them, choosing a path that would take him away from them forever. As they grew, the wound would morph into a different kind of injury—one not of loss but of rejection. Sara would have done anything in her power to spare them this pain. But there was nothing.

The only thing to do was hope that the situation would blow over. Two more days passed, and Sara came home to find Hollis sitting at the table in the kitchen, looking grim. Kate was on the floor playing cards with the girls, but Sara could see this was intended as a distraction; something serious had happened. Hollis showed her the note that had been slid under the door. In blocky handwriting, like a child's, two words: "Adorable girls."

Hollis kept a revolver in a lockbox under the bed. He loaded it and gave it to Sara.

"Anybody comes through that door," he instructed, "shoot them."

He didn't tell her what he'd done, though that was the night Cousin's Place burned to the ground. In the morning, Sara went with Kate to the post office to mail the letter that would, in all likelihood, arrive in Mystic Township many days after she did. *Coming for a visit,* Kate wrote to Pim. *The girls can't wait to see you.*

33

Yes, I am tired. Tired of waiting, tired of thinking. I am tired of myself.

My Alicia: how good you have been to me. *Solamen miseris socios habuisse doloris*: "It is a comfort to the wretched to have companions in misery." When I think of you, Alicia, and what we are to each other, I am reminded of my first trip to a barbershop as a boy. Indulge me—memory is my method in all things, and the story has more bearing than you think. In my boyhood town, there was only one. It was a kind of clubhouse. On a Saturday afternoon, escorted by my father, I entered this sacred masculine space. The details were intoxicating. The odors of tonic, leather, talc. The combs lounging in their disinfecting aquamarine bath. The hiss and crackle of AM radio, broadcasting manly contests upon green fields. My father beside me, I waited on a chair of cracked red vinyl. Men were being barbered, lathered, whisked. The owner of the shop had been a World War II bomber pilot of some renown. Upon the wall behind the cash register hung a photograph of his young warrior self. Beneath his snipping shears and buzzing razor, each small-town cranium emerged a perfect simulacrum of his own, on the day he'd donned his goggles, wrapped a scarf around his neck, and crossed the eaves of heaven to blast the samurai to smithereens.

My turn arrived; I was summoned forth. Many smiles and winks were exchanged among the witnesses. I took my seat—a board balanced upon the chair's chrome arms—as the barber, like a toreador flashing his cape, shook out the curtain with which he meant to dress me, wrapped toilet paper around my neck, and draped my body in decapitating plastic. That was when I noticed the mirrors. One on the wall before me, one behind, and my likeness—a reflection of a reflection of a reflection—caroming down the corridor of cold eternity. The sight brought forth an existential nausea. Infinity: I knew the term, yes, but the world of boyhood is finite and firm. To gaze into the heart of it, and to see my likeness stamped a million-fold upon its face, disconcerted me profoundly. The barber, meanwhile, had set blithely about his task, simultaneously engaged in lighthearted conversation with my father on various adult subjects. I thought that focusing my eyes solely upon the first image might somehow banish the others, but the effect was the opposite: I was made even more aware of the innumerable shadow selves lurking behind him, ad infinitum, infinitum, infinitum.

But then something else happened. My discomfort waned. The lush sensory package of the place, combined with the delicate tickling of the barber's shears upon my neck, eased me into a state of trancelike fascination. The idea came to me: I was not just one small thing. I was, in fact, a multitude. Looking farther, I believed I detected among my infinite fellows certain subtle differences. This one's eyes were a bit closer together, a second's ears were positioned a fraction higher on his head, a third sat just a little lower in his chair. To test my theory, I commenced to make small adjustments—angling my gaze, wrinkling my nose, winking one eye and then the other. Each version of me responded in kind, and yet I discerned the tiniest lag, the barest hitch of time, between my action and its manifold duplication. The barber warned me that if I did not hold still he might accidently cut my ear off—more virile laughter—but his words made no impact, so thoroughly was I enjoying my new discovery. It became a kind of game. Fanning says: Stick out your tongue. Fanning says: Raise one finger. What delicious power I possessed! "Come on, son," my father commanded, "quit your fussing," but I wasn't fussing—far from it. Never had I felt so alive.

Life wrests that feeling from us. Day by day, the sublime glimpses of childhood pass away. It is love, of course, and only love, that restores us to ourselves, or so we hope, but that is taken away. What is left when there is no love? A rope and rock.

I have been dying forever. That is what I mean to say. I have been dying as you are dying, my Alicia. It was you I saw in the mirror, that long-ago morning of boyhood; it is you I see now, as I walk these streets of glass. There is one love, made of hope, and another, made of grief.

I have, my Alicia, loved you.

Now you are gone; I knew this day would come. The look on your face as you strode into the hall: there was wrath in it, yes. How angry you were with me, how your eyes flashed with feelings of betrayal, how the words spat with righteous fury from your lips. *This isn't our deal,* you said. *You said you would leave them alone.* But you know as well as I that we cannot; our purpose is ordained. Hope is none but vapid sweetness to the tongue, without the taste of blood. What are we, Alicia, but the gauntlet through which humanity must pass? We are the knife of the world, clamped between God's teeth.

Forgive me, Alicia, my modest deceit. You made it rather easy. In my defense, I did not lie. I would have told you, had you asked; you believed because you wanted to. You might ask yourself, Who, my dear, was following whom? Who the watcher and who the watched? Night after night you prowled the tunnels like a schoolmarm counting heads. Honestly, your gullibility was a little disappointing. Did you truly believe that all my children are here? That I could have been so careless? That I would be content to bide a meaningless eternity? I am a scientist, methodical in all things; my eyes are everywhere, seeing all. My descendants, my Many: I walk with them, I haunt the night, I see as they see, and what do I behold? The great city defenseless, all but abandoned. The small towns and farms, staking their claim. Humanity bursting with ripeness, flowing over the land. They have forgotten us; their minds have returned to the ordinary concerns of life. How will the weather be? What will I wear to the dance? Whom should I marry? Shall I have a child? What will I name it?

What would you tell them, Alicia?

The heavens toy with me; I will have satisfaction. I have waited long enough for this savior, this Girl from Nowhere, this Amy NLN. She taunts me with her silence, her limitless, tactical calm. To flush me out, that is her aspiration, and so she shall have it. I know what you are thinking, Alicia. Surely I must despise her, for the deaths of my ignoble fellows, my Twelve. Far from it! The day she faced them was one of the happiest of my long, unhappy exile. Her sacrifice was supreme. It was positively God-kissed. It gave me—dare I use the word?—hope. Without alpha, there can be no omega; without beginning, no end.

Bring her to me, I told you. *My quarrel is not with humankind; it is but ransom to the nobler purpose. Bring her to me, my darling, my Lish, and I will spare the rest.*

Oh, I have no illusions. I know what you will do. Always I have known, and I have loved you no less for it—to the contrary. You are the better part of me; each of us must play his role.

Thus the long-awaited day. You asked, Who is the king, whose conscience we must catch? Is it I, or is there another? Shall the creator be moved to pity his creation? Soon we will know. The stage is set, the lights go down, the actors take their marks.

Let it begin.

IV

THE HEIST

MAY 122 A.V.

The jury, passing on the prisoner's life,
May in the sworn twelve have a thief or two
Guiltier than him they try.

—SHAKESPEARE,
MEASURE FOR MEASURE

34

"Everybody, kill your engines."

0440 hours: in darkness they rowed the final fifty yards to shore and dragged the launches onto the sand. A few hundred yards south, the glow of burning butane flickered in the sky. Michael checked his rifle, racked his sidearm, and returned it to its holster. Everyone else did the same.

They broke into three groups and scuttled up the dunes. Rand's squad would take the workers' quarters, Weir's the radio and control rooms. Michael's team, the largest, would rendezvous with Greer's to secure the Army barracks and armory. That's where the shooting would be.

Michael pressed the radio to his mouth. "Lucius, are you in position?"

"Roger that. Waiting on your signal."

The refinery was protected by a two-tiered fence line with guard towers; the remainder of the perimeter was a gauntlet of trip-wire mines. The only access from the north was straight through the gate. Greer would lead the frontal assault using a tanker truck equipped with a plow. A pair of trucks full of men would follow. A pickup at the rear, armed with a fifty-caliber and a grenade launcher, would dispense with the towers if need be. Michael's orders were to avoid casualties if possible, but if it came to that . . .

The teams dispersed at a quick step. Michael and his men took up positions around the barracks, a long Quonset hut with doors front and rear. They were expecting fifty well-armed men inside, perhaps more.

"Team one."

"Good to go."

"Team two."

"Roger that."

Michael checked his watch: 0450. He looked at Patch, who nodded.

Michael raised his flare gun and fired. A popping flash and the compound appeared around them in blocks of light and shadow. A second later, Patch launched the gas canister from its tube. Shouts and gunfire from the gate, and then a crash as the semi plowed through the fence. Gas had begun to sift under the door of the barracks. As it flew open, Michael's men released a barrage of grazing fire into the dirt. The fleeing soldiers lurched backward in confusion. More men were careening into them from behind, choking and coughing and sputtering.

"On your knees! Drop your weapons! Hands on your heads!"

The soldiers had nowhere to run; onto their knees they went.

"Everyone, report."

"Team two, secure."

"Lucius?"

"No casualties. Headed your way."

"Team one?"

Michael's men had moved forward to wrap the soldiers' wrists and ankles with heavy cord. Most were still coughing, a few vomiting helplessly.

"Team one, report."

A grainy crackle of static; then, a voice, not Rand's: "Secure."

"Where's Rand?"

A pause, followed by laughter. "You'll have to give him a minute. That woman sure packs a wallop."

It had been too easy. Michael had expected more of a fight—*any* kind of fight.

"These guns are practically empty."

Greer showed him; none of the soldiers' magazines had more than two rounds.

"What about the armory?"

"Clean as a whistle."

"That's actually not so good."

From Greer, a tight nod. "I know. We'll have to do something about that."

It was Rand who brought Lore to him. Her wrists were bound. At the sight of him she startled, then quickly composed herself.

"I guess you missed me, Michael?"

"Hello, Lore." Then, to Rand: "Take those off."

Rand cut her loose. Lore had nailed him with a hard right cross. His left eye was half-shut, his cheek marked with the imprint of her fist. Michael felt almost proud.

"Let's go someplace and talk," he said.

He led Lore into the station chief's office. *Her* office: for fifteen years, the refinery had been Lore's to run. Michael sat behind the desk to make a point; Lore sat across from him. The day had broken, warming the room with its light. She looked older, of course, aged by sun and work, but the raw physicality was still there, the strength.

"So how's your pal Dunk?"

Michael smiled at her. "It's good to see you. You haven't changed a bit."

"Are you trying to be funny?"

"I mean it."

She glanced away, a furious look on her face. "Michael, what do you want?"

"I need fuel. Heavy diesel, the dirty stuff."

"Going into the oil business? It's a hard life—I don't recommend it."

He took a long breath. "I know this doesn't make you happy. But there's a reason."

"Is that right?"

"How much do you have?"

"You know what I always liked best about you, Michael?"

"No, what?"

"I don't remember either."

It was true: she was just the same. Michael felt a frisson of attraction. Her power had not abated.

He leaned back in his chair, balanced the tips of his fingers together, and said, "You have a major delivery to the Kerrville depot scheduled in five days. Add that to what's in the storage tanks, I'm figuring you've got somewhere in the neighborhood of eighty thousand gallons."

Lore shrugged indifferently.

"So I should take that as a yes?"

"You should take it up your ass, actually."

"I'm going to find out anyway."

She sighed. "Okay, fine. Yes, eighty thousand, more or less. Does that satisfy you?"

"Good. I'm going to need it all."

Lore cocked her head. "I beg your pardon?"

"With twenty tanker trucks, I'm thinking we can move it all in just under six days. After that, we'll release your people. No harm, no foul. You've got my word."

Lore was staring at him. "Move it *where*? What the hell do you need eighty thousand gallons for?"

Ah.

The tanker trucks were being loaded; the first convoy would be ready to move by 0900. For Michael, five days of looking at his watch, yelling at everyone: *Hurry the hell up.*

One wrinkle, maybe small, maybe not. When Weir's men had stormed the communications hut, the radio operator had been in the midst of sending a message. There was no way to know what it was, because the man was dead—the morning's only fatality.

"How the hell did that happen?"

Weir shrugged. "Lombardi thought he had a weapon. It looked like he was drawing on us."

The weapon was a stapler.

"Have any messages come in since?" Michael asked, thinking, *Lombardi, of course it would be you, you trigger-happy asshole.*

"Nothing so far."

Michael cursed himself. The man's death was regrettable, but that wasn't the true source of his anger. They should have taken out the radio first. A stupid mistake, probably not the first.

"Get on the horn," he said, then thought the better of it. "No, wait until twelve hundred. That's when they expect the refinery to check in."

"What should I tell them?"

"'Sorry, we shot the radio operator. He was waving office supplies at us.'"

Weir just looked at him.

"I don't know, something *normal.* 'Everything's peachy, how are you, isn't it a nice day?'"

The man hurried away. Michael walked to the Humvee, where Lore was waiting in the backseat. Rand was handcuffing her to the safety rail.

"You should take somebody else with you," Rand said.

Michael accepted the key to the cuffs and got in the cab. He glanced at Lore through the mirror. "You promise to be good or do you need a babysitter?"

"The man you shot. His name was Cooley. The guy wouldn't squash a bug."

Michael looked at Rand. "I'll be fine. Just get that diesel moving."

The drive to the channel took three hours. Lore barely uttered a word, and Michael made no effort to draw her out. It had been a hard morning for her—the end of a career, the death of a friend, a public humiliation—all at the hands of a man she had every reason to despise. She needed time to adjust, especially considering the things Michael was about to tell her.

They passed through the wires and made their way down the causeway. He brought the truck to a halt behind the machine shed at the edge of the quay. From here, the *Bergensfjord* wasn't visible. He wanted a grand unveiling.

"So why am I here?"

Michael opened Lore's door and unlocked her wrists. As she climbed out of the Humvee, he withdrew his sidearm and held it out to her.

"What's this?"

"A gun, obviously."

"And you're giving it to me?"

"You get to pick. Shoot me, take the truck, you'll be back in Kerrville by nightfall. Stay, and you'll know what this is all about. But there are rules."

Lore said nothing, merely raised an eyebrow.

"Rule one is you can't leave unless I allow it. You're not a prisoner, you're one of us. Once I tell you what's happening, you'll see the necessity. Rule two is I'm in charge. Speak your mind, but never question me in front of my men."

She was looking at him as if he'd lost all sense. Still, the offer had to be made; the woman had to choose.

"Why in hell would I want to join you?"

"Because I'm going to show you something that will change everything you thought you knew about your life. And because, deep down, you trust me."

She stared at him, then laughed. "The comedy never stops, does it?"

"I wasn't fair to you, Lore. I'm not proud of what I did—you deserved better than that. But there *was* a reason. I said you haven't changed, which is true. That's why I brought you here. I need your help. I can see why you'd say no, but I hope you won't."

She eyed him suspiciously. "Where exactly *is* Dunk?"

"This was never about the trade. I needed money and manpower. More than that, I needed secrecy. Five weeks ago, Dunk and all his lieutenants went into the channel. There is no trade anymore. Only me, and those loyal to me." He nudged the gun toward her. "The mag is full, and there's one in the pipe. What you do with it is up to you."

Lore accepted the pistol. For a long moment she looked at it, until, with a heavy sigh, she slid it into the waistband of her jeans at the base of her spine.

"If it's all right with you, I'm keeping this."

"That's fine. It's yours now."

"I must be out of my mind."

"You made the right choice."

"I regret it already. I'm only going to say this one time, but you really broke my heart, you know that?"

"I do. And I apologize."

A brief silence. Then she nodded, just once: case closed. "So?"

"Brace yourself."

He wanted Lore to see the *Bergensfjord* from below. That was the best way. Not just to see her but to *experience* her; only then could her meaning be grasped. They took the stairs to the floor of the drydock. Michael waited as Lore approached the hull. The ship's flanks were smooth and gracefully curved, every rivet tight. Beneath the *Bergensfjord*'s massive propellers, Lore came to a halt, gazing upward. Michael would let her speak first. Above them, the clang of footfalls, men calling to one another, the whine of a pneumatic drill, the ship's vast square footage of metal amplifying every sound like a giant tuning fork.

"I knew there was a boat . . ."

Michael was standing beside her. She turned to face him. In her eyes a struggle was being waged.

"She's called the *Bergensfjord*," Michael said.

Lore spread her hands and looked around. "All this?"

"Yes. For her."

Lore moved forward, extended her right hand over her head, and pressed it against the hull—just as Michael had done on the morning they'd drained the water from the dock, revealing the *Bergensfjord* in all her rusted, invincible glory. Lore held it there, then, as if startled, broke away.

"You're scaring me," she said.

"I know."

"Please tell me you were just keeping your hands busy. That I'm not seeing what I think I'm seeing."

"What do you think you're seeing?"

"A lifeboat."

Some color had drained from her face; she seemed uncertain where to direct her eyes.

"I'm afraid it is," Michael said.

"You're lying. You're making this up."

"It's not good news—I'm sorry."

"How could you possibly *know*?"

"There's a lot to explain. But it's going to happen. The virals are coming back, Lore. They were never really gone."

"This is crazy." Her confusion turned to anger. "*You're* crazy. Do you know what you're saying?"

"I'm afraid I do."

"I don't want anything to do with this." She was backing away. "This can't be true. Why don't people know? They would *know*, Michael."

"That's because we haven't told them."

"Who the hell is 'we'?"

"Me and Greer. A handful of others. There's no other way to say this, so I just will. Anybody who's not on this boat is going to die, and we're running out of time. There's an island in the South Pacific. We believe it's safe there— maybe the only safe place. We have food and fuel for seven hundred passengers, maybe a few more."

He hadn't expected this to be easy. Under ideal circumstances, he would have softened the blow. But Lore would cope, because that was her nature, the meat and marrow of Lore DeVeer. What had passed between them years ago was, for her, a painful memory perhaps, a quick jolt of anger and regret that touched her from time to time, but not for Michael. She was part of his life, and a good part, because she was one of the few people who had ever understood him. There were people who simply made existence more bearable; Lore was one.

"That's why I brought you here. We have a long voyage ahead of us. I need the diesel, but that's not all. The men who work for me, well, you've met them. They're hard workers, and they're loyal, but that only goes so far. I need *you*."

Her struggle was not over. There was more talking to be done. Nevertheless, Michael saw his words taking hold.

"Even if what you say is true," Lore said, "what can *I* possibly do?"

The *Bergensfjord:* he had given her everything. Now he would give her this.

"I need you to learn how to drive her."

35

The funeral was held in the early morning. A simple gravesite service: Meredith had requested that no general announcement of Vicky's death be made until the following day. Despite her high profile, Vicky had been a guarded person, sharing her private life with just a handful of people. *Let it just be us.* Peter offered a few words, followed by Sister Peg. The last to speak was Meredith. She appeared composed; she'd had years to prepare. Still, she said, with a hitch in her voice, one was never really ready. She then went on to tell a series of hilarious stories that left them all weeping with laughter. At the end, everyone was saying the same thing. *Vicky would have been so pleased.*

They adjourned to the house that was now Meredith's alone. The bed in the parlor was gone. Peter moved among the mourners—government officials, military, a few friends—then, as he was preparing to leave, Chase took him aside.

"Peter, if you have a second, there's something I'd like to discuss with you."

Here it comes, he thought. The timing made sense; now that Vicky was gone, the man felt that the path had been cleared for him. They stepped into the kitchen. Chase appeared uncharacteristically anxious, fiddling with his beard. "This is a little awkward for me," he admitted.

"You can stop right there, Ford. It's okay—I've decided not to run again." It surprised Peter a little, how easily the words had come. He felt a burden lifting. "I'll give you my full endorsement. You should have no problems."

Chase looked perplexed, then laughed. "I'm afraid you've got it wrong. I want to resign."

Peter was dumbstruck.

"I was waiting until Vicky . . . well. I knew she'd be disappointed in me."

"But I thought you always wanted it."

Chase shrugged. "Oh, there was a time when I did. When she picked you, I was pretty sore, I won't deny it. But not anymore. We've had our differences along the way, but the woman was right, you were the man for the job."

How could Peter have so badly misjudged? "I don't know what to say."

"Say, 'Good luck, Ford.'"

He did just that. "What will you do?"

"Olivia and I are thinking Bandera. It's good cattle land out there. The telegraphs are in, the town's first on the drawing board for the rail line. I figure fifty years from now, I'll make my grandkids rich."

Peter nodded. "It's a sound plan."

"You know, if you're really not running again, I'd be willing to talk about a partnership."

"You're serious?"

"It was actually Olivia's idea. The woman knows me; I'm all about the details. You want to fix the sewers on time, I'm your guy. But a cattle operation takes more than that. It takes nerve, and it takes capital. Just your name on the operation will open a lot of doors."

"I really don't know anything about cows, Ford."

"And I do? We'll learn. That's what everybody's doing these days, isn't it? We'd be a good team. We have so far."

Peter had to admit it: the notion was intriguing. Somehow, through the years, he had failed to notice that he and Chase had become, of all things, friends.

"But who's going to run if you don't?"

"Does it matter? We're half a government now. Another ten years, this place will be empty, a relic. People will be making their own ways. My guess is, the next guy to sit in that chair will be the one to turn the lights off. Personally, I'm glad it won't be you. I'm your adviser, so let this be my last piece of advice: go out strong, get rich, leave a fortune behind. Have a *life,* Peter. You've earned it. The rest will take care of itself."

Peter couldn't argue the point. "How soon do you need my answer?"

"I'm not Vicky. Take time to think it over. It's a big step, I know that."

"Thank you," Peter said.

"What for?"

"All of it."

From Chase, a grin. "You're welcome. The letter's on your desk, by the way."

After Chase had gone, Peter lingered in the kitchen; he emerged a few minutes later to find that nearly everyone had left. He said goodbye to Meredith and stepped onto the porch, where Apgar was waiting with his hands in his pockets.

"Chase bowed out."

An eyebrow went up. "Did he now?"

"You wouldn't by any chance feel like running for president?"

"Ha!"

A young officer jogged up the path. He was out of breath and sweating hard, evidently having run a great distance.

"What is it, son?" Peter said.

"Sirs," he said between gulps of air, "you need to see something."

The truck was parked in front of the capitol. Four soldiers were standing guard. Peter unlatched the tailgate and drew the canvas aside. Military crates filled the space, packed to the ceiling. Two of the soldiers extricated a crate from the first row and lowered it to the ground.

"I haven't seen one of these in years," Apgar said.

The crates had come from Dunk's bunker. Inside, vacuum-sealed in plastic strips, lay ammunition: .223, 5.56, 9mm, .45 ACP.

Apgar broke the seal on a round, held it up to the light, and whistled admiringly. "This is the good stuff. Original Army." He rose and turned to one of the soldiers. "Corporal, how many rounds do you have in your sidearm?"

"One and one, sir."

"Give it here."

The soldier handed it over. Apgar dropped the magazine, cleared the chamber, and topped the magazine off with a fresh cartridge. He racked the slide and held out the gun to Peter. "You want the honors?"

"Be my guest."

Apgar aimed the pistol at a square of earth ten feet away and pulled the trigger. There was a satisfying boom as dirt leapt up.

"Let's see what else we've got," Peter said.

They removed a second crate. This one contained a dozen M16s with extra thirty-round magazines, similarly sealed, looking fresh as the day they were made.

"Did anybody see the driver?" Peter asked.

Nobody had; the truck had simply appeared.

"So why would Dunk be sending us this?" Apgar asked. "Unless you brokered some kind of deal you didn't tell me about."

Peter shrugged. "I didn't."

"Then how do you explain it?"

Peter couldn't.

36

She crossed into Texas on old Highway 20. The morning of the forty-third day; Alicia had traveled half the breadth of a continent. The going had been slow at the start—cutting her way through the detritus of the coast, working inland across the rocky folds of the Appalachians, then the way had loosened and she'd begun to make good time. The days grew warmer, the trees burst into flower, springtime spread over the land. Whole days passed in heavy rain; then the sun exploded over the earth. Unbelievable nights, wide and starlit, the moon rolling through its cycle as she rode.

But now they stopped to rest. In the shade of a gas station awning Alicia lay on the ground while Soldier grazed nearby. Just a few hours and they'd press on. Her bones grew heavy; she felt herself plummeting into sleep. Throughout her journey, this had been the pattern. Days of wakefulness, her mind so alert it was almost painful, then she'd fall like a bird shot from the sky.

She dreamed of a city. Not New York; it was no city she had ever seen or known. The vision was majestic. In the darkness, it floated like an isle of light. Mighty ramparts surrounded it, protecting it from all danger. From within came noises of life: voices, laughter, music, the delighted shrieks of children at play. The sounds fell upon her like a shimmering rain. How Alicia longed to be among the inhabitants of that happy city! She made her way toward it and walked its perimeter, searching for a way in. There seemed to be none, but then she found a door. It was tiny, fit for a child. She knelt and turned the handle, but the door wouldn't budge. She became aware that the voices had faded. Above her, the city wall soared into blackness. *Let me in!* She began to pound the door with her fists; panic was consuming her. *Somebody, please! I'm all alone out here!* Still the door refused her. Her cries became howls, and then she saw: there was no door. The wall was perfectly smooth. *Don't leave me!* On the far side, the city had fallen silent: the people, the children, all gone. She pounded till she could pound no more and collapsed to the ground, sobbing into her hands. *Why did you leave me, why did you leave me . . .*

She awoke in twilight. Lying motionless, she blinked the dream away, then rose on her elbows to see Soldier standing at the edge of the shelter. He angled one dark eye at her.

"All right already. I'm coming."

Kerrville was four days away.

37

Kate and the girls had been with them a little more than a month. At the start, Caleb hadn't minded. It was good for Pim to have family around, and the girls adored Theo. But as the weeks passed, Kate's mood only seemed to darken. It filled the house like a gas. She did few chores and spent long hours sleeping, or else sitting on the front steps, staring into space.

How long is she going to mope around like that?

Pim was cleaning up the breakfast dishes. She dried her hands on a towel and looked at him squarely. *She's my sister. She just lost her husband.*

She's better off, Caleb thought, but didn't say so; he didn't have to.

Give her time, Caleb.

Caleb left the house. In the dooryard, Elle and Bug were playing with Theo, who had learned to crawl. The boy was capable of astonishing speed; Caleb reminded the girls to keep an eye on their cousin and not wander far from the house.

He was hitching the horses to the plow when he heard a cry of shock and pain. He dashed back to the yard as Kate and Pim came running from the house.

"Get them off! Get them off!"

Elle's bare legs were swarming with ants—hundreds of them. Caleb scooped her up and ran to the trough, the little girl writhing and shrieking in his arms. He plunged her into the water and began frantically stripping the ants from her legs, running his hands up and down her skin. The ants were on him too; he felt the electrical sting of their teeth boring into his arms, his hands, inside the collar of his shirt.

At last Elle quieted, her screams yielding to hiccupy sobs. A dark scrim of ant corpses had floated to the surface of the trough. Caleb lifted her out and handed her to Kate, who wrapped her in a towel. Her legs were covered with welts.

There's ointment inside, Pim signed.

Kate carried Elle away. Caleb drew his shirt over his head and shook it out, sending ants scattering. He had plenty of bites too, but nothing like his niece.

Where are Theo and Bug? he asked.

In the house.

It had been a hard spring for ants. People were saying it was the weather—the wet winter, the dry spring, the early summer, shockingly warm. The woods were bursting with their mounds, some reaching gigantic proportions.

Pim gave him a look of concern. *Is there anything we can do?*

This can't last forever. We should keep the kids inside until it passes.

But it didn't pass. The next morning, the ground around the house was swarming. Caleb decided to burn the mounds. From the shed he retrieved a can of fuel and carried it to the edge of the woods. He chose the largest pile, a yard wide and half as high, splashed it with kerosene, tossed a match, and stepped back to watch.

As black smoke roiled upward, ants exploded from the mound in a massive horde. Simultaneously, the hardened earth of the mound's surface began to bulge volcanically, then split open like a piece of rotten fruit. Soil cascaded down the sides. Caleb lurched back. What the hell was down there? It must have been a gigantic colony, millions of the little bastards, driven to mad panic by the smoke and flames.

The mound collapsed.

Caleb stepped gingerly forward. The last of the flames were sputtering out. All that remained was a shallow indentation in the earth.

Pim came up beside him. *What happened?*

Not sure.

From where he stood, he counted five other mounds.

I'm taking the wagon. Stay inside.

Where are you going? Pim signed.

I need to get more gas.

38

The Possum Man was missing.

The Possum Man, but also dogs—lots of dogs. The city was usually crawling with them, especially in the flatland. You couldn't walk ten paces down there without seeing one of the damn things, all skinny legs and matted fur and gooey eyes, snuffling through a garbage pile or crouched to take a wormy shit in the mud.

But suddenly, no dogs.

The Possum Man lived on the river near the old perimeter. He looked like what he did: pale and pointy-nosed, with dark, slightly bulging eyes and ears that stuck out from the sides of his face. He kept a woman half his age, though not the sort that anyone would want. According to her, they'd heard noise in the yard late at night. They figured it might be foxes, which had gotten into the hutches before. The Possum Man had grabbed his rifle and gone out to look. One shot, then nothing.

Eustace was kneeling by what was left of the hutches, which looked like they'd been hit by a tornado. If there were tracks, Eustace couldn't find any; the earth in the yard was packed too hard. Possum corpses were strewn around, torn to bloody chunks, although a few yards away a pair of them fidgeted in the dirt, staring at him woefully, like traumatized witnesses. They were actually kind of cute. As the closest one loped toward him, Eustace extended his hand.

"Don't want to do that," the woman warned. "They're nasty fuckers. Bite your finger off."

Eustace yanked his hand away. "Right."

He stood and looked at the woman. Her name was Rena, Renee, something like that, as scraggly-looking a thing as he'd ever laid eyes on. It was entirely possible that her parents had given her to the Possum Man in exchange for food. Such bargains were common.

"You said you found the rifle."

She retrieved it from the house. Eustace worked the bolt, kicking out an empty cartridge. He asked her where she'd found it. Her eyes didn't look in quite the same direction; it made her a little hard to talk to.

"Just about where you're standing."

"And you didn't hear anything else. Only the one shot."

"Happened like I said."

He was beginning to wonder if maybe she'd done it—shot the Possum Man, dragged his body to the river, busted up the hutches to cover her tracks. Well, if she had, she probably had a good enough reason, and Eustace sure as hell wasn't going to do anything about it.

"I'll put the word out. He turns up, you let us know."

"You sure you don't want to come inside, Sheriff?"

She was giving him a look. It took Eustace a second to figure out what it was. Her off-kilter gaze traveled the length of his body, then lingered pointedly. The gesture was supposed to be seductive but was more like livestock trying to sell itself.

"Folks say you ain't got a woman."

Eustace wasn't perturbed. Well, maybe a little. But the woman had been treated like property all her life; she had no other way of doing things.

"Don't believe everything you hear."

"But what'll I do he's dead?"

"You've got two possums, don't you? Make more."

"Them there? Them's both boys."

Eustace handed back the rifle. "I'm sure you'll think of something."

He returned to the jail. Fry, at his desk with his boots up, was paging through a picture book.

"She try to poke you?" Fry asked, not looking up.

Eustace sat behind his desk. "How'd you know?"

"They say she does that." He turned a page. "Think she killed him?"

"She mighta." Eustace gestured at the book. "What you got there?"

Fry held it up to show him. *Where the Wild Things Are.*

"That's a good one," Eustace said.

The door swung open and a man entered, banging dust from his hat. Eustace recognized him; he and his wife farmed a patch of ground on the other side of the river.

"Sheriff. Deputy." He nodded at each of them in turn.

"Help you, Bart?"

He cleared his throat nervously. "It's my wife. I can't find her anywhere."

It was nine A.M. By noon, Eustace had heard the same story fourteen times.

39

It was midafternoon by the time Caleb reached town on the buckboard. The place seemed totally dead—no people anywhere. In two hours on the road, he hadn't seen a single soul.

The door of the mercantile was locked. Caleb cupped his eyes to the glass. Nothing, no movement inside. He stilled his body, listening to the quiet. Where the hell was everybody? Why would George close up in the middle of the day? He walked around to the alley. The back door stood ajar. The frame was splintered; the door had been forced.

He returned to the buckboard for his rifle.

He nudged the door open with the tip of the barrel and moved inside. He was in the storeroom. The space was tightly packed—sacks of feed piled high, coils of fencing, spools of chain and rope—leaving only a narrow corridor through which to pass.

"George?" he called. "George, are you in here?"

He felt and heard crunching underfoot. One of the bags of feed had been torn open. As he knelt to look, he heard a high-pitched clicking above his head. He lurched back, swinging the barrel of the rifle upward.

It was a raccoon. The animal was sitting on top of the pile. It lifted onto its hind legs, rubbing its two front paws together, and gave him a look of absolute innocence. *That mess on the floor? Nothing to do with me, pal.*

"Go on, beat it." Caleb poked the barrel of the rifle forward. "Get your ass out of here before I make you into a hat."

The raccoon scampered down the pile and out the door. Caleb took a breath to calm his heart and passed through the beaded curtain into the store. The lockbox where George kept the day's receipts sat beneath the counter in its usual spot. He moved through the aisles, finding nothing amiss. A flight of stairs behind the counter led to the second floor—presumably, George's living quarters.

"George, if you're there, it's Caleb Jaxon. I'm coming up."

He found himself in a single large room with upholstered furniture and curtains on the windows. The homeyness of it surprised him—he had expected a scene of bachelor squalor. But George had been married once. The room was divided into two areas, one for living, the other for sleeping. A kitchen table; a couch and chairs with lace doilies on the headrests; a cast-iron bed with a sagging mattress; an ornately carved wardrobe of a type that usually stayed within a family, traveling the road of several generations. All seemed orderly enough, but as Caleb surveyed the space, he began to notice certain things. A dining chair had been knocked over; books and other objects—a kitchen pot, a ball of yarn, a lantern—were tossed about the floor; a large, free-standing mirror had shattered in its frame, the glass cracked in concentric circles, like a reflective spider's web.

As he moved toward the bed, the odor hit him: the rancid, biological reek of old vomitus. George's chamber pot sat on the floor near the headboard; that was where the smell was coming from. Blankets were bunched at the foot of the mattress as if kicked aside by a restless sleeper. On the bedside table lay George's gun, a long-barreled .357 revolver. Caleb opened the cylinder and pushed the ejection rod. Six cartridges fell into his palm; one had been fired. He turned around and swept the pistol over the room, then lowered the gun and stepped toward the fractured mirror. At the epicenter of the cracks was a single bullet hole.

Something had happened here. George had obviously been ill, but there was more to it. A robbery? But the lockbox hadn't been touched. And the bullet hole was strange. A stray shot, perhaps, though something about it seemed deliberate—as if, lying in bed, George had shot his own reflection.

In the alley, he filled his jugs from the tank and loaded them onto the buckboard. It wouldn't do to leave without paying; he made his best guess and left the bills under the counter with a note: "Nobody here, door unlocked. Took fifteen gallons of kerosene. If the money isn't enough, I'll be back in a week and can pay you then. Sincerely, Caleb Jaxon."

On the way out of town, he stopped at the town office to report what he'd found. At least someone should fix the door of the mercantile and lock the place up until they knew what had happened to George. But nobody was there, either.

Dusk was settling down when he returned to the house. He unloaded the kerosene, put the horses in the paddock, and entered the house. Pim was sitting with Kate by the cold woodstove, writing in her journal.

Did you get what you needed?

He nodded. Strange how Kate was now the silent one. The woman had barely glanced up from her knitting.

How was town?

Caleb hesitated, then signed: *Very quiet.*

They ate corn cakes for supper, played a few hands of go-to, and went to bed. Pim was out like a light, but Caleb slept badly; he barely slept at all. All night his mind seemed to skip over the surface of sleep like a stone upon water, never quite breaking the skin. As dawn approached, he gave up trying and crept from the house. The ground was moist with dew, the last stars receding into a slowly paling sky. Birds were singing everywhere, but this wouldn't last; to the south, where the weather came from, a wall of flickering clouds roiled at the horizon. So: a spring storm. Caleb guessed he had maybe twenty minutes before it arrived. He gave himself another minute to watch it, then retrieved the first jug of kerosene from the shed and lugged it to the edge of the woods.

He didn't know what he was seeing. It simply made no sense. Perhaps it was the light. But no.

The mounds were gone.

40

0600 hours: Michael Fisher, Boss of the Trade, stood on the quay to watch the morning light come on. A thick, cloudy dawn; the waters of the channel, caught between tides, were absolutely motionless. How long since he'd slept? He was not so much tired—he was well past that—as running on some reserve of energy that felt vaguely lethal, as if he were burning himself up. Once it was gone, that would be the end of him; he would vanish in a puff of smoke.

He'd emerged from the bowels of the *Bergensfjord* with some vague intention he couldn't recall; the moment he'd hit fresh air, the plan had fled from his mind. He'd drifted down to the edge of the wharf and found himself just standing there. Twenty-one years: amazing how so much time could slip by. Events grabbed hold of you and in the blink of an eye there you were, with sore knees and a sour stomach and a face in the mirror your barely recognized, wondering how all of it had happened. If that was really your life.

The *Bergensfjord* was nearly ready. Propulsion, hydraulics, navigation. Electronics, stabilizers, helm. The stores were loaded, the desalinators up and running. They'd stripped the ship to the simplest configuration; the *Bergensfjord* was basically a floating gas tank. But a lot had been left to chance. For instance: Would she actually float? Computations on paper were one thing; reality was another. And if she did, could her hull, cobbled together from a thousand different plates of salvaged steel, a million screws and rivets and patch welds, withstand a journey of such duration? Did they have enough fuel? What about the weather, especially when they attempted to round Cape Horn? Michael had read everything he could find about the waters he intended to cross. The news was not good. Legendary storms, crosscurrents of such violence that they could snap your rudder off, waves of towering dimensions that could downflood you in a second.

He sensed someone coming up behind him: Lore.

"Nice morning," she said.

"Looks like rain."

She shrugged, looking over the water. "Still nice, though."

She meant, How many more mornings will we have? How many dawns to watch? Let's enjoy it while we can.

"How are things in the pilothouse?" Michael asked.

She blew out a breath.

"Don't worry," he said. "You'll get it."

A bit of pink was in the clouds now. Gulls swooped low over the water. It really was a fine morning, Michael thought. He felt suddenly proud. Proud of his ship, his *Bergensfjord.* She had traveled halfway around the world to test his worthiness. She had given them a chance and said, *Take it if you can.*

A glow of light appeared on the causeway.

"There's Greer," he said. "I better go."

Michael made his way up the quay and met the first tanker truck just as Greer stepped down from the cab.

"That's the last of it," Greer said. "We tapped out at nineteen tankers, so we left the last one behind."

"Any problems?"

"A patrol eyeballed us south of the barracks at Rosenberg. I guess they just assumed we were on the way to Kerrville. I thought they'd be onto us by now, but apparently they're not."

Michael glanced over Greer's shoulder and signaled to Rand. "You got this one?"

Men were swarming over the tankers. Rand gave him a thumbs-up.

Michael looked at Greer again. The man was obviously worn out. His face had thinned to skull-like proportions: cheekbones ridged like knives, eyes red-rimmed and sunk into their pockets, skin waxy and damp. A frost of white stubble covered his cheeks and throat; his breath was sour.

"Let's get something to eat," Michael said.

"I could go for some shut-eye."

"Have breakfast with me first."

They'd erected a tent on the quay with a commissary and cots for resting. Michael and Greer filled their bowls with watery porridge and sat at a table. A few other men were hunched over their breakfasts, robotically shoveling the gruel into their mouths, faces slack with exhaustion. Nobody was talking.

"Everything else good to go?" Greer asked.

Michael shrugged. *More or less.*

"When do you want us to flood the dock?"

Michael took a spoon of the porridge. "She should be ready in a day or two. Lore wants to inspect the hull herself."

"Careful woman, our Lore."

Patch appeared on the far side of the tent. Eyes unfocused, he shambled across the space, lifted the lid on the pot, decided against it, and took one of the cots instead, not so much lying down as succumbing, like a man felled by a bullet.

"You should catch a few winks yourself," Greer said.

Michael gave a painful laugh. "Wouldn't that be nice?"

They finished breakfast and walked to the loading area, where Michael's pickup was parked. Two of the tankers were already drained and standing off to the side. An idea took shape in Michael's mind.

"Let's leave one tanker full and move it to the end of the causeway. Do we have any of those sulfur igniters left?"

"We should."

No further explanation was necessary. "I'll let you see to it."

Michael got in the pickup and placed his Beretta in the bracket under the steering wheel; a short-barreled shotgun with a pistol grip and a sidesaddle of extra shells was clamped between the seats. His rucksack rested on the passenger seat: more rounds, a change of clothes, matches, a first-aid kit, a pry bar, a bottle of ether and a rag, and a cardboard folder sealed with twine.

Michael started the engine. "You know, I've never been in jail before. What's it like?"

Greer grinned through the open window. "The food's better than it is here. The naps are sensational."

"So, something to look forward to."

Greer's expression sobered. "He can't know about her, Michael. Or about Carter."

"You're not making my job any easier, you know."

"It's how she wants it."

Michael regarded his friend for another few seconds. The man really did look terrible. "Go sleep," he said.

"I'll add it to my to-do list."

The two men shook. Michael put the truck in gear.

41

"Everybody, settle down!"

The auditorium was packed, all the seats taken, with more people crowded into the back and along the aisles. The room stank of fear and unwashed skin. At the front of the room, the mayor, red-faced and sweating, pointlessly banged his gavel on the podium, yelling for silence, while behind him, the members of the Freestate Council—as ineffective a group of individuals as Eustace had ever laid eyes on—found papers to shuffle and buttons to adjust, guiltily averting their gazes like a group of students caught cheating on a test.

"My wife's missing!"

"My husband! Has anybody seen him?"

"My kids! Two of them!"

"What happened to all the dogs? Did anybody else notice that? No dogs anywhere!"

More banging of the gavel. "Goddamnit, people, *please!*"

And so on. Eustace glanced at Fry, who was standing on the other side of the room and sending him a look that said, *Oh boy, ain't this going to be fun.*

Finally the room quieted enough for the mayor to be heard. "Okay, that's better. We know everybody's worried and wants answers. I'm going to bring up the sheriff, who can maybe shed some light. Gordon?"

Eustace took the podium and got to it. "Well, we don't know much more at this point than everybody else. About seventy folks have gone missing over the last couple of nights. Mind, these are the ones we know about. Deputy Fry and I haven't gotten out to all the farms yet."

"So why aren't you out looking for them?" a voice yelled.

Eustace parsed the man's face from the crowd. "Because I'm standing here talking to you, Gar. Now just button it so I can get through this."

A voice barked from the other side of the room: "Yeah, shut your mouth and let the man talk!"

More yelling, anxious voices volleying back and forth. Eustace let it run its course.

"Like I was saying," he continued, "we don't know where these folks have gone off to. What seemed to have happened is that, for whatever reason, these individuals got up in the middle of the night, went outside, and didn't come back."

"Maybe somebody's taking them!" Gar yelled. "Maybe that person is right here in this room!"

The effect was instantaneous; everybody started looking at everybody else. A low murmuring rippled through the room. *Could it be . . . ?*

"We're not ruling anything out at this point," Eustace said, aware of how weak this sounded, "but that doesn't seem so likely. We're talking about a lot of people."

"Maybe it's more than one person doing this!"

"Gar, you want to come up here and run this meeting?"

"I'm just saying—"

"What you're doing is scaring people. I'm not having you start a panic, people looking sideways at each other. For all we know, these folks have gone off on their own. Now, pipe down before I lock you up."

A woman in the front row rose to her feet. "Are you saying my boys ran away? They're six and seven!"

"No, I'm not saying that, Lena. We just don't have any more information than what I'm telling you. The best thing people can do is stay in their homes till we sort this out."

"And what about my wife?" Eustace couldn't see who was talking. "Are you saying she just up and left me?"

The mayor, stepping forward to retake the podium, held up both hands. "I think what the sheriff is trying to express—"

"He's not 'expressing' anything! You heard him! He doesn't know!"

Everybody started shouting again. There was no taking this thing back; it was spiraling out of control. Eustace glanced across the stage at Fry, who tipped his head toward the wings. As the mayor resumed banging his gavel, Eustace slipped backstage and met Fry at the door. The two men stepped outside.

"Well, that was sure productive," Fry said. "Glad to get out before the shooting started."

"I wouldn't joke about that. We're going to be on the top of everybody's list if we don't figure this thing out."

"Think they're still alive?"

"Not really."

"What do you want to do?"

The day was bright and warm, the sun midpoint in a cloudless sky. Eustace remembered a day like this one: spring on the cusp of summer, the earth un-clenching its fist, thick green leaves, rich with fragrance, fattening the trees. A walk by the river, Simon balanced on his shoulders, Nina beside him; the day like a marvelous gift, and then the moment, unmistakable, when the boy had had his fill; returning to the house and putting him down for his nap, Nina beckoning to him from the doorway with her special smile, the one only for him, and the two of them tiptoeing to their room to make quiet, lazy love on a sunny afternoon. Always the joke: *How can you kiss this damn ugly face of mine?* But she could; she did. The last such day; for Eustace, there would never come another.

"Let's find those missing people."

42

Apgar found Peter where he always was: at his desk, wading through a mass of paperwork. Just two days without Chase's organizing presence, and Peter felt completely swamped.

"Got a minute?"

"Make it fast."

Apgar took the chair across from him. "Chase really sandbagged you. You shouldn't have let him off the hook so easily."

"What can I say? I'm too nice."

Apgar cleared his throat. "We've got a problem."

He was filling out a form. "Are you quitting, too?"

"Probably not the moment for that. I got a message from Rosenberg this morning. A lot of tankers moving through there in the last few days, but none of it is showing up here."

Peter raised his head.

"You heard me."

"What does the refinery say?"

"Everything on schedule, blah blah blah. Then, as of this morning, not a peep, and we can't raise them."

Peter leaned back in his chair. *Good God.*

"I've got men on the way to the refinery to check it out," Apgar continued, "but I think I know what we'll find. You've got to hand it to the guy for balls, anyway."

"What the hell would Dunk need our oil for?"

"My bet is, he doesn't. It's a play. He wants something."

"Such as?"

"You've got me there. It isn't going to be small, though. Light and Power says we have enough gas on hand for ten days, a few more if we ration. Even if we can secure the refinery, no way we can get enough slick back into the system to keep the lights burning. In less than two weeks, this city goes dark."

Dunk had them in a vise. Peter had to admit, begrudgingly, that it was sort of brilliant. But one piece didn't fit.

"So he sends us a truck full of guns and ammo, then hijacks all our oil? It seems contradictory."

"Maybe the guns came from somebody else."

"That was bunker ammo. Only the trade has that stuff."

Apgar shifted in his chair. "Well, here's another piece to consider. First you've got Cousin's Place going up in smoke, then there's a rumor going around that one of Dunk's women showed up in the city saying that something happened out there. A lot of shooting."

"A power play by one of his guys, you mean."

"Could be just gossip. And I don't see how it fits, but it's something to consider."

"Where is she now?"

"The woman?" Apgar almost laughed. "Who the hell knows?"

The guns and the oil were connected, but how? It didn't feel like Dunk; holding a city hostage was out of his league, and the Army now had enough weaponry to take the isthmus and put him out of business. It would be a slaughter on both sides—the causeway was a kill box—but once the dust settled, Dunk Withers would find himself either lying dead in a ditch with fifty holes in him or swinging from a rope.

So suppose, Peter thought, the oil wasn't just a play. Suppose it was actually *for* something.

"What do we know about this boat of his?" he asked.

Apgar frowned. "Not a lot. Nobody from the outside has laid eyes on the damn thing in years."

"But it's big."

"So folks say. You think that's got something to do with it?"

"I don't know what to think. But there's something we're missing. Have we spread that ammo around?"

"Not yet. It's still in the armory."

"Get it done. And let's send a patrol to scout the isthmus. How long till we hear from Freeport?"

"A couple of hours."

It was a little after three P.M. "Let's get men on the perimeter. Tell them it's a training exercise. And get some engineers on the gate. The thing hasn't been closed in a decade."

Apgar gave him a look of caution. "Folks will notice that."

"Better safe than sorry. None of this makes sense to us, but it does to someone."

"What about the isthmus? We don't want to wait too long to get a plan in place."

"I won't. Write it up."

Apgar rose. "I'll get it on your desk within the hour."

"That quick?"

"There's only one way in. Not a lot to say." He turned at the door. "This is completely fucked, I know, but maybe it's the opportunity we've been waiting for."

"That's a way of looking at it."

"I'm just glad it isn't Chase sitting in that chair."

He left Peter alone. Just five minutes, and the piles of paper on his desk now seemed completely trivial. He swiveled his chair to face the window. The day had begun with clear skies, but now the weather was turning. Low clouds hovered over the city, a heavy gray mass. A gust of wind tossed the treetops, followed by a flash, whitening the sky. As thunder rolled behind it, the first drops of rain, heavy and slow, tapped the glass.

Michael, he thought, *what the hell are you up to?*

43

Anthony Carter, Twelfth of Twelve, had just shut off the mower when he looked toward the patio and noticed that the tea had arrived.

So soon? Could it be noon again already? He angled his chin to the sky—an oppressive summer Houston sky, pale like something bleached. He removed his hankie and then his hat to mop the sweat from his forehead. A glass of tea would surely hit the spot.

Mrs. Wood, she knew that. Though of course it wasn't Mrs. Wood who brought it. Carter couldn't say just who it was. The same someone who delivered the flats of flowers and bags of mulch to the gate, who fixed his tools when they broke, who made time turn how it did in this place, every day a season, every season a year.

He pushed his mower to the shed, wiped it clean, and made his way to the patio. Amy was working in the dirt on the far side of the lawn. There was some ginger there, it grew like crazy, always needing cutting back, bordered by the beds where Mrs. Wood liked to put some summer color. Today it was three flats of cosmos, the pink ones that Miss Haley loved, picking them and putting them in her hair.

"Tea's here," Carter said.

Amy looked up. She was wearing a kerchief around her neck; there was dirt on her hands and face where she'd wiped the sweat away.

"You go ahead." She batted a gnat from her face. "I want to get these in first."

Carter sat and sipped the tea. Perfect as always, sweet but not too sweet, and the ice made a pleasant tinkling against the sides of the glass. From behind him, in the house, came the bright drifting notes of the girls' playing. Sometimes it was Barbies or dress-ups. Sometimes they watched TV. Carter heard the same movies playing over and over—*Shrek* was one, and *The Princess Bride*—and he felt sorry for the two of them, Miss Haley and her sister, all alone and stuck inside the house, waiting for their mama to come home. But when Carter peeked in the windows, there was never anybody there; the inside and the outside were two different places, and the rooms were empty, not even any furniture to tell that people lived there.

He'd had some time to think on that. He'd thought about a lot of things. Such as, what this place exactly *was*. The best he could come up with was that it was a kind of waiting room, like at a doctor's office. You bided your time, maybe flipping through a magazine, and then when your turn came, a voice would call your name and you'd go on to the next place, whatever that was. Amy called the garden "the world behind the world," and that seemed right to Carter.

How the day got on, he thought. He'd have to get back to work soon; there was a sprinkler head needed replacing, and the pool to skim, and all that edging to do. He liked to keep the yard just so for the day when Mrs. Wood would return. *Mr. Carter, what a beautiful job you've done taking care of the place. You're a godsend. I don't know what I ever did without you.* He liked to think of the things they'd say to each other when that day came. The two of them would have a good talk, just like they used to, sitting on the patio the way any two friends would do.

But for the moment, Carter was content to settle in a spell while the edge came off the heat. He unlaced his boots and closed his eyes. The garden was a place for thinking your thoughts, and that was what he did now. He remembered Wolgast coming to him in Terrell, which was the death house, and then a ride in a van with deep cold and snowy mountains all around, and then the doctors giving him a shot. It made him sick something awful, but that wasn't the worst of it. The worst was the voices in his head. *I am Babcock. I am Morrison. I am Chávez Baffes Turrell Winston Sosa Echols Lambright Martinez Reinhardt . . .* He saw pictures too, horrible things, people dying and such, like he was dreaming someone else's dreams. He'd been to school for a bit, and they'd read a book by Mr. William Shakespeare. Carter hadn't actually read much of it himself. The words in the book were like something chopped up in a blender, that's how confusing it was. But the teacher, Mrs. Coe, a pretty white lady who decorated the walls of her classroom with posters of animals and mountain climbers and sayings like "Reach for the stars" and "Be a friend to make a friend," had showed the class a video. Carter liked it, how everybody was always getting in swordfights and dressed like a pirate, and Mrs. Coe explained that the main guy, who was named Hamlet, and was also a prince, was going crazy because somebody had killed his daddy by pouring poison in his ear. There was more to the story, but Carter remembered that part, because that's what the voices reminded him of. Like poison poured in his ear.

Things had gone on like that for a while, Carter wasn't sure how long. The others were whispering away, saying various things, ugly things, but mostly what they said was their names, over and over, like they couldn't get enough of themselves. Then they fell quiet like the air before a storm and that was when Carter heard him: Zero. "Heard" wasn't exactly the word. Zero could make you think with his own mind. Zero came into his head and it was like taking a step that wasn't there and tumbling down a lightless hole and at the bottom of the hole was a train station. Folks were hurrying in winter coats, and the voice over the loudspeaker was calling out the numbers of the tracks and what was going where. New Haven. Larchmont. Katonah. New Rochelle. Carter didn't know those places. It was cold. The floor was slick with melted snow. He was standing at the kiosk, the one with the four-faced clock. He was waiting for someone, someone important. One train arrived and then another. Where was she? Had something happened? Why hadn't she called, why did she fail to answer? Train after train, the anticipation intense, then, as the last passengers hurried by, the cruelest dashing of his hopes. His heart was shattering, yet he couldn't make himself move. The hands of the clock mocked him with their turning. *She said she would be here, where was she, how he longed to hold her in his arms, Liz you are the only thing that ever mattered, let me be the one to hold you as you slip away* . . .

After that, Carter had gone plain crazy. It was like one long bad dream in which he was watching himself do the worst kinds of things and couldn't stop. Eating folks. Tearing them to bits. Some he didn't kill but only tasted, no rhyme or reason to it, it was just a thing he did because that's what Zero wanted. He remembered a couple in a car. They were driving somewhere in a hurry and Carter had come down on them from the trees. *Leave those people be,* he was telling himself, *what they ever done to you,* but the hungry part of him paid this no mind, it did what it liked, and what it liked was killing folks. He landed hard on the hood and gave them a good long look at him, his teeth and claws and what he was about to do. The two of them were young. There was the man at the wheel and the woman beside him who Carter guessed was his wife. She had short blond hair and eyes that were wide and staring. The car began to fishtail. They were sliding all over the place. The man was yelling *Holy shit!* and *What the fuck!* but the woman barely reacted. Her eyes slid right through Carter, her face as blank as paper, like the sight of a monster on the hood was nothing her brain knew what to do with, and it stopped Carter flat, that's how weird it was, and that was when he noticed the gun—a big shiny pistol with a barrel you could fit your finger in, which the man was trying to aim over the steering wheel. *Now, don't be pointing that,* the one part of him, the still-Carter part, was thinking; *you don't ever point a gun at no one, Anthony;* and maybe it was the memory of his mama's voice or else the way the car was swerving in long looping arcs like a kid on a swing pumping higher and higher and faster and faster, but for a second Carter froze, and as the car began to roll the gun went off in a blast of noise and light and Carter felt a sharp little sting in his shoulder, not much more than a bee might do, and the next thing Carter knew, he was rolling on the pavement.

He came up in time to see the car banging down on its side. It spun in a 360 and crashed down onto its roof with an explosion of glass and a shriek of tearing metal. It began to roll down the asphalt like a log, over and over, bright bits of things hurling away, until it flopped one last time onto its roof and came, at last, to rest.

Everything was very still; they were deep in the country, miles from any town. Debris littered the roadway in a wide, glittering plume. He smelled gasoline, and something hot and sharp, like melted plastic. He knew he should feel something but didn't know what. His thoughts were all mixed up inside him like single frames from a movie he couldn't put in order. He scuttled his way to the car and crouched to look. The two of them were hanging upside down from their seatbelts, the dashboard crunched up against their waists. The man was dead, on account of the big piece of metal in his head, but the woman was alive. She was staring forward, wide-eyed, blood all over her—her face and shirt, her hands and hair, her lips and tongue and teeth. Black smoke was coiling from under the dash. A piece of glass crunched under Carter's foot and her face swiveled toward him, slowly, no other part of her moving, tracing the source of the sound.

"Is somebody there?" Bubbles of blood formed at her lips as they curved around the words. "Please. Is . . . any . . . body . . . there?"

She was looking right at him. That was when Carter realized she couldn't see. The woman was blind. With a soft *whump* the first flames appeared, licking under the dash.

"Oh, God," she moaned. "I can hear you breathing. For the love of God, please answer me."

Something was happening to him, something strange. Like the woman's sightless eyes were a mirror, and what he saw in them was himself—not the monster they'd made him into but the man he used to be. As if he were waking up and remembering who he was. He tried to answer. *I'm here,* he wanted to say. *You're not alone. I'm sorry about what I done.* But his mouth would not make words. The flames were spreading, the cabin filling with smoke.

"Oh God, I'm burning, please, oh God, oh God . . ."

The woman was reaching for him. Not *for* him, he realized. *To* him. Something was clutched in her hand. A hard spasm shook her; she had begun to choke on the blood that was pouring from her mouth. Her fingers opened and the object fell to the ground.

It was a pacifier.

The baby was in the backseat, still strapped in its carrier upside down. Any second the car was going to blow. Carter dropped to the ground and slithered through the back window. The baby was awake and crying now. The carrier would never fit—he'd have to take the baby out of it. He released the buckle, guided the child's shoulders through the straps, and just like that the soft crying weight of a baby filled his arms. A little girl, wearing pink pajamas. Holding her tight to his chest, Carter wriggled free of the car and began to run.

But that was all he remembered. The story ended there. He never did know what became of that baby girl. For Anthony Carter, Twelfth of Twelve, made it all of three steps before the flames found what they were looking for, the gas in the tank ignited, and that car was blown to smithereens.

He never took another one.

Oh, he ate. Rats, possums, raccoons. Now and again a dog, which he always felt sorry about. But it wasn't long before the world went quiet, and there weren't so many people around to tempt him, and then one day after more time had passed, he realized there weren't any people at all.

He'd closed himself to Zero, too—closed it to all of them. Carter wanted no part in what they were about. He built a wall in his mind, Zero and the others on one side and him on the other; and though the wall was thin and Carter could hear them if he chose to, he never sent anything back.

It was a lonely time.

He watched his city drown. He'd made a place for himself in that building, One Allen Center, on account of it was high and at night he could stand on the rooftop, among the stars, and feel close to them for company. Year by year the waters rose around the bases of the buildings, and then one night a great wind came barreling down. Carter had been through a hurricane or two in his day, but this wasn't like any storm he'd ever seen. It set the skyscraper swaying like a drunk. Walls were cracking, windows popping from their frames, everything was in an uproar. He wondered if the end of the world was coming, if God had just grown sick and tired of it all. As the waters rose and the building rocked and the heavens howled, he took to praying, telling God to take him if that's what he wanted, saying he was sorry over and over about the things he'd done, and if there was a better place to go to, he knew he didn't deserve it any but hoped he'd get a chance to see it, assuming God could forgive him, which Carter didn't think he could.

Then he heard a sound. A terrifying, heart-rending, inhuman sound, as if the gates of hell had opened and released a million screaming souls into the whirlwind. From out of the blackness a great dark shape emerged. It grew and grew and then the lightning flashed and Carter saw what it was, though he could not believe it. A ship. In downtown Houston. She was headed straight for him, her great keel dragging along the street, bearing down upon the towers of the Allen Center like God's own bowling ball and the buildings were the pins.

Carter dropped to the floor and covered his head, bracing for the impact.

Nothing happened. Suddenly, everything went quiet; even the wind had stopped. He wondered how this could be so, the sky so furious one minute and still the next. He rose and peered out the window. Above him, the clouds had opened like a porthole. The eye, Carter thought, that's what this was; he was in the eye of the storm. He looked down. The ship had come to rest against the side of the tower, parked like a cab at the curb.

He climbed down the face of the building. How much time he had before the storm returned, Carter couldn't say. All he knew was that the ship being there felt like a message. At length he found himself in the bowels of the vessel, its maze of passages and pipes. Yet he did not feel lost; it was as if an unseen influence was guiding his every action. Oily seawater sloshed around his feet. He chose a direction, then another, drawn by this mysterious presence. A door appeared at the end of the corridor—heavy steel, like the door of a bank vault. T1, it was marked: Tank No. 1.

The water will protect you, Anthony.

He started. Who was speaking to him? The voice seemed to come from everywhere: from the air he breathed, the water sloshing at his feet, the metal of the ship. It enfolded him like a blanket of perfect softness.

He cannot find you here. Abide here in safety, and she will come to you.

That was when he felt her: Amy. Not dark, like the others; her soul was made of light. A great sob racked his body. His loneliness was leaving him. It lifted from his spirit like a veil, and what lay behind it was a sorrow of a different kind—a beautiful, holy kind of sorrow for the world and all its woes. He was holding the wheel. Slowly it turned under his hands. Outside, beyond the walls of the ship, the wind was howling again. The rain lashed, the sky rolled, the seas tore through the streets of the drowned city.

Come inside, Anthony.

The door opened; Carter stepped through. His body was in the ship, the *Chevron Mariner,* but Carter was in that place no more. He was falling and falling and falling, and when the falling stopped he knew just where he was, even before he opened his eyes, because he could smell the flowers.

Carter realized he'd finished his tea. Amy was done with the cosmos and was tidying up the beds. Carter thought to tell her to rest a spell, he'd get to the weeds directly, but he knew that she'd refuse; when there was work to do, she did it.

The waiting was hard for her. Not just because of the things she'd have to face, but for what she'd given up. She never said a word about it, that wasn't Amy's way, but Carter could tell. He knew what it was like to love a person and lose them in this life.

Because Zero would come calling. That was a fact. Carter knew that man, knew he wouldn't rest until the whole world was a mirror to his grief. Thing was, Carter couldn't help but feel a little sorry for him. Carter had been in that station himself. Weren't the question the man had wrong, it was his way of asking it.

Carter got up from his chair, put on his hat, and went to where Amy was kneeling in the dirt.

"Have a good nap?" she asked, looking up.

"Was I sleeping?"

She tossed a weed onto the pile. "You should have heard yourself snoring."

Now, that was news to Carter. Although, come to think of it, he might have rested his eyes there for a second.

Amy rocked back on her heels and held her arms wide over the newly planted beds. "What do you think?"

He stepped back to look. Everything was neat as a pin. "Those cosmos is pretty. Mrs. Wood will like 'em. Miss Haley, too."

"They'll need water."

"I'll see to it. You should get out of the sun for a bit. Tea's still there you want it."

He was hooking the hose to the spigot near the gate when he heard the soft pressure of tires on asphalt and saw the Denali coming down the street. It halted at the corner, then crept forward. Carter could just make out the shape of Mrs. Wood's face through the darkly tinted windows. The car cruised slowly by the house, barely moving but never stopping either, the way a ghost might do, then accelerated and sped away.

Amy appeared beside him. "I heard the girls playing earlier." She, too, was looking down the street, though the Denali was long gone. "I brought you this."

Amy was holding a wand. For a second Carter was unable to connect the idea of it to anything else. But it was for the cosmos, of course.

"Are you okay?" she asked.

Carter responded with a shrug. He threaded the wand to the end of the hose and opened the spigot. Amy returned to the patio while Carter dragged the hose to the beds and began to water them down. It hardly mattered, he knew; autumn would be here soon. The leaves would pale and fall, the garden fade, the wind grow raw. Frost would wick the tips of the grass, and the body of Mrs. Wood would rise. All things found their ends. But still Carter went on with it, passing his wand over the flowers, back and forth, back and forth, his heart always believing that even the smallest things could make a difference.

44

All day long the rain poured down. Everyone was antsy, trapped in the house. Caleb could tell that Pim's patience with her sister was wearing thin, and he felt a row coming. A few days ago, he might have welcomed such a development, if only to get it over with.

Dusk was near when the clouds broke. A radiant sun streamed low across the fields, everything sopping and glinting in the light. Caleb scanned the ground around the house for ants; finding none, he declared that they could go out to enjoy the last of the day. All that remained of the mounds were ovals of depressed mud barely distinguishable from the surrounding earth. Relax, he told himself. You're letting the isolation get to you, that's all.

Kate and Pim supervised the children making mud pies while Caleb went to check on the horses. He'd built an open-sided shelter on the far side of the paddock to give them cover from the weather, and that was where he found them now. Handsome seemed none the worse for wear, but Jeb was breathing hard and showing the whites of his eyes. He was also holding his left rear hoof off the ground. The horse let him bend the joint long enough for Caleb to see a small puncture wound in the raised central structure of the hoof. Something long and sharp was stuck in there. He walked to the shed and returned with a halter, needle-nosed pliers, and a rope. He was fixing Jeb's halter when he saw Kate coming his way.

"He doesn't look so happy."

"Got a pricker in his hoof."

"Could you use an extra set of hands?"

He was fine on his own, but the woman's sudden interest in helping out wasn't anything he was going to say no to. "The ropes should hold him. Just keep a hand on his halter."

Kate gripped the leather near the horse's mouth. "He looks sick. Should he be breathing like that?"

Caleb was crouched at the rear of the animal. "You're the doctor—you tell me."

He lifted the horse's foot. With his other hand, he angled the pliers to the wound. There wasn't much to grab hold of. As the tips made contact, the animal shoved his weight backward, whinnying and tossing his head.

"Keep him still, damn it!"

"I'm trying!"

"He's a horse, Kate. Show him who's boss."

"What do you want me to do, slug him?"

Jeb was having none of it. Caleb left the shelter and returned with a length of three-quarter-inch chain, which he ran through the halter, up and over the horse's nose. He tightened the chain against Jeb's jaw and gave the ends to Kate.

"Hold this," he said. "And don't be nice."

Jeb didn't like it, but the chain worked. Caught in the tips of the pliers, the offending article slowly emerged. Caleb held it up in the light. About two inches long, it was made of a rigid, nearly translucent material, like the bone of a bird.

"Some kind of thorn, I guess," he said.

The horse had relaxed somewhat but was still breathing rapidly. Flecks of spittle hung from the corners of his mouth; his neck and flanks were glossed with sweat. Caleb washed the hoof with water from a bucket and poured iodine into the wound. Handsome was lingering near the shelter, watching them cautiously. While Kate held the halter, Caleb sheathed the hoof in a leather sock and secured it with twine. There wasn't much else he could do at this point. He'd leave the animal tied up for the night and see how he was in the morning.

"Thanks for your help."

The two of them were standing at the door of the shed; the light was just about gone.

"Look," Kate said finally, "I know I haven't been especially good company these days."

"It's fine, forget it. Everybody understands."

"You don't need to be nice about it, Caleb. We've known each other too long."

Caleb said nothing.

"Bill was an asshole. Okay, I get that."

"Kate, we don't have to do this."

She didn't seem angry, merely resigned. "I'm just saying I know what everybody thinks. And they're not wrong. People don't even know the half of it, actually."

"So why did you marry him?" Caleb was surprised at himself; the question had just popped out. "Sorry, that was a little direct."

"No, it's a fair question. Believe me, I've asked it myself." A moment passed; then she brightened a little. "Did you know that when Pim and I were kids we used to have fights over who would get to marry you? I'm talking physical fights—slapping, hair pulling, the whole thing."

"You're kidding."

"Don't look so happy, I'm surprised one of us didn't end up in the hospital. One time, I stole her diary? I think I was thirteen. God, I was such a little shit. There was all this stuff in there about you. How *good-looking* you were, how *smart* you were. Both your names with a big fat heart drawn around them. It was just disgusting."

Caleb found the thought hilarious. "What happened?"

"What do you think? She was older, the fights weren't exactly fair." Kate shook her head and laughed. "Look at you. You love this."

It was true, he did. "It's a funny story. I never knew about any of it."

"And don't flatter yourself, bub—I'm not about to throw myself at your feet."

He smiled. "That's a relief."

"Plus, it would seem a little incestuous." She shuddered. "Seriously, gross."

Night had fallen over the fields. Caleb realized what he'd been missing: the feeling of Kate's friendship. As kids, they'd been as close as any two siblings. But then life had happened—the Army, Kate's medical training, Bill and Pim, Theo and the girls and all their plans—and they'd mislaid each other in the shuffle. Years had passed since they'd really spoken, the way they were doing now.

"But I didn't answer your question, did I? Why I married Bill. The answer is pretty simple. I married him because I loved him. I can't think of a single good reason *why* I did, but a person doesn't get to pick. He was a sweet, happy, worthless man, and he was mine." She stopped, then said, "I didn't come out here to help you with the horses, you know."

"You didn't?"

"I came to ask you what's making you so nervous. I don't think Pim has noticed, but she's going to."

Caleb felt caught. "It's probably nothing."

"I know you, Caleb. It's not nothing. And I have my girls to think about. Are we in trouble?"

He didn't want to answer, but Kate had him dead to rights.

"I'm not sure. We might be."

A loud whinny in the paddock broke his thoughts. They heard a crash, then a series of hard, rhythmic bangs.

"What the hell is *that*?" Kate said.

Caleb grabbed a lantern from the shed and raced across the paddock. Jeb lay on his side, his head tossing violently. His hind hooves were knocking against the wall of the shelter in spasmodic jerks.

"What's wrong with him?" Kate said.

The animal was dying. His bowels released, then his bladder. A trio of convulsions barreled through his body, followed by a final, violent tremor, every part of him stiffening. He held this position for several seconds, as if stretched on wires. Then the air went out of him and he was still.

Caleb crouched beside the carcass, lifting the lantern over the animal's face. A bubbly froth, tinged with blood, was running from his mouth. One dark eye stared upward, shining with reflected light.

"Caleb, why are you holding a gun?"

He looked down; so he was. It was George's revolver, the big .357, which he'd hidden in the shed. He must have grabbed it when he'd retrieved the lantern—an action so automatic as to escape his conscious awareness. He'd cocked the hammer, too.

"You need to tell me what's going on," Kate said.

Caleb released the hammer and swiveled on his heels toward the house. The windows shimmered with candlelight. Pim would be making supper, the girls playing on the floor or looking at books, Baby Theo fussing in his high chair. Maybe not; maybe the boy was already asleep. He sometimes did that, passing out cold at dinnertime only to awaken hours later, howling with hunger.

"Answer me, Caleb."

He rose, slipped the pistol into the waistband of his trousers, and drew his shirt over the butt to conceal it. Handsome was standing at the edge of the light, his head bent low like a mourner's. The poor guy, Caleb thought. It was as if he knew that the job would fall to him to drag the carcass of his only friend across the field to a patch of useless ground where, come morning, Caleb would use the rest of his fuel to burn it.

45

By late afternoon, Eustace and Fry had canvassed most of the outermost farms. Overturned furniture, beds disturbed, pistols and rifles lying where they'd fallen, a round or two fired, if that.

And not a living soul.

It was after six o'clock when they finished checking the last one, a dump of a place four miles downriver, near the old ADM ethanol plant. The house was tiny, just one room, the structure hammered together from scrap lumber and decaying asphalt shingles. Eustace didn't know who'd lived out here. He guessed he never would.

Eustace's bad leg was aching hard; they'd have just enough time to make it back to town before dark. They mounted their horses and turned north, but a hundred yards later Eustace held up.

"Let's have a peek at that factory."

Fry was leaning over the pommel. "We ain't got but two hands of light, Gordo."

"You want to go back without something to show for it? You heard those folks."

Fry thought for a moment. "Let's be quick on it."

They rode into the compound. The plant comprised three long, two-story buildings arranged in a U, with a fourth, much larger than the others, closing the square—a windowless concrete bulk connected to the grain bins by a maze of pipes and chutes. The skeletal husks of rusted vehicles and other machinery filled the spaces between the weeds. The air had stilled and cooled; birds were flitting through the glassless windows of the buildings. The three small structures were just shells, their roofs long collapsed, but the fourth was mostly tight. This was the one Eustace was interested in. If you were going to hide a couple hundred people, that would be a place to do it.

"You got a windup in your saddlebag, don'tcha?" Eustace asked.

Fry retrieved the lantern. Eustace turned the crank until the bulb began to glow.

"Thing won't last more than about three minutes," Fry warned. "You think they're in there?"

Eustace was checking his gun. He closed the cylinder and reholstered the weapon but left the strap off. Fry did the same.

"Guess we're going to find out."

One of the loading dock doors stood partially open; they dropped and rolled through. The smell hit them like a slap.

"I guess that answers that," Eustace said.

"Fuck *me,* that's nasty." Fry was pinching his nose. "Do we really need to look?"

"Get ahold of yourself."

"Seriously, I think I'm gonna puke."

Eustace gave the lantern a few more cranks. A hallway lined with lockers ran to the main work space of the building. The smell grew more intense with every step. Eustace had seen some bad things in his day, but he was pretty sure this was going to be the worst. They came to the end of the hallway, and a pair of swinging doors.

"I'm thinking this might be the time to ask about a raise," Fry whispered.

Eustace drew his pistol. "Ready?"

"Are you fucking kidding me?"

They pushed through. Several things hit Eustace's senses in close order. The first thing was the stench—a miasma of rot so gaggingly awful that Eustace would have lost his lunch on the spot if he'd actually bothered to eat. To this was added a sound, a dense vibrato that stroked the air like the humming of an engine. In the center of the room was a large, dark mass. Its edges appeared to be moving. As Eustace stepped forward, flies exploded from the corpses.

They were dogs.

As he raised his pistol he heard Fry yell, but that was as far as he got before a heavy weight crashed into him from above and knocked him to the floor. All those people gone; he should have seen this coming. He tried to crawl away, but something awful was occurring inside him. A kind of . . . swirling. So this was how it was going to be. He reached for his gun to shoot himself but his holster was empty of course, and then his hands went numb and watery, followed by the rest of him. Eustace was plunging. The swirling was a whirlpool in his head and he was being sucked down into it, down and down and down. *Nina, Simon. My beloveds, I promise I will never forget you.*

But that was exactly what happened.

V

THE MANIFEST

We must take the current when it serves,
Or lose our ventures.

—Shakespeare, *Julius Caesar*

46

It was nearly nine o'clock when Sister Peg walked Sara out.

"Thank you for coming," the old woman said. "It always means so much."

A hundred and sixteen children, from the tiniest babies to young adolescents; it had taken Sara two full days to examine them all. The orphanage was a duty she could have let go of long ago. Certainly Sister Peg would have understood. Yet Sara had never been able to bring herself to do this. When a child got sick in the night, or was down with a fever, or had leapt from a swing and landed wrong, it was Sara who answered the call. Sister Peg always greeted her with a smile that said she hadn't doubted for a second who would be gracing her door. *How would the world get on without us?*

Sara figured that Sister Peg had to be eighty by now. How the old woman continued to manage the place, its barely contained chaos, was a miracle. She had softened somewhat with the years. She spoke sentimentally of the children, both those in her care and the ones who had moved on; she kept track of their lives, how they made their ways in the world, and whom they married and their children if they had them, the way any mother would do. Though Sara knew the woman would never say as much, they were her family, no less than Hollis and Kate and Pim were Sara's; they belonged to Sister Peg, and she to them.

"It's no trouble, Sister. I'm glad to do it."

"What do you hear from Kate?"

Sister Peg was one of the few people who knew the story.

"Nothing so far, but I didn't expect to. The mail is so slow."

"That was a hard thing, with Bill. But Kate will know what to do."

"She always seems to."

"Would it be all right if I worried about you?"

"I'll be fine, really."

"I know you will. But I'm going to worry anyway."

They said their goodbyes. Sara made her way home through darkened streets; no lights burned anywhere. It had something to do with the supply of fuel for the generators—a minor hiccup at the refinery, that was the official word.

She found Hollis dozing in his reading chair, a kerosene lantern burning on the table and a book of intimidating thickness resting on his belly. The house, where they had lived for the past ten years, had been abandoned in the first wave of settlement—a small wooden bungalow, practically falling down. Hollis had spent two years restoring it, in his off hours from the library, which he was now in charge of. Who would have thought it, this bear of a man passing his days pushing a cart through the dusty shelves and reading to children? Yet that was what he loved.

She hung her jacket in the closet and went to the kitchen to warm some water for tea. The stove was still hot—Hollis always left it that way for her. She waited for the kettle to boil, then poured the water through the strainer filled with herbs she'd taken from the canisters that stood in a neat line on the shelf above the sink, each one marked in Hollis's hand: "lemon balm," "spearmint," "rosehips," and so on. It was a librarian's habit, Hollis said, to fetishize the smallest details. Left to herself, Sara would have had to spend thirty minutes looking for everything.

Hollis stirred as she entered the living room. He rubbed his eyes and smiled groggily. "What time is it?"

Sara was sitting at the table. "I don't know. Ten?"

"Guess I fell asleep there."

"The water's hot. I can make you some tea." They always drank tea together at the end of the day.

"No, I'll get it."

He lumbered into the kitchen and returned with a steaming mug, which he placed on the table. Rather than sit, he moved behind her, took her shoulders in his hands, and began, with gathering pressure, to work his thumbs into the muscles. Sara let her head slump forward.

"Oh, that's good," she moaned.

He kneaded her neck for another minute, then cupped her shoulders and moved them in a circular motion, unleashing a series of pops and cracks.

"Ouch."

"Just relax," Hollis said. "God, you're tight."

"You would be too, if you just gave physicals to a hundred kids."

"So tell me. How is the old witch?"

"Hollis, don't be nasty. The woman's a saint. I hope I've got half her energy at her age. Oh, right there."

He continued his pleasurable business; bit by bit, the tensions of the day drained away.

"I can do you next if you want," Sara said.

"Now you're talking."

She felt suddenly guilty. She tipped her face backward to look at him. "I have been ignoring you a little, haven't I?"

"Comes with the territory."

"Getting old, you mean."

"You look pretty good to me."

"Hollis, we're *grandparents*. My hair's practically white; my hands look like beef jerky. I won't lie—it depresses me."

"You talk too much. Lean forward again."

She dropped her head to the table and nestled it into her arms. "Sara and Hollis," she sighed, "that old married couple. Who knew we'd be those people someday?"

They drank their tea, undressed, and got into bed. Usually there were noises at night—people talking in the street, a barking dog, the various small sounds of life—but with the power out, everything was very quiet. It was true: it had been a while. A month, or was it two? But the old rhythm, the muscle memory of marriage, was still there, waiting.

"I've been thinking," Sara said after.

Hollis was nestled behind her, wrapping her in his arms. Two spoons in a drawer, they called it. "I thought you might be."

"I miss them. I'm sorry. It's just not the same. I thought I'd be okay with it, but I'm just not."

"I miss them, too."

She rolled to face him. "Would you really mind so much? Be honest."

"That depends. Do you think they need a librarian in the townships?"

"We can find out. But they need doctors, and I need you."

"What about the hospital?"

"Let Jenny run it. She's ready."

"Sara, you do nothing but *complain* about Jenny."

Sara was taken aback. "I do?"

"Nonstop."

She wondered if this was true. "Well, *somebody* can take over. We can just go for a visit to start, to see how it feels. Get the lay of the land."

"They may not actually want us out there, you know," Hollis said.

"Maybe not. But if it seems right, and everyone's agreed, we can put in for a homestead. Or build something in town. I could open an office there. Hell, you've got enough books right here to start a library of your own."

Hollis frowned dubiously. "All of us crammed into that tiny house."

"So we'll sleep outside. I don't care. They're our *kids.*"

He took a long breath. Sara knew what Hollis was going to say; it was just a matter of hearing him say it.

"So when do you want to leave?"

"That's the thing," she said, and kissed him. "I was thinking tomorrow."

* * *

Lucius Greer was standing under the spotlights at the base of the drydock, watching a distant figure swinging over the side of the ship in a bosun's chair.

"For godsakes," Lore yelled. "Who did this fucking weld?"

Greer sighed. In six hours, Lore had seen very little that she actually approved of. She lowered the chair to the dock and stepped free.

"I need half a dozen guys down here now. Not the same jokers who did these welds, either." She angled her face upward. "Weir! Are you up there?"

The man's face appeared at the rail.

"String up three more chairs. And go get Rand. I want these seams redone by sunrise." Lore looked at Greer from the corner of her eye. "Don't say it. I ran that refinery for fifteen years. I know what I'm doing."

"You won't hear any complaints from me. That's why Michael wanted you here."

"Because I'm a hard-ass."

"Your words, not mine."

She stood back, hands resting on her hips, eyes distractedly scanning the hull. "So tell me something," she said.

"All right."

"Did you ever think it was all bullshit?"

He liked Lore, her directness. "Never."

"Not once?"

"I wouldn't say the thought never crossed my mind. Doubt is human nature. It's what we do with it that matters. I'm an old man. I don't have time to second-guess things."

"That's an interesting philosophy."

A pair of ropes drifted down the flank of the *Bergensfjord,* then two more.

"You know," Lore said, "all these years, I wondered if Michael would ever find the right woman and settle down. Never in my wildest dreams did I imagine my competition was twenty thousand tons of steel."

Rand appeared at the gunwale. He and Weir began to hitch up the bosun's chairs.

"Do you still need me here?" Greer asked.

"No, go sleep." She waved up at Rand. "Hang on, I'm coming up!"

Greer left the dock, got in his truck, and drove down the causeway. The pain had gotten bad; he wouldn't be able to hide it much longer. Sometimes it was cold, like being stabbed by a sword of ice; other times it was hot, like glowing embers tossing around inside him. He could hardly keep anything down; when he actually managed to take a piss, it looked like an arterial bleed. There was always a bad taste in his mouth, sour and ureic. He'd told himself a lot of stories over the last few months, but there was really only one ending he could see.

Near the end of the causeway the road narrowed, hemmed in on either side by the sea. A dozen men armed with rifles were stationed at this bottleneck. As Greer drew alongside, Patch stepped from the cab of the tanker and came over.

"Anything going on out there?" Greer asked.

The man was sucking at something in his teeth. "Looks like the Army sent a patrol. We saw lights to the west just after sundown, but nothing since."

"You want more men out here?"

Patch shrugged. "I think we're okay for tonight. They're just sniffing us out at this point." He focused on Greer's face. "You okay? You don't look too good."

"Just need to get off my feet."

"Well, the cab of the tanker is yours if you want it. Catch a few winks. Like I said, there's nothing going on out here."

"I've got some other things to see to. Maybe I'll come back later."

"We'll be here."

Greer turned the truck around and drove away. Once he was out of sight, he pulled to the side of the causeway, got out, placed a hand against the fender for balance, and threw up onto the gravel. There wasn't much to come up, just water and some yolky-looking blobs. For a couple of minutes he remained in that position; when he decided there was nothing more, he retrieved his canteen from the cab, rinsed his mouth, poured some water into his palm, and splashed his face. The aloneness of it—that was the worst part. Not so much the pain as carrying the pain. He wondered what would happen. Would the world dissolve around him, receding like a dream, until he had no memory of it, or would it be the opposite—all the things and people of his life rising up before him in vivid benediction until, like a man gazing into the sun on a too-bright day, he was forced to look away?

He tipped his face to the sky. The stars were subdued, veiled by a moist sea air that made them seem to waver. He brought his thoughts to bear upon a single star, as he had learned to do, and closed his eyes. *Amy, can you hear me?*

Silence. Then: *Yes, Lucius.*

Amy, I'm sorry. But I think that I am dying.

47

A spring afternoon: Peter was working in the garden. Rain had worked through in the night, but now the sky was clear. Stripped to his shirtsleeves, he jabbed his hoe into the soft dirt. Months of eating from the canning jars while they watched the snow fall; how good it would be, he thought, to have fresh vegetables again.

"I brought you something."

Amy had snuck up behind him. Smiling, she held out a glass of water. Peter took it and sipped. It was ice cold against his teeth.

"Why don't you come inside? It's getting late."

So it was. The house lay long in shadow, the last rays of light peeking over the ridge.

"There's a lot to be done," he said.

"There always is. You can get back to work tomorrow."

They ate their supper on the sofa, the old dog nosing around their feet. While Amy washed up, Peter set a fire. The wood caught with crackling quickness. The rich contentment of a certain hour: beneath a heavy blanket, they watched the flames leap up.

"Would you like me to read to you?"

Peter said he thought that would be nice. Amy left him briefly and returned with a thick, brittle volume. Settling back on the sofa, she opened the book, cleared her throat, and began.

"*David Copperfield,* by Charles Dickens. Chapter One. I Am Born."

> Whether I shall turn out to be the hero of my own life, or whether
> that station will be held by anybody else, these pages must show.
> To begin my life with the beginning of my life, I record that I was
> born (as I have been informed and believe) on a Friday, at twelve
> o'clock at night. It was remarked that the clock began to strike,
> and I began to cry, simultaneously.

How wonderful, to be read to. To be carried from this world and into another, borne away on words. And Amy's voice, as she told the story: that was the loveliest part. It flowed through him like a benign electric current. He could have listened to her forever, their bodies close together, his mind in two places simultaneously, both within the world of the story, with its wonderful rain of sensations, and here, with Amy, in the house in which they lived and always had, as if sleep and wakefulness were not adjacent states with firm boundaries but part of a continuum.

At length he realized that the story had stopped. Had he dozed off? Nor was he on the sofa any longer; in some manner, unaware, he had made his way upstairs. The room was dark, the air cold above his face. Amy was sleeping beside him. What was the hour? And what was this feeling he had—the sense that something was not right? He drew the blankets aside and went to the window. A lazy half-moon had risen, partially lighting the landscape. Was that movement, there, at the edge of the garden?

It was a man. He was dressed in a dark suit; gazing upward at the window, he stood with his hands behind his back, in a posture of patient observation. Moonlight slanted across him, sharpening the angles of his face. Peter experienced not alarm but a feeling of recognition, as if he had been waiting for this nighttime visitor. Perhaps a minute passed, Peter watching the man in the yard, the man in the yard watching him. Then, with a courteous tip of his chin, the stranger turned away and walked off into the darkness.

"Peter, what is it?"

He turned from the window. Amy was sitting up in bed.

"There was somebody out there," he said.

"Somebody? Who?"

"Just a man. He was looking at the house. But he's gone now."

Amy said nothing for a moment. Then: "That would be Fanning. I was wondering when he'd show up."

The name meant nothing to Peter. Did he know a Fanning?

"It's all right." She drew the blanket aside for him. "Come back to bed."

He climbed under the covers; at once, the memory of the man receded into unimportance. The warm pressure of the blankets, and Amy beside him; these were all he needed.

"What do you think he wanted?" Peter asked.

"What does Fanning ever want?" Amy sighed wearily, almost with boredom. "He wants to kill us."

Peter awoke with a start. He'd heard something. He drew a breath and held it. The sound came again: the creak of a floorboard underfoot.

He rolled, reached his right hand to the floor, and took the weight of the pistol in his grip. The creak had come from the front hallway; it sounded like one person; they were trying to keep quiet; they didn't know he was awake; surprise was therefore on his side. He rose and crossed the room to the front window; his security detail, two soldiers stationed on the porch, were gone.

He thumbed off the safety. The bedroom door was closed; the hinges, he knew, were loud. The moment the door opened, the intruder would be alerted to his presence.

He pulled the door open and moved at a quickstep down the hall. The kitchen was empty. Without missing a stride, he turned the corner into the living room, extending the pistol.

A man was seated in the old wooden rocker by the fireplace. His face was turned partially away, his eyes focused on the last embers glowing in the grate. He appeared to take no notice of Peter at all.

Peter stepped behind him, leveling the gun. Not a tall man but solidly built, his broad shoulders filling the chair. "Show me your hands."

"Good. You're awake." The man's voice was calm, almost casual.

"Your hands, damnit."

"All right, all right." He held his hands away from his body, fingers spread.

"Get up. Slowly."

He lifted himself from his chair. Peter tightened the grip on his pistol. "Now face me."

The man turned around.

Holy shit, thought Peter. *Holy, holy shit.*

"You think maybe you could stop pointing that thing at me?"

Michael had aged, but of course they all had. The difference was that the Michael he knew—his mental image of the man—had leapt forward two decades in an instant. It was, in a way, like looking in a mirror; the changes you didn't notice in yourself were laid bare in the face of another.

"What happened to the security detail?"

"Not to worry. Their headaches will be historic, though."

"The shift changes at two, in case you were wondering."

Michael looked at his watch. "Ninety minutes. Plenty of time, I'd say."

"What for?"

"A conversation."

"What did you do with our oil?"

Michael frowned at the gun. "I mean it, Peter. You're making me nervous."

Peter lowered the weapon.

"Speaking of which, I brought you a present." Michael gestured toward his pack on the floor. "Do you mind—?"

"Oh, please, make yourself at home."

Michael removed a bottle, wrapped in stained oilcloth. He uncovered it and held it up for Peter to see.

"My latest recipe. Should strip the lining right off your brainpan."

Peter retrieved a pair of shot glasses from the kitchen. By the time he returned, Michael had moved the rocking chair to the small table in front of the sofa; Peter sat across from him. On the table was a large cardboard folder. Michael cut the wax on the bottle, poured two shots, and raised his glass.

"Compadres," he said.

The taste exploded into Peter's sinuses; it was like drinking straight alcohol.

Michael smacked his lips appreciatively. "Not bad, if I do say so myself."

Peter stifled a cough, his eyes brimming. "So, did Dunk send you?"

"Dunk?" Michael made a sour face. "No. Our old friend Dunk is taking a very long swim with his cronies."

"I suspected as much."

"No need to thank me. Did you get the guns?"

"You left out the part about what they're for."

Michael picked up the folder and untied the cords. He withdrew three documents: a painting of some kind; a single sheet of paper, covered in handwriting; and a newspaper. The masthead said INTERNATIONAL HERALD TRIBUNE.

Michael poured a second shot into Peter's glass and pushed it toward him. "Drink this."

"I don't want another."

"Believe me, you do."

Michael was waiting for Peter to say something. His friend was standing at the window, looking out into the night, though Michael doubted he was seeing much of anything.

"I'm sorry, Peter. I know it's not good news."

"How can you be so damn *sure*?"

"You're going to have to trust me."

"That's all you've got? *Trust* you? I'm committing about five felonies just *talking* to you."

"It's going to happen. The virals are coming back. They were never really gone to begin with."

"This is . . . insane."

"I wish it were."

Michael had never felt so sorry for anyone since the day he'd sat on the porch with Theo, a lifetime ago, and told him the batteries were failing.

"This other viral—" Peter began.

"Fanning. The Zero."

"Why do you call him that?"

"It's how he knows himself. Subject Zero, the first one infected. The documents Lacey gave us in Colorado described thirteen test subjects, the Twelve plus Amy. But the virus had to come from somewhere. Fanning was the host."

"So what's he waiting for? Why didn't he attack us years ago?"

"All I know is, I'm glad he didn't. It's bought us the time we needed."

"And Greer knows this because of some . . . vision."

Michael waited. Sometimes, he knew, that was what you had to do. The mind refused certain things; you had to let resistance run its course.

"Twenty-one years since we opened the gate. Now you waltz in here and tell me it was all a big mistake."

"I know this is hard, but you couldn't know. No one could. Life had to go on."

"Just what would you have me tell people? Some old man had a bad dream, and I guess we're all dead after all?"

"You're not going to tell them anything. Half of them won't believe you; the other half will lose their minds. It'll be pandemonium—everything will fall apart. People will do the math. We only have room for seven hundred on the ship."

"To go to this island." Peter gestured dismissively at Greer's painting. "This picture in his head."

"It's more than a picture, Peter. It's a map. Who really knows where it comes from? That's Greer's department, not mine. But he saw it for a reason, I know that much."

"You always seemed so goddamned *sensible*."

Michael shrugged. "I admit, the whole thing took some getting used to. But the pieces fit. You read that letter. The *Bergensfjord* was headed there."

"And just who decides who goes? You?"

"You're the president—that's ultimately your call. But I think you'll agree—"

"I'm not *agreeing* to anything."

Michael took a breath. "I think you'll agree that we need certain skills. Doctors, engineers, farmers, carpenters. We need leadership, obviously, so that includes you."

"Don't be absurd. Even if what you say is right, which is ridiculous, there's no way I'd go."

"I'd rethink that. We'll need a government, and the transition should be as smooth as possible. But that's a subject for later." Michael removed a small, leather-wrapped notebook from his pack. "I've drafted a manifest. There are some names, people I know who fit the bill, and we've included their immediate families. Age is a factor, too. Most are under forty. Otherwise there are job descriptions grouped by category."

Peter accepted the notebook, opened it to the first page, and began to read.

"Sara and Hollis," he said. "That's good of you."

"You don't have to be sarcastic. Caleb's in there, too, in case you were wondering."

"What about Apgar? I don't see him anywhere."

"The man is what? Sixty-five?"

Peter shook his head with a look of disgust.

"I know he's your friend, but we're talking about rebuilding the human race."

"He's also general of the Army."

"As I said, these are just recommendations. But take them seriously. I've given the matter a lot of thought."

Peter read the rest without comment, then looked up. "What's this last category, these fifty-six spots?"

"Those are my men. I've promised them places on the ship. I won't go back on that."

Peter tossed the notebook onto the table "You've lost your mind."

Michael leaned forward. "This is going to *happen,* Peter. You need to accept it. And we don't have a lot of time."

"Twenty years, and now this is a big emergency."

"Rebuilding the *Bergensfjord* took what it took. If I could have finished faster, I would have. We'd be long gone."

"And just how do you propose we get people to this boat of yours without starting a panic?"

"Probably we can't. That's what the guns are for."

Peter just stared at him.

"There are three options that I can see," Michael continued. "The first is a public lottery for the available slots. I'm opposed to that, obviously. Option two is we make our selections, tell the people on the manifest what's happening, give them the choice of either staying or going, and do our best to keep order while we get them out of here. Personally, I think that would be a disaster. No way we could keep a lid on things, and the Army might not back us. Option three is we tell the passengers nothing, apart from a few key individuals we know we can trust. We round up the rest and get them out in the dead of night. Once they're at the isthmus, we give them the good news that they're the lucky ones."

"*Lucky?* I can't believe we're even talking like this."

"Make no mistake, that's what they are. They'll get to live their lives. More than that. They'll be starting over, someplace that's truly safe."

"And this boat of yours can actually get them there? This derelict?"

"I hope she can. I *believe* she can."

"You don't sound convinced."

"We've done our best. But there aren't any guarantees."

"So those seven hundred lucky people might be going straight to the bottom of the ocean."

Michael nodded. "That might be exactly what happens. I've never lied to you, and I'm not going to start now. But she managed to cross the world once. She'll do it again."

The conversation was broken by a burst of voices outside and three hard bangs on the door.

"Well," Michael said, and clapped his knees. "It looks like our time is over. Think about what I've told you. In the meanwhile, we need to make this look right." He reached into his pack and withdrew the Beretta.

"Michael, what are you doing?"

He pointed the gun halfheartedly at Peter. "Do your best to act like a hostage."

Two soldiers burst into the room; Michael rose to his feet, raising his hands. "I surrender," he said, just in time for the closest one to take two long strides toward him, raise the butt of his rifle, and send it crashing into Michael's skull.

48

Rudy was hungry. *Really* fucking hungry.

"Hello!" he called, pressing his face to the bars to aim his voice down the lightless corridor. "Did you forget about me? Hey, assholes, I'm starving in here!"

Yelling was pointless; nobody had been in the office since early afternoon—not Fry and not Eustace, either. Rudy plopped down on his bunk, trying not to think about his empty stomach. What he would have given for one of those stupid potatoes now.

He rocked back on the cot and tried to get comfortable. There were lots of spots that still hurt; every position Rudy tried made him ache in a different way. Okay, he'd pretty much asked for a beating. He wouldn't say he hadn't. But what would have happened if Fry hadn't gotten the door open? Dead Rudy, that's what.

For a while he drifted. Little squirts of liquid burbled in his gut. He wasn't sure what time it was; late, probably, though without Fry coming back to bring him his meals, the day had lost its rhythm. He wouldn't have minded a book to occupy himself, if there were any light to see by or if he could actually read, which he couldn't, having never understood the point of it.

Fucking Gordon Eustace.

More time slipped by. His mind was floating on the crest of sleep when a jolt of dread aroused him.

Somewhere outside, a woman was screaming.

The window was positioned high on the wall; Rudy had to stand on his tiptoes and grip the bars to keep his nose above the sill. There were lots of sounds now—shots, shouts, screams. A darkened figure tore past the window, then two more.

"Hey!" Rudy yelled after them. "Hey, I'm in here!"

Something was happening, and it was nothing good. He yelled some more, but nobody stopped or even answered. The screaming died down and then picked up again, louder than before, a lot of people at once. Maybe it wasn't such a good idea to be telling everybody where he was, Rudy thought. He released his grip and backed away from the window. Whatever was going on out there, he was trapped like a rat in a can. Better to just shut up.

The world went quiet again. Maybe a minute passed before Rudy heard the front door of the building open. He dropped to the floor and scrambled beneath the cot. The squeak of a chair, a shuffling sound, a drawer being opened: somebody was searching for something. Then Rudy heard it: the jingling of keys.

"Sheriff?"

No answer.

"Deputy Fry? That you?"

A soft green light filled the corridor.

Simultaneously, at the farthest outskirts of Mystic Township, Texas, three virals were emerging from the earth.

Like pupae struggling free of their protective coverings, the members of the pod appeared in stages: first the pearlescent tips of their claws, then the long bony fingers, followed by a busting of soil that laid bare their sleek, inhuman faces to the stars. They rose, shaking off the dirt with a doglike motion, and stretched their slumberous limbs. A moment was required to ascertain their situation. It was night. They were in a field. The field was freshly turned. The first to emerge, the dominant member of the pod, was the widowed shopkeeper, George Pettibrew; the second was the town farrier, Juno Brand; the third was a fourteen-year-old girl from Hunt Township who had been taken up four nights ago when she'd made a midnight run to the outhouse of her family's farm. These identities lay beyond their powers of recollection, for they had none; all they had was a mission.

They saw the farmhouse.

A lazy curlicue of smoke chuffed from its chimney pipe. They circled the structure, taking stock. It possessed two doors, front and rear. Though it was not in their natures to bother with a door, nor with the dainty human custom of turning a handle, such was their task that this was what they did.

They entered. Their senses roamed the space. A sound from above.

Somebody was snoring.

The first viral, the alpha, crept up the stairs. So fine were his movements that not even a floorboard creaked; he barely parted air. The faint glow of a lantern issued from the room at the top, carelessly left burning after the house's inhabitants had retired for the night. In the big bed, two were sleeping, a man and a woman.

The viral bent to the woman. She was on her left side, one arm crooked beneath the pillows, the second exposed upon the blankets. Under the subdued light of the lantern, her skin shimmered deliciously. The viral unlocked his jaws and lowered his face toward her. The barest prick, his teeth delicately sliding into the microscopic spaces of her flesh, and it was done.

She stirred, moaned, rolled over. Perhaps she dreamed that she was pruning roses and got punctured by a thorn.

The viral moved to the other side of the bed. Only the man's head and neck were exposed. The viral sensed as well that the man, whose snores rattled with a phlegmy texture, was not as deeply asleep as the woman. Leaning forward, the viral tilted his head to one side, as if to aim a kiss.

The man's eyes flew open. "Holy fucking shit!"

He shoved the palm of one hand against the viral's forehead to hold him at bay while reaching the other hand beneath the pillow. "Dory!" he bellowed, "Dory, wake up!" The viral was stunned into inaction: this was not how things were supposed to be. And that name, Dory. It jostled his mind. Did he know a Dory? Did he know the man as well? Had the two of them, at one time, been people in his life? And what was the man reaching for beneath his pillow?

It was a gun. With a howl, the man shoved the barrel into the viral's mouth, pressing the muzzle up against his palate, and fired.

A thunder clap, a parabola of blood, the viral's brain matter caroming through the crown of his skull to splatter on the ceiling. The body rocked forward, dead weight. The woman was awake now, immobilized with terror and screaming to beat the band. The other virals vaulted up the stairs. Shoving the corpse aside, the man fired at the first one as it burst through the door. He wasn't really aiming anymore. He was simply squeezing the trigger. The third shot connected in a general way, but that was the extent of it. Two more shots and the hammer fell on an empty chamber. As one of the virals leapt toward him, the man grabbed the only thing he could think of—the kerosene lantern—and hurled it at his attackers.

His aim was true. The viral exploded in flames.

And then everything was on fire.

*   *   *

The feeling hit Amy like a punch to the gut. She doubled over, the trowel falling from her hand, and dropped to her hands and knees in the dirt.

"Amy, are you all right?"

Carter was kneeling beside her. She tried to answer but couldn't; her breath stopped in her chest.

"You hurting somewhere? Tell me what's wrong."

At the same moment, Caleb Jaxon awoke to the disconcerting smell of smoke. He had spent the night in a chair by the door, George's pistol on the table, his rifle cradled in his lap. His first thought was that his own house was burning; he jerked upright, panic pounding through him. But, no, the room was all in order; the smell came from someplace else. He grabbed the pistol and stepped outside. To the west, beyond the ridgeline, the sky was lit with fire.

"Please, Miss Amy," Carter said. "You scaring me."

She was shaking; she could not speak. Such pain they felt, such terror. So many, all at once. Her breath unlocked; air flowed back into her lungs.

"It's started."

VI

ZERO HOUR

The fire which seems extinguished
often slumbers beneath the ashes.

—Pierre Corneille,
Rodogune

49

Just after daybreak, Caleb shook Pim by the shoulder.

Something's happened at the Tatums'.

She sat upright, instantly awake. *What?*

Caleb opened the fingers of both hands and moved them in a rotating motion in front of his chest: *Fire.*

Pim shoved the blankets aside. *I'm coming with you.*

Stay here. I'll look.

She's my friend.

Pim was referring to Dory, of course.

Okay, he signed.

The children were still out cold. While Pim dressed, Caleb awakened Kate to tell her what was happening.

"What do you think it means?" Her voice was groggy, but her eyes were clear.

"I don't know." He pulled the revolver from his waistband and held it out. "Keep this handy."

"Any idea what I'm supposed to be shooting at?"

"If I knew, I'd tell you. Stay inside—we won't be long."

Caleb met Pim in the yard. She was gazing toward the ridgeline, hands on her hips. A thick column of white smoke, the color of a summer cloud, billowed at a distance. The color meant the fire was out.

Jeb? she signed.

The horse was lying where he had fallen. Handsome had wandered to the far end of the paddock, keeping his distance.

He died last night.

Pim's face was all business. *How?*

Maybe colic. I didn't want to upset you.

I'm your wife. She signed these words with brisk anger. *I saw you give Kate a gun. Tell me what's happening.*

Caleb had no answer.

All that remained of the farmhouse was a pile of charred timbers and glowing ash. The heat had been so intense that the glass in the windows had melted. It would be several hours, perhaps a day, before Caleb could look for bodies, though he doubted there'd be anything left but bones and teeth.

Do you think they got out? Pim asked.

Caleb could only shake his head. How had it happened? A loose ember from the stove? A lantern knocked aside? Something small, and now they were gone.

He noticed something else. The paddock was empty. The gate stood open; the ground around it looked scraped, as if someone had killed the horses and dragged the carcasses away. What did it mean?

Let's check the barn, he signed.

Caleb entered first. It took his eyes a moment to adjust to the darkness. At the rear, in deep shadow, was a hump on the floor.

It was Dory. She was lying in a fetal position. Her hair was burned away, brows and lashes gone, her face swollen and scorched. Her nightdress was charred in places, in others fused to her flesh. Her right arm and both legs were blackened to a crisp; elsewhere the skin had bubbled, as if boiled from within.

He knelt beside her. "Dory, it's Caleb and Pim."

Her right eye opened the thinnest crack; the other seemed welded shut. She flicked her gaze toward him. From her throat came a sound, half moan, half gurgle. Caleb couldn't imagine such agony. He wanted to be ill.

Pim brought a bucket and ladle. She knelt beside Dory, cupped the woman's head to lift it slightly, and held the ladle to her lips. Dory managed a small sip, then sputtered the rest from her mouth.

We have to get her back, Pim signed. *Kate will know what to do.*

That the woman was still alive was a miracle; surely she would not survive long. Still, they had to try. A wheelbarrow stood propped against the wall. Caleb rolled it over and fetched a pair of saddle pads from the tack bin and laid them in the bottom.

Take her legs.

Caleb positioned himself behind Dory and hooked his elbows under her shoulders. The woman began to shriek and buck at the waist. After the longest five seconds of his life, they managed to get her into the wheelbarrow. A tacky substance came away on Caleb's bare forearms: pieces of Dory's skin.

Her cries subsided. She was breathing in shallow, rapid jerks. The trip would be unbearable for her; each jostle would bring fresh waves of torture. As Caleb hoisted the bars of the wheelbarrow, he saw another problem. Dory was not a small woman. Keeping the whole thing balanced would take every ounce of his strength.

Give me a side, Pim signed.

Caleb shook his head firmly. *The baby.*

I'll stop if I'm tired.

Caleb didn't want to, but Pim wouldn't be deterred. They rolled Dory to the door. As sunlight fell across her, her whole body recoiled, sending the wheelbarrow tipping dangerously to the side.

It's her eyes, Pim signed. *They must be burned.*

She returned to the barn and came back with a cloth, which she moistened in the bucket and then draped over the upper half of the woman's face. Her body began to relax.

Let's go, Pim signed.

It took almost an hour to get Dory back to the house, by which time the woman had lapsed into a merciful unconsciousness. Kate rushed out to meet them. When she saw Dory, she turned back toward the door, where Elle and Bug were standing watchfully, curious about all the excitement. Theo was nosing through Bug's legs like a puppy.

"Get back in the house," she ordered. "And take your cousin with you."

"We want to look!" Elle whined.

"Now."

They faded inside. Kate crouched next to Dory. "Dear God."

"We found her in the barn," Caleb explained.

"Her husband?"

"No sign of him."

Kate looked toward Pim. *The girls shouldn't see.*

Pim nodded. *I'll take them out back.*

"We need a tarp or strong blanket," Kate said to Caleb. "We can put her in the back room, away from the children."

"Will she survive?"

"She's a mess, Caleb. There's not a lot I can do."

Caleb retrieved one of the heavy wool blankets he used for the horses. They spread it on the ground next to the wheelbarrow, then lifted Dory from the cart and lowered her onto the blanket, tied the corners together, and ran a length of two-by-four through the ends to fashion a makeshift sling. As they hoisted her off the ground, she made a noise from back in her throat that sounded like a strangled scream. Caleb shuddered; he could barely listen to this anymore. That Dory hadn't died seemed a cruelty of immense proportions. They carried her into the house, to the small storage room where the girls had been sleeping, and laid her on the pallet. Caleb nailed a saddle pad to the tiny window as a shade.

"I need to get that nightgown off." Kate gave Caleb a grave look. "This will be . . . bad."

He swallowed. He could barely bring himself to look at the woman, at her charred and bubbled flesh.

"I'm not good with things like this," he admitted.

"Nobody is, Caleb."

He realized something else. He'd waited too long; now they were stranded, waiting for the woman to die. With only one horse, they couldn't use the buckboard to take Dory to Mystic. And Pim would never leave her.

"I'll need clean cloths, a bottle of alcohol, scissors," Kate commanded. "Boil the scissors, and don't touch them afterward, just lay them in a cloth. Then go look after the children. Pim can help me here. You'll want to keep them away from the house for a while."

Caleb didn't feel insulted, only grateful. He retrieved the things she'd asked for, brought them to the room, and traded places with Pim. By the kitchen garden, the girls were playing with their dolls, making beds for them out of leaves and sticks, while Theo toddled around.

"Come on, children, let's go for a walk to the river."

He lodged Theo on his hip and took Elle by the hand. She, in turn, took her sister's, as they had learned to do, making a chain. They were halfway to the river when a scream severed the air. The sound shot through Caleb like a bullet.

Lucius, it's started. I need you now.

Greer had been driving since before dawn. "Just get this boat ready," he'd told Lore. He swung past Rosenberg in the dark, jogged northwest, and hit Highway 10 as the sun was rising behind him.

He would reach Kerrville by four o'clock, five at the latest. What would the darkness bring?

Amy, I am coming.

50

Michael came to consciousness in darkness. Lying on his bunk, he fingered the wound on his head. His hair was rigid with dried blood; he was lucky they hadn't broken his skull. But he supposed an armed criminal in the president's house warranted at least one good blow to the melon. Not an ideal way to get a night's rest, though, on the whole, not entirely unwelcome.

He slept some more; when he awoke, soft daylight was coming through the window. A clunk of tumblers, and a pair of DS officers appeared. One was holding a tray. While the other stood guard, the first placed the tray on the floor.

"Much obliged, guys."

The two walked off. Probably they'd been instructed not to talk to him. Michael lifted the tray and put it on the bunk. A bowl of boiled oats, scrambled eggs, a peach—a better meal than he'd had in days. They'd given him only a spoon—no fork, of course—so he ate the eggs with that, followed by the porridge. He saved the peach for last. Juice exploded over his chin. Fresh fruit! He'd forgotten what it was like.

More time passed. At last he heard footsteps and voices in the hall. Peter, most likely, with someone else in tow. Apgar? Sooner or later, the conversation was going to have to widen.

But it wasn't Peter.

Sara stood in the doorway. She'd changed less than he would have thought. Older, of course, but she'd aged gracefully, the way some women could, the ones who didn't fight it, who accepted the passage of time.

"I don't believe my eyes."

"Hello, Sara."

Michael sat up on his bunk as his sister stepped inside. She was carrying a small leather bag. A guard moved in behind her, holding a baton.

"Goddamnit, Michael." She was standing apart from him.

"I know." An absurd remark: What did it mean? I know I hurt you? I know how this must look? I know I'm the worst brother in the world?

"I am so . . . angry at you."

"You have a right."

An eyebrow lifted. "That's all you have to say?"

"How about, I'm sorry."

"Are you kidding me? You're *sorry*?"

"You look well, Sara. I've missed you."

"Don't even try. And you look like hell."

"Oh, this is one of my better days."

"Michael, what are you *doing* here? I thought I'd never see you again."

He searched her face. Did she know? "What did Peter tell you?"

"Just that you'd been arrested and you had a gash in your head." She lifted the bag a little. "I'm here to sew you up."

"So he didn't say anything else."

She made a face of disbelief. "Like what, Michael? That they'll probably hang you? He didn't have to."

"Don't worry. Nobody's getting hanged."

"Twenty-one years, Michael." Her right hand, the one not holding the bag, was clenched into a fist, as if she might strike him. "Twenty-one years without a message, a letter, nothing. Help me understand this."

"I can't explain right now. But you have to know there *was* a reason."

"Do you know what I had to do? Do you? Ten years ago, I said, That's it, he's never coming back. He might as well be dead. I *buried* you, Michael. I put you in the ground and forgot about you."

"I did some awful things, Sara."

At last the tears came. "I took *care* of you. I *raised* you. Did you ever think of that?"

He rose from the bunk. Sara let the bag drop to the floor, raised her fists, and began to pummel his chest. She was crying in earnest now.

"You *asshole*," she said.

He pulled her into a tight embrace. She struggled in his arms, then let him hold her. The guard was watching them warily; Michael shot him a look: *Back off.*

"How could you do this to me?" she sobbed.

"I never wanted to hurt you, Sara."

"You left me, just like they did. You're no better than they were."

"I know."

"Damn you, Michael, *damn* you."

He held her that way for a long time.

"That's quite a story."

It was late morning; Peter had cleared the office. He and Apgar were seated at the conference table, waiting for Chase. A short retirement for the man, thought Peter.

"I know it is," Peter answered.

"Do you believe him?"

"Do *you*?"

"You're the one who knows the man."

"That was twenty years ago."

Chase appeared in the door. "Peter, what's going on? Where is everybody? This place is a tomb." He was dressed in the jeans, work shirt, and heavy boots of the cattleman he had announced his intention to become.

"Have a seat, Ford," Peter said.

"Will this take long? Olivia's waiting for me. We're meeting some people at the bank."

Peter wondered how many of these conversations he was going to have to have. It was like leading people to the edge of a cliff, showing them the view, and then shoving them off.

"I'm afraid so," he said.

Alicia saw the first mounds just outside of Fredericksburg—three domes of earth, each the length of a man, bulging from the ground in the shade of a pecan tree. Riding on, she came to the outermost farmstead. She dismounted in the packed-dirt yard. No sounds of life reached her from the house. She stepped inside. Furniture overturned, objects strewn about, a rifle on the floor, beds unmade. The inhabitants had been infected as they'd slept; now they slept in the earth, beneath the pecan tree.

She watered Soldier at the trough and continued on her way. The rocky hills rose and fell. Soon she saw more houses—some nestled discreetly in the folds of the land, others exposed on the flats, surrounded by hard-won fields of newly tilled soil. There was no need to look more closely; the stillness told Alicia all she needed to know. The sky seemed to hang above her with an infinite weariness. She had expected it to happen like this, at the outer edges first. The first ones taken up, then more and more, an army swelling its ranks, metastasizing as it moved toward the city.

The town itself was abandoned. Alicia rode the length of the dusty main street, past the small stores and houses, some new, others reclaimed from the past. Just a few days ago, people had gone about their daily lives here: raised families, conducted business and trade, talked of small things, gotten drunk, cheated at cards, argued, fought with their fists, made love, stood on the porches to greet their fellow citizens as they passed. Had they known what was happening? Did the fact creep upon them slowly—first one person missing, a curiosity barely remarked on, then another and another, until the meaning dawned—or had the virals swooped down in a rush, a single night of horror? At the southern edge of town, Alicia came to a field. She began to count. Twenty mounds. Fifty. Seventy-five.

At one hundred, she gave up counting.

51

The day moved on. Still Dory did not die.

From the room where the woman lay, Caleb heard only small sounds—

moans, murmurs, a chair shifting on the floor. Kate or Pim might appear briefly, to fetch some small implement or boil more cloths. Caleb sat in the yard with the children, though he had no energy to amuse them. His mind drifted to undone chores, but then another voice would speak to him, saying it was for naught; they would soon be leaving this place, all his proud hopes dashed.

Kate came out and sat beside him on the stoop. The children had gone down for a nap in the house.

"So?" he asked.

Kate squinted into the afternoon light. A strand of hair, golden blond, was plastered to her forehead; she tucked it away. "She's still breathing, anyway."

"How long will this take?"

"She should be dead already." Kate looked at him. "If she's still alive in the morning, you should take Pim and the kids and get out of here."

"If anybody's staying, it's me. Just tell me what to do."

"Caleb, I can handle it."

"I know you can, but I'm the one who got us into this mess."

"What were you going to do? A horse gets sick, some people go missing, a house burns down. Who's to say any of it's related?"

"I'm still not leaving you here."

"And, believe me, I appreciate the gesture. I never was much of a country gal, and this place gives me the creeps. But it's my *job,* Caleb. Let me do it, and we'll get along fine."

For a while they sat without talking. Then Caleb said, "I could use your help with something."

Jeb's body had swollen and stiffened in the heat. They lashed his hind legs together, set Handsome into his plow harness, and began the slow process of dragging the body to the far edge of the field. When Caleb felt they were far enough away from the house, they led Handsome back to the shelter and brought out one of the jugs of fuel. Caleb dragged some deadfall from the woods and placed it over the corpse, building a pyre; he splashed kerosene over it, recapped the can, and stepped back.

Kate asked, "Why did you call him Jeb?"

Caleb shrugged. "Just the name he came with."

Nothing remained to be said. Caleb struck a match and tossed it forward. With a whoosh, flames enveloped the pile. There was no wind to speak of; the thick smoke rose straight skyward, full of popping sparks. For a while it smelled like mesquite; then it became something else.

"That's that, I guess," he said.

They walked back toward the house. As they approached, Pim appeared in the doorway. Her eyes were very wide.

Something is happening, she signed.

* * *

The room was cool and dark. Only Dory's face was showing; the rest was covered by boiled clothes.

"Mrs. Tatum," Kate said, "can you hear me? Do you know where you are?"

Staring at the ceiling, the woman seemed completely unaware of them. A remarkable change had occurred. Remarkable, but also disturbing. The harsh appearance of the burns on her face had softened. Their color was now pinkish, almost dewy; in other patches, her skin was white as talc. Dory shifted slightly in her bed, exposing her left hand and forearm from under the cloths. Before, it had been a gruesome claw of cooked flesh. In its stead was a recognizable human hand—blisters gone, charred bits flaked off to reveal skin of rosy newness beneath.

Kate looked up at Pim. *How long has she been awake?*

She wasn't. That just happened.

"Mrs. Tatum," Kate said, more commandingly, "I'm a doctor. You've been in a fire. You're at the Jaxons' farm; Caleb and Pim are with me. Do you remember what happened?"

Her gaze, wandering the room in a desultory fashion, located Kate's face.

"Fire?" she murmured.

"That's right, there was a fire at your house."

"Ask her if she knows what started it," Caleb said.

"Fire," Dory repeated. "Fire."

"Yes, what do you remember about the fire?"

Pim stepped forward and knelt by the bed. She gently lifted Dory's exposed hand, placed the tip of her index finger in the woman's palm, and began to form letters.

"Pim," Dory said.

But that was all; the light in her eyes faded. She closed them again.

"Caleb, I'm going to examine her," Kate said. Then, to Pim: *Stay and help.*

Caleb waited in the kitchen. The children, mercifully, were still asleep. A few minutes passed, and the women appeared.

Kate gestured to the back door. *Let's talk outside.*

The light had shifted toward evening. "What's happening to her?" Caleb asked, signing simultaneously.

"She's getting better, that's what."

"How is that possible?"

"If I knew, I'd bottle it. The burns are still bad—she's not out of the woods yet. But I've never seen anybody heal so fast. I thought the shock alone would kill her."

"What about her waking up like that?"

"It's a good sign, her recognizing Pim. I don't think she understood much else, though. She may never."

"You mean she'll stay like this?"

"I've seen it happen." Kate addressed her sister directly: *You should stay with her. If she wakes up again, try to get her talking.*

What about?

Easy stuff. Keep her mind off the fire for now.

Pim returned to the house.

"This changes things," Caleb said.

"I agree. We may be able to move her sooner than I thought. Do you think you can find a vehicle in Mystic?"

He recalled the pickup he'd seen in Elacqua's yard.

Kate seemed surprised. "*Brian* Elacqua?"

"That's him."

"That drunken old cuss. I'd wondered what had become of him."

"That was pretty much my experience of the man."

"Still, I'm sure he'd help us."

Caleb nodded. "I'll ride in in the morning."

Sara was waiting on the porch with their bags when Hollis appeared, sitting atop a sorry-looking mare. With him was a man Sara didn't know, riding a second horse, a black gelding with a back as bowed as a hammock and ancient, runny eyes.

"What's this I see?" Sara said. "Oh, two of the worst horses I ever laid eyes on."

The two men dismounted. Hollis's companion was a squat-looking man wearing overalls but no shirt. His hair was long and white; there was something cunning in his face. Hollis and the man exchanged a few words, shook hands, and the man walked off.

"Who's your friend?" Sara asked.

Hollis was tying the horses to the porch rail. "Just somebody I knew in the old days."

"Husband, I thought we talked about a truck."

"Yeah, about that. Turns out a truck costs actual money. Also, there's no gas to be had. On the upside, Dominic threw in the tack for free, so we are not, technically, one hundred percent penniless at the moment."

"Dominic. Your shirtless friend."

"He kind of owed me a favor."

"Should I ask?"

"Probably best if you don't."

They returned to the house, lightened their gear, loaded the remains into saddlebags, and secured them to the horses. Hollis took the mare, Sara the gelding. She was getting the best of the deal, though not by much. Years had passed since she'd even been on a horse, but the feeling was automatic, touching a deep chord of physical memory. Bending forward in the saddle, Sara gave three firm pats to the side of the horse's neck. "You're not such a bad old guy, are you? Maybe I'm being too hard on you."

Hollis looked up. "I'm sorry, were you addressing me?"

"Now, now," Sara said.

They made their way to the gate and descended the hill. Scattered workers were toiling in the fields beneath a late afternoon sun. Here and there a pennant still hung limply from its pole, marking the location of a hardbox; the watchtowers with their warning horns and sharpshooter platforms jutted from the valley floor, unmanned for years.

At the outer edge of the Orange Zone, the road forked: west toward the river townships, east toward Comfort and the Oil Road. Hollis drew up and took his canteen from his belt. He drank and passed it to Sara. "How's the old boy doing?"

"A perfect gentleman." She wiped her mouth with the back of her hand and gestured eastward with the canteen. "Looks like somebody's in a hurry."

Hollis saw it too: the boiling dust plume of a vehicle, driving fast toward the city.

"Maybe we could see if he'd trade for the horses," Hollis said, not seriously.

Sara examined him for a moment, flicking her eyes up and down. "I have to say, you look rather dashing up there. Takes me back a bit."

Hollis was leaning forward, bracing his weight with both hands on the pommel. "I used to like to watch you ride, you know. If I was on the day shift on the Watch, I'd sometimes wait on the Wall until you came back with the herd."

"Really? I was not aware."

"It was a little creepy of me, I admit that."

She felt suddenly happy. A smile came to her face, the first in days. "Oh, what could you do?"

"I wasn't the only one. Sometimes you drew quite a crowd."

"Then lucky you, things working out like they did." She capped the canteen and handed it back. "Now let's go see our babies."

52

"Hey, good afternoon, everybody."

Two DS officers manned the stockade's outer room—one sitting at his desk, a second, much older, standing behind the counter. Greer recognized the second one immediately; years ago, the man had been one of his jailors. Winthrop? No, Winfield. He'd been just a kid then. As their gazes locked, Lucius could see a series of rapid calculations unfolding behind the man's eyes.

"I'll be damned," Winfield said.

His hand dropped to his sidearm, but the movement was startled and clumsy, giving Greer ample time to raise the shotgun from beneath his coat and level it at the man's chest. With a loud clack, he chambered a shell. "Tut tut."

Winfield froze. The younger one was still sitting behind his desk, staring wide-eyed. Greer nudged the shotgun toward him. "You, weapon on the floor. You too, Winfield. Let's be quick now."

They placed their pistols on the ground. "Who is this guy?" the younger one said.

"Been a while, Sixty-two," Winfield said, using Greer's old inmate number. He seemed more amused than angry, as if he'd run into an old friend of dubious reputation who'd lived up to expectations. "Heard you've been keeping yourself busy. How's Dunk?"

"Michael Fisher," Greer said. "Is he here?"

"Oh, he's here, all right."

"Any more DS in the building? We keep the nonsense to a minimum, this doesn't have to be a problem."

"Are you serious? I don't give a shit one way or the other. Ramsey, toss me the keys."

Winfield opened the door to the cellblock. Greer followed a few paces behind the two men, keeping the shotgun trained on their backs. Michael, lying on his bunk, rose on his elbows as the door to his cell opened.

"This is sudden," he remarked.

Greer ordered Winfield and the other one into the cell, then looked at Michael. "Shall we?"

"Nice seeing you, Sixty-two," Winfield called after them. "You haven't changed a bit, you fucker."

Greer shut the door, turned the lock, and pocketed the key. "Keep it down

in there," he barked through the slot. "I don't want to have to come back here."
He turned to look at Michael. "What happened to your head? That looks like
it hurt."

"Not to sound ungrateful, but I'm thinking your being here is not good
news."

"We're moving to Plan B."

"I didn't know we had one of those."

Greer handed him Winfield's pistol. "I'll explain on the way."

Peter, Apgar, and Chase were looking over Michael's passenger manifest
when shouts erupted in the hall: "Put it down! Put it down!"

A crash; a gunshot.

Peter reached into his desk for the pistol he kept there. "Gunnar, what have
you got?"

"Nothing."

"Ford?"

The man shook his head.

"Get behind my desk."

The handle of the door jiggled. Peter and Apgar took positions against the
wall on either side. The wood shuddered: somebody was kicking it.

The door blew open.

As the first man entered, Apgar tackled him from beind. A shotgun skittered
away. Apgar pinned him with his knees, one hand on his throat, the other
lifted, ready to strike. He stopped.

"Greer?"

"Hello, General."

"Michael," Peter said, lowering his gun, "what the *fuck.*"

Three soldiers charged into the room, rifles drawn.

"Hold your fire!" Peter yelled.

With visible uncertainty, the soldiers complied.

"What was that gunshot outside, Michael?"

The man waved casually. "Oh, he missed. We're fine."

Peter was shaking with anger. "You three," he said to the soldiers, "clear the
room."

They made their departure. Apgar climbed off Greer. Chase, meanwhile,
had come out from behind Peter's desk.

Michael gestured in Chase's direction. "Is he okay?"

"In what sense?"

"I mean does he *know*?"

"Yeah," Chase said tersely, "I know."

Peter was still furious. "The two of you, what do you think you're doing?"

"Under the circumstances, we thought a direct approach was best," Greer replied. "We have a vehicle outside. We need you to come with us, Peter, and we need to leave right now."

Peter's patience was at its end. "I'm not going anywhere. You don't start talking sense, I'll toss your asses in the stockade myself and throw away the key."

"I'm afraid the situation has changed."

"So the virals aren't coming back after all? This is all some kind of joke?"

"I'm afraid it's the opposite," Greer said. "They're already here."

53

Amy was going to miss this place.

They had decided to leave the rest of their chores undone for the day. There seemed no point in finishing them now. *Sometimes,* Carter told her, *you got to let a garden tend itself.*

She felt sick, almost feverish. Could she control it? Would she kill him? And what of the water?

You got to do it the way Zero done, Carter had told her. *Ain't no other way to go back to the way you were.*

The girls were watching a movie in the house. It was one Amy remembered, from being just a girl herself: *The Wizard of Oz.* The movie had terrified her—the tornado, the field of poppies, the wicked witch with her sickly green skin and battalion of airborne monkeys in bellman's hats—but she had also loved it. Amy had watched it in the motel where she and her mother had lived. Her mother would put on her little skirt and stretchy top to go out to the highway, and before she left she'd sit Amy down in front of the television with something to eat, something greasy in a bag, and tell her: *You sit tight now. Mama will be back soon. Don't you open that door for nobody.* Amy could see the guilt in her mother's eyes—she understood that leaving a child by herself wasn't something her mother was supposed to do—and Amy's heart always went out to her, because she loved her, and the woman was so remorseful and sad all the time, as if life was a series of disappointments she could do nothing to stop. Sometimes her mother could barely get out of bed all day, and then night would fall, and the skirt and the top and the television would go on, and she'd leave Amy alone again.

The night of *The Wizard of Oz* had been their last in the motel, or so Amy recalled. She'd watched cartoons for a while and, when these were over, a game show, and then she flipped around the dial until the movie caught her eye. The colors were odd, too vivid. That was the first thing she noticed. Lying on the bed, which smelled like her mother—a mélange of sweat, and perfume, and something distinctly her own—Amy settled in to watch. She entered the story when Dorothy, having rescued her dog from the clutches of the evil Miss Gulch, was racing from the storm. The tornado whisked her away; she found herself in the land of the Munchkins, who sang about their happy lives. But, of course, there was the problem of the feet—the feet of the Wicked Witch of the East, sticking out from beneath Dorothy's tornado-driven house.

It went on from there. Her attention was complete. She understood Dorothy's desire to go home. That was the heart of the story, and it made sense to Amy. She hadn't been home in a long time; she barely remembered it, just a shadowy sense of certain rooms. As the movie drew to a close, and Dorothy clicked her heels together and awoke in the bosom of her family, Amy decided to try this. She had no ruby slippers, but her mother had a pair of boots, very tall, with pointed heels. Amy slid them on. They rose up her skinny, little-girl legs nearly to her crotch; the heels were very high, making it difficult to walk. She took tender steps around the room to get the hang of it, and when she felt comfortable she closed her eyes and tapped the heels together, three times. *There's no place like home, there's no place like home, there's no place like home . . .*

So convinced was she of the magical power of this gesture that when she opened her eyes she was shocked to discover that nothing had happened. She was still in the motel, with its dirty carpet and dull immovable furniture. She yanked off the boots, hurled them across the room, threw herself down on the bed, and began to cry. She must have fallen asleep, because the next thing she saw was her mother's frightened face, looming over her. She was shaking Amy roughly by the shoulder; her top was stained and torn. *Come on now, honey,* her mother said. *Wake up now, baby. We got to go, right now.*

Carter was skimming the pool. The first leaves were falling, crisp and brown.

"I thought we were taking the day off," Amy said.

"We are. Just got to get these here. Bothers me seeing them."

She was sitting on the patio. Inside, the girls had reached the part of the movie where Dorothy and her companions entered the Emerald City.

"They should turn it down a bit," Carter remarked. He was dragging the skimmer along the edges, trying to work some small bit of debris into the net. "Girls are going to wreck their ears."

Yes, she would miss it here. The softness of the place, its cool feeling of green. The small tasks that filled their days of waiting. Carter lay the skimmer on the pool deck and took a chair across from her. They listened to the movie for a while. When the Wicked Witch melted, the girls erupted in happy shrieks.

"How many times they watch that?" Carter asked.

"Oh, quite a few."

"When I was a boy, seemed like it was on TV about half the time. Scared the wits out of me." Carter paused. "I always did like that movie, though."

They loaded the Humvee with cans of fuel. Sitting in the cargo compartment were plastic bins of supplies Greer had brought with him—rope and tackle, a spinner net, a pair of wrenches, blankets, a simple cotton frock.

"I'd be happier if we could bring Sara along," Peter said. "She'd know better than any of us what to do."

Greer heaved a jug over the tailgate. "Not a good idea at this point. We need to keep the number of people to a minimum."

"We have to get word out to the townships," Peter told Apgar. "People need to take shelter. Basements, interior rooms, whatever they've got. In the morning, we can send out vehicles to bring as many back as we can."

"I'll see to it."

Peter glanced at Chase. "Ford? You've got the chair."

"Understood."

Peter addressed Apgar again: "My son and his family—"

The general didn't let him finish. "I'll radio the detachment in Luckenbach. We'll get some men out there."

"Caleb's got a hardbox on the property."

"I'll pass that along."

Greer was waiting at the wheel, Michael riding shotgun. Peter climbed in back.

"Let's go," he said.

It was 1830. The sun would set in two hours.

54

Sara and Hollis were making good time. They had entered the zone everybody called the Gap—a stretch of empty road between Ingram and Hunt Township. They were hugging the Guadalupe now, which gurgled pleasantly in the shallows. Fat live oaks stretched their canopies over the roadway; then they came to an open stretch, the low sun in their faces, then more trees and shade.

"I think this guy needs a break," Sara said.

They dismounted and led the horses to the edge of the river. Standing on the bank, Hollis's mare dipped her long face to the water without hesitation, but the gelding seemed uncertain. Sara removed her boots, rolled up her pants, and led him into the shallows to drink. The water was wonderfully cold, the river bottom made of smooth limestone, firm underfoot.

After the horses had drunk their fill, Sara and Hollis took a moment to let the animals wander. The two of them sat on a rocky outcrop that jutted over the edge of the water. The vegetation on the banks was thick—willows, pecans, oaks, a scrub of mesquites and prickly pears. Evening insects were hatching from the water in ascending motes of light. A hundred yards upstream, the river paused in a wide, deep pool.

"It's so peaceful out here," Sara said.

Hollis nodded, his face full of contentment.

"I think I could get used to this."

She was thinking of a certain place in the past. It was many years ago, when she and Hollis and all the others had traveled east with Amy to Colorado. Theo and Maus were gone by this time, left behind at the farmstead so Maus could have her baby. They'd crossed the La Sal Range and descended to a wide valley of tall grass and blue skies and stopped to rest. In the distance, snow-capped, the peaks of the Rockies loomed, though the air was still mild. Sitting in the shade of a maple tree, Sara had experienced a feeling she'd never really had before—a sense of the world's beauty. Because it really *was* beautiful. The trees, the light, the way the grass moved in the breeze, the mountains' glinting faces of ice: how had she failed to notice these things before? And if she had, why had they seemed different, more ordinary, less charged with life? She had fallen in love with Hollis, and she understood, sitting under the maple tree with her friends around her—Michael had, in fact, fallen asleep, hugging his shotgun over his chest like a child's stuffed animal—that Hollis was the reason. It was love, and only love, that opened your eyes.

"We better go," Hollis said. "It'll be dark soon."

They gathered the horses and rode on.

General Gunnar Apgar, standing at the top of the wall, watched the shadows stretching over the valley.

He glanced at his watch: 2015 hours. Sunset was minutes away. The last transports bringing workers in from the fields were churning up the hill. All of his men had taken up positions along the top of the wall. They had new guns and fresh ammunition, but their numbers were small—far too few to watch every inch of a six-mile perimeter, let alone defend it.

Apgar wasn't a religious man. Many years had passed since a prayer had found his lips. Though it made him feel a little foolish, he decided to say one now. *God,* he thought, *if you're listening, sorry about the language, but if it's not too much trouble, please let this all be bullshit.*

Footsteps banged down the catwalk toward him.

"What is it, Corporal?"

The soldier's name was Ratcliffe—a radio operator. He was badly winded from his run up the stairs. He bent at the waist and put his hands on his knees, taking in great gulps of air between words. "General, sir, we got the message out like you said."

"How about Luckenbach?"

Ratcliffe nodded quickly, still looking at the ground. "Yeah, they're sending a squad." He paused and coughed. "But that's the thing. They were the only ones who answered."

"Catch your breath, Corporal."

"Yes, sir. Sorry, sir."

"Now tell me what you're talking about."

The soldier drew himself erect. "It's just like I said. Hunt, Comfort, Boerne, Rosenberg—we're not getting anything back. No acknowledgment, nothing. Every station except Luckenbach is off-line."

The last bus was passing through the gate. Below, in the staging area, workers were filing off. Some were talking, telling jokes and laughing; others separated themselves quickly from the group and marched away, headed home for the night.

"Thanks for passing that along, Corporal."

Apgar watched him totter away before turning to look over the valley again. A curtain of darkness was sweeping over the fields. *Well,* he thought, *I guess that's that. It would have been nice if it could have lasted longer.* He descended the stairs and walked to the base of the gate. Two soldiers were waiting with a civilian, a man of about forty, dressed in stained coveralls and holding a wrench the size of a sledgehammer.

The man spat a wad of something onto the ground. "Gate should be working fine now, General. I got everything well greased, too. The thing will be quiet as a cat."

Apgar looked at one of the soldiers. "Are all the transports in?"

"As far as we know."

He tipped his face to the sky; the first stars had appeared, winking from the darkness.

"Okay, gentlemen," he said. "Let's lock it up."

Caleb was sitting on the front stoop, watching the night come on.

That afternoon, he'd inspected the hardbox, which he hadn't looked at in months. He'd built it only to please his father; it had seemed silly at the time. Tornadoes happened, yes, some people had even been killed, but what were the chances? Caleb had cleared the hatch of leaves and other debris and descended the ladder. The interior was cool and dark. A kerosene lantern and jugs of fuel stood along one wall; the hatch sealed from the inside with a pair of steel crossbars. When Caleb had shown the shelter to Pim, their second night at the farm, he'd felt a little embarrassed by the thing, which seemed like an expensive and unwarranted indulgence, completely out of step with the optimism of their enterprise. But Pim had taken it in stride. *Your father knows a thing or two,* she signed. *Stop apologizing. I'm glad you took the time.*

Now, looking west, Caleb took measure of the sun. Its bottom edge was just kissing the top of the ridgeline. In its final moments, it appeared to accelerate, as it always did.

Going, going, gone.

He felt the air change. Everything around him seemed to stop. But in the next instant, something caught his eye—a rustling, high in a pecan tree at the edge of the woods. What was he seeing? Not birds; the motion was too heavy. He got to his feet. A second tree shuddered, then a third.

He recalled a phrase from the past. *When they come, they come from above.*

He had levered a round into the chamber of his rifle when, behind him, in the house, a voice cried out his name.

*   *   *

"Hold up a second," Hollis said.

An Army truck was tipped on its side in the roadway; one of its back wheels was still spinning with a creaking sound.

Sara quickly dismounted. "Somebody might be hurt."

Hollis followed her to the truck. The cab was empty.

"Maybe they walked out of here," Hollis said.

"No, this just happened." She looked down the road then pointed. "There."

The soldier was lying on his back. He was breathing in quick bursts, eyes open, staring at the sky. Sara dropped to her knees beside him. "Soldier, look at me. Can you speak?" He was acting like a man who was badly injured, yet there was no blood, no obvious sign of anything broken. The sleeves of his uniform bore the two stripes of a corporal. He rolled his face toward her, exposing a small wound, bright with blood, at the base of his throat.

"Run," he croaked.

Caleb burst into the house. Pim was holding Theo, backing away from the door to Dory's room; Bug and Elle were clustered at her legs.

Kate's voice: "Caleb, come quick!"

Dory was thrashing on the bed, spittle spewing from her lips. With a sound like a sneeze, her teeth flew from her mouth. Kate was standing by the bed, holding the revolver.

"Shoot her!" Caleb yelled.

Kate seemed not to hear him. With a sickening crunch, Dory's fingers elongated, gleaming claws extending from their tips. Her body had begun to glow. Her jaw unlocked; her mouth opened wide, revealing the picketed teeth.

"Shoot her now!"

Kate was frozen in place. As Caleb raised the rifle, Dory jolted upright, rolled into a crouch, and sprang toward the two of them. A confusion of bodies, Dory crashing into Kate, Kate crashing into Caleb; the rifle spat from his hand and skittered across the floor. On his hands and knees, Caleb scrambled toward it. He was yelling for Pim to run, though of course the woman couldn't hear him. His hand found the weapon, and he rolled onto his back. Kate was pushing herself backward toward the opposite wall; Dory stood above her, jaws flexing, fingers extended, strumming the air. Caleb lifted his back off the floor, widened his knees, and leveled the rifle at her with both hands.

"Dory Tatum!"

At the sound of her name, she stiffened, as if struck by a curious thought.

"You're Dory Tatum! Phil is your husband! Look at me!"

She turned toward him, exposing her upper body. *One shot,* thought Caleb, taking the center of her chest into his sights, and then he squeezed the trigger.

*   *   *

The soldier began to shake. The motion began at his fingers, which bent into clawlike shapes, like the talons of a hawk. A groan poured from deep in his throat. The shaking hardened into a whole-body convulsion, his spine arcing, spittle boiling to his lips. Sara was on her feet and backing away. She knew what she was seeing. It seemed impossible, and yet it was happening before her eyes. She sensed movement above her, yet she could not tear her eyes away from the soldier, whose transformation was occurring with unheard-of speed.

"Sara, come on! We have to get out of here!"

One of the horses whinnied and tore past her. It made it all of fifty feet down the road before a glowing shape swooped down and knocked it off its feet. Jaws tore into the horse's neck with a ripping sound.

Sara's mind snapped back into a wider awareness. Hollis was pulling her by the wrist. *The river!* he yelled. *We have to get to the river!* With a hard yank, he hauled her into the cover of the trees; they began to run. Shapes bounded above them, limb to limb. Branches whipped her face and arms. Where was the river, their salvation? Sara could hear it but could not locate it in the dark.

"Jump!"

In midair, she realized what was happening. They had leapt from a cliff. As she hit the surface, a new, deeper darkness, the darkness of water, enveloped her. It seemed she would never stop descending, but at last her feet touched the bottom. She pushed off and shot to the surface.

"Hollis!" She twisted in the water, blindly searching. "Hollis, where are you?"

"Over here. Keep your voice down."

She was spinning frantically, trying to locate the source of the voice. "I can't find you."

"Stay where you are."

Hollis appeared, treading water beside her. "Are you hurt?"

Was she? She took stock of her body. She didn't think she was.

"What's happening? Where did they come from?"

"I don't know."

"Don't leave me."

"Breathe, Sara."

She fought to calm herself. In, out, in, out.

"It looks like there are pockets at the base of the cliff," Hollis said. "We're going to swim there. Can you do it?"

She nodded. The water was freezing; her teeth had begun to chatter.

"Stay close."

With a smooth breaststroke he glided away, Sara following. The cliff took form above her. It wasn't as tall as she'd thought, perhaps twenty feet, and irregularly shaped, with blocky protrusions of pale limestone cantilevered over the pool. The water became shallower; Sara realized she could stand. Hollis guided her beneath an outcrop. A flat-topped boulder rose above the surface of the water. Hollis helped her up.

"We should be safe here for the night," he said.

Shivering, Sara leaned against him; Hollis put his arm around her and drew her close. She thought of her children, out there in the dark. She buried her face in Hollis's chest and began to cry.

Dory melted to the ground like a puppet cut from its strings. Caleb stepped over the body. Kate was still propped against the wall, her body inert, numbed by shock and fear.

"There's more out there," Caleb said. "We have to get to the shelter."

She looked at him with an unfocused gaze.

"Kate, snap out of it."

He couldn't wait. He grabbed her by the wrist and shoved her out the door. Pim was huddled by the hearth with the children. She hadn't heard the shot, but he knew she had felt it, shuddering through the frame of the house.

Caleb signed a single word: *Go.*

He dropped the rifle and scooped Elle and Bug into his arms, balancing them on the points of his hips; Pim was carrying Theo. They raced out the back door into the yard. Pim was ahead of him, Kate behind. The darkness was coming alive. The crowns of the trees tossed as if by the wind of an approaching storm. Pim and Theo reached the shelter first. Caleb dropped the girls to their feet and hauled the door of the hardbox open. Pim scrambled down the ladder and raised her arms to take Theo and then the girls, Caleb following.

At the top of the ladder, he stopped. Kate was standing thirty feet away.

"Kate, come on!"

She drew her collar aside. At the base of her throat, a wound had bloomed with blood. Caleb's stomach dropped; all sensation left him.

"Shut the door," she said.

She was holding the revolver. He couldn't move.

"Caleb, please!" She collapsed to her knees. A deep tremor shook her body. She was cradling the gun in her lap, attempting to lift it. She rocked her head skyward as a second jolt moved through her. "I'm begging you!" she sobbed. "If you love me, shut the door!"

His windpipe clamped; he could barely breathe. Behind her, shapes were dropping from the trees. Caleb reached above his head, taking the handle in his grip.

"I'm sorry," he whispered.

He drew down the door, sealing them in blackness, and shoved the cross-bars into place. The children were crying. He felt for the lantern, took a box of matches from his pocket. His hands were trembling as he lit the wick. Pim was huddled with the children against the wall.

Her eyes grew very wide. *Where's Kate?*

From outside, a shot.

VII

THE AWAKENING

At the round earth's imagin'd corners, blow
Your trumpets, angels, and arise, arise
From death, you numberless infinities
Of souls.

—JOHN DONNE, *HOLY SONNETS*

55

Peter awoke to a clattering of branches dragging against the side of the Humvee. He shook off his sluggishness and sat up.

"Where are we?"

"Houston," Greer said. Michael was asleep in the passenger seat. "Not long now."

A few minutes later, Greer brought the vehicle to a halt. To the east, the darkness had begun to soften.

"Let's be quick now," Greer said.

Peter and Michael unloaded their gear. They were at the edge of the lagoon; to the east, skyscrapers of incredible height cut black rectangles against the diminishing stars. Greer dragged a rowboat into the shallows. Michael sat in the bow, Peter the stern; Greer climbed into the middle, facing backward. The boat sank nearly to the gunwale but remained afloat.

"I was a little worried about that," Greer confessed.

With broad strokes he propelled them across the lagoon. Peter watched the city's core harden into its full dimensions. The *Mariner* soared into view, its great wide stern riding high above the water. Inside One Allen Center they tied off, gathered their supplies, and began to climb.

From a window on the tenth floor, they dropped to the deck. Dawn was a few minutes away. Greer had refurbished a small crane of a type once used to lower cargo over the side of the ship. He spread the net beneath it, tightened the spring on the spinner joint, and attached it to the rope that ran through the block at the end of the boom. A second rope would be used to swing the boom over the water. Greer would manage the first rope, Michael the second. Peter's job was to act as bait—Greer's theory being that Peter was the person Amy was least likely to kill.

Greer handed him the wrench. "Remember, she's not the Amy we know."

They took up their positions. Peter fit the tip of the wrench around the first bolt.

"They're here," said Amy.

Carter was sitting across the table from her. "Feel it, too."

Her heart was racing; she felt a little dizzy. It always came on like this, with a sensation of physical acceleration that culminated in an abrupt expulsion from one world to the next, as if she were a rock hurled from a sling.

"I wish you were coming with me," she said.

"Long as I'm here, they're safe. You know that."

She did. If Carter died, the dopeys, his Many, would die with him. Without them, Amy and Carter stood no chance.

She looked around the garden one last time, saying goodbye. She closed her eyes.

Two bolts to go, one on each side. Peter loosened the first, leaving it in place. As he fit the head of the wrench around the second bolt, a massive force, like a giant fist, struck the hatch from the opposite side. The deck beneath his knees shuddered from the impact.

"Amy, it's me! It's Peter!"

Another *wang;* the loosened bolt popped from the hole and bounced across the deck. He had seconds to spare. With a final yank, he freed the last bolt and began to run.

The hatch blew skyward.

Amy alighted on the deck, compressing to a reptilian crouch. Her body was glossy and compact, annealed with hard muscle beneath the crystalline sheath of skin. Peter was standing just beyond the net. For a moment she seemed puzzled by her surroundings; then her head slanted with a darting motion, taking him into her sights. She scuttled forward. Peter saw no recognition in her eyes.

"Amy." He lifted a hand toward her and spread his fingers. "It's me."

She halted, inches from the net.

"It's Peter."

Rising, Amy stepped forward. Greer pulled the rope; the net engulfed her and shot upward, her weight freeing the spinner from its brake. The net began to twirl, faster and faster. Amy was screaming and thrashing in its grasp. Michael yanked the second rope, swinging the boom over the side of the ship.

Greer let go. The rope holding the net shrieked through the block. Peter ran to the rail. He had just enough time to see the splash before Amy vanished into the oily water.

Darkness.

She was spinning and twisting and falling. Her senses swarmed with the awful, chemical-tasting water. It filled her mouth. It filled her nose and eyes and ears, a grip of pure death. She touched down upon the mucky bottom. The net held her body fast in its tangle. She needed to breathe. To breathe! She was thrashing, clawing, but there was no escaping its grasp. The first bubble of air rose from her mouth. *No,* she thought, *don't breathe!* This simple thing, to open one's lungs and take in the air: the body demanded it. A second bubble and her throat opened and the water slammed into her. She began to choke. The world was dissolving. No, it was she who was dissolving. Her body felt untethered to her thoughts, a thing apart, no longer hers. Her heart began to slow. A new darkness came upon her. It spread from within. *This is what it's like,* she thought. Panic, and pain, and then the letting go. *This is what it's like to die.*

Then she was somewhere else.

She was playing a piano. This was strange, because she'd never learned. Yet here she was, playing not just well but expertly, fingers prancing across the keys. There was no sheet music before her; the song came from her head. A sad and beautiful song, full of tenderness and the sweet sorrows of life. Why did it seem entirely new to her but also remembered, like something from a dream? As she played, she began to discern patterns in the notes. Their relationship was not arbitrary; they moved through discernible cycles. Each cycle carried a slight variation of the song's emotional core, a melodic line that never wholly departed but supported the rest like laundry on a string. How astonishing! She felt as if she were speaking an entirely new language, far more subtle and expressive than ordinary speech, capable of communicating the deepest truths. It made her happy, very happy, and she went on playing, her fingers dexterously moving, her spirit soaring with delight.

The song turned a corner; she could sense its end approaching. The final notes descended. They hung like dust motes in the air, then were gone.

"That was wonderful."

Peter was standing behind her. Amy leaned the back of her head against his chest.

"I didn't hear you come in," she said.

"I didn't want to disturb you. I know how much you like to play. Will you play me another?" he asked.

"Would you like that?"

"Oh, yes," he said. "Very much."

"Pull her up!" Peter yelled.

Greer was looking at his watch. "Not yet."

"Goddamnit, she's drowning!"

Greer continued looking at his watch with infuriating patience. At last he looked up.

"Now," he said.

She played for a long while, song after song. The first was light, with a humorous energy; it made her feel as if she were at a gathering of friends, everyone talking and laughing, darkness thickening outside the windows as the party went on and on into the small hours of the night. The next one was more serious. It began with a deep, sonorous chord at the bass end of the keyboard, with a slightly sour tone. A song of regret, of acts that could not be recalled, mistakes that could never be undone.

There were others. One was like looking at a fire. Another like falling snow. A third was horses galloping through tall grass beneath a blue autumn sky. She played and played. There was so much feeling in the world. So much sadness. So much longing. So much joy. Everything had a soul. The petals of flowers. The mice of the field. The clouds and rain and the bare limbs of trees. All these things and many others were in the songs she played. Peter was still behind her. The music was for him, an offering of love. She felt at peace.

They swung the net over the side and lowered it to the deck. Greer drew a knife and began to slash at the filaments.

In the net was the body of a woman.

"Hurry," Peter said.

Greer hacked away. He was fashioning a hole. "Take her feet."

Michael and Peter drew Amy free and laid her faceup on the deck. The sun was rising. Her body was limp, with a bluish cast. On her head, a scrim of black hair.

She wasn't breathing.

Peter dropped to his knees; Michael straddled her at the waist, stacked his palms, and positioned them on Amy's sternum. Peter slid his left hand beneath her neck, lifting it slightly to open the airway; with his other hand he pinched her nose. He fit his mouth over hers and blew.

"Amy."

Her fingers stilled, bringing a sudden silence to the room. She lifted her hands above the keyboard, palms flat, fingers extended.

"I need you to do something for me," Peter said.

She reached over her shoulder, took his left hand, and placed it against her cheek. His skin was cold and smelled of the river, where he liked to spend his days. How wonderful everything was. "Tell me."

"Don't leave me, Amy."

"What makes you think I'm going someplace?"

"It's not time yet."

"I don't understand."

"Do you know where you are?"

She wanted to turn around to see his face and yet could not. "I do. I think I do. We're at the farmstead."

"Then you know why you can't stay."

She was suddenly cold. "But I want to."

"It's too soon. I'm sorry."

She began to cough.

"I need you with me," Peter said. "There are things we have to do."

The coughing became more intense. Her whole body shook with it. Her limbs were like ice. What was happening to her?

"Come back to me, Amy."

She was choking. She was going to vomit. The room began to fade. Something else was taking its place. A sharp pain struck her chest, like the blow of a fist. She doubled over, her body curling around the impact. Foul-tasting water poured from her mouth.

"Come back to me, Amy. Come back to me . . ."

"Come back to me."

Amy's face was slack, her body still. Michael was counting out the compressions. Fifteen. Twenty. Twenty-five.

"Goddamnit, Greer!" Peter yelled. "She's dying!"

"Don't stop."

"It's not working!"

Peter bent his face to hers once more, pinched her nose, and blew.

Something clicked inside her. Peter pulled away as her mouth opened wide in a throttled gasp. He rolled her over, slipped an arm beneath her torso to lift her slightly, and pounded her on the back. With a retching sound, water jetted from her mouth onto the deck.

There was a face. That was the first thing she became aware of. A face, its features vague, and behind it only sky. Where was she? What had occurred?

Who was this person who was looking at her, floating in the heavens? She blinked, trying to focus her eyes. Slowly the image resolved. A nose. The curving shape of ears. A broad, smiling mouth and, above it, eyes that glittered with tears. Pure happiness filled her like a bursting star.

"Oh, Peter," she said, raising a hand to his cheek. "It is so good to see you."

VIII

THE SIEGE

Thick as autumnal leaves or driving sand,
The moving squadrons blacken all the strand.

—HOMER, *THE ILIAD*

56

All night long, the virals pounded.

It happened in bursts. Five minutes, ten, their fists and bodies slamming against the door—a period of silence, then they would begin again.

Eventually the intervals between the attacks grew longer. The girls gave up their crying and slept, their heads buried in Pim's lap. More time passed with no sounds outside; finally, the virals did not return.

Caleb waited. When would dawn come? When would it be safe to open the door? Pim, too, had fallen asleep; the terrors of the night had exhausted all of them. He leaned his head against the wall and closed his eyes.

He awoke to muffled voices outside; help had arrived. Whoever it was had begun to knock.

Pim awoke. The girls were still asleep. She signed a simple question mark. *It's people,* he replied.

Still, it was with some anxiety that he unbarred the door. He pushed it just a little; a crack of daylight blasted his eyes. He shoved the door open the rest of the way, blinking in the light.

Standing before him, Sara dropped to her knees.

"Oh, thank God," she said.

Hollis was with her; the two were barefoot, soaked to the bone.

"We were coming to see you when they attacked," Hollis explained. "We hid in the river."

Pim lifted the children out and climbed up behind them. Sara embraced her, weeping. "Thank God, thank God." She knelt and drew the girls into her arms. "You're safe. My babies are safe."

Caleb's relief melted away. He realized what was about to happen.

"Kate," Sara yelled. "Come out now!"

Nobody said anything.

"Kate?"

Hollis looked at Caleb. The younger man shook his head. Hollis stiffened, wavering on his feet, the blood draining from his face. For a moment Caleb thought his father-in-law might collapse.

"Sara, come here," Hollis said.

"Kate?" Her voice was frantic. "Kate, come out!"

Hollis grabbed her around the waist.

"Kate! You answer me!"

"She's not in the hardbox, Sara."

Sara thrashed in his arms, trying to break free. "Hollis, let me go. Kate!"

"She's gone, Sara. Our Kate is gone."

"Don't say that! Kate, I'm your mother, you come out here right now!"

Her strength left her; she dropped to her knees, Hollis still holding her around the waist. "Oh, God," she moaned.

Hollis's eyes were closed in anguish. "She's gone. She's gone."

"Please, no. Not her."

"Our little girl is gone."

Sara lifted her face to the heavens. Then she began to howl.

The light was soft and featureless; low, wet clouds blotted the sun. Peter lifted Amy into the vehicle's cargo bay and put a blanket over her. A bit of color had flowed back into her face; her eyes were closed, though it seemed she was not asleep but, rather, in a kind of twilight, as if her mind were floating in a current, the banks of the world flowing past.

Greer's voice was tight: "We better get moving."

Peter rode in the back with Amy. The going was slow, the dirt track crowded by brush. In the dark, Peter had absorbed almost nothing of the landscape. Now he saw it for what it was: an inhospitable swamp of lagoons, ruined structures clawed by vines, the earth vague, like something melted. Sometimes standing water obscured the roadway, its depth unknown; Greer plowed through.

The foliage began to thin; a cyclonic tangle of highway overpasses appeared. Greer threaded through the detritus beneath the freeway, located a ramp, and ascended.

For a time they followed the highway; then Greer veered away. Despite the violent jostling of the Humvee, Amy had yet to stir. They skirted a second region of collapsed overpasses, then climbed up the bank, back onto the highway.

Michael turned in his seat. "Easier going from here."

Rain began to fall, pattering the windshield; then the clouds broke, revealing a strong Texas sun. Amy gave a sigh of wakefulness; Peter looked to find that her eyes had opened. She blinked at him, then, squinting fiercely, covered her eyes with her arms.

"It's bright," she said.

"What was that?" Greer said from the front.

"She says it's bright."

"She's been in the dark for twenty years—the light may bother her awhile." Greer bent forward to reach under his seat. "Give her these."

Over his shoulder, he passed Peter a pair of dark glasses. The lenses were scratched and pitted, the frames made from soldered wire. He slipped the glasses over her face, wrapping the wires gently behind her ears.

"Better?"

She nodded. Her eyes closed once more. "I'm so tired," she murmured.

Peter leaned forward. "How much farther?"

"We should make it before sundown, but it will be close. We're going to need fuel, too. There should be some in the hardbox west of Sealy."

They continued in silence. Despite the tension, Peter felt himself drifting off. He slept for two hours, awakening to find that the truck had stopped. Greer and Michael were toting two heavy plastic jugs of fuel from the hardbox. His thoughts were fuzzy; his limbs, heavy and slow, moved like pooled liquid. Everywhere in his body, he felt his age.

Michael glanced his way as he stepped out. "How's she doing?"

"Still asleep."

Greer was pouring gas through a funnel into the truck's tank. "She'll be okay. Sleep is what she needs."

"Let me take the wheel for a while," Peter offered. "I know the way from here."

Greer bent to cap the can and wiped his hands on his shirt. "Better if Michael does for now. There's a few tricky spots ahead."

They found Kate at the edge of the woods. The gun was still in her hand, her finger curled inside the trigger guard. One shot, through the sweet spot: Kate, thorough to the last, had wanted to be sure.

They had no time to bury her. They decided to take her into the house and lay her in the bed Caleb and Pim had shared, since they would never be coming back here. Hollis and Caleb carried her inside. It did not seem right to leave her in her blood-stained clothes; Pim and Sara undressed her, washed her body, and put her in one of Pim's nightgowns, made of soft blue cotton. They placed a pillow beneath her head and tucked a blanket tightly around her; Pim, weeping silently, brushed her sister's hair. A final question: Should they let the girls see her? Yes, Sara said. Kate was their mother. They needed to say goodbye.

Caleb waited outside. It was midmorning, cruelly bright. Nature mocked him with its disregard. The birds sang, the breeze blew, the clouds scudded overhead, the sun moved in its lazy, fateful arc. Handsome lay dead in the field; a crowd of buzzards jabbed at the banquet of his flesh, flapping their enormous wings. All was a ruin, yet the world did not seem to know or care. In the bedroom, Caleb had told Kate he loved her and kissed her on the forehead. Her skin was shockingly cold, but that was not the most disturbing thing. He realized he was expecting her to say something. *It didn't hurt too much.* Or *It's okay, Caleb, I don't blame you. You did the best you could.* Maybe she would say something sarcastic, such as *Seriously? You're going to tuck me into bed? I'm not a child, you know. I bet this is a lot of fun for you, Caleb.* Yet there was nothing. Her body existed, but all that had made her distinct as a person was absent. Her voice was gone; never would it be heard again.

Pim came out first, with the girls. Elle was crying softly; Bug looked merely confused. A few minutes passed before Sara and Hollis emerged.

"If you're ready, we should get moving," Caleb said.

Hollis nodded. Sara, standing apart, was gazing toward the trees. Her eyes were glassy, her face unnaturally still, as if some essential element of life had left it. She cleared her throat and spoke:

"Husband, will you do something for me?"

"All right."

She looked him in the eye. "Kill every last fucking one of them."

The going was slow. Soon all three children were being carried—Bug on Caleb's shoulders, Elle on her grandfather's back, Theo in his sling, Pim and Sara taking turns. They were deep into the afternoon by the time they reached town. The streets were devoid of life. In Elacqua's yard, they found the truck, still parked where Caleb had seen it. Caleb got in the driver's seat. He'd hoped the key would be in the ignition, but it wasn't. He searched the cab to no avail and climbed back out.

"Do you know how to hot-wire a truck?" he asked Hollis.

"Not really."

Caleb looked toward the house. A window on the top floor was broken, smashed from its frame. Glass and splintered wood littered the ground beneath it.

"Somebody's going to have to go inside to look."

"I'll do it," said Hollis.

"This is my responsibility. Stay here."

Caleb left the rifle with Hollis and took the revolver. The air in the house was so still it felt unbreathed. He crept from room to room, opening drawers and cabinets. Finding no keys, he climbed the stairs. There were two rooms with closed doors on either side of a narrow hall. He opened the first door. Here was where Elacqua and his wife had slept. The bed was unmade; beside it, lace curtains shifted slightly in the breeze coming through the broken window. He searched all the drawers, then stepped to the window and waved down. Hollis gazed up with a questioning look. Caleb shook his head.

One room to go. What if they couldn't find the keys? He'd seen no other vehicles in town. That didn't mean there weren't any, but they were running out of time.

Caleb took a breath and pushed the door with his foot.

Elacqua was lying on the bed fully clothed. The room reeked of piss and rancid breath. At first Caleb thought the man was dead, but then he gave a wet snort and rolled onto his side. An empty whiskey bottle stood on the floor beside the bed. The man wasn't dead, just dead drunk.

Caleb shook him roughly by the shoulders. "Wake up."

Elacqua, eyes still closed, batted clumsily at Caleb's hand. "Leave me alone," he mumbled.

"Dr. Elacqua, it's Caleb Jaxon. Pull yourself together."

His tongue moved heavily in his mouth. "You . . . bitch."

Caleb had a sense of what had occurred. Cast out from his marital bed, the man had anesthetized himself into oblivion and missed the whole thing. Perhaps he'd been drunk to begin with and that was why his wife had sent him packing. In either case, Caleb practically envied him; the disaster had passed him by. How had the virals missed him? Maybe he just smelled too bad; maybe that was the solution. Maybe they should all get drunk and stay that way.

He shook Elacqua again. The man's eyes fluttered open. They roamed blearily, finally landing on Caleb's face.

"Who the hell are you?"

There was no point in attempting to explain the situation; the man was too far gone. "Dr. Elacqua, look at me. I need the keys to your truck."

Caleb might have been asking him the most incomprehensible question in the world. "Keys?"

"Yes, the keys. Where are they?"

His eyes lost focus; he closed them again, his head, with its wild mane of hair, relaxing into the pillow. Caleb realized there was one place he hadn't looked. The man's trousers were soaked with urine, but there was nothing to be done about that. Caleb patted him down. At the base of the man's left front pocket, Caleb felt something sharp. He slid his hand in and pulled it out: a single key, tarnished with age, on a small metal ring.

"Gotcha."

His thoughts were broken by the roar of engines coming down the street. Caleb went to the window. Sara and the others were waving frantically toward the source of the sound, yelling, "Hey! Over here!"

Caleb stepped onto the porch as the trucks, three Army five-tons, halted in front of the house. A broad-chested man in uniform stepped from the cab of the first truck: Gunnar Apgar.

"Caleb. Thank God."

They shook. Hollis and Sara had joined them. Apgar looked the group over. "Is this all of you?"

"There's one more in the house, but we'll need some help getting him out. He's pretty drunk."

"You're kidding." When Caleb said nothing, Apgar addressed a pair of soldiers who had disembarked from the second vehicle: "Haul him out here, on the double."

They trotted up the steps.

"We've been working our way west, looking for folks," Apgar said.

"How many survivors have you found?"

"You're it. We're not even finding any *bodies*. The virals either dragged them off or they've been turned."

Hollis asked, "What about Kerrville?"

"No sign of them yet. Whatever's going on, it's happening out here first." He paused, his expression suddenly uncertain. "There's something else you ought to know, Caleb. It's about your father."

Peter took the wheel east of Seguin. Amy had awakened briefly in midafternoon, asking for water. Her fever was down, and her eyes seemed to be bothering her less, though she complained of a headache and was still very weak. Squinting out a side window, she asked how much farther they had to go. She was wearing the blanket like a shawl over her head and shoulders. Three hours, Greer said, maybe four. Amy considered this answer, then said, very softly, "We should hurry."

They crossed the Guadalupe and turned north. The first township they'd come to was just east of the old city of Boerne. It wasn't much, but there was a telegraph station. Only two hands of daylight remained when they pulled into the small central square.

"Awfully quiet around here," Michael said.

The streets were empty. Odd for this hour, Peter thought. They disembarked into ghostly silence. The town comprised just a few buildings: a general store, a township office, a chapel, and a handful of shoddily erected houses, some half-constructed, as if their builders had lost interest.

"Anybody here?" Michael yelled. "Hello?"

"Feels strange," Greer said.

Michael reached into the Humvee and released the shotgun from the holder. Peter and Greer checked their pistols.

"I'll stay with Amy," Greer said. "You two go find the telegraph station."

Peter and Michael crossed the square to the township office. The door stood open, another oddity. Everything appeared normal inside, but still there were no signs of life.

"So where the hell did everybody go?" Peter said.

The telegraph was in a small room in the rear of the building. Michael sat at the operator's desk and examined the log, a large, leather-bound ledger.

"The last message from here was sent Friday, five-twenty P.M., to Bandera station. The intended recipient was Mrs. Nills Grath."

"What was the message?"

"'Happy birthday, Aunt Lottie.'" Michael looked up. "Nothing after that, at least that anybody bothered to record."

Today was Sunday. Whatever had happened here, Peter thought, it had happened sometime in the last forty-eight hours.

"Send a message to Kerrville," Peter instructed. "Let Apgar know we're coming."

"My Morse is a little rusty. I'll probably tell him to make me a sandwich."

Michael threw a switch on the panel and began tapping the key. A few seconds later, he stopped.

"What's wrong?"

Michael pointed to the panel. "See this meter? The needle should move when the plates touch."

"So?"

"So I'm talking to myself here. The circuit won't close."

Peter knew nothing about it. "Is that something you can fix?"

"Not a chance. There's a break in the line, could be anywhere between here and Kerrville. The storm might have knocked down a pole. A lightning strike could do it, too. It doesn't take much."

They exited through the back door. An old gas generator was crouched like a monster in the weeds, beside a rusted pickup and a buckboard with a broken axle and tall grass poking through the floorboards. Trash of all kinds—construction debris, busted packing crates, barrels with their seams split open—littered the yard. The wreckage of the frontier, flung out the door the moment it had outlived its usefulness.

"Let's check some of the other buildings," Peter said.

They entered the nearest house. It was one story, with two rooms. Dirty dishes were stacked on a table; flies twisted above them in the air. In the back room was a washbasin on a stand, a wardrobe, and large feather bed covered by a quilt. The bed was sturdy and carefully made, with a tableau of interlocking flowers, quite detailed, carved into the headboard; somebody had taken their time with it. A marriage bed, thought Peter.

But where were the people? What had happened that the inhabitants should vanish before they had a chance to clear the dirty dishes from the table? Peter and Michael returned to the main room as Greer came through the door.

"What's the holdup?"

"The telegraph's not working," Michael said.

"What's wrong with it?"

"Break in the line someplace."

Greer leveled his eyes at Peter. "We really have to get moving."

What weren't they seeing? What was this haunted place trying to tell him? Peter's eyes fell upon something on the floor.

"Peter, did you hear me?" Greer pressed. "If we're going to make it back before dark, we need to leave right now."

Peter crouched to get a closer look, simultaneously gesturing toward the table. "Hand me that dishrag."

Using a corner of the cloth, he took hold of the object. The virals' teeth had a way of catching the light, almost prismatic, with a pearlescent, milky luster. The tip was so sharp it seemed to fade into invisibility, too small for the naked eye to discern.

"I don't think Zero's sending an army," Peter said.

"Then what's he doing?" Michael asked.

Peter looked at Greer; the older man's expression said he thought the same.

"I think he's growing one."

57

By the time the convoy reached Kerrville, it was nearly seven o'clock. The group disembarked into a state of siege. Along the top of the wall, soldiers were scurrying back and forth, handing out magazines and other gear. Fifty-caliber machine guns were positioned on either side of the gate. Apgar had exited the cab and was standing with Ford Chase, pointing at one of the spotlights. As Chase moved away, Caleb stepped up.

"General, I'd like my commission back."

Apgar frowned. "I have to say, that's a first. Nobody ever asks to get back in the Army."

"You can bust me to private—I don't care."

The general looked past Caleb's shoulder toward Pim, who was standing with Sara and the children.

"You clear this with your CO?"

"I'd be lying if I said she was happy about it. But she gets it. She lost her sister last night."

Apgar beckoned to a noncom manning the gates. "Sergeant, take this man to the armory and get him suited up. One brass bar."

"Thank you, General," said Caleb.

"You may rethink that later. And your old man's going to have my ass for this."

"Have we heard anything?"

Apgar shook his head. "Try not to worry, son. He's been through worse than this. Report to Colonel Henneman on the platform. He'll tell you where to go."

Caleb went to Pim and hugged her. He placed his palm against the curve of her belly, then kissed Theo on the forehead.

Be careful, she signed.

"We're going to the hospital," Sara said. "There's a hardbox in the basement. We're moving the patients down there."

The sergeant shifted impatiently on his feet. "Sir, we'd better go."

Caleb looked at his family a final time. He felt a gap widening, as if he were viewing them from the end of a lengthening tunnel.

I love you, Pim signed.

I love you, too.

He jogged away.

From Boerne, Greer took the wheel. They were driving into the sun now. Michael was in the passenger seat, Peter in the back with Amy.

They saw no other vehicles, no signs of life at all. The world seemed dead, an alien landscape. The shadows of the hills were lengthening; evening was coming on. Greer, squinting into the harsh light, wore a look of great intensity— his arms and back rigid as wood, his fingers clenching the wheel. Peter saw the muscles of his jaw bunching; the man was grinding his teeth.

They passed through Comfort. The ruins of ancient buildings—restaurants, gas stations, hotels—lined the highway, sand-scoured and scavenged to the bones. They came to the settlement on the west side of the city, away from the wreckage of the old world. Like Boerne, the town was abandoned; they didn't stop.

Fifteen miles to go.

Sara and the others met Jenny at the door to the hospital. The woman was on the verge of wild-eyed panic.

"What's going on? There are soldiers everywhere. A Humvee just rolled by with a bullhorn, telling everybody to take shelter."

"There's an attack coming. We have to get these people to the basement. How many patients are on the wards?"

"What do you mean, an attack?"

"I mean *virals,* Jenny."

The woman blanched but said nothing.

"Listen to me." Sara took Jenny's hands and made the woman look at her. "We don't have a lot of time here. How many?"

Jenny gave her head a little shake, as if trying to focus her thoughts. "Fifteen?"

"Any children?"

"Just a couple. One boy has pneumonia, the other a broken wrist we just set. We've got one woman in labor, but she's early."

"Where's Hannah?"

Hannah was Jenny's daughter, a girl of thirteen; her son was grown and gone. Jenny and her husband had long since parted ways.

"Home, I think?"

"Run and get her. I can handle the situation until you're back."

"God, Sara."

"Just be quick."

Jenny darted from the building. Pim, holding Theo, was standing with the girls. Sara crouched before them. "I need you to go with your Auntie Pim now."

Elle looked fearful and lost; snot was running from her nose. Sara wiped it with the bottom edge of her shirt.

"Where are we going?" the girl asked woefully.

People were scurrying past—nurses, doctors, orderlies with stretchers. Sara glanced up at Pim, then looked at her granddaughter again. "Downstairs to the basement," Sara answered. "You'll be safe there."

"I want to go home."

"It's just for a little while."

She hugged Elle, then her sister; Pim led the girls to the stairs. As they descended, Sara turned to her husband. She recognized the look on his face. It was the same one he'd worn the night after Bill had been killed, when he'd shown her the note.

"It's okay," she said.

"You're sure?"

"I've got things in hand here. Go before I change my mind."

No more words were necessary. Hollis kissed her and strode out the door.

*   *   *

They turned off Highway 10. From here, it was a straight shot south on a gravel road to the city. The truck shook fiercely as they pounded through the potholes. Wind whipped through the open windows; the sun, coming across their right shoulders, was low and bright.

"Michael, take the wheel and keep it steady." Greer reached below his seat. "Peter, give her this."

Peter leaned forward to receive the pistol. A round was already chambered.

"You won't have time to aim," he said to Amy. "Just point and shoot, like you're pointing your finger."

She took the gun from him. Her expression was uncertain, yet her grip seemed firm.

"You have fifteen rounds. You'll have to be close—don't try to shoot them from a distance."

"Unlock the shotgun," Greer said.

Michael freed the weapon. An extended magazine tube ran below the barrel, holding eight shells. "What's in here?" he asked Greer.

"Slugs, big ones. No room for slop, but it'll put one down fast."

The shape of the city emerged in the distance. Standing on the hill, it looked as small as a toy.

"This is going to be tight," Greer said.

The last patients were being brought down from the main floor. Jenny stood at the door of the hardbox with a clipboard, checking names off a list, while Sara and the nursing staff moved among the cots, doing their best to make sure everyone was comfortable.

Sara came to the cot that held the pregnant woman Jenny had spoken of. She was young, with thick, dark hair. While Sara took her pulse, she looked quickly at the girl's chart. A nurse had checked her an hour ago; her cervix had been barely dilated. Her name was Grace Alvado.

"Grace, I'm Dr. Wilson. Is this your first baby?"

"I was pregnant one other time, but it didn't take."

"And how old are you?"

"Twenty-one."

Sara stopped; the age was right. If this was the same Grace, Sara had last seen her when she was just a day old.

"Are your parents Carlos and Sally Jiménez?"

"You knew my folks?"

Sara almost smiled; she might have, on a different day. "This might surprise you, Grace, but I was there the day you were born." She looked toward the girl's companion, who was sitting on a packing crate on the other side of the cot. He was older, maybe forty, with a rough look to him, though like many new fathers he seemed a little overwhelmed by the sudden urgency of events after months of waiting.

"Are you Mr. Alvado?"

"Call me Jock. Everybody does."

"I need you to keep her relaxed, Jock. Deep breaths, and no pushing for now. Can you do that for me?"

"I'll try."

Jenny came up behind Sara. "Everybody's in," she said.

Sara put her hand on Grace's arm. "Just focus on having your baby, okay?"

The basement door was made of heavy steel, set into walls of thick concrete. Sara was about to close it when the room plunged into darkness. An anxious murmuring, and then people began to shout.

"Everybody, settle down, please!" Sara said.

"What happened to the lights?" a voice cried from the darkness.

"The Army's just diverting current to the spots, that's all."

"That means the virals are coming!"

"We don't know that. Everyone, just try to keep calm."

Jenny was standing beside her. "Is that really what they're doing?" she asked quietly.

"Do I know? Go check the storage room for lanterns and candles."

The woman returned a couple of minutes later. Lamps were lit and distributed around the space. The yells had fallen to whispers and, then, in the gloom, a tense silence.

"Jenny, give me a hand."

The door weighed four hundred pounds. Sara and Jenny pulled it closed and turned the wheel to engage the bolts.

A quarter of Apgar's men had taken up positions within five hundred yards of the gate; the rest were spread at regular intervals along the walls and connected by radio. Caleb was in charge of a squad of twelve men. Six of them had been stationed at Luckenbach—part of a small contingent who'd made it to a hardbox as the garrison was overrun. No officers had survived, orphaning them in the chain of command. Now they were Caleb's.

A man came banging down the catwalk toward him. Hollis wore no uniform, but a standard-issue chest pack was cinched to his frame, holding half a dozen spare magazines and a long, sheathed knife. An M4 dangled from its sling across his broad frame, the muzzle pointed downward; a pistol was holstered to his thigh.

He gave a crisp salute. "Private Wilson, sir."

It was absurd, Hollis speaking to him this way. He almost seemed like he was play-acting. "You're kidding me."

"The women and children are secure. I was told to report to you."

His face was set in a way that Caleb had never seen before. This large, gentle man, collector of books and reader to children, had become a warrior.

"I made a promise, Lieutenant," Hollis reminded him. "I believe you were there at the time."

The spots came on, spilling a defensive perimeter of stark white light at the base of the wall. Radios began to crackle; a tremor of energy moved up and down the catwalk.

A call went out: "Eyes up!"

The *clack* of chambering rounds. Caleb pointed his rifle over the wall and flicked off the safety. He glanced to his right, where Hollis stood at the ready: feet wide, stock set, eyes trained down the barrel in perfect alignment. His body was somehow both tense and relaxed, purposeful and at ease with itself. It had the look of an old feeling stitched to the bones, summoned effortlessly to the surface when called upon.

Where would the virals come from? How many would there be? His chest was opening and closing arrhythmically; his vision seemed unnaturally confined. He forced himself to take a long, deep breath. *Don't think,* he told himself. *There are times for thinking, but this isn't one of them.*

A glowing point appeared in the distance, straight north. Adrenaline hit his heart; he hardened the stock against his shoulder. The light began to bob, then to separate like a dividing cell. Not virals: headlights.

"Contact!" a voice yelled. "Thirty degrees right! Two hundred yards!"

"Contact! Twenty left!"

For the first time in over two decades, the horn began to wail.

Greer shoved the accelerator to the floor. The speedometer leapt, the fields flying past in a blur, the engine roaring, the frame of the truck shuddering.

"They're dead behind us!" Michael yelled.

Peter swiveled in his seat. Points of light were rising from the fields.

"Look out!" Greer yelled.

Peter turned around in time to see three virals leap into the headlights. Greer took aim and sliced through the pod. As bodies barreled over the hood, Peter slammed forward and bounced back into his seat. When he looked again, a single viral was clinging to the hood of the truck.

Michael pointed the shotgun over the dash and fired.

The glass exploded. Greer swerved to the left; Peter was thrown against the door, Amy on top of him. They were barreling through a bean field, moving laterally to the gate. Greer swerved the opposite way; the chassis tipped to the left, threatened to roll; then the wheels slammed down. Greer crested a rise and the truck went briefly airborne before spinning back onto the road. An ominous *clunk* from below; they began to decelerate.

Peter yelled to Greer, "What's wrong?"

Smoke was pouring from the grille; the engine roared pointlessly. "We must have hit something—the transmission's blown. On your right!"

Peter turned, took the viral in his sights, and squeezed the trigger, missing cleanly. Again and again he fired. He had no idea if he was hitting anything. The slide locked back; the magazine was empty. The lighted perimeter was still a hundred yards away.

"I'm out!" Michael yelled.

As the truck floated to a halt, flares arced from the catwalk, dragging contrails of light and smoke above their heads. Peter turned to Amy. She was slumped against the door, the pistol, unfired, dangling in her hand.

"Greer," Peter said, "help me."

He pulled her from the cab. Her motions were as heavy and loose as a sleepwalker's. The flares began their lazy, flickering descents. As Amy's legs unfolded from the truck, Greer stepped around the front of the vehicle, shoving fresh shells into the shotgun's magazine. He slapped the gun into Peter's hand and slid his right shoulder under Amy's arm to take her weight.

"Cover us," he said.

Caleb helplessly watched the truck's approach. The virals were still well out of reach for even the luckiest shot. Up and down the wall, voices were yelling to hold fire, to wait until they were in range.

He saw the truck stop. Four figures emerged. At the rear of the group, one man turned and fired a shotgun into the heart of an approaching pod. One shot, two shots, three, flames blooming from the gun's muzzle in the darkness.

Caleb knew that man to be his father.

He had stepped into the harness and clipped in before he was even aware he was doing it. The action was automatic; he had no plan, only instinct.

"Caleb, what the hell are you doing?"

Hollis was staring at him. Caleb hopped to the top of the rampart and turned his back toward the fields.

"Tell Apgar we'll need a squad at the pedestrian portal. Go."

Before Hollis could say anything else, Caleb pushed off. A long arc away from the wall and his boots touched concrete; he shoved himself away again. Two more pushes and he landed in the dirt. He unclipped and swung his rifle around.

His father was running with the others up the hill, just inside the lighted perimeter. Virals were massing at the edges. Some were covering their eyes; others had crouched into low, ball-like shapes. A moment's hesitation, their instincts warring inside them. Would the lights be enough to hold them back?

The virals charged.

The machine guns opened up; Caleb ducked reflexively as bullets whizzed over his head, slicing into the creatures with a wet, slapping sound. Blood splashed; flesh was cleaved from bone; whole pieces of the virals' bodies winged away. They seemed not merely to die but to disintegrate. The machine guns pounded, round after round. A slaughter, yet always there were more, surging into the lights.

"The portal!" Caleb called. He was running forward at a forty-five-degree angle to the wall, waving above his head. "Head for the portal!"

Caleb dropped to one knee and began to fire. Did his father see him? Did he know who he was? The bolt locked back; thirty rounds, gone in a heartbeat. He dropped the magazine, reached into his chest pack for a fresh one, and shoved it into the receiver.

Something crashed into him from behind. Breath, sight, thought: all left him. He felt himself sailing, almost hovering. This seemed extraordinary. In the midst of his flight, he had just enough time to marvel at the lightness of his body compared to other things. Then his body grew heavy again and he slammed into the ground. He was rolling down the incline, his rifle whipping around on its sling. He tried to control his body, its wild tumble down the hill. His hand found the lower unit of the rifle, but his index finger got tangled in the trigger guard. He rolled again, onto his chest, the rifle wedged between his body and the ground, and there was no stopping it; the gun went off.

Pain! He came to rest on his back, the rifle lying over his chest. Had he shot himself? The ground was spinning under him; it refused to be still. He blinked into the spotlights. He didn't feel the way he imagined a shot person would. The pain was in two places: his chest, which had received the explosive force of the rifle's firing, and a spot on his forehead, near the outer edge of his right eyebrow. He reached up, expecting blood; his fingers came away dry. He understood what had happened. The ejecting cartridge, ricocheting off the ground, had pinged upward into his face, narrowly missing his eye. *You are fucking lucky, Caleb Jaxon,* he thought. *I really hope nobody saw that.*

A shadow fell across him.

Caleb raised the rifle, but as his left hand reached forward to balance the barrel he realized the mag well was empty; the magazine had been stripped away. He had, at various times of his life, imagined the moment of his own death. These imaginings had not included lying on his back with an empty rifle while a viral tore him to pieces. Perhaps, he considered, that's the way it was for everybody: *Bet you didn't think of this.* Caleb dropped the rifle. His only hope was his sidearm. Had he racked it? Had he remembered to free the safety? Would the gun even be there, or had it, like the rifle's magazine, been stripped from his person? The shadow had taken the form of a human silhouette, but it wasn't human, not at all. The head cocked. The claws extended. The lips retreated, revealing a dark cave dripping with teeth. The pistol was in Caleb's hand and rising.

A burst of blood; the creature curled around the hole at the center of its chest. With an almost tender gesture, it reached up with one clawed hand and touched the wound. It raised its face with a bland expression. *Am I dead? Did you do that?* But Caleb hadn't; he hadn't even pulled the trigger. The shot had come from over Caleb's shoulder. For a second they studied one another, Caleb and this dying thing; then a second figure stepped from Caleb's right, shoved the muzzle of a shotgun into the viral's face, and fired.

It was his father. With him was a woman, barefoot, in a plain frock, the kind the sisters wore. Her hair was the barest patina of darkness on her skull. In her outstretched hand, she held the pistol she had used to fire the first, fatal shot.

Amy.

"Peter . . ." she said. And melted to her knees.

Then they were running.

No words were passed that Caleb would later recall. His father was carrying Amy over his shoulder; two other men were with them; one of them had the shotgun his father had cast aside. The portal was open; a squad of six soldiers had formed a firing line in front of it.

"Get down!"

The voice was Hollis's. All of them hit the dirt. Shots screamed past them, then ceased abruptly. Caleb lifted his face. Over the barrel of his rifle, Hollis was waving them on.

"Run your asses off!"

His father and Amy entered first, Caleb following. A barrage of gunfire erupted behind them. The soldiers were shouting to one another—*On your left! On your right! Go, go!*—firing their rifles as, one by one, they backed through the narrow doorway. Hollis was the last to enter. He dropped his rifle, swung the door around, and began to close it, clutching the wheel that, once turned, would set the bolts. Just as the lip of the door was about to make contact with the frame, it stopped.

"Need some help here!"

Hollis was bracing the door with his shoulder. Caleb sprang forward and pushed; others did the same. Still, the gap began to widen. An inch, then two more. Half a dozen men were piled against the door. Caleb swiveled his body so his back was braced against it and dug the heels of his boots into the earth. But the end was ordained; even if they could hold the door a few minutes longer, the virals' strength would outlast them.

He saw a way.

Caleb dropped his hand to his belt. He hated grenades; he could not put aside the irrational fear that they would detonate of their own accord. Thus it was with some psychological effort that he freed one from his belt and pulled the pin. Holding the striker lever in place, he angled his face to the edge of the door. He needed more space; the gap between the door and its frame was too narrow. Nobody was going to like what he was about to do, but he had no time to explain. He stepped back; the door lurched inward six inches. A hand appeared at the edge, clawed fingers curling with a searching gesture around the lip. A chorus of yells erupted. *What are you doing? Push the goddamn door!* Caleb relaxed his grip on the grenade, freeing the striker lever.

"Catch," he said, and shoved it through the opening.

He thrust his shoulder against the door. Eyes closed, he counted off the seconds, like a prayer. *One Mississippi, two Mississippi, three Mississippi . . .*

A boom.

The ping of shrapnel.

Dust falling.

58

"We need a corpsman over here right now!"

Peter lowered Amy to the ground. Her lips moved haltingly; then she asked, very softly, "Are we inside?"

"Everyone's safe."

Her skin was pale, her eyes heavy-lidded. "I'm sorry, I thought I could make it on my own."

Peter looked up. "Where's my son? Caleb!"

"Right here, Dad."

His boy was standing behind him. Peter rose and drew him into a fierce hug. "What the hell were you doing out there?"

"Coming to get you." There were scratches on his arms and face; one of his elbows was bleeding.

"What about Pim and Theo?" Peter couldn't help it; he was talking in bursts.

"They're safe. We got here a few hours ago."

Peter was suddenly overcome. Thoughts crowded his mind from all directions. He was exhausted, he needed water, the city was under attack, his son and his family were safe. Two medics appeared with a stretcher; Greer and Michael lifted Amy onto it.

"I'll go with her to the aid station," Greer said.

"No, I'll do it."

Greer took his arm above the elbow and looked at him squarely. "She'll be fine, Peter—we did it. Just go do your job."

They bore her away. Peter looked up to see Apgar and Chase striding toward him. Above them, the gunfire had fallen to random spattering.

"Mr. President," said Apgar, "I would appreciate it if in the future you did not cut it quite so close."

"What's our status?"

"The attack appears to have come only from the north. We've got no sightings elsewhere on the wall."

"What do we hear from the townships?"

Apgar hesitated. "Nothing."

"What do you mean *nothing*?"

"Everybody's off the air. We ran patrols this morning as far west as Hunt, south to Bandera and as far north as Fredericksburg. No survivors, and almost no bodies. At this point, we have to assume they've all been overrun."

Peter had no words. Over two hundred thousand people, gone.

"Mr. President?"

Apgar was looking at him. Peter swallowed and said, "How many people do we have inside the wall?"

"Including military, four, maybe five thousand, tops. Not a lot to fight with."

"What about the isthmus?" Michael asked the general.

"As a matter of fact, we got a call on the radio from them a couple of hours ago. Someone named Lore, wondering where you were. They didn't know anything about last night's attack, so I guess the dracs missed them. That or they were too smart to try to cross that causeway."

Above them, the guns fell silent.

"Maybe that's it for tonight," Chase said. He scanned their faces hopefully. "Maybe we scared them off."

Peter didn't think so; he could tell that Apgar didn't think so, either.

"We need to make some decisions, Peter," Michael cut in. "The window's closing fast. We should be talking about getting people out of here."

The idea suddenly seemed absurd. "I'm not leaving these people undefended, Michael. This thing has started. Right now, I need everybody who can hold a pitchfork on that wall."

"You're making a mistake."

From the catwalk: "Contact! Two thousand yards!"

The first thing they saw was a line of light in the distance.

"Soldier, give me your binoculars."

The spotter handed them over; Peter brought the lenses to his eyes. Standing beside him on the platform, Apgar and Michael were also scanning north.

"Can you tell how many there are?" Peter asked the general.

"They're too far out to tell." Apgar unclipped the walkie on his belt and brought it to his mouth. "All stations, what are you seeing?"

A crackle of static, then: "Station one, negative."

"Station two, no contact."

"Station three, same here. We're not seeing anything."

And so on, around the perimeter. The line of light began to stretch, though it appeared to come no closer.

"What the hell are they doing?" Apgar said. "They're just waiting out there."

"Hang on." Michael pointed. "Thirty degrees left."

Peter followed his aim. A second line was forming.

"There's another," Apgar said. "Forty right, near the tree line. Looks like a large pod. More coming in from the north, too."

The main line was now several hundred yards long. Virals were streaming in from all directions, moving toward the central mass.

"This is no scouting party," Peter said.

Apgar bellowed, "Runners, get ready to move!" He turned to Peter. "Mr. President, we need to get you to safety."

Peter addressed one of the spotters: "Corporal, hand me that M16."

"Peter, please, this is not a good idea."

The soldier passed Peter the weapon. He freed the magazine, blew on the top round to clear any dust, reseated it in the well, and pulled the charging handle. "You know, Gunnar, I think that's the first time in ten years you've called me by my first name."

The conversation ended there. A low, rumbling sound rolled toward them. With each second, it increased in intensity.

"What am I hearing?" Michael said.

It was the sound of feet striking the earth. The mass continued to thicken, its great, heaving volume barreled toward them. In its wake, a cloud of dust boiled high in the air.

"Holy God," Peter said. "It's everyone."

Apgar lifted his voice over the din: "Hold fire till they reach the perimeter!"

The horde was three hundred yards out and closing fast. It seemed less like an army than some great spectacle of nature—an avalanche, a hurricane, a flood. The platform began to hum, its bolts and rivets vibrating in rhythm to the seismic impact of the virals' charge.

"Will that gate hold?" Peter asked Apgar. He, too, had given up his binoculars for a rifle.

"Against this?"

Two hundred yards. Peter pressed the stock of the weapon against his clavicle.

"Ready!" Apgar bellowed.

One hundred yards.

"Aim!"

Everything stopped.

The virals had halted just beyond the edge of the lights. Not just halted—they were frozen in place, as if a switch had been thrown.

"What the *hell* . . . ?"

The mass began to divide into halves, creating a corridor. Starting at the rear, it flowed down the middle with a rippling on either side. The motion seemed somehow reverential, as if the virals were making way for a great king to pass among them, bowing as he passed. A dark shape was pushing forward through the heart of the horde. It appeared to be some sort of animal. It approached the city with painstaking slowness, the corridor unfurling before it. All guns were trained on the spot where it would emerge. A hundred feet, fifty, twenty. The front wall of virals separated, opening like a doorway to reveal the shockingly ordinary figure of a person on horseback.

"Is that him?" Apgar said. "Is that Zero?"

The rider moved forward into the lights. Halfway to the gate, he brought his horse to a halt and dismounted. Not "he," Peter realized. *She.* The glare of the spotlights ricocheted off the lenses of the dark glasses that obscured the upper half of her face. A scabbard containing some kind of weapon, a sword or long gun, lay slantwise across her back; crisscrossing her upper body, she wore a pair of bandoliers.

Bandoliers.

"Holy goddamn," Michael breathed.

Peter's mind was tumbling down a hole in time. "Hold your fire!" He raised his arms high and wide above his head. "Everyone stand down!"

Her back erect, the woman angled her face toward the top of the wall. "I am Alicia Donadio, captain of the Expeditionary! Where is Peter Jaxon?"

59

Thirty minutes had passed; everyone was in position. Standing back from the portal, Peter nodded at Henneman.

"Open it, Colonel."

Henneman turned the wheel and backed away. From inside the tunnel came a slow clop of hooves. A frisson of energy rippled through the line of soldiers facing the portal; all guns were raised, all eyes arrowed over the barrels. A shadow elongated across the wall of the tunnel; then Alicia emerged. One hand held a short rope attached to the horse's bridle; the second lay easily at her side. Her hair, that distinctive red crown, was pulled tight to her scalp, its length corralled into a densely woven braid that fell midway down her back. On her upper body she wore a T-shirt without sleeves, revealing the muscularity of her arms and shoulders; below, loose trousers, cinched at the waist, and a pair of leather boots. A quick scan of the crowd, the lights of the staging area rebounding off the lenses of her goggles like search beams, another step forward, and there she paused, awaiting instructions.

"Move forward," Peter said. "Slowly."

She advanced another twenty feet; Peter ordered her to stop.

"Blades first. Toss them forward."

"That's all you have to say?"

He had a sudden feeling of unreality; it was as if he were talking to a ghost. "The blades, Lish."

She glanced to Peter's right. "Michael. I didn't notice you standing there."

"Hello, Lish."

"And Colonel Apgar." Alicia gave a quick nod from the chin. "It's nice to see you, sir."

"It's 'General' to you, Donadio." The man's arms were folded over his chest; his face was a hard scowl. "Mr. President, say the word and this is done."

"'Mr. President'?" From Alicia, a wry frown. "You've come up in the world, Peter."

The old banter, the jokey tone: was it a trick? "I said, take them off."

In a manner that struck him as leisurely, Alicia unbuckled the straps and tossed her bandoliers to the ground.

"Now the sword," Peter said.

"I'm here to talk, that's all."

Peter lifted his voice toward the top of the wall. "Snipers! Target the horse!" Then, to Alicia: "Soldier, isn't it?"

If he'd rattled her, she didn't show it. Nevertheless, she drew the scabbard over her head and lobbed it forward.

"Now the goggles," Peter said.

"I'm no threat, Peter. I'm just the messenger."

He waited.

"As you like."

Off they came, revealing her eyes. Their orange color had grown stronger, more piercing. Time had not moved for her; she hadn't aged a day. Yet something was different, a quality not so much seen as felt, like the prickling of a storm's approach long before the clouds arrived. Her gaze did not wander but held him straight. A look of challenge, though now that her face was unconcealed, there was something naked about her, almost vulnerable. Her confidence was a ruse; feelings of uncertainty lay beneath.

"Hit the lights."

Three portable banks of sodium vapor lamps were positioned behind him. They went off like a gun, blasting Alicia in the face. As her hands flew upward, half a dozen soldiers charged forward and shoved her face-first to the ground. With a loud whinny, Soldier reared up on his hind legs and pawed violently at the air. One of the soldiers jammed the barrel of a pistol against the base of Alicia's skull while the others covered her body.

"Somebody control that animal," Peter barked. "If it makes any trouble, shoot it."

"Leave him alone!"

"Colonel Henneman, shackle the prisoner."

As two soldiers led the horse away, Henneman holstered his pistol, stepped forward, and chained Alicia's wrists and ankles. A third chain connected the shackles behind her back.

"Rise and face me," Peter said.

Alicia rocked upright into a kneeling position. Her eyes were clamped shut, her face angled down and away from the harsh glare of the lights, like someone dodging a blow.

"I'm trying to save your lives, Peter."

"You have an interesting way of showing it."

"You need to hear what I have to say."

"So talk."

A moment passed; then she began: "There's a man—more than a man, a kind of viral, but he looks like us. His name is Fanning. He's in New York City, in a building called Grand Central. He's the one who sent me."

"So that's where you've been all this time?"

Alicia nodded. "There are things I never told you, Peter. Things I *couldn't* tell you. The viral part of me was always stronger than I let on. The feeling got worse and worse—I knew I couldn't control it for long. Right after Iowa, I began to hear Fanning in my head. That's why I went to New York. I intended to kill him. Or he could kill me. I didn't really care which. I just wanted it all to be over."

"So why didn't you?"

"Believe me, I wanted to. I wanted to slice his damn head off. But I couldn't. The viral that bit me in Colorado wasn't Babcock's. It was Fanning's. It's his virus I carry. I belong to him, Peter."

I belong to him. The phrase was chilling. Peter glanced at Apgar to see if the full meaning had registered. It had.

"Fanning and I had a deal. If I stayed with him, he'd leave you alone."

"Looks like he changed his mind."

She shook her head emphatically. "I didn't have any part in that. By the time I figured out what he was doing, it was too late to stop it. All along he was waiting for you to spread out, your defenses to drop. It's Amy he wants. If I bring her to him, he'll call it off."

So there it was. "What does he want with her?"

"I don't know."

"Don't you lie to me."

"Where is she, Peter?"

"I have no idea. Nobody's seen Amy in over twenty years."

Alicia's tone had shifted; all her bluster was gone. "Listen to me, *please.* There's no stopping this. You've seen what he can do. He's not like the others. The others were *nothing.*"

"We have walls. We have lights. We've fought them before. Go back and tell him that."

"Peter, you don't get it. He doesn't have to *do* anything. You have, what, just a few thousand soldiers? And how much food? How much gas? Give him what he wants. It's your only chance."

"Private Wilson, step forward please."

Hollis moved into the lights.

"You remember Hollis, don't you, Lish? Why don't you say hello."

Her head was bowed. "Why do you even ask me that?"

"How about his daughter, Kate? She would have been a little girl the last time you saw her."

Alicia nodded.

"*Say* it. Say you remember Kate."

"Yes, I remember her."

"I'm glad you do. She grew up to be a doctor, just like her mother. Two little girls of her own. Then one of your friends bit her last night. Want to know what happened next?"

Alicia was silent.

"*Do* you?"

"Just get on with it, Peter."

"All right, I will. That little girl you remember? She shot herself."

Her silence infuriated him. What had happened to her? What had she become?

"You don't have anything to say for yourself?"

"What do you want me to say? That I'm sorry? You can do what you want with me, but that won't stop a thing."

Peter's pulse was pounding; his hands were clenched. He jabbed a finger at her. "*Look at him.* I'll get Sara out here, Kate's daughters, too. You can tell all of them how fucking sorry you are."

Alicia said nothing.

"Two hundred thousand people, Lish. And you come here and talk about surrender? Like he's your *friend*?"

Her shoulders shook. Was she crying?

"I'll ask you again. What does Fanning want with Amy?"

Her head rocked from side to side. "I don't know."

"Gunnar, give me your sidearm."

Apgar drew his pistol, spun it in his hand, and passed it to Peter. Peter released the magazine, checked it, and shoved it back into the well, making a loud show of it.

Michael said, "Peter, what the hell are you doing?"

"This woman is a viral. She's in league with the enemy."

"It's Alicia! She's one of us!"

Peter strode forward and leveled the barrel at Alicia's temple. "Tell me, goddamnit."

"I know she's here," Alicia murmured. "I can hear it in your voice."

He thumbed back the hammer and spoke through gritted teeth. He was running on instinct now, a blind white fury, obliterating all thought. "Answer the question or I am going to put a bullet through your head."

"*Wait.*"

He turned. Amy, clutching Greer's arm for balance, was standing at the edge of the circle.

"Lucius, get her the hell out of here."

Two soldiers moved to block their path. One pressed a hand against Greer's chest. The man tensed, then, apparently changing his mind, permitted this.

"Let me talk to her," Amy said.

The idea was ludicrous. The woman could barely stand; a puff of wind would have knocked her to her knees.

"I mean it, Greer."

"I understand you're angry," Amy said, "but there's more to this than you know."

She spoke to him as one might address a dangerous animal or a man poised at the lip of an abyss. Peter was suddenly conscious of the pistol's slick weight in his hand.

"Lucius can stay where he is," Amy said, "but if you want answers, you need to let me through."

Peter looked back at Alicia. The woman's head hung in submission; she seemed small, frail, broken. Had he really been about to shoot her? This seemed impossible, yet in the moment, something had taken him over, beyond his control.

"Please, Peter."

The moment stretched; everyone was staring.

"All right," he said. "Let her pass."

The soldiers stepped back. Amy's shadow lay long on the ground as she approached Alicia's cowed figure. Using her body to shield Alicia's face from the light, Amy crouched before her.

"Hello, sister. It's good to see you."

"I'm sorry, Amy." Her shoulders shook. "I'm so sorry."

"Don't be." Tenderly, Amy lifted Alicia's chin with the tips of her fingers. "Do you know how proud I am of you? You've been so very strong."

Tears were coursing down Alicia's cheeks, cutting bright streaks in the dirt. "How can you say that to me?"

Amy smiled into her face. "Because we're sisters, isn't that so? Sisters in blood. My thoughts have never been far from you, you know."

Alicia said nothing.

"He comforted you, didn't he?"

Her lips were wet, tears rolling off her chin. "Yes."

"He took you in, cared for you. He made you feel that you were not alone."

Alicia's voice was barely more than a whisper. "Yes."

"Do you see? That's why I'm so proud of you. Because you didn't give in, not in your heart."

"But I did."

"No, sister. I know what it's like to be alone. To be outside the walls. But that's over now." Without breaking Alicia's gaze, Amy lifted her voice to the assembly. "Everyone, are you listening? You can put your guns down. This woman is a friend."

"Hold your positions," Peter commanded.

Amy swiveled her face toward him. "Peter, didn't you hear me? She's with us."

"I need you to step away from the prisoner."

In confusion, Amy looked back at Alicia, then at Peter once more.

"It's okay," Alicia said. "Do as he says."

"Lish—"

"He's only doing what he has to. You really need to back away now."

An uncertain moment passed; Amy got to her feet. Another pause, her expression tentative, and she backed away. Alicia dropped her head.

Peter said, "Colonel, go ahead."

Henneman approached Alicia from behind. He had donned a pair of heavy rubber gloves; in his hands was a metal rod wrapped with copper wire, one end connected by a long cord to the generator powering the lights. As the tip of the rod made contact with the base of Alicia's neck, she jerked upright, her shoulders pulled back and her chest thrust forward, as if she'd been impaled. She made no sound at all. For a few seconds she stayed that way, every muscle taut as wire. Then the air let out of her and she toppled face-first into the dirt.

"Is she out?"

Henneman nudged Alicia's ribs with the toe of his boot. "Looks like it."

"Peter, *why?*"

"I'm sorry, Amy. But I can't trust her."

A truck was backing toward them. Two men jumped down from the cargo bay and dropped the tailgate.

"All right, gentlemen," Peter said. "Let's haul this woman to the stockade. And watch yourselves. You don't want to forget what she is."

60

0530: Peter stood with Apgar on the catwalk, watching the day come on. An hour before dawn, the horde had departed—a vast, silent retreat, like a wave beating back from shore to enfold itself in the dark bulk of the sea. All that remained was a wide swath of trampled earth and, beyond, fields of broken corn.

"I guess that's it for the night," Apgar said.

His voice was heavy, resigned. They waited, not talking, each man alone in his thoughts. A few minutes went by, and then the horn blasted—an expansion of sound like a great intake of breath, followed by the inevitable exhalation, sighing over the valley, then gone. Across the city, frightened people would be emerging from basements and shelters, out of closets and from under their beds. Old people, neighbors, families with children. They would look at each other wide-eyed and weary: Is it over? Are we safe?

"You should get some sleep," Apgar said.

"So should you."

Yet neither man moved. Peter's stomach was sour and empty—he couldn't remember when he'd eaten last—while the rest of him seemed numb, almost weightless. His face felt tight, like paper. The body's demands: the world could end, yet you'd still have to take a piss.

"You know," Apgar said, and yawned into his fist, "I think Chase was onto something. Maybe we should leave this to the kids to sort out."

"It's an interesting idea."

"So, would you have actually shot her?"

The question had plagued him all night. "I don't know."

"Well, don't beat yourself up. I wouldn't have had a problem with it." A pause, then: "Donadio was right about one thing. Even if we manage to hold them back, we don't have the gas to keep the lights burning for more than a few nights."

Peter stepped to the rampart. A gray morning, the light indifferent and worn: it seemed suitable. "I let this happen."

"We all did."

"No, this is on me. We never should have opened those gates."

"What were you going to do? You can't keep people locked up forever."

"You're not letting me off the hook here."

"I'm just pointing out the reality. You want to blame someone, blame Vicky. Hell, blame *me*. The decision to open the townships was made long before you came along."

"I'm the one in that chair, Gunnar. I could have stopped it."

"And had a revolution on your hands. Once the dracs disappeared, this was a done deal. I'm surprised we kept this place running as long as we did."

No matter what Gunnar said, Peter knew the truth. He'd let down his guard, allowing himself to believe that it was all in the past—the war, the virals, the old way of doing things—and now two hundred thousand people were gone.

Henneman and Chase came clomping down the catwalk. Chase looked like he'd slept under a bridge somewhere, but Henneman, always a stickler for appearance, had somehow managed to get through the night with barely a hair out of place.

"Orders, General?" the colonel asked.

It was not the time to drop their defenses, but the men needed rest. Apgar put them on a four-hour rotation: one-third on the wall, one-third patrolling the perimeter, one-third in their racks.

"So what now?" Chase asked, as Henneman moved away.

But Peter had ceased listening; an idea was forming at the back of his mind. Something old; something from the past.

"Mr. President?"

Peter turned to face the two men. "Gunnar, what are our weak points? Besides the gate."

Apgar thought for a moment. "The walls are sound. The dam's basically impregnable."

"So it's the gate that's the problem."

"I'd say so."

Would it work? It just might.

"My office," said Peter. "Two hours."

"Open the door."

The officer keyed the lock; Peter stepped inside. Alicia was sitting on the floor of the cell. Her arms and legs were shackled in front; a third chain connected her hands to a heavy iron ring in the wall. Thick fabric had been used to cover the window, muting the light.

"About time," she said drolly. "I was beginning to think you'd forgotten me."

"I'll knock when I'm done," Peter told the guard.

He left them alone. Peter sat on the cot facing Alicia. A silent moment, the two regarding each other across a distance that felt far vaster than it was.

"How are you feeling?" he asked.

"Oh, you know." A shrug, dismissive. "Beats a bullet to the brain. You had me going for a second there."

"I was angry. I still am."

"Yeah, I sensed that." Her eyes took slow measure of his face. "Now that I have a chance to really look at you, I've got to say, you're holding up nicely. That snow on the roof suits you."

He smiled, just a little. "And you look the same."

She glanced around the tiny box of a room. "And you're really running the show here? President and all that."

"That seems to be the case."

"Like it?"

"The last couple of days haven't been so hot."

These wry exchanges, like a dance to a song that only the two of them could hear: he couldn't help himself; he'd missed them.

"You've put me in a bind, Lish. That was a pretty big splash you made last night."

"My timing wasn't the best."

"As far as this government is concerned, you're a traitor."

She looked up. "And what does Peter Jaxon think?"

"You've been gone a long time. Amy seems to believe you're on our side, but she's not the one calling the shots."

"I am on your side, Peter. But that doesn't change the situation. In the end, you're going to have to give her up. You can't beat him."

"See, this is where I have a problem. I've never heard you talk that way, not about anything."

"This is different. *Fanning* is different. He's been controlling everything from the start. The only reason we were able to kill the Twelve was because he *let* us. We're all pieces on a board to him."

"So why would you trust him now?"

"Maybe I'm not being clear. I don't."

" 'He comforted you.' 'He took care of you.' Am I remembering this correctly?"

"He did, Peter. But that's not the same thing."

"You're going to have to do better than that."

"Why? So you'll believe me? The way I see it, you don't have a choice."

"Who am I talking to here? You or Fanning?"

Her eyes sharpened with anger; his words had hit the mark. "I took an oath, Peter. Same as you, same as Apgar, same as every man on that wall last night. I stayed with Fanning because I believed he'd leave Kerrville alone. Yes, he was good to me. I never said he wasn't. Believe it or not, I actually feel sorry for the guy, until I remember what he is."

"And what's that?"

"The enemy."

Was she lying? For the moment, it didn't matter; that she *wanted* him to believe her was leverage he could use.

"Tell me what we're up against, how many dracs are out there."

"I think what you saw last night."

"The rest of Fanning's forces are in New York, in other words. He's holding them in reserve."

Alicia nodded. "I wasn't followed, if that's what you mean. The rest are in the tunnels under the city."

"And you don't know what he wants with Amy?"

"If I knew, I'd tell you. Trying to understand Fanning is a fool's errand. He's a complicated man, Peter. I was with him for twenty years, and I never figured him out completely. Mostly, he just seems sad. He doesn't like what he is, but he sees a kind of justice in it. Or, at least, he wants to."

Peter frowned. "I'm not following."

Alicia took a moment to form her thoughts. "In the station, there's a clock. Long ago, Fanning was supposed to meet a woman there." She looked up. "It's a long story. I can give you all of it, but it'd take hours."

"Give me the short version."

"The woman's name was Liz. She was Jonas Lear's wife."

Peter was caught short.

"Yeah, it surprised me, too. They all knew each other. Fanning loved her since they were young. When she married Lear, he pretty much gave up on the whole thing, but not really. Then she got sick. She was dying, some kind of cancer. Turns out she loved him, too; she had all along. She and Fanning were going to run away, spend her last days together. You should hear him tell the story, Peter. It'd just about rip your heart out. The clock was where they were going to meet, but Liz never showed. She'd died on the way, but Fanning didn't know that; he thought she'd changed her mind. That night he got drunk in a bar and went home with a woman. She was a stranger, nobody he knew. He killed her."

"So he's a murderer, in other words."

Alicia made an expression of demurral. "Well, it was sort of an accident, the way he tells it. He was half out of his mind; he thought his life was basically over. She pulled a knife on him, they struggled, she fell on it."

"Putting him on death row, like the Twelve."

"No, he got away with it. He actually felt awful about the whole thing. He was plenty mixed up, but he was no hardened killer, at least not yet. It was later that he went to South America with Lear, which is where the virus comes from. Lear had been looking for it for years; he thought he could use it to save his wife, though that was a moot point by then. Fanning describes the guy as totally obsessed."

"Was that how Fanning caught the virus?"

Alicia nodded. "As far as I can tell from Fanning's story, it happened by chance, though in his head Lear was responsible. After Fanning got infected, Lear brought him back to Colorado. He was still hoping to use the virus as a kind of cure-all, but the military got involved. They wanted to use it as a weapon, make some kind of super-soldier out of it. That was when they brought in the twelve inmates."

Peter thought for a moment. Then, his thoughts crystallizing: "What about Amy? Why did the Army make her?"

"They didn't; that was Lear. He used a different virus, not descended from the one Fanning carried. That's why she's not the same as the others. That, plus she was so young. I think he maybe knew that the whole thing had gone bad and was trying to make it right."

"It's a strange way of doing it."

"Like I said, Fanning is pretty much of the opinion that the man was off his rocker. Either way, in Fanning's mind, Amy is the fish that got away. Killing the Twelve was a test—not of us, since we never stood a chance against them. Fanning was testing *her*. I don't know why I didn't think of it at the time, his positioning them all in one place like that. He was never particularly fond of them, to put it mildly. A bunch of psychotics, is how he puts it."

"And he's not?"

Alicia shrugged. "Depends on your definition. If you mean he doesn't know right from wrong, I'd have to say no. He's pretty well versed on the subject, actually. Which is the strangest thing about him, the part I could never really get. Your ordinary drac doesn't care one way or another—it's just an eating machine. Fanning thinks about *everything*. Maybe Michael could keep up with him, but I never could. Talking to him was like being dragged by a horse."

"So why test her? What was he trying to find out?"

Alicia glanced away, then said, "I think he wanted to know if she really was different from the rest of them. I don't think he wants to kill her. That'd be too obvious. If I had to guess, I'd say it all comes down to his feelings about Lear. Fanning hated the guy. Really *hated*. And not just because of what Lear did to him. It goes deeper than that. Lear made Amy as a way to set things straight. Maybe Fanning just can't sit with that. Like I said, he mostly seems miserable. He sits in that station staring at the clock as if time stopped for him when Liz didn't show."

Peter waited for more, but Alicia seemed to end there. "Last night you called him a man."

She nodded. "At least that's how he looks, though there are a few differences. He's sensitive to light, much more than I am. He never sleeps, or almost never. Likes his dinner warm. And"—she used her thumb and forefinger to indicate her incisors—"he's got these."

Peter frowned. "Fangs?"

She nodded. "Just these two."

"Was he always that way?"

"Actually, no. At the start, he was exactly like the rest of them. But something happened, an accident. He fell into a flooded quarry. This was early on, just a few days after he broke out of the NOAH lab. None of us can swim; Fanning went straight to the bottom. When he woke up, he was lying on the shore, looking like he does now." She paused, eyes narrowing on his face, as if struck by a sudden thought. "Is that what happened to Amy?"

"Something like that."

"But you're not going to tell me."

Peter left it there. "Could water change back his Many?"

"Fanning says no, just him."

Peter rose from the cot. A wave of lightheadedness passed through him: he really needed to lie down, even for just a few minutes. But it seemed important not to show her how exhausted he was—an old habit, from the days when the two of them had stood the Watch together, each always trying to best the other. *I can do this, can you?*

"Sorry about those chains."

Alicia lifted her wrists, examining them with a neutral expression—as if they were not her hands but someone else's. She shrugged and let them fall to her lap again. "Forget it. It's not like I'm making this easy for you."

"Do you need anything? Food, water?"

"My diet is a little peculiar these days."

Peter understood. "I'll see what I can do."

A silent moment, each of them acknowledging the awkwardness of the situation.

"I know you don't want to believe me," Alicia said. "Hell, I wouldn't. But I'm telling you the truth."

Peter said nothing.

"We were *friends,* Peter. All those years, you were the one person I could always rely on. We stood for each other."

"Yes, we did."

"Just tell me that still counts for something."

As he looked at her, his mind went back to the night when they had said goodbye to each other at the Colorado garrison, so many years ago—the night before he had ridden up the mountain with Amy. How young they'd been. Standing outside the soldiers' barracks, the cold wind lancing through them, he had loved Alicia fiercely, as he had never loved anyone in his life—not his parents or Auntie or even his brother Theo: no one. It was not the love of a man for a woman, or a brother for a sister, but something leaner, pared to its essence: a binding, subatomic energy that had no words to name it. Peter could no longer recall what they'd said to one another; only the impression remained, like footprints in snow. It was one of those moments when it had still seemed possible to understand life and what was meant by living one—he had been young enough to still believe that such a thing was possible—and the recollection carried a striking vividness of emotion, as if three decades had not passed since that cold and distant hour in which he had stood in the sheltering light of Alicia's courage. But then he blinked the memory away, his mind returned to the present, and what remained was only a great weight of sadness at the center of his chest. Two hundred thousand souls gone, and Alicia at the center of it all.

"Yes," he said. "It counts. But I'm afraid it doesn't change a thing."

He gave three hard bangs on the door. Tumblers turned and the guard appeared.

"Don't be dumb, Peter. Fanning's everything I say he is. I don't know what you're planning, but don't."

"Thank you," he said to the guard. "I'm finished here."

The chain attaching Alicia to the wall rattled as she yanked on it. "Listen to me, goddamnit! It's no good, fighting him!"

But these words barely reached his ears; Peter was already striding down the hall.

61

And now, my Alicia, you reside among them.

How do I know this? I know it as I know everything; I am a million minds, a million histories, a million roving pairs of eyes. I am everywhere, my Alicia, watching you. I have watched you since the beginning, taking measure and stock. Would it be too much to say that I felt your arrival on the day you were born into this world—a wet, squealing nugget, the hot blood of protest already pouring through your veins? Impossible, of course; yet it seems so. Such is the bewitching way of providence: all seems ordained, all known, both in forward and reverse.

What an entrance you made! With what bold declaration, what showmanship, what authoritative poise did you step into the city's lights and stake your claim! How could the occupants of the besieged metropolis fail to swoon under your spell, enchanted by the drama of your arrival? *I am Alicia Donadio, captain of the Expeditionary!* Forgive, Alicia, these windy flights; my mood is grandiose. Not since the great Achilles stood without the battlements of mighty Troy has our pocket of creation seen the likes of you. Within those walls, no doubt, a great parliament commences. Debates, edicts, threats and counterthreats—the customary swordplay of a city under siege. Do we fight? Do we run? Earnest and admirable, yet—and you must pardon the analogy—these discussions are to the outcome what splashing is to drowning: they only make the whole thing go faster.

In your absence, Alicia, I have, so to speak, taken a page from your book. Night after night the dark beckons me; my feet cast me wandering anew into the streets of mighty Gotham. Summer has come at last upon this isle of exile. In the branches the songbirds twitter; the trees and flowers clutter the breeze with their airborne sexual excreta; newborn creatures of every ilk undertake their first uncertain adventures in the grass. (Last night, recalling your concerns for my strength, I devoured a litter of six young bunnies in your honor.) What is this new restlessness inside me? Adrift among Manhattan's maze of glass and steel and stone, I feel closer to you, yes, but something else as well: a sense of the past so glowingly intense it is practically hallucinatory. It was in summer, after all, when I traveled to New York for my friend Lucessi's funeral, when this city first laid its hand of love upon me. I close my eyes and there I am, with her, my Liz, the woman and the place indelible, one and the same. The appointed hour at the clock, and then our exit into the moist human heat of the season's early rush; the abrupt encapsulation of the taxi, with its cracked vinyl bench and feeling of a million prior occupants; the parade of heaving humanity clogging the streets and sidewalks; the impatiently perfunctory honking of horns and the catlike mating shrieks of sirens; the majestic towers of midtown, glazed and shining with the hour's exhausted light; my bright, almost painful awareness of everything, a rush of undifferentiated data to my brain, all of it permanently inseparable from the beloved and eternal *her.* Her shining, sun-blessed shoulders. The faint, womanly aroma of her perspiration in the sealed space of the taxi. Her wan, expressive face, with its touch of mortality, and her myopic gaze, always peering deeper into things. The perfection of her hand in my own as we wandered the dark streets together, alone among millions. It has been said that in ancient times there was only one gender; in that blissful state, humankind existed until, as punishment, the gods divided each of us in two, a cruel mitosis that sent each half forever spinning across the earth in search of its mate, so that it could be whole again.

That was how her hand felt in my own, Alicia: as if, of all men upon the earth, I had found that one.

Did she kiss me that night as I was sleeping? Was it a dream? Is there a difference? That is my New York, as it was once so many's: the kiss one dreams of.

All lost, all gone—as is the city of your love, Alicia, the city of your Rose. *Call Fanning,* my friend Lucessi wrote. *Call Fanning to tell him that love is all there is, and love is pain, and love is taken away.* How many hours did he hang there? How many days and nights did my mother linger, floating in a sea of agony? And where was I? What fools we are. What fools we mortals be.

Thus does the hour of reckoning approach. Unto God I issue my just complaint; 'twas he who cruelly dangled love before our eyes, like a brightly colored toy above a baby's crib. From nothing he made this world of woe; to nothing it shall return.

I know she's here, you said. *I can hear it in your voice.*

And I in yours, my Alicia. I in yours.

62

Two soldiers, rifles dangling, stood at the end of the walkway. As Peter approached, they stiffened, popping quick salutes.

"All quiet here?" Peter asked.

"Dr. Wilson went in a while ago."

"Anyone else?" He wondered if Gunnar had visited, or maybe Greer.

"Not since we came on duty."

The door opened as he mounted the porch: Sara, carrying her small leather satchel of instruments. Their eyes met in a way that Peter understood. He embraced her and backed away.

"I don't know what to say," Peter began. Her hair was damp and pressed to her forehead, her eyes swollen and bloodshot. "We all loved her."

"Thank you, Peter." Her words were flat, without emotion. "Is it true about Alicia?"

He nodded.

"What are you going to do with her?"

"I don't know at this point. She's in the stockade."

Sara didn't say anything; she didn't have to. Her face said it all. *We trusted her, now look.*

"How's Amy?" Peter asked.

Sara heaved a sigh. "You can see for yourself. I'm a little out of my depth here, but as far as I can tell, she's fine. Fine as in *human.* A little malnourished, and she's very weak, but the fever's gone. If you brought her in here and didn't tell me who she was, I'd say she was a perfectly healthy woman in her mid-twenties who'd just come off a bad bout of the flu. Somebody please explain this to me."

As compactly as he could, Peter related the story: the *Bergensfjord,* Greer's vision, Amy's transformation.

"What are you going to do?" Sara said.

"I'm working on it."

Sara seemed dazed; the information had begun to sink in. "I guess maybe I owe Michael an apology. Funny to think about that at a time like this."

"There's a meeting in my office at oh-seven-thirty. I need you there."

"Why me?"

There were lots of reasons; he went with the simplest. "Because you've been part of this from the beginning."

"And now part of the end," Sara said grimly.

"Let's hope not."

She fell silent, then said, "A woman came into the hospital yesterday in labor. Early stages, we might have just sent her home, but she and her husband were there when the horn went off. Along about three A.M. she decides to have her baby. A baby, in the middle of all this." Sara looked at Peter squarely. "Know what I wanted to tell her?"

He shook his head.

"Don't."

The bedroom door was ajar; Peter paused at the threshold. The drapes were shut, bathing the room in a thin, yellowish light. Amy was turned on her side— eyes closed, face relaxed, one arm tucked beneath the pillow. He was about to retreat when her eyes fluttered open.

"Hey." Her voice was very soft.

"It's okay, go back to sleep. I just wanted to check on you."

"No, stay." She cast her eyes groggily around the room. "What time is it?"

"I'm not sure. Early."

"Sara was here."

"I know. I saw her leave. How are you feeling?"

She frowned pensively. "I don't . . . know." Then, eyes widening as if the idea surprised her: "Hungry?"

Such an ordinary want; Peter nodded. "I'll see what I can do."

In the kitchen he lit the kerosene stove—he hadn't used it in months—then went outside to tell the soldiers what he needed. While he waited, he washed up; by the time they returned, carrying a small basket, the fire was ready to go. Buttermilk, eggs, a potato, a loaf of dense, dark bread, and mixed-berry jam in a jar sealed with wax. He set to work, happy to have this small chore to take his mind from other things. In a cast-iron pan he fried the potatoes and then the eggs; the bread he cut into thick slices and smeared with jam. How long since he'd cooked a meal for another person? Probably for Caleb, as a boy. Years ago.

He arranged Amy's breakfast on a tray, added a glass of buttermilk, and carried it all to the bedroom. He'd wondered if she'd fall asleep again in his absence; instead he found her alert and sitting up. She had pulled the drapes aside; evidently the light had ceased to trouble her. A smile blossomed at the sight of him, standing in the doorway like a waiter with his tray.

"Wow," she said.

Peter placed the tray on her lap. "I'm not much of a cook."

Amy was staring at the food as if she were a prisoner released from years in jail. "I don't even know where to start. The potatoes? The bread?" She smiled decisively. "No, the milk."

She drained the glass and set to work on the rest, jabbing the food with her fork like a field hand.

Peter dragged a chair to the bedside. "Maybe you should slow down."

She glanced up, speaking around a mouthful of eggs. "Aren't you going to eat?"

He was famished but enjoyed watching her. "I'll get something later."

Peter went to the kitchen to refill her glass; by the time he returned, her plate was empty. He handed her the buttermilk and watched her polish it off. A healthy color had flowed back into her cheeks.

"Come sit by me," she said.

Peter cleared her tray and perched on the edge of the bed. Amy slipped her hand into his. "I've missed you," she said.

It felt so unreal, to be sitting here, talking to her. "I'm sorry I got old."

"Oh, I think I've got you beat there."

He almost laughed. There was so much he wanted to say, to tell her. She looked just as she did in his dreams; the short hair was the only difference. Her eyes, the warmth of her smile, the sound of her voice—all were the same.

"What was it like, in the ship?"

She dropped her face; her thumb moved gently over the top of his hand. "Lonely. Strange. But Lucius took care of me." She looked at him again. "I'm sorry, Peter. You couldn't know."

"Why?"

"Because I wanted you to live your life. To be . . . happy. I heard Caleb call you 'Dad.' I'm glad, for both of you."

"He's married, you know. His wife is Pim."

"Pim," Amy repeated, and smiled.

"They have a son, too. They named him Theo."

She gently squeezed his hand. "So there's a life, right there. What else made you happy? I want to know."

You did, he thought. *You made me happy. I've been with you every night since you were gone. I've lived a whole life with you, Amy.* But he could not find the words to say this.

"That night in Iowa," he began. "That was real, wasn't it?"

"I'm not sure I even know what real is anymore."

"I mean, it happened. It wasn't a dream."

Amy nodded. "Yes."

"Why did you come to me?"

Amy's eyes darted away, as if the memory pained her. "I'm not sure I know. I was confused, the change had happened so fast. Probably I shouldn't have done it. I was so ashamed of what I was."

"Why would you think that?"

"I was a monster, Peter."

"Not to me."

Their eyes met and held; her hand was warm, though not with fever; it was the warmth of life. A thousand times he'd held it, and yet this was also the first.

"Is Alicia all right?" Amy asked.

"Oh, she's tougher than that. What do you want me to do with her?"

"I don't think that's my decision."

"It's not. But I still need to know what you think."

"This isn't simple for her. She's been with him a long time. I think there's a lot she's not telling us."

"Like what?"

Amy thought for a moment, then shook her head. "I can't tell. She's very sad. But it's like there's a locked box inside her. I can't get past it." Their eyes met again. "She needs you to trust her, Peter. I'm one side of her; Fanning's the other. Between us, there's you. It's you she's really here to see. She needs to know who she is. Not just who she is: *what* she is."

"So what is she?"

"What she always was. Part of this, part of *us.* You're her family, Peter. You have been from the start. She needs to know that you still are."

Peter felt the truth of her words. But knowing something was not the same thing as believing it. That was the hell of it, he thought.

"You're not going with her," he said. "I can't allow it."

"You may not have a choice about that. Alicia's right, the city can't stand indefinitely. Sooner or later, I'll have to face him."

"I don't care. I lost you once. I'm not doing it again."

Footsteps in the hall: Peter turned as Caleb appeared in the doorway, Pim behind him. For a moment, Peter's son appeared dumbstruck. A warm light switched on in his eyes.

"It's really you," he said.

Amy smiled. "Caleb, I believe I would like to hug you."

Peter stepped back; Amy rose on her elbows as Caleb leaned over the bed and the two embraced. When at last they parted, they still held one another by the elbows, each beaming into the other's happy face. Peter understood what he was seeing: the deep bond that Amy and his son shared, forged in the days before Iowa, when Amy had looked after him in the orphanage.

"You look so grown-up," Caleb said, laughing.

Amy laughed, too. "So do you."

Caleb turned to his wife, speaking and signing simultaneously. "Amy, this is Pim, my wife. Pim, Amy."

How do you do, Pim? Amy signed.

Very well, thank you, Pim replied.

Amy's hands were moving with expert speed. *It's a beautiful name. You're just as I pictured you.*

You, too.

Caleb stared at the two women; only then did it occur to Peter that the exchange he had just witnessed was, technically, impossible.

"Amy," Caleb said, "how did you *do* that?"

She frowned at her splayed fingers. "Now, I don't think I know. I suppose the sisters must have taught me."

"None of them can sign."

She dropped her hands to her lap and looked up. "Well, somebody must have. How else could I have done it?"

More footsteps; an atmosphere of official briskness accompanied Apgar into the bedroom.

"Mr. President, I'm sorry for the interruption, but I thought I might find you here." His chin lifted toward the bed. "Pardon me, ma'am. How are you feeling?"

Amy was sitting up now, hands folded in her lap. "Much better, thank you, General."

He narrowed his attention on Caleb. "Lieutenant, aren't you supposed to be in your rack?"

"I wasn't tired, sir."

"That wasn't what I asked. And don't look at your father—he's not interested."

Caleb took Amy's hand and gave it a final squeeze. "Get better, okay?"

"Now, Mr. Jaxon."

Caleb exchanged a hasty, unreadable sign with Pim and exited the room. "If you're done here," Apgar said, "it's time. People will be waiting."

Peter turned to Amy. "I better go."

Amy appeared not to have heard him; her eyes were fixed on Pim's. The seconds stretched as the two women regarded each other with a crackling intensity, as if engaged in a private, inaudible conversation.

"Amy?"

She startled, breaking the circuit. It seemed to take her a moment to assemble her sense of her surroundings. Then she said, very calmly, "Of course."

"And you'll be all right here?" Peter said.

Another smile, but not the same—more of reassurance than something genuine. There was something hollow about it, even forced.

"Perfectly."

63

"Mirrors," Chase repeated.

Around the conference table, clockwise from Peter's left, sat the players, Peter's war cabinet: Apgar, Henneman, Sara, Michael, Greer.

"It doesn't have to be a mirror specifically. Anything reflective will work, just as long as they can see themselves."

Chase took a long breath and folded his hands on the table. "This is the craziest thing I've ever heard."

"It's not crazy at all. Thirty years ago, in Las Vegas, Lish and I were running from a pod of three and got cornered in a kitchen. We were out of ammunition, pretty much defenseless. A bunch of pots and pans were hanging from the ceiling. I grabbed one to use as a club, but when I held it out at the first viral, it stopped the bastard cold, like it was hypnotized. And this was just a copper pot. Michael, back me up here."

"He's right. I've seen it, too."

Apgar asked Michael, "So what does it do to them? Why does it slow them down?"

"Hard to say. My guess would be some kind of residual memory."

"Meaning what?"

"Meaning, they don't like what they see, because it doesn't conform to some other aspect of their self-image." He turned toward Peter. "Do you remember the viral you fought in Tifty's cage?"

Peter nodded.

"After you killed her, you said something to Tifty. 'Her name was Emily. Her last memory was kissing a boy.' How did you know that?"

"It was a long time ago, Michael. I can't really explain it. She was looking at me, and it just happened."

"Not just looking. She was *staring*. You both were. People don't look a viral in the eye when it's about to rip them in half. The natural impulse is to look away. You didn't. And just like the mirror, it stopped her flat." Michael paused, then said, with deeper certainty, "The more I think about this, the more sense it makes. It explains a lot of things. When a person gets taken up, their first impulse is to go home. Dying people feel the same way. Sara, am I right about that?"

She nodded. "It's true. Sometimes it's even the last thing people say. 'I want to go home.' I can't tell you how often I've heard it."

"So a viral is a person infected with a virus, strong, superaggressive. But somewhere deep down, they remember who they were. During the transitional phase, let's say, that memory gets buried, but it doesn't go away, not completely. It's just a kernel, but it's there. Eyes are reflective, just like mirrors. When they see themselves, the memory rises to the surface, and it confuses them. That's what stops them, a sort of nostalgia. It's the pain of remembering their human lives and seeing what they've become."

"That's quite . . . a theory," Henneman said.

Michael shrugged. "Maybe. Maybe I'm just talking out of my exhaust pipe, and it wouldn't be the first time. But let me ask you something, Colonel. How old are you?"

"I'm sorry?"

"Sixty? Sixty-three?"

He scowled a little. "I'm fifty-eight, thank you."

"My mistake. Ever look in a mirror?"

"I try to avoid it."

"Precisely my point. In your mind, you're the same person you always were. Hell, between my ears I'm still just a seventeen-year-old kid. But the reality is different, and it's depressing to look at. I don't see any twenty-year-olds around this table, so I'm guessing I'm not alone."

Peter turned toward his chief of staff. "Ford, what do we have that reflects? We'd need to cover the whole gate, and it's best if we have at least a hundred yards on either side, more if we can do it."

He thought for a moment. "Galvanized roofing metal could work, I suppose. It's pretty shiny."

"How much do we have?"

"A lot of that stuff has moved out to the townships, but we should have enough. We can strip some houses if we come up short."

"Get engineering on it. We also need to reinforce that gate. Tell them to weld the damn thing shut if they have to. The portal, too."

Chase frowned. "How will people get out?"

"'Out' is not the issue right now. For the time being, they won't."

"Mr. President, if I may," Henneman cut in. "Assuming this all works—a big *if*, in my opinion—we still have a couple hundred thousand virals running loose out there. We can't stay inside the walls forever."

"I hate to contradict you, Colonel, but that's exactly what we did in California. First Colony stood for almost a century, with a fraction of the resources. We're down to just a few thousand people, a sustainable population if we manage it right. Within these walls we have enough arable land for planting and livestock. The river gives us a good continuous source for drinking water and irrigation. With some modification, we can still run oil up from Freeport in smaller loads, and the refinery itself is defensible. With careful rationing, using all of our refined petroleum for the lights, we should be fine for a very long time."

"And weaponry?"

"Tifty's bunker can supply us for a while, and probably we can remanufacture more, at least to last for a few more years. After that, we use crossbows, longbows, and incendiaries. We made it work at First Colony. We'll do it here."

Silence from around the table; everybody was thinking the same thing, Peter knew. *It comes to this.*

"All due respect," Michael said, "but this is bullshit, and you know it."

Peter turned toward him.

"So maybe the mirrors slow them down. Fanning is still out there. If what Alicia said is true, the virals we saw last night are just the tip of the spear. He's holding an entire army in reserve."

"Let me worry about that."

"Don't patronize me. I've been thinking about this for twenty years."

Apgar scowled. "Mr. Fisher, I suggest you stop talking."

"Why? So he can get us all killed?"

"Michael, I want you to listen to me very carefully." Peter wasn't angry; he had expected the man to object. What mattered now was making sure everyone stayed on board. "I know your feelings. You've made them very clear. But the situation has evolved."

"The time line has moved up, that's all. We're pissing away our chance sitting around like this. We should be loading buses right now."

"Maybe it would have worked before. But we start moving people out of here now, there'll be a riot. This place will come apart. And there's no way we can move seven hundred people to the isthmus in daylight. Those buses would be caught in the open. They wouldn't stand a chance."

"We don't stand a chance anyway. The *Bergensfjord* is all we have. Lucius, don't just sit there."

Greer's face was calm. "This isn't our decision. Peter is in charge."

"I don't believe what I'm hearing." Michael looked around the room, then back at Peter. "You're just too goddamn obstinate to admit you're beaten."

"Fisher, that's enough," Apgar warned.

Michael turned toward his sister. "Sara, you can't be buying this. Think about the girls."

"I am thinking about them. I'm thinking about everybody. I'm with Peter. He's never steered us wrong."

"Michael, I need to know you're with us," Peter said. "It's that simple. Yes or no."

"Okay, no."

"Then you're dismissed. The door is that way."

Peter wasn't quite sure what was going to happen next. For several seconds, Michael looked him dead in the eye. Then, with an angry sigh, he rose from the table.

"Fine. You make it through the night, you let me know. Lucius, are you coming?"

Greer glanced at Peter, eyebrows raised.

"It's all right," said Peter. "Somebody needs to look after him."

The two men departed. Peter cleared his throat and continued: "The important thing is that we get through tonight. I expect every able-bodied person to man those walls, but we'll need shelters for the rest. Ford?"

Chase rose, crossed to Peter's desk, and returned with a rolled tube of paper, which he unfurled on the table and weighed down at the corners.

"This is one of the builders' original schematics. Hardboxes were constructed here"—he pointed—"here, and here. All three date to the early days of the city, and none has been used in decades, not since the Easter Incursion. I don't imagine they're in very good shape, but with some reinforcement, we can use them in a pinch."

"How many people can we fit?" Peter asked.

"Not many, at most a few hundred. Now, over here," he continued, "you've got the hospital, which can fit, oh, maybe another hundred. Another, smaller box is underneath this building, the old bank vault. Full of files and other junk, but basically in good shape."

"What about basements?"

"There aren't a lot. A few beneath commercial buildings, some of the old apartment complexes, and we can safely assume there are a few in private hands. But the way the city was built, almost everything is on slab or pier. The soil by the river is mostly clay, so no basements at all. That extends from H-town all the way to the southern wall."

Not good, Peter thought. So far, they had accounted for fewer than a thousand people.

"Now, here's the granddaddy." Chase directed everyone's attention to the orphanage, which was marked "HB1." "When they moved the government from Austin, one of the reasons they chose Kerrville is because of this. While the walls were being constructed, they needed a safe place to overnight the workers and the rest of the government. This end of the city sits on top of a large formation of limestone, and it's full of pockets. The largest one is underneath the orphanage, and it's deep, at least thirty feet below the surface. According to the old records, it was originally used by the sisters as part of the Underground Railroad, a place to hide runaway slaves before the Civil War."

"How do we get down there?" Apgar asked.

"I went and looked this morning. The hatch is under the floorboards in the dining area. There's a flight of wooden stairs, pretty rickety but usable, that leads down to the cave. Dank as a tomb, but it's big. If we pack folks in, it can hold another five hundred at least." Chase looked up. "Now, before anybody asks, I went through the census data last night. It's just an estimate, but here's how things break down. Inside the walls, we have about eleven hundred children under the age of thirteen. Not counting military, the remainder divvies up about pretty evenly in terms of gender, but the population skews old. We've got a lot of people over sixty. Some of them will want to fight, but I don't see that they'll be much help, frankly."

"So what about the rest?" Peter asked.

"Of the remainder, we're looking at roughly thirteen hundred men of fighting age. About the same number of women, maybe slightly less. It's safe to assume some of the women will choose to defend the wall, and there's no reason they shouldn't. The problem is armament. We have weapons for only about five hundred civilians. There are probably plenty of guns floating around out there, but there's no way to know how many. We'll just have to wait and see what appears when the time comes."

Peter looked at Apgar. "What about ammunition?"

From the general, a frown. "Not too good. Last night cost us badly. We've got maybe twenty thousand rounds on hand in a mix of calibers, mostly nine-millimeter, forty-five, and five fifty-six. Plenty of shot shells, but they're only good for close quarters. For the big guns, we're down to about ten thousand rounds in fifty-cal. If the dracs charge that gate, our ammo won't last long."

The situation boiled down disconcertingly: maybe a thousand defenders on the wall, enough ammunition to last a few minutes at most, hardboxes for a thousand, and two thousand unarmed civilians with nowhere to hide.

"There's got to be someplace we can put people," Peter said. "Somebody, give me something."

"As a matter of fact," Chase said, "I've got an idea about that." He rolled out another map: a schematic of the dam. "We use the drainage tubes. There are six, each a hundred feet long, so maybe a hundred and fifty people apiece. The downstream openings are barred; no viral has ever gotten through. The only access on the upstream side is through the waterworks, and there are three heavy doors between the tubes and the outside. The beauty of it is, even if the dracs breach the walls, there's no reason they'd think to look there. The people inside would be completely hidden."

It made sense. "Ford, I think you just earned your pay for the month. Gunnar?"

Apgar, lips pursed, nodded. "It's a hell of an idea, actually."

"Everybody else?"

From the room, a murmur of agreement.

"Good, it's settled. Chase, you're in control of the civilian side. We need to start moving people to shelter as soon as possible, no last-minute rushes. Children under thirteen to the orphanage, starting with the youngest. Sara, how many patients do you have in the hospital?"

"Not many. Twenty or so."

"We can use the basement hardbox for some of the overflow, plus the hardboxes on the west side of town. Gunnar, I'll need a security detachment on all of these. Children only, plus mothers with young kids. But no men. If they can walk, they can fight."

"And if they won't?"

"Martial law is martial law. If they don't take your advice, I'll back your decision, but we don't want to stir things up."

Apgar received his meaning with a tight nod.

"The rest who don't want to fight go in the tubes. I want all sheltered civilians in place by eighteen hundred hours, but let's make this orderly to keep panic to a minimum. Colonel, you oversee assembling the civilian force. Send out a couple of squads to go house to house and put out a call for any additional weaponry. People can keep one rifle or pistol of their own, but any extras go into the armory for redistribution. As of this moment, any working firearm is property of the Texas military."

"I'll get it done," Henneman said.

Peter addressed the group: "We don't know how long we'll have to hold them off, people. It might be minutes, it might be hours, it might be all night. They might not attack at all, just wait us out. But if the dracs get in, the orphanage is our fallback position. We protect the children. Is that clear?"

Silent nods passed around the table.

"Then we're adjourned. I'll want everybody back here at fifteen hundred. Gunnar, stay behind a minute. I need a word."

They waited as the room emptied. Apgar, elbows resting on the table, eyed Peter over his meshed fingers. "So?"

Peter rose and stepped to the window. The square was quiet, with no one about, everything becalmed in the summer heat. Where was everybody? Probably hiding in their houses, Peter thought, afraid to come out.

"Fanning will have to be dealt with," he said. "This will never end otherwise."

"This would be the part of the conversation when you tell me you're going to New York."

Peter turned around. "I'll need a small contingent—say, two dozen men. We can use the portables as far north as Texarkana, maybe a little farther before we run out of fuel. On foot, we should reach New York by winter."

"That's suicide."

"I've done it before."

Apgar looked at him pointedly. "And you were fucking lucky, if you'll excuse my saying so. Never mind that you're thirty years older and New York is two thousand miles away. According to Donadio, it's crawling with dracs."

"I'll take Alicia with me. She knows the territory, and the virals won't attack her."

"After last night's performance? Be serious."

"The city won't stand unless we kill him. Sooner or later, that gate will fail."

"I don't disagree. But taking on Fanning with two dozen soldiers doesn't seem like much of a plan to me."

"What do you suggest? That we hand Amy over?"

"You should know me better than that. On top of which, once we give her to Donadio, we've got nothing. No cards to play."

"So what, then?"

"Well, have you given any more thought to Fisher's boat?"

Peter was speechless.

"Don't get me wrong," Apgar continued. "I don't trust the man any farther than I can throw him, and I'm glad you tossed his ass out of here. I don't tolerate division in the ranks, and he was way out of line. Also, I have no idea if that thing will even float."

"I don't believe what I'm hearing."

Apgar let a moment pass. "Mr. President. Peter. I'm your military adviser. I'm also your friend. I know you, how you think. It's served you well, but the situation is different. If it were up to me I'd say sure, go down swinging. The gesture might be symbolic, but symbolism matters to old warhorses like us. I hate these things, and I always have. But by any measure, this isn't going to end well. Like it or not, you're the last president of the Texas Republic. That pretty much leaves you in charge of the fate of the human race. Maybe Fisher's full of shit. You know the man, so that's your call. But seven hundred is better than nothing."

"This place will come apart. There's no way we'll be able to mount a coherent defense."

"No, probably we won't."

Peter turned back to the window. It really was awfully damn quiet out there.

He had the unsettled sense of observing the city from some distant future time: buildings empty and abandoned, dead leaves rolling in the streets, every surface being slowly reclaimed by wind and dust and years—the permanent silence of lives stopped, all the voices gone.

"Not that I'm objecting," he said, "but is this first-name thing going to be a habit?"

"When I need it, yeah."

Below him in the square, a group of boys appeared. The oldest of them couldn't have been more than ten. What were they doing out there? Then Peter grasped the situation: one of the boys had a ball. At the center of the square, he dropped it on the ground and kicked it, sending the rest scurrying after it. A pair of five-tons pulled into the square; soldiers disembarked and began to set up a line of tables. More were hauling out crates of weaponry and ammunition to be distributed among the civilian inductees. The boys took only cursory notice, lost in their game, which appeared to have nothing in the way of formal structure: no rules or boundaries, no objectives or way to keep score. Whoever possessed the ball tried to keep it away from the others, until he was bested by one of his companions, thus starting the mad chase all over again. Peter's thoughts took him back many years, first to the formless contests that had diverted Caleb and his friends for hours and their contagious youthful energy—*just five more minutes, Dad, there's still plenty of light, please just one more game*—and then to his own boyhood: that brief, innocent span in which he had existed in total obliviousness, outside the flow of history and the accumulated weight of life.

He turned from the window. "Do you remember the day Vicky summoned me to her office to offer me a job?"

"Not really, no."

"As I was leaving, she called me back. Asked about Caleb, how old he was. She said—and I think I have this right—'It's the children we're doing this for. We'll be long gone, but our decisions will determine the kind of world they're going to live in.'"

Apgar gave a slow nod. "Come to think of it, maybe I do remember. She was a cunning old broad, I'll give her that. It was a masterpiece of manipulation."

"No chance I could turn her down. It was just a matter of time before I surrendered."

"So what's your point?"

"The point is, this patch of ground doesn't just belong to us, Gunnar. It belongs to *them*. First Colony was dying. Everyone had given up. But not here. That's why Kerrville has survived as long as it has. Because the people here have refused to go quietly."

"We're talking about the survival of our species."

"I know we are. But we need to earn the right, and abandoning three thousand people to save seven hundred isn't an equation I can sit with. So maybe it all ends here. Tonight, even. But this city is ours. This *continent* is ours. We run, Fanning wins, no matter what. And Vicky would say the same thing."

A moment of stalemate passed, the two men looking at each other. Then:

"That's a nice speech," Apgar said.

"Yeah, I bet you didn't know I was such a deep thinker."

"So that's it?"

"That's it," said Peter. "That's my final word. We stay and fight."

64

Sara descended the stairs to the basement. Grace was at the end of the second row of cots, sitting up, her baby resting in her lap. The woman looked tired but also relieved. She offered a small smile as Sara approached.

"He's fussing a little," she said.

Sara took the baby from her, laid him on the adjacent cot, and unwound the blanket to examine him. A big, healthy boy with curly black hair. His heart was loud and strong.

"We're calling him Carlos, after my father," Grace said.

During the night, Grace had told Sara the story. Fifteen years ago, her parents had moved out to the townships, settling in Boerne. But her father had had little luck as a farmer and had been forced to take a job with the telegraph crews, leaving the family alone for months at a time. After he'd been killed in a fall from a pole, Grace and her mother—her two older brothers had long since moved on—had returned to Kerrville to live with relatives. But it had been a hard life, and her mother, too, had passed, though Grace shared no details. At seventeen, Grace had gone to work in an illegal saloon—she was vague about her duties, which Sara didn't want to know—and this was how she'd met Jock. Not an auspicious beginning, although the two were, Grace asserted, very much in love, and when she'd turned up pregnant, Jock had done the honorable thing.

Sara rewrapped the baby and returned him to his mother, assuring her that everything was fine. "He'll complain a bit until your milk comes in. Don't worry—it doesn't mean anything."

"What's going to happen to us, Dr. Wilson?"

The question seemed too large. "You're going to take care of your son, that's what."

"I heard about that woman. They say she's some kind of viral. How could that be?"

Sara was caught off guard—but of course people would be talking. "Maybe she is—I don't know." She put a hand on Grace's shoulder. "Try to rest. The Army knows what it's doing."

She found Jenny in the storage room, taking inventory of their supplies: bandages, candles, blankets, water. More boxes had been brought down from the first floor and stacked against the wall. Her daughter, Hannah, was helping her—a freckled, disarmingly green-eyed girl of thirteen, with long, coltish legs.

"Sweetheart, could your mom and I have a minute? Go see if they need anything upstairs."

The girl left them alone. Quickly, Sara reviewed the plan. "How many people do you think we can fit in here?" she asked.

"A hundred, anyway. More if we really stuff them in, I guess."

"Let's set up a desk at the front door to count heads. No men get in, only women and children."

"What if they try?"

"Not our problem. The military will handle it."

Sara examined four more patients—the boy with pneumonia; a woman in her forties who had rushed in with breathing trouble that she feared was a heart attack but was nothing more than panic; two little girls, twins, who had come down with acute diarrhea and fever in the night—then returned to the first floor in time to see a pair of five-tons roar up to the entrance. She stepped outside to meet them.

"Sara Wilson?"

"That's right."

The soldier turned back to the first truck in line. "Okay, start unloading."

Moving in pairs, the soldiers began carting sandbags to the entrance. Simultaneously, a pair of Humvees with .50-caliber machine guns attached to their roofs backed up to the building and took flanking positions on both sides of the door. Sara watched this numbly; the strangeness of all of it was catching up with her.

"Can you show me the other entrances?" the sergeant asked.

Sara led him around to the back and side doors. Soldiers arrived with sheets of plywood and began hammering them into the molding.

"Those won't keep a drac out," Sara said. They were standing at the front of the building, where more sheets of plywood were being used to cover the windows.

"They're not for the dracs."

Sweet Jesus, she thought.

"Do you have a weapon, ma'am?"

"This is a hospital, Sergeant. We don't just leave guns lying around."

He walked to the first truck and returned with a rifle and pistol. He held them out. "Take your pick."

Everything about his offer went against the grain; a hospital still meant something. Then she thought of Kate.

"All right, the pistol." She tucked it into her waistband.

"You've used one before?" the sergeant said. "I can give you the basics if you want."

"That won't be necessary."

In the stockade, Alicia was gauging the strength of the chains.

The bolt on the wall was negligible—one hard yank should do it—but the shackles were a problem. They were constructed of a hardened alloy of some sort. Probably they had come from Tifty's bunker; the man had made a science of viral containment. So even if she freed herself from the wall, she'd still be as trussed up as a hog for slaughter.

The thought of sleep enticed her. Not merely to obliterate time but to carry her thoughts away. But her dreams, always the same, were nothing she cared to revisit: the brilliantly lit city dissolving to darkness; the happy cries of life within waning, then gone; the pitiless, disappearing door.

And then there was the other issue: Alicia wasn't alone.

The feeling was subtle, but she could tell Fanning was still there: a sort of low-grade hum in her brain, more tactile than aural, like a breeze pushing over the surface of her mind. It made her feel angry and sick and tired of everything, ready to be done with it all.

Get out of my head, goddamnit. Haven't I done what you asked? Leave me the hell alone.

The promised food did not appear. Peter had forgotten, or else he'd decided that a hungry Alicia was safer than a full one. It could be a tactic to make her pliable: *Food is on the way; wait, no, it isn't.* In either event, she was perversely glad; part of her still hated it. The moment her jaws sank into flesh, hot blood squirting upon her palate, a chorus of revulsion erupted in her head: *What the hell are you doing?* Yet always she drank her fill until, thoroughly disgusted with herself, she sank back on her heels and let the lassitude engulf her.

The hours moved sluggishly. At last the door opened.

"Surprise."

Michael stepped into the room. A small metal cage was pressed against his chest.

"Five minutes, Fisher," the guard said, and slammed the door behind him.

Michael put the cage on the floor and took a seat on the cot, facing her squarely. In the cage was a brown rabbit.

"How'd you get in?" Alicia asked.

"Oh, they know me pretty well around here."

"You bribed them."

Michael seemed pleased. "As it happens, a little money changed hands, yes. Even in these troubled times, a man has to think about his family. That, plus nobody else had the stomach to bring you breakfast." He nodded toward the cage. "Apparently, the little bundle of fur is somebody's pet. Goes by Otis."

Alicia allowed herself a good, long look at Michael. The boy she'd known was gone, replaced by a middle-aged man of sinewy hardness, compact and capable. His face had a chiseled look, nothing wasted. Though his eyes still possessed their twinkling, busy alertness, a darker aspect lay within them, more knowing: the eyes of experience, of a man who had seen things in his life.

"You've changed, Michael."

He shrugged carelessly. "This is something I hear a lot."

"How've you been keeping yourself?"

"Oh, you know me." A cockeyed smile. "Just keeping the lights burning."

"And Lore?"

"Can't say that worked out."

"Sorry to hear it."

"You know how it goes. I got the potted plants, she took the house. For the best, really." He angled his head at the floor again, where the caged rabbit was anxiously working its cheeks. "Aren't you going to eat?"

She wanted to, very badly. The intoxicating scent of warm meat, warm life; the swish and throb of the animal's blood surging through its veins, as if she'd cupped a seashell to her ear: her anticipation was intense.

"It's not a pretty sight," she said. "Probably best if I wait."

For several seconds, they just looked at each other.

"Thanks for standing up for me last night," Alicia said.

"No thanks necessary. Peter was way out of line."

She searched his face. "Why don't you hate me, Michael?"

"Why would I do that?"

"Everybody else seems to."

"I guess I'm not everybody else then. You could say I don't have a lot of fans in these parts myself."

"I hardly believe that."

"Oh, trust me. I'm lucky I'm not living down the hall."

A smile, unbidden, rose to her lips; it was good to talk to a friend. "Sounds interesting."

"That would be one word for it." He placed the tips of his fingers together, a man making a point. "I always knew you were out there, Lish. Maybe the others gave up on you. But I never did."

"Thanks, Circuit. That means something. That means a lot."

He grinned. "Now, seeing as it's you, I'll let that nickname slide."

"Talk to him, Michael."

"I've made my opinion known."

"What's he going to do?"

He shrugged. "What Peter always does. Hurl himself at the problem until he bashes his way through it. I love the guy, but he's a bit of an ox."

"It won't work this time."

"No, it won't."

He was watching her intently—though, unlike Peter's, his gaze held no suspicion. She was a confidante, a co-conspirator, a trusted part of his world. His eyes, his tone of voice, the manner in which his body occupied space: all radiated an undeniable force.

"I've thought a lot about you, Lish. For a long time, I believed I was in love with you. Who knows? Maybe I still am. I hope that doesn't embarrass you."

Alicia was dumbstruck.

"I see from your expression that this comes as a surprise. Just take it as a compliment, which is how it's meant. What I'm saying is that you matter a great deal to me, and you always have. When you appeared last night, I realized something. Do you want to know what that was?"

Alicia nodded, still at a loss for words.

"I realized I'd been waiting for you all along. Not just waiting. Expecting." He paused. "Do you remember the last time we saw each other? It was the day you came to visit me in the hospital."

"Of course I do."

"For the longest time I wondered: Why me? Why did Alicia pick me, of all people, at just that moment? I would have guessed Peter would be the one. The answer came to me when I thought about something you said. 'Someday, that boy's going to save our sorry asses.'"

"We were talking about when we were kids."

"That's right. But we were talking about a lot more than that." He leaned forward. "Even then, you knew, Lish. Maybe not knew. But you felt it, the shape of things, just as I did. Just as I do now, sitting here twenty years later talking to you in a jail cell. Now, 'why' is another question. I don't have an answer to that one and I've stopped asking. And as for how this is all going to play out, your guess is as good as mine. Given the general direction of the last twenty-four hours, I'm not especially optimistic. But either way, I can't do this without you."

The sound of tumblers; the guard appeared in the doorway. "Fisher, I said five minutes. You need to get the hell out of here."

Michael reached into his shirt pocket and waved a wad of bills over his shoulder, not even bothering to look as the guard snatched it and skulked away.

"God, they're idiots," he sighed. "Do they actually think money's going to be worth anything this time tomorrow?" He reached into his pocket again and removed a folded sheet of paper. "Here, take this."

Alicia opened it: a map, hastily sketched in Michael's hand.

"When the time comes, follow the Rosenberg road south. Just beyond the garrison, you'll come to an old farm with a water tank on your left. Take the road after it and follow it straight east, fifty-two miles."

Alicia looked up from the paper. Something new was in his eyes: a kind of wildness, almost manic. Beneath Michael's controlled exterior, his aura of self-possessing strength, was a man aflame with belief.

"Michael, what's at the end of that road?"

Alone again, Alicia drifted. So, there had been a woman for Michael, after all. His ship, his *Bergensfjord.*

We are the exiles, he had told her in parting. *We are the ones who understand the truth and always have; that is our pain in life.* How well he knew her.

The rabbit was watching her guardedly. His black eyes, unblinking, shone like drops of ink; in their curved surfaces Alicia could see the ghost of her face reflected, a shadow self. She realized her cheeks were wet; why could she not stop crying? She scooted forward to the cage, undid the latch, and reached inside. Soft fur filled her hand. The rabbit made no attempt to escape; he was either tame, a pet as Michael claimed, or too frightened to react. She lifted the animal free and placed him on her lap.

"It's all right, Otis," she said. "I'm a friend." And she stayed that way, stroking the soft fur, for a very long time.

65

Footsteps, and the creak of the opening door: Amy opened her eyes.

Hello, Pim.

The woman halted in the entryway. She was tall, with an oval face and expressive eyes, and wearing a simple cotton dress of blue fabric. Beneath its soft drape, her belly arced with the bulge of her pregnancy.

I'm glad that you've come back to see me, Amy signed.

A look of deep uncertainty, and Pim stepped to her bedside.

May I? Amy asked.

Pim nodded. Amy cupped her palm against the curving cloth. The force within, being so new, exuded a pure feeling of life—if it were a color, it would be the white of summer clouds—but was also full of questions. Who am I? What am I? Is this the world? Am I everything, or just a part?

Show me the rest, Amy signed.

Pim sat on the bed, facing away. Amy unfastened the buttons of her dress and drew the fabric aside. The stripes on her back, the burns—they were faded, though not erased. Time had given them a ridged and burrowed quality, like roots running under soil. Amy ran the tips of her fingers along their lengths. In the untouched places Pim's skin was soft, with a pulsing warmth, but the muscles were hard beneath, as if forged with remembered pain.

Amy buttoned the dress; Pim swiveled on the mattress to face her.

I've dreamed about you, Pim signed. *I feel like I've known you all my life. And I you.*

Pim's eyes were full of inexpressible emotion. *Even when . . .*

Amy took her hands to quiet them. *Yes,* she replied. *Even then.*

From the pocket of her dress, Pim withdrew a notebook. It was small but possessed the thickness of stiff parchment paper stitched together. *I brought you this.*

Amy accepted it and opened the covers, which were wrapped in soft hide. Here it was, page after page. The drawings. The words. The island with its five stars.

Who else has seen this? she signed.

Only you.

Not even Caleb?

Pim shook her head. A film of tears coated the surface of her eyes; she appeared completely overcome, beyond words. *How do I know these things?*

Amy closed the notebook. *I cannot say.*

What does it mean?

I think it means you will live; your baby will live. A pause, then: *Will you help me?*

In the living room, she found paper and a pen. She wrote the note, folded it into thirds, and gave it to Pim, who hurried away. Alone again, Amy went to the bathroom off the hall. Above the washbasin was a small round mirror. The changes that had occurred to her person had been felt rather than observed; she had yet to see herself. She stepped to the mirror. The face she beheld did not seem to be her own, and yet it was also the person she had long felt herself to be: a woman with dark hair, a well-sculpted though not overtly angular face, pale unblemished skin, and deep-set eyes. Her hair was as short as a boy's, showing the curves of her skull, and bristly to the touch, like the end of a broom. The reflection possessed a disquieting ordinariness; she might have been anyone, just another woman in the crowd, yet it was within this face, this body, that all her thoughts and perceptions—her sense of self—resided. The urge to reach out and touch the mirror was strong, and she allowed herself to do so. As her finger made contact with the glass, her reflection responding in kind, a shift occurred. *This is you,* her mind told her. *This is the one true Amy.*

It was time.

To quiet one's mind, to bring it to a condition of absolute motionlessness—that was the trick. Amy liked to use a lake. This body of water was not imaginary; it was the lake in Oregon where Wolgast, in their first days together at the camp, had taught her to swim. She closed her eyes and willed herself to go there; gradually the scene arose in her thoughts. The cusp of night, and the first stars punching through a blue-black sky. The wall of shadow where tall pines, rich with fragrance, stood regally along the rocky shore. The water itself, cold and clear and sharp-tasting, and the downy duff of needles carpeting the bottom. In this mental construct, Amy was both the lake and the swimmer in the lake; ripples moved outward along its surface in accordance with her motions. She took a breath and dove down, into an unseen world; when the bottom appeared, she began to move along it with a smooth, gliding motion. Far above her, the ripples of her entry dispersed concentrically across the surface. When the last of these disturbances touched their fingers to the shore, and the lake's surface returned to perfect balance, the state she required would be achieved.

The ripples touched. The lake stilled.

Can you hear me?

Silence. Then:

Yes, Amy.

I think that I am ready, Anthony. I think I am ready at last.

Michael had been waiting at the gate for nearly an hour. Where the hell was Lucius? It was nearly 1030; they were cutting it close as it was. Men were welding heavy brackets in place to lay iron beams across the gate. More were hammering sheets of galvanized roofing metal to the outside face. If Greer didn't show up soon, they'd be locked inside like everybody else.

At last Greer appeared, striding briskly through the portal from outside. He climbed into the truck and nodded toward the windshield. "Let's go."

"She's fooling herself."

Greer gave him a look: don't go there.

Michael turned the engine over, angled his head out the window, and yelled to the foreman of the work crew: "Coming through!" When the man failed to turn around, he leaned on the horn. "Hey! We need to get out!"

That got the foreman's attention; he strode up to the driver's window. "The hell you honking at me for?"

"Tell those guys to get out of the way."

He spat onto the ground. "Nobody's supposed to go outside. We're working here."

"Yeah, well, we're different. Tell them to move or get run over. How would that be?"

The man looked like he was about to say something but stopped himself. He turned back toward the gate. "Okay, clear a path for this guy."

"Much obliged," Michael said.

The foreman spat again. "It's your funeral, asshole."

Yours, too, thought Michael.

66

1630 hours: the last of the evacuees were being moved into the dam; the hard-boxes were full; the few remaining civilian inductees were awaiting their assignments. There had been a few incidents—some arrests, even a few shots fired. Yet most people saw the sense of what they were being asked to do; their own lives were on the line.

But processing the inductees was taking longer than expected. Long lines, confusion about weapons and who reported to whom, the distribution of equipment and delegation of duties: Peter and Apgar were trying to assemble an army in half a day. Some barely knew how to hold a gun, much less load and fire it. Ammo was at a premium, but a target range had been set up in the square, using sandbags as a backstop. A crash course for the uninitiated—three shots, good or bad—and off they went to the wall.

Just a few weapons remained, pistols only; the rifles were gone, except for a few that would be held in reserve. Tempers were short; everyone had been standing in the hot sun for hours. Peter was positioned to the side of the processing desk with Apgar, watching the last few men come through. Hollis was checking off names.

A man approached the desk—forties, lean in the manner of someone to whom life had not been kind, with a high, domed forehead and old acne scars on his cheeks. A hunting rifle hung from his shoulder. It took Peter a moment to recognize him.

"Jock, isn't it?"

The man nodded—somewhat sheepishly, Peter thought. Twenty years gone by, yet Peter could tell that the memory of that day on the roof still affected him. "I don't think I ever really thanked you, Mr. President."

Apgar glanced at Peter. "What'd you do?"

Jock said, "He saved my life, is what he did." Then, to Peter: "I've never forgotten it. Voted for you both times."

"What became of you? No more roofs, I'll bet."

Jock shrugged; his regular life, like everyone's, was receding into the past. "Worked as a mechanic, mostly. Just got married, too. My wife had a baby last night."

Peter remembered Sara's story. He gestured toward Jock's rifle, a lever-action .30-30. "Let's see your weapon."

Jock handed it over. The action was jerky, the trigger like mush, the glass of the scope gouged and pitted.

"When was the last time you fired this?"

"Never. Got it from my dad years ago."

Hollis looked up. "We don't have any thirty-thirty."

"How many rounds do you have for this?" Peter asked Jock.

The man held out his open palm, showing four cartridges, old as the hills.

"This thing is worthless. Hollis, get this man a proper rifle."

The gun was produced: one of Tifty's M16s, fresh and gleaming.

"A wedding present," Peter said, passing it off to Jock. "Report to the range. They'll get you ammo and show you how to use it."

The man looked up, blindsided. His face was full of gratitude; no one had ever given him such a present. "Thank you, sir." A crisp nod and he moved away.

"Okay, what was that about?" Apgar asked.

Peter's eyes followed Jock as he made his way to the range. "For luck," he said.

In the orphanage, the last of the women and children were descending into the shelter. It had been decided that only women with children under five would be allowed to accompany their offspring; there had been many tearful scenes of separation, agonizing and awful. Quite a few mothers claimed their children were younger than they obviously were; in those instances that seemed close, or close enough, Caleb let them through. He simply didn't have the heart to say no.

Caleb worried about Pim; the shelter was rapidly filling. At last she arrived, explaining that the children had spent the morning at Kate and Bill's house. For Pim a painful pilgrimage, Kate's ghost everywhere, but a helpful distraction for the girls: a few hours in familiar rooms, playing with familiar toys. They'd bounced on their old beds for half an hour, Pim said.

And yet something was off; Caleb sensed the presence of words unsaid. They were standing by the open hatch. One of the sisters, positioned on the platform below, reached up to assist the children, first Theo, then the girls. As Pim's turn came, Caleb took her by the elbow.

What is it?

She hesitated. Yes, something was there.

Pim?

A flicker of uncertainty in her eyes; then she composed herself. *I love you. Be careful.*

Caleb let the matter rest. Now was not the time, the hatch standing open, everyone waiting. Sister Peg was observing from the side. Caleb had already broached the question of whether or not Sister Peg would be joining the children underground. "Lieutenant," she'd said with a reproachful look, "I'm eighty-one years old."

Caleb hugged his wife and helped her down. As her hands gripped the top rung, she raised her eyes, for a last look. A cold weight dropped inside him. She was his life.

Keep our babies safe, he signed.

More children came through; then, suddenly, the shelter was full. From outside the building a cry went up, followed by a voice from a megaphone, ordering the crowd to disperse.

Colonel Henneman strode into the hall. "Jaxon, I'm putting you in charge here."

It was the last thing Caleb wanted. "I'd be more use on the wall, sir."

"This isn't a debate."

Caleb felt the presence of an unseen hand. "Does my father have something to do with this?"

Henneman ignored the question. "We'll need men on the roof and the perimeter and two squads inside. Are we clear? Nobody else gets inside. How you accomplish that is up to you."

Dire words. Also inevitable. People would do anything to survive.

67

Michael and Greer picked up the first survivors north of Rosenberg, a group of three soldiers—stunned, starving, their carbines and pistols drained. The virals had attacked the barracks two nights ago, they said, tearing through the place like a tornado, destroying everything, vehicles and equipment, the generator and radio, ripping the roofs off the Quonsets like they were opening tins of meat.

There were others. A woman, one of Dunk's girls, with black hair streaked white, walking barefoot along the roadway with her tippy shoes dangling from her fingertips and a story about hiding in a pump house. A pair of men from one of the telegraph crews. An oiler named Winch—Michael recalled him from the old days—sitting cross-legged by the side of the road, carving mean-ingless shapes in the ground with a six-inch knife and babbling incoherently. His face was chalky with dust, his coveralls black with dried blood, though it was not his own. All took their places in the back of the truck in stunned si-lence, not even asking where they were going.

"These are the luckiest people on the planet," Michael said, "and they don't even know it."

Greer watched the landscape flow past, dry scrub yielding to the dense tangle of the coastal shelf. The intensity of the last twenty-four hours had kept the pain at bay, but now, in the unstructured silence of his thoughts, it roared back. An omnipresent, low-grade urge to vomit tossed his gut; his saliva was thick and brassy-tasting; his bladder pulsed with unexpressed fullness, febrile and enormous. When they'd stopped to pick up the woman, Greer had stepped into the scrub with the hope of passing water, but all he'd managed to produce was a pathetic crimson-tinted trickle.

South of Rosenberg, they swung east toward the ship channel. Muddy water sprayed up behind them; each bang of the truck's carriage on the gullied roadway threw fresh punches of pain. Greer wanted a drink of water very badly, if only to clear the taste in his mouth, but when Michael drew his can-teen from under his seat, took a long pull, and offered it to him, all the while staring out the windshield, Greer waved it off. From Michael, a sideways glance—*You're sure?*—and for that moment the man seemed to know some-thing, or at least suspect. But when Greer said nothing, Michael wedged the canteen between his knees and capped it with a shrug.

The air in the truck changed, and then the sky; they were approaching the channel.

"For fucksakes, I only just came from here," said the woman.

Five more miles and the causeway appeared. Patch and his men were waiting at the bottleneck. Barriers of razor wire had been laid across it. As the truck drew to a halt, Patch stepped up to the driver's window.

"Didn't expect you back so soon."

"What has Lore told you?" Michael asked.

"Just the bad parts. No sign of them here, though." Then, glancing into the back of the vehicle, "I see you've brought some friends."

"Where is she?"

"The ship, I guess. Rand says she's driving everybody crazy down there."

Michael turned toward their passengers. "You three," he said to the soldiers, "get out."

They were looking around with bewilderment. "What do you want us to do?" one asked—the highest-ranking among them, a corporal with eyes empty as a cow's and the soft, baby-fatted face of a fifteen-year-old.

"I don't know," Michael said dryly, "be soldiers? Shoot at things?"

"I told you, we haven't got any ammo."

"Patch?"

The man nodded. "I'll fix them up."

"This is Patch," Michael said to the three. "He's your new CO."

They looked blankly at one another. "Aren't you guys, like, criminals?" the one said.

"Right now, do you honestly give a damn?"

"Come on now," Patch cut in, "be good fellows and do like the man says."

Looking askance at one another, the soldiers disembarked. Once Patch and the others had pulled the barrier aside, Michael gunned the engine and roared down the causeway. Rand met them at the shed, shirtless and sweating, a greasy rag knotted around his head.

"What's our status?" Michael asked, stepping down. "Have you flooded the dock?"

"There's a problem. Lore found another bad section. There are soft spots all through it."

"Where?"

"Starboard bow."

"*Fuck.*" Michael gestured toward their remaining passengers, who were standing in a group, staring with befuddlement. "Figure out what to do with these people."

"Where'd you get them?"

"Found them on the way."

"Isn't that Winch?" Rand asked. The man was muttering into his collar. "What the hell happened to him?"

"Whatever it was, it wasn't nice," Michael answered.

Rand's eyes darkened. "Is it true about the townships? That they're all gone?"

Michael nodded. "Yeah, looks like we're it."

Greer interrupted: "Michael, I think we need to take extra men up to the causeway. It'll be dark in a few hours."

"Rand, how about it?"

"I guess we can spare a few. Lombardi and those other guys."

"You two," Rand said to the telegraph men, "come with me. And you," he said to the woman, "what can you do?"

She arched her eyebrows.

"Besides that, I mean."

She thought for a moment. "Cook a little?"

"A little's better than what we've got. You're hired."

Michael strode down the ramp to the ship. A crane with a sling had been moved into place on the dock, near the bow, where six men in bosun's chairs hung over the side. At the far end of the weir, men in welding masks and heavy gloves were using circular saws to cut the replacement from a larger plate, sparks jetting from their blades.

Lore, standing at the rail, saw him and came down. "Sorry, Michael." She was practically yelling to make herself heard over the whine of the saws. "The timing isn't great, I know."

"What the hell, Lore?"

"Did you want her to sink? Because she would have. I'm not the one who missed it. You should be thanking me."

This was more than a delay; it was a catastrophe. Until the hull was tight, they couldn't flood the dock; until they flooded the dock, they couldn't fire the engines. Just flooding the dock would take an additional six hours. "How long do you figure to replace it?" he asked.

"To cut the plates, pull out the old ones, lower them into place, rivet, and weld, I'd say sixteen hours, minimum."

There was no reason to question her; it wasn't something that could be rushed. He turned on his heels and headed down the dock.

"Where are you going?" Lore called after him.

"To cut some fucking steel."

68

The time was 1730; the sun would set in three hours. For the moment, Peter had done all he could. He was well past the need to sleep but wanted a moment to collect himself. He thought of Jock as he walked to the house. He had no particular allegiance to the man; he had been a callow and obnoxious kid who had nearly gotten Peter killed. The rifle was probably wasted on him. But Peter recognized that day on the roof as a turning point, and he believed in second chances.

The security detail was gone.

Peter darted up the stairs and raced into the house. "Amy?" he called.

A silence, then: "In here."

She was sitting on the bed, facing the door, hands folded neatly in her lap.

"Are you all right?" he asked.

She looked up. Her face changed; she gave him a melancholy smile. A peculiar quiet took the room—not merely an absence of sound but something deeper, more fraught. "Yes. I'm fine." She patted the mattress. "Come sit with me."

He took a place beside her. "What is it? What's wrong?"

She took his hand, not looking at him. He sensed she was on the verge of some announcement.

"When I was in the water, I went someplace," she said. "At least, my mind did. I'm not sure I can explain this right. I was so happy there."

He realized what she was saying. "The farmstead."

Her eyes found his.

"I've been there, too." Strangely, he felt no surprise; the words had been waiting to be said.

"I was playing the piano."

"Yes."

"And we were together."

"Yes. We were. Just the two of us."

How good to say it, to speak the words. To know that he was not alone with his dreams after all, that there was some reality to it, though he could not know what that reality was, only that it existed. He existed. Amy existed. The farmstead, and their happiness in that place, existed.

"You asked me this morning why I came to you in Iowa," Amy said. "I didn't tell you the truth. Or, at least, not all of it."

Peter waited.

"When you change, you get to keep one thing, one memory. Whatever was closest to your heart. From all your life, just the one." She looked up. "What I wanted to keep was you."

She was crying, just a little: small, jeweled tears that hung suspended on the tips of her lashes, like drops of dew upon leaves. "Peter, will you do something for me?"

He nodded.

"Please kiss me."

He did. He did not so much kiss her as fall into the world of her. Time slowed, stopped, moved in an unhurried circle around them, like waves around a pier. He felt at peace. His senses were soaring. His mind was in two places, this world and also the other: the world of the farmstead, a place beyond space, beyond time, where only the two of them resided.

They parted. Their faces were inches apart. Amy cupped his cheek, her eyes locked on his.

"I'm sorry, Peter."

The remark was strange. Her gaze deepened.

"I know what you're planning to do," she said. "You wouldn't survive it."

Something came undone inside him. All strength drained from his body. He tried to speak but couldn't.

"You're tired," Amy said.

She caught him as he fell.

Amy laid him on the bed. In the outer room, she pulled her frock over her head and replaced it with the clothing that Greer had fetched for her: heavy canvas pants with pockets, leather boots, a tan shirt, the sleeves torn away, with the insignia of the Expeditionary on the shoulders. They possessed a warm, human odor—a smell of work, of life. Whoever had owned these articles was small; the fit was nearly perfect. On the back porch the soldiers slept soundly, like babies, hands tucked under their cheeks, lost to all cares. Amy gently relieved one of his pistol and tucked it into her trousers, against her spine.

A deep quiet held the street, everyone in hiding, bracing for the storm. As Amy made her way toward the center of town, soldiers began to take notice, yet none spoke to her; their minds were elsewhere, what did one woman matter? The exterior of the stockade was unguarded. Amy strode purposefully to the door and stepped inside.

She counted three men. Behind the counter, the officer in charge glanced up.

"Help you, soldier?"

*　　*　　*

The sound of tumblers: Alicia raised her eyes. Amy?

"Hello, sister."

Alicia looked past her but saw no one; Amy was alone.

"What are you doing here?" she asked.

Amy was unlocking the shackles. She handed Alicia her goggles. "I'll explain on the way."

In the outer room, the guards lay asleep on the floor. Following Greer's directions, Amy and Alicia made their way via backstreets and trash-strewn alleys into H-town. Soon the southern wall rose into view. Amy entered a small house, little more than a hut. There was no furniture at all. In the main room, she drew a threadbare rug aside to reveal a hatch with a ladder. One of the trade's stash houses, Amy explained, though Alicia had already figured that out. They descended into a cool, damp space that smelled of rotten fruit.

"There," Amy said, pointing.

The shelves, stocked with liquor, pulled away to reveal a tunnel. At the far end they came to another ladder and, ten feet up, a metal hatch set into concrete. Amy turned the ring and pushed.

They were outside the city, a hundred yards outside the wall in a copse of trees. Soldier and a second horse were tied up, obliviously grazing. As Alicia climbed free of the hatch, Soldier raised his head: *Ah. There you are. I was beginning to wonder.*

Her sword and bandoliers were hanging from the saddle. Alicia strapped on her blades while Amy covered the hatch with brush.

"You should be the one to ride him," Alicia said. She was also holding out the sword.

Amy considered this. "All right," she said.

She angled the sword over her shoulders and swung up onto Soldier's back. Alicia mounted the second horse, a dark bay stallion, quite young but with a fierce look to him. It was late afternoon, the sun harsh and white.

They rode away.

The dream of the farmstead was different. Peter was lying in bed. The room was full of moonlight, making the walls seem to glow. The sheets were cold; it was this coldness that had aroused him. He had a sense of having slept a long time.

Amy's side of the bed was empty.

He called her name. His voice sounded weak in the darkness, barely a presence. He rose and went to the window. Amy was standing in the yard, facing away from the house. Her posture meant something; panic surged in his heart. She began to walk—away from the house, away from him and the life they had known, her figure silhouetted by the moonlight, growing smaller. Peter could neither move nor cry out. He felt as if his soul were being wrenched from his body. *Don't leave me, Amy* . . .

He awoke with a start; his heart was pounding, his body glazed with sweat. Apgar's face swam into focus.

"Mr. President, something has happened."

He didn't have to say the rest. Peter knew at once. Amy was gone.

IX

THE TRAP

Blood ran in torrents, drenched was all the earth,
As Trojans and their alien helpers died.
Here were men lying quelled by bitter death
All up and down the city in their blood.

—Quintus Smyrnaeus,
The Fall of Troy

69

The saws had silenced; the steel had been cut. On the ship's starboard flank, a gaping hole revealed the hidden decks and passageways within. The sun was receding, sparkling over the channel's waters; the spotlights had been lit.

Rand was operating the crane. From the floor of the dock, Michael watched the first plate descending in its cradle. Voices volleyed through the dock, more from up on deck, where Lore commanded.

The required height was achieved. Men scurried over the surface, hammers and pneumatic guns swaying from their belts; others guided the plate from inside. With a clang, the huge steel sheet made contact. Michael ascended the stairs and crossed the gangway to the deck.

"So far so good," Lore said.

They were, improbably, on schedule. The passing hours were like a funnel, drawing them down to a single moment. Every decision was binding; there would be no second chances.

Lore went to the rail and yelled down a barrage of orders, trying to make her voice heard over the roar of the generators and the whine of the guns; Michael moved beside her. The first plate lay flush against the side. They had six more to go.

"Want to know how they did it?"

Lore looked at him strangely.

"How the passengers killed themselves."

He had not meant to raise the subject. It seemed to have arisen of its own accord, one more secret he wanted to be rid of.

"Okay."

"They'd saved some fuel. Not much but enough. They sealed the doors and rerouted the engine's exhaust back into the ship's ventilation. It would have been like falling asleep."

Lore's face showed no expression. Then, with a small nod: "I'm glad you said something."

"Maybe I shouldn't have."

"Don't apologize."

He realized why he had told her. If it came to that, they could do the same thing.

70

The light was leaving them.

Runners had begun to move; from the command post on the catwalk, Peter felt, with cold clarity, the thinness of their defense. A six-mile perimeter, men without training, an enemy like no other, lacking all fear.

Though Apgar said nothing on the subject, Peter could read the man's thoughts. Maybe Amy had gone with Alicia to give herself up; maybe the dracs wouldn't come, after all. Maybe they would anyway; maybe that was the point. He remembered his dream: the image of Amy in the moonlight, walking away, not looking back. All that kept him going was the certainty of what lay ahead in the next few hours. He had a role to play, and he would play it.

Chase arrived on the platform. Peter almost didn't recognize his chief of staff. The man was dressed in an officer's uniform, though the insignia had been removed, cut away roughly as if in a hurry, perhaps out of respect; he was toting a rifle, trying to seem a certain way with it. The gun looked like it had been hanging over a fireplace for years. Peter was about to say something, then stopped himself. Apgar raised a skeptical eyebrow, but that was the extent of it.

"Where's Olivia?" Peter asked finally.

"In the president's hardbox." Chase seemed uncertain. "I hope that's all right."

The three men listened as the stations called in. All stood ready, braced for attack. The shadows lengthened over the valley. It was a beautiful evening in summer, the clouds ripening with color.

71

Amy did not have to know the place. The place, she knew, would come to her.

They galloped away from the sun, the ground flying beneath them. Dust rose in a gritty cloud; clods of dirt flew up from the horses' hooves. A certain feeling built within her. It magnified with every mile, like a radio signal growing stronger, calling them forward. Soldier's gait was powerful and smooth.

You have taken wonderful care of our friend, Amy told him. *How brave you are, how strong. You will always be remembered. Green fields await you; you will spend a noble eternity among your kind.*

Soldier's gallop faded to a walk. They brought their horses to a halt and dismounted. The rich foam of his efforts boiled from Soldier's mouth; his dark flanks flashed with sweat.

"Here," Amy said.

Alicia nodded but said nothing; Amy detected within her friend an edge of fear. She stepped away and stood in silence, waiting. The wind moved by her ears, through her hair, then faded to nothing. All seemed frozen, sealed in a great calm. The day's last minutes ticked away. On the ground before her, her shadow stretched—longer, longer. She felt the moment of the sun's union with the earth, its first touch upon the line of hills, audible, like a sigh. She closed her eyes and sent her mind diving into darkness; the ripples widened on the lake's tranquil surface high above.

Anthony, I'm here.

First, silence. Then:

Yes, Amy. They are ready. They are yours.

Night was falling.

Come to me, she thought.

Night fell.

72

They were called dopeys. But in their lives, they had been many things.

They hailed from every quarter of the continent, every state and city. Seattle, Washington. Albuquerque, New Mexico. Mobile, Alabama. The toxic chemical swamp of New Orleans and the windswept flatlands of Kansas City and the icebound canyons of Chicago. As a body, they were a statistician's dream, a perfect representative sampling of the inhabitants of the Great North American Empire. They came from farms and small towns, faceless suburbs and sprawling metropolises; they were every color and creed; they had lived in trailers, houses, apartments, mansions with views of the sea. In their human states, each had occupied a discrete and private self. They had hoped, hated, loved, suffered, sung, and wept. They had known loss. They had surrounded and comforted themselves with objects. They had driven automobiles. They had walked dogs and pushed children on swing sets and waited in line at the grocery store. They had said stupid things. They had kept secrets, nurtured grudges, blown upon the embers of regret. They had worshipped a variety of gods or no god at all. They had awakened in the night to the sound of rain. They had apologized. They had attended various ceremonies. They had explained the history of themselves to psychologists, priests, lovers, and strangers in bars. They had, at unexpected moments, experienced bolts of joy so unalloyed, so untethered to events, that they seemed to come from above; they had longed to be known and, sometimes, almost were.

Heirs to the viral lineage of Anthony Carter, Twelfth of Twelve, they were intrinsically less bloodthirsty than their counterparts; it had been remarked many times by human observers that the dopeys satisfied their appetites with an attitude of joyless obligation, and that it was this characteristic, singular among virals, that made them easier to kill. *Dumb as a dopey* was the phrase. This was true, while also concealing a deeper truth. Indeed they did not like it; the butchery of innocents disturbed them. Yet within them lay an unexpressed ferocity, unwitnessed by humankind. For more than a century they had waited, anticipating the day when the call would come to release this hidden power.

In their lives, they had been many things. Then they were another. Now they were an army.

First in twilight, then in blackness, beneath the Texas stars, they roared west, a wall of noise and dust. At the head of the pod, like the point of a spear, a pair of riders led the way. For Alicia, the sensation was one of pure momentum; she was leading as much as she was being led, joined to a primal force. For Amy, the feeling was one of expansion, an internal amassing of souls. The moment Carter had surrendered his forces to her command, they had ceased to be external entities. They had become extensions of her awareness and her will: her Many.

Come with me. Come with me come with me come with me . . .

Ahead, like lights upon a distant shore, the besieged city appeared.

"Weapons up!"

All along the catwalk, the snap of magazines, the clack of bolts, rounds hammering into chambers. The last shadows were gone, drowned in the gloom.

It didn't take long.

A glowing line appeared to the east. Second by second it thickened, spreading over the land. A feeling of fate, of destiny: it hung like a fog. The city seemed meager in its face.

"Here they come!"

The horde rumbled toward them. Its speed was tremendous. Random shots split the air—men adrenalized with terror who could not restrain the urge to fire their weapons.

Peter pressed the radio to his mouth. "Hold your fire! Wait till they're in range!"

The stars were disappearing, blotted out by the great dust cloud that ascended in the virals' wake. The pod had taken the form of an arrowlike wedge.

"Looks like the negotiation phase is over," Apgar said.

More panicked shots; the pod kept coming. They would drive straight through the gate, splitting it like a bull's-eye.

"Hang on a second," Apgar said. He was watching through binoculars. "Something's off."

"What are you seeing?"

He hesitated, then said, "They're moving differently. Short leaps, long strides in between, like the older ones do." He pulled the lenses away. "I think these are dopeys."

Something was happening. The pod was decelerating.

From the spotting platform, a cry went up: "Riders! Two hundred yards!"

Prepare yourselves.

Amy slowed Soldier to a canter, then a trot.

We will defend this city. We will hold this gate, my brothers and sisters of blood.

Flowing like a liquid, her forces spread. Amy moved among them. She dared not show fear; her courage would be theirs. She rode with her back erect, Soldier's reins held lightly in one hand, the other extended in a gesture of blessing, like a priest.

They were people once, like you. But they follow another, the Zero.

A thousand long, three hundred deep, Amy's forces formed a protective barrier along the northern wall and turned to face the field. To the east, the first edge of moon was peeking above the hills.

Do not hesitate, for they will not. Kill them, my brothers and sisters, but always with a blessing of mercy in your heart.

She felt the eyes of the soldiers upon her, the posts and crosshairs of their guns. The great dust cloud was settling. A taste of grit was in her mouth.

Stand tall. Have courage. Show him who and what you are.

They brought their horses to a halt at the front of the line. Amy removed the pistol from her belt, passed it to Alicia, and drew the sword from over her back. The grip possessed a satisfying thickness, comfortable in the hand. She rocked her wrist to turn its blade in the air.

"This is a fine weapon, sister."

"I was sort of guessing when I made it."

Her mind was composed, her thoughts ordered and calm. There was fear, but also relief and, on top of this, curiosity about what would come.

"I've never gone into battle," she said. "What is it like?"

"It's very . . . busy."

Amy considered this.

"Things happen fast. You won't even be aware of them until later. Most will seem like they happened to somebody else."

"I suppose that makes a lot of sense." Then: "Alicia, if I don't survive—"

"One other thing."

"What's that?"

Alicia met her eye. "You're not allowed to say things like that."

On the rampart, chaos reigned. Runners were dashing, fingers were twitching on triggers, nobody knew what to do. *Hold fire? They're virals! And why are they facing the wrong direction?*

"I mean it," Peter barked into the radio, "all stations, stand down now!" He tossed Apgar the radio and turned to the closest runner. "Private, get me a harness."

"Peter, you are *not* going out there," Apgar said.

"Amy can protect me. You can see it for yourself. They're here to defend us."

"I don't care if they're here to fix the plumbing—you've lost your goddamn mind. Do not make me tackle you, because I will absolutely do that."

The soldier darted his eyes to Peter, then the general, then back again. "Sir, should I get the harness or not?"

"Private, you take one step and I'm going to pitch you over that wall," Apgar said.

Another cry from the spotter: "We have movement! The riders are moving away!"

Peter looked up. "What do you mean *away*?"

A face floated over the rail. A quick conferral with someone behind him, then the man pointed due north. "Across the field, sir!"

Peter stepped back to the edge of the rampart and raised his binoculars. "Gunnar, are you seeing this?"

"What are they doing?" Apgar said. "Are they surrendering?"

With a puff of dust, Amy and Alicia brought their horses to a halt. Amy drew and raised the sword. It was not a gesture of capitulation but defiance.

They were setting themselves as bait.

"Fanning, do you hear me?!"

Amy's words dwindled into the gloom.

"If you want me, come and get me!"

"Should we go further out?" Alicia asked.

"If we do, we might not make it back." Then, raising her voice again: "Are you listening? I'm right here, you bastard!"

Alicia waited. Still nothing. Then:

You have done well, Alicia.

She pressed her hands over her ears, a pointless reflex; Fanning's voice was inside her.

Everything I could have wished for, you have accomplished. Her army is nothing, I can whisk it away. You have given me that, and so much more.

"Shut up! Leave me alone!"

Amy was staring at her. "Lish, what is it? Is it Fanning?"

Do you feel it, Alicia? Fanning's voice was smooth, taunting. It was like an oily liquid spreading through her brain. *Of course you do. You always could. Haunting the streets, counting heads. They are a part of you as I am a part of you.*

Alicia heard the sound then. No, not heard: sensed. A kind of . . . scratching. Where was it coming from?

She must come to me in ruins. That will be the truest test. To feel what I feel. What we feel, my Alicia. To know despair. A world without hope, without purpose, everything lost.

"Alicia, tell me what's happening."

I know your dreams, Alicia. The great walled city and its sounds of life within. The music and the happy cries of children. Your longing to be among them, and the door you cannot enter. Did you know even then, Alicia? Did you know what lay in store?

The sound grew more intense. The blood was throbbing in her neck; she thought she might be ill.

My Alicia, it is already done. Can you feel it? Can you feel . . . them?

Her mind slammed back to awareness. She turned in her saddle. Beyond the barrier of Amy's army, the lights of the city shone.

Outside, she thought. I'm outside, just like in the dream.

"Oh, God, no."

* * *

Sara was trying to make herself breathe.

A hundred and twenty souls were crammed in the basement. Candles and lanterns, spread throughout the space, cast odd, animated shadows. Sara's pistol lay in her lap, her hand upon it, loose but ready.

Jenny and Hannah had organized a game of duck, duck, goose to distract some of the children. Others were occupying themselves with smuggled toys. A few were crying, though probably they did not know why; they were channeling the anxiety of the adults.

Sara was sitting on the floor with her back against the door. Its metal face was cool against her skin. Would it hold? Various scenes unfolded in her mind: pounding on the door, the metal bulging, everyone screaming, backing away, then the final crack and death pouring in, engulfing them all.

She was watching Jenny and Hannah. Jenny was terrified—the woman wore her emotions like a coat—but Hannah had a steady streak in her. It was she who had initiated the game. There were people, Sara knew, who were like this, the ones who could not be ruffled or else didn't show it, who possessed great internal reservoirs of calm. Hannah was racing around the circle on her long legs, grinning with conspiracy, pursued by a little boy. Hannah was going to let him catch her, of course; she made a stagy show of her surrender that sent the boy into a fit of happy giggles, which, for a moment, put Sara at ease. She remembered such games, how much fun they were, their object so simple and pure. She had played duck, duck, goose as a girl, then, later, with Kate and her friends. But in the next instant, this thought was replaced by another. Kate, she thought, Kate, where are you, where have you gone? Your body lies in a bed far from home; your spirit has flown. I am lost without you. Lost.

"Dr. Wilson, are you okay?"

Holding Carlos, Grace was standing above her. Sara touched her tears away. "How's he doing?"

"He's a baby—he doesn't know anything."

Sara made a place beside her; Grace lowered herself to the floor.

"Are we going to be safe here?" Grace asked.

"Sure."

A silence; then Grace shrugged. "You're lying, but that's okay. I just wanted to hear you say it." She turned her face toward Sara. "You were the one who transferred your birthright to my parents, weren't you?"

"I guess they told you."

"Just that it was the doctor. I don't see any other women doctors around the place, though, so I figured it had to be you. Why did you do it?"

There was probably an answer, but Sara couldn't think of it. "It just felt like the thing to do."

"My folks were good to me. Things weren't easy, but they loved me as well as anyone could. We always said a prayer for you at supper. I thought you should know."

From baby Carlos, a yawn; sleep was near. For a minute or so, Sara and Grace watched the game together. Suddenly Grace looked up.

"What's that noise?"

"Station six. We have movement."

Peter grabbed the radio. "Say again."

"Not sure." A pause. "Looks like it's gone now."

Station 6 was at the south end of the dam.

"Everyone, maintain readiness!" Apgar yelled. "Hold your positions!"

Peter barked into the mike: "What are you seeing?"

A crackle, and then the voice said, "Forget it, I was wrong."

Peter looked at Chase. "What's below station six?"

"Just scrub."

"Enough for cover?"

"Some."

Peter took up the radio again. "Station six, report. What did you see?"

"I'm telling you, it's nothing," the voice repeated. "Looks like just another sinkhole opening up."

From his post on the roof of the orphanage, Caleb Jaxon did not hear the sound so much as feel it: a disturbance lacking a discernible source, as if the air were bristling with a swarm of invisible bees. He scanned the city with his binoculars. All seemed ordinary, unchanged, yet as his mind stilled, he became aware of other sounds, coming from several directions. The crack of wood splintering. The crash and tinkle of fracturing glass. A rumble, lasting perhaps five seconds, of an unknown type. Around him, and on the ground below, some of his men had begun to sense these things as well; their conversations halted, one man or the other saying, *Do you hear that? What* is *that?* Eyes burning from lack of sleep, Caleb peered into the darkness. From the roof, he had a clear view of the capitol building and the city's central square. The hospital was four blocks east.

He unhitched his radio from his belt. "Hollis, are you there?" His father-in-law was stationed at the entrance to the hospital.

"Yeah."

Another crash. It came from deep within the streets of the city. "Are you hearing this?"

A gap, then Hollis said: "Roger that."

"What are you seeing? Any movement?"

"Negative."

Caleb brought his binoculars to bear on the capitol. A pair of trucks and a long table remained in the square, left behind when the inductions were complete. He took up the radio again. "Sister, can you hear me?"

Sister Peg was waiting by the hatch. "Yes, Lieutenant."

"I'm not sure, but I think something's going on out here."

A pause. "Thank you for telling me, Lieutenant Jaxon."

He clipped the radio to his belt. His grip on his rifle tightened reflexively. Though he knew a round was seated in the chamber, he gently drew back the charging handle to double-check. Through the tiny window, the brass casing gleamed.

The radio crackled: Hollis. "Caleb, come back."

"What have you got?"

"Something's out there."

Caleb's heart accelerated. "Where?"

"Headed for the square, northwest corner."

Caleb pressed the binoculars to his brow again. With vexing slowness, the square came into focus. "I'm not seeing anything."

"It was there a second ago."

Still scanning, Caleb lifted the radio to his mouth to call the command platform.

"Station one, this is station nine . . ."

He stopped in mid-sentence; his vision had grazed something. He swept the lenses back the way they'd come.

The table in the square had been overturned; behind it, the nose of one of the trucks was pointed upward at a forty-five degree angle, its rear wheels sunk deep into the earth.

A sinkhole. A big one, opening up.

Peter turned away from the battlefield. The buildings of the city were shapes against the dark, lit by angled moonlight.

Chase was beside him. "What is it?"

The feeling prickled his skin like static electricity: all eyes. "There's something we're not seeing." He held up a hand. "Hang on. Did you hear that?"

"Hear what?" Apgar's eyes narrowed as he cocked his head "Wait. Yeah."

"Like . . . rats inside walls."

"I hear it, too," Chase said.

Peter grabbed the mike. "Station six, anything out there?"

Nothing.

"Station six, report."

Sister Peg stepped into the kitchen pantry. The rifle was stashed on the top shelf, wrapped in oilcloth. It had belonged to her brother, rest his soul; he had served with the Expeditionary, years ago. She remembered the day the soldier had arrived at the orphanage with the news of his death. He had brought her brother's locker of effects. Nobody had checked the contents, or else the rifle would have been taken back into inventory. Or so Sister Peg had supposed at the time. Most of the belongings in her brother's locker contained no trace of him and did not seem worth keeping. But not his gun. Her brother had held it, used it, fought with it; it stood for what he was. It was more than a remembrance; it was a gift, as if he'd left it behind so that someday she would have it when she needed it.

She moved the ladder into place and, with gingerly steps, brought the gun down and placed it on the table where the sisters kneaded bread. Sister Peg had cared for the weapon meticulously; the action was tight and well lubed. She liked the way it fired, with a decisive trigger and a good, clean snap. Once a year, in May—the month of her brother's death—Sister Peg would remove her frock, don the clothes of an ordinary worker, and take the transport out to the Orange Zone. The rifle rode beside her, concealed in a duffel bag. Beyond the windbreak she would set up a target of cans, sometimes apples or a melon, or sheets of marked paper nailed to a tree.

She carried the rifle, now loaded, to the dining hall. Over the years the gun had grown heavier in her arms, but she could still manage it, including the recoil, which was dampened by a buffer tube with a spring connected to the pad. This was very important for follow-up shots. She chose a position by the hatch with a clear view of the hallway and the windows on either side of the room.

She thought she should take a moment to pray. But, as she was holding a loaded rifle, conventional prayer did not seem entirely suitable. Sister Peg hoped that God would help her, but it was her belief that He much preferred for people to attend to themselves. Life was a test; it was up to you to pass it or not. She raised the gun to her clavicle and angled one eye down the length of the barrel.

"Not my children," she said and pulled the charging handle, snapping the first round into the chamber. "Not tonight."

*   *   *

"Rider inbound!"

A tense new energy shivered along the rampart. Something was shifting. The viral barrier parted, forming a corridor like the one the previous night. Down this hallway a single rider galloped toward them. All along the catwalk, eyes took purchase upon the posts and slots of gunsights; gathering pressure flowed from shoulders to forearms to the padded tips of index fingers. The order to hold fire was clear, yet the urge to do otherwise was strong. Still the rider kept on coming. Raised in the saddle, this person—the gender was as yet unknowable—was yelling incomprehensible words. While one hand clutched the reins, the other swayed in the air over the rider's head, a gesture of ambiguous meaning. Was it a threat? A plea for forbearance?

On the command platform, Peter understood what was about to happen. The inductees had no experience; they lacked the mental muscle memory of military training; they existed in only the most general way within a chain of command. The second Alicia reached the lighted perimeter, he would lose control of the situation. "Hold your fire!" he was yelling. "Don't shoot!" But words went only so far.

Alicia hit the lighted perimeter at a full gallop. "It's a trap!"

Her words made no sense to him.

She pulled up, skidding to a halt. "It's a trap! They're inside!"

A shout came from Peter's left: "It's that woman from last night!"

"She's a viral!"

"Shoot her!"

The first bullet speared Alicia's right thigh, shattering her femur; the second caught her in the left lung. The horse's front legs folded, sending her pitching forward over its neck. The first pops became a full-throated barrage. Dust kicked up around her as she crawled behind the fallen animal, which now lay riddled and dead. Shots were connecting. Bullets were finding their mark. Alicia experienced them like a fusillade of punches. Her left palm, speared like an apple. The ilium of her right pelvis, shrapnelized like an exploding grenade. Two more to the chest, the second of which ricocheted off her fourth rib, plunged diagonally through her thoracic cavity, and cracked her second lumbar vertebrae. She did her best to shove herself beneath the fallen horse. Blood splashed from its flesh as the bullets pounded.

Lost, she thought, as a curtain of darkness fell. *Everything is lost.*

The majority of virals emerged inside the city at four points: the central square, the southeast corner of the impoundment, a large sinkhole in H-town, and the staging area inside the main gate. Others had piloted their way through the pocketed earth to emerge in smaller pods throughout the city. The floors of houses; abandoned lots, weedy and untended, where children had once played; the streets of densely packed neighborhoods. They dug and crawled. They traced the sewage and water lines. They were clever; they sought the weakest points. For months they had moved through the geological and man-made fissures beneath the city like an infestation of ants.

Go now, their master ordered. *Fulfill your purpose. Do that which I've commanded.*

On the catwalk, Peter did not have long to consider Alicia's words of warning. Amid the roar of guns—many of the soldiers, gripped by the frenzy of a mob, were firing upon the dopeys as well—the structure lurched under him. It was as if the metal grate beneath his feet were a carpet that had been lifted and shaken at one end. The sensation shot to his stomach, a swirl of nausea, like seasickness. He looked side to side, searching for the source of this motion, simultaneously becoming aware that he was hearing screams. A second lurch and the structure jolted downward. His balance failed; knocked backward, he fell to the floor of the catwalk. Guns were blasting, voices yelling. Bullets whizzed over his face. *The gate,* someone cried, *they're opening the gate! Shoot them! Shoot those fuckers!* A groan of bending metal, and the catwalk began to tip away from the wall.

He was rolling toward the edge.

He had no way to stop himself; his hands found nothing to grab. Bodies tumbled past, launching into the dark. As he rolled over the lip, one hand seized slick metal: a support strut. His body swung around it like a pendulum. He would not be able to hold on; he had merely paused. Beneath him, the city spun, lit with screams and gunfire.

"Take my hand!"

It was Jock. He had lodged himself under the rail, one arm dangling over the edge. The catwalk had paused at a forty-five-degree angle to the ground.

"Grab on!"

A series of pops: the last bolts were yanking free of the wall. Jock's fingertips, inches from Peter's, could have been a mile away. Time was moving in two streams. There was one, of noise and haste and violent action, and a second, coincidental with the first, in which Peter and everything around him seemed caught in a lazy current. His grip was failing. His other hand flailed uselessly, trying to grasp Jock's.

"Pull yourself up!"

Peter tore away.

"I've got you!"

Jock was gripping him by the wrist. A second face appeared under the rail:

Apgar. As the man reached down, Jock heaved Peter upward; Apgar caught him by the belt. Together they hauled him the rest of the way.

The catwalk began to fall.

The slaughter had commenced.

Freed from hiding, the virals poured over the city. They swarmed the ramparts, flinging men into space. They launched from the ground and rooftops like a glowing fireworks display. They burst through the floors of hardboxes to butcher the occupants and exploded through the floors of buildings to haul the hiding inhabitants from closets and out from under their beds. They stormed the gate, which, although formidable, was not designed to repel an attack from within; all that was required to open the city to invasion was to tear the crossbars from their braces, free the brake, and push.

The pod that emerged near the impoundment was likewise charged with a specific mission. Throughout the day, their delicate sensorium had detected the footfalls of a great number of people, all headed in the same direction. They had heard the roar of vehicles and the barks of bullhorns. They had heard the word "dam." They had heard the word "shelter." They had heard the word "tubes." Those that sought a direct entry to the dam were confounded. As Chase had predicted, there was no way in. Others, like an elite assault force, homed in on a compact building nearby. This was guarded by a small contingent of soldiers, who died swiftly and badly. Jaws snapping, fingers trilling, eyes restlessly roaming, the virals took measure of the interior. The room was full of pipes. Pipes meant water; water meant the dam. A flight of stairs descended.

They arrived in a hallway with walls of sweating stone. A ladder took them deeper underground, a second deeper still. A dense humanity lay near. They were coming closer. They were homing in.

They reached a metal door with a heavy ring. The first viral, the alpha, opened the door and slid inside, the others following.

The room was ripe with the odor of men. A row of lockers, a bench, a table bearing the remains of a hastily abandoned meal. Connected to a complex assembly of pipes and gears was a panel with six steel wheels the size of manhole covers.

Yes, said Zero. *Those.*

The alpha gripped the first wheel. INLET NO. 1 it was marked.

Turn it.

Six wheels. Six tubes.

Eight hundred dying cries.

*　　*　　*

Pistol extended, Sara approached the storage room and gently dislodged the door with her foot.

"Maybe it was just mice," Jenny whispered.

The scratching sounded again. It was coming from behind a stack of crates. Sara placed the lantern on the floor and pushed the pistol out with both hands. The crates were piled four high. One on the bottom began to move, jostling those above it.

"Sara—"

The crates went tumbling. Sara fell back as the viral burst through the floor, twisting in midair to attach itself to the ceiling like a roach. She fired the pistol blindly. The viral seemed not to care at all about the gun or else knew that Sara was too startled to aim. The pistol's slide locked back; the magazine was spent. Sara turned, shoved Jenny from the room, and began to run.

At the base of the wall, Alicia, immobilized, broken, lay alone. Her breathing was labored and damp, punctuated by small, exquisitely painful hitches. Blood was in her mouth. Her vision seemed skewed; images refused to resolve. She had no sense of time at all. She might have been shot thirty seconds ago. It might have been an hour.

A dark shape materialized above her: Soldier, bowing his head to hers. *Oh, see what you've done to yourself,* he said. *I leave you for a minute and look what happens.* His warm breath kissed her face; he dipped closer, nuzzling her, exhaling softly through his nostrils.

My good boy. She raised one bloody hand to his cheek. *My great, my magnificent Soldier, I am sorry.*

"Sister, what have they done to you?"

Amy was kneeling beside her. The woman's shoulders shook with a sob; she buried her face in her hands. "Oh no," she moaned. "Oh no."

The spotlights had gone out. Alicia heard gunshots and cries, but these were distant, dimming. A merciful darkness enveloped her. Amy was holding her hand. It seemed that all that had gone before was a journey, that the road had brought her here and ended. The night slid into silence. She felt suddenly cold. She drifted away.

Wait.

Her eyes flew open. A breeze was pushing over her—dense, gritty—and with it a rumble, like thunder, though the sound did not stop. It rolled and rolled, its volume accumulating, the air swirling with windblown matter. The ground beneath them began to shake; with a whinny, Soldier reared up, his hooves slashing the air.

Her army is nothing. I can whisk it away.

Alicia raised her head just in time to see them coming.

*   *   *

Peter, Apgar, and Jock were racing down the falling catwalk. Its failure proceeded in sections, like dominoes falling in a line. Peter's orders to fall back to the orphanage, the city's last line of defense, went unheeded; a state of panic reigned. The problem was not merely the serial collapse of the catwalk, from which soldiers were falling a hundred feet to their deaths. The virals had also stormed its length. Some men were hurled, others devoured, twitching and screaming as the virals' jaws sank home. Yet a third group were bitten and subsequently left to their own devices. As had been witnessed in the townships, Fanning's virus did its work with unprecedented swiftness; in short order, a growing percentage of Kerrville's defenders were turning on their former comrades.

A hundred yards downstream from the vanished command post, Peter, Apgar, and Jock found themselves boxed in. Behind them, the catwalk's failure continued, span by span; ahead, the virals were coming toward them. No flight of stairs lay within reach.

"Oh, hell," said Apgar. "I always hated doing this."

They unfurled the ropes over the side. Jock was no fan of heights, either; the incident on the mission roof had scarred him for life. Yet it was also true that in the last twenty-four hours a change had occurred. He had always believed himself to be a flimsy man, a chip in the current of life. But since the birth of his son, and the burst of love this had produced, he had discovered within himself a solidity of character he had never thought possible, an expanding sense of life's importance and his place within its web. He wanted to be a man of whom it could be said that he had put others before himself and died in their defense. Thus the newly inducted and personally transformed Private Jock Alvado shoved his terror aside, stepped over the rail, and turned his back on the maw of space below him; Peter and Apgar did the same.

They jumped.

A hundred feet with only the friction of their hands and feet to slow them: they landed hard on the packed dirt. Peter and Apgar came up quickly, but Jock did not. He had sprained, perhaps broken, his ankle. Peter pulled him upright and threw the man's arm over his shoulder.

"Christ, you're heavy."

They ran.

The basement was a death trap.

As Sara ran for the door, a scream volleyed behind her, sharp, like metal being cut, then the room erupted in cries. She was carrying a little girl; she had scooped her up without thinking. She would have carried more if she could; she would have carried them all.

Jenny reached the door first. People were surging behind her. Suddenly the woman couldn't move; the weight of panicked bodies had immobilized her, pressing her against the metal. She was yelling for people to back away but could scarcely be heard. The shrieks of the children were like the highest notes of a scale, impossibly shrill.

The door burst open; a hundred people attempted to cram through at once. Blind instinct had taken hold—to flee, to survive whatever the cost. People were falling, children being trampled underfoot. Virals ricocheted around the room, flinging themselves from wall to wall, victim to victim. Their enjoyment was obscene. One was carrying a child in its mouth and shaking it like a dog with a rag doll. As Sara wedged through the door, a faceless woman wrenched the little girl from her arms and shoved ahead, knocking her to the floor at the base of the stairs. People were thundering past. A familiar face emerged from the chaos: Grace, holding her baby. She was huddled against the wall of the stairwell. Upstairs, guns were popping. Sara gripped the woman by the sleeve to make her look at her. *Stay with me, hold my hand.*

Jenny and Hannah were waving to her from the top of the stairs. Sara half-pulled, half-dragged Grace to the lobby. Beyond the doors, a fierce battle raged. Children were screaming, mothers were huddled with their children, no one knew where to go. A few were running blindly out the door, into the heart of it. The virals were behind them and coming up the stairs.

A huge crash: the front of the building detonated inward. Bricks, shards of glass, splintered plywood went flying. Suddenly an Army five-ton was standing in the lobby. Hollis was at the wheel.

"Everybody, get in!"

Amy covered Alicia's body with her own. Her army was dying; she felt them leaving her, souls draining into the ether. *You did not fail me,* she thought. *It was I who erred. Go peacefully—at last you are free.*

Fanning's virals broke through. Amy buried her face against Alicia's neck, holding her close. It would happen quickly, faster than light. She thought of Peter, then of nothing at all.

It felt as if they were inside a flock of birds; as if the air around them had turned into a million flapping wings.

From the roof of the orphanage, Caleb watched the city die.

He had heard the catwalk collapse, a terrific crash. The scene before him possessed an odd quality of disconnection. It was as if he were observing events that did not wholly pertain to him, unfolding at a great remove. Though when the shooting started, he knew, he would feel differently. Twenty-five men: how long could they last?

The gunshots faded, the flash of fired rounds, the pitiable, anguished screams. The city was sliding into silence, a place of ghosts. A moment of stunning quiet; then a new sound accumulated. Caleb pressed his eyes to the binoculars. An Army five-ton, draped in canvas, was roaring toward them from the square, flanked by a pair of Humvees. The men on the turrets were firing wildly, others shooting through the windows of the cab. Simultaneously Caleb became aware of a second, more compact movement to his right. He swung his lenses around. Impenetrable darkness; then two figures appeared. A third man was being carried.

Apgar.

His father.

They would intersect with the truck near the front of the building. Caleb's feet barely touched the ladder as he descended. One of the Humvees veered away from the other vehicles; virals were clinging to it. It crashed onto its side and began to roll, like an animal trying to shake off a swarm of hornets. The five-ton was moving too quickly; it was going to crash into the building. At the last second, the driver cut the wheel to the left and screeched to a stop.

Hollis leapt from the cab, Sara from the bed. Everyone was grabbing children and hauling them through the door. Caleb vaulted over the sandbags and raced toward his father and the general.

"Take him," his father said.

Caleb threaded an arm around the injured man's back. The situation took shape in Caleb's mind: the orphanage would be their final stand. In the dining room, Sister Peg waited by the open hatch. The woman was holding a rifle. The sight was so odd that Caleb's mind simply rejected it. "Hurry!" Sister Peg yelled. His father and Apgar were ordering men to take positions at the windows. Hands reached up through the opening in the floor to help the children, who funneled into the hatch with a slowness painfully out of sync with everything else that was occurring. People were pushing and shoving, women screaming, babies crying. Caleb smelled gasoline. An empty fuel can lay on its side on the floor, a second by the pantry door. Their presence made no sense—it was in the same category of unaccountable details as Sister Peg's rifle. Men were hurling dining chairs through the windows. Others were upending tables to act as barricades. All the things of the world were colliding. Caleb took a position at the closest window, pointed his rifle into the darkness, and began to fire.

* * *

For Peter Jaxon, last president of the Texas Republic, the final seconds of the night were nothing he had anticipated. Once the catwalk had begun its collapse, and the nature of the situation had become clear to him, he wholly intended to die. This was the only honorable outcome he could foresee. Amy was gone, his friends were gone, the city was gone, and he had only himself to blame. Surviving Kerrville's destruction would be an unthinkable disgrace.

The last of the civilians had descended through the hatch, but would the door hold? Judging from the events of the last ten minutes, Peter could only conclude that, like everything else, it was bound to fail. Fanning, however he'd done it, knew everything.

Still, one had to try. Symbolism counted for something, as Apgar had said. The virals were amassing outside; they would storm the building as a horde. Still firing from the window, Peter ordered the men to fall back to the shelter; they had nothing left to defend except themselves. Many were out of ammo, anyway. A final shot from Peter's rifle and the charger locked back. He cast the gun aside and drew his pistol.

"Mr. President, time to go."

Apgar was standing behind him.

"I thought you were calling me Peter now."

"I mean it. You need to get down that hole right now."

Peter squeezed off a round. Maybe he connected, maybe not. "I'm not going anywhere."

Peter would never be sure what Apgar had hit him with. The butt of his pistol? The leg of a broken chair? A thud at the back of his skull and his legs melted, followed by the rest of him.

"Caleb," he heard Apgar say, "help me get your father out of here."

His body lacked all volition; his thoughts were like slick ice, impossible to hold. He was being dragged, then lifted, then lowered once again. He felt, oddly, like a child, and this feeling morphed into a memory—an impossible memory, in which he was a little boy again, not merely a boy but an infant, being passed from hand to hand. He saw faces above him. They floated enormously, their features bloated and vague. He was being laid upon a wooden platform. A single face came into focus: his son's. But Caleb wasn't a boy anymore, he was a man, and the situation had reversed. Caleb was the father and he the son, or so it seemed. It was a pleasant inversion, inevitable in its way, and Peter felt happy that he had lived long enough to see this.

"It's all right, Dad," Caleb said, "you're safe now."

And then the light went out.

*   *   *

Apgar slammed the hatch and listened as the bolts sealed from inside.

"You could have gone," said Sister Peg.

"So could you." He rose and looked at her. Everything felt suddenly calm. "The gas was a good idea."

"I thought so, too."

"Ready?"

Sounds above: the virals were tearing through the roof. Apgar lifted a rifle from the floor, checked the magazine, and shoved it back into the well. Sister Peg withdrew the box of matches from the pocket of her tunic. She struck one, tossed it. A river of blue flame snaked along the floor, then separated, running in several directions.

"Shall we?" Apgar said.

They walked briskly down the hall. Thick smoke was boiling up. At the door they halted.

"You know," said Sister Peg, "I think I'll stay after all."

His eyes searched her face.

"I think it's best this way," she explained. "To be . . . with them."

Of course that's what she would want. To affirm his understanding, Apgar cupped her chin, leaned his face forward, and kissed her lightly on the lips.

"Well," she managed. Tears rose to her throat. She had never been kissed by a grown man before. "I didn't expect that."

"I hope you didn't mind."

"You always were a lovely boy."

"That's nice of you to say."

She took his hands and held them. "God bless and keep you, Gunnar."

"And you as well, Sister."

Then he was gone.

She faded back into the hall. In the dining room, flames were leaping up the walls; the smoke was dense and swirling. Sister Peg began to cough. She lay down on the hatch. Her time in the physical world was ending. She had no fear of what would come, the hand of love into which her spirit would pass. Fire took the building in its grip. The flames shot up, consuming all. As the smoke snaked inside her, Sister Peg's mind filled up with faces. Faces by the hundreds, the thousands. Her children. She would be with them again.

All around the building, the virals were watching. They stood in abeyance, the glow of the flames glazing their denuded faces. They had been vanquished; fire was a barrier they could not cross. Still they waited, ever hopeful. The hours passed. The building burned and burned and burned some more. The embers were still glowing when dawn came, a blade of light sweeping over the silent city.

X

THE EXODUS

To war and arms I fly.

—RICHARD LOVELACE,
TO LUCASTA,
GOING TO THE WARS

73

"Greer."

He was dead to the world. In a different one, a voice was calling his name.

"Lucius, wake up."

He jerked to consciousness. He was sitting in the cab of the tanker. Patch was standing on the running board by the open door. Through the windshield, a foggy dawn.

"What time is it?" His mouth was dry.

"Oh-six-thirty."

"You should have woken me up."

"What do you think I just did?"

Greer stepped down. The water was still, birds swooping low over its glassy surface. "Anything happen while I was asleep?"

Patch shrugged in his wiry way. "Nothing major. Just before sunrise, we saw a small pod working its way down the shore."

"Where?"

"Base of the channel bridge."

Greer frowned. "And this didn't strike you as important?"

"They never came all that close. It didn't seem worth the trouble to wake you."

Greer got in his truck and drove down the isthmus. Lore was standing on the dock, hands perched on her hips, studying the hull. The repair was nearing completion.

"How long till we fill?" he asked.

"Three, maybe four hours." She raised her voice. "Rand! Watch that chain!"

"Where is he?" Greer asked.

"Quonset hut, I think."

He found Michael sitting at the shortwave.

"Kerrville, come back, please. This is Isthmus station." A momentary pause and he repeated the call.

"Anything?" Greer asked.

Michael shook his head. His expression was blank, his mind far away in worry.

"I have some other news. A viral pod was sighted near the bridge a while ago."

Michael turned sharply. "Did they approach?"

"Patch says no."

Michael sat back. He rubbed his face with a heavy hand. "So they know we're here."

"It would seem so."

The bolts were still too hot to touch. Peter was standing on the platform just below the hatch. His mind had cleared, but his headache felt like an ice pick buried in the back of his skull.

"It's got to be light out," Sara said. "What should we do?"

Caleb and Hollis were there as well. Peter scanned their faces; both wore the same expression: of weariness and defeat, the power of decision beyond them. None had slept a wink.

"Wait, I guess."

An hour or so passed. Peter was dozing on the platform when he heard knocking on the hatch. He reached up to touch the surface; the metal had cooled somewhat. He removed his jersey and wrapped it around his hands; beside him, Caleb did the same. They each took a lever and turned. Cracks of daylight appeared at the edges and, with them, a strong smell of smoke. Water dripped through. They pushed the hatch open the rest of the way.

Chase was standing over them, holding a bucket. His face was black with soot. Peter climbed the ladder, the others following. They emerged into a scene of ruin. The orphanage was gone, reduced to a smoldering wreckage of ashes and collapsed beams. The heat was still intense. Behind Peter's chief of staff stood a group of seven: three soldiers of diverse ranks and four civilians, including a teenage girl and a man who had to be at least seventy. All were holding buckets, their clothes sodden, arms and faces black as coal. They had wetted down a path through the ashes, clearing a way out of the destruction. The fire had leapt to several adjacent buildings, which were burning to various degrees.

"It's good to see you, Mr. President."

As with everyone who had survived the night, Chase's survival was a story of luck and timing. When the catwalk had begun to fail, he had just stepped away from the command deck in search of more ammunition. This placed him near the stairs on the west side of the gate. He had made it to the bottom just in time to see the whole thing come crashing to the ground. Two soldiers had recognized him; they'd hustled him into a truck to get him to the president's hardbox, but they hadn't made it very far before they were attacked, the driver yanked through the windshield. As the vehicle rolled, Chase was thrown clear.

His rifle empty and the hardbox far out of reach, he had run for the closest building, a small wood-framed house that the tax office used for storage. Among the boxes of meaningless paperwork, he was joined over the next two hours by the seven survivors with whom he now stood. For the rest of the night they had remained there, trying not to attract attention to themselves, waiting for an end that never came.

Since daybreak, more survivors had emerged, but not very many. The sight of so many bodies was jarring, sickening. The vultures had begun to alight, pecking at the meat. It was nothing for the children to see. During the night, Sara had counted heads. The shelter contained 654 souls, mostly women and children. Sara descended the ladder to help Jenny organize their removal.

"What about the other hardboxes?" Peter asked.

Chase's face was grim. "They got in through the floors."

"Olivia?"

Chase shook his head.

"I'm sorry, Ford."

He shook his head faintly. None of this was registering completely yet. "What about the tubes?"

"Flooded. I don't know how they did it, but they did."

Peter's stomach dropped; a wave of cold dizziness passed through him.

"Peter?" Chase was gripping his arm; suddenly, he was the strong one.

"No survivors?" Peter asked.

Chase shook his head. "There's something else you need to see."

It was Apgar. The man was alive, though barely. He lay on the ground beside an overturned Humvee. His legs were crushed beneath the frame, though that was not the worst of it; on his left hand, which lay across his chest, was a semicircular imprint of teeth. He was still in the shade, but the sun would soon find him.

Peter knelt beside him. "Gunnar, can you hear me?"

The man's awareness seemed divided. Then, with a faint start, his eyes alighted on Peter's face.

"Peter, hello." His voice was bland, lacking emotion except, perhaps, for a touch of mild surprise.

"Just lie still."

"Oh, I'm not going anywhere." His legs had been crushed to a pulp, yet he seemed to be experiencing no pain at all. He lifted his wounded hand with a vague gesture. "Can you believe this shit?"

"Does anybody have any water?"

Caleb produced a canteen; just an inch or two sloshed in the bottom. Peter cupped the man's neck to lift his head and held the spout to his lips. Peter wondered why Apgar had not yet turned. Of course, there was a range; it varied person to person. A few weak sips, water dribbling from the corners of his mouth, and Apgar leaned back.

"It's true what they say. You can feel it inside you." He took a long, shuddering breath. "How many survivors?"

Peter shook his head. "Not many."

"Don't blame yourself."

"Gunnar—"

"Take this as my last piece of official advice. You've done all you could. It's time to get these people out of here." The general licked his lips and lifted the bloody hand again. "But let's not let this go on too long. I don't want people to see me like this."

Peter turned his face and scanned the group: Chase, Hollis, Caleb, a few of the soldiers. All were staring. He felt benumbed; none of it seemed real yet.

"Somebody give me something."

Hollis produced a knife. Peter accepted its cold weight into his hand. For a moment he doubted he could find the strength to do what was required of him. He crouched beside Apgar again, holding the blade a little behind himself to keep it from view.

"It's been an honor to serve under you, Mr. President."

Through a throat thickened with tears, Peter raised his voice, speaking words no one had said in over twenty years. "This man is a soldier of the Expeditionary! It is time for him to take the trip! All hail, General Gunnar Apgar! Hip hip—"

"Hooray!"

"Hip hip—"

"Hooray!"

"Hip hip—"

"Hooray!"

Apgar took a long breath and let it out slowly. His face became peaceful.

"Thank you, Peter. I'm ready now."

Peter tightened his grip on the knife.

There were two more.

Peter was looking at Apgar's body. The man had died quickly, almost inaudibly. A grunt as the knife went in, his eyes opening wide, death easing into them.

"Somebody get me a blanket."

No one spoke.

"Goddamnit, what's the matter with you people? You—" He jabbed a finger at one of the soldiers. "What's your name, Private?"

The man seemed a little dazed. "Sir?"

"What, you don't know your own name? Are you that stupid?"

He swallowed nervously. "It's Verone, sir."

"Organize a burial detail. I want everyone gathered at the parade ground in thirty. Full military honors, do you read me?"

He glanced at the others.

"Is there a problem, soldier?"

"Dad—" Caleb gripped him by an arm and made his father look at him. "I know this is painful. We all understand how you felt about him. I'll get a blanket, all right?"

The tears had begun to flow; his jaw trembled with confined fury. "We're not just leaving him here for the birds, goddamnit."

"There are a lot of bodies out here. We really don't have time."

Peter shook him off. "This man was a hero. He's the reason any of us are still alive."

Caleb spoke in measured tones: "I know that, Dad. Everyone does. But the general was right. We really have to think about what comes next."

"I'll tell you what comes next. We bury this man."

"Mr. President—"

Peter turned: Jock. Someone had wrapped his ankle and found him a pair of crutches. He was sweating and a little out of breath.

"What the hell is it now?"

The man seemed uncertain.

"For God's sake, just say it."

"It looks like . . . somebody's alive outside."

The gate was gone: one of the doors had been knocked askew and was hanging from a single hinge; the other lay on the ground a hundred feet inside the wall. As they moved through the opening, Peter's first, impossible impression was that it had snowed in the night. A fine, pale dust coated every surface. A moment passed before he grasped the meaning. Carter's army lay dead; their bones, now in sunlight, had begun their dissolution.

Amy was sitting near the base of the wall, arms wrapping her knees, gazing across the field. Covered in ash, she looked like a ghost, a specter from a children's story. A few feet beyond her, beside Soldier's body, lay Alicia. The horse's throat was torn open, among other things. Flies were buzzing around him, dipping in and out of his wounds.

Peter strode forward with gathering speed. Amy turned her face toward him.

"He didn't kill us," she said. She spoke as if in a daze. "Why didn't he kill us?"

Her presence barely registered in Peter's mind; it was Alicia he wanted. "You knew!" He barreled past Amy, seized Alicia by the arm, and rolled her faceup. "You fucking knew all along!"

Amy cried, "Peter, stop!"

He dropped to his knees and straddled Alicia's waist; his fingers wrapped her throat. His eyes and mind filled with the loathsome sight of her. "He was my friend!"

More voices, not just Amy's, were yelling at him, but this was a matter of no importance. They might just as well have been calling to him from the moon. Alicia was making a gurgling sound; her lips were paling to a bluish color. She was squinting into the morning light. Through these narrow slits, their gazes met. In her eyes, Peter saw not fear but fatalistic acceptance. *Go ahead,* her eyes said. *We've done everything else together, why not this?* Beneath the pads of his thumbs, he felt the stringy gristle of her trachea. He shifted them downward, positioning them in the spoonlike depression at the base of her throat. Hands had grabbed him. Some were tugging at his shoulders, others attempting to pry his fingers from her neck. "He was my friend and you killed him! You killed all of them!" One hard push to crush her larynx and that would be the end of her. "Say it, you traitor! Say you knew!"

A tremendous force yanked him away. He crashed onto his back in the dust. Hollis.

"Take a breath, Peter."

The man had positioned himself between Peter and Alicia, who had begun to cough. Amy was kneeling beside her, cradling her head.

"We all heard her," Hollis said. "She was trying to warn us."

Peter's face was burning; his hands, clenched into fists, shook with adrenaline. "She lied to us."

"I understand your anger. We all do. But she didn't know."

Peter's awareness expanded. The others were watching him in mute incomprehension. Caleb. Chase. Jock, leaning on his crutches. The old man, who was, for some reason, still carrying his bucket.

"Now, do I have your agreement to leave her be—yes or no?" Hollis said.

Peter swallowed. The fog of fury had begun to dissipate. Another moment and he nodded.

"All right, then," said Hollis.

He extended a hand and pulled Peter to his feet. Alicia's coughing had eased somewhat. Amy looked up. "Caleb, run and get Sara."

Amy waited by Alicia until Sara arrived. At the sight of Alicia, she startled.

"You're kidding me." Her voice was dispassionate, lacking all pity.

"Please, Sara," said Amy. There were tears in her eyes.

"You think I'm helping *her*?" Sara scanned the others. "She can go to hell."

Hollis took her by the shoulders to make her look at him. "She's not our enemy, Sara. Please believe me. And we're going to need her."

"What for?"

"To help us get out of here. Not just you and me. Pim. Theo. The girls."

A moment passed; Sara sighed and broke away. She crouched beside Alicia, passing her eyes quickly over her without expression, then looked up. "I'm not doing this with an audience. Amy, you stay. The rest of you, a little space, please."

The group backed away. Caleb took Peter aside.

"Dad? Okay?"

He wasn't sure what to say. His anger had faded, but not his doubt. He glanced past his son's shoulder. Sara was moving her hands over Alicia's chest and stomach, pressing with her fingertips.

"Yeah."

"Everybody understands."

Caleb said nothing more; neither did anyone else. A few more minutes went by before Sara rose and went to them.

"She's broken up pretty badly." Her tone was indifferent; she was doing a job, that was all. "I can't really tell the full extent. And in her case, things will probably happen differently. A couple of the gunshot wounds have closed up already, but I don't know what's happening inside. She's got a broken back, and about six other fractures I can detect."

"Will she live?" Amy asked.

"If she were anyone else, she'd be dead already. I can sew her up and set her leg. She needs to be immobilized. As for the rest . . ." She shrugged without feeling. "Your guess is as good as mine."

Caleb and Chase returned with a stretcher; they carried Alicia inside. All the survivors had been brought out of the shelter and had gathered in the staging area. Jenny and Hannah were moving through the group with buckets of water and ladles. Here and there, a person was sobbing; others were talking quietly or just gazing into space.

"So what now?" Chase asked.

Peter felt unattached to everything, almost floating. Particles of ash, bitter-smelling, drifted down. The fires had begun to spread. Leaping from building to building, they would sweep down to the river, consuming everything in their path. Other parts of the city, spared from the flames, would take longer— years, decades. Rain, wind, the devouring teeth of time—all would do their work. Peter could see it in his mind. Kerrville would become one more ruin in a world of them. He was suddenly crushed by the simplicity of it all. The city had fallen; the city was gone. He felt it keenly: the stab of defeat.

"Caleb?"

"Here, Dad."

Peter turned. His son was waiting; everyone was. "We need vehicles. Buses, trucks, whatever you can find. Fuel, too. Hollis, you go with him. Ford, what do we have for power?"

"Everything's out."

"The barracks have a backup generator. See if we can get it running. We need to get a message to Michael, tell him we're coming. Sara, you'll be in charge here. People will need food and water, enough for the day. But everybody needs to stay put. No wandering off, no looking for family or retrieving belongings."

"What about a search party?" Amy asked. "There could still be people out there."

"Take two men and a vehicle. Start on the other side of the river and work your way back. Stay clear of shaded areas, and keep out of the buildings."

"I'd like to help," Jock said.

"Fine, do your best but be quick about it. You've got one hour. No passengers unless they're injured. Anyone who can walk can make it here on their own."

"What if we find more infected who haven't turned yet?" Caleb asked.

"That's up to them. Make the offer. If they don't take it, leave them where they are. It won't make any difference." He paused. "Is everyone clear?"

Nods and murmurs passed around the group.

"Then that's it," Peter said. "We're done here. Sixty minutes, people, and we're gone."

74

They were 764 souls.

They were dirty, exhausted, terrified, confused. They rode in six buses, three to a seat; four five-tons, crammed with people; eight smaller trucks, both military and civilian, their cargo beds full of supplies—water, food, fuel. They had only a few weapons, and barely any ammunition. Among their numbers, they counted 532 children under the age of thirteen, 309 of these below the age of six. They included 122 mothers of children three and younger, including 19 women who were still nursing infants. Of the remaining 110, there were 68 men and 42 women of various ages and backgrounds. Thirty-two were, or had been, soldiers. Nine were over the age of sixty; the oldest, a widow who had sat in her house through the night, muttering to herself that all the noise outside was just a bunch of goddamn nonsense, was eighty-two. They included mechanics, electricians, nurses, weavers, shopkeepers, bootleggers, farmers, farriers, a gunsmith, and a cobbler.

One of the passengers was the drunken doctor, Brian Elacqua. Too inebriated to comprehend the orders to relocate to the dam, he had found himself, as night had fallen, wondering where everyone had gone. He had passed the twenty-four hours since his return to Kerrville drinking himself into oblivion in the abandoned house that had once been his—a miracle he had managed to find it—and awakened to a silence and darkness that disturbed him. Departing his house in search of more liquor, he reached the square just as gunfire erupted along the wall. He was profoundly disoriented and still quite drunk. Dimly he wondered, Why were people shooting? He decided to head for the hospital. It was a place he knew, a touchstone. Also, maybe someone could tell him what in the hell was going on. As he made his way there, his apprehension mounted. The gunfire had continued, and he was hearing certain other sounds as well: vehicles racing, cries of distress. As the hospital came into sight, a shout went up, followed by a barrage of shooting. Elacqua hit the dirt. He had no idea what to make of any of this; it seemed entirely unconnected to him. Also, he wondered, with sudden concern, what had become of his wife? It was true that she despised him, yet he was accustomed to her presence. Why was she not here?

These questions were shoved aside by the sound and shock of a tremendous impact. Elacqua peeled his face off the ground. A truck had crashed into the front of the building. Not just into: it had rammed straight through the wall. He got to his feet and stumbled toward it. Perhaps someone was injured, he thought. Perhaps they needed help. "Get in!" a man yelled from the cab. "Everybody in the truck!" Elacqua wobbled his way up the steps and beheld a scene of such disorder that his addled brain could not compute it. The room was full of screaming women and children. Soldiers were shoving and tossing them into the cargo bed while simultaneously shooting over their heads in the direction of the stairwell. Elacqua was caught in the crush. From the chaos, his mind distilled the image of a familiar face. Was that Sara Wilson? He had a sense that he'd seen her rather recently, though he could not pull the memory into shape. Either way, getting into the truck seemed like a good idea. He fought his way through the melee. Children were scrambling all around and underfoot. The driver of the vehicle was racing the engine. By this time, Elacqua had reached the tailgate. The truck was packed with people, barely any room at all. Also, there was the problem of getting one foot onto the bumper to hoist himself into the cargo compartment, an act requiring a degree of physical coordination he didn't think he could muster.

"Help me," he moaned.

A hand, heaven-sent, reached down. Up and into the truck he went, tumbling over bodies as the vehicle shot forward. A syncopation of bone-jarring bangs followed as the truck sailed out of the building and down the steps. Through the fog of terror and confusion, Brian Elacqua experienced a revelation: his life had been unworthy. It might not have begun that way—he'd meant to be a good and decent man—but over the years he had strayed far from the path. If I get out of this, he thought, I won't ever touch a drink again.

Which was how, sixteen hours later, Brian Elacqua came to find himself on a school bus of 87 women and children, deep in the physical and existential sorrows of acute alcohol withdrawal. It was still early morning, the light soft, with a golden color. He had, with many others, watched from the window as the city faded, then disappeared from sight. He wasn't completely sure where they were going. There was talk of a ship that would take them to safety, though he found this difficult to fathom. Why had he, of all people, a man who had squandered his life, the most worthless of worthless drunks, survived? Seated on the bench beside him was a little girl with strawberry-blond hair, tied in back with a ribbon. He supposed she was four or five. She was wearing a loose dress of thick woven fiber; her feet were dirty and bare, covered with numerous scratches and scabs. At her waist she clutched a ratty stuffed toy, some kind of animal, a bear or maybe a dog. She had yet to acknowledge him in any manner, her eyes staring forward. "Where are your parents, honey?" Elacqua asked. "Why are you alone?" "Because they're dead," the little girl stated. She did not look at him as she spoke. "They're all dead."

And with that, Brian Elacqua dropped his face to his hands, his body shaking with tears.

At the wheel of the first bus, Caleb was watching the clock. The hour was approaching noon; they had been on the road a little more than four hours. Pim and Theo sat behind him with the girls. He was down to half a tank; they planned to stop in Rosenberg, where a tanker from the isthmus would meet them to refuel. The bus was quiet; no one was talking. Lulled by the rocking of the chassis, most of the children had fallen asleep.

They had passed through the last of the outer townships when the radio crackled: "Pull over, everyone. Looks like we've lost one."

Caleb brought the bus to a halt and stepped down as his father, Chase, and Amy emerged from the lead Humvee. One of the buses, the fourth in line, was parked with its hood open. Steam and liquid were pouring from its radiator.

Hollis was standing on the bumper, slapping at the engine with a rag. "I think it's the water pump."

"Can you do anything about it?" Caleb's father said. "It'd have to be fast."

Hollis jumped down. "No chance. These old things aren't built for this. I'm surprised it's taken this long for one to conk out."

"As long as we're stopped," Sara suggested, "probably the children need to go."

"Go where?"

"To the bathroom, Peter."

Caleb's father sighed impatiently. Any minute of delay was a minute they'd be driving in darkness at the other end. "Just watch for snakes. That's all we need right now."

The children filed off and were led into the weeds, girls on one side of the buses, boys on the other. By the time the convoy was ready to move again, they had been stopped for twenty minutes. A hot Texas wind was blowing. It was 0130 hours, the sun poised above them like the head of a hammer in the sky.

The patch was complete, the dock ready to fill. Michael, Lore, and Rand, in one of six pump houses along the weir, were preparing to open the vents to the sea. Greer was gone, headed with Patch to Rosenberg in the last tanker truck.

"Shouldn't we say something?" Lore asked Michael.

"How about 'Please open, you bastard'?"

The wheel had not been turned in seventeen years.

"That'll have to do," said Lore.

Michael wedged a pry bar between the spokes; Lore was holding a mallet. Michael and Rand gripped the bar and leaned in.

"Hit it now."

Lore, positioned to the side, swung the mallet. It glanced off the top of the rim.

"For God's sake." Michael's jaws were clenched, his face reddened with effort. "Hit the bastard."

Blow after blow: still the wheel refused to turn.

"This isn't great," Rand said.

"Let me try," said Lore.

"How's that going to help?" Then, when Lore just stared at him, he stepped aside. "Suit yourself."

Lore left the pry bar where it was, gripping the wheel instead.

"You've got no leverage," Rand said. "That'll never work."

Lore ignored him. She planted her feet wide. The muscles in her arms tightened, thick ropes stretched over bone.

"This is pointless," Michael said. "We have to think of something else."

Then, miraculously, the wheel began to turn. An inch, then two. They all heard it: water had begun to move. A fine spray shot through the vent on the floor of the dock. With a jolt, the wheel released. Below them, the seas began to pour in. Lore backed away, flexing her fingers.

"We must have loosened it," Rand said lamely.

She gave them a droll smile.

The time was fast approaching.

His army was gone. Carter had felt the dopeys leaving him: a scream of terror, and a blast of pain, and then the letting go. Their souls had passed through him like wind, a whorl of memories, waning, then gone.

He did the last of his chores for the day with a solemn feeling. A deck of low clouds moved over the sky as he rolled his mower to the shed, padlocked the door, and turned to face the yard so that he might survey his handiwork. The crisp lawn, every blade just so. The tailored edges along the walkways with their bit of monkey grass to mark them. The trees all limbed up and the flowers, banks of them, like a carpet of color beneath the hedges. That morning, a dwarf Japanese cut-leaf maple had appeared by the gate. Mrs. Wood had always wanted one. Carter had rolled it in its plastic pot to the corner of the yard and set it in the ground. Cut-leafs had an elegant feel to them, like the hands of a beautiful woman. It felt like an act of completion to plant it there, a final gift to the yard he'd tended for so long.

He wiped his brow. The sprinklers came on, scattering a fine mist over the lawn. Inside the house, the little girls were laughing. Carter wished he could see them, talk to them. He imagined himself sitting on the patio while watching them play in the yard, tossing a ball or chasing each other. Little girls needed time in the sunshine.

He hoped he didn't stink too bad. He sniffed his armpits and supposed he'd pass all right. At the kitchen window, he inspected his reflection. It was a long time since he'd bothered to do that. He supposed he looked like he always had, which wasn't really one thing or the other, just a face like most people's.

For the first time in over a century, Carter opened the gate and stepped through.

The air wasn't any different here; he wondered why he'd thought it might be. The busy city made a whooshing sound in the background but the street was otherwise quiet, all the big houses staring back at him with no particular interest. He walked to the end of the drive to wait, fanning himself with his hat.

It was the hour when everything changes. The birds, the insects, the worms in the grass—all know this. Cicadas were buzzing in the trees.

75

1700: Greer and Patch had been waiting in the tanker truck for two hours. Patch was reading a magazine—reading or perhaps just looking at it. It was called *National Geographic Kids;* the pages were brittle and popped out when he turned them. He nudged Greer on the shoulder and held it out to show him a picture.

"Think it'll be like that?"

A jungle scene: fat green leaves, brightly colored birds, everything wreathed in vines. Greer was too preoccupied to look very closely.

"I don't know. Maybe."

Patch took it back. "I wonder if there's people out there."

Greer used binoculars to scan the horizon to the north. "I doubt it."

"Because if there is, I hope they're friendly. Seems like a lot to go through if they're not."

Another fifteen minutes passed.

"Maybe we should go look for them," Patch suggested.

"Hang on. I think this is them."

A cloud of dust had formed in the distance. Greer watched through the binoculars as the image of the convoy took shape. The two men climbed down from the cab as the first vehicle drew up.

"What kept you?" Greer asked Peter.

"We lost two buses. A busted radiator and a broken axle."

All of the vehicles took diesel except the smaller pickups, which carried their own extra fuel. Greer organized a team to pour the diesel off into jugs; they began moving down the line to refill the buses. The children were allowed off but told not to wander far.

"How long is this going to take?" Chase asked Greer.

It took almost an hour. The shadows had begun to stretch. They had fifty more miles to go, but these would be the hardest. None of the buses would be able to travel more than twenty miles per hour over the rough terrain.

The convoy began to move again.

The dock had been filling for seven hours. Everything was ready—batteries charged, bilge pumps on, engines ready to fire. Chains had been fixed to hold the *Bergensfjord* in place. Michael was in the pilothouse with Lore. The sea had risen a yard past the waterline—within a reasonable margin of error but disturbing nonetheless.

"I can't stand this," Lore said.

She was pacing around the tiny space, all her energy suddenly having nowhere to go. Michael picked up the microphone from the panel. "Rand, what are you seeing down there?"

He was moving through the corridors belowdecks, checking seams. "All good so far, no leaks. She seems tight."

Higher and higher the water rose, wrapping the hull in its cold embrace. Still the ship refused to budge.

"Flyers, this is killing me," groaned Lore.

"That's not an expression I've ever heard you use," Michael said.

"Well, I kind of see the sense of it now."

Michael held up a hand; he'd felt something. He willed all his senses to focus. The sensation came again: the tiniest shudder, rippling through the hull. His eyes met Lore's; she'd detected it, too. The great creature was coming to life. The deck shifted beneath him with a deep moan.

"Here we go!" Lore cried.

The *Bergensfjord* began to lift from her braces.

At the end of the block, the Denali appeared, turning the corner with painstaking care. Carter stepped into the road and positioned himself in its path. He did not hold up his hand or in any way indicate his wish that it should stop. He stepped aside as the car came to a halt in front of him. With a hushed, mechanical purr, the driver's window drew down. Crisp air and a smell of leather flowed out onto his face.

"Mr. Carter?"

"It's good to see you, Mrs. Wood."

She was wearing her tennis clothes. The silver packages in back, the baby seat with its mobile of plush toys, the sunglasses perched on her head: all the same as the morning they'd met.

"You're looking well," he said.

Her eyes narrowed on his face, as if she were attempting to read small print. "You stopped me."

"Yes, ma'am."

"I don't understand. Why did you do that?"

"Why don't you pull into the driveway? We can have us a talk."

She glanced around in confusion.

"You go on now," he assured her.

Rather reluctantly, she turned the Denali into the driveway and shut off the engine. Carter stepped to the driver's-side window again. The motor was making a quiet ticking sound. Hands locked on the steering wheel, Rachel stared straight out the windshield, as if afraid to look at him.

"I don't think I'm supposed to be doing this," she said.

"It's all right," Carter said.

Her voice sharpened with panic. "But it's *not* all right. It's not all right at all."

Carter opened her door. "Why don't you come and see the yard, Mrs. Wood? Kept it nice for you."

"I'm *supposed* to drive the car. That's what I *do.* That's my *job.*"

"Just this morning planted one of those cut-leaf maples you like. You should see how pretty it is."

For a moment she was silent. Then: "A cut-leaf maple, you say?"

"Yes, ma'am."

She nodded pensively to herself. "I always thought it would be just the right thing for that corner. You know the one I mean?"

"Absolutely I do."

She turned to look at him. For a moment she studied his face, her blue eyes slightly squinted. "You're always thinking of me, aren't you, Mr. Carter? You always know just the thing to say. I don't think I've ever had a friend like you."

"Oh, I expect you have."

"Oh, please. I have people, sure. Lots of people in Rachel Wood's life. But never anyone who understands me the way you do." She looked at him kindly. "But you and me. We're quite a pair, aren't we?"

"I'd say we are, Mrs. Wood."

"Now, if I've said it once, I've said it a thousand times. It's Rachel."

He nodded. "Anthony, then."

Her face opened as if she'd discovered something. "Rachel and Anthony! We're like two characters in a movie."

He held out a hand. "Why don't you come on now, Rachel? It'll all be fine, you'll see."

Accepting his hand for balance, she exited the car. By the open door she paused with great deliberateness and filled her lungs with air.

"Now, that's a wonderful smell," she said. "What is that?"

"Cut the lawn just now. I suspect that's it."

"Of course. Now I remember." She smiled with satisfaction. "How long has it been since I smelled new-mown grass? Smelled anything, for that matter."

"Garden's waiting on you. Lots of good smells there."

He made a circle with his arm; Rachel let him lead the way. The shadows were stretching over the ground; evening was about to fall. He steered her to the gate, where she came to a stop.

"Do you know how you make me feel, Anthony? I've been trying to think how to say it."

"How's that?"

"You make me feel *seen*. Like I was invisible until you came along. Does that sound crazy? Probably it does."

"Not to me," said Carter.

"I think I sensed it right away, that morning under the overpass. Do you remember?" A feeling of distance came into her eyes. "It was all so upsetting. Everyone honking and yelling and you there with your sign. 'HUNGRY, ANY-THING WILL HELP. GOD BLESS YOU.' I thought, that man means something. He's not just there by accident. That man's come into my life for a purpose."

Carter opened the latch; they stepped through. She was still clutching his arm, the two of them like a couple walking down the aisle. Her steps were solemn and measured; it was as if each one required a separate act of will.

"Now, Anthony, this really *is* lovely."

They were standing by the pool. The water was perfectly still and very blue. Around them, the yard made an effulgent display of color and life.

"Honestly, I can hardly believe my eyes. After all this time. You must have worked so hard."

"Wasn't any trouble. I had some help, too."

Rachel looked at him. "Really? Who was that?"

"Woman I know. Named Amy."

Rachel pondered this. "Now," she declared, raising a finger to her lips, "I believe I met an Amy not too long ago. I believe I gave her a lift. About so tall, with dark hair?"

Carter nodded.

"A very sweet girl. And what skin. Absolutely *glorious* skin." She smiled suddenly. "And what have we here?"

Her eyes had fallen on the cosmos. She separated from him and walked across the lawn to the beds, Carter following.

"These are just beautiful, Anthony."

She knelt before the flowers. Carter had planted two shades of pink: the first a deep solid, the second softer with green flares, on long, tippy stems.

"May I, Anthony?"

"You go on and do as you like. Planted them for you."

She selected one of the deeper pink and pinched off the stem. Holding it between thumb and forefinger, she rotated it slowly, breathing softly through her nose.

"Do you know what the name means?" she asked.

"Can't say I do."

"It's from the Greek. It means 'balanced universe.'" She rocked back onto her heels. "It's funny, I have no idea how I know that. Probably I learned it in school."

A quiet passed.

"Haley loves these." Rachel was looking at the flower, gazing at it as if it were a talisman or the key to a door she couldn't quite unlock.

"That she does," Carter answered.

"Always putting them in her hair. Her sister's, too."

"Miss Riley. Cute as a bug, that one."

A soft night was coming on between the branches of the trees. Rachel pointed her face to the sky.

"I have so many memories, Anthony. Sometimes it's all so hard to sort out."

"Things will come to you," he assured her.

"I remember the pool."

It was happening. Carter crouched beside her.

"That morning, how terrible everything was. The air so raw." She took a long, mournful breath. "I was so sad. So incredibly sad. Like a great black ocean and there you are, floating in it, drifting, no land anywhere, nothing to want or hope for. It's just you and the water and the darkness and you know it will always be like that, forever and ever."

She fell silent, lost in these old, troubled thoughts. The air had cooled; the lights of the city, coming on, reflected off the cloud deck, making a pale glow. Then:

"That was when I saw you. You were in the yard with Haley. Just . . ." She shrugged. "Showing her something. A toad, maybe. A flower. You were always doing that, showing her little things to make her happy." She shook her head slowly. "But that was the thing. I *knew* it was you, I *believed* it was you. But that wasn't who I saw."

She was staring at the ground, dry-eyed, beyond feeling. It would all pour forth now, the memories, the pain, the horrors of that day.

"It was Death, Anthony."

Carter waited.

"I know that's an old idea. A *crazy* idea. And you so sweet to me, to all of us. But I saw you standing there with Haley and I thought, Death has come. He's here, he's outside right now with my little girl. It's all a mistake, a horrible mistake, I'm the one he wants. *I'm* the one who needs to die."

The day was fading, colors draining, the sky releasing the last of its light. She raised her face; her eyes were beseeching, moist and wide.

"That's why I did what I did, Anthony. It wasn't fair. It wasn't right, I know that. There are things that can never be forgiven. But that is why."

Rachel had begun to cry. Carter put his arms around her as she collapsed into his weight. Her skin was warm and sweet-smelling, just a hint of her perfume lingering. How small she was, and he not a big man in the slightest. She might have been a bird there, just a little bit of a thing cupped in his hand.

The girls were laughing in the house.

"Oh God, I left them," Rachel sobbed. She was clutching his shirt in her fists. "How could I leave them? My babies. My beautiful baby girls."

"Hush now," he said. "Time to let go of all the old things."

They stayed like that for a time, holding each other. Night had descended in full; the air was still and moist with dew. The little girls were singing. The song was sweet and wordless, like the songs of birds.

"They waitin' on you," said Carter.

She shook her head against his chest. "I can't face them. I can't."

"You be strong, Rachel. Be strong for your babies."

She let him slowly draw her to her feet and took his arm, gripping it tightly with both hands, just above the elbow. With small steps, Carter led her around the pool toward the back door. The house was dark. Carter had expected it to be this way but could not say why that should be so. It was simply a part, another part, of the way things were in this place.

They stopped before the door. From deep in the house, more laughter and the creaking of springs: the girls were jumping on the beds.

"Aren't you going to open it?" Rachel asked.

Carter didn't answer. Rachel looked at him closely; something shifted in her face. She understood that he would not be going with her.

"Have to be this way," he explained. "You go on, now. Tell them hello for me, won't you? Tell them I've been thinking on them, every day."

She regarded the knob with a deep tentativeness. Inside, the girls were laughing with wild delight.

"Mr. Carter—"

"Anthony."

She placed a palm upon his cheek. She was crying again; come to think of it, Carter was crying a little himself. When she kissed him, he tasted not just the softness of her mouth and the warmth of her breath but also the saltiness of their tears conjoining—not a taste of sorrow, strictly speaking, though there was sorrow in it.

"God bless you, too, Anthony."

And before he knew it—before the feel of her kiss had faded from his lips—the door had opened and she was gone.

76

2030 hours: the light was almost gone, the convoy moving at a creep.

They were in a coastal tableland of tangled scrub, the road pocked with potholes in places, in others rippled like a washboard. Chase was driving, his gaze intent as he fought the wheel. Amy was riding in back.

Peter radioed Greer, who was driving the tanker at the rear of the column. "How much farther?"

"Six miles."

Six miles at twenty miles per hour. Behind them, the sun had been subsumed into a flat horizon, erasing all shadows.

"We should see the channel bridge soon," Greer added. "The isthmus is just south of there."

"Everyone, we need to push it," Peter said.

They accelerated to thirty-five. Peter swiveled in his seat to make sure the convoy was keeping pace. A gap opened, then narrowed. The cab of the Humvee flared as the first bus in line turned on its headlights.

"How much faster should we go?" Chase asked.

"Keep it there for now."

There was a hard bang as they rocketed through a deep hole.

"Those buses are going to blow apart," Chase said.

A scrim of light appeared ahead: the moon. It lifted swiftly from the eastern horizon, plump and fiery. Simultaneously, the channel bridge rose up before them in distant silhouette—a stately, vaguely organic figure with its long scoops of wire slung from tall trestles. Peter took up the radio again.

"Drivers, anybody seeing anything out there?"

Negative. Negative. Negative.

Through the windscreen of the pilothouse, Michael and Lore were watching the drydock doors. The portside door had opened without complaint; the starboard was the problem. At a 150-degree angle to the dock, the door had stopped cold. They'd been trying to open it the rest of the way for nearly two hours.

"I'm out of ideas here," Rand radioed from the quay. "I think that's all we're going to get."

"Will we clear it?" Lore asked. The door weighed forty tons.

Michael didn't know. "Rand, get down to engineering. I need you there."

"I'm sorry, Michael."

"You did your best. We'll have to manage." He hung the microphone back on the panel. *"Fuck."*

The lights on the panel went dead.

Twenty-eight miles west, the same summer moon had risen over the *Chevron Mariner.* Its blazing orange light shone down upon the deck; it shimmered over the oily waters of the lagoon like a skin of flame.

With a bang like a small explosion, the hatch detonated skyward. It seemed not so much to fly as to leap, soaring into the nighttime sky of its own volition. Up and up it sailed, spinning on its horizontal axis with a whizzing sound; then, like a man who's lost his train of thought, it appeared to pause in midflight. For the thinnest moment, it neither rose nor fell; one might easily have been forgiven for thinking it was charged with some magical power, capable of thwarting gravity. But, not so: down it plunged, into the befouled waters.

Then: Carter.

He landed on the foredeck with a *clang,* absorbing the impact through his legs and simultaneously compressing his body to a squat: hips wide, head erect, one splayed hand touching the deck for balance, like an offensive tackle preparing for the snap. His nostrils flared to taste the air, which was imbued with the freshness of freedom. A breeze licked at his body with a tickling sensation. Sights and sounds bombarded his senses from all directions. He regarded the moon. His vision was such that he could detect the smallest features of its face—the cracks and crevices, craters and canyons—with an almost lurid quality of three dimensions. He felt the moon's roundness, its great rocky weight, as if he were holding it in his arms.

Time to be on his way.

He ascended to the top of One Allen Center. High above the drowned city, Carter took measure of the buildings: their heights and handholds, the fjord-like gulfs between them. A route materialized in his mind; it had the force, the clarity of a premonition, or something absolutely known. A hundred yards to the first rooftop, perhaps another fifty to the second, a long two hundred to the third but with a drop of fifty feet that would expand his reach . . .

He backed to the far edge of the platform. The key was, first, to create an accumulation of velocity, then to spring at precisely the right moment. He lowered to a runner's crouch.

Ten long strides and he was up. He soared through the moonlit heavens like a comet, a star unlocked. He made the first rooftop with room to spare. He landed, tucked, rolled; he came up running and launched again.

He'd been saving up.

*　　*　　*

In the cargo bay of the third vehicle in the convoy, among the other injured, Alicia lay immobilized. Thick rubber cords strapped her to her stretcher at the shoulders, waist, and knees; a fourth lay across her forehead. Her right leg was splinted from ankle to hip; one arm, her right, was pinned across her chest. Various other parts of her were bandaged, stitched, bound.

Inside her body, the rapid cellular repair of her kind was under way. But this was an imperfect process, and complicated by the vastness and complexity of her wounds. This was especially true of the winglike flange of her right hip, which had been pulverized. The viral part of her could accomplish many things, but it could not reassemble a jigsaw puzzle. It might have been said that the only thing keeping Alicia Donadio alive was habit—her predisposition to see things through, just as she had always done. But she no longer had the heart for any of it. As the bone-banging hours passed, that she had failed to die seemed more and more like a punishment, and proof enough of Peter's words. *You traitor. You knew. You killed them. You killed them all.*

Sara was sitting on the bench above her. Alicia undestood that the woman hated her; she could see it in her eyes, in the way she looked at her—or, rather, didn't—as she went about attending to Alicia's injuries: checking the bandages, measuring her temperature and pulse, dribbling the horrible-tasting elixir into her mouth that kept her in a pain-numbed twilight. Alicia wished she could say something to the woman, whose hatred she deserved. *I'm sorry about Kate.* Or *It's all right, I hate myself enough as it is.* But this would only make things worse. Better Alicia should accept what was offered and say nothing.

Besides, none of this mattered now; Alicia was asleep, and dreaming. In this dream, she was in a boat, and all around was water. The seas were calm, covered in mist, without a visible horizon. She was rowing. The creak of the oars in their locks, the swish of water moving under their blades: these were the only sounds. The water was dense, with a slightly viscous texture. Where was she going? Why had the water ceased to terrify her? Because it didn't; Alicia felt perfectly at home. Her back and arms were strong, her strokes compact, nothing wasted. Rowing a boat was something she did not recall ever doing, yet it felt completely natural, as if the knowledge had been inscribed into her muscles for later use.

On she rowed, her blades elegantly slicing through the inky murk. She became aware that something was moving in the water—a shadowy bulk gliding just beneath the surface. It appeared to be following her, maintaining a watchful distance. Her mind did not register its presence as menacing; rather, it merely seemed to be a natural feature of the environment, one she might have anticipated if she'd thought about it in advance.

"Your boat is very small," said Amy.

She was sitting in the stern. Water was running from her face and hair.

"You know we can't go," Amy stated.

The remark was puzzling. Alicia continued to row. "Go where?"

"The virus is in us." Amy's voice was dispassionate, without any perceptible tone. "We can't ever leave."

"I don't understand what you're talking about."

The shape had begun to circle them. Great bulges of water began to rock the boat from side to side.

"Oh, I think you do. We're sisters, aren't we? Sisters in blood."

The motion increased in intensity. Alicia drew the oars into the boat and clutched the gunwales for balance. Her heart turned to lead; bile bubbled in her throat. Why had she failed to foresee the danger? So much water all around them, and her little boat, so small as to be nothing. The hull began to rise; suddenly they were no longer in contact with the water. A great blue bulk emerged under them, water streaming from its encrusted flanks.

"You know who that is," Amy said impassively.

It was a whale. They were balanced like a pea atop its immense, horrible head. Higher and higher it lifted them into the air. One flick of its monstrous tail and it would send them soaring; it would crash down upon them and smash their boat to pieces. A hopeless terror, that of fate, took her in its grasp. From the stern, Amy issued a bored sigh.

"I'm so . . . tired of him," she said.

Alicia tried to scream, but the sound stopped in her throat. They were rising, the sea was falling away, the whale was looming up . . .

She awoke with a slam. She blinked her eyes and tried to focus. It was night. She was in the back of the truck, and the truck was bouncing hard. Sara's face floated into view.

"Lish? What is it?"

Her lips moved slowly around the words: "They're . . . coming."

From the rear of the convoy, the sound of guns.

Shit. Shit shit shit.

Michael took the stairs from the pilothouse three at a time; he raced across the deck, his feet barely touching steel, and down the hatch. He was yelling into his radio, "Rand, get down here right now!"

He hit the engineering catwalk at a sprint, grabbed the poles of the ladder, and slid the rest of the way. The engines were quiet, everything stopped. Rand appeared above him.

"What happened?"

"Something tripped the main!"

Lore, on the radio: "Michael, we're hearing shots up here."

"Say again?"

"*Gunshots,* Michael. I'm looking down the isthmus now. We've got lights coming this way from the mainland."

"Headlights or virals?"

"I'm not sure."

He needed current to trace the problem. At the electrical panel, he switched diagnostics over to the auxiliary generator. The meters jumped to life.

"Rand!" Michael bellowed. "What are you seeing?"

Rand was positioned at the engine-control array on the far side of the room, checking dials. "Looks like its something in the water jacket pumps."

"That wouldn't trip the main! Look farther up the line!"

A brief silence; then Rand said, "Got it." He tapped a dial. "Pressure's flat-lined on the starboard-side charger. Must have shut down the system."

Lore again: "Michael, what's going on down there?"

He was strapping on his tool belt. "Here," he said, tossing Rand the radio, "you talk to her."

Rand looked lost. "What should I say?"

"Tell her to get ready to engage the props straight from the pilothouse."

"Shouldn't she wait for the system to repressurize? We could blow a header."

"Just get on the electrical panel. When I tell you, switch the system back over to the main bus."

"Michael, talk to me," Lore said. "Things are looking very fucking serious up here."

"*Go,*" Michael told Rand.

He raced aft, plugged in his lantern, dropped to his back, and wedged himself under the charger.

This goddamn leak, he thought. It's going to be the death of me.

The convoy hit the isthmus doing sixty miles an hour. Buses were bounding; buses were going airborne. The tanker, last in the line, had failed to keep up. The virals were close behind and massing. The barrier of razor wire appeared in the headlights.

Peter yelled into the radio, "Everyone keep going! Don't stop!"

They careened straight through the barrier. Chase stamped the brakes and pulled to the side as the convoy roared past with inches to spare, pushing a wall of wind that buffeted the vehicle like a howling gale. Peter, Chase, and Amy leapt from the cab.

Where was the tanker?

It lumbered into view at the base of the causeway—lamps blazing, engine roaring, traveling toward them like a well-lit rocket in slow motion. Past the turn it began to accelerate. Two virals were crouched on the roof of the cab. Chase raised his rifle and squinted through the scope.

"Ford, don't," Peter warned. "You hit that tank, it could blow."

"Quiet. I can do this."

A bullet split the air. One of the virals tumbled away. Ford was taking aim at the second when it dropped to the hood: no shot.

"Shit!"

From the cab, a pair of shotgun blasts came in rapid succession; the windshield shattered outward into the moonlight. There was a hissing groan of brakes. The viral flopped backward into the conical glare of the truck's headlights and disappeared beneath the front wheels with a wet burst.

Suddenly the cab was at a right angle to the causeway; the tanker was jackknifing. The whole thing began to swing crosswise. As its back wheels touched the water, the rear of the truck abruptly decelerated, swinging the cab in the opposite direction like a weight on a string. The truck was less than a hundred yards away now. Peter could see Greer fighting the wheel for control, but his efforts were now pointless; the vehicle's angular momentum had assumed command.

It flopped onto its side. The cab separated from its cargo, which rammed it from behind in a second crunch of glass and metal. A long, screeching skid, and the whole thing came to rest, lying driver side up at a forty-five-degree angle to the roadway.

Peter dashed toward it, Chase and Amy close behind. Fuel was gushing everywhere; black smoke billowed from the undercarriage. The virals were funneling onto the isthmus; they would arrive within seconds. Patch was dead, his head crushed from behind; what was left of him was spread-eagled over the dashboard. Greer was lying on top of him, soaked in blood. Was it Patch's or his own? He was staring upward.

"Lucius, cover your eyes."

Peter and Chase began to kick what was left of the windshield. Three hard blows and the glass caved inward. Amy climbed inside and took the man by the shoulders while Peter took his legs. "I'm okay," Greer muttered, as if to apologize. As they hauled him out, the first fingers of flame appeared.

Chase and Peter each took a side. They ran.

Passengers had massed at the narrow gangway, attempting to shove their way through the bottleneck. Cries of panic stabbed the air. Men were scrambling over the deck of the ship to free the chains that held it in place. Many of the children seemed dazed and uncertain, drifting on the dock like a herd of sheep in the rain.

Pim and the girls were already on the ship. At the top of the gangway, Sara was lifting the smallest children aboard, pulling others by the hand to hasten them; Hollis and Caleb were shepherding the children from the rear. A man charged from behind, nearly knocking Hollis over. Caleb grabbed him, threw him to the pavement, and shoved a finger into his face.

"You wait your goddamn turn!"

They weren't going to make it, Caleb thought. People had resorted to using the chains, attempting to drag themselves hand over hand to the ship. A woman lost her grip; with a cry, she plunged into the water. She came up, her face visible for only a moment, arms waving over her head: she didn't know how to swim. She sank back down.

Where were his father and the others? Why hadn't they come?

From the causeway, an explosion; all faces turned. A ball of fire was rising in the sky.

Wedged under the charger, Michael was trying to trace the faint hiss of leaking gas. Keep cool, he told himself. Do this by the numbers, joint by joint.

"Anything?" Rand was standing at the base of the charger.

"You're not helping."

It was no use. The leak was too small; it must have bled for hours.

"Get me some soapy water," he called. "I need a paintbrush, too."

"Where the hell am I going to get that?"

"I don't care! Figure it out!"

Rand darted away.

The blast hit them like a slap, hurling them forward, off their feet. Debris whizzed past: tires, engine parts, shards of metal sharp as knives. As a wall of heat soared over him, Peter heard a scream and a great crunch of metal and splintering glass.

He was lying facedown in the mud. His thoughts were disordered; none seemed related to any of the others. A raglike bundle lay to his left. It was Chase. The man's clothes and hair were smoking. Peter crawled to him; his friend's eyes stared sightlessly. Cradling the back of the man's head, he felt something soft and damp. He turned Chase onto his side.

The back of the man's skull was gone.

The Humvee was totaled, crushed and burning. Greasy smoke clotted the air. It coated the insides of Peter's mouth and nose with its rancid taste. With every breath it drilled into his lungs, deeper and deeper.

"Amy, where are you?" He staggered toward the Humvee. "Amy, answer me!"

"I'm here!"

She was pulling Greer clear of the water. The two of them emerged covered in gooey mud and collapsed to the ground.

"Where's Chase?" She had pink burns on her face and hands.

"Dead." Crouched, he asked Greer, "Can you walk?"

The man was holding his head in his hands. Then, glancing up: "Where's Patch?"

The burning truck would hold the virals at bay, but once the fires died, the horde would come streaming down the isthmus. The three of them had nothing to fight with except Amy's sword, which still lay in its scabbard over her back.

A harsh white light raked their faces; a pickup was racing down the roadway toward them. Peter hooded his eyes against the glare. The driver skidded to a stop.

"Get in," Caleb said.

Alicia saw only the sky. The sky and the back of a man's head. She sensed the presence of a crowd. Her stretcher jostled beneath her, there were voices, people crying, everything rushing around her.

Don't take me. Her body was broken; she lay loose as a doll. *I'm one of them. I don't belong.*

Clanging footsteps: they were crossing the gangway. "Put her over there," someone said. The stretcher-bearers lowered her to the deck and hurried away. A woman was sitting beside her, her body curled around a blanketed bundle. She was murmuring into the bundle, some kind of repeated phrase that Alicia could not make out, though it possessed the rote rhythm of prayer.

"You," Alicia said.

One syllable; it felt like lifting a piano. The woman failed to notice her.

"You," she repeated.

The woman looked up. The bundle was a baby. The woman's grip on it was almost ruthless, as if she feared someone might snatch it away at any moment.

"I need you . . . to help me."

The woman's face crumpled. "Why aren't we moving?" She bent her face to the baby again, burying it in the cloth. "Oh, God, why are we still here?"

"Please . . . listen."

"Why are you talking to me? I don't even know you. I don't know who you are."

"I'm . . . Alicia."

"Have you seen my husband? He was here a second ago. *Has anybody seen my husband?*"

Alicia was losing her. In another moment, she'd be gone. "Tell me . . . her name."

"What?"

"Your baby. Her . . . name."

It was as if nobody had ever asked her such a question.

"Say it," Alicia said. "Say . . . her name."

She shook with a sob. "He's a boy," she moaned. "His name is Carlos."

A moment passed, the woman weeping, Alicia waiting. There was chaos all around, and yet it felt as if they were alone, she and this woman she did not know, who could have been anyone. *Rose, my Rose,* Alicia thought, *how I have failed you. I could not give you life.*

"Will you . . . help me?"

The woman wiped her nose with the back of a wrist. "What can *I* do?" Her voice was utterly hopeless. "I can't *do* anything."

Alicia licked her lips; her tongue was heavy and dry. There would be pain, a lot of it; she would need every ounce of strength.

"I need you . . . to untie . . . my straps."

Soaring leap after soaring leap, Carter made his way down the channel toward the isthmus. The mushroom shapes of chemical tanks. The rooftops of buildings. The great, forgotten debris fields of industrial America. He moved swiftly, his power inexhaustible, like a huge heaving engine.

A great backlit shape rose before him: the channel bridge. He unleashed his body skyward; up he flew, seizing a handhold just below the bridge's shattered surface. A moment of calibration and he hurled himself upward again, grabbed a guy wire with one hand, and somersaulted to the deck.

Below, the unfolding battle was laid out before him like a model. The ship and the mob of people funneling aboard; the truck roaring down the causeway; the barricade of flames and the viral horde amassed behind it. Carter cocked his head to calculate his arc; he needed more height.

Using one of the support wires, he climbed to the top of the tower. The water shone below him still as glass, like a great smooth mirror to the moon. He felt some uncertainty, even a bit of fear; he pushed it aside. The tiniest fleck of doubt and he would fail, he would plummet into the abyss. To traverse such a distance—to master its breadth—one needed to enter an abstract realm. To become not the jumper but the jump, not an object in space but space itself.

He compressed to a crouch. Energy expanded outward from his core and gushed into his limbs.

Amy, I am coming.

From the pilothouse, Lore was watching the viral horde through binoculars. Blockaded by the flaming wreckage, it appeared as a column of thrumming light that stretched far back onto the mainland and beyond, widening to encompass virtually all of the far shore.

She raised the radio to her mouth. "I don't want to rush you, Michael, but whatever's wrong, you have got to fix it *right the fuck now.*"

"I'm trying here!"

Something was happening to the horde, a kind of . . . rippling. A rippling but also a compacting, like the gathering action of a spring. Beginning at the rear, the motion slithered forward, gathering speed as it proceeded down the causeway toward the flames. The truck was lying lengthwise across the roadway. What was she seeing?

The head of the column crashed into the burning tanker like a battering ram. Gouts of smoke and fire shot into the sky. The tanker began to creep forward, scraping along the roadway. Burning virals peeled off into the water as more were propelled from behind into the destruction.

Lore looked down from the rail. The chains connecting the hull to the dock had been released; dozens of people were splashing helplessly in the water. At least a hundred, including some children, remained on the dock. Panicked cries knifed the air. *"Get out of my way!" "Take my daughter!" "Please, I'm begging you!"*

"Hollis!" she cried.

The man looked up. Lore pointed toward the isthmus. She realized her mistake: others on the dock had seen her. The mob surged forward, everyone attempting to wedge themselves onto the narrow gangway simultaneously. Blows were thrown, bodies hurled; people were trampled in the crush. From the center of the melee came the crack of a gunshot. Hollis rushed forward, arms swinging like a swimmer's, carving a path through the chaos. More shots; the crowd scattered, revealing a lone man with a pistol and two bodies on the ground. For a second the man just stood there, as if amazed by what he'd done, before he turned and charged up the gangway. Too late for him: he made it all of five steps before Hollis grabbed him by the collar, pulled him backward, placed his other hand under the man's buttocks, hoisted him over his head—the man flailing his arms and legs like an overturned turtle—and hurled him over the rail.

Lore grabbed the radio: "Michael, it's getting ugly up here!"

A froth of bobbles appeared. Rand passed Michael a three-foot length of pipe and a tub of grease. Michael wrenched the old pipe free, greased the threads of its replacement, and fitted it into place. Rand had returned to the panel.

"Switch it over!" Michael yelled.

The lights flickered; the mixers began to spin. Pressure flowed into the lines.

"Here we go!" Rand cried.

Michael wriggled free. Rand tossed him the radio.

"Lore—"

Everything died again.

She had failed; her army was gone, scattered to dust. With all her heart Amy wanted to be on that ship, to depart this place and never come back. But she could never leave, not on this boat or any other. She would stand on the dock as it sailed away.

How I wanted to have that life with you, Peter, she thought. *I'm sorry, I'm sorry, I'm sorry.*

The truck was racing east, Caleb at the wheel, Peter, Amy, and Greer in the cargo bed. Ahead the lights of the dock loomed; behind them, across the widening distance, Amy saw the burning tanker pivoting. The first virals appeared through the breach. Their bodies were burning. They staggered forward, man-sized wicks of flame. The gap continued to widen, opening like a door.

Amy turned to the window of the cab. "Caleb—"

He was looking through the mirror. "I see them!"

Caleb floored it; the truck shot forward, sending Amy tumbling. Her head impacted the metal floor with a *clang* and a burst of disorienting pain. Lying on her back, her face to the sky, Amy saw the stars. Stars by the hundreds, the thousands, and one of them was falling. It grew and grew, and she knew what this star was.

"Anthony."

Carter's aim was true; as the truck zoomed past, he landed behind it on the causeway, rolled, and came up on his feet. The virals were careening toward him. He drew himself erect.

Brothers, sisters.

He sensed their confusion. Who was this strange being who had dropped into their path?

I am Carter, Twelfth of Twelve. Kill me if you can.

"What the hell happened?"

"I don't know!"

The radio squawked: Lore. "Michael, we have *got* to go *right now.*"

Rand was madly checking gauges. "It's not the charger—it has to be electrical."

Michael stood before the panel in utter desolation. It was hopeless; he was beaten. His ship, his *Bergensfjord,* had denied him. His paralysis became anger; his anger turned to rage. He slammed a fist against the metal. "You bitch!" He reared back, struck again. "You heartless bitch! You do this to me?" With tears of frustration brimming, he grabbed a wrench from the deck and began to slam it against the metal, again and again. "I've . . . given . . . you . . . *everything!*"

A sudden rumble, like the roar of a great caged beast. Lights came on; all the gauges leapt.

"Michael," said Rand, "what the hell did you do?"

"That's got it!" Lore cried.

The sound increased in intensity, humming through the ship's plating. Rand yelled over the din: "Pressure's holding! Two thousand rpm! Four! Five! Six thousand!"

Michael snatched the radio from the floor. "Engage the screws!"

A groan. A shudder, deep in the bones.

The *Bergensfjord* began to move.

They skidded into the loading area. Amy leapt from the back of the truck before it stopped moving.

"Amy, stop!"

But the woman was already gone, racing toward the causeway. "Caleb, take Lucius and get on that boat."

Standing by the cargo bed, his son seemed stunned.

"Do it!" Peter ordered. "Don't wait!"

He took off after her. With every step he willed himself to go faster. His breath was heaving in his chest, the ground flying beneath him. The gap between them began to narrow. Twenty feet, fifteen, ten. A final burst of speed and he grabbed her around the waist, sending both of them rolling on the ground.

"Let me go!" Amy was on her knees, fighting to break free.

"We have to leave *right now.*"

There were tears in her voice. "They'll kill him!"

Carter coiled. He flexed his fingers, claws glinting. He flexed his toes, feeling the taut wires of ligaments. Blueing moonlight doused him like a benediction.

Reaching one hand forward, Amy released a wail of pain. "Anthony!"

He charged.

They had to clear eight hundred feet.

At the rear of the vessel, a wall of foam churned up. Shouts rose from the dock: *"They're leaving without us!"* The last of the passengers rushed forward, shoving themselves onto the ramp, which had begun to scrape along the pier as the *Bergensfjord* pulled away.

Standing at the rail, Pim watched the scene unfold in silence. The bottom lip of the gangway was inching toward the edge; soon it would fall. Where was her husband? Then she saw him. Supporting Lucius, he was racing at a quick-step down the pier. She began to sign emphatically to any who might see: *That's my husband!* And: *Stop this ship!* But, of course, no one could make sense of her.

The gangway was clotted with people. Crammed between the guardrails, they squeezed forward onto the deck of the ship only one or two at a time, ejected from the squirming mass. Pim began to moan. She was not aware that she was doing this at first. The sound had emerged of its own volition, an expression of violent feeling that could not be contained—just as, twenty-one years ago, in Sara's arms, she had wailed with such ferocity that she might have been mistaken for a dying animal. As the volume increased, the sound began to form a distinctive shape altogether new in the life of Pim Jaxon: she was about to make words.

"Caaay . . . leb! Ruuuuunnnn!"

The lip of the gangway halted. It had lodged against a cleat at the edge of the pier. Under the pressure of the ship's accelerating mass, it began to twist on its axis. Rivets were popping, metal buckling. Caleb and Greer were steps away. Pim was waving, shouting words she couldn't hear but felt—felt with every atom of her body.

The gangway began to fall.

Still chained to the ship, it cantilevered into the side of the hull. Bodies plunged into the water, some wordlessly, their fate accepted, others with pitiful cries. At the bottom of the ramp, Caleb had hooked an elbow through the rail while simultaneously holding on to Greer, whose feet were balanced on the lowest rung. The *Bergensfjord* was gathering speed, dragging a roiling whirlpool. As the stern passed by, the ones in the water were dragged under, into the propeller's froth. Perhaps a cry, a hand reaching up in vain, and they were gone.

In the bowels of the *Bergensfjord,* Michael was running. Deck by deck he ascended, legs flying, arms swinging, heart pumping in his mouth. With a burst he flung himself into open air. The point of the bow was passing the end of the drydock door.

They weren't going to clear it. No goddamn way.

He took the stairs to the pilothouse three at a time and charged through the door. "Lore—"

She was staring out the windscreen. "I know!"

"Give it more rudder!"

"You don't think I did that?"

The gap between the door and the ship's right flank was narrowing. Twenty yards. Ten. Five.

"Oh, shit," Lore breathed.

Peter and Amy were racing down the dock.

The ship was departing; she was gliding away. Gunfire spattered from the fantail, bullets whizzing over their heads; the virals had broken through.

A crash.

The side of the hull had collided with the end of the drydock door. A long scraping sound followed, the irresistible force of the ship's momentum meeting the immovable object of the door's weight. The hull trembled even as it failed to decelerate, thrusting forward.

The great wall of steel slid heartlessly by. In another few seconds, the *Bergensfjord* would be gone. There was no way to board. Peter saw something hanging off the side of the ship: the fallen gangway, still attached at the top. Two people were clinging to it.

Caleb. Greer.

With one arm crooked around the gangway rail, his son was calling to them while pointing at the end of the pier. The drydock door had been nudged away from the ship; it now stood at an acute angle to the moving hull. When the gangway passed the end of the door, the gap between them would narrow to a jumpable distance.

But Amy was no longer beside him; Peter was alone. He spun and saw her, standing a hundred feet behind him, facing away.

"Amy, come on!"

"Get ready to jump!" Caleb yelled.

The virals had reached the far end of the pier. Amy drew her sword and called to Peter over her shoulder, "Get on that ship!"

"What are you doing? We can make it!"

"Don't make me explain! Just go!"

Suddenly he understood: Amy did not intend to leave. Perhaps she never had.

Then he saw the girl.

Far out of his reach, she was crouched behind a giant spool of cable. Strawberry hair tied with a ribbon, scratches on her face, a stuffed animal gripped tightly to her chest with arms thin as twigs.

Amy saw her, too.

She sheathed her sword and dashed forward. The virals were charging down the dock. The little girl was frozen with terror. Amy swung her onto her hip and began to run. With her free hand she waved Peter forward. "Don't wait! I'll need you to catch us!"

He raced down the drydock door. The bottom of the gangway was thirty feet away and closing fast. Caleb yelled, "Do it now!"

Peter leapt.

For an instant it seemed he had jumped too soon; he would plunge into the roiling water. But then his hands caught the rail of the gangway. He pulled himself up, found his footing, and turned around. Amy, still holding the girl, was running down the top of the wall. The gangway was passing them by; she was never going to make it. Peter reached out as Amy took five bounding strides, each longer than the last, and flung herself over the abyss.

Peter could not remember the moment when he grabbed her hand. Only that he'd done it.

They had cleared the dock. Michael ran down from the pilothouse and dashed to the rail. He saw a deep dent, fifty feet long at least, though the wound was high above the waterline. He looked toward shore. A hundred yards aft, at the end of the dock, a mass of virals was watching the departing ship like a crowd of mourners.

"Help!"

The voice came from the stern.

"Someone's fallen!"

He raced aft. A woman, clutching an infant, was pointing over the rail.

"I didn't know she was going to jump!"

"Who? Who was it?"

"She was on a stretcher, she could barely walk. She said her name was Alicia."

*   *   *

A coiled rope lay on the deck. Michael pushed the button on the radio. "Lore, kill the props!"

"What?"

"Do it! Full stop!"

He was already wrapping the rope around his waist, having shoved the radio into the hand of the woman, who stared at him in confusion.

"Where are you going?" the woman asked.

He stepped over the rail. Far below, the waters swirled in a maelstrom. *Kill them,* he thought. *Dear God, Lore, kill those screws now.*

He jumped.

Toes pointed, arms outstretched, he pierced the surface like a spike; instantly the current grabbed him, shoving him down. He slammed into the mucky bottom and began to roll along it. His eyes stung with salt; he could see nothing at all, not even his hands.

He fell straight into her.

A confusion of limbs: they were both tumbling, spiraling along the bottom. He grabbed her belt and drew her body into his and wrapped his arms around her waist.

The slack ran out.

A hard yank; Michael felt as if he were being sliced in two. Still holding Alicia, he vaulted upward at a forty-five-degree angle. Michael had already been in the water for thirty seconds; his brain was screaming for air. The screws had stopped turning, but this no longer mattered. They were being pulled along by the boat's momentum. Unless they broke the surface soon, they'd drown.

Suddenly, a whining sound: the screws had reengaged. *No!* Then Michael realized what had happened: Lore had reversed the engines. The tension on the rope began to soften, then was gone. A new force gripped them. They were being sucked forward, toward the spiraling props.

They were going to be chopped to bits.

Michael looked up. High above, the surface shimmered. What was the source of this mysterious, beckoning light? The sound of the screws abruptly ceased; now he understood Lore's intentions. She was creating enough slack in the line for them to ascend. Michael began to kick. *Alicia, don't give up. Help me do this. Unless you do, we're dead.* But it was no use; they were sinking like stones. The light receded pitilessly.

The rope went taut again. They were being pulled.

As they broke the surface, Michael opened his mouth wide, sucking in a vast gulp of air. They were beneath the stern, a mountain of steel soaring above them; the light he'd seen was the moon. It shone down upon them, fat and full, spilling across the surface of the water.

"It's all right, I've got you," Michael said. Alicia was coughing and sputtering in his arms; from high above, a lifeboat floated down. "I've got you, I've got you, I've got you."

77

Carter's eyes were full of stars.

He lay on the causeway, bloodied and broken. Some parts of him felt as if they were absent, no longer attached. There was no pain; rather, his body felt distant, beyond his command.

Brothers, sisters.

They stood around him in a circle. Toward them, he felt only love. The ship was gone; it was streaming away. He felt a great love for everything; he would have wrapped the world with his heart if he could. At the edge of the causeway, moonlight skittered across the water, making a glowing road for him to travel.

Let me do this. Let me feel it coming out of me. Let me be a man again, before I die.

Carter began to crawl. The virals stepped back, allowing him to pass. There was in their comportment a feeling of respect, as if they were pupils, or soldiers accepting the sword of their enemy. Across the roadway, Carter made his passage. His left hand, reaching out, was the first part of him to touch the sea. The water was cool and welcoming, rich with salt and earth. A billion living things coursed through it; to them he would be joined.

Brothers, sisters, I thank you.

He slipped beneath the surface of the water.

XI

THE CITY OF MIRRORS

I wear the chain I forged in life. . . .
I made it link by link, and yard by yard;
I girded it on of my own free will,
and of my own free will I wore it.

—CHARLES DICKENS,
A CHRISTMAS CAROL

78

Dawn at sea.

The *Bergensfjord* lay at anchor, her great engines at rest. The sky was low, the water blank as stone; far away, a screen of rain fell into the Gulf. Most of the passengers were sleeping on the deck. Their bodies lay in disorder, as if felled all at once. They were a hundred miles from land.

Amy stood at the bow, Peter beside her. Her mind was drifting, refusing to attach to any thought but one. Anthony was gone. She was all that remained.

The little girl's name was Rebecca. Her mother had died in the attack, her father years ago. Amy's feeling of her—her body's weight and heat, the desperate force with which she'd clung to her as they had soared through space—was still palpable. Amy did not think it would ever depart; the sensation had become a part of her, stitched to her bones. It had defined the moment, making the choice for her. It was not only Rebecca that Amy had seen on the pier but her own little-girl self, who had, after all, been just as alone, abandoned by the great heaving engine of the world and in need of saving.

For some time, perhaps ten minutes, neither she nor Peter spoke. Like her, Peter was only half present, staring into space—the pale dawn sky, the sea, limitlessly calm.

It was Amy who broke the silence. "You better go talk to her."

In the small hours of the night, a decision had been reached. Amy could not go; neither could Alicia. If the survivors were going to make a new life for themselves, all traces of the old terrors needed to be left behind. What mattered now was for others to accept it.

"She didn't do this, Peter."

He glanced at her but said nothing.

"Neither did you," she added.

Another silence. With all her heart she wanted him to believe this, yet she knew it was impossible for him to think otherwise.

"You need to make peace with her, Peter. For both your sakes."

The sun was rising unremarkably behind the clouds; the sky was devoid of color, its edges blended imperceptibly into the horizon. The rain kept its distance. Michael had assured them that the weather wouldn't be a problem; he knew how to read these things.

"Well," Peter said with a sigh, "I suppose I better do this."

He left her and descended to the crew's quarters. The air belowdecks was cooler, smelling of wet metal and rust. Most of Michael's men were snoring in their racks, using this brief hiatus to rest and prepare themselves for what lay ahead.

Alicia lay on a lower bunk at the far end of the corridor. Peter pulled up a stool and cleared his throat. "So."

Staring upward, she had yet to look at him. "Say what's on your mind."

He wasn't entirely sure what that was. *I'm sorry I tried to strangle you?* Or *What were you thinking?* Perhaps he meant *Go to hell.*

"I'm here to offer a truce."

"A truce," Alicia repeated. "Sounds like Amy's idea."

"You tried to kill yourself, Lish."

"And it would have worked, too, if Michael hadn't decided to be the hero. I've got a bit of a bone to pick with the guy."

"Did you think the water would change you back?"

"Would it make you feel better if I did?" She blew out a breath. "I'm afraid that's not an option for me. Fanning was pretty clear on that score. No, I'd have to say that drowning was pretty much the goal."

"I can't believe that."

"Peter, what do you want? If you're here to pity me, I'm not interested."

"I'm aware of that."

"What you mean to say is that you need me."

He nodded. "That would be fair."

"And, under the circumstances, it's best if we bury the hatchet. Comrades, brothers-in-arms, no division within the ranks."

"More or less, yes."

With painful slowness, she turned her face toward him. "Want to know what I was thinking? While your hands were around my throat, I mean."

"If you want to tell me."

"I was thinking, Well, if anybody's going to strangle me, I'm glad it's my old friend Peter."

She'd spoken these words without bitterness; she was merely stating a fact.

"I was wrong," he said. "You didn't deserve it. I don't know what's between you and Fanning. I doubt I'll ever get it, frankly. But I sold you short."

She weighed his words, then shrugged. "So, you screwed up. Short of an outright apology, I guess I'll have to take that."

"I guess you will."

She gave him a look of warning. "I said I can get you in there, and I can. But you're throwing your life away."

"I'd say it's the opposite."

Alicia made a sound that began as a laugh but turned into a cough—deep, hacking. Her eyes clamped shut with pain. Peter waited for it to subside.

"Lish, are you all right?"

Her cheeks were flushed; spittle flecked her lips. "Do I look all right?"

"On the whole, you've seemed better."

She shook her head indulgently, the way a mother might with a hopeless child. "You never change, Peter. Fifty years I've known you, and you're still the same guy. Maybe that's why I can't stay mad at you."

"And I'll take that." He stood. "Need anything before we leave?"

"A new body would be nice. This one seems to have run its course."

"Short of that."

Alicia thought for a moment, then smiled. "I don't know—how about another rabbit?"

He found his son on deck, sitting on a wooden crate and watching Michael making his preparations on the fantail.

"You mind?" he asked.

Caleb scooted over.

"Where's Pim?"

"Asleep." His son turned and gave him a hard look. "Help me understand this."

"I'm not sure I can."

"Then why? What difference could it possibly make now?"

"People will come back someday. If Fanning's still alive, it starts all over again."

"You're going because of her."

Peter was speechless.

"Oh, don't look so surprised," Caleb went on. "I've known about it for years."

Peter didn't know how to respond. In the end, he could only admit the truth. "Well, you're right."

"Of course I'm *right*."

"Let me finish. Amy does have something to do with this, but she's not the only reason." He brought his thoughts into focus. "Here's the best way I have to explain it. It's a story about your father. At the Colony, we had a tradition. We called it standing the Mercy. When a person was taken up, a relative would wait for them each night on the city wall. We'd set out a cage with a lamb inside as bait. Seven nights, waiting for them to come home, and if they did, it was that person's job to kill them. It was usually the responsibility of the closest male relative, so when your father disappeared, I had to stand for him."

Caleb was watching his face closely. "How old were you?"

"Twenty, twenty-one? Just a kid."

"But he didn't come back. He'd been taken to the Haven."

"Yes, but I didn't know that. Seven nights, Caleb. That's a lot of time to think about killing a person, especially my own brother. At the start, I wondered if I actually could. Our parents had died, Theo was the only person I had left in the world. But as the nights passed, I came to understand something. There was something worse than killing him, and that would be letting somebody else do it. If the situation were reversed, if I had been the one taken up, I wouldn't have wanted it any other way. I didn't want to do it, believe me, but I owed him that much. The responsibility was mine and no one else's." Peter gave his words a moment to sink in. "That's what this is like, son. I don't know why it has to be me. That's a question I can't answer. But it doesn't matter. Pim and the kids—those are your responsibilities. You were put on earth to protect them till your last breath. That's your job. This is mine. You need to let me do it."

Aboard the *Nautilus,* Michael was issuing instructions to the crewmen who would assist in launching her. The hull had been wrapped in thick rope webbing; a steel boom and a system of blocks would be used to lift her from her cradle and lower her over the side. Once she was in the water, they would cut her free, raise the mast, and set sail for New York.

"He'll kill you," Caleb said.

Peter said nothing.

"And if you succeed? Amy can't leave. You said so yourself."

"No, she can't."

"So what then?"

"Then I live my life. Just like you're going to live yours."

Peter waited for his son to say more; when he didn't, he put his hand on Caleb's shoulder. "You have to accept this, son."

"It's not easy."

"I know it's not."

Caleb tipped his face upward. He swallowed, hard, and said, "When I was a kid, my friends always talked about you. Some of what they said was true, a lot of it was total bullshit. The funny thing was, I felt bad for you. I won't say I didn't like the attention, but I also knew you didn't want people to think of you like that. It kind of stumped me. Who wouldn't want to be a big deal, some kind of hero? Then one day it hit me. You felt that way because of me. I was the choice you'd made, and the rest didn't matter to you anymore. You would have been perfectly happy if the world just forgot about you."

"It's true. That's how I saw it."

"I felt so goddamn *lucky.* When you started working for Sanchez, I thought things might change, but they never did." He looked at Peter again. "So now you ask me if I can just let you go. Well, I can't. I don't have that in me. But I do understand."

They sat without speaking for a time. Around them, the ship was waking up, passengers rising, stretching their limbs. *Did that really happen?* they thought, their eyes blinking against an unfamiliar, oceanic light. *Am I really on a ship? Is that the sun, the sea?* How stunned they must be, thought Peter, by the infinite calm of it all. Voices accumulated—mostly the children, for whom a night of terror, abruptly and in a manner completely unforeseen, had opened a door to an entirely new existence. They had gone to sleep in one world and awakened in another, so dissimilar as to seem, perhaps, an alto-gether different version of reality. As the minutes passed, many of the passen-gers were drawn magnetically to the rail—pointing, whispering, chattering among themselves. As he listened, memories poured through him, as well as a sense of all the things he would never see.

Michael walked toward them. The man's eyes darted toward Caleb, quickly sizing up the situation, then back to Peter. Shuffling his hands in his pockets, he said, gently, almost as if he were apologizing, "The supplies are all aboard. I think we're about ready here."

Peter nodded. "Okay." But he made no move to do anything about this.

"Do you . . . want me to tell the others?"

"I think that would be good."

Michael walked away. Peter turned to his son. "Caleb—"

"I'm all right." He rose from the crate, holding himself stiffly, like a man with a wound. "I'll get Pim and the children."

Everyone gathered at the *Nautilus*. Lore and Rand operated the winch that hoisted Alicia, still strapped to her stretcher, to the cockpit. Michael and Peter carried her down to the boat's small cabin, then descended the ladder to join the others: Caleb and his family; Sara and Hollis; Greer, who had rebounded well enough from the crash to join them on deck, though his head was ban-daged and he stood unsteadily, one hand braced against the hull of the *Nauti-lus*. Everywhere on the ship, people were watching; the story had spread. It was 0830 hours.

The final goodbyes: no one knew where to start. It was Amy who broke the stalemate. She embraced Lucius, the two of them exchanging quiet words that no one else could hear, then Sara and then Hollis, who, of everyone, more so even than Sara, seemed undone by the weight of it all, hugging Amy tightly against his chest.

But, of course, Sara was steeling herself. Her composure was a ruse. She would not go to Michael; she simply could not bear to. Finally, as the various farewells proceeded around them, it was he who went to her.

"Oh, damn you, Michael," she said miserably. "Why are you always doing this to me?"

"I guess it's my talent."

She wrapped her arms around him. Tears squeezed from the corners of her eyes. "I lied to you, Michael. I never gave you up. Not for a day."

They parted; Michael turned to Lore. "I guess this is it."

"You always knew that you wouldn't be going, didn't you?"

Michael didn't answer.

"Oh, hell," Lore said. "I guess I kind of knew it, too."

"Take care of my ship," Michael said. "I'm counting on you."

Lore took his cheeks in her hands and kissed him, long and tenderly. "Stay safe, Michael."

He climbed aboard the *Nautilus*. At the base of the ladder, Peter shook Greer's hand, then Hollis's; he hugged Sara long and hard. He had already said goodbye to Pim and the children. His son would be the last. Caleb was standing to the side. His eyes were tight, withholding tears; he would not cry. Peter felt, suddenly, as if he were marching to his death. Likewise was he struck, as never before, by a sense of pride. This strong man before him. Caleb. His son, his boy. Peter pulled him into a firm embrace. He would not hold on long; if he did, he might not let go. It's children, he thought, that give us our lives; without them we are nothing, we are here and then gone, like the dust. A few seconds, recording all he could, and he stepped back.

"I love you, son. You make me very proud."

He climbed the ladder to join the others on the deck. Rand and Lore began to crank the winch. The *Nautilus* rose from her cradle and swung over the side. With a soft splash, the boat settled into the water.

"Okay, hold us there!" Michael called up.

They used their knives to cut the net. It passed beneath their stern, half-floating, then was dragged under the surface by its weight. Peter and Amy attached the guy wires while Michael set the lines that would pull the mast erect. They had begun to drift away from the *Bergensfjord*. When everything was ready, Michael commenced turning the winch. The mast rose into position; he locked it in place and unstrapped the sail from the boom. The distance to the *Bergensfjord* had increased to fifty yards. The air was warming, with a gentle breeze. The great ship's engines had come on. A new sound emerged, one of chains. Beneath the *Bergensfjord*'s bow, the anchor appeared, water streaming as it ascended. The ship's rail was lined with faces; people were watching them. Some began to wave.

"Okay, we're ready," Michael said.

They raised the mainsail. It flapped emptily, but then Michael pulled the tiller to one side and the bow veered slowly off the wind. With a pop, the canvas filled.

"We'll raise the jib once we're clear," said Michael.

Their velocity was, to Peter, quite startling. The boat, heeling slightly, possessed a stable feel, the point of its bow slicing cleanly through the water. The *Bergensfjord* receded behind them. The sky seemed infinitely deep.

It happened gradually, then all at once: they were alone.

79

Log of the *Nautilus*

Day 4: 27°95'N, 83°99'W. Wind SSE 10–15, gusts to 20.
  Skies clear, seas running 3–4 feet.
After three days of light air, we are finally making decent headway, running at 6–8 knots. I expect we will reach Florida's west coast by nightfall, just north of Tampa. Peter seems to be finally getting his sea legs. After three days vomiting over the side, he announced today that he was hungry. From Lish, not very much; she sleeps most of the time and has said virtually nothing. Everyone is worried about her.

Day 6: 26°15'N, 79°43'W. Wind SSE 5–10, shifting.
  Partly cloudy. Seas running 1–2 feet.
We have rounded the Florida peninsula and turned north. From here we will leave the coast behind and make a straight shot for the Outer Banks of North Carolina. Heavy clouds all night but no rain. Lish is still very weak. Amy finally talked her into eating, and Peter and I drew straws. He was the winner, though I guess it depends on how you look at it. I was a little nervous about Sara's instructions and I'm no good with needles, so Amy took over. One pint. We'll see if it helps.

Day 9: 31°87'N, 75°25'W. Winds SSE 15–20, gusts to 30.
  Skies clear. Seas running 5–7 feet.
A horrible night. The storm hit just before sunset—huge seas, high winds, driving rain. Everyone was up all night working the bailers. Blown way off

course, and the self-steerer is shot. We've taken on water, but the hull seems tight. Running reefed in heavy air, no jib.

Day 12: 36°75'N, 74°33'W. Winds NNE 5–10.
Patchy clouds. Seas running 2–3 feet.
We have decided to head west for the coast. Everyone is exhausted and needs to rest. On the bright side, Lish seems to have turned a corner. Her back is the issue; she's still in a lot of pain and can barely bend at all. My turn with the needle. Lish seemed to have a little fun with that. "Oh, buck up, Circuit," she said. "A girl's got to eat. Maybe your blood will make me smarter."

Day 13: 36°56'N, 76°27'W. Winds NNE 3–5. Seas running 1–2 feet.
Lying at anchor at the mouth of the James River. Fantastic wreckage everywhere—huge naval vessels, tankers, even a submarine. Lish's mood has improved. At sunset she asked us to bring her up on deck.

A beautiful starlit night.

Day 15: 38°03'N, 74°50'W. Winds light and variable. Seas 2–3 feet.
Under way again with fair winds. Running at 6 knots. Everyone feels it—we are getting closer.

Day 17: 39°63'N, 75°52'W. Winds SSE 5–10. Seas 3–5 feet.
Tomorrow we reach New York.

80

The four of them sat in the cockpit in the gathering dusk. They were lying at anchor; off the port bow, a long sandy line. The southern edge of Staten Island, once populated by a dense humanity, now exposed, swept clean, a wilderness.

"So, we're all in agreement?" Peter said, scanning the group. "Michael?"

Seated by the tiller, he was fingering a pocketknife, opening and closing the blade. His face had been crisped by salt and wind; through his beard, the color of sand, his teeth shone white. "I told you before. If you say that's the plan, then that's the plan."

Peter turned to Alicia. "Last chance to weigh in here."

"Even if I said no, you wouldn't listen."

"I'm sorry, that's not good enough."

She looked at him guardedly. "He's not going to just surrender, you know. 'I'm sorry, I guess I was wrong after all.' Not really the man's style."

"That's why I need you in the tunnel with Michael."

"I belong in the station with you."

Peter looked at her pointedly. "You can't kill him—you said so yourself. You can barely walk. I know you're angry and you don't want to hear this. But you need to put your feelings aside and leave that part to me and Amy. You'd only slow us down, and I need you to protect Michael. Fanning's virals won't attack you. You can give him cover."

Peter could see that his words had stung. Alicia glanced away, then back, her eyes narrowed with warning. "You realize that he knows we're coming. I seriously doubt any of this has escaped his attention. Waltzing into the station plays straight into his hands."

"That's the idea."

"And if this doesn't work?"

"Then we all die and Fanning wins. I'm willing to hear a better idea. You're the expert on the man. Tell me I'm wrong and I'll listen."

"That's not fair."

"I know it's not."

A brief silence passed. Alicia sighed in surrender. "Fine, I can't. You win."

Peter looked toward Amy. After two weeks at sea, her hair had grown out somewhat, softening her features while also making them seem clearer somehow, sturdier and more defined. "I think it all depends on what Fanning wants," she said.

"From you, you mean."

"Maybe he just intends to kill me, and if so, there's not a lot to stop him. But he's gone to a lot of trouble to get me here if that's all he has in mind."

"What do *you* think he wants?"

The light was nearly gone; from the shore, the long shushing of waves.

"I don't know," she said. "I agree with Lish, though. The man has something to prove. Beyond that . . ." She trailed off, then continued: "The important thing is to make sure he's in that station. Get him there and keep him there. We shouldn't wait for Michael. We need to be there when the water hits. That's our moment."

"So you agree with the plan."

She nodded. "Yes. I think it's our best chance."

"Let's look at that drawing."

Alicia had sketched a simple map: streets and buildings, but also what lay beneath them and points of access. To this she added verbal descriptions: how things looked and felt, certain landmarks, places where their passage would be obstructed by forest growth or collapsed structures, the sea's margins where it lapped over the southern tier of the island.

"Tell me about the streets around the station," Peter said. "How much shade is there for the virals to move in?"

Alicia thought for a moment. "Well, a lot. Midday you'd get more sun, but the buildings are all very tall. I'm talking sixty, seventy stories. It's like nothing you've ever seen in your life, and it can get pretty dark at street level any time of day." She drew their attention to the drawing again. "I'd say your best bet would be here, at the station's west exit."

"Why there?"

"Two blocks west, there's a construction site. The building's fifty-two stories tall, not huge by the standards of what's around it, but the top thirty stories are only framed in. There's good sun around the base, even late in the day. You can see it from the station—there's an external elevator and a crane up the side of the building. I used to spend a lot of time up there."

"On the crane, you mean?"

Alicia shrugged. "Yeah, well. It was kind of a thing with me."

She offered no more explanation; Peter decided not to press. He pointed to another spot on the map, a block east of the station. "What's this?"

"The Chrysler Building. It's the tallest thing around there, almost eighty stories. The top is made of this kind of shiny metal, like a crown. It's highly reflective. Depending on where the sun is, it can throw a lot of light."

The day was over; the temperature had dropped, drawing dew from the air. As a silence settled, Peter realized they had come to the end of the conversation. In a little under eight hours they would raise the sails, the *Nautilus* would make the final leg to Manhattan, and whatever was bound to happen there would happen. It was unlikely that all of them would survive, or even that any of them would.

"I'll take the watch," said Michael.

Peter looked at him. "We seem well protected here. Is that necessary?"

"The bottom's pretty sandy. The last thing we need is a dragging anchor right now."

"I'll stay, too," Lish said.

Michael smiled. "Can't say I'd mind the company." Then, to Peter: "It's fine, I've done it a million times. Go sleep. You two are going to need it."

Night spread her hands over the sea.

All was still: only the sounds of the ocean, deep and calm, and the lap of waves against the hull. Peter and Amy lay curled together on the cabin's only bunk, her head resting on his chest. The night was warm, but belowdecks the air felt cool, almost cold, chilled by the water encircling the bulkhead.

"Tell me about the farmstead," Amy said.

Peter needed a moment to gather his answer; lulled by the boat's motion and the feeling of closeness, he had, in fact, been skating on the edge of sleep.

"I'm not sure how to describe it. They weren't like ordinary dreams—they were far more real than that. Like every night I went someplace else, another life."

"Like . . . a different world. Real, but not the same."

He nodded, then said, "I didn't always remember them, not in detail. It was mostly the feeling that lasted. But some things. The house, the river. Ordinary days. The music you played. Such beautiful songs. I could have listened to them forever. They seemed so full of life." He stopped, then said, "Was it the same for you?"

"I think so, yes."

"But you're not sure."

She hesitated. "It only happened the one time, when I was in the water. I was playing for you. The music came so easily. As if the songs had been inside me and I was finally letting them out."

"What happened then?" Peter asked.

"I don't remember. The next thing I knew I woke up on the deck, and there you were."

"What do you think it means?"

She paused before answering. "I don't know. All I know is that for the first time in my life, I was truly happy."

For a while they listened to the quiet creaking of the boat.

"I love you," Peter said. "I think I always have."

"And I love you."

She drew herself closer against him; Peter replied in kind. He took her left hand, slipped her fingers through his, pulled it to his chest, and held it there.

"Michael's right," she said. "We should sleep."

"All right."

Soon she felt his breathing slow. It eased into a deep, long rhythm, like waves upon the shore. Amy closed her eyes, although she knew it was no use. She would lie awake for hours.

On the deck of the *Nautilus,* Michael was watching the stars.

Because a person could never grow tired of them. All his many nights at sea, the stars had been his most loyal companions. He preferred them to the moon, which seemed to him too frank, always begging to be noticed; the stars maintained a certain cagey distance, permitting the mystery of their hidden selves to breathe. Michael knew what the stars were—exploding balls of hydrogen and helium—as well as many of their names and the arrangements they made in the night sky: useful information for a man alone at sea in a small boat. But he also understood that these things were an imposed ordering that the stars themselves possessed no knowledge of.

Their vast display should have made him feel tiny and alone, but the effect was exactly the opposite; it was in daylight that he felt his solitude most keenly. There were days when his soul ached with it, the feeling that he had moved so far away from the world of people that he could never go back. But then night would fall, revealing the sky's hidden treasure—the stars, after all, weren't gone during the day, merely obscured—and his loneliness would recede, supplanted by the sense that the universe, for all its inscrutable vastness, was not a hard, indifferent place in which some things were alive and others not and all that happened was a kind of accident, governed by the cold hand of physical law, but a web of invisible threads in which everything was connected to everything else, including him. It was along these threads that both the questions and the answers to life pulsed like an alternating current, all the pains and regrets but also happiness and even joy, and though the source of this current was unknown and always would be, a person could feel it if he gave himself a chance; and the time when Michael Fisher—Michael the Circuit, First Engineer of Light and Power, Boss of the Trade and builder of the *Bergensfjord*—felt it most was when he was looking at the stars.

He thought of many things. Days in the Sanctuary. Elton's blind, rigid face and the hot, cramped quarters of the battery hut. The gassy stink of the refinery, where he had left boyhood behind and found his course in life. He thought of Sara, whom he loved, and Lore, whom he also loved, and Kate and the last time he had seen her, her compact youthful energy and easy affection for him on the night when he had told her the story of the whale. All so long ago, the past forever retreating to become the great internal accumulation of days. Probably his time on earth was reaching its end. Maybe something came after, beyond one's physical existence as a person; on this subject, the heavens were obscure. Greer certainly thought so.

Michael knew that his friend was dying. Greer had tried to conceal it, and nearly had, but Michael had figured it out. No one thing in particular had told him this; it was simply his sense of the man. Time was outstripping him—as, sooner or later, it did everyone.

And, of course, he thought about his ship, his *Bergensfjord*. She would be far away now, somewhere off the coast of Brazil, churning south beneath the selfsame starry sky.

"It's beautiful out here," Alicia said.

She was sitting across from him, reclining lengthwise on the bench, a blanket covering her legs. Her head, like his, was tipped upward, her eyes glazed by starlight.

"I remember the first time I saw them," she continued. "It was the night the Colonel left me outside the Wall. They absolutely terrified me." She pointed toward the southern horizon. "Why is that one so bright?"

He followed her finger. "Well, that's not a star, actually. It's the planet Mars."

"How can you tell?"

"You'll see it most of the summer. If you look closely, you can see that it has a slight red tint. It's basically a big, rusty rock."

"And that one?" Directly overhead this time.

"Arcturus."

In the dark, her expression was hidden from his view, though he imagined her frowning with interest. "How far away is it?"

"Not very, as these things go. About thirty-seven light-years. That's how long it takes the light to get here. When the light you're seeing left Arcturus, we were both a couple of kids. So when you look at the sky, what you're actually seeing is the past. But not just *one* past. Every star is different."

She laughed lightly. "That kind of messes with my head when you put it that way. I remember you telling me about this stuff when we were kids. Or trying to."

"I was pretty obnoxious. Probably I was just trying to impress you."

"Show me more," she said.

He did just that; Michael traced the sky. Polaris and the Big Dipper. Bright Antares and blue-tinted Vega and her neighbors, the small cluster known as Delphinius the Dolphin. The broad galactic band of the Milky Way, running horizon to horizon, north to south, bisecting the eastern sky like a cloud of light. He told her all he could think of, her interest never wavering, and when he was done, she said, "I'm cold."

Alicia scooted forward from the transom; Michael crossed over and wedged himself behind her, his legs positioned on either side of her waist. He pulled the blanket up, wrapping the two of them, drawing her in for warmth.

"We haven't talked about what happened on the ship," Alicia said.

"We don't have to if you don't want."

"I feel like I owe you an explanation."

"You don't."

"Why did you come in after me, Michael?"

"I didn't really give it a lot of thought. It was a heat-of-the-moment thing."

"That's not an answer."

He shrugged, then said, "I guess you could say I don't much like it when people I care about try to kill themselves. I've been down that road before. I take it kind of personally."

His words stopped her flat. "I'm sorry. I should have thought—"

"And there's absolutely no reason you would have. Just don't do it again, okay? I'm not such a great swimmer."

A silence fell. It was not uncomfortable but the opposite: the silence of shared history, of those who can speak without talking. The night was full of small sounds that, paradoxically, seemed to magnify the quiet: each shifting touch of water against the hull; the pinging of the lines against the spars; the creak of the anchor line in its cleat.

"Why did you name her *Nautilus*?" Alicia asked. The back of her head was resting against his chest.

"It was something from a book I read when I was a kid. It just seemed to fit."

"Well, it does. I think it's nice." Then, quietly: "What you said, in the cell."

"That I loved you." He felt no embarrassment, only the calm of truth. "I just thought you should know. It seemed like a big waste otherwise. I've kind of had it with secrets. It's okay—you don't have to say anything about it."

"But I want to."

"Well, a thank-you would be nice."

"It's not that simple."

"Actually, it's exactly that simple."

She fit the fingers of one hand into his, pressing their palms together. "Thank you, Michael."

"And you are most welcome."

The air was damp, mist falling, beads clinging to every surface. At an indeterminate distance, waves were hissing on the sand.

"God, the two of us," she said. "We've been fighting our whole lives."

"That we have."

"I'm so . . . tired of it." She drew his arm tighter around her waist. "I thought about you, you know. When I was in New York."

"Did you now?"

"I thought: What is Michael doing today? What is he doing to save the world?"

He laughed lightly. "I'm honored."

"As you should be." A pause; then she spoke again. "Do you ever think about them? Your parents."

The question, though unexpected, did not seem strange. "Once in a while. It was a long time ago, though."

"I don't really remember mine. They died when I was so young. Just little things, I guess. My mother had a silver hairbrush she liked. It was very old; I think it belonged to my grandmother. She used to visit me in the Sanctuary and brush my hair with it."

Michael considered this. "Now, that sounds right to me. I think I recall something like that happening."

"You do?"

"She'd put you on a stool in the dormitory, by the big window. I remember her humming—not a song exactly, more like just notes."

"Huh," Alicia said after a moment. "I didn't know anyone was paying attention."

They were quiet for a time. Even before she said the words, Michael sensed their approach. He did not know what she was about to tell him, only that she was.

"Something . . . happened to me in Iowa. A man raped me there, one of the guards. He got me pregnant."

Michael waited.

"She was a girl. I don't know if it was what I am or something else, but she didn't survive."

When Alicia fell silent, Michael said, "Tell me about her."

"She was Rose. That's what I named her. She had such beautiful red hair. After I buried her, I stayed with her awhile. Two years. I thought it would help, make things easier somehow. But it never did."

He felt, suddenly, closer to Alicia than he had to anyone in his life. Painful as this story was, telling him was a gift she had given him, the heart of who she was, the stone she carried and how love had happened in her life.

"I hope it's okay I told you."

"I'm very glad you did."

Another silence, then: "You're not really worried about the anchor, are you?"

"Not really, no."

"That was nice, what you did for them." Alicia tipped her head upward. "It's such a beautiful night."

"Yes, it is."

"No, more than beautiful," she said and squeezed his hand, nestling against him. "It's perfect."

81

So, at the last, a story.

A child is born into this world. She is lost, alone, in due course both befriended and betrayed. She is the carrier of a special burden, a singular vocation that is only hers to bear. She wanders in a wasteland, a ruin of grief and tormented dreams. She has no past, only a long, blank future; she is like a convict with an unknown sentence, never visited in the cell of her interminable imprisonment. Any other soul would be broken by this fate, and yet the child abides; she dares to hope that she is not alone. That is her mission, the role for which she has been cast at heaven's cruel audition. She is hope's last vessel on the earth.

Then, a miracle: a city appears to her, a bright walled city on a hill. Her prayers have been answered! Shining like a beacon, it has the aspect of a prophecy fulfilled. The key turns in the lock; the door swings open. Ensconced within its walls she discovers a wondrous race of men and women who have, like her, endured. They become hers, after a fashion. In the eyes of this wordless child, the most prescient among them perceive an answer to their most persistent questions; as they have relieved her loneliness, so has she relieved theirs.

A journey commences. The world's dark arrangement is revealed. The child grows; she leads her companion to a glorious victory. By her hand, seeds of hope are scattered over the land, promise bubbles forth from every spring and stream. And yet she knows this flowering is an illusion, the merest respite. There can be no safety; her triumphs have but scratched the crust. Below lies the dark core, that great iron ball beneath all things. Its compressed weight is fantastic; it is older than time itself. It is a vestige of the blackness that predates all existence, when a formless universe existed in a state of chaotic un-creation, lacking awareness even of itself.

She falters. She has doubts. She becomes indecisive, even fearful. Hers is the greatest of all errors; she has grown attached to life. She has dared, unwisely, to love. In her mind a contest rages, that of one who questions fate. Is she merely a lunatic's puppet? Is she destiny's slave or its author? Must she turn away from all the things and people she has grown to love? And is this love a reflection of some grand design, a taste of an ordered and divine creation? Is it truth or a departure from the truth? Romantic love, fraternal love, the love of a parent for a child and the love returned in kind—are they a mirror to God's face or the bitterest gall in a cosmos of sound and fury, signifying nothing?

As for me: there was a time in my life when I put aside all doubt and supped at the flower of heaven. What sweet juice was there! What balm to all suffering, the soul's holy ache! That my Liz was dying did not countermand my joy; she had come to me like a messenger, in the hours when all is laid bare, to reveal my purpose on the earth. All my days, I had scrutinized the tiniest workings of life. I had gone about this task blandly, never fathoming my true motive. I gazed upon the smallest shapes and processes of nature, seeking divinity's fingerprints. Now the evidence had come to me not at the end of a microscope but in the face of this slender, dying woman and the touch of her hand across a café table. My long, lonely hours—like yours, Amy—seemed not an exile or imprisonment but a test that I had passed. I was loved! Me, Timothy Fanning of Mercy, Ohio! Loved by a woman, loved by a god—a great, fatherly god, who, measuring my trials, had found me worthy. I had not been made for nothing! And not just loved; I had been charged as heaven's escort. The blue Aegean, where ancient gods and heroes were said to dwell; the whitewashed house one climbed a flight of stairs to reach; the humble bed and homespun furnishings; the workaday sounds of village life, and a terrace with a view of olive groves and the wild sea beyond; the soft white light of eternal mornings, growing brighter and brighter and brighter still. In my mind's eye I saw it, saw it all. In my arms she would pass from this life to the next, which surely existed after all, love having come to me—to both of us—at last.

Not an hour would have gone by, her body grown cold in my embrace, before I would have followed her from this world. That, too, was part of my design. I would take the last pills, the ones I'd saved for myself, and slip away in silence, so that together we would be bound eternally to each other and to an invincible universe. My resolve was implacable, my thoughts lucid as ice. I possessed not an iota of doubt. Thus at the anointed hour of our rendezvous I took my position at the kiosk, waiting for my angel to appear. In my suitcase, the instruments of our mortal deliverance slept like stones. Little did I know that this was but a foretaste of the wider ruin—that the hurrying travelers flowing around me possessed no inkling that death's prince stood among them.

Thrice have I been fathered; thrice betrayed. I will have satisfaction.

You, Amy, have dared to love, as once I did. You are hope's deluded champion, as I am sworn to be its enemy. I am the voice, the hand, the pitiless agent of truth, which is the truth of nothing. We were, each of us, made by a madman; from his design we forked like roads in a dark wood. It has ever been thus, since the materials of life assembled and crawled from nature's muck.

Your band approaches; the time grows sweeter by the hour. I know that he is with you, Amy. How could he fail to stand at your side, the man who made you human?

Come to me, Amy. Come to me, Peter.

Come to me, come to me, come to me.

82

It emerged like a vision, the great city, soaring from the sea like a castle or some vast holy relic. A ruin of staggering dimensions: it boggled the senses, its scope too massive to hold in the mind. The morning sun, low, slanting, blazed off the faces of the towers, ricocheting from the glass like bullets.

Peter joined Amy at the bow. She seemed almost preternaturally calm; a profound intensity radiated off her like heat from a stove. Minute by minute the metropolis loomed higher.

"Good God, it's enormous," Peter said.

She nodded, though this was only half the truth. Fanning's presence saturated the city. It was as if a background hum she'd been hearing all her life, so omnipresent as to be barely noticeable, were increasing in volume. She felt a heaviness. That was the only word. A terrible exhausted heaviness with everything.

They had decided to come in from the west. On tepid air they sailed up the Hudson, searching for a place to dock. Daylight was everything; they needed to move quickly. The tide was strong, pushing against them like an invisible hand.

"Michael . . ."

He was working the lines and tiller, seeking to harness any breath of wind. "I know."

The river was dark as ink; its force was immense. The day turned toward afternoon. At times they seemed stopped cold.

"This is impossible," said Michael.

By the time they found a place to tie off, it was four o'clock. Clouds had moved in from the south; the air was sultry, smelling of decay. Four, perhaps five hours of daylight remained. From the cabin, Michael retrieved the backpack of explosives, as well as a long spool of cable and the detonator, a wooden box with a plunger. It seemed primitive, but that was the point, he explained. The simple things were always the most reliable, and there would be no second chances to get this right. In the cockpit, they armed themselves and reviewed the plan a final time.

"Make no mistake," Alicia said, "this island is a deathtrap. It gets dark, we're done."

They disembarked. They were in the West Twenties. The roadway was choked with the skeletons of cars; glassless windows stared at them like the mouths of caves. Here they would diverge, Michael and Lish south to Astor Place, Peter and Amy across midtown to Grand Central. Michael had fashioned a crude crutch for Alicia from a boat oar.

"Sixty minutes," Peter said. "Good luck."

They parted cleanly, no goodbyes.

Peter and Amy walked north along Fifth Avenue. Block by block, the vertical core of the city rose, fashioning narrow fjords between the buildings. In places the pavement was buckled with the roots of trees, in others collapsed into craters that varied in size from a few yards to the width of the street, forcing them to creep along the edge. As they moved up the island, Peter took note of the landmarks: the Empire State, dizzyingly tall, like a single imperious finger pointing to the sky; the Chrysler Building, with its curved crown of burnished metal; the library, sheathed in a feathery cloak of vines, its broad front steps guarded by a pair of pedestaled lions. At the corner of Forty-second and Fifth, the half-constructed tower Alicia had described came into view. The exposed girders of its upper floors possessed a reddish appearance—the product of decades of slow oxidation. An exterior elevator ascended to the top of the structure; from there, the crane rose another ten or fifteen stories, its horizontal boom parallel to the building's west flank, high above Fifth Avenue.

So far, they had seen no trace of Fanning's virals—no scat or animal carcasses, no sounds of movement from the buildings. Except for pigeons, the city seemed dead. Each of them had a semiautomatic rifle and a pistol; Amy also carried the sword. She had offered it to Alicia, but the woman had refused. "Peter's right," Alicia said. "I've got no use for it. Just do me a favor and cut the bastard's head off."

They approached from the west, via Forty-third to Vanderbilt; between the buildings, a view of Grand Central emerged. Compared to what was around it, the structure seemed modest in its dimensions, nestled like a heart in the bosom of the city. The streets around it were open to the sun, though an elevated roadway encircled the perimeter at balcony level, creating a zone of darkness beneath.

Amy checked her watch: twenty minutes to go. "We need to scout that door," she said.

A risk, but Peter agreed. If they moved cautiously and kept low, maintaining an upward line of sight, they would be able to detect any virals beneath the overpass before they got too close.

Which was, Peter later realized, precisely what Fanning had intended them to do: to look *up*. Never mind Alicia's warnings not to underestimate their adversary. Never mind that the street was suspiciously carpeted in vines, or that with each step forward the air thickened with the damp, septic odor of an open sewer. Never mind the faint sound of rustling, which might have been caused by rats but wasn't. One careless moment was all it took. They crept beneath the overpass, every ounce of their attention focused on the empty ceiling.

Peter and Amy never even saw them coming.

Michael watched the numbers of the streets decline. A few were impassable, choked with vegetation or debris, others empty, as if forgotten by time. In some of the buildings, trees were growing; flocks of startled pigeons burst forth in their path, wheeling upward in huge, flapping clouds.

At the corner of Eighteenth and Broadway, they paused to rest. Alicia was breathing hard, her face glazed with sweat. "How much farther?" Michael asked.

She coughed and cleared her throat. "Eleven blocks."

"I can do this on my own, you know."

"Not a chance."

The crutch was too unstable; they left it behind and went on, Michael supporting Alicia from one side. A rifle dangled over her shoulder. Her steps were labored, more hobble than walk. From time to time, she issued a tiny gasp he knew she was trying to hide. The minutes dripped away. They came to a small shelter of elaborate iron scrollwork, painted white with pigeon guano. The smell of the sea had grown strong.

"This is it," she said.

From his pack, Michael removed a lantern and lit the wick. As they descended the stairs, he detected small movements along the floor. He paused and raised the lantern. Rats were scurrying everywhere, long brown ropes of them hugging the edges of the walls.

"Yuck," he said.

They reached the bottom. Arched brick columns supported the roof above the tracks. On the tiled wall, a sign in gold lettering read ASTOR PLACE.

"Which direction?" Michael felt turned around in the dark.

"This way. South."

He dropped onto the rail bed. Alicia handed him her rifle, and he helped her down. As they passed into the tunnel, the air became colder. Water sloshed at their feet. He counted their steps. At one hundred, the light of his lantern caught a frisson of movement: the hissing spray of water that shot from the edges of the bulkhead. He stepped forward and pressed his hand against the thick metal. Behind it lay untold tons of pressure, the weight of the sea, like an unfired cannon.

"How much time?" Alicia asked. She was leaning against the wall, scanning the tunnel with the rifle.

They had used forty-five minutes. He stripped off his pack and removed his supplies. Alicia was keeping watch on the far end of the tunnel. He twisted the wires of the blasting caps together, then clipped the end to the cable from the spool. Keeping everything dry would be a challenge; he had to prevent water from contacting the fuses. He returned the dynamite to his pack and searched the door for something to hang it on. Its surface was absolutely smooth.

"There," Alicia said.

Beside the bulkhead, a long rusty screw jutted from the wall. Michael hung his pack on it, handed Alicia the detonator, and began to pull out the cable from the spool.

"Let's go."

They emerged into the Astor Place station and scrambled onto the platform. Unspooling the cable behind them, they headed for the stairs and ascended to the first landing. A particle-filled daylight filtered down from street level. Kneeling, Michael placed the plunger on the floor, split the cable with his teeth, and threaded one wire into each of the two slotted screws on the top of the box. Alicia was sitting on the step below him, goggles pushed up onto her forehead, her rifle pointed into the blackness below. Circles of sweat drenched her shirt at the throat and armpits; her jaw was tight with pain. As he tightened the wing nuts, their eyes met.

"That ought to do it," Michael said.

Ten minutes to go.

Amy in darkness: First came the pain, a sharp-edged thudding at the back of her skull. This was followed by the sensation of being dragged. Her thoughts refused to organize. Where was she? What had occurred? What force was pulling her along? Solitary pictures drifted by, pushed by mental winds: a television screen of spitting static; fat, feathered snowflakes descending from an inky sky; Carter's garden, a carpet of living color; the tossing, blue-black sea. There was the floor—dirty, scuffed. Her tongue was dense and heavy in her mouth. She tried to make a sound, but none would come. The floor passed by in aortal jerks, timed to the rhythm of the tugging pressure on her wrists. The idea of resistance took hold, but when she attempted to move her limbs, she found she had no power to act; her body had been sundered from her will.

She sensed, then saw, a light, a kind of filtered glowing, and in the next instant everything changed: how the air moved on her skin, the way sound behaved, her intuitive sense of the physical parameters around her. Noises expanded and leapt away; the air smelled different, less confined, with a bio-logical tang.

"Leave her there, please."

The voice—nonchalant, even a little bored—came from someplace ahead. The pressure on her wrists released; her face slammed into the floor. A hot, glowing ball ricocheted around the interior of her skull like an ember spat from a fire.

"*Gently,* for God's sake."

Consciousness ebbed, then, like a dark wave returning to shore, broke upon her again. She tasted blood in her mouth; she had bitten her tongue. The floor was cool against her cheek. The light, what was it? And the sound? A low-grade murmuring, not made by voices per se but by a volume of breathing bodies. She sensed the presence of faces. Faces and also hands, lurking in a fog. Her brain told her: *Look harder, Amy. Focus your eyes and look.*

It wasn't good. It wasn't good at all.

She was surrounded by virals. The first layer was crouched around her at a distance of just a yard or two—jaws clicking, throats amphibiously bobbing, hooked fingers caressing the air with small, syncopated movements, as if tapping the keys of invisible pianos. This was bad, but not the worst of it. The room writhed and throbbed, a population of hundreds. They carpeted the walls. They gazed down from the balconies like spectators at a contest. They filled each nook and corner and perched atop every ledge. The space was squirming like a pit of snakes.

"That all went rather smoothly," the voice drolly continued. "I'm a little bit amazed, actually. I was worried that their enthusiasm might get the better of them. They do that."

She was still having difficulty bringing her mind and her body into align-ment, to forge the proper chain of command. Everything seemed delayed and out of sync. The voice seemed to emanate from everywhere around her, as if the air were speaking. It flowed over and into her like slick oil, lodging with cloying, buttery sweetness at the back of her throat.

"Would it be too obvious to say how long I've waited to meet you? But I have. Since the day Jonas told me of your existence, I've wondered, When will we meet? When will my Amy come to me?"

"My Amy." Why was the voice calling her that? She discovered the sky. No, not the sky: the ceiling, far above, and on it the image of the stars with gilded figures floating among them.

"Oh, you should have heard the man. How *guilty* he felt. How *sorry* he was. 'Jesus, Tim, you should see her. She's just a little kid. She doesn't even have a proper last name. She's just some girl from nowhere.'"

The backward stars, thought Amy. As if the heavens were being viewed from without, or were reflected in a mirror. She felt her thoughts attaching to this notion, and as they did, new ideas began to form. As if stumbling from a dream, her mind began to open to her circumstances; memories were rising to the surface. An image entered her mind: Peter, his body airborne, crashing through a plate-glass window.

A dark chuckle. "Not really funny, I suppose, when you put it in the context of a few billion corpses. Still, the whole thing was quite a performance. Jonas missed his true calling. He should have been an actor."

Fanning, she thought.

The voice was Fanning.

And everything came slamming back.

"I waited so long, Amy." A heavy sigh. "Always hoping that my Liz would be on the next train. Do you know what that's like? But how could you. How could anyone?"

She struggled onto all fours. She was in the west end of the hall. To her right, the ticket windows, barred like cells in a jail; to her left, the shadowy recesses of train platforms. Shrouded windows, both behind her and to her right, pulsed with a febrile glow. Ahead, at a distance of perhaps a hundred feet, stood the kiosk, topped by its pearlescent clocks. A man was standing there. An altogether unremarkable-looking man, wearing a dark suit. He was positioned in profile, back erect and chin tipped slightly upward, left hand tucked casually in the pocket of his suit coat, his attention aimed at the dark maws of the tunnels.

"How alone she must have felt at the end, how afraid. No words of comfort. Not the touch of a hand for company."

Still he did not look at her. All around her, the virals trilled and stroked, flexed and snapped. She had the sense that they were kept at bay only by the thinnest of invisible barriers.

"'I have known the evenings, mornings, afternoons, I have measured out my life with coffee spoons.' That's T. S. Eliot, in case you were wondering. An oldie but a goodie. When it came to existential exhaustion, the man was one smart cookie."

Where was Peter? Had the virals killed him? What of Michael and Alicia? She thought: Water. She thought: Time. How much had passed? But the answer to this question was like an empty drawer in her brain. Moving just her eyes, she scanned for something to use as a weapon. But there was nothing, only the virals and the inverted heavens and her heart beating in her throat.

"Oh, I had my books, my thoughts. I had my memories. But those things only take a man so far." Fanning paused, then said, with more directness, "Consider this place, Amy. Imagine it as it once was. Everyone hurrying, rushing here, rushing there. The appointments. The assignations. The dinners with friends. How gloriously alive it was. All our lives, the one thing we never seem to have enough of is time. Time to work. Time to eat. Time to sleep. Time to love and be loved before it's time to die." He shrugged. "But I digress. You came to kill me, wasn't it?"

He turned to face her. His right hand, now revealed, held the sword.

"Just to clear the decks, let me say that I don't hold it against you in the least. *Au contraire, mon amie.* That's French, by the way. Liz always said it was the mark of a truly cultured person. I never had much of a knack for languages, but with a century to kill, you get around to trying new things. Any preference? Italian, Russian, German, Dutch, Greek? How about Latin? We could do this whole thing in Norwegian if you'd like."

Close your mouth, Amy's brain commanded her. *Use the silence, because it's all you have.*

Fanning's face soured. "Well, your choice. I was only trying to make a little small talk." He gave a backhanded wave. "Let's have a look at you."

More hands upon her: a large, smooth male and a slightly smaller female, with a wispy diadem of white hair on her otherwise featureless skull. They seized her by the upper arms and whisked her forward, her feet skimming the tile, and dumped her unceremoniously to the floor.

"I said gently, for fucksake!"

Looming like a thundercloud, Fanning stood above her, his aura of merry confidence replaced by jaw-clenched rage.

"You." He pointed the sword at the large male. "Get over here."

A spark of hesitation in the creature's eyes—or did she imagine this? The viral scuttled forward. It dropped to its knees at Fanning's feet and bowed its head submissively, like a subdued dog.

Fanning raised his voice to the room. "Everyone, are you listening? Are you hearing my words, goddamnit? This woman is our guest! She is not a piece of luggage for you to toss around as you please! I expect you to treat her with respect!"

As he raised the sword, Amy covered her head. A crack, followed by a grinding sound and then the thump of something heavy hitting the floor. A wet stickiness splashed the side of her face and, with it, a rotten smell, as if a door had blown open onto a room of corpses.

"Oh, for the love of God."

The viral was still on its knees, its headless torso folded forward to the floor. Dark, rhythmic spurts were convulsing from its severed neck, forming a glossy pool on the floor. Fanning was staring at the front of his pants with revulsion. His suit, Amy realized, was rotten and threadbare. It hung on his body with the unstructured looseness of rags.

"Look at this," he moaned. "This is never going to come out. They're like pets, the mess they make. And the stink. Just god-awful."

It was absurd, all of it. What had she expected? Not this. Not this whirlwind of instantly changeable moods and thoughts. This man before her: there was something almost pathetic about him.

"Well, now," he said, and smiled nonsensically. "Let's get you to your feet, shall we?"

She was hauled upright. Fanning stepped forward; from his pocket he produced a handkerchief, flapped it open with a flourish, and dabbed the blood from her face. His eyes seemed both close and far away, peculiarly magnified, as if she were observing them through a telescope. On his cheeks and chin was a dusting of whitish beard; his teeth were gray, dead-looking. He hummed tunelessly as he went about this chore, then took a step back, lips pursed, brow furrowed, examining his handiwork with a slow nod.

"Much better." He regarded her at uncomfortable length, then declared, "I have to say, there's something very appealing about you. A certain innocence. Though I'm guessing there's more there than meets the eye."

"Where's Peter?"

His eyes widened. "She speaks! I was beginning to wonder." Then, dismissively: "Not to worry about your friend. Delayed in traffic, I expect. As for me, I'm glad the two of us can have this chance to talk amongst ourselves. I hope this doesn't seem too forward, but I feel a certain kinship with you, Amy. Our journeys are not so very different when you think about it. But first: where, pray tell, is my friend Alicia? This specimen of overgrown table cutlery tells me she's around here someplace."

Amy didn't answer.

"Nothing to share on the subject? Have it your way. Do you know what you are, Amy? I've given it a lot of thought."

Let him talk, she told herself. Time was what she needed. Let him use the minutes.

"You're . . . an apology."

Fanning said nothing further. The virals held her fast. He stepped away toward the train tunnels, where he resumed his original position, gazing forlornly into the blackness.

"For a long time, I wanted to kill you. Well, perhaps not 'wanted.' You can't help being what you are, any more than I can. It wasn't anything personal. You were merely a symbol, a stand-in for the thing I hated most." He turned the sword in his hand, studying the blade. "Imagine it, Amy. Imagine the folly of the man. He actually *believed* he could make everything all right, that he could atone for his crimes. But he couldn't. Not after what he did to Liz. To me, to you." He looked up. "She was nothing to me, the other one. Just some woman in a bar, looking for a night of fun, a bit of company in her lonely little life. I regret that intensely."

Amy waited.

"I thought I could forget about it. But that was the night. I see that now. It was the night the truth of the world opened to me. It wasn't the woman that did it. No, it was the child. The little girl in the crib. Do you know that I can still smell her, Amy? That sweet soft odor that all babies have. It's practically holy. Her little fingers and toes, the smoothness of her skin. Her whole life was in her eyes. All of us begin that way. You, me, everyone. Full of love, full of hope. I could see it: she trusted me. Her mother lay dead on the kitchen floor, but here was this man, come to answer her cries. Would I give her a bottle? Change her diaper? Perhaps I would pick her up, take her on my lap and read her a story. She had no idea what I'd done, what I *was*. I felt so sorry for her. But that wasn't the reason. I felt sorry because she'd had to be born in the first place. I should have killed her right then. It would have been a mercy."

A silence caught and held. Then:

"I see from your expression that I appall you. Believe me, I appall myself sometimes. But the truth is the truth. There's no one watching over us. That's the cold heart of it, the grand delusion. Or if there is, he's the cruelest kind of bastard, letting us believe he cares. I'm nothing, compared to him. What kind of God would allow her mother to die like that? What God would let Liz be all alone at the end, not the touch of a hand or a single word of kindness to help her leave her life? I'll tell you what kind, Amy. The same one who made me." He turned toward her again. "Your friends on the boat will be back, you know. Don't be surprised—I know all about it. I practically watched them sail away from the pier. Oh, maybe not soon. But eventually. Their curiosity will get the better of them. It's simple human nature. All of this will be dust by then, but here I'll be, waiting."

Do it, Alicia, she thought. *Do it, Michael. Do it now.*

"What do I want, Amy? The answer is quite simple: I want to save you. More than that. I want to teach you. To make you see the truth." His expression darkened. "Hold her tightly, please."

The clock had run down. Michael glanced at Alicia. "Ready?"

She nodded.

"You might want to cover your ears."

He shoved down the plunger.

"What the hell, Circuit?"

He drew up the bar and tried again. Nothing. He pulled the positive wire, touched it lightly to the contact, and pressed the plunger a third time. A spark leapt.

He had current; the problem was at the other end.

"Stay here."

He unscrewed the second wire, grabbed the plunger box and lantern, and tore down the stairs.

The strength of the virals' grip increased with a hot jab. The pain was eye-watering; bits of confettied light danced in her vision.

"Bring him in, please."

Peter.

Two virals dragged him from the direction of the tunnels. His body hung floppily, facedown, the tips of his boots skimming the floor.

"It's the only way, Amy. I wish there were another, but there simply isn't."

Amy could barely think. The slightest movement ignited shrieks of agony. It felt as if the bones of her upper arms were about to shatter under the pressure of the virals' hands, to crumble into dust.

"Ah, here we are."

The virals halted, still holding Peter by the shoulders. Blood was dripping from his hair, flowing down the creases of his face. Fanning stepped toward him, sword extended. Amy's breath stopped in her throat. He positioned the flat of the blade beneath Peter's chin and, with cruel slowness, tilted his face upward.

"You care about this man, do you not?"

Peter found Amy with his eyes but seemed unable to focus. His mouth was moving soundlessly, with what might have been a sigh or groan.

"Answer the question."

"Yes," she said.

"So much that you would do anything to save him, in fact."

Her vision swam. To be undone so easily; that was the cruelest thing.

"Say it, Amy. Let me hear the words."

Her answer came out with a choking sound: "Yes, I'd do anything to save him." Her head rolled forward in defeat; she had nothing left. "Please, just let him go."

One flick of the wrist and his throat would open like paper. Peter's eyes were closed, preparing for death. That or he had slipped back into a merciful unconsciousness.

"Let me show you something," Fanning said. "It's a little talent I've discovered. Jonas would get a real kick out of this."

He did something strange: he began to undress. First the suit coat, which he folded in half and lay neatly on the floor with the sword, then his shirt, unbuttoning it to reveal a fan of downy white chest hair and a smooth, leanly muscled trunk.

"I have to say, it's good to finally get out of these clothes." He had knelt to untie his shoes. "To put aside these *trappings.*"

Shoes, socks, pants. The air around him had begun to change. It fluttered like waves of heat above a desert road. He rocked his head toward the ceiling; a sheen of oily sweat appeared on his skin. He licked his lips with a slow tongue and began to roll his shoulders and neck, his eyes half-lidded, lost in sensation.

"God, that's good," he said.

With a bony pop, Fanning arced his back and moaned with pleasure. His hair was ejecting in clumps; fat, throbbing veins pulsed beneath the skin of his face and chest, tatting a bluish web. He rocked his jaw, showing his fangs. His fingers, from which long, yellowish nails now protruded, flexed restlessly.

"Isn't it . . . wonderful?"

Michael hit the tunnel, Alicia shouting his name behind him. Rats were suddenly everywhere, an undulating wave of them, flowing toward the bulkhead.

The screw had torn loose; the pack lay in the water. The fuses were soaked and useless.

"Fuck!"

His eyes fell on a small electrical panel, at eye level, just to the right of the bulkhead. The ground was boiling with rats. They were swarming around his ankles, brushing against his legs with their soft, nauseating weight. With the tip of a screwdriver, he popped the door and waved the lantern over the interior.

"Get back!"

Alicia was standing a few yards behind him. Thirty feet away, a viral was crouched on the floor of the tunnel; a second clung to the ceiling, its inverted head rocking side to side. The long, bald tail of a rat was whipping from its mouth.

"Go on, beat it!" The virals merely looked at her. "Get out of here!"

The inside of the panel was a tangled mess of wires connected to a breaker board. Give me an hour, Michael thought, and I can do something with this, no problem.

"These guys look hungry, Circuit. Tell me you've figured this out."

God, how he hated that name. He was pulling wires free, attempting to separate them into some kind of coherence, to trace them back to their source.

"More coming!"

He glanced over his shoulder. The walls of the tunnel had begun to glow green. There was a skittering sound, like dry leaves rolling on pavement. "I thought these guys were your friends!"

Alicia fired at the viral on the ceiling. Her aim was unsteady; sparks flew up. The viral skittered backward, dropped, and came up on all fours. "I don't think it's me they're interested in!"

He sliced off a length of cable, stripped the ends, and screwed them to the plunger. Holding the wire, he gave a final look into the panel. He would have to take a wild guess. This one? No, that.

A barrage of fire behind him. "I'm not kidding, Michael, we've got about ten seconds!"

With four quick turns, he spliced the ends of the wires together. Alicia was backing toward him, firing in short bursts. The sound reverberated off the walls of the tunnel, hammering his eardrums. Good God, he was tired of this sort of thing. Tired of guesswork and laboring in the dark, tired of leaking valves and bad circuits and busted relays—tired of things not working, things that refused to bend to his will.

"Need some help here!" Alicia yelled.

Her rifle drained, Alicia tossed it aside and drew a pair of blades from her belt, one for each fist. Michael grabbed her around the waist and pulled her into him.

The tunnel was a squirming mass.

They fell backward as the first viral careened forward. Michael drew his sidearm and fired two shots, the first sparking off its shoulder, the second catching it in the left eye. A splash of blood and with a shriek it skidded to the floor. They were scooting backward toward the bulkhead, Michael firing his pistol, shoving his heels against the concrete, one arm encircling Alicia's waist to drag her with him through the fetid water. He had fifteen rounds in the gun, another two magazines stashed in a pocket, useless and out of reach.

The slide locked back.

"Oh, shit, Michael."

So: the end of the line. How slow its approach, how sudden its arrival. We never truly believe it's coming, he thought, and then before we know it, it's here. All the things we've done in our lives, and the undone things as well, extinguished in an instant. He dropped the gun and pulled Alicia tight against him. His hand was on the plunger.

"Close your eyes," he said.

The change was complete.

Fanning's face was still tipped upward, lips parted, eyes shut. A sigh of satisfaction heaved from deep in his chest. The being before her was not one Amy had ever seen or imagined—still recognizable as himself but neither wholly man nor wholly viral. An amalgam, half one and half the other, as if a new version of the species had been born into the world. There was something of the rodent about him, the nose snoutlike and full-nostriled, the ears triangulated at the top and swept back from the curve of his skull. His hair was gone, replaced by pinkish natal fuzz. His teeth were the same, though the mouth itself had enlarged into a kind of windblown grin, giving a full view of his fangs, which dripped from the corners. His limbs possessed a thin-boned delicacy; the index fingers of both hands had elongated to curve-tipped points.

Amy thought of a giant wingless bat.

He stepped toward her. His eyes locked on hers; she dared not look away, no matter how much she wanted to. Fear had paralyzed her limbs. They felt far away and useless, loose as liquid. As Fanning neared, his right hand rose. The digits were webbed with a translucent membrane. The daggered index finger, jointed in the middle, unfurled toward her face. Her eyes clamped shut instinctively. A prick of pressure on her cheek, not quite hard enough to break the skin: every molecule in her body shuddered. With lascivious slowness the nail traced downward, following the curve of her face. As if he were tasting her flesh through his finger.

"How good it is to let the truth come out."

His voice, too, had altered, possessing a high, hidden note with a squeaking sound. The air around him smelled of animals. The small, burrowing things of the world.

"Open your eyes, Amy."

Fanning was standing beside Peter. The virals had hauled him upright.

"This man, he is your curse, as Liz was mine. It's love that enslaves us, Amy. It is the play within the play, the stage on which the tragic drama of our human lives unfolds. That is the lesson I have to teach you."

And with these words, Fanning opened his jaws wide, tipped Peter's face upward on the end of one long, webbed digit—tenderly, like a mother with her child—and clamped his jaws around Peter's neck.

The squeak of current from the plunger was not enough to open the bulkhead all the way; but it was enough to get things started. As the door's counterweights jolted downward, creating a gap between the door and the floor of the tunnel, Michael and Alicia were blasted by a jet of water. In less than a second, the tunnel became a roaring river. Michael attempted to rise, but the force was too great, he could find no traction, and then they were tumbling, hurtled downstream in the roiling water.

They plunged into the station, going like a shot. There was no real light, only a vague glow from the stairway, glimpsed fleetingly as they passed. Water filled his nose and mouth, foul-tasting—he imagined this to be the taste of rats—and threatening to choke him. They were riding just beneath the platform. Gripping Alicia by the wrist, Michael reached out with his free hand and made a desperate lunge for the edge. His fingers touched but tore away.

They passed through the station. The water was rising fast; soon it would be over their heads. The next station would come at Fourteenth Street—much too far. Ahead, a faint glow appeared. As they neared, the light congealed into a discrete shaft—an opening in the roof of the tunnel.

"There's a ladder!" Alicia cried. Her head went under again.

"What?"

Her face reemerged; she was fighting for breath. She pointed. "A ladder on the wall!"

They were sailing straight for it. Alicia grabbed hold first. Michael spun around her body, then, using his left hand, reached out, seized a rung, and hooked an elbow through it. At the top of the ladder was a metal grate, daylight beyond it.

"Can you make it?" Michael said.

They were being pummeled by the current. Lish shook her head.

"Try, damn it!"

Her strength was gone; she had nothing left. "I can't."

He would have to pull her up. Michael reached above her head and drew himself free of the water. The grate presented a different problem; unless he could find a way to open it, they were going to drown anyway. At the top of the ladder, he raised one hand and pushed. Nothing, not the slightest tremor. He reared back and shoved the heel of his palm into the slatted metal. He punched the grate again, and again. On the fourth blow, it burst open.

He shoved it aside, climbed out, and pressed his body to the pavement. The rising water had lifted Alicia halfway up the ladder. The light seemed to make a kind of halo around her face.

He reached down. "Take my hand—"

But that was all he said, his words cut short as a wall of water slammed into her—into both of them—bursting like a geyser through the open grate and blowing Michael halfway across the street.

The collapse of the bulkhead just south of the Astor Place station—one of eight retention dams protecting the subway lines of Manhattan from the greedy Atlantic—was the first in a series of events that no person, Michael included, could have anticipated. Freed from incarceration, the water shot through the tunnel with the hammering power of a hundred locomotives. It ripped and tore. It blasted to bits. It detonated and crushed and destroyed, plowing through the structural underpinnings of lower Manhattan like a scythe through wheat. Eight blocks north of Astor Place, at Fourteenth Street, the water jumped the tracks. While the main body churned straight north beneath Lexington Avenue, toward Grand Central, the rest veered west on the Broadway line, roaring toward the bulkhead at Times Square, which would subsequently fail as well, flooding everything beneath the pavement south of Forty-second Street between Broadway and Eighth Avenue and opening the whole West Side to the sea.

And it was only just getting started.

In its thundering wake, the water left a trail of destruction. Manhole covers blew sky-high. Sewers exploded. Streets buckled and collapsed. Beneath the ground, a chain reaction had commenced. Like the ocean of which it was a part, the raging water sought only the expansion of its domain; the prize was the island itself, which, after a century of sodden neglect, was rotten to the core.

On the corner of Tenth Street and Fourth Avenue, Michael returned to consciousness with the unsettled sense that the world's relationship to gravity had altered. It was as if every object were moving away from every other in a state of general repulsion. He blinked his eyes and waited for this feeling to stop, but it did not. A great font of water was jetting from the grate, high into the air, dissolving at the top into a sparkling mist that cast a rainbow above the flooded street. In his mentally fogged state, Michael stared at it in astonishment, not yet connecting the sight to anything else, while also noting, rather blandly, that other things were occurring: loud things, concussive things, things that warranted further consideration if only he could marshal his thoughts. The street seemed to be sinking—either that or everything else was getting taller—and bits of material were sailing off the faces of the buildings.

Wait a second.

The structure he was looking at—a nondescript, mid-rise office building of dark tinted glass—was doing something peculiar. It appeared to be . . . breathing. A deep respiratory flexing, like a baby's first breaths of life. It was as if this anonymous structure, one of thousands like it on the island, had awakened after decades of abandoned slumber. Spidering cracks materialized in its reflective face. Michael sat upright, balancing on his palms. The pavement had begun to undulate disturbingly beneath him.

The glass exploded.

Michael rolled and flattened himself to the ground, covering his head as a million shards rained down. Whole plates detonated on the pavement. He was yelling at the top of his lungs. Nonsensical words, vile curses, an aural vomitus of terror. He was about to be diced to ribbons. There wouldn't be enough of him left to bury, not that there would be anybody around to do that. The seconds passed, glass cascading all around him, Michael waiting, for the second time that day, to die.

He didn't.

He lifted his face from the pavement. The sun was gone, the air grown dim. Tiny, twinkling shards covered his body, clinging to his arms and hands and hair and the fabric of his clothing. A gritty wind swirled the air. The sky, it seemed, had begun to issue snow. No, not snow. Paper. A single page dropped lazily into his hands. "Memo," it read at the top. And, beneath that, "From: HR Department. To: All employees. Re: Benefits enrollment period." Michael was momentarily transfixed by the strangeness of these words. They felt like a code. Within their mysterious phrasing lay an entire reality, a world lost in time.

Suddenly the paper was gone; a gust of air had stripped it from his hand. The street was darkening. A roaring sound came from his left. Second by second it increased, as did the wind. He turned his head to look uptown, toward the source of the noise.

A great gray monster was roaring toward him.

He scrambled to his feet. His head was swimming; his legs felt like wet sand.

He ran, nonetheless, like hell.

The first building to fall was not the one Michael saw. By this time, the collapse of midtown Manhattan was several minutes old. From the south edge of Central Park to Washington Square, edifices large and small were in the process of acute structural liquefaction, melting and toppling into the gobbling sinkhole that the island's central core was on its way to becoming. Some fell independently, crumpling vertically into their foundations like prisoners felled by a firing squad. Others were encouraged by their neighbors, as building after building teetered and toppled into others. A few, such as the great glass tower on the east side of the trapezoidal city block at Fifty-fifth and Broadway, appeared to succumb entirely through the power of suggestion: *My fellows are giving up the ghost—why don't I do that also?* The process might have been likened to a swiftly moving metastasis; it leapt across the boulevards as if from organ to organ, it churned through the avenues of blood, it wrapped its lethal fingers around the bones of steel. Dust clouds roared in a great carcinogenic regurgitation, blackening the skies.

An ersatz night fell over Manhattan.

Beneath Grand Central Station, the water arrived from two directions: first via the Lexington Avenue subway line from Astor Place, then, a few seconds later, through the Forty-second Street shuttle line from Times Square. The currents converged; like a tsunami compressing as it approached the shore, the water's power magnified a thousand-fold as it tore up the stairs.

"You ungrateful bitch!" Fanning cried. "What have you done?"

He said no more; the water arrived, a pounding wall, blasting them off their feet. In a blink, the main hall was subsumed. Amy went under. She was rolling, tossing, her sense of direction obliterated. The water was six feet deep and rising. Glass was shattering, things were falling, everything was in a tumult. She broke the surface in time to see the hall's high windows burst inward; the current grabbed her, sending her under again. She flailed helplessly, searching for something to grasp. The body of a viral careened into her. It was the female with the hair. Through the roaring murk, Amy glimpsed her eyes, full of terrified incomprehension. She sank and was gone.

Amy was being swept toward the balcony stairs. She impacted hard—more bells, more pain—but she managed to grab hold of the rail with her right hand. Her lungs cried out for air; bubbles rose from her mouth. The urge to breathe could not be forestalled much longer. The only thing to do was let the current take her, in the hope that she would be carried to safety.

She let go of the rail.

She smashed into the stairs again, but at least she was moving in the right direction. If she'd been carried into the tunnels, she would have drowned. A second shock wave hit her, squirting her upward.

She landed on the balcony, clear of the water at last. On her hands and knees, she coughed and retched, foul-tasting water spewing from her mouth.

Peter.

Hurled up the stairs by the same current, he was lying just a few feet behind her. Where was Fanning? Had he been pulled under like the other virals, carried to the bottom by his weight? As she thought this, the floor lurched. The air cracked. She looked up to see a large chunk of the ceiling detach and tumble to the water.

The building was coming down.

Peter's chest was moving rapidly. The change had yet to begin. She shook him by the shoulders, called his name; his eyes fluttered open, then squinted at her face. She saw no recognition in them, only vague puzzlement, as if he could not quite place her.

"I'm going to get you out of here."

She drew him up by his arms and folded his body over her right shoulder. Her balance wavered, but she managed to hold on. The floor was sliding and undulating like the deck of a boat. Hunks of ceiling continued to break away as the building's structural underpinnings failed.

She looked around. To her right, a door.

Run, she thought. *Run and keep on running.*

Then they were outside, though it hardly seemed so. The sky was dark as night, the sun eclipsed by dust, the great city unrecognizable. A vast immolation, everything rushing to ruin. The noise hammered her ears, roaring from all directions. She was on the elevated roadway on the west side of the station. It was tipped at a precarious angle; cracks were spreading, whole sections collapsing. Amy picked a direction; under Peter's weight, the best she could manage was a jog. Instinct was her only guide. To run. To survive. To carry Peter away.

The road sloped down to street level. She could go no farther; her legs were giving way. At the base of the ramp, she eased Peter to the ground. He was trembling—shaking with small, sharp spasms, like the chills of a fever, but growing stronger, more defined. Amy knew what he would want. He would want to die while still a man. The mortal instruments lay everywhere among the wreckage: segments of rebar sharp as knives, hunks of twisted metal, shards of glass. Suddenly she knew: this was what Fanning had intended, all along. That she should be the one. *It's love that enslaves us, Amy.* She was beaten; it was all for nothing in the end. She would be alone again.

As she knelt beside him, a great sob shook her, the pain of her too-long life, forestalled for a century, unleashed. The glimpse of life she'd been given: how fleeting it was. Better, perhaps, never to have had it. Peter had begun to moan. The virus churned inside him; it bore him away.

She made her choice: a three-foot length of steel with a triangulated tip. What function had it served? Part of a signpost? The frame of a window that had once gazed out upon the busy world? The underpinnings of a mighty tower soaring to the sky? She knelt again by Peter's body. The man inside was leaving. She bent and touched his cheek. His skin was damp and feverish. The blinking had commenced. Blink. Blink, blink.

A voice from behind: "Goddamn you!"

She went hurling through the air.

Michael sprinted down Fourth Avenue, the debris cloud roaring behind him. There would be no outrunning it. He turned right onto Eighth Street. At the ends of the block, both in front and behind, the cloud roared past with a tornadic whoosh, then, as if suddenly recalling his presence—*Oh, Michael, sorry I forgot you*—turned the corners, barreling toward him from two directions.

He dove through the nearest door and slammed it behind him. Some kind of clothing shop, coats and dresses and shirts hanging disembodied on the racks. A wide window with mannequins propped upon an elevated platform faced the street.

The cloud arrived.

The window burst inward; Michael's hands shot up to protect his eyes. Dust engulfed the room, blasting him backward. Pricks of pain announced themselves all over his body—his arms and hands, the base of his throat, the parts of his face that had been exposed—as if he'd been attacked by a swarm of bees. He tried to rise; only then did he discover the long shard of glass embedded in his right thigh. It seemed strange that it didn't hurt more—it should have hurt like hell—but then the pain arrived, annihilating his thoughts. He was coughing, choking, drowning in the dust. He scrambled back from the window and crashed into a clothing rack. He yanked a shirt from its hanger. It was made of some kind of gauzy material. He wadded it in his fist and pressed it to his mouth and nose. Breath by hungry breath, oxygen flowed back into his lungs.

He tied the shirt around the lower half of his face. With stinging eyes, he looked out upon the dark street. He was inside the cloud. Everything was silent except for a faint pattering: the sound of airborne particles falling upon the pavement and the roofs of abandoned cars. His hands and arms were slick with blood; his leg, where the long piece of glass was buried, screamed with the slightest motion. He drew his blade and cut, then tore, the leg of his trousers away. The glass, a long, narrow splinter, irregularly edged and slightly curved, had entered at an angle; the wound was roughly halfway between his groin and his knee on the inside flank of his leg. *Good Christ,* he thought. *Another few inches higher and that thing would have sliced my nuts off.*

He reached over his head to yank another shirt from the rack and used it to wrap the exposed end of the shard. He supposed it was possible that removing the glass would open the wound wider, but the pain was unendurable. Unless he removed it, he wouldn't be going anywhere. To do it quickly: that was the best way.

He took the wrapped shard in his fist. He counted to three. He pulled.

All up and down the block, man-sized figures, moving in the dust, halted in their tracks and swiveled their faces toward the sound of Michael's scream.

"This was a temple!"

Fanning's hand caught her across the cheek. The blow sent her careening backward.

"You do this to *me*? To *my* city?"

She raised her hands to protect her face. Instead Fanning yanked her by the collar, hauled her up until her feet left the pavement, and tossed her away.

"I am going to take my time with you. You're going to *want* me to kill you. You are going to *beg.*"

He came at her again, and again. Tosses, slaps, kicks. She discovered herself lying facedown. She felt detached from everything. Her thoughts possessed a lazy, unmoored quality. They seemed on the verge of some permanent and final severing, as if with the next blow they would sail up and away from her body, swallowed into the sky like a balloon cut from its string.

Yet, to yield, to accept death: the mind forbade it. The mind demanded, against all sense, to go on. Fanning was somewhere behind her. Amy's awareness of him was less as a physical presence than an abstract force, like gravity, a well of darkness into which she was being relentlessly sucked. She began to crawl. Why wouldn't Fanning just kill her? But he'd said so himself: he wanted her to feel it. To feel life leaking out of her, drip by drip.

"Look at me!"

A crack to her midriff lifted her off the ground; Fanning had kicked her. The wind sailed from her chest.

"I said, look at me!"

He kicked her again, burying his foot below her sternum and flipping her onto her back.

He was holding the sword over his head.

"We were supposed to meet at the kiosk!"

We?

"You said you would be there! You said we would be together!"

What was he seeing? Who was she to him? The transformation: it had done something to his mind.

"I never should have loved you!"

She rolled away as the sword came down. It struck the pavement with a single-noted clang. Fanning howled like a wounded animal.

"I wanted to die with you!"

She was on her back again. Fanning had raised the sword above his head, ready to swing. She raised her arms in forbearance. One chance was all she had.

"Tim, don't."

Fanning froze.

"I wanted to be there. To be with you. That was all I ever wanted."

His arms tensed. At any second, the blade would fall. "I waited all night! How could you do that to me? Why didn't you come, why?"

"Because . . . I died, Tim."

For a moment nothing happened. *Please,* she thought.

"You . . . died."

"Yes. I'm sorry. I didn't mean to."

His voice was numb. "On the train."

Amy spoke cautiously, keeping her voice even. "Yes. I was coming to see you. They carried me off. I couldn't stop them."

Fanning's eyes floated away from her face. He glanced around uncertainly. "But I'm here now, Tim. That's what matters. I'm sorry it took me so long."

How long could she sustain the lie? The sword was everything. If she could convince Fanning to give it to her . . .

"We can still do it," she said. "There's a way we can always be together, just like we planned."

He looked back at her.

"Come with me, Tim. There's a place we can go. I've seen it."

Fanning said nothing. She sensed her words gaining traction in his mind.

"Where?" he asked.

"It's the place where we can start over. We can do it right this time. All you have to do is give me the sword." She extended her hand. "Come with me, Tim."

Fanning's eyes were locked on hers. Everything was inside them, the whole history of the man he'd been. The pain. The loneliness. The interminable hours of his life. Then:

"You."

She was losing him. "Give me the sword, Tim. That's all you have to do."

"You're not her."

She felt it all collapsing. "Tim, it's me. It's Liz."

"You're . . . Amy."

Fifty yards away, lying faceup on the ground, the man known as Peter Jaxon had begun to disappear.

His mind straddled two worlds. In the first, one of darkness and commotion, Fanning was hurling Amy through the air. Peter sensed this rather dimly; he could not recall why it should be so. Nor could he intervene, his powers to act, even to move at all, having abandoned him.

In the other was a window.

A shade, drawn over it, glowed with summer light. The image felt familiar, like déjà vu. *The window,* Peter thought. *It means I must be dying.* As he fought to focus his eyes, to bring himself back to reality, the light began to change. It was becoming something else: not a window in his mind but something physical. Through the dust-filled darkness was an opening, like a corridor ascending to a higher world, and through this tunnel a shining shape appeared. It teased at his memory; he knew what it was, if only he could summon the image forth. The picture sharpened. It resembled a crown, multilayered, each layer arched as it narrowed to a spiked peak. Sunlight flared upon its mirrored face, shooting a bright beam down the corridor, which was a hole in the clouds, into his eyes.

The Chrysler Building.

The corridor collapsed; darkness folded over him again. But now he knew: the night in which he dwelled was false. The sun was still up there. Above the cloud of dust it shone, bright as day. If he could get to the sun, if he could somehow lead Fanning into its light . . .

But this thought was lost as a great force gripped him, like a vortex. Its power was colossal. He felt himself being pulled, down and down and down. What lay at the bottom he did not know, only that when he reached it, he would be forever lost. Somewhere distant, his body was changing. Racked with convulsions, it hammered on the pavement of the broken city. Bones elongated. Teeth showered from his gums. He was sinking into a sea of everlasting darkness in which no trace of himself would remain. *No! Not yet!* He searched for something, anything, to hold on to. In his mind's eye, Amy's face appeared. The picture was not imagined but taken from life. They were sitting on his bed. Their faces were close, their hands entwined. Teardrops hung upon her eyelashes like beads of light. *You get to keep one thing,* she told him. *What I wanted to keep was you.*

Was you, thought Peter.

You.

He fell.

The pain in Michael's leg exploded. Removing the glass had peeled the skin back like the rind of an orange, exposing the fibrous, subtly pulsating muscle beneath. Another backward reach above his head produced a long, silk scarf. He twirled it into a thick rope and tied it tightly around the wound. The fabric was instantly saturated. Was he doing this right? He wished Sara were here. Sara would know what to do. The things that came into your mind at a time like this: the brain was not kind, it had no sense of fairness, it taunted you with thoughts of the things you did not have or couldn't do.

The noise outside had subsided as the destruction marched north. The air had an unnatural chemical smell, bitter and burnt. For the first time since he'd awakened on the street, his mind went to Alicia, the look on her face as the water crashed into her and swept her away. She was gone. Alicia was gone.

From the street, a crunch of glass.

Michael froze. The noise came again.

Footsteps.

Pushing with her heels, Amy scrambled backward. "Tim, don't! It's me!"

"Don't call me that!"

She had lost him; the spell was broken. In his eyes, the look of white-hot fury had returned. Suddenly Fanning raised his head. A new emotion came into his face, one of unanticipated pleasure.

"And what have we here?"

It was Peter. The transformation was complete; his body, sleek, powerful, had joined the anonymous horde.

"There's a good fellow." Fanning's lips pulled back into a smile, showing his fangs. "Why don't you join us?"

Peter moved toward them through the rubble, legs bent, arms held away from his body. His steps seemed uncertain; his back and shoulders rippled with an undulating motion, like a man stretching after a long night of sleep or adjusting himself inside a new suit of clothes.

"Allow me, Amy, to make a point."

With a flick of his wrist Fanning tossed the sword, handle first, to Peter, who snatched it robotically from the air.

"Let's see who's in there, shall we?" Fanning strode toward him, straightened his back and tapped the center of his chest. "Right about here, I should think."

Peter was staring at the sword, as if puzzling over its function. What was this alien object in his hand?

"Come on, now. I promise I won't move a muscle."

Peter took another step forward. His movements were jerky, as if the parts of his body could not completely coordinate. The muscles of his arms and shoulders tightened as he attempted to lift the blade.

"Getting heavier, I see."

Another step and Peter stopped. He was within striking distance now. Fanning made no effort to defend himself; his batlike face radiated confidence, almost amusement. The sword, at a forty-five-degree angle to the ground, refused to rise.

"Here, let me help you."

With the long-nailed tip of his index finger, Fanning guided the blade to a horizontal position. He moved slightly forward until the point made contact with his chest, just below the sternum.

"One good thrust should do it."

A growl of effort rose from deep in Peter's throat. The seconds stretched, every part of his body drawn taut. A pop of air expelled from his lungs; he melted to his knees, the sword clanging on the pavement.

"You see, Amy? It is simply not possible. This man belongs to me now."

Like the viral in the hall, Peter had bowed his head in abject surrender. Fanning placed a hand on his shoulder. It was as if he were patting an especially obedient dog. "Do me a favor, won't you?" Fanning asked him.

Peter raised his head.

"Would you please kill her?"

Michael pushed backward from the window on his palms, leaving a wide trail of blood on the floor. There was more than one viral out there, he could sense it; they were like wraiths, there and not there, shadowy figures gliding and shifting in the dust.

Searching. Hunting.

Once they found him, he wouldn't make it two steps. He scooted to the rear of the room, where there was a long counter and, behind it, a doorway half-hidden by a curtain. As he slipped behind the counter, the floor began to shake again. The feeling gathered in intensity like a revving engine. Clothes racks toppled. Mirrors shattered and burst outward. Chunks of plaster severed from the ceiling and detonated on the floor. Curled into a ball, arms wrapped around his head, Michael thought, *God, whoever you are, I am sick of your shit. I am not your plaything. If you're going to kill me, please stop screwing around and get it over with.*

The shaking subsided. From all up and down the street, Michael heard the crack of windows popping free of their frames and crashing on the pavement. The virals still lurked out there, but maybe the commotion had put them off his trail. Maybe they were cowering in some dark corner, as he was. Maybe they were dead.

He peeked around the counter. The place looked like a wrecking ball had hit it, nothing left intact except for a free-standing, full-length mirror, which stood anomalously on the right side of the room like a bewildered survivor surveying the wreckage of some terrible catastrophe. Angled slightly toward the front of the store, the mirror's face gave him a partial view of the street.

A pod of three emerged in the murk. They seemed to be drifting aimlessly, looking around as if lost. Michael willed his body into absolute stillness. If they couldn't hear him, maybe they'd pass him by. For several seconds they continued their confused wandering, until one of them stopped abruptly. Standing in profile, the viral rotated its face from side to side, as if attempting to triangulate the source of a sound. Michael held his breath. The creature paused and angled its chin upward, holding this position for another several seconds before swiveling toward the storefront. Its nose was twitching like a rat's.

Peter stepped toward her. There was no point in trying to get away; the outcome would be the same. Time had given up its customary course. Everything seemed to happen in a manner both rushed and strangely sluggish; her vision had narrowed, the city around her fading to a collection of shadows.

She was crying, though not for herself. She couldn't have said what she was crying for; her tears possessed an abstract quality of sadness, though something else as well. Her trials were ended. In a way, she was glad. How strange, to put down life like a heavy load she had been too long forced to carry. She hoped she would go to the farmstead. How happy she had been there. She remembered the piano, the music flowing forth, Peter's hands resting on her shoulders, the joy of his touch. How happy they had been, together.

"It's all right," she murmured. Her voice felt distant, not quite her own. It spilled from her lips on shallow, rapid breaths. "It's all right, it's all right."

Peter positioned the sword so that the tip was pointed at the base of her throat. The gap narrowed, then stopped, flesh mere inches from steel. His head cocked to the side; in another second he would strike.

"Well?" Fanning said.

Their gazes met and held. To know and be known: that was the final desire, the heart of love. It was the one thing she could give him. A huge force was bursting open inside her. It was a kind of light. She would have beamed it straight into his heart if she could.

"You're Peter," Amy whispered, and went on whispering, so that he would be hearing these words. "You're Peter, you're Peter, you're Peter . . ."

The blood, thought Michael.

They can smell my blood.

He wasn't sure he could stand, let alone run. He had painted a road of red on the floor, leading them straight to him. He pressed his back against the counter and drew his knees to his chest. The virals had entered the store. He heard a kind of wet snuffling, like the noise of hogs rooting in mud; they were sucking the blood off the floor. Michael felt a weird surge of protectiveness. *Hey, leave my blood alone!* On and on went their lascivious slurping. So intense was their focus that Michael began to think about the curtained door. What lay beyond it? Was it a dead end or was there, perhaps, a hallway that led deeper into the building—to the street, even? The doorway was only partially concealed by the counter. For some interval of time, depending on how fast he was able to go, he would be exposed.

He peeked around the corner, using the angled mirror to survey the room. The virals, on their hands and knees, were busily pressing their mouths to the floor, their tongues swirling like mopheads. Michael scooted down the length of the counter so he was as close as possible to the door, which was positioned ten feet behind him and to his right. If he could move the virals to the opposite corner of the room, the counter would obscure him completely.

Michael unwound the scarf from his leg. The fabric was bloated with blood. He formed it into a ball, tied off the ends to hold the shape, and rose on his knees, keeping the top of his head just below the lip of the counter. Pulling back his arm, he counted to three. Then he lobbed the scarf across the room.

It impacted the far wall with a splat. Michael dropped to his stomach and began to crawl. From behind him, he heard scurrying, then a series of clicks and snarls. It was better than he'd hoped; the virals were fighting over the rag. He slipped beneath the curtain and kept going. Now he couldn't see a goddamn thing. He crawled another few feet, until he was away from the door, and attempted to rise. The instant the foot of his injured leg touched the ground was one he was pretty sure he would always remember. The pain was simply spectacular. He reached into his shirt pocket for a box of matches. Fumbling in the dark, he managed to remove one without dumping out the rest, and scraped it on the striker.

He was in a narrow hallway of high brick walls that led deeper into the building. Metal racks of empty hangers lined the walls. The air was clearer here, less dust-choked. He pulled the kerchief down from his face. An opening to his left dead-ended in a small room of curtained booths. He looked down; drops of blood had followed him like a trail of crumbs. More blood sloshed in his boot. The match burned down; he flicked it away, lit another, and went on.

Eight matches later, Michael concluded that there was no way out. Branching hallways always led him back to the central corridor. Who designed a building like this? How long before the virals' interest in the rag exhausted itself and they followed the blood?

He came to a final room. It appeared to be a kitchen, with a stove and sink and cabinets lining two of the four walls; in the center was a small square table covered with open cans and plastic bottles. Two brown-boned skeletons lay on a cratered mattress, curled together. In all of New York, these were the first human remains Michael had encountered. He crouched beside them. One of them was much smaller than the other, who appeared to be a grown woman, with a desiccated tangle of long hair. A mother and her child? Probably they had holed up together during the crisis. For a century they had lain here, their last loving moment captured for all time. It made him feel like an interloper, as if he had violated the sanctity of a tomb.

A window.

It was covered by a cage, hinged shutters of crisscrossing wire, held in place by metal bars bolted to the wall. The two halves were joined with a padlock. The match burned down, scorching his fingertips; he flung it away. As his eyes adjusted he realized a faint glow was coming through the window, just enough to see by. He looked around the room for something to use as a lever. *Think, Michael.* On the table was a butter knife. The floor lurched again with a single, horizontal bang. Plaster dust rained down. He wedged the knife into the curved arm of the lock. His hands felt cold and slightly numb, at the edge of his ability to command them; the loss of blood was catching up to him. He tightened his arms and shoulders and twisted the blade, hard.

It snapped in two.

That was it; enough already. Michael was done. He sank to the floor and braced his back against the wall so that he could see them coming.

Peter was standing in a field of knee-high grass. The color of everything was peculiar, possessing an unnatural, off-kilter vividness that accentuated the smallest movements in the landscape. A breeze was blowing. The land was perfectly flat, though in the far distance mountains jostled the horizon. It was neither day nor night but something in between, the light soft and shadowless. What was this curious place? How had he come to be here? He searched his memory; only then did he realize that he did not, in fact, know who he was. He felt vaguely alarmed. He was alive, he existed, yet he seemed to have no history he could recall.

He heard the sound of running water and walked toward it. The action was automatic, as if an invisible intelligence were piloting his body. After some time had passed, he came upon a river. The water moved lazily, murmuring around scattered rocks. Leaves spiraled in its current like upturned hands. He followed the river downstream to a bend where it gathered in a pool. The surface of the water was still, almost solid-looking. He felt a peculiar agitation. It seemed that within the pool's depths lay an answer, though the question eluded him. It was on the tip of his tongue, yet when he tried to focus on it, it darted up and away from his thoughts like a bird. He knelt at the edge of the pool and looked down. An image appeared: a man's face. It was disturbing to look at. The face was his, yet it might as well have been a stranger's. He reached out and with his index finger broke the surface. Concentric rings bloomed outward from the point of contact; then the image reassembled. With this came the sense, distant at first, but growing stronger, of recognition. He knew who he was, if only he could manage to recall. *You're . . .* It was as if he were attempting to lift a boulder with his mind. *You're . . . you're . . .*

Peter.

He lurched backward. A dam was bursting in his mind. Images, faces, days, names—they poured forth in a torrent, almost painful. The scene around him—the field and the river and the flat light of the sky—began to disperse. It was washing away. Behind it lay a wholly different reality, of objects and people and events and ordered time. *I am Peter Jaxon,* he thought, and then he said it:

"I am Peter Jaxon."

Peter stumbled backward; the sword fell from his hand.

"What do you think you're doing?" Fanning barked. "I said, kill her."

Peter's head swiveled; his eyes narrowed on Fanning's face. It was happening, thought Amy. He was remembering. The muscles of his legs compressed.

He sprang.

He rammed Fanning headlong. Surprise was on his side: Fanning went sailing. He crashed back down and rolled end over end, coming to rest against a concrete pylon. He rose onto all fours but his movements were sluggish. He gave his head a horsey shake and spat on the ground.

"Well, *this* is unexpected."

Then Amy was being lifted; Peter had gathered her into his arms. Together they raced down Forty-third Street on soaring strides. Where was he taking her? Then she understood: the partially constructed office tower. She tipped her face skyward, but the dust was too thick to see if the building's upper floors rose above the cloud deck. Peter halted at the base of the elevator shaft. He swung her onto his back, scrambled ten feet up the shaft's outer structure, guided Amy back around his waist, lowered her through the bars to the elevator's roof, and followed her down. His purpose in all this was unknown to her. He hoisted her onto his back again, using his elbows to compress her legs around his waist to tell her to hold on to him as tightly as possible. All of this had transpired in just a matter of seconds. The elevator's cables, three of them, were set into a steel plate affixed to a crossbar on the elevator's roof. Peter gathered the cables into his fists and set his feet wide. Amy, her arms hooked around his shoulders and her legs squeezing his waist like a vise, felt a gathering pressure in his body. Peter began to groan through his teeth. Only then did she grasp his intentions. She closed her eyes.

The plate tore free; Amy and Peter launched skyward, Peter gripping the cables, Amy riding his back like the shell of a turtle. Five stories, ten, fifteen. The elevator's counterweight plunged past. What would happen when they reached the top? Would they shoot through the roof into space?

Suddenly the whole cage shuddered; the counterweight had reached the bottom. The tension on the cable was instantly gone. Hurled upward, Amy found herself looking down at the base of the shaft. She was alone in the air, unattached to anything. Her body slowed as she approached the apogee of her ascent and for a second seemed to hover. *I am going to fall,* she thought. How far away the ground was. She would hit it going a hundred miles an hour, maybe more. *I am falling.*

A jolt: Peter, still gripping the cable, had seized her by the wrist. He pumped his legs, shifting his center of gravity to swing Amy in progressively wider arcs. Amy saw his target, an opening in the wall of the shaft not far below them.

He flung her away.

She landed on the floor and rolled to a halt. They were still inside the dust cloud. The adrenaline of their ascent had sharpened her thoughts. Everything was coming into a fine, almost granular focus. She scrambled to the edge and looked down into a dizzying maw of space.

Fanning was climbing up the side of the building.

The air concussed with a titanic roar. The building on the opposite side of Forty-third Street began to melt straight down into itself like a man felled at the knees. The floor under Amy began to shake. The vibration deepened; sounds of buckling metal rippled through the structure as the floor tipped abruptly toward the street. Loose materials—rusted tools, sawhorses, moisture-swollen pieces of drywall, a bucket of nails—slid past her and sailed into the abyss. She was on her stomach, pressing herself to the floor. The angle was increasing. She was slipping, her hands and feet could gain no traction, gravity was taking hold . . .

"Peter, help!"

The sweet pressure of his hand on her arm halted her slide; he was lying on his stomach, the crowns of their heads just touching. The floor gave another downward lurch, yet he held on, his toes digging into the concrete. With gathering force, he drew her back from the edge.

"Ah," said Fanning. His face had appeared above the lip of the floor. "*There you are.*"

Michael heard a faint metallic ringing from the hallway—the sound of hangers jostling on racks. A short silence ensued; the trail of his blood, crisscrossing the various hallways and doubling back, had momentarily perplexed them. The delay was excruciating. If only he would just pass out. If anything, he felt more alert than ever.

Maybe he should make a noise. Call out to them, to get the whole thing over with. *Hey, I'm in here, idiots! Come and fucking get it!*

Such a stupid, arbitrary place to die. He'd never thought he'd die in bed; it wasn't that sort of world, and he wasn't that sort of person. But some damn kitchen?

A kitchen.

Standing up was out of the question. But the top of the stove lay within his reach. Vertigo sloshed through his brain as he rocked onto his knees; straining forward, he grabbed hold of the skillet. He spat on the underside and wiped the metal with the hem of his shirt. His reflection was vague and undetailed, more a general outline of a human face than any particular person, but it was what he had.

The sounds were coming closer.

They raced up the stairs. Two flights brought them to the roof. The dust was as thick as ever, though in the western sky a paler region, weak but discernible, showed the sun's location.

They had to get higher. They had to get above the cloud.

Amy looked up. The boom of the crane was rocking like the neck of a pecking bird. A long, hooked cable swayed from its tip. A stairway inside the crane's mast ascended to the top.

They began to climb. Where was Fanning? Watching them, no doubt—enjoying himself, choosing his moment.

They clanged the rest of the way to the top. The swaying was getting worse. The whole thing felt unstable, as if at any moment the crane might peel away from the side of the building. They were still inside the cloud. The skyline of midtown Manhattan was a smoldering wreckage, the destruction continuing to extend outward from its epicenter. A rumble, a cloud, and another building toppled. Broad gaps existed where whole blocks had once stood.

"Hello up there!"

Fanning was halfway up the mast. Gripping a bar with one hand, he leaned out and waved to them with merry confidence. "Not to worry, I'll be there soon!"

A narrow catwalk led to the end of the boom. Amy crawled along it, Peter following. The boom was slamming up and down. She kept her eyes aimed forward; she didn't dare look down into the void. Even a glimpse would paralyze her.

They reached the end; there was no place else to go.

"God*damn* I like a view."

Fanning had reached the top of the mast and was now standing fifty feet behind them. Back arched, chest puffed out, he let his gaze travel over the ruined city.

"You've really made a mess of things, haven't you? Speaking as a New Yorker, I have to say, this brings back some very unpleasant memories."

A sudden warmth touched Amy's cheek. She looked to her left, across Fifth Avenue. The glass facade of the building on the far side shone with a faint orange color. Which made no sense; the building faced east, away from the sun. The light, she realized, was a reflection.

Fanning huffed a sigh. "Well. Looks to me like we've reached the end of the line. I'd ask you to stand aside, Peter, but you don't seem to be a very good listener."

The violence of the crane's movement intensified. Far below, the hooked chain was swaying like a pendulum. The glow of the glass was growing brighter. Where was the light coming from?

"What do you say? Perhaps the two of you could hold hands and throw yourselves off. I'll be glad to wait."

There was a flash. A ray of intense sunlight, angling off the steel crown of the Chrysler Building, had broken through the murk.

It shot Fanning directly in the face.

Suddenly the crane tipped away from the side of the building. The bolts attaching the mast to the structure's outer girders were breaking away. With a groan, the boom began to arc over Fifth Avenue, slowly at first, then with gathering velocity. The mast was tipping from its base. They were moving both down and away, the boom falling like a hammer toward the glass tower across the street. It would spear the building at a forty-five-degree angle, going like a shot.

Oh please, thought Amy. She was hugging the edges of the catwalk. *Make it stop.*

Glass exploded around them.

The virals did not so much enter as pop into the room. The first one, the alpha, bounded straight over the table, landing in front of him. Michael thrust the pan out toward its face.

It froze.

The other two seemed confused, unable to decide what to do. It was as Michael had hoped; he had disrupted their chain of command. He moved the pan a little to the side; the viral's gaze tracked it unerringly. This discovery would have intrigued him if he weren't so terrified. Hardly daring to breathe, Michael slowly drew the pan toward himself. The viral obediently followed; it seemed utterly entranced. Inch by inch, the gap between them closed. Michael shifted the pan to the left, making the viral turn its face.

A broken butter knife, thought Michael. *I better get this right.*

He struck.

The end of the crane's boom speared the glass tower at the northwest corner of Forty-third and Fifth at the thirty-second floor. Such was the force of impact that it continued its downward course through two more floors, while also embedding itself deeper within the structure. Here it came to rest in precarious balance, mast and boom forming the upper legs of an isosceles triangle suspended three hundred feet above the street.

Amy returned to consciousness with only partial recollection of these events: a sensation of wild descent, culminating in a chaos so total that her mind could not sort its components. She was lying on the floor, her body twisted and her knees drawn up, her left arm extended past her head. Ahead lay a region of light and wind and swirling dust, which, after a moment, showed itself to be a gaping hole in the side of the building. To her left, the end of the boom sloped downward into the floor, swaying from side to side with a soporific creaking sound. The air was otherwise weirdly still. Something rough and bulky lay beneath her: the chain. It was still attached to the tip of the boom. She felt profound puzzlement at having survived, at the mere fact of being alive. That was her only emotion. As she rolled onto her stomach, her center of gravity, distorted by her long plunge through space, swayed nauseatingly inside her. Nevertheless, she managed to push herself onto her hands and knees and crawled toward the end of the boom.

Peter was lying facedown on the catwalk. He did not, at first, appear to be living. There was blood everywhere, and his neck was bent away from her at an unnatural angle. One arm dangled over the edge. But as Amy inched forward, calling his name, she detected a faint respiratory stirring, followed by a twitch of his exposed hand. I'm coming, she cried, I'm coming to get you. Just hang on.

She didn't have much time; the crane's tenuous state of balance would not last long. At any moment the whole thing would wrench free and topple to the street below. Kneeling on the catwalk, Amy slid her hands beneath Peter's shoulders. She was panting for air; perspiration dripped into her mouth and eyes. In a series of jerks, she drew him to the end of the boom and slid him onto the floor.

She rolled him onto his back. His body seemed completely inert, yet his eyes were open. Amy cupped his chin to make him look at her. His tongue swished behind his teeth with a gurgling sound; he was attempting to speak.

"You're hurt," she said. "Don't try to talk."

The muscles of his face compressed. His eyes were open very wide. She realized he wasn't looking at her. He was looking *behind* her.

A single word, the last one of his life, burst from Peter's lips: *"Fanning."*

The fractured end of the butter knife sank into the creature's eye with a spurt of clear fluid. Michael tried to hold on, but the metal slipped from his fingers as the creature emitted a high-pitched squeal and staggered backward, the blade still embedded. Now Michael had nothing but the pan to work with. As one of the others shot forward, he swung it as hard as he could, connecting with the side of the creature's skull. He fell onto his side, still pressed to the wall. He raised the pan before his face.

The viral batted it away.

Michael rolled onto his stomach and buried his head in his arms.

Roaring with rage, Fanning blasted into her. A second of confusion and she was on her back, Fanning straddling her waist, claws coiled around her neck. The skin of his face was blackened and charred, the flesh separated in long, puckered slits that exposed the musculature beneath; his lips were gone, transforming his mouth into a skeleton's grin of naked teeth. Bits of damp, stringy material dangled from his eye sockets; the orbs within had burst. She tried to breathe, but no air passed the knot of pressure on her throat. Jets of spittle flew from Fanning's mouth into her eyes. Her hands batted at his arms and face, but her efforts were weak and vague. The floor began to shake; the crane was breaking loose. The walls of her vision were compacting around her like a narrowing tunnel. She abandoned her flailing and swept her hands along the floor. *He's blind,* she told herself. *He can't see what you're doing.* The shaking deepened; with a shriek of torquing metal, the boom jerked upward.

There it was, in her hand. The chain.

As she wound it around Fanning's neck, his face and body startled; Amy felt a momentary easing of the pressure on her windpipe. The boom had begun to back out the side of the building. She quickly formed a second loop and tossed it over his head.

Fanning released her and sat upright. He raised a searching hand to his throat. The slack was running out.

"Look for her," said Amy.

He made no cry. He exited the world in a blink. He was there one second and gone the next, plucked into the whirling dust, his body thus to join the ashes of the vanished city.

And then it was over.

For a long time Michael waited. The silence seemed like a trick. But as the seconds passed and nothing happened, he realized something had changed. There was, all around him, a deep stillness, as if he were alone in the room.

He uncovered his eyes and looked.

The virals were dead. The one that had knocked the pan away lay at his feet, curled in a fetal position. The other two were on the far side of the room in a similar posture—even the one with the blade in its eye, from which still issued a trail of blood-tinged fluid. There was something tender about their postures. It was as if, overcome by a sudden exhaustion, they had lain on the floor and gone to sleep.

He used the stove to pull himself upright and limped down the hall, following the trail of his own blood. He took a scarf from one of the racks, rebandaged his leg, and ventured outside. A low evening sun, punching through the dust, flared the clouds with color. He made his way east to Lafayette Street and turned north. It wasn't until he'd traveled another block that he knew for certain what had happened.

The virals lay everywhere. On the sidewalks. On the street. On the roofs of old cars. All in the same fetal posture, curled like children in their beds, worn out by a too-long day. A sight less of death than of a vast, collective repose. Their bodies, like the city of which they had so long been a part, were crumbling to dust. It was a scene of wonder. A great, sad, and joyous wonder, too heavy for one mind to bear. He stumbled forward. Uptown, the rumbling of destruction persisted. For months, years, centuries even, the immolation would continue, the great metropolis finally folding itself into the sea. But now, as Michael moved among the bodies, an infinite quiet prevailed, the world pausing in acknowledgment, history held in time's cupped hand.

And Michael Fisher did the only thing he could. He fell to his knees and wept.

Peter had begun to die.

Amy felt his spirit fade; Fanning was leaving him. His eyes were open, yet the light inside was dimming. Soon it would be gone.

Don't leave me. She lifted his hand and pressed it to her cheek; his flesh was growing cold. The muscles of his face relaxed toward death. *Please,* she said, and shuddered with a sob, *don't leave me alone.*

The time had come to let him go, to say goodbye, yet the prospect was unendurable; it could not be accepted. There was a way, perhaps. The gravest act—a betrayal, even. She momentarily had the sensation of being outside her body, watching herself, as she took the shard of glass from off the floor and slashed the edge across her palm. Blood rose from the wound and swiftly gathered in a rich, crimson puddle. She took Peter's hand and did the same. A last flicker of doubt, then she placed his palm against her own and meshed their fingers together. She felt a tiny twitch; with accumulating pressure, Peter folded his fingers over the back of her hand.

She closed her eyes.

XII

THE WILD BEYOND

Though my soul may set in darkness,
it will rise in perfect light;
I have loved the stars too fondly
to be fearful of the night.

—SARAH WILLIAMS,
"THE OLD ASTRONOMER TO HIS PUPIL"

83

At the top of Central Park, away from the destruction, Amy and Michael pitched their camp. It had taken them nearly a week to find each other; the center of the island was blocked by impenetrable mountains of debris. It was on the morning of the sixth day that Amy had heard him calling. Michael emerged from the rubble, a ghostly figure, covered with ash. By this time, Amy knew Alicia was gone; her presence, her spirit, these were nowhere in the world. Still, when Michael told her what had happened, the reality undid her. She sat on the ground and wept.

—And Peter? Michael asked tentatively.

Not looking up, Amy shook her head. No.

They remained there for three weeks to rest and gather supplies. Michael slowly regained his strength. Together they constructed a simple smokehouse and set snares to catch small game. Elsewhere in the park they found a variety of edible plants, even some apple trees, fat with glossy fruit. Michael worried that the water in the reservoir would be tainted by seawater, but it wasn't; they retrieved the water filter from the *Nautilus* to clean it of debris. From time to time they would hear the rumble of another building's collapse, followed by a silence that seemed somehow deeper in the aftermath. At first this unnerved them, but eventually the noise became commonplace, nothing even to acknowledge.

The days were long, the sun hot. One early morning they awoke to a blast of thunder. Storm after storm crashed through the city. When at last the sun returned, the air was different. A sparkling freshness lay upon the park, dust washed from the leaves of the trees.

It was on their final night that Michael produced the bottle of whiskey. He had found it in an apartment building when he'd gone to scavenge tools and clothes. The cap was sealed, the glass caked with dust so thick it was like a layer of soil. Sitting by the fire, Michael was the first to try it. "Absent friends," he said, raising the bottle, and took a long swallow. As his throat bobbed, he began to cough while also, somehow, wearing an expression of triumph.

"Oh, you're going to like this," he wheezed, and handed it to her.

Amy took a small sip, to get the feel, then, as Michael had done, tipped her head back and let the whiskey fill her mouth. A rich, smoky taste bloomed on her tongue, filling her sinuses with tingling warmth.

Michael looked at her inquisitively, eyebrows raised. "You might want to go easy," he warned. "That's a hundred-and-twenty-year-old Scotch you're drinking."

She took a second pull, savoring the flavor more deeply.

"It tastes . . . like the past," she said.

In the morning they broke camp and headed south, through the park and down Eighth Avenue. At the water's edge they loaded the last of Michael's supplies into the *Nautilus*. He would head first for Florida, where he would restock, then make the long jump to the coast of Brazil, hugging the land until he reached the Strait of Magellan. Once through, a final stop to rest and resupply and he would set sail for the South Pacific.

"Are you sure you can find them?" Amy asked.

He shrugged carelessly, though they both understood the danger of what he was attempting. "After all this, how hard can it be?" He stopped, looked at her, then said with a note of caution, "I know you don't think you can come with me—"

"I can't, Michael."

He hunted for words. "It's just . . . how will you get along? All alone."

Amy did not have an answer, at least not one she believed would make sense to him. "I'll have to manage." She looked at his sad face. "I'll be all right, Michael."

They had agreed that a clean break would be best. Yet as the moment of separation arrived, this seemed not just foolish but impossible. They embraced, holding each other for a long time.

"She loved you, you know," Amy said.

He was crying a little; they both were. He shook his head. "I don't know that she did."

"Perhaps not the way you wanted. But it was the way she knew how." Amy drew back a little and placed a hand to his cheek. "Hold on to that, Michael."

They parted. Michael stepped down into the cockpit; Amy cast off the lines. A snap of the sail and the boat streamed away. Michael waved once over the transom; Amy waved in reply. *God bless and keep you, Michael Fisher.* She watched the image recede into the vastness.

She put on her pack and hiked north. By the time she reached the bridge, it was early afternoon. A strong summer sun gleamed upon the surface of the water, far below. She made her way across and on the opposite side stopped to drink and rest, then donned her pack once more and continued on her journey.

Utah was four months away.

* * *

From the observation deck of the Empire State Building—one of the last intact structures between Grand Central and the sea—Alicia watched the *Nautilus* sail down the Hudson.

It had taken her most of two days to make the climb. Two hundred and four flights of stairs, most in total darkness, an agonizing ascent on her makeshift crutch and, when the pain became too great, her hands and knees. For hours she had lain on various landings, perspiring and breathing hard, wondering if she could go on. Her body was broken; her body was done. In those places where there was no pain, she felt only a creeping numbness. One by one, the lights of life were winking out inside her.

But her mind, her thoughts: these were her own. No Fanning, no Amy. How she'd escaped the subway tunnel she possessed no memory of; somehow she had been ejected onto dry land. The rest was fragments, flashes. She remembered Michael's face, backlit by sunshine, and his hand reaching down; the water slamming into her, its power immeasurable, large as a planet's; all volition gone, her body plunging and tumbling; the first involuntary gulp, making her choke, her throat opening instinctively to take a second breath, pulling the water deeper into her lungs; pain, and then a merciful lessening of pain; a feeling of dispersal, her body and her thoughts losing their distinctiveness, like a radio signal fading from range; and then nothing at all.

She'd awakened to find herself in the most perplexing circumstance. She was sitting on a bench; around her, a small park of overgrown trees and a playground deep in tall, feathered grass. Slowly her awareness expanded. Vast crags of debris surrounded the perimeter although the park itself was miraculously untouched. The sun was out; birds twittered in the trees, a peaceful sound. Her clothing was soaked and her mouth tasted of salt. She sensed a gap in time between remembered events and her present situation, the calm of which seemed wholly anachronistic, like nothing she had ever known. She wondered, somewhat dully, if she was dead—if she was, in fact, a ghost. But when she attempted to stand, and the pain volleyed through her body, she knew this wasn't so; surely death would bring an absence of bodily sensation.

That was when she realized it. The virus was gone.

Not transmuted into some new state, as it had been in Fanning and Amy, restoring their human appearance while leaving other traits intact. The virus was nowhere inside her at all. Somehow the water had killed it, and then returned her to life.

How was this possible? Had Fanning lied to her? But when she searched her memory she realized he had never told her, in so many words, that the water would kill her, she who was neither wholly viral nor wholly human but poised between the two. Perhaps he had sensed the truth; perhaps he simply hadn't known. What irony! She had hurled herself off the fantail of the *Bergensfjord* intending to die, yet it was the water that had been her salvation in the end.

But to be alive. To smell and hear and taste the world in proper proportion. To be alone in one's mind at last. She inhaled the sensation like the purest air. How amazing, how wondrous and unexpected. To be purely and simply *a person* again.

Fanning was dead. The wreckage of the city told her so first, then the bodies, curled and crumbling to ash. She took shelter in a ruined bodega. Perhaps the others were searching for her; perhaps they weren't, believing her dead. On the morning of the second day she heard someone calling. It was Michael. "Hello!" His voice ricocheted through the becalmed streets. "Hello! Is anybody there?" *Michael!* she answered. *Find me! I'm here!* But then she realized that she had not, in fact, spoken these words aloud.

It was very puzzling. Why would she not call out to him? What was this impulse to be silent? Why could she not tell him where she was? His calls faded, then were gone.

She waited for the meaning of this to become clear, so that a plan might emerge. The days moved by. When it rained, she set pots outside the store to catch the drops, and in that manner she slaked her thirst, though she had neither food nor the means to locate it, a fact that seemed oddly unimportant; she wasn't hungry at all. She slept a great deal: whole nights, many days as well. Long, deep states of unconsciousness in which she dreamed with fascinating emotional and sensory vividness. Sometimes she was a little girl, sitting outside the wall of the Colony. At others, a young woman, standing the Watch with cross and blades. She dreamed of Peter. She dreamed of Amy. She dreamed of Michael. She dreamed of Sara and Hollis and Greer and, quite often, of her magnificent Soldier. Whole days, whole episodes of her life replayed before her eyes.

But the greatest of these dreams was the dream of Rose.

It began in a forest—misty, dark, like something from a childhood tale. She was hunting. On cautious, nearly floating steps she progressed beneath the trees' dense canopy, bow at the ready. From all around came the small noises and movements of game in the brush, yet her targets remained elusive. No sooner would she identify the location of a particular sound—a cracking twig, the rustle of dry leaves—than it would swing behind her or shift to the side, as if the woodland's inhabitants were toying with her.

She emerged into an area of rolling fields of open grassland. The sun had set, but darkness was yet to fall. As she walked, the grass grew taller. It rose to her waist, then to her chest. The light—soft, faintly glowing—remained uniform and appeared to have no source. From somewhere ahead she heard a new sound. It was laughter. A bright, bubbly, little-girl laughter. *Rose!* she cried, for she knew instinctively that the voice was her daughter's. *Rose, where are you!* She tore forward. The grass whipped her face and eyes. Desperation gripped her heart. *Rose, I can't see you! Help me find you!*

—Here I am, Mama!

—Where?

Alicia caught a flicker of movement, ahead and to the right. A flash of red hair.

—Over here! the girl teased. She was laughing, playing a game. Can't you see me? I'm right here!

Alicia plunged toward her. But like the animals in the forest, her daughter seemed to be everywhere and nowhere, her calls coming from all directions.

—Here I am! Rose sang. Try to find me!

—Wait for me!

—Come find me, Mama!

Suddenly the grass was gone. She found herself standing on a dusty road sloping upward toward the crest of a small hill.

—Rose!

No answer.

—Rose!

The road beckoned her forward. As she walked, she began to have a sense of her environment, or at least the kind of place it was. It was beyond the world she knew while also a part of it, a hidden reality that could be glimpsed as if from the corner of the eye but never wholly entered into in this life. With each step, her anxiety softened. It was as if an invisible power, purely benevolent, was guiding her. As she mounted the hill, she heard, once again, the bright, distant music of her daughter's laughter.

—Come to me, Mama, she sang. Come to me.

She reached the top of the rise.

And there Alicia awakened. What waited in the valley beyond the hilltop was not yet hers to see, though she believed she knew what it was, as she also knew the meaning of the other dreams, of Peter and Amy and Michael and all those whom she had loved and been loved by in return.

She was saying goodbye.

A night came when Alicia dreamed no more. She awoke with a feeling of fullness. All she had meant to do had been accomplished; the work of her life was complete.

On the crutch she had fashioned from scrap wood she made her way through the debris, three blocks north and one block west. Even this short distance left her gasping with pain. It was midmorning when she began her ascent; by nightfall she had reached the fifty-seventh floor. Her water was nearly gone. She slept on the floor of a windowed office, so that the sun would wake her, and at dawn she resumed her climb.

Was it coincidence that this was the very same morning that Michael set sail? Alicia preferred to think it wasn't. That the sight of the *Nautilus,* pulling away on the wind, was a sign, and meant for her. Could Michael feel her? Did he, in some manner, sense that she was observing him from above? Impossible, and yet it pleased Alicia to think so—that he might suddenly look up, startled, as if touched by a sudden breeze. The *Nautilus* was departing the inner harbor, headed for open sea. Sunlight glimmered dazzlingly upon the water. Clutching the balustrade, Alicia watched as the tiny shape became smaller and smaller, fading into nonexistence. *Of all people, Michael,* she thought. And yet he had been the one. He had been the one to save her.

A tall fence, curved inward at the top, fixed into the top of the balustrade, had once formed a barricade around the perimeter of the platform; many sections remained, but not all. Alicia had saved a little water. She drank it now. How sweet it was, the scavenged rain. She experienced a profound sense of the interconnectedness of all things, the eternal rising and falling of life—how the water, which had begun as the sea, had ascended, gathered into clouds, and descended from the sky as rain, to be gathered in the pots she'd laid. Now it had become a part of her.

Alicia sat on the balustrade. Below, on the outer side, was a small ledge. She rotated her body, using her hands to assist her disobedient legs over the rail. Faced away from the building, she scooted a few inches forward on the concrete until her feet touched the ledge. How did one do it? How did one say farewell to the world? She took a long breath and let the air out slowly. She realized she was crying. Not with sadness—no, not that—although her tears did not seem unrelated to sadness. They were tears of sadness and happiness conjoined, everything over and done.

My darling, my Rose.

Pushing with her palms, she drew herself erect. Space jumped away beneath her; she pointed her eyes to the sky.

Rose, I am coming. I will be with you soon.

Some might have said she fell. Others, that she flew. Both were true. Alicia Donadio—Alicia of Blades, the New Thing, Captain of the Watch and Soldier of the Expeditionary—would die as she had lived.

Always soaring.

* * *

Night came on.

Amy was somewhere in New Jersey. She had left the main thoroughfares behind, moving into the wild backcountry. Her arms and legs were heavy, full of a deep, almost pleasurable exhaustion. As darkness fell, she made her camp in a field of winking fireflies, ate her simple supper, and lay down beneath the stars.

Come to me, she thought.

All around her, and all above, the small lights of heaven danced. A stout full moon rose from the trees, sharpening the shadows.

I'm waiting for you. I'll always wait. Come to me.

A pure silence; not even the air was moving. Time passed in its languid course. Then, like the brush of a feather inside her:

Amy.

At the far edge of the field, in the boughs of the trees, she saw and heard a rustling; Peter dropped down. He had just eaten, a squirrel or mouse perhaps, or some small bird; she could feel his contentment, the rich satisfaction he had taken in the act, like waves of warmth washing through her blood. Amy rose as he moved toward her, passing among the fireflies. There were so many, it was as if he—as if the two of them—were swimming together in a sea of stars. *Amy.* His voice like a soft wind of longing, breathing her name. *Amy, Amy, Amy.*

She raised her hand; Peter did the same. The gap between them closed. Their fingers meshed and fell together, the soft pressure of Peter's palm against her own.

Am I . . . ?

She nodded. —Yes.

And . . . I'm yours? I belong to you?

She sensed his confusion. The trauma was still fresh, the disorientation. She tightened her fingers, pressing their palms together, and held his eyes with hers.

—You are mine, and I am yours. We belong to each other, you and I.

A pause, then: *We are each other's. You are mine and I am yours.*

—Yes, Peter.

Peter. He held the thought for a moment. *I am Peter.*

She cupped his cheek.

—Yes.

I am Peter Jaxon.

Her vision swam with tears. The moonlit night was fantastically still, everything held in abeyance, the two of them like actors on a stage of dark wings with a single spotlight falling upon them.

—Yes, that is who you are. You are my Peter.

And you are my Amy.

As she made her way west—and then for many years after—he was to come to her each night in this manner. The conversation would be repeated countless times, like a chant or prayer. Each visit was as if it were the first; at the start he retained no memory, either of the previous nights or of the events that had preceded them, as if he were a wholly novel creature in the world, born anew each night. But slowly, as the years became decades, the man inside the body—the essential spirit—reasserted itself. Never would he speak again, though they would talk of many things, words flowing through the touch of their hands, the two of them alone among the stars.

But that came later. Now, standing in the field of fireflies, beneath the summer moon, he asked her:

Where are we going?

She smiled through her tears.

—Home, said Amy. My Peter, my love. We are going home.

Michael had cleared the harbor. Over the transom, the image of the city grew faint. The moment of decision was upon him. South, as he'd told Amy, or a new direction entirely?

It wasn't even a question.

He tacked the *Nautilus,* turning in a northeasterly direction. The wind was fair, the seas light, with a gentle green color. The following afternoon he rounded the tip of Long Island and leapt into open sea. Three days after leaving New York, he made landfall at Nantucket. The island was arrestingly beautiful, with long beaches of pure white sand and crashing surf. There appeared to be no buildings at all, or none he could see; all traces of civilization had been swept away by the ocean's hand. Anchored in a sheltered cove, he made his final calculations, and at dawn, he set sail again.

Soon the ocean changed. It grew darker, with a solemn look. He had passed into a wild zone, far from any land. He felt not fear but excitement and, beneath this, a thrilling rightness. His boat, his *Nautilus,* was sound; he had the wind and sea and stars to guide him. He hoped to reach the English coast in twenty-three days, though perhaps that wouldn't happen. There were many variables. Maybe it would take a month, or longer; maybe he'd end up in France, or even Spain. It didn't matter.

Michael Fisher was going to find what was out there.

84

Fanning came to awareness of his surroundings slowly, and in parts. First there was a sensation of cold sand on his feet; this was followed by the sound of waves, gently pushing upon a tranquil shore. After an unknown interval of time had passed, other facts emerged. It was night. Stars thick as powder lay across a sky of velvety blackness, immeasurably deep. The air was cool and still, as after a daylong rain. Above and behind him, atop a steep bluff of eelgrass and beach plum, were houses; their white faces shone faintly with the reflected light of the moon, which was ascending from the sea.

He began to walk. The hems of his trousers were damp; he seemed to have mislaid his shoes, or else he had arrived in this place without them. He had no destination in mind, merely a sense that walking was something the situation called for. The unanticipated nature of his circumstances, its feeling of elastic reality, aroused in him no anxiety. Quite the contrary: everything felt inevitable, reassuringly so. When he tried to recall anything that might have happened prior to his being in this place, he could think of nothing. He knew who he was, yet his personal history seemed devoid of narrative coherence. There was a time, he knew, when he had been a child. And yet that period of his life, like all others, registered only as a collection of emotional and sensory impressions with a metaphoric aspect. His mother and his father, for example, resided in his memory not as individuated beings but as a feeling of warmth and safety, like being cradled in a bath. The town where he'd grown up, whose name he did not recall, was not a discrete civic unit of buildings and streets but a view through a window screen of rain pattering upon summer leaves. It was all very peculiar, not unsettling but simply unexpected, especially the fact that his adult life seemed almost completely unknown to him. He knew that in his life he had been happy, also sad; for a long time he had been very, very lonely. Yet when he tried to reconstruct the circumstances, all he remembered was a clock.

For a great while, in this unforeseen and generally pleasant state of un-remembering, he made his way down the broad boulevard of sand at the water's edge. The moon, having cleared the horizon, had ceased its upward arc. The tide was high, boastfully so, the sky immense. At length he became aware of a figure in the distance. For a time the figure grew no closer; then, with a telescoping quality, the gap began to narrow.

Liz was sitting on the sand with her arms wrapped around her shins, gazing over the water. She was wearing a white dress of some diaphanous material, light as a nightgown; her feet, like his, were bare. He vaguely recalled that something had happened to her, very unfortunate, though he couldn't say what that thing might have been; she had gone away, that was all, and now she had returned. He was happy, very happy to see her, and although she indicated no awareness of his presence, he felt very much as if she were expecting him.

"Liz, hello."

She looked up; her eyes twinkled with starlight. "Well, there you are," she said, smiling. "I was wondering when you'd get here. Do you have something for me?"

In fact, he did. He was holding her glasses. How curious this fact was.

"May I have them, please?"

She accepted the glasses, turned her face once again toward the water, and put them on. "There," she remarked, with a nod of satisfaction, "that's much better. I can't see a damn thing without them. All of this beauty was practically wasted on me, if you want to know the truth. But now I can see everything just fine."

"Where are we?" he asked.

"Why don't you sit?"

He lowered himself onto the sand beside her.

"That is an excellent question," Liz said. "The beach, would be the answer. This is the beach."

"How long have you been here?"

She touched a finger to her lips. "Now, isn't that funny. Even just a few minutes ago, I think I would have said for quite some time. But now that you're here, it doesn't seem like very much at all."

"Are we alone?"

"Alone? Yes, I should think so." She paused; a look of mischief came into her face. "You don't recognize any of this, do you? That's all right; it takes a little while to adjust. Believe me, when I first got here, I didn't have a clue what was going on."

He looked around. It was true; he had been in this place.

"I always wondered," Liz continued. "What would have happened if you had kissed me that night? How would our lives have been different? Of course, you might well have, if I hadn't gotten so drunk. What a self-pitying fool I made of myself. The whole thing was totally my fault from the get-go."

At once he remembered. The beach below her parents' house on Cape Cod: that's where they were. The place where, long ago, he had let life pass by, failing to say what his heart knew.

"How are we . . . here?"

"Oh, I think 'how' is not the question."

"What's the question, then?"

"The question, Tim, is 'why.'"

She was looking at him absorbedly. It was a gaze meant to comfort, as if he were ill. She had taken his hand in hers without his quite being aware of it. It felt warm as a cup of tea.

"It's all right," she said softly. "You can let it out now."

Suddenly his mind seemed to plunge. He remembered everything. The past reared up inside him, complete. He saw faces; he inhabited days; he lived the hour of his birth and each that followed. He felt as if he were choking; his lungs could find no air.

"That's all you have to do, is let it out."

She had put her arms around him. He was trembling, weeping, such tears as he had never wept in his life. All his sorrows, all his pain, the terrible things he'd done.

"Everything is forgiven, my darling, my love. All is forgiven, nothing is lost. Everything you have loved will come back to you. That is why you have come."

He moaned and shook. He cast his cries upward to the heavens. The waves moved in and out in their ancient rhythm; the stars poured down their primordial light upon him.

I'm here, Liz, his Liz, was saying. *It's over now, everything will be all right. Oh, beloved, I am here.*

It took some time. It took days, weeks, years. But this was unimportant. It would pass in a blink, not even. All things fell into the past but one; and what that was, was love.

XIII

THE MOUNTAIN AND THE STARS

And thence we came forth, to see again the stars.

—DANTE ALIGHIERI, *INFERNO*

85

"Shut it off," Lore said.

Rand stared at her, expressionless. They were on the engineering deck—heat stifling, air throbbing with the engines' rhythmic roar. Rand's broad, bare chest shone with sweat.

"You're sure about this?"

They were down to their last ten thousand pounds of fuel.

"Please," Lore said, "don't argue with me. It's not like we have a choice."

Rand raised the radio to his mouth. "That's it, gents. We're powering down. Weir, switch the generator to the auxiliary bus—bilges, lights, and desalinators only."

A crackle, then Weir's voice came through: "Lore said that?"

"Yeah, she said it. I'm looking right at her."

A moment passed; the thrumming ceased, replaced by a low electrical hum. Above them caged bulbs flickered, failed, then, as if with reluctance, sparked back to life.

"So that's it?" Rand asked. "We're dead in the water?"

Lore had no answer to that.

"I'm sorry, I shouldn't have said it that way."

She made some vague gesture. "Forget it."

"I know you did your best. Everyone does."

She had nothing to say. They were twenty thousand tons of steel, drifting in the ocean.

"Maybe something will still work out," Rand offered.

Lore ascended through the ship to the deck and climbed the stairs to the pilothouse. It was the morning of their thirty-ninth day at sea, the equatorial sun already blazing like a furnace. Not a breath of wind moved the air; the sea was absolutely flat. Many of the passengers were camped on deck, huddled in the shade of canvas shelters. On the charting table were the sheets of thick, fibrous paper on which Lore had run her final computations. The currents when they'd rounded the Horn had nearly stopped them cold; running at full throttle, they had barely powered through, huge waves blasting over the deck, everybody vomiting helplessly. They had made it eventually, but day by day, as Lore watched the fuel gauges drop, the cost grew painfully evident. They had stripped everything they could and jettisoned it into the sea: pieces of bulkhead, doors, the loading crane. Anything to reduce weight, to buy one more mile with the fuel they had. It wasn't enough. They had come up five hundred miles short.

Caleb entered the pilothouse. Like Rand, he was shirtless, the skin of his shoulders and cheeks flaking with sunburn. "What's going on? Why did we stop?"

From the helm, Lore shook her head.

"Jesus." For a second he seemed dazed, then looked up. "How long?"

"We can keep the desalinators running about a week."

"And then?"

"I really don't know, Caleb."

He had the look of a man who needed to sit down. He took a place on the bench by the chart table. "People are going to figure it out, Lore. We can't just turn off the engines and not tell them anything."

"What do you want me to say?"

"We could lie, I guess."

"There's an idea. Why don't you come up with something?"

Her sense of failure was overwhelming; she had spoken too curtly. "Sorry, you didn't deserve that."

Caleb took a long breath. "It's all right, I get it."

"Tell everyone it's just a minor repair, nothing to worry about," Lore said. "That should buy us a day or two."

Caleb stood and put one hand on her shoulder. "It's not your fault."

"Who else is there?"

"I mean it, Lore. It's just bad luck." He tightened his grip, giving her a sharp squeeze that offered no comfort at all. "I'll put the word out."

After he'd gone, she sat alone for a time. She was exhausted, filthy, beaten. Without its engines, the ship felt soulless, inert as stone.

I'm sorry, Michael, she thought, *I did everything I could, but it wasn't enough.*

She dropped her face to her hands.

It was late in the day when she descended into the hull. She met Sara as the woman was closing the door to Greer's cabin.

"How is he?"

Sara shook her head tersely: not well. "I don't see how things can go on much longer." She paused, then said, "Caleb told me about the engines."

Lore nodded halfheartedly.

"Well, let me know if I can do anything to help. Maybe it just wasn't meant to be."

"You're not the first to say that."

When Lore said nothing else, Sara sighed. "See if you can get him to eat. I left a tray by his cot."

She watched the woman move down the passageway, then quietly turned the handle and stepped inside. The air had an unwashed smell of sweat and urine and sour breath and something else, like fermenting fruit. Greer was lying faceup on his bunk with a sheet pulled to his chin, his arms lying at his sides. At first Lore thought he was dozing—he slept most of the time now—but at the sound of her entry, he rotated his face toward her.

"I wondered when I'd see you."

Lore drew a stool to the edge of the cot. The man was a shadow of a shadow, a shell of bones. His flesh, a sickly yellow, possessed a damp, translucent appearance, like the inner layers of an onion.

"I guess you noticed," she said.

"Hard not to."

"Don't try to cheer me up, okay? A lot of people are doing that, and it's already getting old. Now, what's this I hear about you not eating?"

"Hardly seems worth the bother."

"Nonsense. Let's scoot you up."

He was too weak to rise off the mattress on his own; Lore drew him to a sitting position and wedged a pillow between his back and the bulkhead.

"All right?"

He offered a faint, courageous smile. "Never better."

On the tray were a cup of water and a bowl of porridge, also a spoon and cloth. She draped the cloth over Greer's chest and began to spoon the porridge into his mouth. He worked his lips and tongue hesitatingly, as if these simple actions required tremendous concentration. Still, he managed a good amount before waving her off. She wiped his chin and held the cup of water to his lips. He took a small sip; she could tell he was humoring her. She had noticed, while feeding him, a basin at the foot of the bed, stained with blood.

"Happy now?" he asked, as she put the cup aside.

She almost laughed. "What a question."

"Michael picked you for a reason. That's no less true now than it was thirty-nine days ago."

Suddenly the tears came. "Oh, goddamnit, Lucius. What am I going to tell people?"

"You're not going to tell them anything yet."

"They're going to figure it out. Probably a lot of them already have."

Greer gestured to the bedside table. "Open that drawer," he said. "The top one."

Inside she found a single sheet of heavy paper, folded into thirds and sealed with wax. For several seconds she just looked at it, dumbfounded.

"It's from Michael," Greer said.

She took it in her hand. It weighed almost nothing—it was only paper—but it felt like far more; it felt like a letter from the grave. She wiped her face with the back of her wrist. "What does it say?"

"That's between the two of you. All he told me was that you weren't supposed to open it until we arrived at the island. His orders."

"So why are you giving it to me now?"

"Because I think you need it. He believed in you. He believed in the *Bergensfjord*. The situation is what it is; I won't tell you different. But things may work out yet."

She hesitated, then said, "He told me how the passengers died. How they killed themselves, sealing the ship and channeling back the engines' exhaust."

"Don't get ahead of yourself, Lore."

"I'm only saying he knew it was a possibility. He wanted me to be ready."

"We're not there yet. A lot of things can happen between now and then."

"I wish I had your faith."

"Feel free to use mine. Or Michael's. God knows I borrowed his lots of times. We all did. None of us would be here if we hadn't."

A brief silence passed.

"Tired?" Lore asked.

His eyes were heavy-lidded. "A little, yeah."

She put her hand on his arm. "You just rest, all right? I'll come check on you later."

She rose and went to the door.

"Lore?"

She turned at the threshold; Greer was looking at the ceiling.

"A thousand years," he said. "That's how long."

Lore waited for more but there was none. Finally she said, "I don't understand."

Greer swallowed. "In case Amy and the others fail. That's how long before anybody can go back." He took a deep breath and let the air out slowly, closing his eyes. "I'm only saying this because I might not be around to tell you later."

She let herself into the passageway and returned to the pilothouse, where she sat at the chart table. The sky beyond the windscreen showed evening coming on. A mass of clouds, as thick and textured as wads of unspun cotton, had moved in from the south; perhaps they'd be lucky and get some rain. She watched as the sun dipped to the horizon, flaring the sky with its final light. A sudden weariness enfolded her. Poor Lucius, she thought. Poor everyone. The world could do without her for a while, she decided, and she laid her head on the table, cradling it with her arms, and soon was fast asleep.

She dreamed of many things. In one dream, she was a girl again, lost in a forest; in another, she was stuck inside a closet; in a third, she was carrying a heavy object of unknown type and could not put it down. These dreams were not pleasant, but neither were they nightmares. Each unfolded seamlessly into the next, depriving them of their full power—no climax was reached, no mortal moment of terror—and as sometimes occurred, she was also aware that she was dreaming, that the landscape she inhabited was harmlessly symbolic.

The final dream of Lore's thirty-ninth night at sea was hardly a dream at all. She was standing in a field. All was quiet, yet she knew a danger was approaching. The color of the air began to change, first to yellow, then to green. The hair on her arms and the back of her neck rose, as if with a static charge; simultaneously, a great wind swirled up around her. She tilted her face to the sky. Clouds of black and silver had begun to form a whirlpool overhead. With a crackling explosion and a biting smell of ozone, a bolt of lightning jagged the ground in front of her, blinding her utterly.

She began to run. Sheets of rain commenced to fall as, above her, the furious, whirlpooling clouds congealed into a single, fingerlike cone. The ground was shaking, thunder crashing; trees were bursting into flames. The storm was pursuing her. It would sweep her into oblivion. As the finger touched down behind her, the air was rent by a deafening, animal roar. Its power seized her like a fist; suddenly the ground was gone. A voice, far away, was calling her name. She was lifting into the air, she was soaring higher and higher, she was being hurled off the face of the earth . . .

"Lore, wake up!"

Her head jerked from the table. Rand was staring at her. Why was he so wet? And why was everything moving?

"What the hell are you doing?" Rand barked. Rain and seawater were pelting against the windscreen. "We're in real trouble here."

As she attempted to rise from the bench, the deck heaved sideways. The door flew open with a bang, rain and wind blasting into the pilothouse. Another groan from deep within the hull and the deck began to heel in the opposite direction. Lore went tumbling, sliding down the deck and smacking into the bulkhead. For a moment it seemed that they would just keep going, but then the motion reversed. Gripping the edge of the table for balance, she fought her way upright.

"When the hell did this start?"

Rand was clutching the edge of the pilot's seat. "About thirty minutes ago. It just whipped up from nowhere."

They were taking the sea broadside. The lightning flashed, the heavens shook; huge waves were crashing over the rails.

"Get below and fire the engines," she ordered.

"That'll use the rest of our fuel."

"No choice." She strapped herself into the pilot seat; water was sloshing over the floor. "Without helm control, this is going to pound us to pieces. I just hope we have enough left to get through this. We'll need all the thrust you've got."

As Rand exited, Caleb appeared out of the storm. The man's face was white as a ghost's, whether with terror or seasickness, Lore couldn't tell.

"Is everyone below?" she asked.

"Are you kidding me? It's like a screaming contest down there."

She yanked the straps tight. "This is going to be rough, Caleb. We need every hatch sealed. Tell people to tie themselves down however they can."

He nodded grimly, turned to go.

"And shut that fucking door!"

The ship heeled into the next trough, listing at a perilous angle before rolling up the other side. With nearly all of their fuel gone, they had no ballast; it wouldn't take much to capsize them. She looked at her watch; it was 0530. Dawn would soon be breaking.

"Goddamnit, Rand," she muttered. "Come on, come on . . ."

The pressure gauges leapt; power flowed through the panel. Lore set the rudder, gripped the throttle control, and opened it wide. The compass was spinning like a top. With excruciating slowness, the bow began to turn into the wind.

"Come on, girl!"

The bow bit and held, plummeting into the next trough as if down a mountainside. Spray blasted over the deck. For a second, the front of the ship was almost fully submerged; then it ascended, the hull rearing upward like a great rising beast.

"That's the way!" Lore shouted. "Do it for Mama!"

She drove into the howling darkness.

For twelve full hours, the storm raged. Many times, as giant waves crashed over the bow, Lore believed the end had come. Each time, the foredeck plunged into the abyss; each time, it rose again.

The storm did not so much fade as simply stop. One second the wind was howling, the rain lashing; in the next it was all over. It was as if they had simply passed from one room into the next, one of violence, the other of almost perfect calm. With cramped hands, Lore unfastened her straps. She had no idea what was going on belowdecks, nor did this question, at that moment, concern her very much. She was tired and thirsty and badly needed to pee. She squatted over the pot she kept in the pilothouse and stepped outside to toss the contents over the side.

The clouds had begun to break apart. She stood at the rail for a moment and watched the evening sky. She had no idea where they were; she hadn't been able to read the compass since the storm had begun. They had survived, but at what cost? Their fuel was nearly exhausted. Beneath the stern of the *Bergens-fjord,* the screws were softly churning, pushing them through the motionless sea.

Rand emerged from the main hatch and ascended the stairs toward her. He took a place beside her at the rail.

"I've got to admit, it sure is pretty out here," he said. "Funny how it's like that after a storm."

"What's the situation belowdecks?"

His shoulders were slumped, his eyes rimmed with dark circles of fatigue; a bit of something, vomit perhaps, was caught in his beard. "We've got the bilges working—we should be dry pretty soon. You have to hand it to Michael, the guy knew how to build a boat."

"Any injuries?"

Rand shrugged. "Few broken bones, I heard. Some cuts and scrapes. Sara's taking care of it. Lucky thing no one's going to want to eat for a week, seeing as how we're so low on food. The smell is pretty bad down there." He looked at her for a moment, then said, carefully, "Want me to shut down the engines? It's your call."

She considered this question. "In a minute," she said.

For a while they stood together without talking, watching the sun descend over the starboard side. The last of the clouds were separating, lit from within by a purpling light. An area of water near the port bow had begun to boil with fish, feeding near the surface. As Lore watched, a large bird with black-tipped wings and a yellowish head swooped low over the surface, reached down with its bill—a quick, sharp jab—hauled a fish free, tossed it backward into its gullet, and began to climb away.

"Rand. That's a bird."

"I know it's a bird. I've seen birds before."

"Not in the middle of the ocean you haven't."

She darted into the pilothouse and returned with the binoculars. Her pulse was racing, her heart was in her mouth. She pressed the lenses to her eyes and scanned the horizon.

"Anything?"

She held up a hand. "Quiet."

She made a slow circle. Facing due south, she stopped.

"Lore, what are you seeing?"

She held the image in the lenses for an extra few seconds to be sure. Holy damn, she thought. She lowered the binoculars.

"Get Greer up here," she said.

By the time they were able to bring him up on deck, darkness was falling. Lucius did not appear to be in pain; that part had passed. His eyes were closed; he did not seem to know where he was or what was happening. With Sara supervising, Caleb and Hollis served as stretcher-bearers. Others had gathered around; word had spread throughout the ship. Pim was there, with Theo and the girls; Jenny and Hannah; Jock and Grace, holding their infant son; the men of the crew, weary after the long battle of the storm. All stood aside as the stretcher passed.

They carried him to the bow and lowered the gurney. Lore crouched beside him and wrapped one hand with her fingers. His skin was cold and dry, loose on the bones.

"Lucius, it's Lore."

From deep in his throat, a soft moan.

"I have something to show you. Something wonderful."

She slipped the palm of her left hand beneath his neck and gently tipped his face forward, toward the bow.

"Open your eyes," she said.

His lids separated to make the thinnest slits, then a little more. It was if he were using the last of his strength to perform this tiny act. All stood silent, waiting. The island was well within sight now, directly ahead: a single mountain, lushly green, soaring from the sea, and, above it, a cross of five bright stars, punching through the twilight.

"Do you see?" she whispered.

The breath in his chest was barely a presence; death was in his face. A long moment passed as he struggled to focus. At last the faintest of smiles curled his lips.

"It's . . . beautiful," Greer said.

86

Lucius Greer lived three more days, thus earning the distinction of being the first settler on the island, as yet unnamed, to die upon its soil. He spoke no more words; it could not have been said that he regained full consciousness. Yet from time to time, as Sara or one of the others attended to him, the smile would reappear, as if rising from a happy dream.

They buried him in a clearing surrounded by tall palms with a view of the sea. Apart from the men who had worked on the boat, few of the ship's complement knew the man or even who he was, least of all the children, who had heard only vague rumors of a dying man in a cabin, and whose shouts of play could be heard throughout the ceremony. Nobody minded; it seemed suitable. Lore was the first to speak, followed by Rand and Sara. They had decided in advance that each would tell a story. Lore spoke of his friendship with Michael; Rand, the tales Greer had told him about his life in the Expeditionary; Sara, the day she and Greer had met, so many years ago, in Colorado, and all that had happened there. When this was done, they formed a line so each could place a stone upon the grave, which bore a simple marker Lore had fashioned from pieces of driftwood:

LUCIUS GREER

SEER, SOLDIER, FRIEND

It was the next morning that a small group used two of the dinghies to return to the *Bergensfjord,* which waited at anchor a thousand yards offshore. There had been some disagreement on the matter—the ship contained all manner of usable materials—but Lore was firm and, as captain, had final say. We let her rest, she told them. It's what Michael wanted.

She had not, in fact, opened Michael's letter until their second day on the island, by which time she had begun to suspect what it said. She could not say why this should be so; perhaps it was merely her sense of the man. Thus it was without undo surprise, only a pleasant sense of hearing his voice, that she read the three simple sentences the letter contained.

> *Look in aft storage locker #16.*
> *Scuttle the ship.*
> *Start over.*
>
> > *Love, M*

The storage locker contained a crate of explosives, as well as spools of cable and a radio detonator. Michael had left instructions for their proper distribution. Caleb and Hollis ran the cables through the passageways while Lore and Rand distributed the explosives throughout the hull. The fuel tanks, now nearly empty, were full of highly combustible diesel fumes. Lore turned on the mixers, opened the valves, and set the final charge.

There was no further discussion about what would happen next; the job was Lore's. The men returned to the dinghies. Lore took a final tour through the ship, its silent rooms and passageways. She thought of Michael as she walked, for the two, Michael and the *Bergensfjord,* were one and the same in her mind. She was sad but also full of gratitude, for all he had given her.

She ascended to the deck and headed aft. The detonator was a small metal box operated by a key. She removed the key, which she wore on a chain around her neck, and carefully inserted it into the slot. Rand and the others were waiting below in their boats.

"Goodbye, Michael."

She turned the key and dashed for the stern. Beneath her, explosions were ripping through the hull, headed toward the fuel tanks. She hit the fantail at a dead sprint, took three long steps, and launched.

Lore DeVeer, captain of the *Bergensfjord,* airborne.

She entered the water cleanly, with barely a splash. All around her, a beautiful blue world appeared. She rolled onto her back and gazed upward. A few seconds passed; then a flash of light lit the surface. The water shook with a muffled boom.

She emerged just a few yards from the boats. Behind her, the *Bergensfjord* was in flames, a huge cloud of black smoke soaring skyward. Caleb helped her in.

"That was a nice dive," he said.

She sat on the bench. The *Bergensfjord* was sinking from the stern. As its bow lifted clear of the water, exposing its massive, bulbous nose, shouts went up from the beach; the children, thrilled by the marvelous display, were cheering. When the hull reached a forty-five-degree angle, the ship began to slide backward, accelerating with astonishing speed. Lore closed her eyes; she did not want to witness the final moment. When she opened them, the *Bergensfjord* was gone.

They rowed back toward shore. As they approached the beach, Sara came jogging down the sand to meet them.

"Caleb, I think you'd better come," she said.

Pim's membranes had ruptured. Caleb found her underneath a tarp hung between trees on one of the thin mattresses they'd stripped from the *Bergensfjord.* Her face was calm, though damp in the tropical heat. During the last few weeks, her hair had grown incomparably thick, its color deepening to a rich chestnut that flared with red in the sun.

Hey, he signed.

Hey yourself. Then, with a smile: *You should see your expression. Don't worry, I'll be done in no time.*

He looked at Sara. "How is she really?" He was signing simultaneously; no secrets, not now.

"I don't see any problems. She's only a little short of her due date. And she's right: for a second birth, things tend to go faster."

Theo's birth had taken forever, nearly twenty hours from the first contraction to the last. It had just about crushed Caleb with worry, though less than a minute after Theo hit the air, Pim was all smiles, demanding to hold him.

"Just hang around," Sara told him. "Hollis can look after Theo and the girls."

Caleb could tell that there was something the woman wasn't saying. He moved away, Sara following.

"Out with it," he said.

"Well. The thing is, I'm hearing two heartbeats."

"Two," he repeated.

"Twins, Caleb."

He stared at her. "And you didn't know this until now?"

"Sometimes it happens." She reached out and took him by the upper arm. "She's strong—she's done this before."

"Not with two."

"It's not so very different until the end."

"Good God. How am I going to tell them apart?" A foolish concern, and yet it was the first thought to enter his mind.

"You'll figure it out. Plus, they might not be identical."

"Really? How does *that* work?"

She laughed lightly. "You don't know the first thing about this, do you?"

His stomach churned with anxiety. "I guess not."

"Just stay with her. The contractions are still far apart, there's really nothing for me to do at this point. Hollis will keep the kids amused." She gave him a parental look. "Okay?"

Caleb nodded. He felt completely overwhelmed.

"Attaboy," she said.

He watched her head down the beach and returned to the shelter. Pim was jotting in her notebook. It was one he hadn't seen before, handsomely bound with leather. A bottle of ink sat on the sand beside her, as well as a pile of books from Hollis's stash. Pim looked up, closing the diary with a muffled clap as Caleb sat on the sand.

She told you.

Yes.

Pim, too, was grinning at him in a manner that verged on laughter. He felt like he'd wandered into the wrong room at a party, one in which everybody knew everybody else and he knew exactly no one.

Relax, she signed. *It's no big deal.*

How do you know?

Because women know. She drew a sharp breath, her face scrunching with pain. Caleb saw it in her eyes: her lighthearted attitude was a cover. His wife was steeling herself for what would come. Hour by hour, she would go further away from him, into the place where all her strength came from.

Pim? Okay?

A few seconds went by; her face relaxed as she expelled a long breath. She tipped her head at the pile of books. *Read to me?*

He lifted the first volume from the pile. Caleb had never been much for reading; he found it tedious, no matter how much his father-in-law had attempted to persuade him otherwise. At least the title made sense to him: *War and Peace.* Perhaps, contrary to all his expectations, it would actually be interesting. The book was enormous; it felt like it weighed ten pounds. He opened the cover and turned to the first page, which was covered in dispiritingly minuscule print, like a wall of ink.

You're sure about this? he signed.

Pim's eyes were bright, her hands folded together over her belly. *Yes, please. It's one of my father's favorites. I've been meaning to read it for ages.*

Full of dread, yet anxious to please her, Caleb sat on the sand, balanced the book on his lap, and began to sign:

"*'Well, prince, Genoa and Lucca are now no more than private estates of the Bonaparte family. No, I warn you, that if you do not tell me we are at war, if you again allow yourself to palliate all the infamies and atrocities of this Antichrist (upon my word, I believe he is), I don't know you in future, you are no longer my friend, no longer my faithful slave, as you say.'*"

And so on. Caleb was totally baffled; nothing seemed to be happening, just obscure conversations that went nowhere, full of references to places and characters he couldn't keep track of, even a little. The signing was laborious; many words he did not know and had to spell out. Yet Pim seemed to be enjoying herself. At unforeseen moments, she would issue small sighs of pleasure, or her eyes would widen with anticipation, or she would smile at what Caleb supposed was the book's equivalent of a joke. It wasn't long before his hands were exhausted. Pim's contractions continued, the gaps between them shortening over time while their durations increased. When this happened, Caleb would pause in his reading, waiting for the pain to end; Pim would nod to tell him it was over, and he would begin reading again.

The hours moved by. Sara visited at regular intervals, taking Pim's pulse, touching her belly here and there, reporting that all was well, things were moving normally. Of *War and Peace,* she only remarked, eyebrows raised, "Good luck."

Others came by: Lore and Rand, Jenny and Hannah, as well as several people Pim had befriended on the ship. In midafternoon, Hollis brought Theo and the girls. The boy could have cared less, sitting on the ground beside his mother and attempting to fill his mouth with sand, but for the girls, the birth of a cousin—not just one but, magically, a pair of them—was a long-anticipated excitement, like a present waiting to be unwrapped. During their weeks on the ship with little to amuse them, Elle's signing had improved. No longer was she limited to the most elementary phrases. With Pim she chattered away, oblivious to the woman's discomfort, though Pim didn't seem to mind or, if she did, managed not to show it.

"All right," Hollis said finally, clapping his hands together, "your aunt needs her rest. Let's go look for shells, shall we?"

The girls complained, but off they went, Theo riding his grandfather's hip. Pim's eyes followed them. *She looks so much like Kate,* she signed.

Which one?

She paused. *Both of them.*

The afternoon faded. Caleb had become aware of a certain energy being directed at the tent from multiple directions. Word had gone around: a baby was being born. Eventually Pim told him to stop reading. *Let's save the rest for later,* she said, by which she meant: nothing besides having these babies is going to happen for a while. The contractions intensified, long and deep. Caleb called for Sara. A quick exam, then she looked at him pointedly.

"Go wash your hands. We'll need a couple of clean towels, too."

Jenny had heated a pot of water. Caleb did as Sara instructed and returned to the tent. Pim had begun to make a great deal of noise. The sounds she made were different than other people's. There was something more raw about them, almost animalistic. Sara hiked up Pim's skirt and laid one of the towels beneath her pelvis.

Ready to push?

Pim nodded.

"Caleb, sit next to her. I need you to translate what I say."

The next contraction seized her. Pim clamped her eyes tight, raising her knees and bending her chin to her chest.

"That's the way," Sara said. "Keep going."

Another few seconds, torturous to Caleb, and then Pim relaxed, gasping for breath, her head falling back onto the sand. Caleb hoped for some respite, but virtually no time passed before the next contraction. The long, listless afternoon had become a battle. Caleb took one of her hands and began to write in her palm. *I love you. You can do this.*

"Here we go," said Sara.

Pim coiled and bore down. Sara had placed her hands beneath Pim's pelvis with her palms open, as if to catch a ball. A dark, round cap of hair appeared, slithered back inside, then emerged once more. Pim was puffing rapidly through pursed lips.

"One more time," Sara said.

Caleb signed the words, though Pim took no notice. It hardly mattered; her body was in control now—she was merely following its commands. She gripped Caleb's arm for balance, rose up, and buried her fingers into his flesh as every part of her compressed.

The head appeared again, and then the shoulders; with a slippery sound the baby slid free, into Sara's hands. A girl. The baby was a girl. Sara passed her to Jenny, who was kneeling beside her. Jenny quickly snipped the cord and balanced the baby along her forearm; cupping the baby's face with her palm, she began to rub her tiny, blue-skinned back with a tender, circular motion. The air of the shelter had a smoky smell, as well as a note of something sweet, almost floral.

The baby made a small, wet sound, like a sneeze.

"Piece of cake," Jenny said with a smile.

"We're not done here, Caleb," Sara said. "The next one's yours."

"You're kidding."

"You have to earn your keep around this place. Just follow Jenny's lead."

Pim rocked forward again. Her last push seemed less effortful; the path had been cleared. A single sustained straining and the second child arrived.

A boy.

Sara passed him to Caleb. The cord, a glistening rope of veins, was still attached. The boy was warm against Caleb's skin, his color dull, almost gray. He placed his son along his arm as Jenny had done and began to rub. The lightness of his body was stupendous; how astounding that a person could grow from this small thing, that not just people but every living creature upon the earth had begun this way. Caleb felt swept into a miracle. Something soft and wet filled his palm; the baby's chest expanded with a gulp of air.

One life had left them; now two had entered. Pim, her face glazed with relief, was already holding their daughter. Sara cut the cord, washed the little boy with a damp cloth, wrapped him in a blanket, and gave him back to Caleb. An unanticipated longing washed over him; how he wished his father were here. For weeks he had kept this feeling at bay. Holding his son in his arms, he could no longer.

Tears poured from his eyes.

87

They named the girl Kate; the boy was Peter.

Two months had passed. Quickly the joy of the settlers' arrival had been put aside as everyone turned to the concerns of making the island a home. Hunting parties were organized, food gathered, fishing nets laid, vines harvested and trees felled for the construction of shelters. The island seemed eager to fulfill their needs. Many things were new. Bananas. Coconuts. Huge tusked boars, nasty as hell and not to be messed with but which, when taken, provided bountiful meat. In the jungle, less than a hundred yards from the beach, a mountain stream, descending in a dazzling waterfall, filled a rocky grotto with water so cold and fresh it made their heads pound.

It was Hollis who suggested that the first civic structure should be a school. This seemed sensible; without something to organize their days, the children would run wild as mice. He selected a site, organized a party, and got to work. When Caleb happened to mention that they had very few books, the big man laughed. "Seems to me we're starting over in more ways than one," he said. "I guess we'll just have to write some."

It did not take long for the memories of their old life to recede. That was, perhaps, the most amazing thing. Everything was new: the food they ate, the air they breathed, the sound of the wind in the palm fronds, the rhythm of days. It was as if a blade had fallen onto their lives, carving it into a time before and a time after. Ghosts were always with them, the people they had lost. Yet everywhere, on the beach and in the jungle, was always the sound of children.

The mantle of leadership had naturally fallen to Lore. At first she'd demurred: *What do I know about running a town?* Yet the precedent had been set; that she'd been captain was hard to put aside in people's minds, and she commanded the respect not only of the crew, who had served under her, but of the people she had brought safely to shore. A vote was held; over her objections, which had come to seem only halfhearted, she was elected by acclaim. Some discussion followed as to what her title should be; she opted for "mayor." She organized a cabinet of sorts: Sara would be in charge of all medical matters; Jenny and Hollis would oversee the school; Rand and Caleb would supervise construction of all the residential structures; Jock, who'd turned out to be a fine shot with a bow, would organize the hunting parties; and so on.

They had yet to investigate much of the island, which was far bigger than it had originally appeared. It was decided that two scouting parties would set out, circling the mountain in opposite directions. Rand led one party, Caleb the other. They returned a week later, reporting that the island, rather than standing alone, was the southernmost of what appeared to be a chain. Two more were visible from the high cliffs of the island's northern side, with a third, perhaps, lurking in the far distance. They had also found no traces of prior inhabitation. That did not mean it wasn't there; perhaps one day they would discover evidence that people had been here before. But for now, the island's unspoiled quality, its wildness and beneficence, spoke in tones of solitude.

It was a hopeful time. Not without cares; there was much to do. But they had begun.

For many weeks, Pim had been considering what to do with her book. The work was complete, the words polished. Of course, the story it told went only so far; the end was unknown to her. But she had done all she could.

The decision to bury it, or in some similar manner conceal it, had come upon her slowly, and with some surprise. She had long supposed that eventually she would show it to other people. Yet day by day the idea grew that these writings were not, in fact, for anyone still living but served a grander purpose. She attributed this intuition to the same mysterious influence that had led her to write these pages in the first place, and to write them as she had. One early morning, not long after Caleb's return from scouting the island, she awoke to a feeling of great calm. Caleb and the children were still asleep. Pim rose quietly, gathered her journal and shoes, and stepped outside.

The first rays of dawn were crawling upward from the horizon. Soon the settlement would awaken, but for now, Pim had the beach to herself. The world had a way of speaking to you if you let it; the trick was learning to hear. She stood for a moment, savoring the quiet, listening for what the world was telling her this morning.

She turned away from the water and headed into the jungle.

She had no destination; she would let her feet carry her where they chose. She found herself walking beneath thick foliage roughly parallel with the beach, perhaps two hundred yards inland. All of this had been explored, of course. Dew was dripping from the leaves; the rising sun saturated the jungle canopy with a warm green light. The ground became uneven, folded into rocky ridges. At times she was forced to crawl on her hands and knees. At the top of a ridge she saw, below her, a gentle depression, guarded on three sides by rock walls roped with vines. Jeweled beads of water trickled down the face of the farthest wall, collecting at the base in a pool. She carefully descended. Something about this place felt new and undiscovered; it possessed a feeling of sanctuary. Crouched by the pool, she filled her cupped hands and drank. The water was clean and tasted like stone.

She rose and surveyed her surroundings. Something was here; she could sense it. Something she was meant to find.

As she scanned the rocky perimeter, her eyes fell upon a zone of shadow within the dense vegetation. She made her way toward it. It was a cave, the opening curtained by vines. She drew them aside. Here was a likely place—indeed, an ideal place—in which to conceal her journal. She reached down into the pocket of her dress; yes, a box of matches, one of the last. She scraped a match on the striker and extended it into the cave's mouth. The space was not especially large, more like the room of a house. The match burned down to her fingertips. She extinguished it with a flick of her wrist, struck a second, and followed its light inside.

At once Pim became aware that she had entered not merely a natural formation but somebody's home. The space was furnished with a table, a large bed, and two chairs, all fashioned from rough-cut logs roped together with vines. Other objects, similarly primitive in their manufacture, littered the floor: simple stone tools, baskets of dried fronds woven together, plates and cups of unfired clay. She lit another match and approached the bed. Shadows stretched before her, revealing a human form beneath the brittle blanket. She drew it aside. The body, what persisted of it—dried bones the color of wood, a whorl of hair—lay curled on its side, its arms tucked protectively against its chest. Whether male or female, Pim could not discern. Carved into the wall beside the bed were a series of marks, small slashes cut into the stone. Pim counted thirty-two. Did they represent days? Months? Years? The bed was unnecessarily large for one person; there were two chairs, not one. Somewhere, probably not far, would be the grave of the cave's other inhabitant.

Pim stepped outside. That she was meant to conceal her journal in this place was apparent; the cave was a repository of the past. Still, she longed to know more. Who were these people? Where had they come from? How had they died? Standing at the edge of the pool, she could feel the presence of these silenced lives. She made her way around the walls. Gradually, as if a veil had lifted from her eyes, other artifacts emerged. Shards of pottery. A wooden spoon. A circle of stones where a fire had once been laid. On the far side of the pool, she came to a tangle of bushes with thick, waxy leaves. Something lurked behind it—a curved shape, bulging from the ground.

It was a boat—more precisely, a lifeboat. The fiberglass hull, about twenty feet long, was settled deeply into the soil. Vines entwined it, rendering it nearly invisible; a thick duff of organic matter carpeted the bottom, small plants growing from it. How long had it rested here, slowly sinking into the jungle floor? Years, decades, even more. She circled the hull, hunting for clues. It yielded nothing until she reached the stern. Affixed to the transom, partially obscured by vegetation, was a wooden plaque—faded, brittle, riven with rot. Spectral letters were etched into its surface. She crouched and pulled the vines aside.

For a time she did not move, so profound was her astonishment. How could it be so? But as the minutes passed, a new feeling rose within her. She remembered the storm, the great wind howling down, carrying them to shore when all seemed lost. Destiny was too small a word; there was a force at work that ran far deeper, a thread woven into the fabric of all things. When more time had elapsed she rose and returned to the clearing. She had no intentions; she was acting by instinct. At the edge of the pool she knelt once more. There, in the water's placid surface, she beheld the image of her face: a young face, smooth and unlined, though this, she knew, would change. Time would have its way, as it did for everyone. Her babies would grow; she, and all the people she loved, would recede, becoming memories, then memories of memories, and finally nothing at all. It was a sad thought, but it also made her happy in a way that felt new. This island of refuge: It was meant to be theirs. It had waited for them all along, so that history could begin again. That's what the words on the plaque had told her.

Perhaps a time would come when it would feel right to share this with the others. On that day, she would lead them to the boat and show them what she had discovered. But not just yet. For now—like her journals and the story they told—it would be her secret, this message from the past, engraved upon the transom of a derelict lifeboat.

BERGENSFJORD

OSLO, NORWAY

88

Carter held his breath as long as he could. Bubbles rose around his face; his lungs were screaming for air. The world above seemed miles away, though in fact it was only a few feet. Finally he could endure it no longer. He pushed off and zoomed to the surface, exploding into the summer sunshine.

"Do it again, Anthony!"

Haley was clinging to his back. She was wearing a pink two-piece suit and cobalt-blue goggles that made her look like an enormous bug.

"All right," he laughed, "just give me a second. Besides, it's Riley's turn."

Haley's sister was sitting on the pool deck, dangling her feet in the water. Her bathing suit was one piece, green, with a flouncy skirt and a single plastic daisy appliquéd onto one shoulder strap; she was wearing orange water wings. Carter could toss her into the water for hours without her getting bored.

"Again! Again!" demanded Haley.

Rachel walked toward them from the garden. She was dressed in shorts and a white T-shirt streaked with dirt; on her head, a broad straw hat. In one gloved hand she held a pair of shears, in the other a basket of freshly cut flowers of various types and colors.

"Girls, let Anthony catch his breath."

"I don't mind," Carter said. He was clinging to the side. "It's no bother."

"See?" said Haley. "He says he doesn't mind."

"That's because he's being polite." Rachel removed her gloves and dropped them into the basket. Her face shone with sweat and sun. "How about some lunch?"

"What do we have?" Haley asked.

"Let me think." Her mother frowned theatrically. "Hot dogs?"

"Yay! Hot dogs!"

Rachel broke into a smile. "I guess that decides it. Hot dogs it shall be. Do you want one, Anthony?"

He nodded. "I can always take a hot dog."

She returned to the house. Carter climbed from the pool and got towels for himself and the girls.

"Can we swim more?" Haley asked, as he was rubbing her hair. It was blond, with flecks of a copper color. Riley's was a soft, heathery brown, quite long. She liked to wear it in pigtails when she swam.

"Depends on what your mama says. Maybe after lunch."

She made her eyes grow wide. That was the kind of girl she was, always putting on a show to get what she wanted. It was the funniest thing. "If you say yes, she'll have to say it, too."

"Don't work that way, you know that. We'll just have to see."

He squeezed the last of the water from her hair, sent the two of them off to play, and sat at the wrought-iron table to catch his breath and watch. There were toys all over the yard—Barbies, stuffed animals, a brightly colored plastic play set Haley was too big for but still liked to fool with, the two of them pretending it was other things, such as the counter at a store. Haley had gone off in one direction, her sister in another.

"Look!" Riley yelled. "I found a toad!"

She was crouched over the path by the garden gate.

"Is that right?" Carter said. "You go on and bring that over here and let me have a look."

She walked to the patio with cupped palms extended before her, her big sister following.

"Now, that there is one handsome toad," Carter declared. The creature, a mottled tan color, was breathing rapidly, loose skin flapping along its sides.

"I think it's disgusting," Haley said with a sour face.

"Can I keep him?" Riley asked. "I want to name him Pedro."

"Pedro," Carter repeated with a slow nod. "Sounds like a fine name. Now, of course," he went on, "he may already got one. That's something to consider. Something he goes by with the other toads."

The little girl's face pinched with a frown. "But toads don't have names."

"Now, how you know? Do you speak toad?"

"That's silly," the older girl stated. She was tugging at the bottom of her suit. "Don't listen to him, Riley."

Carter leaned forward in his chair and raised a finger, drawing their attention to his face. "I'm going to tell you something true now, both of you," he said. "And that is this: everything got a name. It's got a way to know itself. That's an important lesson in life."

The smaller girl stared at him. "Trees?"

"Sure," he replied.

"Flowers?"

"Trees, flowers, animals. Everything living."

Haley looked at him askance. "You're making this up."

Carter smiled. "Not in the least. Grown folks know things, you'll see."

"I still want to keep him," Riley insisted.

"Maybe so. And I'm sure Mr. Toad would like that just fine. But a toad belongs in the grass, with the other toads who know him. Plus, your mama would pitch a fit she knew I let you keep him."

"I *told* you," Haley moaned.

Carter sat back. "You two go on now. You can play with him a bit if you like, but leave him be after that."

They scampered away. Carter rose to put on his shirt and sat back down. The sun was mild on his face in the dappled shade of the live oaks; from far away, he heard a quiet wash of traffic. A few minutes passed before Rachel came out the back door, bearing a tray of the promised hot dogs. Riley's had ketchup and cheese, Haley's mustard; Carter's had all three. For herself, Rachel had made a salad. She returned to the kitchen and came back out with paper plates and a bag of chips, then once more with drinks: milk for the girls, a pitcher of tea for the grown-ups.

"Riley found a toad," Carter remarked. "Wanted to keep it as a pet."

Rachel put the hot dogs onto plates and laid out napkins. "Of course she did. I'm assuming you said no." She looked up and raised her voice. "Girls, come for lunch!"

They ate their hot dogs and chips and drank their tea and milk. Afterward, cherry popsicles for dessert. By the time they finished, the girls were starting to fade. Usually Riley took a nap after lunch; Haley would put up a fuss but wasn't too old for one, especially after the morning they'd had, hours and hours of playing in the pool in the hot sun. With promises of more swimming later, they ushered the girls into the house, Carter carrying Riley, who was already half asleep. In the girls' bedroom, he passed her off to Rachel, who removed Riley's damp suit, replaced it with a T-shirt and underpants, and tucked her into bed. Haley was already under the covers.

"Now, I want you two to sleep," Rachel said from the door. "No fooling around." She closed the door with a quiet click. "Come to think of it," she said, "I could go for a nap myself."

Carter nodded. "I was thinking the same thing. Girls just about wore me out."

In the bedroom, he traded his bathing suit for an old pair of shorts he liked, soft from laundering, and lay down on top of the comforter. Rachel moved in beside him. He put his arm around her and pulled her close. Her hair had a clean, sweet smell he loved. It was just about the nicest thing there was.

"You know," she said softly, "I was thinking."

"What's that now?"

She shrugged against his chest. "Just how wonderful this morning was. The garden was so beautiful."

Carter pulled her tighter against him to say he thought the same.

"I could do this forever," she said.

Forever was what they had. Soon her breathing steadied, long and low, like waves upon a placid shore. Its rhythm moved into him in a soft current, taking him with her.

What happiness, thought Carter, and closed his eyes. What happiness at last.

XIV

THE GARDEN BY THE SEA

343 A.V.

This bud of love, by summer's ripening breath,
May prove a beauteous flower when next we meet.

—SHAKESPEARE, *ROMEO AND JULIET*

89

She had chosen a spot in sight of the river. The earth was softer here, but that was not the only reason. As dawn broke over the ridgeline, Amy began to dig. The river was low, as it always was in summer; mist floated atop the water like smoke. She dug first to the calls of birds, then, as the heat built, to the stillness spreading over the land.

Stopping now and then to rest, she finished at midday. At the river's edge she splashed her face and cupped her palms to drink. She was sweating profusely in the heat. For a time she sat on a rock to gather herself, her shovel resting above her on the bank. In the shallows she detected the shapes of trout, tucked behind rocks. Protected from the current, they held themselves in place with small flicks of their tails, lying in wait for the insects that washed downstream to their open mouths.

The body was swathed in a sheet. Amy used a wooden bier and ropes, tackled to a sturdy tree limb, to lower it. Her thoughts were ordered and calm; she'd had years to prepare for this moment. But at the first pattering of soil upon the shroud, she experienced a rush of emotion, an upwelling of feeling she had no name for. It seemed like many things at once; it came not from her mind but from a deeper place, almost physical. Tears mixed with the perspiration streaming down her face. One shovelful at a time, the body disappeared, becoming one with the earth.

She tamped the surface and knelt by the grave. She would erect no marker; the proper memorial would be made in due course. Perhaps an hour passed; she possessed no sense of time, nor had the need to. Her heart felt heavy and full. As the sun touched the line of the hills, she pressed one palm to the freshly turned earth.

"Goodbye, my love," she said.

Peter had died, as he had long believed he would, on a summer afternoon. Four nights ago, he had failed to return to the house. This had happened before, when his wanderings took him too far to make it back before first light. But when he didn't appear the next night, Amy went to look for him. She found him curled beneath an overhang on the east side of the mesa, his body wedged tightly against the rocks. He was only partially conscious. His breathing was quick and thin, his skin pallid, his hands dry and cold. She wrapped him in a blanket and lifted him into her arms; the lightness of his body shocked her. She carried him back to the house and upstairs to the bedroom. She had already closed the shutters. She laid him in the bed and got in next to him, holding him as he slept, and the next morning she sensed something, a presence. Death had entered the house. He seemed to experience no pain, just a kind of fading. He did not regain awareness of his surroundings, or did not seem to. The hours passed. She would not leave him, not for a moment. At midday, his breathing slowed until it was barely perceptible. Amy waited. A moment came when she realized he had slipped away.

Now, her task complete, she returned to the house and made a simple dinner for herself. She tidied the kitchen and put her dishes away. The quiet of eternity had settled over the rooms. Darkness came on. The stars wheeled above the silent land. She had preparations to make, but these could wait until morning. She did not want to go upstairs—those days were over. She bedded down on the sofa, curled beneath a blanket, and soon was fast asleep.

Dawn's soft glow in the windows awakened her. Standing on the porch, she took measure of the day, then returned to the house to prepare her supplies. She had fashioned a simple pack with a wooden frame she could carry on her back. Into this went the things for her journey: a blanket, some simple tools, extra clothing, food for a couple of days, a plate and cup, a tarp, a coil of rope, a sharp knife, bottles of water. That which she lacked or had failed to anticipate, she could find along the way. Upstairs, she washed and dressed. In the mirror above the stand, she saw her face. She, too, had aged. She might have been a woman of forty, perhaps forty-five. Ribbons of gray, almost white, threaded through her long hair. Crinkles fanned from the corners of her eyes; her lips had thinned and paled, becoming almost colorless. How much time would go by before this face, her face, was observed by another living soul? Would this even happen, or would she pass from the world unseen?

In the living room, Amy sat at the piano. Its existence was nothing she'd ever been able to account for; when she and Peter had arrived at the farmstead, all those years ago, the piano was waiting, a gift from beyond. Every night, Amy played it; the music was the force that summoned Peter home. Now, placing her hands above the keys, she waited for something to come to her; with a quiet chord she began, letting her hands tell her where to go. Bright notes filled the house. Within the song's phrases lay all that she felt. It passed through her in waves, rising and falling, circling and returning, a language of pure emotion. *I never grow tired of it,* Peter always told her. He would stand behind her, placing his hands on her shoulders with the gentlest touch to feel the music as she did, as a force that flowed from within. *I could listen to you play forever, Amy.*

Every song is a love song, she thought. Every song is for you.

She came to the end. Her hands stilled above the keys; the last notes hovered, faded, and were gone. So, the moment of parting. A lump had lodged in her throat. She cast her eyes a final time about the room. It was just a room, like any other—simple furnishings, a hearth blackened with long use, candles on the tables, books—but it meant vastly more. It meant everything. Here they had lived.

She rose, put on her pack, and strode out the door, not looking back.

She reached California in the fall. First the deserts, scorched by the sun, then mountains emerged from the haze, their great blue backs surging above the arid valley. Two more days in sight of them and she began to climb. The temperature declined; cool green woodlands waited at the top. Beneath her, the valleys and mountains of the high Mojave undulated in the haze. The wind was fierce and dry on her face.

At length, the Colony Wall appeared. It was still towering in places, in others crumbled to ruin, barriers of vegetation poking through the rubble. Amy scrambled over the detritus and made her way to the center of town. Great trees stood where none had grown before; most of the buildings were gone, collapsed into their foundations. Yet a handful of the larger ones remained. She came to the structure that had been known as the Sanctuary. The roof had caved in; the building was a shell. She mounted the steps to look through a window that had, miraculously, remained unbroken. It was caked with grime; she used a dampened cloth to make a small porthole and cupped her eyes to the glass. Open to the sky, the interior had become a forest.

It took her some time to get her bearings, but eventually she located the stone. It had settled into the earth somewhat; many of the names inscribed into its face had washed away to mere depressions, scarcely legible. Still, she was able to discern certain surnames. Fisher. Wilson. Donadio. Jaxon.

Evening was approaching. She removed her pack and withdrew her tools: chisels and gouges of various sizes, picks, and two hammers, one large, one small. For a time she sat on the ground, surveying the stone. Her eyes traveled over the stoic surface as she planned her attack. She could have waited until morning, but the moment seemed right. She selected a spot, took up her chisel and hammer, and began.

She finished on the morning of the third day. Her hands were bloody and raw. The sun was high in the sky as she stood back to examine her handiwork. The quality of the inscription was unpracticed but, on the whole, better than she'd hoped. She slept that day and all the next night and, in the morning, refreshed, packed her camp and descended the mountain. She headed west, first away from the sun and then toward it. The land was empty, without history, devoid of life. The days passed in windswept silence, until, one morning, Amy heard the sea. On the air was the scent of flowers. The sound, a low roaring, expanded; suddenly the Pacific appeared. Its blue expanse seemed infinite; she felt as if she were beholding an entire planet. White-tipped waves crashed upon the shore. She made her way through banks of wild roses and eelgrass down to the wide beach at the water's edge. She felt uneasy but also consumed by a sudden urge. She stripped off her pack and then her clothes and sandals. As the first wave broke across her body, its power nearly knocked her off her feet; a second claimed her, and rather than resist, she dove down into the surging water. She could no longer touch the bottom—it had happened that fast. She experienced no fear, only a wild, startled joy. It was as if she had rediscovered a wholly natural condition in which she was connected to the forces of creation. The water was wonderfully cold and salty. With the barest motions of her arms and legs, she could keep herself afloat. She allowed herself to bob freely in the swells, then dove down again. Beneath the surface she opened her eyes but could see virtually nothing, just vague shapes; she rolled her body to look up. Brilliant sunshine ricocheted off the face of the water, making a kind of halo. Gazing at this heavenly light, she held her breath as long as she could, hidden in this unseen world beneath the waves.

She decided to remain awhile. Every morning she swam, each time moving farther out. She was not testing her resolve; rather, she was waiting for a new impulse to emerge. Her body felt clean and strong, her mind rinsed of all care. She was entering a new phase of life. She spent her days just sitting and watching the waves or taking long walks up and down the sandy expanse. Her needs were simple and few; she discovered a grove of oranges and, near that, great banks of blackberries, and these were what she ate. She missed Peter, but the feeling was not the same as missing something she had lost. He was gone but would always be a part of her.

Content as she was, she realized over the months that her journey had not ended. The beach was a way station, a place of preparation for the final leg. When spring came, she broke camp and made her way north. She had no destination in mind; she would let the land speak to her. The terrain grew more rugged: rocky promontories, the heart-stopping beauty of the California coast, towering trees blasted by the salted winds into strange, grasping shapes that cantilevered over the sea. She passed her days walking, the sun's hands pressing on her shoulders, the ocean beside her, curling and falling; at night she bedded down beneath the stars or, if it was raining, a tarp suspended on a cord between the limbs of a tree. She saw animals of every type: the small ones, squirrels and rabbits and groundhogs, but also larger, statelier creatures, antelope and bobcats and even bears, great dark shapes shambling through the brush. She was alone on a continent that man had conquered and then left. Soon no trace of his long habitation would remain; it would all be new again.

Spring became summer, summer fall. The days were crisp and cool, and at night she built a fire for warmth. She was north of San Francisco, she didn't know quite where. One morning she awoke under her tarp and knew at once that something had changed. She emerged into a world of soft white light and silence; snow had fallen in the night. Fat flakes floated soundlessly down from the sky. She tipped her face upward, receiving them. Flakes clung to her lashes and hair; she opened her mouth to taste them on her tongue. A flood of memories engulfed her. It was as if she were a girl again. She lay on her back and extended her legs and arms, moving them back and forth to carve a shape in the snow: a snow angel.

She understood, then, the nature of the force that was drawing her north. She did not arrive until spring and even then was caught by surprise. It was early morning, the forest air thick with mist. The sea, far below, at the base of a tall cliff, was heavy and dark. In the dense shade of trees, she was cresting a rise when all of a sudden a feeling of completeness overwhelmed her, so arresting that it froze her in her tracks. She ascended the rest of the way and emerged into a clearing with a view of the ocean, and there her heart seemed to stop.

The field was carpeted with the most lustrous show of wildflowers she had ever seen—flowers by the hundreds, the thousands, the millions. Purple irises. White lilies. Pink daisies. Yellow buttercups and red columbines and many others she knew no names for. A breeze had arisen; the sun had broken through the clouds. She shrugged off her pack and walked slowly forward. It was as if she were wading into a sea of pure color. The tips of her fingers brushed the petals of the flowers as she passed. They seemed to bow their heads in salutation, welcoming her into their embrace. In a trance of beauty, Amy moved among them. Corridors of golden sunshine fell over the field; far away, across the sea, a new age had begun.

Here she would make her garden. She would make her garden, and wait.

EPILOGUE

THE MILLENNIALIST

INDO-AUSTRALIAN REPUBLIC
POP. 186 MILLION
1003 A.V.

The past is never dead. It's not even past.

—William Faulkner,
Requiem for a Nun

90

Third Global Conference on the North American Quarantine Period
Center for the Study of Human Cultures and Conflicts
University of New South Wales, Indo-Australian Republic
April 16–21, 1003 A.V.
Transcript: Plenary Session 1

Welcoming Address by Dr. Logan Miles
Professor and Chair of Millennial Studies, University of New South Wales, and Director of the Chancellor's Task Force on North American Research and Reclamation

Good morning and welcome, everyone. I'm happy to see so many esteemed colleagues and valued friends in the audience today. We have a busy schedule, and I know everyone is eager to get started with the presentations, so I will keep these opening remarks brief.

This gathering, our third, brings together researchers from every settled territory, in virtually every field of study. Among our numbers, we count scholars in disciplines as various as human anthropology, systems theory, biostatistics, environmental engineering, epidemiology, mathematics, economics, folklore, religious studies, philosophy—and on and on. We are a diverse group, with a range of methodologies and interests. But we are united by a common purpose, one that runs far deeper than any specific field of study. It is my hope that this conference will serve not only as a springboard for innovative scholarly collaboration but also as an occasion for reflection—the opportunity for all of us, individually and collectively, to consider the broader, humanistic questions that lie at the heart of the North American Quarantine and its history. This is especially important now, as we pass the millennial mark and the project of North American reclamation, under the authority of the Trans-Pacific Council and the Brisbane Accord, moves into its second phase.

A millennium ago, human history very nearly came to an end. The viral pandemic we know as the Great Catastrophe killed over seven billion people and brought humanity to the edge of extinction. Some among us would assert that this event was an arbitrary occurrence—nature's way of shuffling the deck. Every species, no matter how successful, eventually encounters a force greater than itself, and it was simply our turn. Others have postulated that the wound was self-inflicted, the consequence of mankind's rapacious assault upon the very biological systems that sustained our existence. We made war on the planet, and the planet fought back.

Yet there are many—and I count myself among them—who look at the history of the Great Catastrophe and see not merely a tale of suffering and loss, arrogance and death, but also one of hope and rebirth. How and where the virus originated is a door that science has yet to unlock. Where did it come from? Why did it vanish from the earth? Is it still out there, waiting? We may never know the answers, and in the last instance, I pray we never do. What *is* known is that our species, against the greatest odds, endured. On an isolated island in the South Pacific, a pocket of humanity survived, eventually to spread the seeds of a reborn civilization across the Southern Hemisphere and establish a second age of humankind. It has been a long struggle, fraught with peril, and we have far to go. History teaches us that there are no guarantees, and we ignore the lessons of the Great Catastrophe at our peril. But the example of our forebears is no less instructive. Our instinct for survival is indomitable; we are a species of unconquerable will and the capacity for hope. And should that day come again when the forces of nature rise up against us, humanity will not go quietly.

Until very recently, very little of substance was known about our ancestors. Scripture tells us that they made their passage to the South Pacific from North America, and that they carried with them a warning. North America, it was said, was a land of monsters; to return was to bring death and ruin down upon the world once more. Until a thousand years had passed, no man or woman should set foot there. This injunction has been a central tenet of our civilization, encoded as law by virtually every civic and religious institution since the foundation of the republic. No scientific evidence has heretofore existed to support this claim or, even, its source. We have, so to speak, taken the matter on faith. But it lies at the core of who we are.

Much has changed in the last few years. With the discovery of the ancient writings we know as "The Book of Twelves," new light has been shed on the past. Concealed in a cave on the southernmost of the Holy Isles, this text, of unknown authorship, has for the first time lent historical credence to our common lore, even as it has deepened the mysteries of our origins. Dating from the second century A.V., "The Book of Twelves" recounts an epic contest on the North American continent between a small band of survivors and a race of beings called virals. At the center of this struggle is the young girl Amy—the Girl from Nowhere. Possessing unique powers of body and spirit, she leads her fellows—Peter, the Man of Days; Alicia of Blades; Michael the Clever; Sara the Healer; Lucius the Faithful; et al.—in the fight to save humanity. The tale and its cast of characters are familiar to all, of course. No document in our history has been the subject of as much study, speculation, and, in many cases, outright skepticism as this manuscript. Certainly elements of the narrative are far-fetched, more the province of religion than science. Yet from the moment of its discovery, nearly everyone has agreed that it is a document of extraordinary importance. That it should be found in the Holy Isles, the cradle of our civilization, forges the first tangible link between North America and the lore that has shaped and guided us for nearly a millennium.

I am a historian. I deal in facts, in evidence. My professional creed dictates that only through the prisms of doubt and patient scholarship can the truth of the past be revealed. But one thing my various travels in the past have taught me, ladies and gentlemen, is that behind every legend lies an element of truth.

May I have the first slide please?

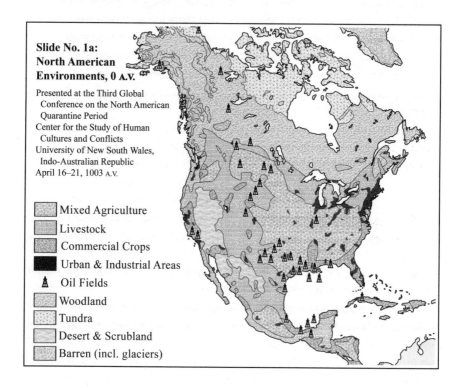

Since our return to North America, thirty-six months ago, a great deal has been learned about the state of the continent both before and during the Quarantine Period. These two images represent two very different North Americas. The contrast could not be more vivid. On the top we see a reconstruction of the continent as it stood in the final years of the American Imperial Period. Cities of millions dominated both coasts. Unsustainable agricultural practices had decimated virtually all of the continent's interior plains. Heavy industry, powered by fossil fuels, had rendered vast swaths of land virtually uninhabitable, the soil and water fouled by heavy metals and chemical by-products. Though some wilderness remained, primarily in the alpine regions of the Appalachian uplift, the northern Pacific coast, and the Intermountain West, there is little doubt that the image represents a continent, and a culture, consuming itself.

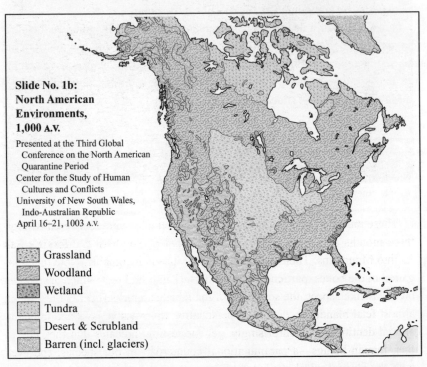

Slide No. 1b:
North American
Environments,
1,000 A.V.

Presented at the Third Global
  Conference on the North American
  Quarantine Period
Center for the Study of Human
  Cultures and Conflicts
University of New South Wales,
  Indo-Australian Republic
April 16–21, 1003 A.V.

- Grassland
- Woodland
- Wetland
- Tundra
- Desert & Scrubland
- Barren (incl. glaciers)

On the bottom we see North America as it now stands. Airship reconnaissance, conducted from floating platforms situated beyond the two-hundred-mile quarantine line, has revealed a pristine wilderness stunning in its organic diversity. Virgin forests now rise where once stood huge cities and poisonous industrial complexes. Gone are the tamed fields of the continent's interior plains, replaced by grasslands of incomparable biological richness. Most significantly, a majority of the great coastal metropolises, including New York, Philadelphia, Boston, Baltimore, Washington, D.C., Miami, New Orleans, and Houston, have all but disappeared, subsumed by rising sea levels. Nature, as is its wont, has reclaimed the land, wiping away the leavings of the imperialistic power that once radiated from its shores.

Powerful images, indeed—but hardly unexpected. It is at ground level that our most startling findings have occurred.

Next slide?

These mummified remains, one male, one female, were recovered twenty-three months ago in an arid basin at the foot of Southern California's San Jacinto Mountains. Their monstrous appearance is inarguable. Note the elongation of the bones, particularly those of the hands and feet, which have taken on a clawlike aspect; the softening of the facial support structure, creating an almost fetal blandness, devoid of personality; the massive jaws and radically altered dentition. Yet, surprisingly, genetic testing indicates that they are, in fact, human beings—a paramutational counterpart of our species, endowed with the physiological attributes of nature's most fearsome predators. Excavated at a depth of just under two meters, these remains were found in the midst of many others, suggesting a mass die-off of some kind, probably occurring at or near the end of the first century A.V.—the same time frame to which carbon dating has attributed the writing of "The Book of Twelves."

Are these the "virals" that our forebears warned us of? And if they are, how did these dramatic changes come about? To this there appears to be an answer.

Next slide?

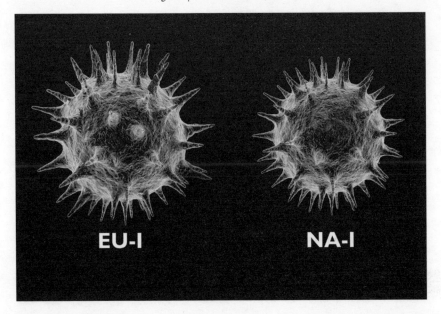

On the left we see the EU-1 strain of the GC virus, taken from the body of the so-called "frozen man," a polar researcher who succumbed to the infection a millennium ago. This virus, we believe, was the primary biological agent of the Great Catastrophe, a microorganism of such robustness and lethality that it was able to kill its human host within hours and virtually wiped out the world's population in fewer than eighteen months.

I draw your attention now to the virus on the right, which was extracted from thymus tissue of one of the two corpses found in the Los Angeles basin. We now believe this to be a precursor to the EU-1 strain. Whereas the virus on the left contains a considerable quantity of genetic material from an avian source—more specifically, *Corvus corax,* known as the common raven—the one on the right does not. In its stead we find genetic material linking it to an altogether different species. Though our teams have yet to identify this organism's genetic author, it bears some resemblance to *Rhinolophus philippinnensis,* or the large-eared horsehoe bat. We are calling this virus NA-1, or North America–1.

In other words, the Great Catastrophe was caused not by a single virus but by two: one in North America and a second, descendant strain that subsequently appeared elsewhere in the world. From this fact, researchers have built a tentative chronology of the epidemic. The virus first emerged in North America, infiltrating the human population from an unknown vector, though in all likelihood a species of bat; at some later point, the NA-1 virus changed, acquiring avian DNA; this new, second strain, far more aggressive and lethal, subsequently made its way from North America to the rest of the world. Why the EU-1 strain failed to bring about the physical changes caused by NA-1 we can only speculate. Perhaps in some instances it did. But by and large, the consensus of opinion is that it simply killed its victims too quickly.

What does this mean for us? Put succinctly, the "virals" of "The Book of Twelves" are not fiction. They are not, as some have claimed, a mere literary device, a metaphor for the predatory rapaciousness of North American culture in the B.V. period. They existed. They were real. "The Book of Twelves" describes these beings as a manifestation of an almighty deity's displeasure with mankind. That is a matter for each of us to weigh in the privacy of his or her own conscience. So, too, is the story of the man known as Zero and the twelve criminals who acted as the original vectors of infection. Speaking for myself, the jury is still out. But in the meantime, we know who and what the virals were: ordinary men and women, infected with a disease.

But what of humanity? What of the story of Amy and her followers? I turn now to the matter of survivors.

Next slide?

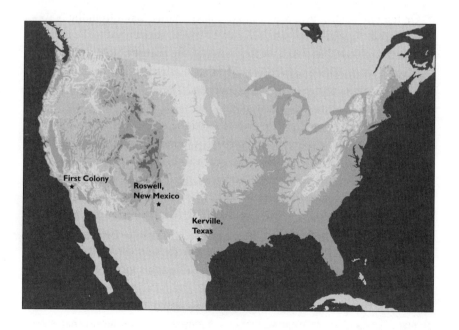

As everyone here certainly knows, it has been an exciting year in the field—very exciting, indeed. Excavations of several newly discovered human settlements in the North American West, dating from the first century of the Quarantine Period, have begun to bear fruit. Much of this work is still in its infancy. Yet I think it's no overstatement to say that what we've uncovered in the last twelve months alone has signaled a truly radical reconceptualizing of the period.

Our understanding of the early Quarantine Period has long presupposed that no human inhabitants remained in North America between the Equatorial Isthmus and the Hudson Frontier Line following the year zero. The disruption to the continent's biological and social infrastructures was believed to have been so complete as to render the continent incapable of supporting human life, let alone any kind of organized culture.

We now know—and once again, the last year has been extraordinary—that this view of the Quarantine Period is incomplete. Indeed, there were survivors. Just how many, we may never know. But based on the findings of the last year, we now think it possible, indeed very likely, that they numbered in the tens of thousands, living in a number of communities throughout the Intermountain West and the Southern Plains.

The size and configuration of these settlements varied considerably, from a mountaintop village housing just a few hundred inhabitants to a city-sized compound in the hills of central Texas. But all give evidence of human habitation well after the continent was thought to have been depopulated. These communities also share a number of distinctive traits, most significantly a culture that was both classically survivalist and, paradoxically, deeply attentive to the social practice of being *human*. Within these protected enclaves, the men and women who survived the Great Catastrophe, and generations of their descendants, went about their lives, as men and women do. They married and had children. They formed governments and engaged in trade. They built schools and places of worship. They kept records of their experience—I am speaking, of course, about the documents known to everyone in this room, indeed to people throughout the settled territories, as "The Book of Sara" and "The Book of Auntie"—and, perhaps, even sought contact with others like themselves, beyond the walls of these isolated islands of humanity.

Using "The Book of Twelves" as a road map, research teams on the ground have identified three such settlements, all named within those writings. These include Kerrville, Texas; Roswell, New Mexico, the site of what has been called the "Roswell Massacre"; and the community we know as First Colony, in the San Jacinto Mountains of Southern California.

May I have the next image, please?

The photograph we see here provides an aerial view of the layout of the First Colony site, which might, for our purposes today, be considered a "typical" human settlement of the Quarantine Period. Situated on an arid plateau two thousand meters above the Los Angeles coastal formation, and guarded to the west by a granite ridge rising an additional fifteen hundred meters, the settlement presents itself very like a walled medieval city—roughly five square kilometers, irregularly shaped, with high ramparts defining the outer perimeter. These steel-and-concrete fortifications, which stood twenty meters high, appear to have been constructed right around the time of the Great Catastrophe. This conforms to "The Book of Twelves," which asserts that First Colony was constructed to house children evacuated from the eastern coastal city of Philadelphia. Beyond these fortifications, the terrain now presents a mixture of alpine forest and high desert chaparral, but soil samples taken both within and outside the walls indicate that the mountainside was decimated by fire as recently as fifty years ago, and during the first century of the Quarantine Period, the terrain was almost entirely denuded.

The entire settlement seems to have been surrounded by banks of high-pressure sodium vapor lamps. These were powered, we believe, by a stack of proton exchange membrane fuel cells, connected by a buried cable to an array of wind-powered turbines, also dating from the pre-Q period, located forty-two kilometers to the north, in the San Gorgonio Pass. Seismic activity has substantially altered the northern slope of the mountain, and we have yet to locate the power trunk connecting First Colony to its primary energy source. But we hope this will happen in due course.

Inside the walls, we find several discrete zones of human activity, arranged in a ringlike formation and leading to a central core. The outer ring, which has received the most extensive excavation, seems to have served as a staging platform for defense. From these areas we have recovered a range of artifacts, including, at the lowest levels, a variety of conventional firearms of the pre-Q period, yielding at the upper levels to more homemade weaponry, such as knives, longbows, and crossbows. Though more primitive, these armaments were surprisingly sophisticated in their design and manufacture, with arrow points honed to a width of just fifty microns—sufficient, we believe, to pierce the crystalline-silicate breastplate of an infected human.

Moving farther in, we find discrete regions for sanitation, agriculture, live-stock, commerce, and housing. Structures in the eastern and northern quadrants of the interior appear also to have served as domiciles, perhaps for married couples or families. The exposed foundation we see near the center seems to have been some kind of school dating from the pre-Q period but converted by the citizens of First Colony to perform a variety of civic functions. We believe that this building, the most substantial structure on the site, could have been employed as a final refuge in the event that the colony's outer defenses were penetrated. But in daily life, it seems to have served as a kind of communal nursery or hospital.

On their own, these findings are remarkable enough. But there is more. "The Book of Twelves" speaks of First Colony as the place from which Amy and her fellows traveled east, eventually coming into contact with other survivors, including an armed force from Texas, known as the Expeditionary. Is there any archaeological record to support these claims?

I draw your attention now to the large, open area at the center, and in particular to the object located on the northwest corner.

May I have the next image?

This object, which we are calling the First Colony Stone, sits adjacent to the settlement's central public space. The stone itself is an ordinary granitic boulder of the type found throughout the San Jacinto uplift, standing three meters high, with a basal radius of about four meters. Etched into its surface we find three distinct groups of writings. The first group, by far the most extensive, begins with a date, 77 A.V., followed by a list of what appears to be 206 names in four columns. As we can see, they are presented in family groups and include seventeen different surnames. Though there is some debate on this point, the arrangement suggests that these individuals may have perished in a single event, perhaps one associated with the massive earthquake that struck California at about that time.

Below this we see a second group of three names, also legible: Ida Jaxon, Elton West, and a person named as "The Colonel," evidently a military leader of some stature. Beneath these markings we see the single word "Remembered." Our best guess is that these individuals may have perished in some kind of battle, perhaps one in which the fate of the Colony itself was determined.

It is the third grouping, however, that is the most provocative. As we can see, the etching is much less sophisticated, and exposure to the elements has rendered the names unreadable to the naked eye. Significantly, wear-pattern analysis indicates that these markings date to about 350 A.V., well after the settlement was abandoned. Again, there's some disagreement on this point, but prevailing opinion holds that these markings are, like the others, a memorial of some kind. Digital enhancement reveals names well known to all.

May I have the final slide?

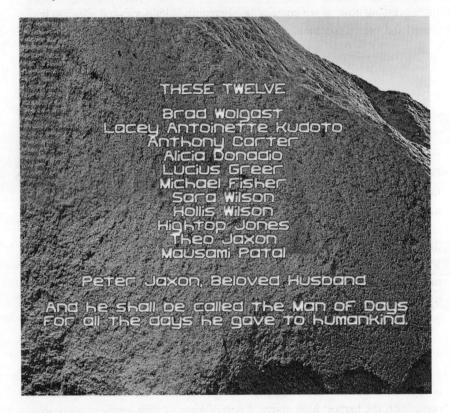

THESE TWELVE

Brad Wolgast
Lacey Antoinette Kudoto
Anthony Carter
Alicia Donadio
Lucius Greer
Michael Fisher
Sara Wilson
Hollis Wilson
Hightop Jones
Theo Jaxon
Mausami Patal

Peter Jaxon, Beloved Husband

And he shall be called The Man of Days
for all the days he gave to humankind.

Of Amy, the Girl from Nowhere, there is no mention. Perhaps we shall never learn who she was, if she existed at all.

There is much we do not understand. We don't know who these people were. We don't know what role they may have played, if any, in the extinction of the paramutational race known as virals. And we don't know what became of them, how they died. This gathering, I hope, will open the door to addressing some of these mysteries. But even more, what I wish is for all of us to come away with a deeper appreciation of the most fundamental questions that define us. History is more than data, more than facts, more than science and scholarship. These things are merely the means to a greater end. History is a *story*—the story of ourselves. Where do we come from? How have we survived? How can we avoid the mistakes of the past? Do we matter, and if we do, what is our proper place upon the earth?

I shall put the question another way: Who are we?

In a very real and pressing sense, the study of the North American Quarantine Period is far more than an academic investigation of the past. It is—and I think everyone in the room would echo this notion—a crucial step toward safeguarding the long-term health and survival of our species. This is all the more pressing now, as we contemplate humanity's long-awaited return to that feared and vacant continent.

91

For Logan Miles, age fifty-six, professor of millennial studies and director of the Chancellor's Task Force on North American Research and Reclamation, it has been a good morning. A very good morning, indeed.

The conference is off to a roaring start. Hundreds of scholars are in attendance; press interest is intense. Before he reaches the door of the ballroom, a wall of reporters surrounds him. What does it all mean, they want to know, these names on the stone? Were the twelve disciples of Amy real people? What will be the effect on North American reclamation? Are the first settlements going to be delayed?

"Patience, everyone," Logan says. Flashbulbs fire into his face. "You know what I do, neither more nor less."

Free of the crowd, he departs the building via a rear exit off the kitchens. It is a pleasant autumn morning, dry and blue-skied, with an easterly breeze coming off the harbor; high above, a pair of airships float serenely, accompanied by the vibrato buzzing of their massive propellers. The sight always brings his son to mind; Race, a pilot in the air service, has just been promoted to captain, with a ship of his own—a great achievement, especially for a man so young. Logan pauses to take in the air before making his way around the corner of the building toward the campus's central quadrangle. The usual protestors linger by the steps, forty or fifty of them, holding their signs: "NORTH AMERICA = DEATH," "SCRIPTURE IS LAW," "THE QUARANTINE MUST STAND." Most are older—country people, adherents to the old ways. Among them are perhaps a dozen Ammalite clergy, as well as a scattering of Disciples, women dressed in plain gray robes tied with a simple cord at the waist, their heads shorn in the manner of the Savior. They have been there for months, always showing up at precisely eight A.M., as if clocking in for a job. At the start, Logan found them irritating, even a little disturbing, but as time went by, their presence acquired a quality of doomed listlessness, easily ignored.

The walk to his office takes ten minutes, and he is both pleased and surprised to find the building practically empty. Even the department secretary has flown the coop. He makes his way to his office, on the second floor. In the past three years, he has become an infrequent visitor; most of his work is now in the capitol, and he sometimes doesn't set foot on campus for weeks at a stretch, not counting his visits to North America, which have devoured whole months. With its walls of bookshelves, enormous teakwood desk—a splurge to mark his promotion to department chair, fifteen years ago—and overall atmosphere of professorial seclusion, the room always reminds him of both how far he's come and the unlikely role that has been thrust upon him. He has reached a kind of pinnacle; yet it is still true that from time to time he misses his old life, its quiet and routine.

He is sorting through a file of papers—a tenure committee report, graduation forms requiring his signature, a caterer's bill—when he hears a knock and looks up to see a woman standing in the doorway: thirty or perhaps thirty-five and quite striking, with auburn hair, an intelligent face, and energetic hazel eyes. She wears a tailored suit of dark navy and high, somewhat tippy heels; a well-used leather satchel hangs from her shoulder. Logan senses that he has seen her before.

"Professor Miles?" She does not wait for permission to enter but insinuates herself into the room.

"I'm sorry, Miss . . ."

"Nessa Tripp, *Territorial News and Record.*" As she steps to his desk, she extends her hand. "I was hoping I might have a minute of your time."

A reporter, of course; Logan recalls her from the press conference. Her grip is firm—not masculine but meant to convey a message of professional seriousness. Logan catches the high note of her perfume, subtly floral.

"I'm afraid I'm going to have to disappoint you. This is quite a busy day for me. I've really said all I have to say for one morning. Perhaps you could call my secretary to schedule an appointment."

She ignores the suggestion, knowing full well that it's a dodge; nobody would schedule anything. She offers a smile, rather coquettish, meant to charm. "I promise, it won't take long. I have only a few questions."

Logan doesn't want to. He dislikes dealing with the press, even under the most scripted of circumstances. Many times he has opened the morning paper to find himself misquoted or his words taken entirely out of context. Yet he can tell that this woman can't be brushed off so easily. Better to face the music now, quickly, and move on.

"Well, I suppose . . ."

Her face beams. "Wonderful."

She takes a chair across from him and digs into her bag for a notebook, followed by a small recorder, which she places on the desk. "To start, I was wondering if I could get a little bit of personal information, just for background. There's very little about you that I could find, and the university press office wasn't much help."

"There's a reason. I'm a very private person."

"And I can respect that. But people want to know about the man behind the discovery, wouldn't you agree? The world is watching, Professor."

"I'm really not very interesting, Miss Tripp. I think you'll find me rather boring."

"I hardly believe that. You're just being modest." She flips quickly through her notebook. "Now, from what I can gather, you were born in . . . Headly?"

A softball question, to get things started. "Yes, my parents raised horses."

"And you were an only child."

"That's correct."

"Sounds like you didn't much care for it."

His tone, evidently, has betrayed him. "It was a childhood like any other. There were some good points, some bad."

"Too isolated?"

Logan shrugs. "When you're my age, these sorts of feelings soften a great deal, though at the time I probably saw it that way. In the end, it wasn't the life for me—that's really all there is to say."

"Still, Headly is a very traditional place. Some would even say backward."

"I don't think the people there would see it that way."

A quick smile. "Perhaps I misspoke. What I mean is, it's a long way from a horse farm in Headly to heading the chancellor's task force on resettlement. Would that be fair to say?"

"I suppose. But I never had any doubts that I would go to university. My parents were country people, but they let me chart my own course."

She looks at him warmly. "So, a bookish boy, then."

"If you like."

This is followed, once again, by a brief trip to her notes. "Now," she says, "I have here that you're married."

"I'm afraid your information is a little out of date. I'm divorced."

"Oh? When was that?"

The question makes him uncomfortable. Still, it is a matter of public record;

he has no reason not to answer. "Six years ago. All very amicable. We're still good friends."

"And your ex-wife, she's a judge, yes?"

"She was, with the Sixth Family Court. But she's left that now."

"And you have a son, Race. What does he do?"

"He's a pilot in the air service."

Her face brightens. "How marvelous."

Logan nods. Obviously she knows all of this.

"And what does he have to say about your discoveries?"

"We haven't really talked about it, not recently."

"But he must be proud of you," she says. "His own father, in charge of an entire continent."

"I think that's a bit of an overstatement, don't you?"

"I'll rephrase. Going back to North America—you'd have to concede it's pretty controversial."

Ah, thinks Logan. *Here we go.* "Not to most people. Not according to the polls."

"But certainly to some. The church, for instance. What do you make of their opposition, Professor?"

"I don't make anything."

"But surely you've thought about it."

"It's not my place to hold one voice above any other. North America—not just the place but the *idea* of the place—has sat at the center of humankind's sense of itself for a millennium. The story of Amy, whatever the truth is, belongs to everyone, not just the politicians or the clergy. My job is simply to take us there."

"And what do *you* think the truth is?"

"It doesn't matter what I think. People will have to judge the evidence for themselves."

"That sounds very . . . dispassionate. Detached, even."

"I wouldn't say that. I care a great deal, Miss Tripp. But I don't leap to conclusions. Take these names on the stone. Who were they? All I can tell you is that they were people, that they lived and died a very long time ago, and that somebody thought well enough of them to make a memorial. That's what the *evidence* says. Maybe we'll learn more, maybe we won't. People can fill in the blanks however they like, but that's faith, not science."

For a moment she appears nonplussed; he is not being a cooperative subject. Then, reviewing her notes again: "I'd like to go back to your childhood for a moment. Would you say you come from a religious family, Professor?"

"Not especially."

"But somewhat." Her tone is leading.

"We went to church," Logan concedes, "if that's what you're asking. It's hardly unusual in that part of the world. My mother was Ammalite. My father wasn't really anything."

"So she was a follower of Amy," Nessa says, nodding along. "Your mother."

"It's just the way she was raised. There are beliefs, and there are habits. In her case, I'd say it was mostly a habit."

"What about you? Would you say you're a religious man, Professor?"

So, the heart of the matter. He feels a growing caution. "I'm a historian. It seems like more than enough to occupy myself."

"But history could be said to be a kind of faith. The past isn't something you can actually *know,* after all."

"I wouldn't say that."

"No?"

He settles back to gather his thoughts. Then: "Let me ask you something. What did you have for breakfast, Miss Tripp?"

"I beg your pardon?"

"It's a straightforward question. Eggs? Toast? A yogurt, perhaps?"

She shrugs, playing along. "I had oatmeal."

"And you're quite certain? No doubts in your mind."

"None."

"How about last Tuesday? Was it oatmeal or something else?"

"Why this curiosity about my breakfast?"

"Indulge me. Last Tuesday. It wasn't very long ago, surely you ate something."

"I haven't the foggiest."

"Why not?"

"Because it's not important."

"Not worth remembering, in other words."

She shrugs again. "I suppose not."

"Now, how about that scar on your hand?" He gestures toward the one holding the poised pen. The mark, a series of pale, semicircular depressions, runs from the base of her index finger to the top of her wrist. "How did you get that? It looks to be quite old."

"You're very observant."

"I don't mean to be impertinent. Merely demonstrating a point."

She shifts uncomfortably in her chair. "If you must know, I was bitten by a dog. I was eight years old."

"So you *do* remember that. Not what you ate last week, but something that happened long ago."

"Yes, of course. It scared the hell out of me."

"I'm sure it did. Was it your dog or a neighbor's? A stray, perhaps?"

Her expression grows irritated. Not irritated: exposed. As he watches, she reaches with her other hand to the scar and covers it with her palm. The gesture is involuntary; she isn't aware that she is doing it, or is only partly cognizant.

"Professor, I fail to see the point in all this."

"So it was *your* dog."

She startles.

"Forgive me, Miss Tripp, but if it wasn't, you wouldn't be so defensive. The way you covered your hand just now? It tells me something else."

She moves her hand away deliberately. "And what's that?"

"Two things. One, you believe it was your fault. Perhaps you were playing too roughly. Perhaps you teased him, not meaning to, or maybe a little. Either way, you were part of it. You did something, and the dog responded by biting you."

She shows no reaction. "And what's the other?"

"That you never told anyone the truth."

The look on her face tells Logan that he has hit the mark. There is a third thing, of course, that has gone unstated: the dog was put down, perhaps unjustly. Nevertheless, after a moment passes, she breaks into a grin. *Two can play at this game.*

"That's quite a trick, Professor. I'll bet your students love it."

Now he's the one who smiles. "Touché. But it's not a trick, Miss Tripp, not entirely. The point is a meaningful one. History isn't what you had for breakfast. That's meaningless data, gone with the wind. History is that scar on your hand. It's the stories that leave a mark, the past that refuses to stay past."

She hesitates. "You mean . . . like Amy."

"Exactly. Like Amy."

Their eyes meet. Over the course of the interview, a subtle shift has occured. A barrier has unexpectedly fallen, or so it feels. Logan notes yet again how attractive she is—the word he thinks of, somewhat old-fashioned, is "lovely"—and that she wears no ring. It has been a while for him. Since his divorce, Logan has dated only occasionally and never for long. He does not still love his ex-wife; that isn't the problem. The marriage, he has come to understand, was really a kind of elaborate friendship. He isn't sure quite what the problem is, though he has begun to suspect that he is simply one of those people who is destined to be alone, a creature of work and duty and not much else. Is his interlocutor's flirtatious manner merely a tactic, or is there more to it? He knows that he is, for his age, passably appealing. He swims fifty laps each morning, is still blessed with a full head of hair, favors pricey, well-tailored suits and somewhat splashy ties. He is aware of women and maintains a certain courtly style—holding doors, offering his umbrella, rising when a female companion excuses herself from the table. But age is age. Nessa calls him "Professor," the appropriate mode of address, yet the word also carries a reminder that he is at least twenty years older than she is: old enough, technically, to be her father.

"Well," he says, rising from his chair. "If you'll excuse me, Miss Tripp, I'm afraid I'll have to stop there. I'm running late for a lunch engagement."

She seems caught off guard by this announcement—jarred from some complex mental state by this ordinary detail of a day. "Yes, of course. I shouldn't have kept you so long."

"May I show you out?"

They make their way through the silent building. "I'd like to talk more," she says, as they are standing on the front steps. "Perhaps once the conference is over?"

She retrieves a card from her bag and hands it to him. Logan glances at it quickly—"Nessa Tripp, Features, *Territorial News and Record*," with both home and office numbers—and slips it into the pocket of his suit coat. Another silence; to fill it, he offers his hand. Students flow by, singly and in groups, those on bicycles weaving through the stream like waves around a pier. The air is alive with the buzz of youthful voices. Nessa lets her hand linger an extra second in his, though perhaps it is he who does this.

"Well. Thank you for your time, Professor."

Her watches her walk down the steps. At the bottom, she turns.

"One last thing. Just for the record, the dog wasn't mine."

"No?"

"He was my brother's. His name was Thunder."

"I see." When she says nothing else, he asks, "If you don't mind my asking, what became of him?"

"Oh, you know." Her tone is casual, even a little cruel. She raises her index fingers to make air quotes. "My father took him to 'a farm.'"

"I'm sorry to hear it."

She laughs. "Are you kidding? Couldn't have happened to a nastier son of a bitch. I was lucky he didn't bite my hand off." She hikes her bag higher on her shoulder. "Call me when you're ready, okay?"

She smiles as she says this.

Logan takes a streetcar to the harbor. By the time he arrives at the restaurant, it is nearly one o'clock, and the hostess directs him to the table where his son is waiting. Tall and rangy, with pale blond hair, he takes after his mother. He is wearing his pilot's uniform—black slacks, a starched white shirt with epaulets on the shoulders, and a dark, narrow tie clipped to the front of his shirt. At his feet rests the fat briefcase he always carries when he flies, emblazoned with the insignia of the air service. When he catches sight of Logan, he puts down his menu and rises, smiling warmly.

"Sorry I'm late," Logan says.

They embrace—a quick, manly hug—and settle in. It is a restaurant they have been coming to for years. The view from their table embraces the busy waterfront. Pleasure boats and larger commercial craft ply the water, which sparkles in the bright autumn sunshine; offshore, wind turbines stand in echelon, propellers spinning in the ocean breeze.

Race orders a chicken sandwich and tea, Logan a salad and sparkling water. He apologizes once again for his lateness and the short time they will have together, their first visit in months. Their talk is light and easy—his son's twin boys, his travels, the travails of the conference and Logan's next trip to North America, scheduled for late winter. It is all familiar and comfortable, and Logan relaxes into it. He has been away too long, depriving himself of the enjoyment of his son's company. He has certain regrets about Race's childhood. Logan was too absent, too distracted by work, and much was left to the boy's mother. This capable, handsome man in uniform: what has Logan done to deserve such a prize?

As the waitress takes their plates, Race clears his throat and says, "There's something I've been meaning to talk to you about."

Logan detects a note of anxiety in his son's voice. His first impulse, born of his own experience, is that there is trouble in the marriage. "Of course. Say what's on your mind."

His son folds his hands on the table. Now Logan is certain: something is wrong. "The thing is, Dad, I've decided to leave the air service."

Logan is stunned beyond words.

"You're surprised," his son tenders.

Logan searches frantically for a response. "But you love it. You've wanted to fly since you were young."

"I still do."

"Then why?"

"Kaye and I have been talking. All this travel is hard on us, hard on the boys. I'm gone all the time. I'm missing too much."

"But you were just promoted. An airship captain. Think what that means."

"I have thought about it. This isn't easy, believe me."

"Is this Kaye's idea?"

Logan is aware that his words sound somewhat accusing. He is fond of his son's wife, an elementary school art teacher, but has always found her a bit too fanciful—the effect, he supposes, of her spending so much time around children.

"It was, at first," Race answers. "But the more we discussed it, the more it made sense. Our life is just too chaotic. We need things to be simpler."

"Things will get easier, son. It's always hard, with young children. You're just tired, that's all."

"My mind's made up, Dad. There really isn't anything you can say to change it."

"But what will you do instead?"

Race hesitates; Logan realizes the core of his announcement is coming. "I was thinking of the ranch. Kaye and I would like to buy it from you."

He is speaking of Logan's parents' horse farm. After his father died, Logan sold off a quarter section to pay the estate taxes; for reasons he cannot quite name, he kept the rest, though he hasn't visited it for years. The last time he saw it, the house and outbuildings were a wreck, falling down and full of mice. Weeds were growing in the roof gutters.

"We've saved the money," Race says. "We'll give you a fair price."

"You can have it for a dollar, as far as I'm concerned. That's not the issue." He regards his son for a moment, utterly nonplussed. The request makes no sense to him at all. "Really? This is what the two of you want?"

"It's not just me and Kaye. The boys love the idea."

"Race, they're four years old."

"That's not what I meant. They spend half their time in daycare. I see them two weeks out of four if I'm lucky. Boys like that—they need fresh air, room to roam."

"Trust me, son, country life is much more appealing in the abstract."

"You turned out fine. Take it as a compliment."

He feels a growing frustration. "But what will you do out there? You don't know anything about horses. Even less than I do."

"We've thought about that. We're planning on starting a vineyard."

It is a pie-in-the-sky plan if ever he heard one; it has dreamy Kaye written all over it.

"We had the land checked out," Race continues, "and it's close to ideal— dry summers, damp winters, the right kind of soil. I have some investors, too. It won't happen overnight, but in the meantime, Kaye can teach at the township school. She already has an offer. If we're careful with money, that should tide us over until we're up and running."

Gone unspoken, of course, is the underlying criticism: Race wants to be around for his boys, a deep part of their lives, as Logan failed to do for him.

"You're really *certain* about this?"

"We are, Dad."

A brief silence passes as Logan searches for something to say that might dissuade his only child from this ludicrous plan. But Race is a grown man; the land is just sitting there; he has expressed the desire to sacrifice something important on behalf of his family. What can Logan do but agree?

"I guess I can call the lawyer to get the ball rolling," he concedes.

His son seems surprised; for the first time, it occurs to Logan that Race expected he might say no. "You mean it?"

"You've made your case. It's your life. I can't argue with it."

His son looks at him earnestly. "I meant what I said. I want to pay you what it's worth."

Logan wonders: What is something like that worth? Nothing. Everything.

"Don't worry about the money," he insists. "We'll figure that out when the time comes."

The waitress arrives with the bill, which Race, in jocular spirits, insists on paying. Outside, a car is waiting to take him to the airfield. Race thanks his father again, then says, "So I'll see you Sunday at Mom's?"

Logan is momentarily confused. He has no idea what his son is talking about. Race senses this.

"The party? For the boys?"

Now Logan remembers: a birthday party for the twins, who are turning five. "Of course," he says, embarrassed by the lapse.

Race waves this away with a laugh. "It's fine, Dad. Don't worry about it."

The driver is standing by the door. "Captain Miles, I'm afraid we really have to be going."

Logan and his son shake hands. "Just don't be late, okay?" Race admonishes him. "The boys are excited to see you."

The next morning, back from his morning swim, Logan sees Nessa's article in the paper. Page 1, below the fold; it is neutral, as these things go. The conference and his opening address, mention of the protestors and "the ongoing controversy," snippets of their conversation in his office. Curiously, this disappoints him. His words seem wooden and performed. The article contains a perfunctory stiffness; Nessa has described him as "professorial" and "reserved," both of which are true enough but feel reductive. Is that all he is? Is that what he's become?

For two days the conference occupies him utterly. There are panels and meetings, lunches and, in the evenings, gatherings for drinks and dinner. His moment of triumph, and yet he feels a growing depression. Some of this is Race's announcement; Logan does not like to think of his son abandoning his accomplishments to eke out a living in the middle of nowhere. Headly cannot even be said to be a proper town. There is a mercantile, a post office, a hotel, a farm supply store. The school, which includes all grades, is housed in a single, ugly building made of concrete and possesses neither playing fields nor a library. He thinks of Race wearing a broad-brimmed hat, a sweat-sodden kerchief encircling his neck and insects buzzing around his face, shoving a spade into the unforgiving earth while his wife and children, bored beyond measure, fidget in the house. Scenes of provincial life: Logan should have sold the place years ago. It is all a terrible mistake he is powerless to correct.

On Thursday night, his conference duties concluded, he returns to the courtyard apartment where he has lived since his divorce. It was, like many things in life, meant to be temporary, but six years later, here he is. It is compact, tidy, without much character; most of the furniture was purchased in haste during the confusing early days of separation. He makes a simple dinner of pasta and greens, sits down to eat in front of the television, and the first thing he sees is his own face. The footage was taken immediately after the conference's closing ceremonies. There he is, microphones hovering around his head, his face washed to corpselike whiteness by the harsh glare of the television crew's lights. "STUNNING REVELATIONS," the banner at the bottom of the screen reads. He turns it off.

He decides to call Olla, his ex-wife. Perhaps she can shed some light on their son's perplexing plans. Olla lives at the edge of the city in a small house, a cottage really, that she shares with her partner, Bettina, a horticulturalist. Olla insisted that the relationship did not overlap with the marriage, that it began later, though Logan suspects otherwise. It makes no difference; in a way, he is glad. That Olla should take up with a woman—he had always known her to be bisexual—has made things easier for him. It would be more difficult for him if she were married to a man, if a man were in her bed.

Bettina is the one who answers. Their relationship is wary but cordial, and she fetches Olla to the phone. In the background Logan can hear the chirps and squawks of Bettina's collection of caged birds, which is voluminous—finches, parrots, parakeets.

"We just saw you on TV," Olla starts off.

"Really? How did I look?"

"Quite dashing, actually. Confidence-inspiring. A man at the top of his game. Bette, wouldn't you agree? She's nodding."

"I'm glad to hear it."

This light, easy banter. Very little has changed, in a way. They were always friends who could talk.

"How does it feel?" Olla asks.

"How does what feel?"

"Logan, don't be modest. You've made quite a splash. You're *famous*."

He changes the subject. "By any chance, have you talked to Race lately?"

"Oh, that," Olla sighs. "I wasn't really surprised. He's been hinting at it for a while, actually. I'm surprised you didn't see it coming."

Just one more thing he has missed. "What do you make of it?" he says, then adds, jumping the gun, "I think it's a huge mistake."

"Maybe. But he knows his own mind—Kaye, too. It's what they want. Are you going to sell it to them?"

"I didn't really have a choice."

"There's always a choice, Logan. But if you're asking my opinion, you did the right thing. The place has been sitting there too long. I always wondered why you didn't let it go. Maybe this was the reason."

"So that my son could toss his career away?"

"Now you're being cynical. It's a nice thing, what you're doing. Why not let yourself just look at it that way?"

Her voice is even, careful. Her words, not rehearsed exactly, are nonetheless things that have been imagined in advance. Logan has the unsettling sense, yet again, that he is a step behind everyone, a quantity to be managed by those who know better than he does.

"Your feelings are complicated, I know that," Olla goes on, "but a lot of time has passed. In a way, it's not just a new start for Race. It's a new start for you."

"I wasn't aware I needed one."

A pause at the other end of the line; then Olla says, "I apologize. That didn't come out right. What I mean to say is that I worry about you."

"Why would you worry about *me*?"

"I know you, Logan. You don't let go of things."

"I'm just afraid that our son is about to make the worst error of his life. That this is all some romantic whim."

In the silence that follows, Logan thinks of Olla standing in her kitchen, telephone receiver pressed to her ear. The room is cozy, low-ceilinged; copper pots and dried herbs, tied into bunches with twine, hang from the beams. She will be twirling the phone cord around her index finger, a lifelong habit. Other images, other memories: the way she pushes her eyeglasses up to her forehead to read small print; the reddish spot that flares on her forehead whenever she is angry; her habit of salting her food without tasting it. Divorced, but still the keepers of shared history, the inventory of each other's lives.

"Let me ask you something," Olla says.

"All right."

"You're all over the news. You've been working toward this your whole life. The way I see it, you're getting more than you ever could have asked for. Are you enjoying *any* of this? Because it doesn't sound as if you are."

The question is peculiar. Enjoying it? Is that what one is supposed to do? "I haven't thought about it that way."

"Then maybe it's time you should. Put aside the big questions for a while and just live your life."

"I thought I was."

"Everyone does. I miss you, Logan, and I liked being married to you. I know you don't believe that, but it's true. We had a wonderful family, and I'm very proud of all you've accomplished. But Bettina makes me happy. This *life* makes me happy. In the end, it isn't very complicated. I want you to have that, too."

He has nothing to say; she has him dead to rights. Does he feel hurt? Why should he? It is only the truth. It occurs to him suddenly that this is precisely what Race is asking from him. His son wants to be happy.

"So we'll see you Sunday?" Olla asks, steering the conversation back to firmer ground. "Four o'clock—don't be late."

"Race told me the same thing."

"That's because he knows you the same as I do. Don't be insulted—we're all used to it by now." She pauses. "Come to think of it, why don't you bring someone?"

He's not sure what to make of this curious suggestion. "That isn't the province of ex-wives, generally speaking."

"I'm serious, Logan; you have to start somewhere. You're a celebrity. Surely there's someone you can invite."

"There isn't. Not really."

"What about what's-her-name, the biochemist."

"Olla, that was two years ago."

Olla sighs—a wifely sound, a sound of marriage. "I'm only trying to help. I don't like to see you like this. It's your big moment. You shouldn't do it alone. Just think about it, all right?"

The call over, Logan broods. The sun has set, darkening the room. "Like this"? What is he like? And "celebrity": the word is strange. He is not a celebrity. He is a man with a job who lives alone, who comes home to an apartment that looks like a suite at a hotel.

He pours himself a glass of wine and walks to the bedroom. In the closet he finds his suit coat and, in an outer pocket, Nessa's card. She answers on the third ring, slightly breathless.

"Miss Tripp, it's Logan Miles. Am I disturbing you?"

She seems unsurprised by the call. "I just came back from a run. Give me a moment, will you? I need to get a glass of water."

She puts down the phone. Logan listens to her footsteps, then hears a tap running. Is he hearing anything—anyone—else? He doesn't think so. Thirty seconds and she returns.

"I'm glad you called, Professor. Did you see the article? I suppose you must have."

"I thought it was very good."

She laughs lightly. "You're lying, but that's all right. You didn't give me very much to work with. You're a secretive man. I wish we could have spoken longer."

"Yes, well, that's the reason I called, you see. I was wondering, Miss Tripp—"

"Please," she interrupts, "call me Nessa."

He feels suddenly flustered. "Nessa, of course." He swallows and wades in. "I know it's short notice, but I was wondering if, perhaps, you'd like to join me for a party this Sunday at four o'clock."

"Why, Professor." She sounds coyly amused. "Are you asking me on a date?"

Logan knows it at once: he is making a fool of himself. He has no idea if she is even available. The invitation is preposterous.

"I have to warn you," he says, backing away, "it's a birthday party for a couple of five-year-olds. My grandsons, actually." How smooth of you, he thinks, telling her you're a grandfather. With every word, he feels like he is digging his own grave. "Twins," he adds, rather pointlessly.

"Will there be a magician?"

"I'm sorry?"

"Because I'm very fond of magicians."

Is she making fun of him? This was a terrible idea. "Of course, I understand if you're not free. Perhaps another time—"

"I'd love to," she says.

Sunday arrives, sunny and bright. Logan passes the morning buying presents for the boys—a hop-a-long for Noa; for his brother, Cam, the more cerebral of the duo, a construction set—takes a swim to settle his nerves and waits for the hour to come. At three o'clock he retrieves his car from the garage—undriven for many weeks, it is, to his dismay, rather dusty—and drives to the address Nessa has provided. He finds himself in front of a large, modern apartment complex three blocks from the harbor; Nessa is waiting by the entrance. She is dressed in white slacks, a peach-colored top, and low-heeled, open-toed sandals. Her hair is loose and freshly washed. She is holding a large package wrapped in silver paper. Logan disembarks to open her door.

"That's very thoughtful of you," he says of the parcel, "but you didn't need to bring a present."

"It's a tether ball," she says, pleased. She places the box on the backseat with the others. "You don't think they're too young? My nephews play with theirs for hours."

This is the first mention of her family, which is, Logan learns, quite large. Raised in a northern suburb, where her parents still live—her father is a postmaster—she is the fourth of six children. Three of them, her older sisters and a younger brother, are married with families of their own. So, Logan thinks, she is alone but not unacquainted with the life he has led, that customary life of children and duty and never enough time. Logan has already explained that the party will be held at his ex-wife's house, a fact on which Nessa has made no comment. He wonders if this is a reportorial habit, withholding her thoughts so that others will reveal more of themselves, then chastises himself for being suspicious; maybe it makes no difference to someone of her generation, raised in a more ethically malleable world of constantly changing partners.

The drive to Olla's takes thirty minutes. Their talk comes easily. Little mention is made of the conference. He questions her about her work, if she enjoys it, which she says she does. She likes the travel, meeting new people, learning about the world and trying to shape it into stories. "I was always like that, even as a kid," she explains. "I'd sit in my room and write for hours. Silly stuff mostly, elves and castles and dragons, but as I got older, I got more interested in real things."

"Do you still write fiction?"

"Oh, once in a while, just for fun. Every reporter I know has a half-written novel in their desk somewhere, usually pretty awful. It's like a disease we all have, this wish to get below the surface somehow, to find some kind of larger pattern."

"Do you think that's possible?"

She considers the question, looking out the windshield. "I think there is one. Life *means* something. It's not just going to work and making dinner and taking your car to the repair shop. Wouldn't you agree?"

They are passing through an outer neighborhood: tidy houses set far back from the road, mailboxes standing at attention at the curb, dogs barking from the yards as they drive by.

"I think most people would," Logan says. "At least, we hope so. It can be very hard to see, though."

She seems pleased with his answer. "So you have your way, and I have mine. Some people go to church. I write stories. You study history. They're not really so very different." She glances over at him, then returns her gaze to the passing world. "I have a friend who's a novelist. He's rather famous—maybe you've heard of him. The man's a total mess, drinks a liter a day, barely bothers to change his clothes, the whole cliché of the tortured artist. I asked him once, Why do you do it if it makes you feel so awful? Because seriously, the man's not going to make it to forty the way he lives. His books are thoroughly depressing, too."

"What did he say?"

" 'Because I can't stand not knowing.' "

They arrive. The door stands open in welcome; the road in front of the house is lined with cars. Parents and children of various ages are making their way up the path, the youngest ones dashing ahead, bearing the presents they cannot wait to see opened, their magical contents revealed. Logan hadn't realized the party would be so large; who are all these people? Companions of the boys from play school, neighbors, colleagues of Race and Kaye and their families, Olla's sisters and their husbands, a few old friends Logan recognizes but in some cases hasn't seen for years.

Olla greets them as they enter. She is wearing a willowy dress, a large, somewhat clumsy necklace, neither shoes nor makeup. Her hair, gray since her early forties, falls unmanaged to her shoulders. Gone forever is the barrister in a polished suit and heels, replaced by a woman of simpler, more relaxed habits and tastes. She kisses Logan on both cheeks and turns to Nessa to shake hands, her eyes bright with barely concealed surprise; never did his ex-wife imagine that her dare would be accepted. Nessa goes to the kitchen to fetch drinks while Logan and Olla carry their presents to the spare room off the hall, where a huge pile of gifts rests on the bed.

"Who is she, Logan?" Olla says enthusiastically. "She's lovely."

"You mean young."

"That's entirely your business. How did you meet her?"

He tells her about the interview. "It was kind of a shot in the dark," he admits. "I was surprised she said yes, an old codger like me."

Olla smiles. "Well, I'm glad you asked her. And she certainly seems to like you."

In the living room he moves among the adults, greeting those he knows, introducing himself to those he doesn't. Nessa is nowhere to be found. Logan exits through the patio doors onto the ample, sloped lawn, which is flanked by elaborate gardens, Bettina's handiwork. The children are madly dashing around according to some secret code of play. He spies Nessa seated with Kaye at the edge of the patio, the two of them locked in animated talk, but before he can go over, Race grips him by the arm.

"Dad, you should have told me," he says with mischievous delight. "Holy moly."

"Blame your mother. It was her idea, me bringing a date."

"Well, good for her. Good for you. Boys," he calls, "come say hello to your grandfather."

They break away from their game and trot toward him. Logan kneels to gather their small, warm bodies in his arms.

"Did you bring us presents?" Cam asks, beaming.

"Of course I did."

"Come play with us," Noa begs, tugging at his hand.

Race rolls his eyes. "Boys, let your grandfather catch his breath."

Logan glances past his grandsons and sees that Nessa has already joined the children. "What, do I look too old?" He smiles at the boys. He is full of memories of other parties, when Race was small. "What are the rules?"

"You freeze when you get tagged," Noa explains, wide-eyed. It is as if he is announcing a discovery that will change the fate of mankind. "When everybody freezes, you win."

"Show me the way," he says.

The party roars forward, riding the children's energy, which seems inexhaustible, an engine that can't run down. Logan allows himself to be tagged as quickly as possible, though Nessa does not, dodging and weaving until, with a shriek, she succumbs. A pair of ponies arrive by trailer, swaybacked and balding, like moth-eaten clothes. They are so docile they seem drugged; the man in charge looks like he slept under a bridge. Never mind: the children are thrilled. Cam and Noa take the first rides, while the rest form a line to wait their turns.

"Having a good time?" Logan, approaching Nessa from the side, hands her a glass of wine. Her brow is damp with perspiration. Parents are snapping pictures, hoisting their children onto the backs of the mangy ponies.

"Loads," she says with a smile.

"Fun comes so naturally to them. Children, I mean."

Nessa sips the wine. "Your daughter-in-law is adorable. She told me about their plans."

"You approve?"

"Approve? I think it's marvelous. You must be thrilled for them."

Is it simply the mood of the afternoon that he suddenly feels this way? Not thrilled, perhaps, but certainly more comfortable with the notion. Yes, why not, he thinks. A vineyard in the country. Open spaces, cool, moist dawns, a night sky exploding with stars. Who wouldn't want that?

"*And* you can keep the land in the family," Nessa goes on. She lifts her glass in a little toast. "A bit of history, no? Sounds to me like that would be right up your alley."

The great ceremony comes: the presents are unwrapped. The boys barely acknowledge each one before tearing into the next. Hamburgers and hot dogs, chips, strawberries and slices of melon, cake. Among the children, heads begin to droop, minor disagreements flare, eyes grow heavy-lidded. As evening comes on, they make their departures while some of the adults linger, drinking on the patio. Everyone seems to acknowledge Nessa as an important new presence, especially Bettina, who in the gathering dusk gives Nessa a tour of her gardens.

By the time they leave, there are almost no cars out front. Nessa, exhausted and perhaps a little drunk, leans back in her seat as they pull away.

"You have a wonderful family," she says sleepily.

It's true, Logan thinks; he does. Even his ex-wife, who, despite their difficulties, has emerged at this late stage of life as an advocate for his happiness. Under the influence of the day he feels something long-clenched relaxing inside him. Life is not so bad, so purely dutiful, as he has thought. As they drive, his mind travels to the ranch. He has already spoken to his lawyer to set the paperwork in motion. Soon his son and his family will be there, infusing it with fresh life, fresh memories.

"I was thinking," Logan begins, "perhaps I should drive out and have a look at the old place. I haven't been there for years."

Nessa nods dreamily. "I think that's a good idea."

"Would you like to come? It would only be for a couple of days. Next weekend, say."

Nessa's eyes are closed. Another mistake; he has gotten ahead of himself. She is drunk; he is taking advantage of this moment of warm feeling. Perhaps she has fallen asleep.

"It could be useful to you," he offers quickly. "Another article, perhaps."

"An article," Nessa repeats neutrally. Another moment lapses. "So, just to be clear, you're asking me to go away with you for the weekend to help me write an article."

"Yes, I suppose. If that's what you want."

"Pull over."

"Are you feeling ill?" The worst is upon him. The night is ruined.

"Please, just do it."

He draws the car to the side of the road. He expects her to burst from the door, but instead she turns to face him.

"Nessa, are you all right?"

She seems about to laugh. Before he can utter another word, she takes his cheeks in her hands and draws him toward her, crushing his mouth with a kiss.

They have lunch together on Tuesday, see a film the following night, and on Saturday depart in the early morning. The city falls away as they drive deep into the heart of the country. The day is cool, with fat white clouds, though the temperature begins to rise as they make their way west, away from the sea.

It is just noon when they arrive in Headly. The town has improved somewhat. More commercial concerns now line the dusty main street, and the school has expanded. A new municipal hall stands at the top of the square.

They check in to the inn—Logan has booked separate rooms, not wanting to assume too much—and, with a picnic lunch, drive on to the ranch.

The sight is dispiriting. The land, untended for years, is weedy and wild; the barn has caved in, as well as many of the outbuildings. The house is only a little better—paint peeling, porch tipping to one side, gutters languishing off the eaves. Logan stands in silence for a moment, taking it in. The house was never large, but like all revisited places it seems a lesser version of the one held in memory. Its degraded condition disturbs him. Yet he also feels the upwelling of an emotion he hasn't experienced in years: a sense of homecoming, of home.

"Logan? All right?"

He turns to Nessa. She is standing slightly apart from him. "Strange to be back," he says and shrugs diffidently, though the word "strange" hardly does the situation justice.

"It's really not so bad, you know. I'm sure they can fix it up."

He does not want to enter the house yet. They put their blanket on the ground and lay out their picnic: bread and cheese, fruit, smoked meat, lemonade. The site they have selected has a view of the parched hills; the sun is hot but clouds scud past, creating brief intervals of shade. As they eat, Logan points out the sites, explaining the history: the barns, the paddocks, the fields where horses once grazed, the thickets where he spent idle hours as a boy, lost in worlds of his own imagining. He begins to relax; the tension between what he remembers and what he now sees softens; the past flows forth, wanting to be told—though there is, of course, more to the story.

The moment comes when the house can no longer be avoided. Logan takes the key from his pocket—it has lain in his desk drawer, untouched, for years—and lets them in. The door opens directly onto the front parlor. The air is stale. Some of the furnishings remain: a couple of armchairs, shelves, the desk where his father did his accounts. A thick layer of dust coats every surface. They move deeper into the house. All the kitchen cabinets stand open, as if explored by hungry ghosts. Despite the staleness, smells assault him, tinged with the past.

They press on to the back room. Logan is drawn to it as if by a magnetic force. There, covered by a tarp, is the unmistakable shape of the piano. He pulls the cloth aside and raises the fallboard, exposing the keys, which are as yellow as old teeth.

"Do you play?" Nessa asks.

They are the first words either of them has spoken since entering the house. Logan depresses a key, expelling a sour note. "Me? No." The sound hovers in the air, then is gone. "I'm afraid I haven't been completely honest with you," he says, looking up. "You asked me if I came from a religious family. My mother was what used to be known as an 'Amy dreamer.' Are you familiar with the term?"

Nessa frowns. "Isn't that a myth?"

"You mean, hasn't modern science rebranded the phenomenon? In conventional terms, I suppose you could say she was crazy. Schizophrenic with a tendency toward grandiosity. That's more or less what the doctors told us."

"But you don't think so."

Logan shrugs. "It's not really a yes-or-no question. Sometimes I do, sometimes I don't. At least she came by it honestly. Her maiden name was Jaxon."

Nessa is visibly taken aback. "You're First Family?"

Logan nods. "It's not something I like to talk about. People make assumptions."

"I hardly think these days anyone would make much of it."

"Oh, you'd be surprised. Out here, folks put stock in a thing like that."

Nessa pauses, then asks, "What about your father?"

"My father was a simple man. *Straightforward* would be the term. If he had a religion, it was horses. That, and my mother. He loved her a great deal, even when things got bad. When they married, according to him, she was just like anybody else. Perhaps a little more devout than most, but that wasn't so unusual in these parts. It wasn't until later that she started having spells. Visions, episodes, waking dreams, whatever you like to call them."

"Was the piano hers?"

Nessa has correctly intuited this. "My mother was a country girl, but she came from a musical family. From an early age she was quite good. Some people said she was a prodigy, even. She could have gone on to a real career, but then she met my father, and that was that. They were very traditional in that way. She still played sometimes, though I think she had mixed feelings about it."

Logan takes a steadying breath before continuing: "Then one night I woke up and heard her playing. I was very young, six, maybe seven. The music wasn't like anything I'd heard before. Incredibly beautiful, hypnotic almost. I can't even describe it. It swept me up completely. After a while, I went downstairs. My mother was still playing, though she wasn't alone. My father was there, too. He was sitting in a chair with his face in his hands. My mother's eyes were wide open, but she wasn't looking at the keys or anything else. Her face had a kind of erased blankness to it. It was as if some outside force was borrowing her body for its own intentions. It's hard to explain—maybe I'm not telling it right—but I knew instinctively that the person playing the piano wasn't my mother. She'd become someone else. 'Penny, stop,' my father was saying—pleading, really. 'It's not real, it's not real.'"

"It must have been terrifying."

"It was. There he was, this proud man, strong as a bull, completely helpless, shaking with tears. It rocked me to the core. I wanted to get the hell out of there and pretend the whole thing had never happened, but then my mother stopped playing." Logan snaps his fingers for emphasis. "Just like that, right in the middle of a phrase, as if somebody had thrown a switch. She stood up from the piano and marched right past me like I wasn't even there. 'What's happening,' I asked my father, 'what's wrong with her?' But he didn't answer me. We followed her outside. I didn't know what time it was, though it was late, the middle of the night. She stopped at the edge of the porch, looking out over the fields. For a little while nothing happened—she just stood there, the same empty look on her face. Then she began to mutter something. At first I couldn't tell what she was saying. One phrase, over and over. 'Come to me,' she was saying. 'Come to me, come to me, come to me.' I'll never forget it."

Nessa is watching his face intently. "Who do you think she was talking to?"

Logan shrugs. "Who knows? I don't remember what happened after that. I suppose I went to bed. A few days later, the same thing happened. Over time it became a kind of nightly ritual. *Oh, Mom's playing the piano again at four A.M.* During the day she seemed fine, but then that changed, too. She became harried, obsessive, or else wandered around the house in a kind of daze. That's when the painting started."

"'Painting'?" Nessa repeats. "You mean, pictures?"

"Come on, I'll show you."

He escorts her upstairs. Three tiny bedrooms, tucked under the eaves; in the ceiling of the hallway is a hatch with a cord. Logan pulls it down and unfolds the rickety wooden stairs that lead to the attic.

They ascend into the cramped, low-ceilinged space. Standing a dozen deep, his mother's paintings line nearly a whole wall. Logan kneels and draws the protective cloth aside.

It is like opening a door onto a garden. The paintings, of various sizes, depict a landscape of wildflowers, the colors burning with an almost supernatural brightness. Some show a background of mountains; others, the sea.

"Logan, these are beautiful."

They are. Bound up in pain, they are, nevertheless, creations of stunning beauty. He takes the first one and brings it to Nessa, who holds it in her hands.

"It's . . ." she begins, then stops. "I'm not even sure how to say it."

"Unearthly?"

"I was going to say haunting." She looks up. "And they're all the same?"

"Different viewpoints, and her style improved over time. But the subjects are identical. The fields, the flowers, the ocean in the background."

"There are hundreds."

"Three hundred and seventy-two."

"What do you think this place is? Was it someplace she'd been?"

"If it is, I never saw it. Neither did my father. No, I think the image came from inside her head someplace. Like the music."

Nessa considers this. "A vision."

"Perhaps that's the word."

She examines the painting again. A long silence follows.

"What became of her, Logan?"

He takes a long breath to steady himself. "It eventually got to be too much. The spells, the craziness. I was sixteen when my father had her committed. He visited every week, sometimes more, but he wouldn't let me see her; I gather her state was rather bad. My junior year in college, she killed herself."

For a moment, Nessa says nothing. And, really, what is there to say? Logan has never known. One minute there, in another one gone. All of it far in the past, nearly forty years ago.

"I'm sorry, Logan. That must have been very hard."

"She left a note," he adds. "It wasn't very long."

"What did it say?"

The rope, the chair, the silent building after everyone had gone to bed: this is where his imagination ends. He has never permitted it to go further, to envision the mortal moment.

"'Let her rest.'"

They return to the inn. There, for the first time, in Nessa's room, they make love. The act is unhurried; they conduct it without words. Her body, firm and smooth, is extraordinary to him, as wondrous a present as he has ever received. In the aftermath, they sleep.

Night is falling when Logan awakens to the sound of running water. The shower shuts off with a groan and Nessa emerges from the bathroom in a soft robe, a towel wrapping her hair. She sits on the edge of the bed.

"Hungry?" she asks, smiling.

"There aren't a lot of choices. I thought we'd go to the restaurant downstairs."

She kisses him on the mouth. The kiss is brisk, but she allows her face to linger close to his. "Go dress."

She returns to the bathroom to finish her preparations. How swiftly life can change, Logan thinks. There was no one, now there is someone; he is not alone. Telling the story of his mother was, he realizes, his intention from the start; he has no other way of explaining who he is. That is what two people must give to each other, he thinks: the history of themselves. How else can we hope to be known?

He puts on his trousers and shirt to go next door to change for dinner, but as he enters the hallway he hears his name being called.

"Dr. Miles, Dr. Miles!"

The voice belongs to the hotel proprietor, a small, deeply tanned man with jet black hair and a nervously formal manner, who bounds up the stairs. "There is a phone call for you," he says with excitement. He pauses to catch his breath, waving air into his face. "Someone has been trying to reach you all day."

"Really? Who?" As far as Logan is aware, nobody knows he's here.

The proprietor glances at the door to Nessa's room, then back again. "Yes, well," he says, and clears his throat self-consciously, "they are on the phone now. They say it is quite urgent. Please, I will show you the way."

Logan follows him downstairs, through the lobby, to a small room behind the check-in desk, where a large black telephone rests on an otherwise empty table.

"I will leave you to it," the proprietor says with a curt bow.

Alone, Logan picks up the receiver. "This is Professor Miles."

A woman's voice, unknown to him, says, "Dr. Miles, please hold while I patch you through to Dr. Wilcox."

Melville Wilcox is the on-site supervisor at First Colony. Such calls happen only rarely, and always with considerable advance planning; only by positioning a chain of airships across the Pacific, a tenuous and expensive arrangement, can a signal be relayed. Whatever Wilcox wants, it's bound to be important. For a full minute, the line crackles with empty static; Logan has begun to think the call's been lost when Wilcox comes on the line.

"Logan, can you hear me all right?"

"Yes, I can hear you fine."

"Good, I've been trying to set this up for days. Are you sitting down? Because you might want to."

"Mel, what's happening there?"

His voice grows excited. "Six days ago, an unmanned reconnaissance airship surveying the coast of the Pacific Northwest took a photo. A *very* interesting photo. Do you have access to an imager?"

Logan scans the room. To his surprise, there is one.

"Give me the number," Wilcox says. "I'll have Lucinda send it over."

Logan fetches the proprietor, who enthusiastically provides the information and offers to man the machine.

"Okay, they're sending it," Wilcox says.

The imager emits a shriek. "The connection has been made, I believe," the proprietor declares.

"Why don't you just tell me what it is?" Logan asks Wilcox.

"Oh, believe me, it's better if you see this for yourself."

A series of mechanical clunks and the machine draws a piece of paper from the tray. As the print head moves noisily back and forth, Logan becomes aware of a second sound, coming from outside—a kind of rhythmic beating. He has only just realized what he is hearing when Nessa enters the room, dressed for dinner. She looks animated, even a little alarmed.

"Logan, there's a lifter out there. It looks like it's about to land on the front lawn."

"And here we are," the proprietor announces.

With a triumphant smile, he places the transmitted picture onto the desk. It is the image of a house, seen from above. Not a ruin—an actual house. It is encircled by a fence; within this perimeter are a second, smaller structure, a privy perhaps, and the neatly planted rows of a vegetable garden.

"Well?" Wilcox says. "Did you get it?"

There is more. In the field adjacent to the house, rocks have been arranged on the ground to make letters, large enough to be read from the air.

"What is it, Logan?" Nessa asks.

Logan looks up; Nessa is staring at him. The world, he knows, is about to change. Not just for him. For everyone. Outside the walls of the inn, the racket reaches a crescendo as the lifter touches down.

"It's a message," he says, showing Nessa the paper.

Three words: COME TO ME.

92

Six days have passed. Logan and Nessa, in the observation lounge, sit in silence.

On an airship, time moves differently. The excitement of travel quickly wanes, replaced by a kind of mental and physical hibernation; the days seem shapeless, the ship itself barely to move at all. Logan and Nessa, the only passengers, the objects of obscene fussing by a staff that far outnumbers them, have passed the time sleeping, reading, playing cards. In the evening, after eating by themselves in the too-large dining room, they have their pick of movies from the ship's collection and watch alone or with members of the crew.

But now, with their destination in view, time snaps back into line. The ship is headed north, tracing the northern California coastline at an altitude of two thousand feet. Towering cliffs wreathed by morning fog, mighty forests of ancient trees, the indomitable greatness of the sea where it collides with the land: Logan's heart stirs, as it always does, at the sight of this wild, untouched place.

"Is it what you thought it would be?" he asks Nessa.

Looking raptly out the window, she has barely spoken a word since breakfast.

"I'm not sure what I thought." She turns her face toward him, lips pressed together and eyes slightly squinted, like someone puzzling out a problem. "It's beautiful, but there's something else to it. A different feeling."

Not much later, the platform appears. Standing a hundred meters above the ocean's surface, it has the appearance of a rigid structure, though it is, in fact, floating at anchor. The airship moves gracefully into place and attaches at the nose to the docking tower; ropes and chains are lowered; the vessel is drawn slowly downward to the deck. As Logan and Nessa disembark, Wilcox strides toward them with a rolling gait: a heavyset man with an untidy beard peppered with gray, his face and arms bronzed by sun and wind.

"Welcome back," Wilcox says as they shake. "And you," he says, turning, "must be Nessa."

Wilcox is aware of Nessa's role, although he is, Logan knows, not entirely comfortable with it, believing it is too soon to involve the press. But that is part of Logan's design. Security is never as tight as it should be; word will get out, and once it does, they will lose control of the narrative. He'd rather get ahead of the situation by giving the story to one person, someone they can trust.

"Do you need to eat, clean up?" Wilcox asks. "The bird's fueled and ready whenever you want."

"How long will it take to get to the site?" Logan asks.

"Ninety minutes, about."

Logan looks at Nessa, who nods. "I see no reason to delay," he says.

The lifter waits on a second, slightly elevated platform, its props pointed upward. As they walk to it, Wilcox brings Logan up to speed. Per Logan's instructions, no one has approached the house, although the building's inhabitant, a woman, has been sighted several times, working in the yard. Wilcox's team has moved equipment to the camp in order to bag the house, if that's what Logan wants to do.

"Does she know she's being watched?" Logan asks.

"She'd have to, with all those lifters going in and out, but she doesn't act like it." They take their seats in the bird. From the portfolio under his arm, Wilcox removes a photo and hands it to Logan. The image, taken from a great distance, is grainy and flattened; it shows a woman with a nimbus of white hair, hunched before a vegetable patch. She is wearing what appears to be a kind of thickly woven sack, almost shapeless; her face, angled downward, is obscured.

"So who is she?" Wilcox says.

Logan just looks at him.

"I know what you're thinking," Wilcox says, holding up a hand in forbearance, "and pardon me, but no fucking way."

"She's the sole human inhabitant of a continent that's been depopulated for nine hundred years. Give me another theory and I'll listen."

"Maybe people came back without our knowing it."

"Possible. But why just her? Why haven't we found anybody else in thirty-six months?"

"Maybe they don't want to be found."

"She has no problem with it. 'Come to me' sounds like an engraved invitation."

The conversation is drowned out by the roar of the lifter's engines; a lurch and they are airborne again, rising vertically. When a sufficient altitude is achieved, the nose tips upward as the rotors move to a horizontal position. The lifter accelerates, coming in low over the water and then the coast. The ocean vanishes. All below them is trees, a carpet of green. The noise is tremendous, each of them encased in a bubble of their own thoughts; there will be no more talking until they land.

Logan is drifting at the edge of sleep when he feels the lifter slowing. He sits up and looks out the window.

Color.

That is the first thing he sees. Reds, blues, oranges, greens, violets: extending from the forested base of the mountains to the sea, flowers paint the earth in an array of hues so richly prismatic it is as if light itself has shattered. The rotors tilt; the aircraft begins to descend. Logan breaks his gaze from the window to find Nessa staring at him. Her eyes are full of a mute wonder that is, he knows, a mirror to his own.

"My God," she mouths.

The camp is situated in a narrow depression separated from the wildflower field by a stand of trees. In the main tent, Wilcox presents his team, about a dozen researchers, some of whom Logan is acquainted with from previous trips. In turn, he introduces Nessa to the group, explaining only that she has come as "a special adviser." The house's resident, he is told, has been working in the garden since morning.

Logan issues instructions. Everybody is to wait here, he says; under no circumstances should anyone approach the house until he and Nessa report back. In Wilcox's tent, they strip to their underclothes and don their yellow biosuits. The afternoon is bright and hot; the suits will be sweltering. Wilcox tapes the joints of their gloves and checks their air supplies.

"Good luck," he says.

They make their way through the trees, into the field. The house stands about two hundred meters distant.

"Logan . . ." Nessa says.

"I know."

Everything is perfect. Everything is just the same, without the slightest deviation. The flowers. The mountains. The sea. The way the wind moves and the light falls. Logan keeps his eyes forward, lest he be consumed by the powerful emotions roiling inside him. Slowly, in their bulky suits, he and Nessa make their way across the field. The house, one story, is homey and neat: wide-planked siding weathered to gray, a simple porch, a sod roof, from which a haze of green grass grows.

As promised, the woman is working in the dooryard, which is planted in rosebushes of several colors. Logan and Nessa halt just outside the picket fence. Kneeling in the dirt, the woman doesn't notice them, or appears not to. She is profoundly old. With gnarled hands—fingers bent and stiffened, skin puckered in folds, knuckles fat as walnuts—she is plucking weeds and placing them in a bucket.

"Hello," Logan says.

She offers no reply, just continues her work. Her movements are patient and focused. Perhaps she has not heard him. Perhaps she is hard of hearing or deaf.

Logan tries again: "Good afternoon, ma'am."

She stops in the manner of someone alerted by a distant sound; slowly she raises her face. Her eyes are rheumy, damp and faintly yellow. She squints at him for perhaps ten seconds, fighting to focus. Some of her teeth are gone, giving her mouth a pursed appearance.

"So, you've decided to come up, then," she says. Her voice is a coarse rasp. "I was wondering when that would happen."

"My name is Logan Miles. This is my friend Nessa Tripp. I was hoping we could talk with you. Would that be all right?"

The woman has resumed her weeding. She has also begun, faintly, to mutter to herself. Logan glances at Nessa, whose face, behind her plastic mask, drips with sweat, as does his own.

"Would you like some help?" Nessa asks the woman.

The question appears to puzzle her. The woman shifts backward onto her haunches. "Help?"

"Yes. With the weeding."

Her mouth puckers. "Do I know you, young lady?"

"I don't believe so," Nessa replies. "We've only just arrived."

"From where?"

"Far away," says Nessa. "*Very* far away. We've come a great distance to see you." She points toward the field of rocks. "We got your message."

The woman's yellowed eyes follow Nessa's gesture. "Oh, that," she says after a moment. "Set that up a long time ago. Can't really remember the reason for it. You say you want to help with the weeding, though—that's fine. Come on through the gate."

They enter the yard. Nessa, taking the lead, kneels before the rose beds and begins to work, scooping the dirt aside with her thick gloves; Logan does the same. Best, he thinks, to let the woman get used to their presence before pressing her further.

"The roses are lovely," Nessa says. "What kind are they?"

The woman doesn't answer. She is scraping the ground with a metal claw. She appears to take no interest in them whatsoever.

"So, how long have you been here?" Logan asks.

The woman's hands stop, then, after a beat, resume working. "Started work early this morning. Garden doesn't rest."

"No, I meant in this place. How long have you lived here?"

"Oh, a long time." She plucks another weed and, unaccountably, places the green tip between her front teeth and nibbles on it, her jaws working like a rabbit's. With a sound of dissatisfaction, she shakes her head and tosses it in the bucket.

"Those suits you're wearing," she says. "I think I've seen those before."

Logan is perturbed. Has someone else been here? "When was that, do you think?"

"Don't remember." She purses her lips. "I doubt they're very comfortable. You can wear what you like, though. It's not really my business."

More time passes. The pail is nearly full.

"Now, I don't believe we got your name," Logan says to the woman.

"My name?"

"Yes. What are you called?"

It is as if the question makes no sense to her. The woman lifts her head and angles her gaze toward the sea. Her eyes narrow in the bright oceanic light. "No one around here to call me anything."

Logan glances at Nessa, who nods cautiously. "But surely you have a name," he presses.

The woman doesn't answer. The murmuring has returned. Not murmuring, Logan realizes: humming. Mysterious notes, almost tuneless but not quite.

"Did Anthony send you?" she asks.

Once again, Logan looks at Nessa. Her face says that she, too, has made the connection: Anthony Carter, the third name on the stone.

"I don't believe I know Anthony," Logan tenders. "Is he around here?"

The woman frowns at the absurdity of this question, or so it seems. "He went home a long time ago."

"Is he a friend of yours?"

Logan waits for more, but there is none. The woman takes a single rose between her thumb and forefinger. The petals are fading, brittle and brown. From the pocket of her dress she removes a small blade and clips the stem at the first tier of leaves and drops the wilted bloom in the pail.

"Amy," Logan says.

She stops.

"Is that you? Are you . . . Amy?"

With painstaking, almost mechanical slowness, she swivels her face. She regards him for a moment, expressionless, then frowns as if puzzled. "You're still here."

Where would they have gone? "Yes," says Nessa. "We came to see you."

She shifts her eyes to Nessa, then back to Logan. "Why are you still here?"

Logan senses a deepening presence in her gaze. Her thoughts are taking clearer form.

"Are you . . . real?"

The question stops him. But of course it makes sense that she would ask this. It is the most natural question in the world, when one has been alone so long. *Are you real?*

"As real as you are, Amy."

"Amy," she repeats. It is as if she is tasting the word. "I think my name was Amy."

More time goes by. Logan and Nessa wait.

"Those suits," she says. "They're because of me, aren't they?"

It surprises him, the thing he does next. Yet he experiences not the slightest hesitation; the act feels ordained. He removes his gloves and reaches up to the clasp that holds his helmet in place.

"Logan—" Nessa warns.

He pulls the helmet over his head and places it on the ground. The taste of fresh air swarms his senses. He breathes deeply, enriching his lungs with the scents of flowers and the sea.

"I think this is much better, don't you?" he asks.

Tears have risen at the corners of the woman's eyes. A look of wonder comes. "You're really here."

Logan nods.

"You've come back."

Logan takes her hand. It is nearly weightless, and alarmingly cold. "I'm sorry it took us so long. I'm sorry you have been alone."

A tear spills down her weathered cheek. "After all this time, you've come back."

She is dying. Logan wonders how he knows this, but then the answer comes: his mother's note. "Let her rest." He has always assumed she was speaking of herself. But now he understands that the message was for him, for this day.

"Nessa," he says, not breaking his gaze from Amy, "go back to camp and tell Wilcox to gather his team and call for a second lifter."

"Why?"

He turns his face to look at her. "I need them to leave. All their gear, everything except a radio. Deliver the message and then come back. I would be very grateful if you could do that for me, please."

She pauses, then nods.

"Thank you, Nessa."

Logan watches as she passes through the flowers, into the trees, and out of sight. So much color, he thinks. So much life everywhere. He feels tremendously happy. A weight has lifted from his life.

"My mother dreamed of you, you know."

Amy's head is bowed. Tears fall down her cheeks in glistening rivers. Is she happy? Is she sad? There is a joy so powerful it is like sadness, Logan knows, just as the opposite is also true.

"Many people have. This place, Amy. The flowers, the sea. My mother painted pictures of it, hundreds of them. She was telling me to find you." He pauses, then says, "You were the one who wrote the names on the stone, weren't you?"

She gives the barest nod, grief flowing, rising out of the past.

"Brad. Lacey. Anthony. Alicia. Michael. Sara. Lucius. All of them, your family, your Twelve."

Her answer comes in a whisper. "Yes."

"And Peter. Peter most of all. 'Peter Jaxon, Beloved Husband.'"

"Yes."

Logan cups her chin and gently raises her face. "It was a world you gave us, Amy. Do you see? We are your children. Your children, come home."

A quiet moment passes—a holy moment, Logan thinks, for within it he experiences an emotion entirely new to him. It is the feeling of a world, a reality, expanding beyond its visible borders, into a vast unknown; and likewise does he believe that he—that everyone, the living and the dead and those yet to come—belong to this greater existence, one that outstrips time. That is why he has come: to be an agent of this knowledge.

"Will you do something for me?" he asks.

She nods. Their time together will be brief; Logan knows this. A day, a night, perhaps no more.

"Tell me the story, Amy."

DRAMATIS PERSONAE

(In chronological order)

B.V., OHIO, CAMBRIDGE, AND NEW YORK

Timothy Fanning, a student
Harold and Lorraine Fanning, his parents
Jonas Lear, a student
Frank Lucessi, a student
Arianna Lucessi, his sister
Elizabeth Macomb, a student
Alcott Spence, a ne'er-do-well
Stephanie Healey, a student
Oscar and Patty Macomb, parents of Elizabeth Macomb
Nicole Forood, an editor
Reynaldo and Phelps, police detectives

A.V., TEXAS REPUBLIC

Alicia Donadio, a soldier
Peter Jaxon, a laborer
Amy Bellafonte Harper, the Girl from Nowhere
Lore DeVeer, an oiler
Caleb Jaxon, adopted son of Peter Jaxon
Sara Wilson, a physician
Hollis Wilson, her husband; a librarian
Kate Wilson, their daughter
Sister Peg, a nun
Lucius Greer, a mystic
Michael Fisher, an explorer
Jenny Apgar, a nurse
Carlos and Sally Jiménez, expectant parents
Grace Jiménez , their daughter
Anthony Carter, a gardener

Pim, a foundling
Victoria Sanchez, president of the Texas Republic
Gunnar Apgar, general of the Army
Ford Chase, president's chief of staff
The Maestro, an antiquarian
Foto, a laborer
Jock Alvado, a laborer
Theo Jaxon, infant son of Caleb and Pim Jaxon
Bill Speer, a gambler
Elle and Merry ("Bug") Speer, daughters of Kate Wilson Speer and Bill Speer
Meredith, partner of Victoria Sanchez
Rand Horgan, a mechanic
Byron "Patch" Szumanski, a mechanic
Weir, a mechanic
Fastau, a mechanic
Dunk Withers, a criminal
Phil and Dorien Tatum, farmers
Brian Elacqua, a physician
George Pettibrew, a shopkeeper
Gordon Eustace, a lawman
Fry Robinson, his deputy
Rudy, an Iowan
The Possum Man's wife, an Iowan
Rachel Wood, a suicide
Haley and Riley Wood, her daughters
Alexander Henneman, an officer
Hannah, a teenage girl, daughter of Jenny Apgar

A.V., INDO-AUSTRALIAN REPUBLIC

Logan Miles, a scholar
Nessa Tripp, a reporter
Race Miles, a pilot, son of Logan and Olla Miles
Kaye Miles, a teacher, wife of Race Miles
Olla Miles, ex-wife of Logan Miles
Bettina, a horticulturalist, partner of Olla Miles
Noa and Cam Miles, twin sons of Race and Kaye Miles
Melville Wilcox, an archaeologist

ACKNOWLEDGMENTS

Thanks and yet more ponies to the usual suspects: Mark Tavani, Libby McGuire, Gina Centrello, Bill Massey, and the spectacular editing, marketing, production, sales, and publicity teams at Ballantine, Orion, and my many publishers around the world. Y'all are going to need a bigger barn.

To Ellen Levine, my agent and friend of twenty years: you are a true treasure in my life.

In the course of writing the Passage trilogy, I've called upon the expertise of many individuals on subjects ranging from epidemiology to military strategy. My gratitude to all. A special shout-out to Dr. Annette O'Connor of La Salle University, who has advised me on scientific questions since the beginning.

Although I generally adhere to a policy of strict realism in matters of geography and landscape, this is not always possible. Respectful apologies to the fine citizens of Kerrville, Texas, for liberties taken with the area's topography. Similar adjustments have been made to the Houston Ship Channel and environs.

To Leslie, I say again: Without you, nothing.

Finally, special thanks to my daughter, Iris, who challenged me ten years ago to write a story about "a girl who saves the world."

Darlin', here it is.

ABOUT THE AUTHOR

Justin Cronin is the *New York Times* bestselling author of *The Passage, The Twelve, The City of Mirrors, Mary and O'Neil* (which won the PEN/Hemingway Award and the Stephen Crane Prize), and *The Summer Guest*. Other honours for his writing include a fellowship from the National Endowment for the Arts and a Whiting Writers' Award. A Distinguished Faculty Fellow at Rice University, he divides his time between Houston, Texas, and Cape Cod, Massachusetts.

Facebook.com/justincroninauthor
@jccronin